SAGACIOUS BLADE

Books set in the Thousand Isles Empire

The Phoenix Feather Arc:

Fledglings

Redbark

Firebolt

Dragon and Phoenix

The Sagacious Arc:

Tribute

Sage Empress I

Sage Empress II

Sagacious Blade

SAGACIOUS BLADE

SHERWOOD SMITH

BOOK VIEW CAFE

BOOK VIEW CAFE

FOREWORD

"WE ARE ALL," AFAN Arikanda once told her children, "made up of a number of identities. Sometimes these even have names."

She managed to keep from admitting that of her own identities, the one she liked best to lay aside was Empress of the Thousand Isles. By the time those children reached adulthood, they'd become aware how much their mother liked to cast aside the rich, heavy embroidered silken layers of her exalted rank and pull on the simple, much-worn smock and trousers OF the gallant wanderer Firebolt of Redbark Sect.

It was invariably spring when she left; though she had deeply appreciated the splendor of the imperial Journey to the Cloud Empire, in which the imperial court on their sumptuous barges enjoyed some of the most exquisite orchids in the empire as the best musicians played to them from rocks and grottos, between poetry contests and scholarly debates. That was an experience she appreciated infrequently, inclining more to the freedom and festival chaos of the commoners' Kraken Boat Festival at the same time.

The Journey to the Clouds was the high point of the year for her otherworldly brother Yskanda, who went each year in companionship with her husband Jion, Emperor Shiyan, beloved to both.

She and Jion kissed with all the tenderness of their first embrace, and he used the mysterious bronze Sagacious Blade to inscribe a door in the air. She was very careful not to let a strand of hair nor a fold of the fabric of her travel-worn cloak touch those shimmering edges, stepped through to Te Gar Harbor, and happily breathed in the heady scents of brine, incense, and the delicious aromas of street food.

She ducked around celebrating subjects and sailors and gallant wanderers, paused to watch a hundred-footed kraken weave its way in dance down the street to the sound of clashing gongs and screeling pipes, then entered the Blue Hibiscus Inn, a portion of a sectioned staff visible above each shoulder as she paused to take in the busy room.

Bing Feg, the middle-aged innkeeper, recognized her at once. His mouth rounded, but before he could speak, Ari put her finger to her lips, and so Bing Feg only clasped his hands in respectful greeting of an elder, then returned to tending his counter.

Ari had watched Feg grow from a small boy tagging at his parents' heels to a gangling youth wrangling tables, and to his present position as boss of the floor, which permitted Bing Petal and Ki Matu to occasionally visit Matu's home island far to the northwest.

"Are your esteemed parents here?" Ari asked as after she greeted Feg.

"They left for Ten Leopards," Feg replied, bowing respectfully. "Ma wanted to be there for the birth of Rose's child." Rose being Feg's younger sister, who had taken the Ki name when she chose the gallant wanderer life at a very young age. "Mother left a message for you with my wife," he added with another clasp of his hands.

Feg was already the father of three hopeful boys, but Petal had almost given up hoping that her daughter Rose, now rising forty, might ever bring home a grandchild.

"I hope that means she got her granddaughter at last," Ari murmured to herself, and as she threaded among the tables, she breathed a short prayer to Suanek, for never would granddaughter be as spoiled and loved as this one, were she to come into being.

Madam Bing, Feg's wife, was supervising two stringbean sons in collecting dirty dishes. Seeing Ari, she clasped her hands in cheery greeting.

"Feg said you had a message? Is it a girl?"

"No pigeon yet about that," Madam Bing said, and made a sign to Suanek. "Mother Petal sent a note that they arrived safely, and I was to tell you, if you came, that Waoji Lion's Mane was seen going up to the mountain."

That sounded ominous.

Ari had met with Waoji Lion's Mane from time to time over the past fifty years. He was a tall, gaunt man whose shock of wild white hair resembled a great dandelion. In his youth it had been likened to a lion's mane; there had been many legends about him when she was a teenager. But he was quite a bit older—he'd been a man in his forties when she was a teen. Why, he must have reached ninety easily. He'd reminded her of a fine old tree, gnarly, but one in which the sap still ran vigorously, powerful in branch and leaf even in autumn.

After the death of his beloved wife, Bi the Whirlwind—treacherously killed while defending their two children—he had retreated to grieve alone in those mountains, only visiting Grandfather Ki in his own retreat, from time to time.

If he had gone back there, after all these years, it was for a reason. "Mother Petal said that she sent notes to Waoji Reckless to try to find you, but who knows where he's wandering? She also sent a letter to the local imperial navy to pass up to you as empress, but she didn't know if they would send it on."

Petal was thoroughly a gallant wanderer in outlook, though a respected merchant in this garrison town. She didn't trust the imperial navy much more than the generality of gallant wanderers did.

"Thank you," Ari said. "Ayah, here I am. Do you have my usual room?"

"We always keep it free during the warm months," Madam Bing assured her proudly.

Ari didn't actually need it, but it was easier to hire a room than to explain stepping through glittering doors between islands weeks and even months apart by sea.

In the room, she lit a candle, and gazed into it, reaching mentally, with the ease of years of practice, for Jion. As she expected, he'd been listening for her, and there he was, smiling out of the bright flame. "Ryu?"

She adored his using her Redbark name when they were in private, a reminder of their days together before she became the famed Firebolt. Just as he liked her using his gallant wanderer name, Shigan.

"It's Waoji Lion's Mane." She explained Petal's message. The air scintillated, then he stepped through a shimmering door, wearing a fabulous robe of crimson embroidered with dancing golden dragons. The air he brought with him filled the chamber with the fragrance of beeswax candles and incense.

"It's the middle of a concert," he said. "I have a moment."

To recover, she translated to herself. She knew he hated to admit that there was any personal cost to his forcing invisible doors between one location and another. But she, having studied Essence matters most of her life, understood.

"I wouldn't ask—I'd love the journey north—but I'm worried that I will arrive and whatever his purpose is, I might get there too late," she finished. "I can't forget that Master Ki withdrew to the mountain before he died. And I was never able to see him again."

"I'll take you there," Jion said. "And you can enjoy the journey back. And incidentally, turn up here and there, a salutary reminder to any officials who might need it."

Ari laughed. He was far too vigilant for bad governors to last long.

He had Sagacious Blade with him, of course. The white stone in the hilt winked and glittered as he carefully described a door, then with his free hand, he clasped hers, and they stepped through. Wind whirled around them, and with it a fine rain. The far north was appreciably colder, the slant of light different, as they stood on the edge of the lake below that mountain retreat. Jion could only go to places he knew by sight, and Ari had brought him there once or twice before.

"Are you sure you don't want me to try the little valley?" he asked. "I remember it quite well."

"But things do grow fast there, and I'm always afraid that your door might open onto a tree or worse, a creature."

He accepted that. Neither of them understood this potentially dangerous method of transfer. The rules of the physical world that constrained humans did not work the same in the mysterious realm of the demons and gods.

"Besides, the walk will be good for me," she finished.

They kissed again, and then he returned to Yskanda on the imperial barge. She watched the shimmering line vanish like the spangles of the sun on water smothered by a cloud crossing the sun, and began to trot up the mountain toward Waoji Lion's Mane.

Now that great tree seemed very near the winter of life. He still sat with his back to a corner so that he could see in all directions. She folded down onto the mat opposite him.

His smile quirked, and she knew he had seen her shock in her face. "Be at peace, young Ari," he said—he had called her that for more than fifty years, to her enjoyment. "Bi has often spoke to me in my dreams of late. It probably won't be long before I join her."

Ari listened with sympathy, hiding question—if not quite skepticism. For in all her years, no one had spoken to her in dreams. That is, if they were even recognizable, they were usually within a context that seemed nonsensical in the light of day. On the other hand, her brother Yskanda regularly spoke to the dead in his dreams—whether real or symbolic seemed irrelevant to him.

"I thought that this would be the appropriate place," Lion's Mane continued. "I have finally finished something I have been preparing for many years."

"Oh?" she prompted.

He reached into the worn travel satchel at his side, and with both hands, withdrew a scroll.

There was an air of finality in Lion's Mane's manner that drew her attention to the scroll. She did not recognize the neat handwriting, but she noted that the ink was not the brown of great age.

"It is the life of Ki Mek—he whom you knew as your master, Grandfather Ki. He knew I was writing it; it was, in fact, with you in mind that he talked long with me those evenings when you slumbered so peacefully on the cave floor all those years ago. He knew that after far longer a life than most humans are granted, his was coming to a close. He had prayed he would find the right person to inherit Sagacious Blade—and that was you."

Ari was not sure what to say. She had only studied martial arts, combined with Essence, for scarcely a year under Grandfather Ki, then he had sent her out to experience the world. She still thought of him wistfully from time to time, wishing she'd had longer with him.

"Though he often told me stories during the year I cultivated with him, he never said very much about his own life, even when I asked," Ari said slowly. "I finally figured he did not want it known. Or, he did not want me knowing."

Lion's Mane smiled a little. "On his first meeting you, you were accompanied by someone whose features were very familiar," he said, surprising Ari even more. "He decided it was better to wait upon events, in spite of the fact that he recognized in you the person he had been waiting for."

"Oh?" Ari said, running her mind past her fellow Redbark gallant wanderers—only the four of them at that time. Surely his ambivalence had not been about Matu, whose unfortunate tendency toward seasickness kept him from much travel. Nor could it have been Petal—

Of course. "It was Shigan," Ari said. "Shigan Fin, he called himself at that time. He really did think he was going to spend his life as a gallant wanderer." Those instantly recognizable, obsidian-black, long phoenix eyes under slanted brows, the proud nose, the beautifully defined bones were seen in variation in the pictures of the Jehan Dynasty, and in Ari's and Shigan's own progeny, to greater or lesser degree.

"Grandfather Ki recognized the Jehan features."

"Ayah," Ari exclaimed. "And Grandfather Ki tested him, a little. Not with just martial arts, but with his music. And Shigan danced."

"Yes."

"Though dancing well doesn't prove one is a good future emperor. Or even a good person. I understand why he might have been wary, when I think of a couple of Shigan's forefathers! But he's an excellent emperor—furthermore, he is aware of his dynastic history."

Lion's Mane clasped his hands in agreement. Ari was used to the skepticism with which gallant wanderers regarded the imperial government. The tension between their desire to wander freely, everyone equal to everyone else, their loose hierarchy based on skill, not on birth or accumulated merit, was centuries old. She and Shigan understood the gallant wanderer world as an escape door for the young, the strong, the skilled, who fretted under the constrains of Kanda's ancient rules. "An empire that did not allow for escape doors too easily became a tyranny," he had said, waving at the imperial archive. "But a proper government is there to protect those who are not young, and strong, and skilled. Which is usually the first thing tyrants forget," he added with a sour smile.

Lion's Mane went on, "Grandfather Ki's only regret, he said shortly before he died, was that he was not to have more time training you in the higher Essence matters."

Though it had been many decades since her days with Grandfather Ki, Ari found her eyes stinging. The memories of Grandfather Ki's little pocket valley, where animals came and went freely, were precious. "I was never going to be a great

Essence wielder by myself. In defeating the White Dragon, I needed us all to work together."

"I think he would have agreed," Lion's Mane said. "Also. You might not have reached that conclusion if you had remained with him and learnt his solitary ways. I believe he sensed that when he let you go."

Ari clasped her hands in the gallant wanderer bow.

He bowed back, then held out a scroll with both hands. "Here it is. I make no claims for its poetry or elegance of language, only that it is as true as I could make it. Go ahead. Read it. Ask questions. I'll wait."

ONE

WHEN TELLING THE STORY of a life, I have to determine the right place to begin—after first deciding what constitutes "right." After reading all the records about the legendary Sagacious Blade, and weaving the two with countless reminiscences, I think it best to begin with the Ki clan on a spring evening during the last reign of the Tan Dynasty.

The elders circled Little Twelve, a baby midway between one and two years, typically round of face and body, under a soft thatch of flyaway dark hair. He sat on the grass, fat little hands trying to touch slowly darting fireflies. As they watched he gave up, and in his palm a light glowed into being, though no actual object could be seen there. He seemed to be offering it to the fireflies, and frowned in perplexity at their obliviousness.

The boy's mother, looking worn and anxious, said softly, "He *is* good, you understand, Elder Ki. A very easy child. Except for *that*. And, ah, entering my dreams when he's hungry."

That was all she could bring herself to say in mixed company, for it was startling and perhaps even unseemly, that her baby son could puncture her dreams and present her with a highly realistic and somehow emphatic image of the milk-source he sought. Right down to the little mole on one side.

Elder Ki said, "Little Twelve appears to be a Talent."

No one spoke, but signified agreement in sidelong glances, shifting of feet, and the nervous rubbing of the mother's hands.

"Talent," observed the child's father with an uneasy expression, "seems to me to be much like dragons. Everyone admires them from afar, but no one seems prepared to have one in the house."

The mother was quick to defend her child, in a timorous voice utterly unfamiliar, as she was as fierce on a ship's deck when pirates attempted boarding as she was tough during practice. "He's very good. Other than these...other things." She fought a yawn until her jaw ached—for she had had scant sleep since the day Little Twelve made his appearance into the world.

"Things," the baby's Second Uncle said in stiff, disapproving tones, "like creating fires out of nothing."

"Not fires," objected Twelve's father. "Light only."

"That is even less desirable. There is something of the ghost about light which does not burn," retorted Second Uncle. "Inauspicious." *His* two boys, Five and Eight, did not trespass in so outrageous a manner—which he began to expatiate with superficially humble words belied by a hortatory tone until a significant harrumph from Elder Ki caused him to halt mid-word.

"*I'll* take him," Elder Ki stated. "He will learn strict discipline with me, until we can find someone to train a wild Talent into useful pursuit."

The exhausted mother heard that word "strict" and said doubtfully, "I'd willingly give up the luck of my next five lives to have so esteemed a person take an interest in our troublesome son." She clasped her hands and bowed. "But, though he's troublesome, he is no wolf cub. When he was little more than a hundred days old, he was trying to put food in *my* mouth. He never minds when the older children pinch his date cakes—"

Elder Ki, who understood very well what the mother was trying to say, commented, "By strict I mean firm, not harsh. You married into our family. You could not know that never have I raised a hand in anger to any of my children." And after accepting another heartfelt bow made in silent apology, "You must do your part, too, Twelve's Mother; if he comes into your dreams tonight, you are to turn over and go back to sleep."

All heads turned toward the Headman, Elder Ki's second son, who had remained silent through this discussion. He gave a short nod, and it was decided.

Elder Ki was as good as her word.

To Little Twelve, she became Grandmother. As the seasons blended and one year, two, then three passed, Little Twelve stayed in Grandmother's courtyard. There were birds to watch, kittens to play with, a dog to curl up with on his mat at night, tasty noodles to eat, and stories to be heard as he performed the exercises that Ki children learned from the time they could walk.

He was firmly guided in Ki household rules, which did not hold with ghosts, demons, or arcane powers, much less trespassing in dreams. Power, to the Ki clan, was a matter of skill at arms.

Still, talent was talent. Perhaps his could be guided into a useful form; Elder Ki debated within herself, then began to teach him acupoints. He was like a dried sea sponge immersed in water. He retained all she taught him, and so she kept teaching, explaining to Twelve's mother, who, once he was weaned, still brought treats now and then, "It won't harm him to begin on defense early. I'm thinking that he'll need plenty to work on so that he will forget that Essence foolery with ghost lights. Has he ceased to trouble you at nights?"

"He has. I think he understands now that trespass in dreams is like entering a closed door without invitation."

"There, now," Elder Ki said, pleased. "What did I tell you? He's quick and willing to learn what's proper."

At five, he was deemed ready to go among his many cousins and siblings—by that time, both his parents had remarried, bringing an elder brother and a small sister into the family. He had learned to shut away the unwelcome Essence, and to emulate the others (all of whom were larger save the baby sister) lest he find himself sat on until he learned his place in their order.

His was a happy life, if somewhat rough-and-tumble, for to become trade ship defenders, Ki children had to learn to be resilient.

Nothing changed until his sixth spring, when he pattered into the courtyard, eyes round, to report that the oddest sight had appeared from the harbor road. "Grandmother! It's a monk! I think, though he is not bald atop. There is an *owl* nesting in his hair! He has a donkey, but a hen is riding on it, and he walks beside it with a staff! I'm to say, might he come in?"

"Aish! That is Master Root, here at last. Is there a snake in his beard?"

Little Twelve shook his head, his eyes even rounder. "No snake, Grandmother. I should like to see a snake in his beard," he offered tentatively.

"Then you would be a fool as well as uncouth. Ki men do not put snakes in their beards. No ship captain will accept a man with a snake in his beard, however famed he is with the knives."

Twelve, used to his opinion being summarily squashed, clasped his hands in wordless acknowledgment, then added, "He has two pigeons on one shoulder. On the other his carryall."

"You are to make your very best bow to Master Root," Grandmother Ki stated. "And then you are to say, very politely, if he has a snake anywhere about him, we shall drink tea in the court. If he has no snake, then he may leave the donkey and the birds and enter the house," she added, and she set about boiling water for tea.

"The donkey can come into the court, Grandmother?" Little Twelve asked.

"Yes. If it's the same one he's had for the past twenty-five years, it is a very polite donkey. It will not misbehave in the court. I wish I could say the same for the birds."

Feeling very important, Little Twelve ran out, tough bare feet smacking the tiles, to fetch up before the startling figure, a tall, white-bearded man wearing a robe that might have been that of a monk, or of a traveling scholar, but was so threadbare and sun-dyed and shapeless that color and purpose had diminished to the rags of poverty long ago. The donkey looked as lean and shabby as he did. Only the hen, the pigeons, and the owl were plump.

Master Root entered the courtyard. He and Elder Ki exchanged the bows of gallant wanderers, then Master Root leaned on his staff to admire the peach tree in the center.

"Master Root," Elder Ki said, "please come within."

Master Root tipped his head, then uttered a soft laugh as the owl spread wing and glided up over the roof. "Perhaps we can sit out here under the leaves of this noble tree?"

Elder Ki eyed him. "You *do* have a snake. And I told the boy—"

"Not *a* snake. I did not lie, for I have two, actually," Master Root said. "I'd thought to tease you, but you have treated the sapling I gave you with such care—a reminder of years we will never see again in this life—that I cannot bring myself to it. Though I will remind you that snakes deserve the same respect as any creature."

"And I will maintain that I will respect them anywhere else in the world but in my house, or in my sight," Elder Ki declared.

They sat on the little platform under the tree, Master Root not troubling to wait for a cushion, but dropping with a grunt and a certain crackling of knees to the clean-swept tile. The hen flapped to the ground and began to hunt for bugs and seeds. The pigeons eyed the table as Elder Ki set out the tea and some small cakes, and, seeing nothing appealing, they took off together with a coo and a flutter of feathers to forage for themselves.

The two old friends made ritual enquiries after relations and friends both had known half a century before, and toasted each departed soul with sips of tea, as the donkey nosed the grasses springing up at the edge of the court. The snakes did not appear, but Elder Ki was certain she saw the curve of one around Master Root's arm as he reached for a cake, and she shuddered. At least it was not visible.

Besides, she had a request to make.

"And so we come to the present," she began. "I troubled you with a letter on behalf of the boy there. His mother's great-great-grandmother was a Kwai, and while we Kis are undistinguished, the Kwai family has an ancient and illustrious—"

"Yes," Master Root interrupted with the ease of decades' acquaintance.

"Eh?"

"Yes, I will tutor the boy," Master Root said patiently. "I could feel his Essence potential from down in there in Dawn's Placid Sea. Kwai or no Kwai—though in this instance I believe the claim of inheritance might actually be justified—you were right to send for me. It is time, nearly past time, to train him before he reaches the age to experiment on his own. That much Talent could be disastrous."

"I thought that was only in fire attributes, or metal," Elder Ki protested. "The shaman after he was born insisted he's mainly earth."

"The shaman was correct at the time," Master Root stated, thinking to himself that that shaman had perhaps been tempted to tell these wary Kis what they wanted to hear. Earth talents were always acceptable to those who distrusted Essence abilities, though the Kwai clan's affinities usually tended toward air and fire. "Earth, air, and some wood. Imagine a tree sprouting in the middle of the house. Perhaps an avalanche of soil if someone troubles his temper."

"No," Elder Ki exclaimed, as moral authority shifted from her (still miffed about the snakes) to him. "But...it would be very hard to take him away at so young an age," she added humbly.

"I think so, too. Fear not. I was looking for a place to winter over," Master Root explained. "Master Long-Ears here is getting old, and dislikes being chilled. It isn't good for him to be trudging through snow up here in the north."

Elder Ki gave a nod. "There's a snug cottage back of the bakehouse. It's been empty since Fourth Great-Aunt died in the last Dolphin Year. I can send the older children to scour it out and bring in fresh bed things and dishes. But those birds..."

Little Twelve watched with intense hope as her eyes strayed upward, for though the birds were to her mere vexations whose habits were intolerably untidy, Little Twelve looked upon them with a wild desire for wings.

Master Root raised a hand. "The pigeons prefer the eaves, for choice. And Owl the chimney."

"Then it is yours," Elder Ki promised, with the conviction of a clan elder. "And now we come to what is most important."

"I have to admit some surprise at your writing to me instead of to one of the Essence sects, for you well know I have no interest in the martial skills. My staff, with a little Essence, can send a brigand on the way, but that is the extent of it."

"That is exactly why I thought of you," she said, lowering her voice. "When he goes out, as he must in a few years, I want it to be solely with the skills all the others have. His talent can be used for other ends. Or forgotten altogether, for all of me."

Master Root said, "This much talent is not conveniently stuffed into a jade jar, however much we might wish to have it so."

"Nevertheless," she returned sturdily.

"You know I am no friend to violence," was his answer. "Should you object to it being turned toward music?"

"Music would suffice," she said, contented again as she poured out more of her best Two Moons' Silver Leaf, only used for special occasions. "You know we like to train our youth to a second skill, whether to earn money if stranded, or simply to entertain the company on long voyages. Our Ki defenders are much sought not only for their ability to put away the bow when the wolf is gone, but to pick up a broom or a drum if needed."

"I will do my best," Master Root promised, and after contemplation, decided on a course that would content the wary Ki clan—and also encourage the boy to develop his weakest skills. The strongest would see to themselves.

Two

Like temples, scrapes, villas, palaces and so on, the Ki clan houses were constructed around a square in which training and other activities took place.

In such a small community, it's common to find that what one person knows, everyone knows. There are spheres within that square — the women know things not necessarily shared with the men, and the opposite is true — and children are vitally interested in one another's great affairs, while the doings of the adults to them are as the patterns of the great birds up against the clouds, or the krakens in the sea.

Word spread by nightfall that an Essence master had come, and would teach Little Twelve, who everyone knew had been a bit odd as a baby. That night, many of the children debated including themselves in these lessons, for to them Essence suggested great doings from the legends.

The first night, before Little Twelve slept, the kindly master traced a talisman on his forehead, murmuring words about safety, as a cool sense of fog spread through the boy, an Essence binding against a dangerous affinity for air.

The next afternoon, Little Twelve was accompanied by several siblings and a miscellany of cousins up the path past clumps of graceful, starry clematis, blooming rhododendrons, and the sharp green lines of bamboo stands through which filtered green, autumnal light. The line was led by Twelve's elder brother, and included Fourth Cousin, whose inquisitiveness was unsurpassed on the entire island of Mountain Peony, or so the elders said.

Master Root accepted without comment this sudden

swelling of his instructional responsibilities. "Sit down, youngsters."

They did so expectantly, waiting for demonstrations of fireworks and storms, splintered trees and other Essence spectacles.

"We begin with the definitions," he said. "Now, repeat after me. 'Essence governs the five elements, in both the sun phase—action—and in the moons phase, resting. In light and in darkness.'"

All voices repeated the words obediently. Repetition was not unfamiliar, for the Ki clan insisted that all their defenders be able to read a chart and to write their names, writing being taught through reciting the long poem that covered the first thousand characters.

"Without Essence, no object can exist. Repeat."

"Without Essence, no object can exist," restated the treble voices, though few paid attention to the meaning.

"Essence has no shape or shadow, but everything is made of it. Everything, from the butterfly on a flower to the stars overhead. And so, its fundamental nature is often called Purpose."

They repeated that, too, and waited for the fiery examples and power displays.

There was none. Instead, everyone had to repeat those lines until the smallest of them could stumble through with only a hint or two.

"Living things as well as non-living things, at the moment of their making, receive Essence, so that they may have a form and a nature of their own."

Fewer voices as some blundered over words or concepts, and others' minds wandered: when would they get to see Essence used?

"…and so we come to right. Who can define right?"

Most children looked to Eight, who regarded himself as an authority. "The one who follows the family rules," he stated.

"That is certainly a valuable definition. Is there another?"

"Pardon, Master Root, but how can there be another?" Fourth Cousin asked, rising to clasp her hands and bow. "Is there not one definition?"

"Some may think so," Master Root said. "Which is how you get wars, more often than not. But for our purpose here, permit me to give you my own definition, which is to live in harmony with nature, the seen and the unseen world, and with one another. Repeat that."

And when they had, Eight rose, clasped his hands, bowed, and asked, "What is wrong, then? For if you have a right you have to have a wrong, which in the Ki family is breaking rules."

Master Root clasped his gnarled hands to Eight, then said, "Wrong is to destroy that harmony. We therefore learn how to use Essence and remain in harmony with the world."

They grimly got that out, repeated it—and then had to put together the whole. It took many, many repetitions until the smallest of them had stumbled tediously through it.

And once that was done?

"Now," Master Root said, "we learn to breathe correctly."

At this, Seven rose and clasped his hands. "We already do breathing for our knife forms."

"You do. But that is the breathing used by warriors, which gives you more air for your movements. This is Essence breathing, which is akin, but not the same. Now. Begin with your tongue at the back of your mouth roof, so…"

The following afternoon was more repetition and Essence breathing. After that they learned, line by line, how the realms seen and unseen are connected by ever greater circles within circles, eternally wheeling with the stars overhead.

Master Root talked about bees and butterflies, plants, flowers, fruit, and seeds, explaining how every living thing contains its meed of Essence, from the lowly worm to the immense fire dragons beneath the island. "This is in part why this island is now the empire's capital, did you know that? Because the imperial dragon below Mt. Lir began breathing smoke, until the city was eternally in night."

"*Everyone* knows *that*," Fourth Cousin piped. "It has nothing to do with *us*."

The rest agreed, though not out loud. They were martial artists, and they wanted to see Master Root flying about on his staff, or even without it. They wanted to see him wave up a whirlwind, or throw fire from his fingertips. Best of all would be the dispatch of a demon!

Master Root eyed them sternly. "It's said that Heaven was displeased with the emperor's forebears, which is why the dragon is angry, and there are droughts on some islands, and floods on others. These are things you ought to know, for such things affect trade, and trade has everything to do with you."

Perhaps. But such matters had little to do with sitting quietly, concentrating on their breathing as they tried to sense Essence pooling within them. Especially as most had no more Essence within them than the spark of life shared by all living things. Except for Little Twelve, who had learned early to close the Essence firmly into a box inside him. Of them all, only he and Seven did not stir restlessly.

"Now, back to breathing..."

There were fewer the following day. And the number of children had halved by the time Master Root declared them ready to put what they were learning into practice. Seven and Eight vanished when this first exercise proved to be tootling a flute. After all that talk and talk and talk. Typical of your adult—holding up a honey-cake while handing you medicine!

Little Twelve was now alone. Day after day he struggled with fingering and breath control. But at the end of each lesson, he got to feed a carrot to Long Ears, or to observe Owl, who delighted him by sometimes running on unexpectedly long, feathered legs. And as the days chilled, sometimes he sat very quietly while practicing with the little green snake snug and warm next to his tummy. He learned to move smoothly and gently so as not to startle the snakes.

His days settled into a new routine.

Each morning he stood at the back of the lines of clan members, doing forms in ever increasing difficulty, then sparring with wooden knives, building his spindly, six-year-old strength, stamina, and skill. After other lessons, the youngsters played games that enhanced their training, such as pitch pot, Circle, and stickball. On festival days, they were free to go exploring or down to the lake to play.

No one interfered if a child changed their extra lessons, as long as they chose one. Only Little Twelve remained with Master Root. He struggled to get his fingering correct, playing patterns of notes over and over, just as in the mornings, his body worked through patterns over and over. But Master Root altered the hard lessons with delightful new things, such as describing the ways Owl saw the world, which was different from the pigeons' view.

Twelve learned how to care for Long Ears, and to distinguish among snakes—which ones might be friends and which to leave be—and he learned about lizards and salamanders, both earth ones and fire salamanders, and he even learned something of dragons. "I only know a bit," Master Root said. "Dragons are as hard for us to know as we humans are hard to know for the busy ant. We share the world, but not our lives."

All the while, the boy tried to get unruly fingers to cooperate with the bamboo flute. "This is how you'll learn to use Essence without harming yourself or the world," Master Root said, when his student knotted up, discouraged with fingering and lip-controlled breathing.

One dismal, dripping day, as Twelve swallowed sobs of frustration, Master Root took the bamboo, and played a rippling chord so clean and so pure that the boy's spirits combed smooth again as Owl glided silently overhead. Even the evergreens seemed to listen, stilling their rustle.

"Owl likes music. Many living things respond to music imbued with joyful Essence," Master Root explained. "Essence expressed this way is harmony in sound. Did you feel the Essence in the music?"

"Oh, yes, I did, Master Root! It was like the hottest day, when I fall into the stream by Five Old Stones."

"Very vividly put, my boy. Perhaps one day you might rework the concept into a poem. If it is clever enough, you're sure to earn at least one meal, especially if your handwriting is good enough to inscribe it on a wall to benefit all travelers." He sighed with reminiscence. "Many of my best meals left poems behind me."

Twelve bowed.

Master Root's obedient student applied himself with renewed vigor to his flute—and by New Year's Two Moons, he at last achieved something that he recognized as music, as opposed to a series of laborious notes.

By late spring, Master Root was ready to move on for the warm seasons, leaving Twelve with strict instructions about what he was to achieve on his own. Elder Ki knew that he seldom remained in one place as long as he had, but he made exceptions for pupils who interested him.

She exulted when he returned after harvest; as she had surmised, her Little Twelve was truly a qilin, a wild Talent very rare. Properly trained, he would bring merit to the Ki clan—and with merit came wealth.

Master Root saw that Twelve had practiced assiduously, and awarded him with a Hulusi that he had found on his travels. "I am no professional musician," Master Root explained. "I know no other instruments. I only play the simplest rhythms. But you can safely leave prodigious feats of musical arts to those who play for kings and courts. The rest of the world loves a tune to which one can sing and dance, and which brings cheer and good fellowship for a little while."

Master Root returned three more times. During these half-years, Twelve began to comprehend a little of the language of animals, of birds, and of trees, and even of clouds. Master Root's ever-changing menagerie was the result of coming across creatures needing healing. Once they were restored to health, all except Long Ears and Owl went away again, but there were always more to learn from. The last autumn, when Twelve was approaching his tenth year, Master Root brought with him a shaggy three-footed dog, who promptly burrowed his way into the hearts of all the younger Ki children.

Master Root explained what he did to heal animal, bird, or reptile, and Twelve learned how arm differed from wing, and wing from jointed insect leg; though he had not the vocabulary for such wonders—indeed, many of these lessons occurred without a word spoken—he watched, and listened, and his mind hummed with delight in the intricacies of life, a delight that communicated itself clearly to Master Root, soul to soul.

"I might even get him interested in healing," the old man gloated over tea to Elder Ki, who also gloated at the value such a defender would be aboard a great trader in future. "At least he knows now how to detect natural poisons, and to draw them, and he might soon be able to set a bone in a simple break, easing pain through the acupoints you have taught him. But for real training, you must find a physician."

Elder Ki reflected that these were often to be found on larger ships. Yes, it was time to send Twelve for his first voyage, though he was a couple of years younger than usual.

Meanwhile the lessons extended to herbs and roots and leaves, the feel, the smell, the method of grinding and making medicine, with simple charms to bind and strengthen.

As for Twelve's martial arts, he was slowly working his way along the back of the ranks. Though it seemed he was destined to be short and neat in build, as was his mother and her kin, he made up for that with his quickness and a calmness of temper honed after a lifetime of having to rein and even to suppress his natural instincts. Within his own mind, he had firmly established two separate modes: his martial skills, and his Essence, which he only used when he played his flute, or in making a simple medicine. For the latter, he had no vocabulary outside the spoken charms that helped his mind to bind Essence to ingredients.

When his tenth birthday came and went, he tested with the others deemed ready. The family lit incense to the earth, sea, and sky gods as the Elders formally introduced the family to those who had passed the test, using their birth names. Twelve was now Ki Mek. A good, sturdy, unpretentious name common to those with earth affinities, with its connotation of fertile soil.

And so, Master Root stayed long enough to see his former student cavorting with his age mates as they celebrated the prospect of venturing into the wide world. Then, with some regret, for he'd become fond of the boy, he said his farewell.

Mek bowed to the ground in thanks for his teachings, then offered Master Root a pretty piece on the hulusi to emulate the courtship song of the painted-eye bird; it would not do before a court, but his melody pleased both master and kin.

Then Master Root, Owl, and Long-Ears made their way down the path for the last time, and out of Ki Mek's life—but not out of his memories, as the elders and the chosen cousins and siblings prepared to journey to the harbor at Dawn's Placid Sea.

THREE

MEK WAS MORE DISTRESSED at leaving the dogs than at leaving his family, as his parents and older siblings had been coming and going all his life—in fact Father had been away for half a year, and Mother for longer. Elder Ki had been brisky astringent, having inured her heart to the entirely natural departures of the young since her firstborn had turned her back at sixteen and ventured down the road, then reappeared ten years later with two children at her heels.

For Mek, going into the world also meant getting accustomed to straw shoes even when it was not winter, and having to mind his own clothing. When the departure day dawned, Mek cried a little to leave Yellow and Three-Leg, but he knew that the dogs liked other warm beds to crawl into of a cold night, and other children's kisses on their soft ears, and so he marched off with three uncles, one aunt, and a gaggle of cousins plus one sister. As usual he was the youngest and shortest, his chief thought, as he left his home behind, to wonder how tall he would be when he returned.

When they reached the last bend in the mountain road, below lay most of the northeast coast of Mountain Peony, along with a string of small islands seaward, glinting in the sun like green jade as they stretched away to the east.

"There are the Tiger Isles," Fourth Uncle pointed out. Luckily dour Second Uncle was away in the western sea, along with Twelve's father and the best warriors, so there would be no long lecture about the perfidious Ji family, who governed the Tiger Isles. "Beyond them, the Great Ocean."

"Do the Easterners really have fire instead of hair?" piped

up a twelve-year-old cousin, who had been put up to it by some snickering young teens.

"Fire for hair! How could you show such ignorance? You'd be laughed off your ship! Come, come. You ought to recognize a poetical image by now? How often have you urchins been likened to three rats with four eyes when you squabble among yourselves?"

Resigned, the first timers among the children reflected that once again, nothing the older cousins or siblings told them ought to be believed without testing, and they lost all interest in this uncle's ramblings about his own journeys on the eastern route, in favor of a silent finger game, played as they hopped and skipped along the path.

They camped for the night, and set out at dawn, the children looking forward to the sight of the great harbor, and the delights to be discovered. But as it happened, the trade convoy was nearly complete. To the children's disgust, everything was hurry, hurry, hurry, so as to be well south when the dragon storm season struck.

The result? Mek and his siblings and cousins barely got a sniff of the harbor and its delicious street snacks before they were summarily separated and bundled aboard the various ships, with final exhortations about manners and duty ringing in their ears. His eldest sister Zar was with him along with Cousin Hu, nearly eighteen, both exhorted to keep watch over their younger cousin.

Mek looked about his first ship in curiosity. Talismans streamed from the masts, which were also hung with banners belonging to the convoy as well as the wide-winged blue bird denoting their ship, the *Blue Albatross*. It was a splendid array of colors.

Loud instruments screeched and gongs clashed from the wharf as the anchor was hauled up and the sails raised. Wind filled the battened sails with a clatter, and Mek watched the shore slide away as the wake behind them widened and the ship began to tip and roll. He had his medicinal ginger root ready to hand, but it turned out he had no need for it.

They were putting out to sea!

The elders often repeated that a ship was like a small empire, its captain the emperor, but Ki Mek had by age ten begun to believe that there were emperors everywhere you looked, just called by some other name. Such as brigand captains or mighty heroes in stories, and Second Uncle at home.

He had discussed this once with Master Root, who stroked his beard (momentarily disturbing a pretty striped snake that had been slumbering there) and exclaimed, "Ayah, you have discovered a truth of living in groups. Every wolf pack must have its leader, and every pride of lions its king. Humans are exactly the same."

"Even in temples?"

"Even in temples. No matter how small the group, there is always someone, and sadly, sometimes, more than one someone, who appoints himself the emperor. The matter for contemplation is why others will follow them, even when they display no merit whatsoever. If you do not wish to fall afoul of such persons, or to fall in with them, there are ways to protect your roots while the winds sweep past."

Before the shipmaster beckoned to the newcomers to sort them out, Mek surveyed those his age—and sure enough, he soon spotted the one who wanted to be the emperor. This brawny boy lounged aft, where he could see everything, his expression pugnacious. All the other apprentices faced him.

He spotted Mek the newcomer at once, of course, but waited until the shipmaster brought him over. "Ki Mek, this is Little Tiger, apprenticed to Cargo Boss Shu. He will show you where to stow your things, and explain how we do things aboard the *Blue Albatross*. Little Tiger, this is Ki Mek, son of Defender Ki of the Salamander Convoy on the western route. Saved at least two ships, he did—I was there in the previous Rat Year, when Western raiders tried to take us. Look out well for his boy."

The master then waved Mek toward Cargo Boss Shu's apprentice, and trod forward again to far more important matters.

"I'm *Tiger*," the elder boy stated truculently, scorning the *Little*. "How old are you? Six?"

"Ten," Mek said, remembering Zar's warnings: watch for insults just to see if they can get a rise out of you.

"I'm *fifteen*." Tiger eyed this runty Mek: short, light, but unafraid. You'd expect that of a Ki. Nor had he showed any reaction to being likened to a six-year-old. Tiger knew—as did the entire trade world—that the Ki clans were ship defenders, and lucky the ship to get them. So, though this boy was the youngest of them all, and probably only carried wooden knives, those knives would be sharp, and he would be trained well before being permitted on board.

Best to test right now, and get him in his place.

He lunged forward, aiming a slap at Mek, who stepped out of range, and when Tiger followed the slap with a blow from the other hand, Mek ducked that, too. But he didn't attack.

Two or three more exchanges, Mek always a finger's breadth out of reach, and Tiger halted, scowling. "Aren't you going to try to hit me?"

"If you want me to," Mek said.

Tiger's thick brow met over his flat nose. Tiger did not shout in rage or try to leap on Mek; there was little glory in that, as Mek was so much smaller. This was solely a matter of place.

The boy waited, straw-shod feet well planted, hands loose at his sides.

"I dare you," Tiger stated, clarifying matters: this was going to go on until one or the other made contact.

Mek did not want to be on the receiving end if he could avoid it. This time, when Tiger came on, Mek whirled, blocked, and sidestepped, then added a finger-flick to the exact spot on the elbow joint that sent stars shooting across Tiger's vision as pain seized up his arm for a few heartbeats.

Tiger regarded Mek warily, hazily reflecting that Mek could have just as easily flicked his nose—even more painful—or another more vulnerable body part. Both boys were aware that a serious fracas among the apprentices would not be welcomed by their elders, and decided at the same time to tolerate the other, unless Mek were to offer a challenge that he had no intention of giving.

"Come along. You'll be belowdecks in the hole with the rest of us," Tiger said, pointing to the hatch. On their way, Tiger pointed out people and things of importance, that is, from the perspective of fifteen.

The "hole" was a narrow compartment with a platform much like the one Mek had slept in. The boys had one side and the girls the other, with a thin partition between.

Back on deck, Tiger passed by a boy roughly between their ages, who hung head and shoulders over the side of the rail.

"Sick?" Mek asked, pointing.

Tiger lifted a shoulder in the gesture that meant, *who cares?* "He's a passenger," Tiger said dismissively. "We treat them like ghosts."

A girl ran by, skipping up the stairs to the command structure. "That's Ha Nua, the navigator's daughter." She ignored the boys.

Next was a comprehensive tour of the ship. Mek learned by sight the three most important beings aboard the ship: the captain, the navigator, and the ship's master.

When that was over, a gong clanged, announcing mealtime. Passengers joined the captain and his officers first, after which the crew was fed, and finally the youngsters. If most of the tasty treats like candied haws and fruit desserts were scant pickings by then, there were plenty of noodles, swimming in a sauce filled with greens and slivers of grilled fish. In any case, the fruit things would be the first to vanish from the board until they touched at the next harbor, Mek had been told. "Get used to going without," Cousin Hu had advised. "You'll get a part of your pay for your liberty watch, and you'll be able to stuff yourself sick on sweets then."

Mek accepted with resignation the sight of the empty bowl with mere scrapings of plum sauce, and later, heard without demur that he was expected to run messages, fetch, and carry for the morning watch, which began at the last Tiger Hour, before Phoenix First Hour. That meant rising well before dawn.

Thus his first voyage began pretty much as predicted. Cousin Hu made sure he was on deck for drill each morning at Last Phoenix, and Zar kept a distant but watchful eye to make certain that he was eating well, keeping himself tidy, and comporting himself properly.

Two gongs past noon, he was free.

He noticed within a day or two that that same silk-clad boy was invariably at the side, bent so far over Mek had yet to see his face. He finally asked Ha Nua who the boy was; Ha Nua ignored the boys generally, but Mek had seen that the girl unbent if asked specific questions.

"He's Je Tai."

"Tye?" Mek repeated, unsure of her slurring accent.

"*Ta. Ee.* A two-character personal name, as he's a cousin to the Ji family of Tiger Islands," Ha Nua said with a slight emphasis on each name. "The 'ee' is a generational name from their patriarch's clan poem," she went on rather self-importantly. "He was home for mourning, but now he's on his way back to White Jade, where the augurs now train." She scurried off.

When Mek's watch was over, he made his way to the side, and poked Tai, whose head turned. He was taller than Mek (everybody in the world was), with a sharp chin and a long body much like a noodle.

Mek said diffidently, "I have a ginger twist my grandmother made, against sea sickness. I won't need it. If you'd like it, you can have it."

Tai said in a flat voice, "I'm not sick." He turned back to his perusal of the waves splashing against the hull.

Mek shrugged, and when he was summoned to take a jug of water up to the captain, ran off.

Clear sailing, with every day warmer than the one before as they scudded southward. One stop, two, always out in the bay, which meant merely a tide's stay, and the only liberty the important people. Then word spread that the next stop would be at Te Gar. This time the ship paid for a berth, which meant a ramp to a pier instead of waiting on a boat to row to shore.

When the island rose on the horizon, Zar swooped out of nowhere, grabbing him by the topknot. "Mek, if you're wise, you'll keep your tinnies until we get to the Jade Islands, which are far better than Te Gar. But you'll probably waste your pay in this stupid place. All the babies do, once."

With that, she was off again, laughing and whispering with Ha Nua.

The captain declared that the night watch would be permitted to go ashore first. Mek toiled with the unlucky watch in hauling bales and barrels off the ship to the shore, then bringing aboard more goods as passengers came and went. He heard scraps of talk about dragon skies to the southeast, and blood sunsets, never an auspicious sign.

The morning watch was permitted the remainder of the afternoon for liberty. And, as promised, the shipmaster's apprentice gave him ten tinnies toward his earnings. With this wealth in his inner pocket, he ignored Zar's advice and followed a party ashore, for he wanted land beneath his feet, a feeling he could scarcely put words to. The sense of solid ground beneath him heartened him greatly as he walked up Prince Ratha's Miracle Victory Way, the main street running parallel to the shoreline.

So many sights! Acrobats tumbling, musicians playing and singing, street vendors crying their wares. He squandered three tinnies on a stick of candied haws, which he'd never had before, but saw in the hands of many children. They were as delicious as they looked. He munched them slowly, getting at least ten silver taels' worth of pleasure out of the candy as he viewed the parading approaches of the grand carriages of the wealthy, and gazed at bowing scholars with their long sleeves and the breeze-tossed ribbons in their hair as they conversed in tea shops.

When the great drums boomed from the garrison, followed by the bong of an unseen bronze bell, he ran back to the wharf, and joined the last of the liberty crew and passengers before the *Blue Albatross* lifted anchor and sailed out to rejoin the rest of the convoy bobbing on the sea. Exulting, he deposited his remaining seven tinnies in his carryall, along with his other set of clothes, his bamboo flute, and his practice knives.

By nightfall, he became aware of frowns and harsh words among many of the adults. He waited until the evening meal bell, and caught Cousin Hu on his way to the crew's mess down below. "What's wrong?"

Cousin Hu scowled. "We've a *week* added on. A week at least, depending on the wind, all because some rabbit was bleating about demon storms south of the imperial island. We're to go the long way about, then beat back eastward again to the Jades."

"Oh."

Cousin Hu turned away abruptly, leaving Mek standing on the gangway. He shrugged inwardly. A week or even more made no difference to him—he was far from bored. Though the ship's world was even smaller than the Ki enclave had been, the ship's routine was still interesting. There was so much to see, and to hear!

He was especially enchanted to discover that a person could climb to the roof of the superstructure, where he could sit and practice his flute without disturbing anyone; by now he'd discovered that there were far more facile players aboard, whose melodies made his own sound simple. He was far too shy to offer to play for the company.

He could also work on his forms up there, balancing on his hands in the continual rocking, without catching scornful comments by the ship's boys. He could view the sea and the sky in all directions unimpeded, and best of all, he could lie flat and relish the exhilaration of seabirds in flight. How they soared! They seemed to hang in the air, except for a minute flick of a tail feather here, then there, before suddenly banking and shooting down alongside the hull to catch a flying fish. If he concentrated on them, his body felt oddly light, almost as if he might be able to fly with them.

Once he watched a pair of enormous albatrosses riding the glowing air currents, their gray wings outstretched, feathers barely lifting. They were so close and for a time one was so still that he could see a sapient eye surrounded by white feathers viewing him with calm complacence, before the bird veered away and dove down toward the sea.

Mek followed its dive, catching sight of Je Tai below — and it was then that he discovered what the other boy had been doing all this time. He was feeding sea creatures. *Big* ones.

Mek was so surprised that he gave in to impulse and leaped down, still feeling that deceptive lightness. Deceptive as for one heart-stopping instant he began to fall, but then instinct flared through him, airy as a fresh and powerful breeze, and he landed lightly on the gangway three stories below — after which he clutched at the rail, dizzy for a shuddering breath or two.

Tai recoiled a step back. "Where did you come from?" he uttered flatly.

Mek ignored the question. "That fish! The one you were throwing food to. It's too big to be a dolphin!" And too blunt of face, he was going to add, standing on the tips of his toes as he tried to look down over the rail. Annoyingly, he was exactly a finger's breadth too short.

Tai said, "It's a baby scholar whale."

"Scholar whale?"

Tai gestured toward his forehead, mimicking a bulge. "A scholar's brain. Or so our forebears thought. Gray, for the robe of the untested scholar. Other whales have different faces. Some are black. Some white. Or spotted." He said all this in a monotone.

Je Tai turned back to the rail as his hand dipped into a pouch at his side, then his shoulders slumped. "You scared it away."

"Won't it come back?" Mek guessed. "That is, is it the same one that you've been feeding?"

"I share with anyone who comes alongside," Tai said.

"They're curious. Mostly dolphins," he added. "And there's an orca. Keeps coming back. Likes to catch anchovies." Tai mimed tossing something into the air.

"I want to throw an anchovy to an orca," Mek said at once.

"Pay the net crew. Same as I do." Tai said this with no animosity, but no encouragement, either. "But if you get caught at it, the ship master will scold. They don't like drawing the big whales. Say they bump the ships. They call it an attack."

"Why do you do it?"

"Because I don't believe whales attack unless you attack them first." There was almost feeling in that declarative, then Tai was back to his flat monotone. "That orca knows me. That is, he knows to come when he sees me. Why would he attack when he likes to catch anchovies?"

"You know a lot about the deeps?" Mek guessed.

"At home." Tai was definitely morose, now. "When we visited Tiger Island in summer, I mostly watched the dolphins play. Before I was sent to White Jade."

"Mek! Water to the cabin!"

"The cabin" meant the captain's cabin, up on the third story. Mek ran off to replenish the water always kept on the boil, and then he asked one of the net crew who caught the fish for the cooks how much for a bowl of anchovies — to discover that he hadn't half the amount.

He turned away, thinking that he could watch, at least, even if he couldn't toss the anchovies himself. But the next time he was free, and saw Je Tai at his place by the rail, Tai merely stood there. Since Mek couldn't see over the rail, he hustled to the roof — and it was clear that no fishes, big or small, were rising to the surface.

One more day, the same. Mek sat back on the roof, disappointed with the lack of fish, and with the color of the sea, which to him seemed a sickly sort of greenish gray, with very dark undertones. The waves were coming in low triplets, how very odd. The sky remained blue, though hazy in the east, as if a thumb had smudged the air between sea and the heavens.

He didn't want to practice hand-walking. Or even playing his flute. It was very hot all of a sudden. Even the fretful wind seemed hot. By the time the last meal of the day had been served, he found himself catching at bowls and cups to keep them from sliding off the table, and when he went up to the deck, it was to witness so lurid a sunset, streaked with layers of bruise-colored clouds, that the light itself seemed poisoned. Everyone's complexion looked bleached, or perhaps that was worry, as the crew went about tying everything firmly down.

He retired with the other apprentices, his ears ringing with the harsh warning that they ought to "Get what sleep you can. All hands might be summoned earlier than later."

So far, no one under fifteen had been expected to respond to "all hands," people his size being regarded as mostly in the way. The news that every pair of hands might be required sobered Mek—especially as the rolling slant of the ship was sharper than it had ever been.

He was deep in a dream when the world dissolved into omnipresent roar, as if a thousand dragons bellowed from heavens to deep in the sea. The ship jolted and shuddered, its slant so steep that the boys slid off their platform to fall in a heap.

They disentangled themselves in the total darkness, feeling for clothing. Mek was shocked to discover water washing about their feet. His hands shook as he pulled on sodden clothing. He gave up trying to find his straw shoes, and followed Tiger by hanging onto the back of his clothes. Slam! Smack! The pitch flung them against hard surfaces; no longer could he discern up and down.

He tried to quiet the frantic tattoo of his heart by feeling the solidity of the wood around him. Wood floats, he reminded himself. This ship has weathered storms. He'd listened to how many stories about that, mere days ago?

He could hear nothing but the roar. Someone put a mouth to his ear, shouting, "All hands!" and then lurched away.

Where was he to go now? Tiger had shaken him violently off, or maybe that was the motion of the sea-tossed ship. He tried to find his place by feel, until a jittering lance of blue-white lightning revealed the ladder to the hatch over that way, but on its side. No, he was crawling over a wall, and sliding constantly...

He finally reached the ladder, just to be shoved back again. In another flare of lightning he barely recognized Cousin Hu's face, distorted by his effort to be heard over the roar, as shattered light glittered in his wet skin, hair, and clothes: "No! Go below, forward compartment! Wind will snatch you away if you come on deck—"

Someone shoved past, and Mek bounced painfully off a

surface, and landed with a splash in the swirling water. A hard hand hauled him upright and flung him out of the way as two unknown figures dashed for the ladder—which was again sideways in the flickering glare.

Someone else elbowed him into a space. He remembered then that he could think a light into the cup of his palm. By its light he caught sight of Tai's frightened face as he lay sprawled against barrels shifting and bumping one another. He recognized this space, from helping with loading and unloading. At least he'd managed to reach the proper place: they were the only two under fifteen.

He doused the light again, and felt his way toward a barrel to lean against when a rending crash flung Mek on top of Tai, then the two recoiled into the compartment door as the world splintered around them, hurling them upward.

In purple-white light Mek saw barrels tumble slowly end over end down toward the black sea as he hung in the air, fingers scraping the door so hard that splinters drove beneath his nails. Awareness flashed over him: his hand, numb lips, a grip on his ankle, Tai's face lengthened in a soundless scream.

We mustn't fall, Mek thought—and so strong was his conviction that with a long, shuddering indrawn breath, he pulled at the wind rushing under the compartment door, spinning him high, then higher into the air, with Tai rigid at his feet.

Water dragons streamed around and over them, drawing screeching strings of wind imps thinned to ghost-glow by the racing gusts. Higher still they spun. A jerk on Mek's clothes, and Tai grasped a handful of Mek's tunic. Then his arm, and held there, gripping so tight Mek's arm tingled as his body thumped against the spinning wood.

"We're in the air," he said, or tried to say, but his lips were too numb, and whirling imps snatched away the sound of his voice.

"We'll fall," he bleated.

And they did.

FOUR

A TICKLE AGAINST MEK'S nose roused him. Everything hurt. Including breathing. Strong morning light stabbed when he tried to open his eyes, and his gritty eyelids closed again.

He groaned. Memory: falling end over end as he tried to find that wind again, but it pushed and pulled and writhed like an angry snake, and he tumbled harder, until he crashed into mighty-boled trees whose broken, rain-wet leaves filled his nose with the strong scent of cold medicine.

He'd slammed through branches until he thumped to the sand in a shower of wind-driven leaves…

Another tickle against his nose was accompanied by a tiny bump against his forehead.

He cracked an eye open, to find himself eye to eye with a…
Turtle?

He sat up slowly, ignoring the crashing in his head as he looked down at several small turtles heading in various directions, little feet barely making an imprint in the sand.

He stared at them, scarcely aware of hunger amid his many hurts. What did Master Root say about baby turtles? They go down to the sea as soon as they hatch, which happens at night. But many of these little turtles made their frantic, unsteady way along the beach, up a nearby sand dune from which tufts of grass grew, and one was heading for the woods farther up on land. Mek blinked at utterly unfamiliar trees, then carefully thumbed the sand from his eyelids.

"Turtles," he muttered.

"Uhn."

Mek turned, and there, maybe thirty paces away, lay a

huddle of torn silk. Only the top of his head was visible, black hair escaping from a jade clasp. Mek recognized that silk, and the jade. That was Je Tai! Alive?

Mek crawled painfully over the white sand toward Tai, who groaned, then pushed himself slowly up on one hand. He blinked around, lifting a shaking finger to touch the side of his face, cruelly scraped by twigs. Blood glinted sluggishly through a rent in his silk sleeve.

Mek looked down at himself, and discovered tears, scrapes, and his fingernails rimed with dark red. As soon as he looked, the wounds began to throb to the same rhythm as the pounding in his head.

"No!" Tai croaked suddenly, and lunged up, flapping one arm. He fell back as an enormous bird veered away, squawking, and glided slowly around, head moving minutely as it surveyed the beach.

"It's going to eat the little turtles," Tai said, with more expression than Mek had ever heard from him. "They ought to've come out at night."

Mek said, "I thought so, too."

Tai turned a pained expression his way. "You don't understand. It was us. When we fell. We—our impact. Must have shaken the ground. Hard enough to crack the shells?" As he spoke, he roused himself to hands and knees, then stood, swaying. "We must make a trail."

Still fuzzy in mind, Mek looked about at the little turtles going off in all directions. A couple had even fallen over, tiny legs wiggling in the air. To be just born, and then snapped up to death before living so much as a day? Je Tai was right.

Mek rolled to hands and knees, rose, tottered a few steps, and reached down to turn the nearest turtle proper side to. It seemed a long, long downward reach, as if his legs had grown tall as a tree. He lifted his head and gazed slowly around to steady himself, to see a number of huge birds circling in the air, or perched on branches farther up the strand. Then he turned over the two other turtles that had managed to flip themselves belly-side up

"Go! Eat something else," Tai shouted, flapping his sleeves, then he stooped over and began scraping the still-wet sand in a long line toward the lapping waves.

"What are you doing?" It even hurt to speak.

Tai looked up, his forehead puckered against his own

headache. Though he was taller, at nearly fourteen, in those sodden silks he seemed less of a noodle and more of a twig. "Put...the turtles...here."

Mek began to gather up the little wanderers. He set them down on the path Tai scraped, aimed small heads toward the sea, then stumbled up the dunes to catch those fleeing in the wrong direction. Tai had finished his makeshift path, and lurched about, nudging turtles in the right direction with finger and embroidered toe.

Mek did the same, until they got them all pattering onto the wet sand at last, and swarming down to the water. Small heads and shells bobbed, then the turtles vanished, as the two boys stood on the sand watching.

"They'll swim now," Tai said, and added reflectively, "They are born knowing how to swim, whereas we have to learn and it takes ages."

It was a statement reflecting the precise and benign dispositions of Order, but to Mek it was merely stating the obvious. "Will sharks get them? Or do they have aunties and uncles to watch for them?"

"Don't know what happens now—I've only seen the great turtles that are years old, and that merely twice. I do think we ought to go away from this sand." Tai mopped at his face with his salt-encrusted sleeve, then winced. "There's got to be more nests along here. We shook that one loose with our impact. We shouldn't be here."

They began walking slowly up the beach toward the larger dunes. Now that the excitement of turtle rescue was over, Mek's various hurts clamored anew. Along with thirst and hunger. He was still a little dizzy. Slivers of memory intruded, of turning end over end through the air. Abruptly he sat down on a dune, his empty stomach heaving.

When that passed, leaving him clammy and miserable, he looked away, fighting tears. There was no lesson for being thrown into the sky, then falling down again somewhere unknown. But he'd learned very early that crying was useless. "Ki defenders don't cry," Elder Ki had said many times in those early days. "They do their duty. That's why we are first in demand by all the most prestigious trade companies."

What was his duty now? "Water," he muttered. At least there was a lesson for that. Look for the tallest trees closest together, Master Root had said.

Thirst, worsened by the vile taste in his mouth, forced Mek to rise again. He stumbled wearily in the direction of those tall, bright green trees over there, until Tai—heading for the shade of the trees—called, "Where are you going?"

Mek tried to answer, but speaking took too much effort.

Tai changed direction to follow uncertainly. It seemed to take forever to trudge up the strand, then to thread among the huge rocks until he reached firm ground. A little strength seemed to seep up from that familiar solid ground, and he began his Essence breathing, semi-conscious of reaching for more Essence from the deep, patient earth beneath his spread toes.

There it was! Essence tingled from soles to legs and upward until it cleared his head a little, though it didn't do anything for the cuts and bruises. At least his stomach settled enough for him to move again, gradually working up the land toward a cluster of trees not far distant.

When they drew near, they heard the rushing of water, a tumbling stream full after the storm that had brought them. Mek ran down and splashed into the cold water, dipped his hands, and drank. Dip, drink, dip, drink, until he had drunk enough. Tai had stopped a little way along, his fine embroidered shoes with the toes turned up muddy and wet. He leaned out on a flat rock, his sleeves dragging over it as he dipped his hands to drink.

Mek said, "You didn't hear any of the others around us?"

Tai swung about to stare at him. "What others?"

"The ship's people." Mek sat on the bank of the stream. He was shivering now. "Do you think the ship broke up into pieces and everybody drowned?" He thought of his sister, and his cousin, and even Tiger, who wasn't any worse than Eight and his ready slaps and kicks.

"No." Tai stared into the air. "Unless another ship struck, too."

"Too? What do you mean, too?"

Tai considered what to say. His craving for order had been shaped by rigorous tutoring in the heavenly stems and phases, the twelve Houses, the weaving patterns of the two moons, counterpoint to one another, balanced by the sun, and by the spheres of seasons, days, the five elements that governed those seasons and days. Hours within the days. The entire world a perfect, pure order—except when the underworld burst through, flinging ghosts and demons and elements of chaos like rocks hurled into a placid lake.

Within that framework, Tai had fitted the ceaseless calculation going on in his head, a calculation so quick and so constant he could seldom find the words to express a small part of it.

He tried. "The other ship struck at an angle. Or we would be dead. You and I were in the farthest forward compartment. The ship striking sheered off the bow."

Mek remembered the utter bewilderment of that darkness. "How do you know? I was there with you. No one told us that."

"By the impact. By how the splinters flew." Tai's cold-mottled hand chopped vaguely, his nails, Mek saw for the first time, bitten down, the skin around them reddened and rough. "By the direction. That side, then that way." He waved a hand.

"Then…everyone on deck at the front end. That is, forward. They must have…"

Tai said, "They would have seen it coming. We couldn't. They put us where they thought we were safest." He turned to eye Mek. "The ship that struck us might have been another in our convoy. But I can't explain the air."

"Air?"

"The compartment door is what we landed on. It whirled up into the *air*. That might have been the impact. But then it *flew*. With. The. Wind." Tai bit off every word to emphasize the effrontery of a door that flew, against all proper order. Inanimate things' first property was to go down if dropped, not up. "Unless that door had charms worked in, there isn't a way that happens. Unless you did it."

"I—I don't know," Mek said finally, though he was aware of a pulse of memory, of wanting to rise above the crashing, smashing world, and pulling on the wind the way he pulled Essence into his flute to make harmony. But thinking about that made his head throb worse. "Where do you think we are? How will they find us?"

Tai heard the wobble in his voice, but said nothing. He had learned very early that when people tried to hide crying, they did not want it to be pointed out. It was one of the countless little signs in the art of augury that made him most uneasy: how to read humans. Reading stars was so very much easier.

As always, he took refuge in what he knew. "Those were camphor laurels we crashed through. Did you smell them?"

"Like medicine and incense," Mek said. "But we don't have them in Mountain Peony."

"On the northern slopes of the larger island some grow," Tai countered. "They're mostly known in the north. And also in the far west, where the barbarian galleys plague the seas, our schoolmaster once said."

"West. I remember my Cousin Hu saying we had to sail west. Then back again."

"We did sail west. The storm pushed us more west. I don't know how far we were carried on that wind." Tai pointed toward the tangle of roots and trees farther downstream. "Those are redbark trees."

The telltale bark did look familiar. "I thought redbarks only grew on mountains," Mek said, remember Master Root's lessons.

"That is the mountain species. Those are the water species." Tai lifted his chin. "Redbarks always grow in families, which is why Kanda calls them sacred. But we won't find anything to eat on them. I think I smell persimmon…" He halted.

Mek also stopped, head cocked slightly. Voices! "They've come back for us," he breathed, filled with joy.

Tai was going to protest, but hesitated. Just because it felt as if that dragon wind had blown them across the sky from rim to rim didn't mean it had actually happened, without trustworthy evidence to support the impression. Human senses could be fooled.

Anyway, Mek was scrambling back up the little ridge, waving his arms. "Here we are!" he shrilled.

With Tai trailing him, he tumbled down toward the white sand beach, then stopped when he saw a group of adults, some hauling a cart. Their dark heads looked odd, too small and too round; as they neared, he realized that they were bareheaded, with their hair cut short about their ears. His worried gaze stayed on the wicked curves of the glinting spear blades that some held.

But then the leader of the party took the two of them in — two battered, sodden youngsters — and made a sign with her hand. The spears lowered.

Mek blinked at a grandmotherly woman who had a livid mark on her forehead. In fact, they all did. Those were tattoos! Some much larger than others. The woman's looked kind of like a character and kind of like a flower.

She barked something at the boys, as they stared back uncomprehending.

The woman looked around, and called something else in a question-tone, her hands open as she swept it toward the sea and around.

"I think she might be asking if there is anyone with us," Tai stated as he joined Mek.

"What language is that?" Mek asked. "Is it a dialect?"

A pair of husky men reached them then. They were each hoisted up under a muscular arm, and dropped into the cart. Mek saw a basket of blankets, a jug, and caught a whiff of something spicy that made his stomach waken. But no one offered them any of these things. And when Mek reached for a blanket, he was pushed to the back of the cart.

"I think," said Tai, "these are Westerners. And we are now prisoners."

FIVE

THE CART BUMPED AND jolted through the aromatic camphor forest, cold drops splat-splatting from ancient branches tangled overhead, until the party reached a smooth road. The spear men marched next to those pulling the cart via ropes attached to yokes worn over their shoulders.

Mek and Tai shivered as the sun dropped westward, taking with it the mild warmth. Tai looked longingly at the things in the baskets, but after having been dissuaded, he did not try again, used as he was to the sharp-honed, subtle tortures of his cousins in the primary family. Mek looked about him with interest. They seemed to be heading toward a mountain. No, a palace. No, a...

He nudged Tai, and the tired, bewildered boys stared, trying to make sense of their first sight of a Dragon Empire fortress. These were built in burnt-out volcanos wormed by ancient lava tubes that had been smoothed out centuries before. All the tubes that opened to the air had balconies built around them, topped by lanterns now glowing in the twilight. At the very top, a building emerged from the long-dead cone with upturned corners at the eaves, though these were exaggerated, so that the entire eave formed a curve, resembling the horns of a beast.

The whole looked intimidatingly alien to the salt-bleared eyes of the two boys, for this fortress was neither wholly building nor landscape but an incomprehensible combination of both.

That impression intensified as they drew near. Both were startled by the sudden appearance of huge birds—taller than the men pulling the cart — who ran by on long legs. Mek turned to watch them, fascinated. They had three toes, and a single feathery curl sticking up from the short feathers on their small heads. Their necks were a deep blue, the feathers shading lighter and longer toward their big bodies, whose shape resembled a rutabaga turned on its side. Their wings were very short, fluttering as the birds crossed the path and vanished beyond ferny plants and date trees.

When the cart reached the fortress, the main company separated off, including the woman in charge. That left the carters and a single pair with spears to escort the boys through a barred gate and well-guarded tunnel, down and down into a vast cavern about whose walls platforms had been chiseled, along with doors.

Mek sensed someone outside the Essence door in his mind. Master Root had taught him during their first winter together that it wouldn't be so hard to keep from dream-traveling if he made a good, sturdy door inside his head. He could be on one side, and on the other, the rest of the world. When he went to sleep at night, he would remind himself of that closed door. If someone waited outside to speak to him, he could open the door if he chose.

They'd practiced that. If he wanted to talk to Master Root on the other side, he only had to knock on the door, thinking of Master Root. Then, perhaps, Master Root would open his own door. Or not. If Master Root did not answer, Mek had to leave the door alone, exactly as he must not trouble an elder in a house who did not wish to be disturbed.

For the first time in his life, somebody was outside his mental door. He was curious, but that word "prisoners" was a weight in his middle. He wouldn't open the door.

The cart stopped and people wearing dull brown appeared. Their clothes didn't fold over and tie at the hip, another reminder to the apprehensive boys that they were far beyond home.

The crowd parted for an emperor, from the look of her. Because everybody, even the ones with spears, bowed their heads and crossed their hands over their chests as this woman said something. She, unlike the others, wore a tall hat. Her brown clothes had gold worked in down the arms, and there was a golden glint in a carved wooden tally that she carried.

She snapped her fingers, and from a tunnel scurried a wiry

old man with more wisps of hair coming out of his ears than grew on his head. He had a very faded forehead tattoo that looked like a character, though not one Mek knew.

At a gesture from the hat woman, this old man said in a heavy accent, "You're to be examined by the Heir." At least they understood him.

They climbed many stairs, flanked by the spear bearers and the old man, until they stopped outside a door carved with figures of warriors, weapons, and symbols. Some of these wiggled in a sickening way. Mek sensed Essence in them.

He took in the chamber, which had been carved from living rock—still very much a part of earth, as opposed to stones that had been cut out. His inner balance steadied. This had to be a chamber belonging to a very important person. Beautiful golden candleholders shaped like elongated swans sat at either side of very low couch whose edges had been carved with racing hounds, also elongated, and gilt. Most of the decorative designs were squares and circles doubled and overlaid in pleasing patterns.

On the couch, amid a welter of richly embroidered fabrics, sat a girl who appeared to be Tai's age. One hand rested against a half-sized staff carved of wood, with a golden oriole at the top, its wings swept back. Her wide blue eyes gazed somewhere between Tai and Mek as she spoke to the old man.

The man's eyes were seamed at the corners, his bushy eyebrows lifted in question as he said with a very heavy accent, "You boys are Muds? What they call the imperials. How did you arrive on this island?"

"We are from the Empire of the Thousand Isles," Tai said. "There was a shipwreck and we were thrown clear."

"You fell out of the sky?" the man asked, his voice wheezy.

"I guess we did," Mek said, wincing at a vivid image of crashing through layers of leaves.

"The Heir wishes to know if Dragon Father sent you."

"Who?"

With a quick look toward the hat woman, the old man said, "What they here in the Dragon Empire call the Jade Emperor." He glanced skyward. "Heaven."

"We were in the wind," Tai said. "Not heaven."

Mek wondered if he ought to say he remembered water and air dragons in the wind with them, but the girl was talking.

The old man bowed very low to her, hands crossed on his

breast, then turned back to the boys. "The Heir wishes to know if you come from families of important rank among the barbarians." He added very quickly, in almost a whisper, "There will be another seer, who detects lies."

"I am Je Tai. My father is a magistrate," said Tai. Then, "We're a side branch, separated by six generations, from the Ji family, whose title is prince of the third rank." His hand rose and he bit absently at his raw, reddened thumbnail, then he seemed to recollect himself and lowered his hand.

"Is that important enough for you to be ransomed?" the old man asked.

Tai's gaze dropped; he would not be so unfilial as to trouble his father, who might have to borrow from their Ji relatives. Who might humiliate Father by refusing to lend him the fortune that no doubt these wicked folk would demand. "No. I think it unlikely that anyone will ransom me."

The old man turned to Mek, who said, "I'm Ki Mek, and we in the Ki clan don't recognize imperial rank. We work on traders," he added, remembering Second Uncle saying, *If you are ever captured by the Ghost-Eyes, if you tell them you're a warrior, they will either kill you outright, or put you in their fighting ring and lay wagers on how long it takes for you to die. You always say you're a sailor, or a cook, or a farmer.* "I don't know about ransom. But my cousin or my sister on the *Blue Albatross* will know for certain," he added doubtfully.

"Is that a warship?"

"No, a trader." Both boys' voices clashed.

The old man translated, and the tall hat woman murmured something to the Heir, who tapped the short staff on the carpeted floor. The hat woman pointed her tally at someone behind Mek and Tai, who ran out as if chased.

The Heir spoke, and then the old man: "We shall find that ship."

For the third time, Mek sensed someone at his mind's inner door, almost a pressure. But he was very well practiced at keeping the door shut.

One more short speech, then the old man said, "I am to say, the law is clear. If you cannot be ransomed, then you become slaves."

Mek and Tai both stared witlessly. Slaves!

They were then turned over to the spearmen, who took them back down that long tunnel, down and down to a dank-smelling stone environment. Presently they were shut into a barred cell. It was bare, with a drain hole in one corner, below which they could hear the trickle of running water. It clearly emptied to a night soil collection of some sort. The light was very dim and uneven, a reflection from a torch out of sight.

They sank down side by side with their backs to the rough stone wall. Mek was trying not to cry, though his chest shuddered and his chin wobbled. Tai's mind had frozen in some vast shadow place, with no escape, no succor. It was too much like the first time his Ji First Cousin had closed him into a wardrobe and locked the door.

There was no sound other than the tiny click of Tai's teeth as he worried at his cuticles. Mek ground his chin into his knees, his toes spread on the rough, somewhat mossy floor of the cell. Master Root spoke in memory, *Trying to resolve a problem with a knotted heart and mind is like boiling dumplings in a teapot: you will never get them out in order to eat them.*

This was the time he needed Essence breathing the most, he reminded himself. And made himself begin. One. Two, three, softly at first. Ayah! Even in the fortress of the enemy, he could still find the unending quiet of the earth! Down and down his awareness sank. There was no dragon below, but before going wherever dragons go, it had left a pool of molten rock that worked its way up in heat and steam.

Cradled by that unchanging peace, he sank into slumber and slept hard until noise outside the barred cell shocked him to wakefulness. In came someone bearing a jug of water and a couple of steamed buns that turned out to be cold, hard, and stale.

They were left alone again. They shared the water, then Tai sat back, his eyes closed. His hands fell to his lap, one holding his bun.

Mek looked down at his, which was slippery with residue fish oil. Small bits of spiced fish had been mixed into it, along with egg. Not unfamiliar. He bit into it. Hard and stale, but his stomach roared for something to be put in it, and he began to chew determinedly at the bun as Tai just sat.

When Mek had finished his, he looked at Tai, who hadn't moved. "You ought to eat. We have to be ready for whatever comes next."

Tai looked at the younger boy, who came from defenders. "What ought we to do?"

Mek said, "I don't know." Elder Brother had said once, *Even when there are tigers in the walls and rats in the temples a Ki fights to the end.* Second Uncle had exhorted them time after time, *If you see the Lord of the Underworld coming for you, why go easy?* Mek added, trying to bolster his own resolve, "If they try to execute us, I'll fight."

If he might have to try to defend himself, he had to be ready. He got up, and in spite of his healing bruises and cuts, began to move very slowly. Yes, this was the right thing to do, and not only because of the threat. It hurt to move, but it was the good kind, the one that comes after effort. That ache made you stronger.

There was not much space in the cell, but the Ki clan had a drill for shipboard that accounted for lack of space. The knots smoothed as his muscles warmed up, and he began knife practice with the utmost vigor until his breath came short and he'd warmed all over. Since he couldn't spar—Tai didn't look like he could stand up for very long—Mek tried walking on his hands from bars to wall and back again, until his arms trembled.

When he sat down again, he said, "May I finish the water? Half."

Tai turned his head slowly. Stiffly. As if that took all the strength he had in him. "Drink it all. I can't move. Everything hurts."

Mek could hear the strain in his voice. "Maybe you need more sleep?"

"Sleep!" Tai's breath whooshed out in a trembly sort of laugh with no amusement in it. He'd almost hated Mek for the ease with which he'd slept. "I don't—I can't," he finished shortly.

"If you ate?"

"My stomach has closed. I'll get sick if I try. Here. You take it." He thrust the cold bun into Mek's hand. Maybe three small bites had been scraped out of it.

Mek was about to take a huge bite, then an idea occurred to him. This might be a situation he could practice what Master Root had taught him!

"I know some healing charms. Not many," he added in haste. "But the ones I know are about breaks, and poisons. And aches. Those happen all the time. Aye, not poison. Not sure why I had to learn that, because, as my sister said, pirates don't usually come on board and start poisoning everybody. Anyway, might I try something my tutor taught me?" he asked diffidently. "It won't hurt. That is, he doesn't use needles, or fire, or bleeding."

Tai looked up in question, too miserable for hope. It was Mek's diffidence that enabled him to say, "If you can. I would be very grateful."

Mek set aside the bun and closed his eyes, resuming his Essence breathing. He pulled up a ball of Essence, like digging his fingers into sun-warmed, spring-fresh soil. Then he said, "Sit with your back toward me."

Tai turned sideways, his bony back bowed.

Mek took a moment to review the acupoints, and how they connected to the limbs and the internal organs. He pinched the nails of his forefinger and thumb together to approximate a needle, then flicked Essence into the space between two specific knobs on Tai's upper back—so very sharply defined, those— and midway between the knobs in line with bottom of Tai's ribs and his tailbone.

A weird zing jolted Tai's nerves. He sat upright, then drew in a cautious breath. "Oh!" It was like a blanket of snow over the burning cinders of pain. The cinders were still there, but not worsening. No, definitely not worsening. He stretched out a hand cautiously. "It still hurts. But not like before. I don't feel as sick in my stomach."

"Good. Eat this." Though Mek could have eaten two more of those buns, even stale, he thrust Tai's bun back into his hand.

Tai began to gnaw at it with a grim, determined air, as Mek got up and did some more handstands.

At least that took time, which otherwise lay heavily on them both.

Mek didn't think about the future. He never had. He did what he was told, and day followed day. He was still going to do what he'd been told by his elders on Mountain Peony, which was to fight as hard as he could if the Westerners came at him with knives or swords, as he had only the haziest idea what it meant to be slaves—except that this was very bad. And so, as time stretched slowly on, whenever he felt restless, he got up and did the Ki practice patterns over and over, as hard as he could, until he could sit quietly and do Essence breathing with his flute fingering exercises.

Tai finally fell asleep, driven by exhaustion. Again they

woke to the appearance of water and this time, a fish cake baked with seagrass and cabbage, mixed with egg. Stale. Probably left from everybody else in the Westerners' fortress getting their share first.

Mek finally threw off his grimy, salt-encrusted clothes and did his practices in his drawers, his bare feet hissing and slapping lightly on the stone floor. Tai shut his eyes, trying to move as little as possible, for he could not bear the feel of his own clothing chafing his skin.

Some days passed in this manner, Mek a whirl of strenuous action and Tai motionless in a corner, picking his nail beds raw as his mind sank ever deeper into the beautiful interlocking majesty of the Heavenly Houses, sending his mind ranging over the stars.

At last arrived a day when, instead of food and water coming in, they were bade to follow. Mek hastily threw on his clothes, which had served as his pillow.

They followed a new pair of spear carriers, both with short dark hair and fish-belly pale eyes, and that same old man. Tai was short of breath and trembling by the time they reached the chamber of the Heir.

That same girl sat on her low divan, still wearing silk. The old man bowed low, arms crossed over his chest. The spear carriers also bowed. The girl spoke, and the old man turned to the boys. "What was your place among the imperials? You said your rank. What was your apprenticeship?"

"I am a student in the fifth class of Imperial Divination," Tai said.

And Mek said, "I'm learning to play the flute."

Tai was too miserable to react, though he was aware of mild surprise.

Mek's heart thumped as he said it, but no one seemed to question. The old man spoke, the girl spoke, and then the old man said, not without sympathy in his wheezy voice, "The search went all the way out beyond the east waters, and in all other directions. There was no ship. You have been abandoned, or given up as dead, and you are now slaves of Angja Island. The heir has decreed that you will work in the laundry until you understand the Dragon tongue. Then, perhaps, you might be put to translate books and scrolls." That to Tai, and to Mek, "And the Music Chief will examine your skills, then decide if you can be taught our ways."

The girl spoke again.

The old man said, "We are dismissed." As the spear carriers gave the boys narrow glances, the old man said quickly, "You must learn to bow." He crossed his arms over his chest, and bowed very low toward the heir.

Tai seemed uncertain, then stiffly copied the movement, echoed by Mek, who thought sourly, stupid bowing, just like the imperials.

They were led out and back down through another long, curving tunnel. Essence lights had been placed along the walls at the upper level. Down below there were fewer lights, mostly torches that smelled of burned honey.

Here, new figures in brown took hold of their arms and marched them along. It hurt to walk that fast. Tai winced along until a tunnel widened into a cavern full of steam. That at least was familiar: a bath.

Two men bare except for undyed loincloths, one young, one old, stripped the boys down to the skin, ignoring feeble protests, and pushed them into a pool. Hot water swirled around Mek, searching out his scrapes and cuts. A strong hand grabbed his wobbly topknot, yanked out his wooden hairpin, and then the other hand came up with a knife.

Before Mek could protest, the knife sawed, and his shorn hair flopped onto his forehead. The hand grabbed at the sides and back of his hair and slashed at that, too, then tossed what it had cut onto the pile of Mek's clothes. Which someone else picked up, making a face as if it was crawling with maggots, and turned to collect Tai's things. Some of Tai's things. Mek caught sight of someone carefully folding the soggy, stained silk over robe, and another hand palmed Tai's jade hair clasp.

The older bath man plunged in beside Mek. He said something incomprehensible before shoving Mek's head beneath the water. Mek gasped, choking, then was pulled up by his now short hair.

Cold something that smelled of strange herbs was rubbed into the top of his scalp. A vigorous scrub-down heedless of his cuts. After that, another duck. The cuts throbbed as he was hauled out of the hot bath into cold air and briskly toweled before more hands pulled a coarse brown something over his head. He fumbled to get his hands into sleeves. The front gaped, but a yank brought laces to close the front. Loose trousers were next, and his feet left bare.

Then a push in one direction. Mek stumbled forward, catching sight of Tai, whose scrawny body was lost in a long, brown shirt much too large. His wet hair hung on his forehead, barely reaching his up-slanted eyebrows—slanted not unlike those of several of the men around them. But except for the man who had known their language, most of these others had eyes of various watery shades.

Unsettled, Mek tried to keep up with the fast pace, then was aware of that someone once again outside his Essence door. He kept the door firmly shut as he toiled behind the fast-walking leaders, hearing the wheezing of that old man behind him. They certainly were not very respectful toward elders here. Or, was the old man a slave, too?

Mek's wet, short hair flopped coldly at his ears and forehead at each step. He resented it. Not the missing hair itself—the only time he'd ever thought about hair was to hate combing it out—but the fact that they cut it without saying anything, which was so disrespectful to the parents who had given him life.

They stopped outside a cavern from which emanated the smell of close-packed humanity. Darkness lay beyond; somewhere in that inky darkness someone coughed. Prison? But this archway was not gated.

They were pushed into a side-chamber lit by a single oil lamp, whose circle of light revealed baskets of folded clothing, racks of hempen shoes, and blankets.

They were alone, except for the old man. He motioned for them to sit as he slowly lowered himself to the rough, uneven ground.

"I am to teach you the Dragon tongue. I'm Daldi. I was a fisher, caught in a storm when one of their raiders found me. I was a galley slave for thirty years before they brought me inside to translate for them, and to tend the birds."

"Can't we go home?" Mek asked, his throat aching.

Tai whispered, "We were in a trader. We are no part of the navy."

"This is your fate," Daldi said, with tired sympathy. "As it was mine. You are now a slave. As am I. When the Cobra Sage next visits, you'll get a tattoo on your forehead, like mine. The charm in it will keep you obedient. If you try to run before, they'll cut you down and throw your body to the sharks."

Mek's stomach abruptly closed.

Daldi glanced upward. "Bar means lord. You must learn the language. Address anyone with a staff as 'bar' unless they have a higher title. Bar-Than Ardal of Angja — that's the heir's formal title. 'Than' means heir. Ardal is her name, but do not dare to use it. Angja is the name of this island. It is also her family name, though the other Dragon's Chosen only go by island name, not clan. Bar Ardal is one of a very long line. Angja Island is the last of the ancient Golden Island People. Those islands were always passed mother to daughter, while the men ventured out looking for islands to trade with, until the Dragon's Chosen came…"

"Dragon's Chosen," Mek repeated. "Does that mean us? Isn't our emperor called the dragon, and his throne the dragon throne?"

Daldi looked around, and though no one was there, he rubbed callused, gnarled hands over his shiny scalp, then said, "Here, they say heaven is ruled by Father Dragon rather than the Jade Emperor. The language is the Dragon tongue, spoken by the Dragon's Chosen. And you'll know their raiding galleys by the black dragons on the banners, against whatever color their clan comes from. The warriors use obsidian blades." He looked around again. "Slaves are not even allowed to touch obsidian, which is also used by the Cobra Sages. Obsidian is more important than gold or jade. Though gold is important, too. I tell you this, because how else am I to teach you?"

The boys asked no more questions about dragons. Mek didn't care, and Tai was so furious he remained silent.

Daldi wiped his forehead again. "As I said, the Heir is Bar Than Ardal, and her sister is Bar Odval."

Daldi waited for comprehension. Rumor insisted that the boys had fallen from the sky; there had only been two pairs of footprints, leading from Coral Inlet to the Eastwater Stream and back. Also, there'd been broken tree branches off Coral Inlet. Branches unreachable by any but birds. However, they certainly did not look as if they'd dropped out of heaven. Light skills flying? But neither had a sword or a staff…

He shrugged away vaguely remembered tales from his youth. These boys were surely too young for such rare skills. "Bow to everyone. That will keep you out of trouble. We'll begin on the language first thing in the morning. The call to waken will come early," he warned.

"Where do we sleep?"

"In the chamber there. I'll give you each a blanket."

Daldi hoisted himself to his feet with a grunt of effort. He went to the pile of blankets, which were woven of coarse, undyed cloth, but stuffed with a layer of feathers or down that seemed softer than the goose feather-stuffed covers used during winter at home, and gestured for them to follow.

He led the way inside the cavern, which was warm from all those bodies. The sleepers lay in rows on bare stone, each cocooned by his blanket.

There was a space for two right up against the wall. Mek wrapped up in his blanket, and stretched full length gratefully. He dropped immediately into Essence breathing, pulled up Essence from the rock below him, and the firm earth beneath that. Slowly the worst of his aches began to ease.

He began to drift toward sleep when Tai turned over yet again next to him.

Mek turned his head. "Are you chilled, with a wet head? Do you want my blanket? I don't really need it. It's warm enough in here."

Tai whispered. I can't—"

"Shut up," someone muttered drowsily nearby.

They did. Mek sensed Tai's ambivalence, and solved it by pulling his blanket free and putting it on top of Tai. Who lay still, then slowly sat up and wrapped both blankets about himself. He was actually shivering.

Mek stretched out again. Another deep breath—and there was a presence at his inner door. Only this time it was familiar enough for him to peek out—and in rushed the presence, nearly overwhelming him.

It was the Heir, Bar Thann Ardal.

SIX

THIS WAS NOT AT all like Master Root's inner visits, conducted in quiet, controlled words. This was a sudden inrush awareness and question, distorted images too quick to catch amid an intense sensory stream. It was a bit like someone had dashed into Grandmother's cottage and begun picking things up and putting them down, sniffing under the lids of the pots on the stove, and rummaging through the clothes trunk, then rubbing fabrics between fingers. It was wordless—or rather, the images carried words, all utterly incomprehensible.

Dizzied by a sensory onslaught so different from his own perception, Mek threw up the inner wall again, with the door firmly closed. The whelm ended abruptly, leaving question, curiosity, and passionate expectation. He had to do more Essence breathing before he slid into sleep.

It seemed two heartbeats later when a foot knocked into his side, and he jolted awake to discover the smack of bare feet around him, and the rustle of blankets being folded.

Tai sat up slowly, wincing.

"Sore? I can fix you a little," he whispered. "Like before."

Tai obediently turned his scrawny back, and Mek pushed Essence into the acupoints. "Can you get up now? We're the last."

Tai rose, and though his body complained, the ache was muted. He bundled his blanket in his arms and shuffled awkwardly next to Mek. At the storage place, under the hard eyes of a waiting adult slave, Mek quickly taught Tai how to fold his blanket before adding it to the neat piles.

There followed a race to the privy, then to the baths,

occasional elbows and bumps knocking into them. Tai endured it in mute misery; he had learned to discern intent from the direction of eye, the tension in hands, the tight shoulder of the imminent slap. Last night's clothes went into a gigantic pile, and they rooted among the last of the clean clothes. To be expected, left were the most threadbare—not that Mek noticed.

Mek then reached up to make a tidy topknot, to discover a ruff of short, flyaway curls sticking up. Weird. He dropped his hands as Tai flushed with humiliation and suppressed anger.

Daldi bustled up, red and gasping. "Good, good, good, you've come this far. The quicker you learn, the better, the quicker the better, for the lord ought to be back at any time now that spring is here." His voice dropped on the word bar, or lord.

Breakfast was a bowl of congee made of wheat rather than rice, an imperial feast to the boys who had existed the past few days on a single stale bun or fish cake apiece. The congee, mixed with goat milk, egg, and a trace of honey, was somewhat familiar for Mek, but Tai struggled from shock to shock as they were enjoined to get the meal down, given a small dish of tea obviously third or fourth brew, and then Daldi hurried them to laundry duty.

There were ten or twelve others, including some girls who appeared from somewhere. Everyone gathered up the baskets of dirty, smelly clothes from the baths, and lugged them further down to where a stream had been diverted.

Mek loathed doing laundry, but it was nothing new to him. Tai had never even seen a laundry paddle. It seemed simple enough, at least, except that his hands were soon aching, not quite numb from the cold water, and his arm cramped painfully—he was unaccustomed to lifting anything heavier than an inkstone. He covertly watched Mek, who seemed inexhaustible in smacking brown shirt-tunics one after another. Daldi labored right alongside them as he talked.

If it hadn't been for the language lessons interspersed with bits of information, Tai might have been tempted to throw himself head first into the stream and end his pain and shame, for he was now very certain that he and Mek were lost forever, and he was a mere burden, worse than a basket trying to hold water. But he was quite sure that it would be unfilial to send them demanding a ransom to his father, who would be forced to go to the Ji family on his knees. And most likely be turned down; judging by his cousins' bullying whenever they met for the New Year's Two Moons, the Ji family would consider Tai not worth the trouble.

"…that's the word for 'mud.' And that's also what they call us imperials, Muds, for the color of our eyes. Get used to hearing it. If you hear the shout Mud!, you answer the call at once …"

In spite of his gloom, Tai still listened, the calculating, cataloguing part of his mind divorced completely from the clamors of his physical being. In a constant stream, Daldi gave them words from a slave's day, with cautionary words added in. The lessons were haphazard outside of that—verbs mixed with nouns, plural forms then back to words of respect denoting rank, then a hop over to descriptors. Interspersed with names. So many names.

Moth. Seagrass. Freckle. Raincloud, Phoenixtail-Cloud, Lambkin-Cloud. Beetle. Popper-Kelp. Names both practical and also obviously whim—though some names were reused if a slave who had lived long enough to be considered part of a specific job died. The new slave was expected to become the new name for the convenience of those used to calling it; so it was always a Rosemary, regardless of gender, who mended the lords' shoes.

Tai's mind tried separate categories for words and names. Finally he had enough verbs as distinguishable from nouns to form some useful categories for those, at least.

Daldi, though kind and patient, was no teacher. Mek was very soon lost.

That night, Tai slept from sheer exhaustion; Mek's empty arms ached for Yellow-dog or Three Leg. He tried to scold himself out of tears—useless, Elder Ki had admonished him— but his middle quaked, and he turned his face into the blanket and tried to keep his crying quiet, until at last he slept.

The next day was much the same, though Mek's head ached. Grandmother was right about crying, how useless it was! He slammed that paddle into the defenseless fabric over and over as Daldi flooded them with a stream of words.

By the third day, as Tai taught Mek the trick of reciting the lists, Mek began to feel less like he was drowning in a whirlpool of names and words. They were two grasshoppers on the same twig. Though every bone and muscle still hurt, Tai now had something to offer—he was not a mere burden.

They tried to master the 'th' sound, which came out a buzz

or a hiss or a splutter, which caused endless entertainment to the other children doing laundry with them. Completely ignoring Old Daldi, the bolder of these children began offering insults and crude remarks to the ignorant Muds, just to hear them say these words uncomprehendingly, until a roaming slave with a knotted rope appeared, drawn to the sound of laughter. Silence fell, except for Daldi's wheezing voice.

The two began putting together simple sentences. Mek stumbled over tense and number, but Tai was very careful, very slow, and very precise, and he actually got out a correct sentence in a comprehensible accent.

One day, two, three more passed this way.

The Westerners in the sleeping chamber began addressing Mek as Mushroom, because of this round face topped by that cap of feathery curls. Tai was Spider, for his scrawny limbs. So far, no one had physically attacked them, but both Mek and Tai began to suspect that when they did not have the relative protection of Daldi, there might be trouble.

If they finished laundry before the bell, they were supposed to take any cloth that the slave in charge had deemed too thin to be worn anymore—usually after much mending—to be cut into strips, dipped in honey, and bound to sticks for torches. There was always a need for torches.

Or they could go out to weed in the garden.

By then, Mek had discovered that there were odd alcoves here and there along the way that he could duck into and do at least one practice. He felt better doing these familiar movements. He could close his eyes and pretend he was home.

Tai felt slightly better to be clean, and given clean food, and he bent his mind to eliciting the secrets of this new language. He was soon far ahead of Mek in comprehension; Mek figured out how to navigate the lower reaches of the fortress.

Tai was used to being alone, for he'd learned to avoid the oil-tongued augury students who'd tried to get him to do their calculations for them. But Mek would not leave Tai. Protection was the context in which he'd been raised. That dragon wind had thrown two of them here, and so two of them must escape. And though Tai was older and bigger, he clearly was as ignorant as a babe in arms about protecting himself.

Mek mulled this for a few days, as they fell into the fortress rhythm. But how to escape? First, Tai had to be able to!

One afternoon, Daldi left them at the vegetable garden,

having been summoned away. They were harvesting turnips at the end of a row when Mek made sure no one was around, then said, "I'll show you how to defend yourself."

Tai gave him a skeptical glance. "I can't do any of those things you do."

"You can learn."

"I'm too old."

"My master taught me that no one is too old to cultivate themselves. And you're better than I at remembering all the new words. I know you can learn!"

Tai retorted, "Because I've been learning reading, writing, and the old forms from the time I first took a writing brush in hand. That puts me in mind of a question. You heard Daldi warn us about seers who see truth. But you told them you are a musician. Why?"

"I really am learning the flute," Mek protested. "I like playing the flute. I wish I had mine now, though maybe they wouldn't let me play it. I notice we haven't heard any music so far. Anyway, our elders said, never to admit to being in warrior training if we get taken prisoner."

Tai considered this as he plopped another turnip into the basket, then leaned back to sit on his heels. "If you get in a fight, won't they know at once?"

A rustle caused them to look up, but it was only a troop of bluenecks walking delicately among the planted rows, long necks bent as the creatures nipped insects off the vegetables. That's why there were no worms or caterpillars to pick off. Mek looked after one of the birds, wondering if it was as soft to the touch as it seemed. But he was not going to approach a bird that was taller than old Daldi by two palms, even though some small children roamed close behind the birds, gleaning the gossamer-like feathers that they dropped as they molted their winter plumage.

Tai had gone back to carefully pulling turnips, trying to keep his fingers as clean as he could. Mek could fill a basket in the time it took Tai to choose and pull five vegetables, but that was habit. He thought hard. Tai was right. If he squared up into a fighting stance, wouldn't that give him away?

What was he to do? Not fight back?

He mulled this dilemma over the rest of the day, until he lay awake in the night, aware of that oppressive sense of longing.

No, he decided. *A spooked horse will jump the fence*, Father had taught him: anyone, seeing an attacker coming, might react. Father also said, the best fight was the quickest. Especially if you're younger and weaker. You need surprise on your side, which only lasts for the first exchange. Make it be effective.

And! If a pack of wolves comes at you, you take out the leader. So…to hide his training, it seemed that the thing to do was to deflect, disable the leader, and make it look like it was an accident?

He didn't want to kill anybody. He could touch one of the acupoints that would make his foe stumble, or even freeze. And the only way to do that and have a strong effect would be to shove Essence in, the way he did when he did a healing charm.

Would it work? Master Root had only spoken about using Essence in healing—but he wasn't a warrior. The elders had never talked about using Essence in fighting because they didn't trust Essence, outside of charms to ward demons and the like. Not everybody could even sense it. Some could, but the elders insisted that in the real world, Essence wasn't of any practical use.

That was decided, then. He'd fight back. That meant he had to find more time to do his practice forms!

As often happens, even if you think you are prepared, the actuality can still take you by surprise.

They did not even see the initiating incident, when one of the older teens deliberately tripped another as they were laboriously bumping barrels of fish oil up to be delivered to the weaving wing. The target tumbled down several stairs until he caught the rail, thereby managing not to break a bone, but the barrel bounded agonizingly off one of his knees, hit the next stair with a resonant *tunk*, then—spinning—smashed to splinters halfway down, sending a river of fishy oil splashing across the floor.

Voices rose—accusations—and a couple of spear guards appeared. Both had knotted ropes at their waists. These young men, Tai had discovered from Daldi's rambles, had reached the age to be sent to the galleys, but had so pleased the household steward that they were entrusted to guard the fortress instead, which they did with unremitting zeal. *Nobody wants to go to the galleys*, Daldi had wheezed, slowly shaking his shiny bald head. *Most will even prefer the ring.*

The line of slaves froze, including the feuding two. "What happened here?" a slave guard demanded, pulling his rope free and swinging it.

"Hand slipped," hoarsely cried the one whose knee was swelling visibly under the brown cloth of his trousers. "Oily." He held up shiny palms.

"Get the rest of those barrels up," the other said to the older teens. And then, turning to the younger ones, "The rest of you get that mess cleaned."

Having delivered these orders, the two guards walked off on their round.

And now, the one Mek had identified as an emperor among the younger boys turned to Tai and Mek, and with a cruel grin, snarled, "A job for you Muds."

The rest of the boys immediately and enthusiastically agreed.

"He say, says, *all*," Tai responded, indicating the circle of younger boys. To him it made sense—if everyone worked, the noisome job would be done the quicker.

Though he had been the target of highly competitive cousins, it had mostly been verbal, calculated, covert. Rarely physical. So the slap seemed to come out of nowhere, and if he hadn't been on the bottom step, because by now nobody expected him to be able to lift much beyond a cup, he would have flown backward down the stairs.

He landed painfully, aware of the whisk of cloth past him as Mek ducked, seemed to lose balance as if tripping over him, and slammed into the would-be emperor, fingers striking the acupoint below the breast bone. Lightning flashed painfully through the bully's nerves, and he let out a yell.

Unfortunately, the noise had drawn attention. From the landing above, the tall hat woman (the steward, Mek and Tai had learned) appeared in time to see the emperor's assistant take a swing at Mek. Who eased just out of reach.

"Halt!" Steward Hathi commanded. Then, "You. Mud. Why are you on the ground?" She pointed at Tai.

Mek stepped in front of Tai and made the slave bow. Five of his ten years had been spent in the tumble of life among cousins and siblings training as warriors. Win or lose, the worst thing you could do is become a telltale, which made you a white-eyed wolf, a rat, a demon.

Mek said, pointing, "Oil slop! Slip."

Steward Hathi knew very well that this was unlikely, but she had been an instant too late to actually witness the taller foreign slave knocked down. Therefore she said only, "The Heir wishes to interview the foreigners. The rest of you, get this area cleaned up now!"

Everybody bowed, except Tai, still sprawled on the hard stone floor. He got to his hands and knees, then to his feet as Mek held out a hand in case he needed it.

Tai avoided the hand, and together they trod up the steps. Midway along, as the other slave boys faced the mess, Tai leaned toward Mek. "Teach me," he breathed.

SEVEN

FOR THE THIRD TIME, the boys entered the Heir's interview chamber. She sat on her divan, as before. Two men stood there, one tall and gaunt, the other short and round. At the side Steward Hathi, the woman with the hat watched everything.

Bar Ardal said very slowly and distinctly, "Kimek and Jetai. I am told you progress. We will place your skills."

Tai got that. Mek was still trying to remember the word for progress as the gaunt man gestured to Tai, and pointed to a low writing desk, where ink, brush, and paper waited. The brush was somewhat heavier than that Tai was used to, and the ink smelled odd, but it clung to the brush properly.

"Write," the man said. "In Mud language."

Tai began to write the beginning of the Thousand Characters primer that every child must begin with: "Heaven above, earth below, vast is the world between" — the characters being heaven, earth, vast, world.

As he executed this in his best calligraphy, the short man opened a beautifully carved flat box, to display several flutes. Some were reed flutes, blown from one end, but there were also two of the side-hole flutes Mek was used to. The one on the right was even a bamboo flute, a little larger than his, but instantly familiar.

Mek worked his lips, glad he'd practiced fingering. He planted his bare feet wide, breathed in Essence, and began to play one of his favorite pieces. He tried to infuse it with joy, but there was no joy in him.

At the end of a phrase, he paused to draw breath — and there was Bar Ardal in his mind again. Busy with music and Essence, he'd forgotten his door. He winced at the intensity of her inner presence, a weird mixture of sensory brilliance infused with words, though this time he picked out, "You! You! It was you!"

"Door," he thought firmly—and once again, slammed her out.

He sensed her outside the door. She waited there. Master Root had had a way of seeming to knock, though of course there was no hand or wood involved. Bar Ardal did not do that, but waited, and he could sense curiosity, eagerness. Excitement. And…worry?

So, even though she was an enemy, he opened the door. He sensed her struggling to slow her words to one at a time, though they came with a rush of sensory impressions, of not-quite-sound echoes that he found confusing.

He recollected his early lessons with Master Root and presented Bar Ardal with the image of a door, and of Master Root knocking, and of Mek opening the door to let him in. They'd gone through the motions with the door to Master Root's cottage over and over while Mek associated them with the Essence world in his head.

Unfortunately, Bar Ardal seemed bewildered. She was older than he was! He knew she could talk. He'd heard her! But she seemed puzzled and intrigued by the concept of knocking at a door. Why? They had doors here! He'd seen them! Didn't they knock?

"Learn. More. Words," he offered tentatively.

This time, she vanished—no image of a door. She was just gone.

Mek opened his eyes, to see the man gazing at him with a slight frown. He was waiting for Mek to finish his piece. Mek moistened his lips, and played the rest of his song, into which seeped his yearning to be home. He could see that his song had an effect, though he interpreted the expression on their faces as doubt. Hadn't he played well enough?

Bar Ardal and Steward Hathi spoke. Mek picked two or three words out of that quick stream, but no sense. Tai was told that he was to commence writing lessons under the scribe students, led by the gaunt man.

Daldi appeared, received orders from Steward Hathi and turned to Mek. "You're to join me with the bluenecks, until you can speak and understand. Come along!"

For the first time, the two boys were separated. Mek was

taken across the kitchen gardens to a stretch of land marked by wild date trees and strange ferny plants, sloping away toward more marshy land bordered by what appeared to be a solid wall of redbark trees whose roots interlocked. Beyond, at a distance, sparkled the sea. At first, it seemed that the entire area was dotted with snow. But that was wrong. The air, though not as warm as at home at this time of year, was much too sunny for snow.

"The children begin by gathering down," Daldi explained. "Children your age wash it and sort it, and eventually it gets sewn into jackets, quilting, bolsters, and the like. I'm told it was this island's ancient trade, far more precious than the gold back then. The birds are busy shedding their winter padding to be ready for the warmth of summer."

Mek bent down to pick up some fluff clinging to an early thistle. It was so soft to the touch, and the smell was mild, a little musty at most. Not as pungent as goats or sheep. No wonder even the slaves got those soft blankets. It looked like there was enough down right here to stuff mattresses for an army.

Fortress children in brown tunics flapping about bare knees swarmed over the entire area, gathering the down. Mek spent the rest of the day with Daldi at his side, talking and repeating words until he said, "Tomorrow, I must be over on the other side, as the hatchlings are beginning to come. You'll be here. Some responsible children will teach you." Daldi waved a hand. "You'll eat with the children now. And one of Steward Hathi's assistants will show you where you two will now sleep."

The children had their own eating hall nearer the baths and farther from the kitchens, and as slave children were served last, the food was usually cold. Mek was bombarded with questions. They laughed at his accent, and his errors, but none of that mattered to him. The children already knew he was strong—his paddle-wielding had been seen and reported days ago. They were no threat.

At night, he was taken to a sort of crevasse that seemed as high as a mountain, honeycombed with round little chambers big enough for one or two, made by bubbles in the molten rock millennia ago. Some were larger than others, and nearly complete, that is, an entire bubble except for a small opening; these, it turned out, were highly prized as they afforded slightly more privacy once one climbed inside. They went to adults. Some were too small, or too shallow, to be used except to hold lamps.

These bubble-chambers were reachable by very narrow rails cut into the stone, and some by rope ladders. He found Tai already in theirs, halfway up the slab of rock. It was accessible to anyone who wanted to look in, except for a shallow curve at either side of the round opening. There were two blankets, and a shelf for tools of whatever trade they'd been assigned. Tai had been issued brushes and an odd, round inkstone that was like a wine jar, narrow at the top, with a stopper to keep the ink from drying. They apparently did not grind ink for each use here, but kept it somehow in liquid form.

Mek grabbed his blanket, and lay down to do Essence breathing, drawing strength from deep in the ground, as the mighty chasm between the two slabs of stone whistled softly from a constant breeze off the ocean. Far off, the underground river rushed.

"You look mad. Was it terrible?" Mek asked at last in a whisper. "Mine isn't so bad, picking bird fluff off thistles and sticky plants. Tomorrow we have to go down to the redbark trees, because the birds go there to pick off insects. I didn't see you at dinner."

"I was with the scribe students."

"Oh. I'm with everybody my age and smaller, I guess. Some of them tried to teach me, aside from trying to get me to say that I'm a butt, or a rabbit. But some didn't make sense. Like, certain words you have to know but you can't say. And others you have to use."

"Slave pronouns," Tai whispered tightly. "We had something similar in our language, but long ago, before the Sage Empress outlawed slavery."

"They said you can get *killed* here, just for saying 'I' in the wrong way."

"I hate this language," Tai murmured, soft but with fierce sibilants. "*Slave* language. I hate that writing is reserved for the lords, or for a few scribes. There are a thousand terms for punishment. More. And nothing about civilization. And their buildings make no sense. Rooms scattered about like chicken scraps, as if we are ants crawling aimlessly."

"Master Root says ants are never aimless."

"Really? Aish, I don't want to learn about ants now. There is no order in this fortress. You can go into any building in the empire, and know where the hall is, and which side is for men, and which for women, and where the ancestral hall is, or the altar, at least. Here?"

"I don't care where anything is," Mek whispered back, his eyelids drifting down. "All I want is to escape."

Tai muttered, "That's another terrible thing. Remember what Daldi told us? There is something called a Cobra Sage coming. Who will burn their brand into our foreheads, and put charms in to kill us if we are not obedient."

That chilled Mek into wakefulness.

Tai sighed. "In the morning. Teach me some martial skill?"

"Morning," Mek promised, made certain his inner door was firm, then sank into restless, troubled sleep.

In the morning, the distant clang of the early bell reverberated through the chasm, waking them. Weak morning light shafted in, pale against the stone. There was even less space in their little shelter than had been in their cell, but in the beginning, Tai wouldn't be moving much. Mek guessed that learning a horse stance was going to take him weeks—if he even stuck with it past two days.

"Quick," Mek said. "I'll show you the correct stance. Practice it whenever you can."

He pushed Tai against the inner wall at one side of the opening, which would make him difficult to spot at a casual glance. By dint of pushing and shoving, he managed to get Tai into a horse stance, though his noodle legs shook before he even got halfway down. Then they folded their blankets and raced out to join the others going to the baths.

Tai did stick with it past two days, then two weeks.

In fact, he practiced every moment he chanced to find himself alone. When he could hold a true horse stance for the count of fifty, Mek began showing him his first form, a bit at a time.

Spring ripened, and the rains came. The fortress seemed emptier as the general labor pool shifted out to the fields for planting.

Tai was deep in language studies, and already given tasks for translation. It was a completely haphazard collection of imperial books and scrolls, letters, sometimes lists of goods. There were also a couple of adventure tales, and one play, the scroll rough from a dip in salt water, as well as a herbal written for the rice island of Lan, far to the southeast. Would they even have some of those plants here?

Mek's language was gained piecemeal, gleaned from the

slave children. As there was no space in their open cubicle, he and Tai met when they could, and Tai slowly, painfully, learned his first martial form. When they whispered late at night, it was invariably of escape.

From a distance, the Heir, Bar Ardal, waited with increasing impatience for the day she could actually speak to the mystery-ous boy named Kimek.

One day, as rain pounded the island, her sister Odval ran all the way to the aerie—the very top of the fortress—having not found her elder sister in her usual places. "Here you are! Does that mean the fleet is back?" Odval pressed her fists together at her breastbone.

"I thought," Ardal said slowly. "But it was another raider pack, going north. Away. How is the boy doing?"

Odval flopped down beside her sister, and helped herself to a date cake. The fortress was filled with boys, but ever since the strange appearance of the two Muds—still unexplained—there was only one boy on Ardal's mind.

"He makes sense, mostly, now," Odval reported. "In a babyish way. At least he only has to ask 'what did you say' a few times a day. As long as you keep it simple. His word order is worse than that Mud accent, but really, if you must talk to him, you could do it now."

Ardal frowned, musing, "But does he have the vocabulary?"

Odval said, "Who does, when it comes to what you do? And how much is he going to learn about that from those brats down there? I've used exercising the dogs as an excuse to be there, listening. I could tell you the silly things they had him repeating, just to hear him say it in that funny accent, without knowing what he said. They never get tired of it."

"Perhaps I ought to get Steward Hathi to put Old Daldi back with him. Someone else can manage the eggs this year. We have plenty of bluenecks," Ardal finished bitterly, thinking of lost trade—once so important to the Golden Islands. But now Angja was the only one left, the old ways being replaced by Dragon's Chosen customs more and more.

Odval considered her sister's frown as she straightened out a tangle of brightly colored silk-fringed shawls that Ardal had cast aside. The sun shone directly through the open windows, and the room was quite warm. "That boy probably learns more from the slave children than he does from Old Daldi, because

Daldi kept talking at him more than actual teaching."

"Then he won't need Old Daldi," Ardal said.

"You don't want to order the children to teach him properly?" Odval asked.

"No. Let them just talk. Even if it's slow." Grandmother had repeated many times, *Learn from our foremothers, who led by example, and corrected by encouragement. Let them be as happy as they can be, and you won't need the rope.*

Tell Uncle Gatslan that!

Reminded of the imminent threat of their uncle's return with the fleet, Ardal said, "Maybe I should try to talk to him anyway. But his Hearing is so *different!*"

"He's only ten," Odval pointed out, from the lofty pinnacle of nearly thirteen. "I still don't understand why you trouble yourself."

Ardal ran her hands over the golden oriole crowning her staff of rank. "He's the only one who Hears that I've ever met outside of Grandmother and Mother. The only one! With Grandmother gone, and Mother required to attend on the obsidian throne, I thought I was alone in the world. Maybe he knows things that will help me to hold Angja!" Her voice was high and breathy with strain.

Odval did not believe a foreign boy of ten would be the lease use to Ardal, but she'd do anything for her sister. She patted Ardal's taut hand. "Call him up here. Any time he doesn't understand something, you tell me and I'll make a list. Then *I'll* teach him the words?"

"Except there aren't words for so much of Hearing," Ardal said. "Even using the word 'hear' is wrong. I have to ignore my ears. It's why I come up to the aerie when I Hear something very faint and far. Grandmother said there'd never had to be a word, because our foremothers Heard each other without words. But is that true in the Mud empire? Grandmother insisted that their flying around was merely demons mistaken for human, and that Muds don't Hear, or they'd know when raider packs were descending on them. That boy is evidence that at least one Mud can Hear. And he knows how to hide his thoughts! I can't even imagine doing that! Clearly someone taught him. I have to *know*, Odval!"

The urgency in Ardal's voice convinced Odval. "I'll go fetch him. It's nearly time for the bell anyway." She ran off.

EIGHT

SADLY, THE UNDER-TWELVES were confined to feather-gleaning, and to keeping the birds' nesting areas tidy. With all the rain, and the frequency of the big birds' droppings, that was a constant, pungent toil in muck that somehow managed to be both slimy and sticky.

This particular gray, humid afternoon, Mek's hands and bare feet were covered in that greenish muck after raking out then putting fresh hay in the hen houses where the hens laid their eggs. These huge green eggs were not the kind that had chicks in them—those nests were off in an area that only Old Daldi and a couple of other older slaves tended. The father birds, not the mothers, sat on the eggs for a surprisingly long time before they hatched little striped babies.

Mek tried to shake his sour mood by using all that space for a fast set of martial forms until his shapeless brown tunic whipped about his legs. But the sound of voices on the hill at the back end of the vegetable gardens caused him to pick up his tools to carry back to storage for the night.

He saw the gleaners and others stopping and making the slave bow. Mek copied them, groaning inside. He didn't want anything postponing dinner.

The "bar" who appeared was the youngest, Bar Odval. The golden chimes at the end of her many long braids jingled sweetly as she skirted past the mound of guano composting into fertilizer. She wore a headband with a small oriole embroidered in gold. Tiny chains dangled from it in the back, mingling with the braids.

She pinched her nose and raked Mek with a glance. "You!

Kimek," she called. "Go clean up, then come up to the aerie!"

Postpone it was. Mek sighed, but not where the roaming boss with his rope could hear. To his surprise, he found Bar Odval waiting impatiently outside the men's bathing area. Just as well he'd hurried.

"She's waiting," Odval said to Mek. "Come, come, come!"

Mek raced up the stairs behind her fluttering, brightly embroidered robe. They went all the way to the top of the fortress. He cast a quick glance through the many windows that afforded a broad view of the southern tip of the island, the nearest inlet, and on the other side, the spine of the island fading into the cloudy haze in the north west.

"Kimek," Odval exclaimed. "My sister is *here*."

The sharpness in her voice was immediately undercut by Ardal's low, "Let it rest. You know Grandmother always said respect comes from the heart, not the bended knee."

Odval flushed. To her, every sign she saw as disrespect for Ardal was a sign that they were going to lose the island forever.

Mek turned around, remembered his slave bow, which was just a meaningless action to him, and waited.

Ardal gazed at Mek, somewhat dismayed, for the boy who glowed nearly as bright as a sun was so small and so young. But she remembered how skilled he was and said slowly, "How do you hide your Hearing?"

Mek repeated each word to himself. They still made no sense. "I hear fine," he said. "Anyway, nobody can hide hearing. Can they?" This last in doubt, as once again he sensed her presence beyond his inner door.

Oh! Could she mean his inner door?

He said, "I tell you. I told you. The door."

"Tell me again?" She relinquished the visible world, turning with relief to Hearing.

He explained in the mental realm, twisting back and forth as he struggled to think the words in the Dragon tongue. Finally, he thrust an image of a door at Ardal, and said out loud, "Maybe we have to practice here." He pointed at the aerie's carved door, inlaid with golden ships on stylized waves.

Ardal's wide blue gaze remained on him. Or rather, where he'd been standing until he stepped toward the carved door. He turned to Odval and whispered, "Is she..." What was their word for blind? "Not-see?" He covered his eyes with his hands.

Odval was not unfamiliar with this mistaken assumption —

one her grasping relations had made, or pretended to make, as proof that Ardal could not perform the Heir's chief duty. "She can see just fine. It's just that she has to stop seeing in order to Hear." And at a slight gesture from her sister, she said less truculently, "Or she gets very very dizzy. Grandmother did, too. And Mother, also, Grandmother told us."

Most of that was too fast for Mek, and confusing. Someone who had to not see in order to hear? But Ardal caught enough of his confusion to force the shift once again, though it gave her lingering vertigo.

She rose, made sure she was steady on her feet, and crossed the distance, her blue outer robe embroidered in gold and crimson trailing behind her. She was nearly as tall as Tai.

"I'll show you," Mek said, and taught her the same way that Master Root had taught him: step outside the real door. Make the inner door. Knock on the real door, then inwardly knock on the imagined door. Open the real door—and inwardly, permit her presence to meet his.

"Ah, ah, ah, ah," Ardal breathed as she stood within the door frame. "Yes! This is possible. It is almost simple!"

Mek stared. Her Essence presence was so strong—stronger than Master Root's—and yet she was acting as if this, his very first lesson when he was five or six, was her toughest lesson and the newest.

His stomach growled loudly, and Ardal blinked at him. "You're hungry?"

"Yes," he said, with passionate truth.

She pointed at a side table, where last year's peaches, conserved in salt and sugar, sat in a golden bowl, alongside date cakes and food he didn't even recognize, though it smelled interesting. "Eat any of those you wish. I must try again. And again."

The slaves in the labor pool did not get delicacies like date cakes or preserved fruits. Mek flung himself down at the low table and began stuffing himself. He'd cleared the date cakes and was working on the spice-pickled cabbage when Ardal said at last. "I must practice. I will *knock at the door* if I have questions."

Mek fled—arriving in time to catch the last of the stragglers going in for the slaves' dinner. Here was a rare piece of luck!

Later on, he and Tai were settling into their blankets when he sensed Ardal outside his Essence door. He opened the door and there she was, clearly trying very hard to constrain herself to simple language. Which he didn't understand.

He said, "Je Tai knows more of your words than I do. I'll ask him." He turned to Tai. "Do you know what these words mean?" He repeated what he remembered.

Tai sat up, his brow wrinkled. "First, what is the context?"

"The what?"

"What is the circumstance behind her asking?"

"Oh! It's Essence. Didn't I tell you? Maybe I didn't. She can hear me, and I can hear her." Mek tapped his head. "Her way is very different, but—oh, I don't even know how to say it. I did teach her how to make a door."

"What does that mean?" Tai asked, then, very quickly, "Can she heard us now?"

"No. I shut the Essence door when I use regular speech. I don't like the echoes in my head if I have the door open, and someone talks there, then someone talks to me, here, like you are now—ayah! I think I understand now why she makes herself blind when she does Essence things."

Tai frowned. "She can't hear us, then?"

"No."

Tai leaned forward, lowering his voice. "First, remember, she's an enemy. We are prisoners, forced to be slaves. Anything you teach her might be used to keep us from escape."

"Oh." Mek considered this, aware of Ardal still waiting for an answer. He was going to point out that she didn't feel like an enemy—she'd let him eat the best dinner he'd had since leaving home—but he suspected that Tai would scorn that as a reason to trust her.

Finally he said, "Master Root only taught me peaceful things. I don't see how her being able to close someone out would hurt our chance of escape, if I teach her this one thing."

Tai nodded slowly. Then said, even slower, "Tell her that I don't understand the context, and must learn more of their language. That ought to give me time to investigate the situation here."

Mek said, "I know that everybody seems afraid of Bar Gatslan, the Heir's uncle, who is supposed to be returning soon."

"There's also some kind of seer coming," Tai reminded him. "Perhaps that is the Cobra Sage? Ay! I don't know what that means for us."

Mek sighed, suddenly very tired. He closed his eyes, opened the inner door, and told Ardal that Tai understood the words but not the context. She exhorted him to learn more words, and she was gone.

Mek carefully strengthened his door, and stretched out to sleep.

The next day, there was Odval waiting for Mek out in the yard, next to the rake, bucket, and wheelbarrow that meant he was stuck mucking out more blueneck nests. It had rained hard in the night, and the ground had turned to soup, rendering the toil extra nasty.

Odval followed him to the first nest. "I know you're a little boy," she began, "but you've got to understand how important it is to teach my sister everything you know."

Mek said nothing as he attacked the mess. He didn't like being called a little boy by someone Seventh Brother's age, but he could hear beneath her voice how earnest she was. More than earnest, worried. There was no mean intent here.

"First I need the…the context," he said, testing the word. To Mek, context sounded a bit like the way Master Root saw the world, contrasted, say, with the way Second Uncle saw the world. In Master Root's context, all the animals, the birds, the insects, the sea life, were of equal importance to humans. In Second Uncle's context, animals were like landscape, important only as useful or obstacles.

Odval followed him as he began raking the ruined hay into a pile. "This is how she explained it to me. She Hears—that means she detects… things… coming near the island. Mother can do it. She has to do it for the throne, far away at Baris Tharan. That's the treaty, you see."

"What treaty?"

"The treaty between the obsidian throne and us, here, that lets us keep Angja," Odval said impatiently. "Thirteen generations, our foremothers kept watch over the Golden Islands. Until the Black Dragon raiders came—but never mind that. They didn't think my sister could Hear when Grandmother died. She was my age then. But she *can*. And to prove it, she Heard you two, when you came. But she needs to be able to Hear farther out. And then be able to… do something. Grandmother said it would come in time, but she wasn't able to teach her. Grandmother was very old. Very old."

Mek got about half of that. "But I don't even know what it

is your sister does," he said as he began piling the dirty straw in the wheelbarrow.

"That's what she wants to teach you, you silly boy," Odval exclaimed. "So you can teach her what *you* know."

He looked as puzzled as he was, and meanwhile he had hen houses to muck out. Then the Heir was outside his door. He groaned, and leaned on his rake.

"What's wrong?" Odval demanded.

He opened the inner door, and there was the sensory whelm again, but in a heartbeat Ardal contained it, and asked with care, "Is my sister with you?"

"Right here," he responded inwardly, proud of being able to think in the Dragon tongue.

"Tell her to leave at once!" And she was gone.

Mek turned to Odval, who stared at him wide-eyed. "Your sister says to come at once," he said.

In the aerie, Ardal said to her sister, "I know you want to help, but you *can't* draw any more attention to that boy. Not with Uncle due at any time."

"Why not?"

"If they find out what he can do, they're sure to throw him to the snakes! You know the Cobra Sages' laws!"

Odval hung her head, chimes tinkling. "I forgot. I never see them, not since I failed their snake test," she reminded her sister. "And I'm never sick. "Would they even take a foreigner?"

"I think so. Or kill him. I don't want that to happen, Odval. Right now everyone thinks I sent for the boys to translate confiscated Mud documents. But if we're calling for either of those boys every day, it's sure to raise questions."

"I'll stay away from him," Odval promised, flushing with remorse.

"Besides, I know now how to talk to him without anyone knowing," Ardal said. "And it can only get easier as he learns more."

Odval said, "As to that, I can hear my tutor talking to the other one over in the library, when I'm doing lessons. He's already translating documents."

"Is he," Ardal said. "I wonder when the Chief Scribe was going to report that to me." *If at all.*

NINE

TAI WAS MUCH GIVEN to reflection, though seldom about himself. Those rare times, he saw himself as a lacquered cabinet, similar to the one that a very wealthy merchant had brought as a gift.

This cabinet was made of the finest parasol tree wood, stored for a hundred years (it was said) in fragrant herbs, then fashioned with many, many tiny drawers, cleverly constructed so that a section of these hid another set of drawers entirely. But one had to employ a golden key and at the same time, depress a tiny carved rosebud set among gaudier flowers entwined with gold, to reveal the secret compartment.

He hadn't been permitted to touch the cabinet, but his pleasure derived entirely from seeing the little drawers slide easily in and out, disclosing their treasures — rings in one, jade ornaments in another, in a third silver coins struck before such things were regulated during the Era of Peaceful Rectification early in the Yslan Dynasty. Beautiful long silken tassels lay in a shallow, lengthy drawer that could as easily have held a dagger. Once it might have, for the cabinet was a treasure of the troubled Dai Dynasty.

Tai likened himself to such a cabinet because he strove to lock up fear in one drawer, decorated with dancing rabbits. Anger in another drawer, on whose front was painted a crimson fall of lava from a fire mountain. Regret, hatred, sadness, mortification in the secret drawers behind the other drawers. If he could lock those secret drawers, he could regain the clarity of mind he so envied in monks and hermits, the serenity promised by Kanda, though it seemed to recede like a mirage.

It was when his cabinet was locked, its front smooth, that he could do his best work. And he was working very hard now, determined to master the hated Dragon tongue, initially to wipe the scorn from the faces of the other scribe apprentices. But now he strove to master everything in order to figure out how to get back home. To that end, he read everything in reach. Which wasn't much — until Mek woke one day, and in that odd way of his, said suddenly, "The Heir wants you to go up in the aerie to translate things. I think what she really wants is to teach you some words that you can then teach me."

A day without those other scribe apprentices around? Tai made certain he was very clean, the humiliating short hair slicked back as firmly as he could make it, his clothing tidy before he trod barefoot up and up to the aerie. He noted with bleak satisfaction that though he barely knew one of Mek's martial forms, and was exactly as hopeless at "sparring" as ever, he no long was fighting for breath, though he'd climbed more stairs than ever before.

The Heir was alone in the topmost floor, with an unimpeded view of the island. "What have you translated so far?" she asked.

As always, Tai mentally constructed his sentences before speaking. "I finished one, a trader's bill of lading. Unfinished, an herbal. A play…" He listed them off.

Ardal listened closely. None of these were vital. This was therefore not evidence that the Chief Scribe was supporting Uncle Gatslan behind her back. And yet that list had not been checked with her before being given to him to translate. That would not have happened in Grandmother's day.

Steward Hathi was impeccable in her execution of her duties, but Ardal could not determine where her loyalties truly lay. Which was why, when Ardal was in the interview room below, Steward Hathi standing by, every word she spoke was uttered as if Uncle Gatslan was listening in the next room.

Last night, with Odval watching from the door, Ardal had gone through Grandmother's trunks, locating a very old scroll written in the Mud language. This, she handed to Tai.

He glanced at it, and said, with some surprise, "This is a copy of Ar Laq's *The Sacred Seasons* poems."

"I know," Ardal murmured. "It was at the bottom of a very old trunk full of ritual clothes. We don't have those rituals anymore. I first found it when I went through my grandmother's things after she died. I don't think it's been touched since she went through *her* grandmother's things. I burned Grandmother's copy of the translation this morning. So I can say that we require a translation."

Tai knew that slaves were not supposed to put questions. But she was his age, and she needed something illicit. More as a test than because he wanted the answer, he said, "I can translate it. That is, I know most of the poems by heart, though I might not know all your words yet. But why do you want me to translate it?"

"Because I don't want you, or Kimek, to catch the eye when my uncle returns," she whispered fiercely. Then, in a low, urgent voice, "They seldom trouble with scribe apprentices, as many are short-sighted like you. And Kimek is small."

"Short-sighted like me?" Tai repeated.

"Yes. It's clear at a glance, the way you bend over your writing, and your squint just now when you looked through the window. I could try to teach Kimek this way." She tapped her head. "But it takes me so very long to…to Hear-speak to him one word at a time. It's like trying to run in water. I can tell you. And anyone listening will assume that what I say relates to the poetry. You can tell Kimek."

He held the fragile scroll with both hands, satisfied that her intent did not seem to be to endanger either Mek or himself. Besides, a glance around this chamber and its many books and scrolls was a severe temptation. Proximity might not mean access, he scolded himself: to assume it would be easy to peruse those for a means of escape was like counting on rain at the first breath of wind.

But here, he was wrong. Because nothing could be easier.

Once he'd begun his work, the Heir settled on her divan, then stilled in a way that had to be her going blind in order to "Hear" at a distance.

He tried reaching for a book from a shelf adjacent to his writing desk.

He took it down.

Opened it.

Turned a page.

Ardal never stirred.

He rejoiced, resolving to do a certain amount of work, listen for people coming up the stairs, and ransack these scrolls for what he could learn.

Several days passed.

Tai's diligence broadened his skill in the Dragon tongue. He sampled a bit of each book and scroll, one by one, until he reached one labeled:

TO SHE WHO COMES AFTER ME: WHAT MY FOREMOTHERS TAUGHT ME ABOUT OUR ISLAND.

The other slave children liked Mek. He didn't look like much, but he was strong, friendly, he was curious about the birds and grateful to learn—and his speech was often hilariously wrong. But he didn't mind being laughed at.

One day, Old Daldi summoned him. "The birds now know you. They know your smell. They've accepted you. I can put you in with those assigned to help train the chicks."

Delighted, Mek followed Old Daldi's shining bald head toward the far enclave. The little striped chicks—new, fuzzy ones, unsteady on their twig-like legs, appearing every day— were to be played with, and coaxed into groups. This, he learned, was centuries-old practice.

The day had never passed so fast—and that night, after the meal, he was directed to another tunnel entirely. It seemed that the Westerners didn't have professional musicians. At least on this island. Everyone summoned to practice had other jobs, and the master he'd met the once was one of the bolster embroilderers by day.

"We must be ready for the return of the Angja raider fleet," the master said. "We expect them at any time. There is always triumphal music to celebrate their return. You flutes play the cascades. The bili carry the melody." Here, he played a double-reeded bamboo flute whose sound reminded Mek of the suona.

The rest of the musicians played clappers, drums, and little tinkling bells. At first, very raggedly, making it clear that weeks, more like months, had passed since the last time they had gathered.

They were dismissed so late that Tai was asleep when he made his way back to their alcove.

The fourth day, a fierce rainstorm kept the blueneck tenders inside, and Tai was told, "Your work was given to Grasshopper there when you were called up to serve the Heir. Go to the laborers."

Tai was halfway there when he encountered Mek, who was about to slip outside. "Where are you going?"

"To practice by the hen houses. No one will be there in this rain."

"I will come," Tai said. And as they threaded the kitchen garden, empty of people, Tai said, "How short-sighted am I?"

"I don't know. Can you see those trees there?"

"Of course. They're *trees*."

"Can you tell them apart?"

"The rain is too hard for me to smell them," Tai admitted, his long, tilted eyes narrowing to a squint.

"You mean, you can't see the individual leaves?"

"No one can at this distance!"

"You can't tell the gingko from the mimosa?"

"I take it you can," Tai observed.

Mek jumped up, pulled a spring green leaf, and splashed down. He laid the leaf in Tai's hand. "Look, gingko leaves are like fans. See? And..." Another jump, another splash. "Mimosa are like feathers."

Tai brought the leaves to chin level, then his somber expression changed. "I've always differentiated trees by shape. Color. Smell. Ay!"

"You're a little short-sighted." Mek shrugged, his curls plastered to his skull and neck like writhing worms. "Have you found anything that'll help us escape?"

Dripping wet, the two began the warmups that now had become habit for Tai, though he still clomped with heavy feet.

"I've learned plenty about these Westerners. It seems they are two different peoples. Each claims the other speaks a dialect."

"Fist straight," Mek said. "Don't bend it. Think of a straight line from your middle finger's knuckle all the way to your shoulder."

"Middle finger," repeated Tai, and tried the block and strike again.

"Better," Mek said. "Dialects? Is any of it going to matter to us getting away?"

"Perhaps," Tai said, midway between the curiosity of the scholar and impatience at his awkward body. How was it that he made so much effort, and Mek seemed to float through the movements, like the spin of a wheel? "One of the Heir's foremothers wrote a history to be passed down from Guardian to Guardian. It's mostly a collection of memories of what they have lost. It's in archaic language. I'm still trying to puzzle it out. Bar Thranis, the Heir's grandmother, was the previous Guardian. She added to it, meant for the eyes of her successor. I'm careful to ask for words if I can relate them to the Ar Laq poems, so she won't guess I'm reading it, in case we're not supposed to," he added in a low voice.

"Back leg solid before you kick," Mek said, recognizing that blank stare. Once again, Tai was paying little heed to what his body was doing. Never a good idea in martial arts cultivation.

"Unh! Is that a good kick?"

"Yes," Mek encouraged, adding to himself, *for a child just getting front teeth.*

Tai concentrated on two, three moves, then continued. "This island, with its gold mines, was once the capital of the Golden Islands. The gateway to the rest of the archipelago. It was the one the Black Dragon galleys had to take if they wanted the rest. Also, it was the place where the other island chiefs met twice a year, to celebrate Two Moons and No Moons, and to agree on island matters."

"Midwinter and midsummer," Mek said, not the slightest bit breathless, though Tai was breathing hard. "Got it."

"They don't seem to have had a government in the way we do. No emperor. No one declared to be Heaven's Chosen. No army. The clan chiefs gathered in a circle and couldn't leave it until all agreed on trade matters, or conflicts between clans. Guardian seems to be the title for the one who listens." He tapped his head.

"Kick!"

Tai kicked, without much force. "The Golden Islanders were traders. Not raiders. They didn't live in fortresses inside these hollow mountains, but on houses along the shore. This island wasn't trading gold so much as bolsters, made with blueneck feathers. They traded a lot with us, in fact, which is I think why there are so many imperial words in their dialect, pronounced differently."

"Let's do this form again, this time faster."

"I need to catch my breath first. This mud, and the rain, make it so difficult. How do you do it?"

"Practice," Mek said. "We cultivate outside every day,

whatever the weather. Pirates won't wait for a balmy day to attack."

"Ay! I should probably start at the beginning. If this is truly a beginning. The Golden Islanders didn't follow the Black Dragon Father, and they didn't regard obsidian as sacred, as the Dragon's Chosen do. They regarded birds as emissaries from heaven. The big birds—the ones that fly highest—being those closest to heaven, and therefore the most sacred."

"Like our Crane God?"

"I think so."

"The Heir has an oriole on her staff," Mek said, his attention wandering to his form. Was he leaping higher than before? Or was it just the splash of his feet that made it seem so?

"The golden oriole is the symbol of the Guardian, which was the other important thing in this island. Mek, this concerns you, now. I really think it's an Essence skill that comes down through Bar Ardal's family, mothers to daughters."

"What Ardal calls Hearing? I'm pretty sure you're right. Only girls get it?"

"Only girls could inherit," Tai corrected. "I don't know what happened to boys born with the skill before the Black Dragon raiders came against them, but now, it seems, the Cobra Sages take any boys with the skill away. Before the raider galleys came to conquer the Golden Islands, the Golden Island men went out in fishers to harvest fish and seagrass and kelp, and the women stayed on the island."

"Oh. Like in the far south," Mek said. "I remember that from lessons."

"Yes. One last thing. The raiders never actually conquered them in battle. I can't quite get how the Islanders managed to keep them away, but they did. For generations. Until something happened and they had to make a treaty, and give concessions, and in return, the Heir's ancestors through the mothers govern this island. But over the generations, the obsidian throne has been taking over. Slaves. Boys taken away for the mines and the galleys, and the fighting circles. Girls get taken by the Cobra Sages as well as boys—except for the Heir."

Mek scowled. "I hate that. And hearing it is not going to get us out of here."

Tai had to squash down the urge to *know*. He reframed what he'd intended to say. "It might, because this is what the Heir seems to want to learn from you: whatever you know that might keep the Dragon galleys from taking Angja Island away from her entirely, their excuse being that she's so young."

Mek's ready sympathy sparked. "All my lessons with Master Root were peaceful lessons. They aren't lessons for her in this situation."

Tai agreed. But! "I need to learn more."

The next day, Steward Hathi caught him at the stairs. "Go to the labor chamber. It is time to ready for the fleet. They are coming."

TEN

PART OF READYING THE fortress was making sure the slaves looked like Dragon's Chosen's slaves. Everyone knew that Bar-Than Ardal held to Guardian Bar Thranis's rules: though she could not change the state of the slaves, she saw to it that they were treated as humanely as she could contrive within the treaty that kept the obsidian throne from taking the island entirely.

It was well known that Bar Gatslan favored northern ways, and one of those ways was making certain that slaves were identifiable as slaves at first glance, not just by the slave tattoo on their foreheads.

A pair of steady oldsters inspected the boys and girls from the labor chambers up through the skilled workers, trimming slaves' hair and seeing that no one wore shoes — and that the straw shoes slaves wore in winter were stored with winter things.

The children in Mek's peer group were used to this. One of the apprentice weavers brought a pair of scissors, which were passed from hand to hand; though they were forbidden to touch anything that could be construed as a weapon, these scissors were permitted for this occasion.

The apprentices in Tai's group were sent down as well. Tai refused to cut his hair, his fists tight as he tried to hide his fury and shame. He would not do something so unfilial, even if they beat him for it. But he did want to stay alive. He forced himself to submit to being shorn along with the others who had grown shaggy.

When the scissors reached Mek's hand, it cost Mek a slight pang, mostly because he didn't like the erosion of home customs. He knew that his parents would approve his doing everything possible to come home alive. If that meant cutting his hair, so be it—and he attacked his head with such vigor that he ended up looking dreadful, with two great bald spots where he'd cut too close, and everything else uneven. Made worse by the stubborn, downy curls sticking up in every direction.

The children got a good laugh at him, as well as at a hapless boy named Coral who had managed to make one side far shorter than the other, and a girl who, in her nervous haste, nicked the top of an ear. The exasperated woman who came to inspect them did what she could to neaten them up with snips and clips, scowled at the girl, and moved on.

Mek waited for the girl to be seen to, then saw that they didn't seem to have a healer. That is, he knew that the Westerners wrapped broken limbs, because he'd seen bandages on a young man injured in a fall.

"Stop the nick?" he asked the girl, making a motion of stanching a wound.

She glowered at him, suspicious. "How is anyone to do that?"

"Press turmeric finger there," Mek said, as if it was obvious. He'd learned the Western word for turmeric from Old Daldi while weeding.

"Turmeric?" she repeated, even more suspicious, as she wiped at her bleeding ear with her fingers, and then bent to clean them on the grass lest she drip on her clothes and risk a beating. "Isn't that an herb for flavoring the bars' vegetables? Are you making game of me, Mud?"

"No. My family use it for cuts," Mek said. "Not a cure. Helps the scab."

She looked unsure, as if she thought he was lying.

"I get." Mek dashed off, skirting the main vegetable garden, and headed for the area bordering the herb garden.

He reached the turmeric at the top of the rise, then peered past a ragged line of mimosa toward a slope that at first glance seemed covered with weeds and wildflowers, but there was a puzzling sense of order. Was that bright yellow arnica?

Arnica was poisonous to eat, Master Root had taught Mek, but it was good for helping to heal bruises faster. He spotted ginger, and honeysuckle—good for sore throats…

His gaze returned to the mimosa, and the significance of that ragged line began to dawn: mimosa bark was another medicine. Was that whole area beyond the mimosa, now long neglected, once the healers' garden?

He remembered the girl, snatched up some tender turmeric fingers and pelted back. "This should be cooked. Dry." He crushed the rhizome, which the Ki clan called a finger. "Press on cut."

She stared at her palm in doubt a heartbeat before a long arm thrust through the welter of children and fingers and pinched him by the ear.

The music master exclaimed, "There you are! We must rehearse!"

The musicians had foregathered with a shared grim determination. They commenced a rehearsal that would take them into the middle watch of the night.

Upstairs, the girls' personal slaves were busy setting out golden candlesticks, fine woven rugs, and all the decorations befitting their ancestry. Last, Ardal had to endure having her long river of dark brown hair brushed out of its usual single braid and plaited into many, along with the most beautiful of the beads her grandmother had left for her. At the ends, the braids were tied off with the delicate golden ornaments called courting chimes. Odval adored these, but Ardal found them annoying. "They make my head heavy," she grumbled. "And the noise distracts me when I want quiet for Hearing."

"And have Grandmother's spirit wailing in shame?" Odval protested. "You know what is due to her. To us! And you know that Jathyam will be doing his best to outshine us."

Ardal stuck her tongue out at the mention of their cousin, who had been their favorite playmate when they were all small. But ever since his hands and feet started growing and his voice changed, each year he was less like that boy and more like the raider warriors he so admired. On his last visit, he'd strode about snapping orders, sending the slaves scurrying to fetch things he could have fetched himself, and bragging about his wins in the ring and how many enemy ships the raiders chased, took, or sank.

Jathyam and his father were both on the watch the next day.

As the tide carried the fleet in toward the southeast inlet, it was clear that there really was some mysterious way that Ardal — younger than Jathyam by two years! — somehow knew that they were coming.

The flagship drifted in on the flood, and as it kissed up to the wharf, easy as a feather dropping, the galley slaves smartly lifted oars and pulled them in as one. On the wharf, a gaggle of slave musicians began playing "The Black Dragon Commands the Skies, the Lands, and the Seas" until their faces were crimson.

What was that skill that Ardal had, anyway? Jathyam's father had forbidden him to talk about it. "You don't have it," he'd said shortly. "Consider yourself lucky."

Eh, there was that! Any sign of mysterious powers and the snakes got you, and then you lost your name altogether, much less anything you might have been heir to. You belonged to the snakes forever.

There were two Cobra Sages behind him now, one old and one his age, on his first voyage. His circle-shaped forehead tattoo was new and sharp.

Jathyam looked away quickly, lest their eyes meet. He did not know what this boy's skills were, but he did not want to risk having his mind ransacked.

Gatslan of Angja did not notice his son. His attention was on the black dragon banners against a gold background, the kneeling slaves in lines, heads down except for the musicians toiling away with their noise. Everything proper—clearly they were expected, though he'd sent scouts out to the widest perimeter, under orders to sink and burn any craft whatsoever. Which they had done. No one could possibly have warned that girl, and yet here she was, with the younger brat, waiting at the gate in the correct place for an heir to greet an elder.

An heir! A teen, and heir for almost three years, when he ought to rule here. Unlike every other island in the Empire of Father Dragon's Chosen, in which potential heirs competed against one another until they faced off in the ring. That was the way the best and strongest ought to be chosen. But there was that accursed treaty, and when that girl reached eighteen, she would become Guardian Bar Angja for life.

Unless something happened to her…

But then her mother would know.

Gatslan's mind shied away from that road, and he ordered his thoughts. Everything was correct; at least the girl knew what was due to his position, weird powers or not. *Some* things were almost as they should be on this island.

He stepped from ship to land. The musicians switched instantly to the "Family Reunited" screeching and drumming as the old shaman—still alive—doddered out and called down Father Dragon's blessing on them all.

The lord acknowledged the sisters' polite bows, and they passed the lower wall and proceeded up into the fortress. It looked quite fine with black dragon banners draped over every balcony, along with luck talismans.

They separated inside with all the proper words, agreeing to meet again at the family banquet, and he retired to his suite to hear reports from his people among the staff. The only thing in the steady stream of news that caught his ear was Steward Hathi's precise account of the Heir's report of something falling out of the sky, two months previous. When they sent out searchers, prepared for anything, they discovered two Muds, considerably battered from the storm that had blown the two days before.

"Muds? Are they in the prison? Spies?"

Steward Hathi said, "They're mere boys. The younger can't be more than ten. He's an apprentice musician. He was on the dock today."

Gatslan thought back. Ten? He recollected a small slave blowing away at a flute, noticeable only because of a huge bald spot in his hair above one eyebrow. If that boy was a Mud spy, then Gatslan was a blueneck. "The other?"

"A little older. A short-sighted weed who was a scribe apprentice to the Muds."

"Short-sighted? Has he been castrated?"

"It's very slight. He is quite adept at writing, and is mastering our tongue so that he can be put to translation."

"Hai-yoo," Gatslan said. "A *little* short-sightedness in a slave is no bad thing. Perhaps we can breed him one day, if it doesn't worsen—it might be worth raising a few half-Muds to send back against them."

Steward Hathi bowed, expressionless as always.

Gatslan said, "How did they end up here? This island is weeks from Great Ran, even with the wind at our back."

"They don't know anything beyond their ship—both insisted it was a trader—crashing into another ship, and the wind whirled them up and away. It was a true dragon storm."

"I remember that storm." Gatslan narrowed his eyes. "Did you search for ships that might have landed them in secret, under its cover?"

"The Heir sent our fast scouts out in line-of-sight search for three days' distance in all directions. There was nothing."

"Unlucky fate, then," Gatslan said, losing interest. "Probably *was* traders, crashing into one another like drunken beggars—their navy would be positioned better to ride out storm winds. Do you think her talent is increasing?"

Steward Hathi said woodenly, "I cannot gauge that, my lord. But she works diligently each day, after doing her duties for the island."

"You are dismissed—wait. There's a letter here for each of my nieces, from their mother. Take them." He snapped his fingers at a waiting slave, who retrieved said letters, handed them off, and the steward bowed herself out, leaving the lord feeling virtuous in having bestirred himself in the matter. "Now, send for the horses. Jathyam! Let's scout the hunting grounds, shall we, before dinner?"

The musicians played at the banquet, as slaves did decorous dances meant for exalted company, between exhibitions of skill. Then Odval came out to dance in honor of her relations, after which Jathyam performed the latest knife dance popular among the boys of rank in the capital.

There were a few ballads recited to the drums, and then the long evening came to a close amid the ritual toasts for health, success, and luck to those far away.

The next day, the lord, after issuing his orders for the Cull, took his son, his elite warriors, and a few favored lower ranking individuals from among his fleets to go hunting up in the wilds of the north.

Ardal learned early that the Cull was the first item on the treaty mandate—a custom vitally important to the Dragon's Chosen. Here, she had no more influence than Grandmother had had.

She watched from above as the Cobra Sages and the battle master caused all the slaves to be lined up in the court between the kitchen storage and the outer buildings. Behind the battle master walked the lord's own executioner and interrogator, obsidian knife held in the ritual position up the inside of his forearm, blade out; his purpose today was to cull any weak or sickly slaves with the "merciful end," a swift stroke with the obsidian knives that were so sharp that supposedly the child didn't even know it was cut until its blood had rushed from its body.

It was well known that the old Guardian Bar Thranis had

not approved of this custom any more than her foremothers had. Weak babies could grow into strong adults. Though it had been a few generations since the Golden Island Guardians had displayed their legendary skills—all the more mysterious for not requiring bloodshed—Bar Gatslan still erred on the side of prudence when issuing orders to his battle master.

But the slaves did not know that. And there had been culls in the past. Even the smallest tried to look strong and alert as the four passed along the kneeling rows.

At the end of the line, the battle master grunted as he flicked a hand, and Steward Hathi raised her voice. "All those under five years, return to the nursery."

The tension remained with those over five. Mek and Tai were added to this group, standing immediately out. Terror flared in both when the Cobra Sages in their black and red cowled robes approached, carrying finely carved boxes of ebony.

Slave guards followed them, ropes at the ready at the slightest sign of struggle, even whimpering. But Mek scarcely noticed them. His hands had gone clammy at the sight of those Cobra Sages, and he shut his eyes, mentally rebuilding his wall not with wood or brick but imagining it as thick as a mountain. No hint of Essence must leak!

He was so inwardly focused that he missed the first few tattoos, until the wail of a child rose, sharply cut off by a hard pinch and a hissed warning from one of the slave guards.

The two Cobra Sages began. Mek forced himself to watch, so that he would know what to expect. The old Cobra Sage was fast, whispering some kind of ritual words that blurred in his ears as his blade, nearly as thin as a needle, quickly marked the circle-and-curved-line character on a child's forehead. Two slave guards stood at either side, the child's head pressed tight between bolsters to keep him from moving.

The young Cobra Sage was slow and in his earnest determination to do well, cut too deeply, leaving his tattooed children with blood dripping down their foreheads, wiped quickly by the caretakers as the children were whisked away, where—according to long-standing orders from the Guardians—they were permitted to lie down after drinking some hoarded calming tea, a strictly Angjan drink made from pineapple weed, lemon balm, and lavender.

Tai looked about wildly, and Mek held his breath at the way Tai's face flushed then paled, his entire body as taut as the string of a zither. Was he going to run? He'd be cut down before he got three steps! Maybe he wanted that?

Mek yearned to reassure him, to remind him of their escape pact. Though how they were to escape when constrained by whatever Essence charms were put on those tattoos, he did not know. Escape had always seemed possible, hovering there in the distance, like the great seabirds. But suddenly, the threat of the tattoos was here. Now.

The Cobra Sages approached Tai and Mek, then one of the guards said, "Wasn't this one to be castrated?" He grabbed the front of Tai's tunic.

"No," stated the battle master. "The lord said, only if his short-sightedness worsens. Leave him be this year."

The guard let go the fabric and pressed his bolster to the side of Tai's head. The second guard came at the other side, and a third bent over Tai from the back, hands gripping his shoulders to hold him absolutely still.

Powerless, wretched with humiliation, Tai was forced to endure the quick strokes. The old Cobra Sage stepped back, frowning down at him. "You Muds are notoriously stupid. Do you understand what will happen if you are disobedient?" He made some kind of Essence sign in the air, and Tai let out a choked cry of pain, and sagged, his complexion gray. "That's what will happen to you if you venture past the shoreline without permission."

It was Mek's turn. The three adult slaves took firm hold of him, keeping his head immovable and his shoulders steady. Mek watched the young Cobra Sage dip his needle-blade in a golden vessel as he whispered words. Mek tried to listen, but the words blurred horribly, making him slightly dizzy.

Then a finger braced itself against his cheek and the blade sliced, cold then hot; Mek detected something in that heat, and all his poison lessons rushed back. He tried to kill the poison at the site, but Master Root had taught him how to ward ingested poison. His blood moved too fast to catch the invader. But he'd identified it.

Those holding him released him. He fell forward in a face-down bow, mostly to hide his face lest it betray any sign of the Essence that he yearned to loose against the invader.

The Cobra Sages saw the movement as an abject bow, and the young one said, "Shall I administer the warning penalty?"

The old one murmured, "No, that one looks obedient

enough. And he saw what happened to the other Mud."

The Cobra Sages moved away, for their task was not yet done.

One of the slave guards said, "Back to work, now." And, lower, "We all had to endure it. You'll live."

Mek wasn't so sure about Tai, as they started to cross the court. Mek wanted to run, to get out of sight of those Cobra Sages, but Tai was trembling so much he had trouble walking. His face had gone ghost pale, and tears showed beneath his lashes. His breath shuddered and he fell to his knees, then his head dropped forward onto them. Had he fainted?

Mek looked around. They were now alone. The children had all gone. The Cobra Sages moved toward the far end of the court, the wind toying with their long robes. The older slaves knelt in silent, rigid rows. Some would be chosen out for guard training, either here or on the raiders. Mek saw one of the hot-tempered youths he and Tai had learned to avoid flash a fierce smile as he and a handful of the bigger, stronger slaves were sent in one direction.

"Tai," he whispered, shaking the other boy's bony shoulder. "We should go. We don't want to be killed for weakness."

"I'm going to be sick," Tai muttered into his knee.

"Do it inside?"

Mek glanced warily toward the other end of the court, where the battle master was choosing out a second group. The worst bully in the labor pool was sent to this one—he looked toward the small group still trying to hide their smiles, and began a loud protest, but the slave guards were on him in a heartbeat, the rope ends rising and falling.

The Cobra Sages were busy doing something to the first group's tattoos. Mek turned away. If he understood right, some of those in that larger group looking so stunned and defeated would be condemned to the galleys, and the rest to the mines.

Would the Cobra Sages or the battle master look this way? "We have to go," Mek said urgently.

Tai lifted his head, shuddering hard. "I want to die."

Mek whispered, "We want to escape. Not die."

Tai turned his blood-smeared face toward Mek. "Didn't you understand what they did to me? To you? What they said?"

Mek looked around one more time before putting his lips close to Tai's ear. "I know the poison they put in us. It carries the charm. I'm going to find a way to get it out."

ELEVEN

THEY MADE IT TO the privy before Tai was very sick.

Mek waited with him, unsure what else to do. He knew he was supposed to return to the blueneck nests. Old Daldi wouldn't fuss at him too much—he knew that, too. But who else might be roaming around, counting people? An image of that bully, his face streaked with blood from the violence of those blows, made him shudder. Anything could happen.

"Drink some water, Tai. Then let's go. We don't want them looking for us."

"My mouth tastes vile."

The stale tea for rinsing mouths had long since been emptied. "I'll get you a willow twig," Mek offered, and was relieved to see Tai's face relax a little, under the slow trickle of blood. "Keep rinsing your face. The cold water ought to slow the bleeding, and numb it a little. I'll get some more turmeric fingers, too."

Tai leaned against the wall, eyes closed. "Can you really take out the charm?"

"I believe so. I need to experiment. But I'll do that on me."

Mek hoped to see Tai recover, but there was little reaction other than Tai muttering under his breath. All Mek caught was "shamed for life."

Mek hadn't thought about affinities and suchlike for a long time. He was not adept at sorting them, unless they were distinct. Tai's Essence was small, but his affinity was as distinct as a knife-edge: pure metal. Very rare, pure metal, Master Root had said. Mek didn't remember much about general characteristics common to metal affinities, except that long memories was one. And stubbornness.

"Go and lie down. I'll tell the Heir that they cut extra deep and you're bleeding too much to risk dripping on the good paper."

Mek ran out, skirting the extremity of the kitchen garden, until he found an old willow alongside a bend in the stream that fed the garden. He plucked a twig or two, concealed them in the waistband of his underclothes, then sped up to the Heir's wing to report Tai's absence.

As he expected, she said, "Tell him that's quite responsible, and to stay away until tomorrow."

He bowed, and there she was again, this time at the inner door. But he did not dare answer. Not with those Cobra Sages around. One of them had glowed with Essence when Mek had taken a tiny peek as the raiders approached.

He hurried away, stopping once to rinse his own forehead. He took the willow to Tai, then returned to the bluenecks, where he mucked and tidied sedulously until the bell.

The following day, Steward Hathi reported that most of the slaves tattooed by the younger Cobra Sage were still bleeding. Ardal gave instructions to the nursery caretakers for them to have calming tea if they needed it, and she looked with sympathy at the appearance of the elder Mud, Jetai, his forehead swollen around the gaping cuts. *Compromise,* Grandmother had said. *When you haven't the strength to carry your will, try to win compromise. I can't overturn slavery. I regret the rope's end, but that is preferable to the Cobra Sage charms that burn you from the inside.*

Ardal busied herself by rereading her mother's letter, until Jathyam turned up, his braids more ornamented than Odval's. A glance and Ardal saw in his restless manner that he was bored, and wanted to be entertained. As his gaze drifted toward Jetai bent over his work, bony shoulder blades sticking up from his shapeless slave garment, instinctively she moved to block him from sight. Though Jathyam had never been a bully, life in the north might have changed him even more than it had so far.

Resigning herself to a wasted day, she said, "I was going to take a ride. Would you like to visit the rainbows at Five Falls?"

"Hai-yoo, so I haven't." He snapped his fingers at one of the many hovering slaves. "Horses."

During the walk to the stable, he bragged about tedious things—what he'd killed, the distance of his shots, how many contests he won in archery, knife fighting, and the like.

She responded with the expected praise, but it was so calm and so kindly that he began to feel almost as if he shouted into a wind. He cast around for a different subject as they trotted through the three succeeding gates, sentries saluting and slaves bowing low — everything reassuringly proper — then said, "Did you get your letters from Aunt?"

"We did, our thanks to Uncle Gatslan," Ardal said.

Never would she mention that neither she nor Odval expected any real communication in these letters. They knew these were read by other eyes before ever reaching Angja. Just the sight of Mother's dear hand was more important than the bland words about great doings around the obsidian throne.

"I saw her right before we sailed. She looked well. She had a lot of new ornaments. Means she's earned merits, you know." He brushed his hand over his breast — bare now of his own merit necklace.

"She mentioned them, along with her gratitude to the empress," Ardal said, remembering Grandmother's admonishment to always express gratitude with your flattery, when in doubt about someone.

"She always asks me to embrace you two, but we're too old for that," Jathyam added with a bark of a laugh.

"We are, thank you," Ardal said with firm cordiality.

"And she always asks if we've caught sight of your brother. As we see more snakes than she does, I guess. I don't want to tell her that I probably wouldn't recognize him if I saw him."

"No, I expect not," Ardal said, sparing a rare thought for her unknown elder brother who had been taken by the Cobra Sages before she was even born. That, she reflected now, argued for a tremendous amount of innate skill. Like —

"Let's race," he said, having run out of subjects.

They kicked the animals into a gallop. Of course he must win. Why? He was Uncle Gatslan's heir. His sisters had both been betrothed at birth, so he had no need to compete with them. But he could never have Angja while she lived. Unlike all his supposed friends, who might win the competition for lordships without the constraints of a treaty.

And here they were, out here quite alone.

That brought a chilling thought: *Does he want me dead?*

She glanced at him. He was armed with the obsidian knife he'd fought so hard to earn, there in pride of place at his side.

Two knives of plain metal in each boot top. And that golden thing stuck through the knot holding his braids high on his head might even be a weapon, though Ardal had read that poisoned hairpins were the common weapons of princesses and noble girls. He wasn't wearing his merit necklace, which was of course strictly for formal rituals, but also—so she had read—was worn when going into battle or facing a duel. But he wouldn't consider killing her a true duel...

He glanced over, looking puzzled. She said quickly, "I thought we were lost—it has changed since I was here last." She pointed to last year's landslide. "There's the fall, beyond that slope. I can hear it now." She was aware that she was speaking too quickly, but he only shrugged, and peered under his hand.

"I always forget just how big it is," he said as they descended the last of the trail onto the shoreline. "Too bad when that mountain exploded, or broke, it didn't have more gold at the center."

Ardal agreed, knowing that Uncle Gatslan was always worried that the gold mine would run out. They were already delving dangerously deep—but the gold mine was part of the treaty that he controlled, as senior man of the family. She could do nothing about the danger and horror of sending more slaves there.

The falls were now in view.

Sometime in the unimaginable past, a great portion of a fire mountain had either slid into the sea, forming the little islands out there scarcely big enough for all the birds perched on the naked rocks, or had exploded in such a way that caused nearly half the mountain to leap into the air and land out there. Either way, since then, water had found its way from the higher mountains further north where the gold mines lay, and divided into five streams. The falls resounded the loudest all spring, when the snows atop the highest mountains melted. And if you rode to a certain promontory on land, beyond where the shaman had his cottage, you could see rainbows in interlocking arches.

Jathyam put back his head to stare, his mouth a little open, and in his profile Ardal caught a glimpse of the happy little cousin who had loved drawing horses and warriors when he was small.

"Dragon Father must be pleased with us," he said finally, a palm turned heavenward as he grinned.

She did not know what pleased Dragon Father—besides bloodshed, apparently—and did not want to know, but she hummed assent, and presently they turned back.

On the raiders' arrival, Bar Gatslan had witnessed once again the undeniable proof that his niece really had inherited his mother's ability, which confirmed another generation in the long line of Guardians. He would not inherit, he reflected as they sailed away two days later.

But after all, this island was where his wealth came from. So many had to strive and struggle to maintain their prestige, yet with every visit there awaited him a cargo of gold and of the exquisitely embroidered, cloud-soft blueneck-eider bolsters unmatched by any other island, and prized exceedingly by the emperor, the empress, and especially the First Prince.

Beyond that, this island was boring. The Guardians forbade the establishment of a fighting ring, there was no one worth speaking to, and hunting was fun only in good weather. This was why it was wise to arrive late in spring, which placed a limit on his stay. Everyone understood that he must be back in the capital for Father Dragon's Birth at the end of Sixth Mother Moon Month, and its all-important competitions and sacrificial rituals to the heroic ancestors of old, imploring them to bring glory to this generation.

As Angja sank below the horizon, it sank from the forefront of his thoughts.

And, as the raiders sank out of view from the islands, they diminished from the attention of the inhabitants.

The black dragon banners were hauled in and folded away for the next visit. The newly tattooed began to heal, all except Tai regarding the episode as an expected part of life.

During the succeeding days, Mek kept himself busy in the bluenecks' territory. He had decided to explore that herbal garden, though beyond the ten or so most common herbs used for medicine, he was not at all certain if he'd be able to identify anything. At least he could harvest some arnica. Bruises were a fact of life here. Why not ease them?

Wait…hadn't Tai said something about translating an herbal?

"Of course I remember everything I read," Tai stated later,

slightly offended, when Mek asked.

He began to recite the herbal.

"Hold, hold, slow down," Mek pleaded, when he realized that Tai really did know it all. As would someone with a metal affinity.

"I'll bring you the original." Tai fingered the fresh scabs on his forehead; he could not seem to keep his hands from them, though it hurt more when he touched them. And sometimes they oozed. "No one would ever look at it, as it's written in old imperial. I don't even know if they will look at my translation."

"It'll take forever to read it." Mek sighed; he knew how to read, but once he'd learned, he'd seldom had to do it.

"Learn," Tai said, and yanked his fingers away from his face. He could not suppress yet another memory of that guard grabbing for his privates and throwing the word *castration* into the air so casually. He added seriously, "Promise me. We will find a way to escape this island before those Cobra Sages return with that four-eyed rat Bar Gatslan."

Mek also remembered that threat, coming so suddenly from that slave guard. It could only have meant that the lord was considering it. "I said I'd figure it out, and I will. But you have to continue to cultivate forms. That includes learning sparring."

He'd expected Tai to scoff at that, but instead, Tai gave him a strange look, the sort of fervent unblinking stare of someone uttering a vow, and said, "I have not forgotten. And I will cultivate diligently." He meant every word.

It was Tai who shook Mek awake very early the next morning, so they could go out to the hens, in the rain, to take up where they had stopped.

Mek had discovered that once his chores were done, kindly Daldi left him largely alone, now that the old man was free from having to teach him the Westerners' tongue. A week after the departure of the raider fleet, he decided he was safe enough to run over the hill toward that abandoned herbal garden and this time, explore it thoroughly.

As he ran, he filled with questions about the Essence winds that had brought them all this way. Had *he* done that, somehow, or had those wind dragons he'd sensed been real? "Are there demons around me now?" He turned his gaze up and around.

No answer.

As he tore down the slope toward the stream, joy rushed back, strong and sure. How he loved to run and leap! Fast as a jackrabbit! Why did these people disparage rabbits? Aish, they did at home, too, which was just as stupid. Rabbits are fast! They're smart! They don't attack anybody else in going about their lives.

He needed to be fast to cover all that ground. But when he drew strength into his lightened heart, why, the ground seemed to push him up and away! That last one, he was certain he'd leaped twice the length of a tall man. Another thing to experiment with—but again, he could not do it where he risked being seen.

He leaped over the stream with plenty of air between himself and the water, and reached the garden. It spread all across a southeast-facing slope, at the apex of which grew a clump of mountain redbark trees, so familiar from home. Sheltered beneath their leaves, in dappled light, grew longevity root. He crouched down to touch it reverently when he sensed the Heir outside his massive inner door.

He dissolved that door for the first time since the morning the raiders arrived.

"Where are you?" she asked.

He considered a lie. Except she, or Odval, might have looked for him. Anyway, she had not betrayed him to those Cobra Sages. He knew that Tai did not trust the sisters, but Mek sensed no falseness in Ardal when she opened her door, and all her emotions flooded his senses.

"I am in medicine garden," he thought carefully in her language.

To his surprise, she responded, "Healer's garden. Healer. Gives medicine. Hai-yoo! You must learn faster! If you know some healing, it is good. But...slow."

He had already figured out from well-meant whispers after his tattooing that the Dragon way was to "cull weakness." How ridiculous! He wished the gut gripes on the lord and especially those Cobra Sages.

In the immediate sense, he was free to explore that garden. He'd take Tai with him, if they were supposed to be translating that old herbal from imperial to the westerners' tongue. And *that* meant, he could really start cultivating with Tai.

But that was counting on rain at the first breath of wind.

TWELVE

I WILL PASS QUICKLY over the rest of that spring.

Tai was discovering that any physical activity built strength. He was astonished the first time he was able to maintain a handstand, after uncounted ignominious flops. He ground away at it whenever he could, often until his muscles trembled with fatigue, and the next day he sat to his tasks aching all over. But he drank the strengthening herbs that Mek added to his tea, no matter how bitter the taste.

Mek didn't keep his medicine a secret. He hated seeing a rash, an infected cut, the greenish complexion of internal distress, when he knew how to fix those. He kept experimenting with the medicines on himself or on those who sometimes sidled to him during work and asked if he knew any nostrums for itches in armpits, or rashes, or a cough that wouldn't stop. "Freckle told me your family had a medicine garden. Do you have a weed that can fix me?"

He constructed drying racks that summer, and Freckle, who tended bluenecks with him, after Mek cured a nasty rash, asked his father in the kitchen for an old grinding wheel so that Mek could make powders to be added to tea. As the weather warmed, and the lizards came out to sun themselves along the wooden slats of their herb racks, Mek taught Freckle as much as he knew about the properties of plants.

It became general knowledge among the slaves that Mushroom, that is, Kimek, knew a lot of Mud nostrums that cleared up runny noses, eased aches, calmed tempestuous insides, and so on.

When he found the right combination of bark and honey to

ease the ache in the music master's hands so that he could get back to his weaving, the music master let him take his flute to practice with.

At the beginning of Phoenix sixth month (or what the Westerners called Mother Moon sixth month, the smaller moon being Ghost Moon, as at home) the labor slaves, apprentices included, were sent to the tea plantations to harvest leaves, as their masters celebrated Father Dragon's Birth. They camped outside at night, the weather being clear. Mek brought the flute along, and played as his group lay staring up at the stars before slumbering.

When they returned with their fragrant bushels and baskets, Mek spent many a pleasant twilight out among the bluenecks, playing his old songs, and learning new. Daldi was convinced the birds liked his music. They certainly clustered around a lot. Whatever kept the birds happy kept him content.

Summer ripened and waned. Autumn crept like the steadily lengthening shadows, bring the promise of cold winds.

Mornings, either before or after Mek and Tai did their cultivation in the hollow below the medicine garden, Mek experimented alone with poisons, easily winning cooperation with various cobras he met. He was getting to be very fast at identifying and encapsulating snake poison, but that got him no closer to clearing the Cobra Sages' charmed poison from his blood.

"It's a different..." He began to say to Tai, and drifted, not having the vocabulary in either tongue.

"Different type of cobra?" Tai asked. "Or is it the charms that are different?"

"It could be?"

"My grandmother showed me how to Hear," Ardal said the day that Tai finished translating the imperial herbal, late that autumn. "She promised there was more to learn, and once she even said she might write it down, but all she had time for was her share of the memoir." She gently touched the slim sheaf of pages. "I can see, now that you've translated that old imperial herbal, some of which she copied."

Ardal held the precious document to her breast before tenderly laying it on a shelf. "I don't know if anyone besides Kimek will be able to use it while I live, but at least it's here."

"It's a stupid rule, that medicine panders to weakness, and therefore must be forbidden," Tai stated, irked to see all his hard work effectively tucked away. "And like stupid rules, of course those who have the power to enforce them make exceptions for themselves?"

"Hai-yoo!" Odval exclaimed. "When Jathyam was here last, he mentioned that the emperor had been ill during winter, and not just the Cobra Sages but the shamans had been puzzled."

"They call in shamans for illness?" Tai asked.

"Yes. Everyone knows that shamans also do healing, though it's said to be part of the propitiation rituals," Ardal stated. "Grandmother told us that only the very powerful dare to summon them for illness, though. They always call illness something else, usually a curse. Or an omen. 'Send for the shaman, as this or that lord has been cursed,' if there is a rash, or an internal pain. Father Dragon's Chosen People are supposed to use their own strength to expel inner injuries or illnesses."

Mek understood that—in a way. He said, working his way through his still-sparse vocabulary, "But it's all right to wrap wounds from knives or swords?"

"Yes, because it's from an outside source, and also it's deemed part of the risk the strong take for achieving merit. There is no merit without bloodshed."

"But they don't see being sick from bad water, or too much cold, or by other things we don't understand…they don't see those as outside sources?" Mek asked, distracted by the wheel and dive of a flock of gulls on the shore below the fortress.

"No. All is seen in terms of the strength of arms. This proves you are the best. And that proves that you are Father Dragon's Chosen."

That sounded familiar to Tai. If someone seized the throne of the Thousand Islands and held it, the scribes all wrote that that indicated that the Jade Emperor had chosen that emperor.

But he said nothing. Over the waning of autumn, though these occasional summonses to the Heir's interview room had resulted in sharing ideas, he had only to glimpse the girls' foreheads innocent of these obscene tattoos to recollect the invisible divide between westerner and imperial. Enemy and trust.

"What are you pondering so seriously?" Odval asked him one day.

She had entered behind him, as she so often did of late. It seemed she had little to do besides offer to deliver or fetch something for her sister, though she chattered about lessons preparatory to practicing her courting dance, whatever that was.

"What am I to translate next?" Tai said, turning to the Heir. "If you've nothing more, the scribe will be expecting me back among the apprentices." He had already read everything he wanted to in the interview chamber, and was curious about the greater library behind the scribe area. And since the Cull, the male scribe apprentices had largely ignored him — and the three girls had actually become helpful.

Odval said to Ardal in a coaxing tone, "Surely there's something for him to do up here?"

Her sister looked surprised. "If there are Mud books that we have that you want translated, you've only to speak up." To Ardal, Tai had been primarily useful in teaching Mek the Dragon language.

"Yes," Odval said. "That is, how will I know unless they do get translated? There is always something new to learn," she added breezily, her gaze sliding toward Tai.

Who sat impassively, but then part of that was what made him so… interesting.

Ardal promised to speak to the scribe on the morrow, and they separated for the night — the two girls to their comfortable, warm chambers, where slaves waited to serve them, and the two boys to their cramped alcove that was now very chilly until they cocooned themselves in their winter blankets.

The next morning, the boys discovered the first freeze of winter. Mountain Peony got cold in winter. Snow was frequent. But the boys were not accustomed to deep freezes. They slipped and slid out to the blueneck yard, which was too treacherous for cultivation. Even if their feet in their straw shoes had not been going dangerously numb.

"We can't do this out here," Mek said finally.

Tai expelled a breath — which froze and began to fall in minute dots of white snow.

"The slaves' clothes storage room?" Tai asked presently.

"We'll go back to blindfolded sparring, since it's so small a space."

Tai agreed.

Winter deepened. The bluenecks huddled in their huts, mostly sleeping. Angja celebrated the turn of the year in some familiar ways and some strange ones. There was the same vigorous sweeping of every single surface to rid the fortress of any lingering bad luck, then the shaman walked through, wearing a robe covered in long, curling talismans as he waved an incense censor and uttered summons meant to bring good luck, health, and prosperity through the coming year.

For the festival meal, the slaves were given three dishes instead of the usual one, after which the stewards awarded those of the three divisions (children, apprentices, general labor) who had produced the most, or been deemed the most obedient, with the fragrant hot wine left from their masters' feast, and their choice of delicacies also left.

Afterward, the slave musicians played (no rehearsal for that) and the slaves were allowed to dance until midnight, when the two moons touched. The shaman returned to invoke a blessing, and everyone retired: work as usual on the morrow.

As the two boys bent against the freezing wind in crossing the court to their area, they looked up at the two moons in the ice-sharp, clear sky. Both longed for home, but neither spoke until they reached their alcove. Mek lifted his flute to his lips and played, putting such unspoken yearning into his melodies that most of those in the other alcoves stopped their conversations, listening. Some looked out at the sliver of the silvery sky visible, trying to catch sight of those paired moons before they sank.

Mek played until a guard appeared on the narrow catwalk, scolding. Mek put away the flute. And for the remainder of winter, if he couldn't sleep, he played, sitting back against the wall and knees up, barely blowing across the hole so that the flute whispered as he worked his fingering. One night he noticed that if he played this way when Tai was asleep, Tai's breathing relaxed and deepened.

Did that mean good dreams? He could actually check on Tai's dreams! But Master Root had made it very clear that that was a trespass, a betrayal of trust, unless permission was granted.

He put away the flute and burrowed in his blanket to sleep.

THIRTEEN

BLIZZARD, FREEZE, BLIZZARD, FREEZE, blizzard freeze melt, blizzard freeze, then another brief melt, and after an eternity of an increasingly dirty white world, the sky low and bleak, the plum trees burst out in blossoms. The cruel, cold winter was weakening at last, but for the slaves, every day was the same. Only the weather and its resultant chores changed.

As soon as the boys could tolerate it, they resumed their secret cultivation in the yard. Hibernating creatures ventured forth, blinking and hungry. Including the snakes.

Spring ripened. Tai found himself waking some mornings, having been scratching at the healed-over tattoo on his forehead during his uneasy sleep—he dreaded the return of the lord, and he worked hard to hide his very mild short-sightedness, lest someone think it had worsened.

Mek was assigned to help with the planting. Then there was weeding, until the bluenecks began to molt in earnest, and the days filled with chasing down and gleaning the precious down and feathers.

Days passed, cold, warm, cold, warm, warm, then warmer—and before they knew it, the large moon's sixth month had come, and no visit. "It happens, some years. They are probably on war maneuvers, ordered by the obsidian throne," Ardal said, and gave the order for the banners to be laid away in storage again.

Everyone in the fortress returned to the normal tread of days. Mek kept toiling away at reading and experimenting with the imperial herbal, between occasional experiments with pois-on donated by snake friends from the herbal garden and charms.

His reading improved. He located in that overgrown heal-er's garden quite a number of plants described in the imperial herbal. He harvested a precious longevity root, though he knew that he would not be able to gather dew on full moon days, and many of the other requirements to make the strongest elixir. But at least he could infuse what he had with Essence. He saw with inward delight that his infusion gave some relief to Old Daldi's gnarled hands, and to the other old slaves, who had been shift-ed to easier duties—for Angja Islanders of all ranks knew that the lord could slit the slaves' throats at any time if they became entirely useless, as it was rumored they did in the capital. Calling it a mercy.

The seasons fed one into the other, Mek having passed his eleventh year and was fast closing on twelve.

Tai tried not to think about those unacknowledged birth-days passing.

He tried to keep busy. Doing forms and sparring with Mek helped. To the amazement of both, he was actually becoming an adequate sparring partner. For a twelve-year-old partner.

He never gave up yearning for escape.

Summer waxed and waned, work in the blazing heat exhausting, then the sun began its slow descent, and the days cooled, with intermittent, incessant rain. The snakes would be hibernating soon.

Mek became aware of Tai's intense, painfully expectant gaze as the pages of the herbal slowly turned over the succeed-ing days. Few pages were left. One cold night, Mek took the herbal out, tipped it toward the ever-burning torch farther up the catwalk, and strained his eyes as he skimmed ahead.

As he'd expected, at this end of the herbal, the larger concern was the alleviation of the many aches and pains of old age. There was not going to be anything more about poisons of the blood than he'd already found: *ground cicada wings. Peach seed and safflower. Ginseng. Peony root.* None of these were going to touch that invader he could feel coursing through his body if he concentrated inwardly on his blood.

He looked over at slumbering Tai, who was now a palm and a half taller than Mek. Somehow that had happened without them noticing, until Mek found himself having to brace against Tai's sparring blows. There were even a couple of tiny dark hairs on his sharp-cut chin. Tai was so learned, so meticulous and honest, and yet in some ways Mek couldn't explain, he seemed like a little brother. Only in some ways. In other ways, Mek didn't think he'd ever catch up with Tai's scholarship.

Mek knew how much Tai dreaded the next appearance of Bar Gatslan. One careless point of a finger, and his life would be forever changed. Ruined, so Tai thought: neither ever forgot that careless reference to castration. Tai could never bear to refer to it, but Mek had asked Freckle and some of the other boys if that really happened. "Is that a punishment, too?"

Freckle shrugged uncomfortably. One of the slightly older boys looked about to make sure no girls were listening, and muttered, "It's so they won't have weak children."

The idea of having children seemed to Mek a very remote one, far in the future. "You say, slaves can have children?"

That caused a laugh. "Where do you think we came from?"

Stolen, or prisoners, like us, Mek thought, but didn't say.

"You can earn time alone," the older boy said. "Good production. Good behavior. The slave steward has a list. Some earn marriage. But the children belong to the masters."

"Aish!"

Aish, the others repeated after Mek pelted off. They thought the Mud expressions hilarious.

Unconcerned, Mek reported what he'd learned to Tai, who maintained the resolute silence that Mek knew by now meant he was deeply disturbed. It was better to concentrate on escape.

This old imperial herbal was not going to teach him—he knew that now. What about that grandmother herbal? Mek ought to look at it himself.

Having resolved that, he settled down to sleep.

The next morning, as they worked through the third form, he said, "Can you borrow that grandmother herbal from the Heir?"

Tai glanced his way. "It's not an herbal so much as family rules. What there is just replicates some of the imperial herbal."

"I know. But now that I can read some of their language, I'd like to take a look. Maybe I know enough to get any useful variations in recipes and prescriptions that you might have missed, if nothing else."

Tai gave a short nod. "She won't let me take it. I'm certain of that. All her grandmother's things are precious to her. But she might summon you to the aerie to see it."

Mek shrugged. Even though he was a gallant wanderer,

he'd learned here to be aware of who went before whom, and where they stood in a room, and how much space they commanded around them.

Tai did not see the Heir for several days. He could not go unless summoned, and he did not want to beg unless put to it. He was fighting that inner battle still when Odval encountered him coming back from morning practice with Mek. Though her words claimed that the encounter was accidental, it was clear that she had been seeking them.

Mild alarm chilled both boys. Though Odval had been increasingly friendly over the past year, even offering to smuggle treats to Tai (which he turned down, aware that her idea of "smuggling" would draw even more attention to these forbidden delicacies that no one else got to taste), they knew that getting caught cultivating martial arts was a death sentence.

It was Mek who blurted, "Bar Odval." He bowed. "I was asking Tai. If you might ask the Heir. Might I be permitted to see the grandmother herbal?"

Odval's gaze shifted to Tai. She smiled. "I'll go ask her now," she said in a sprightly voice.

A short time later, both were summoned to the aerie.

Ardal had not yet begun her day's tasks. Her gaze went straight to Mek, hope crowding her heart. "Why do you need to see it?"

Mek could not tell her the truth, of course. The Westerners must never know about his attempts to nullify the Cobra Sage poison! "There might be something useful that you or Tai missed," he said, and at her dubious look, "Could I ask what your esteemed grandmother said about those recipes and charms she copies. When she gave it to you."

Ardal gazed back in memory. "It was right before she died. She put my hand on it. Patted my hand. How hers trembled, it struck me to the heart! *Progress*, she whispered. No, it was *Purpose*, that's right. As if I'd *ever* forget my purpose, knowing that I was about to inherit all the things she had done so well, and I not prepared! But that was a reference to our family rules, I am sure." Ardal sighed out the lingering pain of grief, and added, "She died not long after."

She rose, felt among the golden keys hanging from her belt, and knelt at a cedarwood trunk carved with a complexity of cranes in flight, each bird enhanced with a thread of gold as if sunlight limned its feathers. "I keep it here. I like to think of the things she touched keeping me company through the day."

She lifted out the slim sheaf and laid it down. "Careful," she admonished Mek—remembering her cousin at that same age and the way he'd flung about impatiently.

Mek scarcely heard her. Was that thing glowing with Essence? He approached. It was! He looked up. "Didn't you notice the glow? Or did you put a charm on it?"

"No. I know no charms to lay upon it." Ardal gazed at him in question. "Everything of hers burns in my heart with the light of memory."

He gave his head a shake, laid his hand on the first page, then snatched it back as ice snapped through his nerves. "Ow!"

All three stared at him.

He popped his fingers in his mouth. "Didn't you feel that?" He turned to Tai accusingly. "You didn't tell me it had a warning charm on it."

In response, Tai touched the top page, then looked back in silent question.

Mek wondered if the charm only burned those with Essence skill. But who would the grandmother want to keep from looking at it? Cobra Sages?

"There's a..." What had Master Root called such things? "There's a binding on it." Making a connection, "Like on these." He tapped his forehead tattoo.

"But my grandmother loathed Cobra Sages," Ardal protested. "She would never have permitted one near her things."

Mek put his palm out. "You said. She had Essence skills."

"Such things are forbidden to anyone but the Cobra Sages, and the shamans," Odval said, turning from Mek to Tai.

Mek spoke up. "This charm might prevent them from touching it. A binding charm. I think there's something that breaks the charm. Think of it as a lock, needing a key to turn in it."

"Does it have to be an actual key?" Ardal looked doubtfully at the papers.

"No. It can be anything. Like a ring. Or some secret object. Or even a word. That's harder."

Then he heard an echo of Ardal's earlier words: Progress. Purpose. What if she wasn't just reminding Ardal to study hard? A girl who always studied hard?

In mind, Master Root spoke, as they combed twigs out of the goat's fur: *Remember, Kanda told us in his earliest writings that the world of Heaven and Earth is good, and that goodness is born into human hearts. Kanda's Way teaches us that Purpose is the stuff of which Essence derives...*

He looked up. "You said she kept patting it. Though she couldn't lift her hand much. Try touching it, and think, *Purpose.*"

Ardal bent over the paper lying on the top of the trunk, closed her eyes, and her lips moved.

A little snap briefly zinged in the air, and faded writing in brown ink leaped into clarity, written between the lines of the herbal at the front of the memoir. There were two handwritings here, one in newer ink, and the old one with a slightly different lettering.

Ardal turned to Mek. "I did not know...I thank you." She put her palms together, then crossed her palms over her chest.

Mek blushed. "Can I look at the herbal now? There might be some Essence procedures here. For some of the plants in the healer garden?"

Ardal turned back to the faded writing. There, she read in growing amazement: *The easiest spell is to raise vapor in a thick enough fog to hide ships from one another....*

Elements to regain their properties of origin...

Break the blood spells, such as —

She slammed her hand down on the paper, fingers spread, and then picked up the whole, and stuffed it in the trunk again. Then locked it. "This is meant only for my eyes," she said, sharp and even shrill. "It is instructions only for the Guardian."

She was trembling, her knees like water. With difficulty, she mastered herself, and turned to Mek. "I thank you again. But I cannot show you this now. Not until I have read it all, and I can figure out what can be shared with...". She paused. "With you," she finished.

The divide between slave and master, Westerner and Thousand Islander yawned between them. The boys bowed and left.

They didn't speak until late that night, alone in their alcove. "Ayah, that was a kick in the butt," Mek said. "Here I gave her what she wanted, and we won't get a sniff of those papers!"

"Not so," Tai whispered. "While you were talking to her, I read the top two pages. There are two parts to what is written, one part the formations the Guardians passed one to another. And the second part is Cobra Sage secrets."

FOURTEEN

He PAUSED, THE WORDS *Cobra Sages* a sinister hiss in the air.

Mek muttered, "I think we better wait for morning. When we can see in all directions."

He could wait. He knew how to wait. He also needed to think about what had happened. The glow in the paper that Ardal couldn't perceive, though she sensed things way out over the waters. She'd told Mek during one of their conversations last spring, "Once I could Hear without having to limit myself to what my eyes could see, Grandmother said to think myself higher. With the birds. First, looking down at the roof of the aerie, so that I would not lose my balance."

Mek understood losing balance, remembering his wild fall from the sky.

"And when I am steady in the air, to look out, and the horizon is so much farther away. That is what I practice and practice, but I have reached my limit, for I must always be able to see the top of the fortress. I cannot go higher than that, into the clouds."

Even so, that was a *very* powerful Essence power!

He needed sleep.

He turned over, brought to mind his favorite dream, home in the summer with Yellow-dog, Three-Leg, Long Ears, Owl, and Master Root, as they peeled lychee nuts and the old man talked about the living things of the world…

Tai heard Mek's breathing deepen, and for the thousandth time he envied Mek for being able to fall asleep instantly. He lay awake, gnawing at his thumbs and fighting the urge to pick at the cursed tattoo. He knew it was an imaginary itch, or burn.

Eventually he slept in fits until at stirrings from outside the alcove permitted him to give it up altogether. Mek woke, and they left.

The ground was cold under their feet, bearable as yet. Their breath clouded as they began warmups, and Tai said, "Don't interrupt, and I will give you exact words that I read on that top page. Then if you need translation into imperial, I can try from that memory, but it won't be exact."

Mek didn't care about exactitude.

Tai shut his eyes as his body swept into the first form, and he recited softly:

My dear child: I have been seeing signs in my body that I will not live to my hundredth year after all. I will not tell you this, as I know you will fret, and you must learn as fast as you can.

I ought not to have waited so long, but you are so young! Need demands I repair my delay, and so, while I have the strength, I shall write out my thoughts first, and if I have time after, begin with each step.

This will be divided into two sections. First, the defensive charms that I inherited from our foremothers — those with the skill to wield them. I did not have enough skill, for many of these though I believe you might. You are already farther than I was at twice your age, which is what gives me hope for Angja.

The first set of charms are simply stated: the altering of elements, such as water — which can be raised in vapor. Our foremothers kept the invaders at bay by enfogging them, and then drawing them away from our island, out to sea. They could restore nitre, brimstone, and charcoal to their natural forms, which rendered their gunpowder inert. These are just two examples.

Alas, I cannot quite compass these skills, but you might, eventually.

Mek was so startled that for the first time since he was small, he tripped in the middle of a difficult passage in the third form. He fell, and rolled to his feet, ignoring the load of mud clinging to his body and clothes. "Go on, go on!"

Tai resumed his recitation:

The second set is the most secret, and the most dangerous, which is why I have not burdened you, a child of barely ten. This is dream-walking. I visit your mother when it is safe for her to do so. But I also visit the dreams of your brother. Alas, you will not be able to walk in the dreams of your brother, because you have never met him. But I had the raising of him after he was weaned, and your mother was required to go to the capital to Listen for threat whenever the imperial family travels.

Because I knew him so well, and he me — he appeared in my dreams before I even knew he was doing it — I learned through him how to sustain these dreams through an object we both have grasped, and through that, distance becomes nothing. I have been witnessing his memories as he dreams them, ever since he was taken away by the Cobra Sages before he turned five.

This knowledge is forbidden, as you can imagine, therefore I will be binding these pages to your hand. (I learned that from the Cobra Sages, too.)

Most of what they have taught him I would never use, though there are some healing techniques at fundament, twisted to afford greater control.

The spells (that is the word they use) I list here I believe will be necessary, if you are ever able to achieve Angja's freedom…

Tai's voice dropped the recitation tone. "That is as far as I read."

"What was that about 'something' dreams through an object?"

"'Sustaining.'" Tai looked over. "What use is that?"

"Because *I* can visit in people's dreams. I used to do it. When I was little. I guess this brother of Ardal's and Odval's did, too. What did she say about an object? Need it be charmed, somehow?"

"I was not able to read that far before she put the text away."

They began to spar lightly, both remembering Ardal's reaction. Fear, foremost. "She sees us as the enemy," Tai stated. "I always expected that to happen sooner or later."

"I think she was too afraid. We are enemies, yes. But I think…" Mek snapped strikes and blocks as he struggled for words to express an amorphous idea — more of an impression. "Not *attacking* enemies."

"Slaves," Tai said, his teeth flashing briefly, the word an expletive on his tongue.

"Do you mean, we're slaves who can be tortured until we reveal all we know?"

"Yes. Even if she believed in our intent to keep her secret, we would still be a weakness, if her uncle or those Cobra Sages become suspicious of us for any reason."

"You can't tell her you saw that stuff, then, or ask for more?" Mek said.

"No." The word was an exhale.

A few more martial exchanges, then Mek said, "Maaaayyy-be, if you are alone up there again..."

Tai smiled bitterly. "If she hasn't already locked that trunk away in her private rooms, I would be astonished."

"Aish, you have it right," Mek muttered. Then, as the bell rang to begin the day, he dropped his hands. "I'll have to try with what you saw."

"Is there anything I said that you can use?"

"It's new ways to think," Mek said uncertainly. He needed to consider that paper, bound to Ardal's touch, and the focus on Purpose. "I'd forgotten all about bindings—a subject Master Root only knew about from a distance."

"The great bindings are studied in augury. Only Essence masters can keep the islands from quaking so violently they kill everything that lives," Tai said. "I've a great-aunt who is one—it was she who got me into my school. Anyway. Purpose."

"One of Kanda's explanations of the way to civilization," Mek recited.

"Something Ardal's grandmother might have taught, but not the Dragon's Chosen," Tai stated, sure of himself now. "For them, Purpose was 'merit through skilled arms' instead of 'civilization.'"

Mek pressed tentative fingers to that tattoo on his forehead and concentrated on Purpose. His fingertips buzzed in that peculiar way of very strong Essence. The harder he concentrated, the stronger the buzz, until he got a sense of heat in the skin of the tattoo. Something was resisting him.

A voice calling in the distance separated them.

He went back through the imperial herbal for clues over the following days. They only saw Ardal at a distance. Odval still turned up, bringing Tai lotus root, Jade Palm, hundred-flowers candied petals, "embroidered courting ball" scallops—all festival dishes—and offering fresh tea, rather than the usual third and fourth steepings given to the slaves before the leaves were thrown to compost. When he kept refusing with grave thanks, she took to leaving these things with the scribes for him—which Tai promptly shared with the others. Which increased his steadily growing popularity—not that he paid it the least attention.

He was bemused by these friendly overtures. He worked so hard to keep his emotions shut and locked away in their lacquered cabinet that Odval's persistence seemed baffling. He was always scrupulously deferential, but returned short answers to her attempts to return to the more casual footing they had all been on during the early days of the boys' stay.

"I'm sure her questions might go in dangerous directions," he told Mek one afternoon, after sharing her latest gift, pressed on him as he left the scribes' chamber to fetch new ink. Candied petals, this time. Tai disliked such sweet dishes, but Mek ate everything with voracious appetite.

Mek looked up from crunching petals. "You think Ardal is afraid we saw those words?"

"Yes. Otherwise, why would she send Odval around like this?"

"Are you sure Ardal is sending her?" Mek asked. "Seems to me Odval was bringing snacks and coming around to talk before the thing happened with the grandmother herbal."

Tai frowned, then gave a short nod. "That is correct. I hadn't thought about that. But yes, that is correct."

They pondered a bit longer—Mek twelve, and still oblivious to lingering glances between older slaves. And Tai, who considered such matters utterly irrelevant.

They returned to their routine, as up in the interview room, Ardal compounded with new worries. There, in those pages, Grandmother had not only written down what Ardal had been too young to comprehend at ten, but she also gave her the means to rid the island of the Dragon raiders by making it inaccessible.

Ardal was very certain that she would be able to execute the spells and the constellations. That was a new word. It meant interlocked spells, as the stars interlocked in heavenly constellations. But ought she to do it?

She could never let those Mud boys even catch a hint of the danger of those papers. They had no protection. A mere gesture from a Cobra Sage, and they would be thrown into so much pain they would surely blurt out everything they knew. And why not? They were effectively prisoners, enslaved. They could not be expected to hold a pinch of loyalty to the Dragon's

Chosen. She ought to have found a way to put them on a boat and sent them back to the east, before Uncle Gatslan came, bringing the Cobra Sages. Except she was so desperate to learn from Kimek…

No, no, she had to dismiss *what might have happened* musings. Useless.

But what about this dream-walking? Grandmother had said that Ardal's unknown brother had begun it. Might Kimek possibly know anything about it? After all, he had taught her the inner door… Oh, to be able to communicate directly with Mother!

The elements seemed deceptively simple: Grandmother said that first, you must know the person, so that you could reach them within the vast world of the spirit. And if you had an object that the both of you had touched, you could use it to bridge the distance. She did not know how it worked. Only that it did.

As for the Cobra Sages' spells and constellations…

But. Grandmother had said before describing them in detail: *You must not throw away your one chance to use them. Because you will only have one chance. If they find out you have that much power, they will throw all the Cobra Sages against you in order to get that power for themselves. They would begin with your innocent sister.*

Ardal agonized, wavering.

As the days slipped past, she withdrew more and more, alternating between working on extending her reach, experimenting with spells before attempting a formation, and…debating within herself.

Suddenly it was the dawn of a new year, and Odval insisted they had to look through their ritual clothes. "We both have grown," Odval said, hands on her hips as she twitched this way and that, flirting with her reflection in the polished brass. "We can't host the provincial chiefs or our relations while wearing outgrown clothes. Especially now that you're old enough for courting fashions."

"I'm not courting anyone yet," Ardal said quickly. "Grandmother said to wait until I'm at least twenty-five before I think about heirs."

"Heirs!" Odval exclaimed, as if *she* were twenty-five, and not barely fifteen. "Who said anything about heirs? You can drink milkweed tea now, and flirt and have fun. I can hardly wait till *I'm* sixteen! I already know who I will begin with. I'm practicing my courting now!"

Ardal had scarcely been heeding Odval's chatter, but a tone in her sister's voice—a new tone—caused her to turn to look at her. Really look at her.

Odval had taken to courting chimes at a young age, but apparently that was the fashion now, though it had been strictly forbidden in Grandmother's day. But her clothes fit different-ly—the bamboo-shaped little sister now tied her sash in a way that nipped in her waist, emphasizing her shape above and below. Still very slim—she was scarcely fifteen—but it was there. And so, obviously, was her interest.

"As long as whoever you choose is not a slave," Ardal ventured at bowshot.

And to her considerable surprise, struck the mark. Odval whirled to face her, braid chimes tinkling. "Why?"

"You know Grandmother's laws: slaves left to slaves, and we with our own kind."

Odval's arms thumped across her chest. "Do you really think slaves are not human, like Jathyam's horrible sisters?"

"Jathyam's horrible sisters were horrible, but really, they only parroted what they were told. What the Dragon's Chosen believe."

Odval lifted a shoulder. "Forget them! About slaves…"

"Grandmother says, slaves cannot truly say no."

Odval's lips moved as she repeated these words, then she still looked puzzled. Ardal said, "As for new clothes, order whatever you think will suit me. I'm still studying Grandmother's instructions."

"More instructions," Odval muttered. "I really thought you'd had enough of that! But I know, I know, it's duty. I'll take a look. A regret that Uncle didn't turn up last spring—we could really use some silk."

"We could," Ardal said, striving to make her voice easy. "Which puts me in mind of an idle question. Supposing Uncle decided we were too boring, and he never came back?"

Odval clapped her hands in delight, then her mouth twisted skeptically. "That will never happen. Even I know he mainly comes for the Cull. And the gold."

"If he didn't. If, say, we ended up cut off from the capital. Permanently."

"Wouldn't that mean war?" Odval asked, all the mirth

fading from her face. "And with Mother locked up there? They say it's mutual honor, and the treaty, but even I know Mother is a hostage for what we do here."

"That's true."

"What caused this question?"

"Nothing but a wild dream," Ardal said as carelessly as possible, horrified at herself for having forgotten the danger to her mother. Momentarily!

"A wild dream more like a nightmare." Odval tossed her hair. "Imagine being betrothed at birth! What if he's a shark? Just as well the treaty forbids the obsidian throne from making matches for *us*. I want to go to the capital to see for myself." With that, she flounced away.

Ardal returned to her tasks, brooding intermittently.

The weather cooperated with her plans on the eve of the new year. Though it was cold, the winter sun a tenuous disk riding low in the milky sky, they were able to play games in the front court, which had been decorated with colored lamps and aromatic cedar boughs.

The girls played on the jumping board, a game that Odval had always excelled at—jumping girl after girl off. A few of the younger boys insisted on taking a turn, striving mightily, as the board teetered up and down. Then they played at Casting the Sticks, guessing at the combinations as the sticks fell within the ribbon-tied grid, and pasting a strip of paper depicting an animal to their faces when they lost. The fun, of course, came in judging the animal charades and noises the losers had to make in hopes the others would clap in approval, allowing them to remove the papers one by one.

The elders looked on, sipping hot wine and chatting, until it was time for the banquet. Ardal caught sight of Kimek among the musicians summoned to play for the dancing. Oh, how she wished she dared to speak to him—except the questions she wanted to ask were the ones most directly dangerous to her, to her family, to the entire island.

When the dancing ended at last, Ardal waited for her moment. She commented to her great-aunt, Grandmother's cousin, "I was just thinking about how the jumping game is popular in the capital, my cousin Jathyam once told me. But the box game comes down from the Golden Island days. If we *could* go back to those days, would we? Is it possible?"

Before her aunt could answer, Adal's great-uncle—raised in

the capital, and sent to marry into the family — laughed, his eyes mere slits in merriment. "What an extraordinary idea! We might be proud that there is no returning to those ignorant days!"

Ardal's aunt said more slowly, "I don't know if we could, assuming the obsidian throne decided to abandon this island. The northern customs are so intermixed with what my elders said was old Golden Island custom."

And another cousin muttered, when the great-uncle turned to address someone else, "We'd get a new king in a matter of days. Whoever has the weapons wins." She rolled her eyes toward their mutual relative-by treaty marriage.

Great-Aunt hushed her with a glance. "The families are so intermixed."

Ardal went to bed that night wondering bleakly if there was ever any going back. It seemed that Grandmother's wisdom had been proved yet again. If she were to use those constellations to cut Angja free from the reach of the Dragon's Chosen, she would have to first convince the islanders that going back to the old ways would be better, or what was the use?

But that would mean no slaves at all. And if there were no slaves, who would do the necessary work, she fretted as she settled into her clean, aired bed, warmed ahead of time, as soft-footed slaves tidied the room and carried her festival clothes off to be cleaned and stored away.

FIFTEEN

THE NIGHT OF THE last snowstorm of the year, Ardal closed her doors, and commenced her first experiment, Restoring an Element. Grandmother had said that raising fog was the simplest, but how to do that without anyone seeing? So Ardal turned to the second of the Restoring the Elements spells: wood.

She took an old writing brush, its goat-hair sparse and misshapen from so much use. She concentrated, drawing warmth from the sun, then bent over the wood, touched it, and threw all that warmth down her arm, through her finger into the wood…

At first nothing happened.

Was that a tiny dot on the brush?

She bent over, her nose nearly touching the wood. The dots swelled slightly. Then the tiniest light green nub appeared.

Frantic with joy and wonder, she repeated the entire exercise—thrust the warmth into the wood—and a second nub broke through. Both green nubbins stretched slowly, and one threw off a tightly curled leaf.

It *worked!*

She knew from Grandmother's paper that if she wanted this wood to truly take life on its own, she must keep at it until it began to root, then get it to soil and sunlight. Like acorns or walnuts or other seeds. But that could wait.

She stared down at it, her heart a-swim with the intensity of joy, and instinctively she reached for Kimek.

And there he was.

Her joy overflowed, pouring out image and emotion until

her mind caught up. She must be careful! With an effort, she shuttered the images, rather like throwing a net to catch up a thousand dispersing fireflies, and constrained them into one image, then words: "I learned how to Restore an Element."

Kimek responded with delight, "Good! Very good!"

"The next lesson is to visit through dreams. My grandmother used to visit my mother through her dreams. I would so love to do that, but her instructions are vague."

"I know how to do that," he responded promptly.

"Can you teach me?" she asked. "Grandmother says I need an object that both people have touched. Might I be able to use my mother's letter for that?"

"It can be anything. I think. I did it when little. I was told it was wrong."

He waited. She waited, twisting painfully between asking him to demonstrate, and fear that her dreams might reveal the secrets that she had to guard. That would be terrible! He hesitated, afraid she might sense his experiments with the slave tattoo.

They both shut the mental door.

The next day, Mek made sure he was at the far end of the medicine garden—under the sheltering foliage of the redbark trees—when he sent a gust of wind up to rustle the leaves. It was fun, but not really useful for anything.

That night, when he and Tai were alone in their alcove, he pulled his blanket over his head, making a kind of tent by drawing his knees up, and traced the tattoo, while drawing Essence from deep beneath the fortress, and thinking of smothering a fire with snow as he pressed the Essence in…

And he felt the binding begin to disintegrate.

He stopped, his heart thundering in his chest.

"Tai?"

"I'm awake."

"I found it."

Tai sat up, his face a dim shape. He breathed, "The binding?"

"Yes."

Tai dropped his head back as his breath hissed harshly. Then he got hold of himself. "Save it. Till we find a way to get off the island."

He mulled these new lessons as their work doubled, a sense of fearful anxiety forming like a cloud over the fortress at the possibility of Bar Gatslan showing up early. The possibility became probability when Steward Hathi summoned all the stewards below her to inform them that the Heir had spotted a raider fleet perhaps four days out.

Work was already hard, but now became a frenzy of effort. Tai was sick with apprehension. He worked zealously, partly to still the yammer of fear in his mind, and partly in hopes of earning the approbation of the master scribe in order to prove that his sight was good. Better!

This, he did not tell Mek, who seemed free of all troubling emotions in that regard. Tai struggled mightily to get all those emotions thrust firmly into their boxes, to be locked away in the secret compartment, never to be let out.

Four days became two, as a great wind rose, favoring the approaching ships. The air filled with the scent of burnt honey as the exhausted slaves labored by torchlight. Equally exhausted but vigilant slave guards roamed about, waking with the rope's end those who leaned for a few moments' brief slumber.

Utterly unaware of the consternation his approach caused (not that it would have disturbed him had he known) Bar Gatslan prowled his flagship impatiently, wishing the wind would push them faster yet. Though they already knifed through long rollers, spray reaching halfway up the lacquered battens of the sail as they plunged down.

The song of the wind about the masts and the thump of the drums that kept the galley slaves' oars in rhythm would have exhilarated him at any other time. Hai-yoo, to be flying north to join the First Prince, to spend the summer in practicing fleet maneuvers!

A maddened dash all night, warriors armed with poles to boom off any floating ice they encountered. This far south, at least, they were unlikely to encounter any of the ship-destroying ice mountains glowing malevolent blue and green in the moonslight.

At dawn, the welcome hail came, "Land in sight!"

They were all on deck, Jathyam behind his father as they sailed into the little harbor. Gatslan had resolved that no more than two days would be spent here, as long as the gold was ready. And it ought to be, as he hadn't come the previous spring.

Everyone was lined up properly, slaves on their knees, musicians noisily figuring away, which he took as a sign that he'd have his gold in the hold by nightfall. He smiled grimly to himself, and was going to warn Jathyam not to be riding on any hunting overnights when he caught sight of his son's fixed gaze.

"Jathyam," he breathed.

His son didn't stir. Gatslan turned his head to see what had so transfixed his eye. The Heir, her sister, the stewards, all were as always—and Jathyam did not seem to notice them. His attention lay behind, where the slaves knelt. Several years' experience caused Gatslan to look past the cluster of young slave girls to the boys, for Jathyam definitely had a taste for the boys—and there he was.

Gatslan blinked, startled. Blue-black hair like silk, kept brutally short; long phoenix eyes, cheeks and jaw cut as if by a blade, straight shoulders and arms beginning to gain definition and power, evident even in the flapping brown sacks the slaves all wore. Where had *that* young dragon come from?

He forced his gaze back to the gate, where the Heir stood, and then Gatslan noticed the younger niece's attention also fixed in the direction of that same black-eyed dragon.

He suppressed his impatience as the shaman did the ritual blessing in spite of spitting rain. Then they progressed up to the fortress under the dripping banners.

Presently he was alone with the head steward, who stood rigidly before him. When she was done with her report, he waved off the papers containing the numbers of bars of gold, bolsters of silver thread and so forth, and said, "Who is that handsome dragon's spawn among the slaves? When did you find him?"

Steward Hathi knew immediately who was meant. Behind Jetai's back, he had begun to be referred to as a phoenix, a dragon in training, a five-tailed leopard—a symbol of beauty, wit, and luck.

"He was here at your last visit," the steward replied. "The Mud scribe apprentice, Jetai."

"A Mud?" Gatslan repeated. "All I recollect was a short-sighted weed and a blob of a boy."

"The first is he," Steward Hathi replied in her flat voice,

hands crossed before her. "The short-sightedness is minimal; his calligraphy is superlative. Finished translating several Mud documents for the Heir, and now recopies reports for the archive."

"Is he active in the pens?"

"Never," the steward replied firmly.

"Really?" Gatslan barked with disbelief. "Then he's sneaking off."

"I," the steward replied rigidly, "would know. The only time he goes outside is to help the other Mud sweep the blueneck yard."

With a lifetime of experience, Gatslan drawled, "That boy did not get those arms and a warrior's bearing dipping a brush in ink, or wielding a broom."

Steward Hathi just waited, since she had not been asked a question.

Gatslan's mind reached in another direction. "And he sees all the fortress's..." He stopped before he said, "private reports." A calligrapher would see the island's accounts, and that girl would think nothing of it. Angja was isolated. Remote. If the Heir took that Mud dragon on as a lover, a very patient, very clever dragon could effectively take over the island from within.

His fists tightened. Then he reminded himself that nothing of the sort had actually happened. Yet.

"The other boy?"

"He also has nothing but meritorious report from Old Daldi. He cures the slaves around him of minor ills, using farm remedies known among the Muds."

"Cures..." Gatslan frowned, remembering Jetai's downturned face on the wharf. The two might very well be exemplary slaves now, but what about in five years? They were too young, too lightly built for the ring, but narrow tunnels always needed small, lithe bodies. And best of all, they couldn't raise any trouble *there*.

Impatiently, he decided to cut trouble before it could attack his flank later.

He turned to the slave assistant to the battle master, and said, "The Muds to the mines."

SIXTEEN

ARDAL HATED THE CULL. She always kept herself busy until it was over. The first sign that something was amiss was finding Odval sobbing in her suite.

"Odval, Uncle Gatslan speaks of leaving on tonight's tide. We must all be at the farewell feast."

"No."

"Are you…"

It never did to say "ill" for they were supposed to be above mere bodily weakness. But the two were alone, and Grand-mother had been very frank about illness, especially at the end. And no one could have called her weak. "Are you ill?" There. She said it.

"No. I *hate* him. I'll *tell* him I hate him, if he says anything."

"Why?"

"Go away! *You'll* just say I'm wrong!"

"Wrong? About what?" Ardal asked, truly upset. Odval had always been her best ally, especially since they'd lost Grandmother. Which was also the last time she heard Odval weep.

But Odval refused to speak, or even to look at her. Ardal returned to her interview chamber, doing her best to remain serene and competent in manner. Presently Steward Hathi appeared. "I have the list of goods Bar Gatslan has ordered taken aboard. And here is the list of those taken in the Cull."

"Give the tribute list to the master scribe. And the Cull list to the slave steward," Ardal said wearily. "How many of our skilled people did they take?"

"Five. The two Muds, Stolid from the carpentry, Rathis

from—"

"What?" Ardal interrupted, shocked. "The two *Muds*? He took the *Muds*? But they can't fight!"

"They're to go to the mines," the steward replied.

Ardal eyed the steward. "Why? What did you say to him?"

"No more than he asked, Bar Ardal." Steward Hathi did not show how unexpectedly painful she found this dart. "If this steward may be permitted to speak…"

"Speak!" Ardal commanded. "I would rather hear it than find out it was said behind my back."

Steward Hathi's thin cheeks mottled with spots of color. "Then, from my loyalty to the memory of Bar Thranis, I will observe that in most respects you are still a child. In spite of your dedication to the welfare of this island. Others might be dedicated, too, I might point out, and work hard in their own ways. And if those others see a possible dangerous course, and an easy way to avoid it, they are obliged to act."

"Dangerous course?"

"Bar Odval's preoccupation with the Mud Jetai," the steward said flatly.

"Preoccupation—" Ardal was going to deny it, but hesitated. Was that true?

"Where are they?" Ardal asked—but she knew she could not interfere. The men were Uncle Gatslan's to cull or not, as his needs required.

"They are on board the galley now," Steward Hathi replied. "The Cobra Sages have just finished marking all those culled."

Ardal's shock was great, but a minnow to the whale of shock the boys had sustained when the battle master barely looked at them, and said to the slave guards, "The mines for those two."

Tai was too controlled to let anything escape, but Mek squawked, "What?"—and was knocked down.

He scrambled to his feet, his joints like water and his heart drumming in his chest as they were shoved into the small, wretched group intended for the mines. They were regarded with scorn and pity by those chosen to go off to the ring fighting training, before a Cobra Sage approached.

Mek's mind had already formed another mountainous, earthen door, which still held. The Cobra Sage murmured, the word again a weird blur, as he made a single stroke, changing the character of the slave tattoo. *I can defeat it, I can defeat it,* Mek sang in his mind over and over. This litany enabled him to walk with the others down through the ringed walls, and to one of the smaller boats.

This craft was long and narrow, with a covered platform at the back. Mek and Tai were shoved toward the narrow, open boat with benches bisecting it; as they stood uncertainly, a burly shipmaster plunked Mek on a bench beside an enormous, muscled man next to a wizened graybeard gnarled as a crabapple tree, both of whom eyed him grimly. Tai was placed next to a couple of somewhat smaller young men.

"Don't think you're going to get out of pulling," Mek's bigger seatmate grumbled.

Mek was far too afraid to respond; he was intensely aware that that man's massive thigh was bigger around than Mek's entire body.

The tide being on the flood, they were the first to depart. The shipmaster barked something, and Mek's seatmate thumped him behind the ear with a huge, scar-ridged palm.

"Clap on," he muttered, planting enormous feet as he braced. His sheer size seemed to expand, and Mek found himself bumped to the edge of the bench so that he was half off. "Pull!"

It took a couple of turns before Mek caught on to the rhythm. He braced his feet against the bottom of the galley, which was dank and moldy. Very soon his arms ached along both front and back, and his shoulders strained. Even his stomach muscles quivered. But that was a candle to the sun of a steadily building thirst—in spite of a cold wind and a spattering of rain.

When he tried to slacken to ease the agony, both his seatmates glared at him.

Tai was just as confused and terrified, though he was surprised to discover that he was able to bring some strength to bear, due to all those handstands, martial forms, and sparring. Even so, he, too, soon ached from the unaccustomed strain. And thirst was soon a torment.

As a rain shower passed, a gust of wind caught the sail, sending the galley plunging. The master bawled for them to lift and ship the oars, as dippers of water were brought down the rows. When the wind began to slacken, the order came again to "Pull!"

Mek glanced up at that sail, then all around him at the sea.

Was that what it took to gain a respite from the murderous toil of those oars, a driving wind from behind? He knew what to do about that! But…Master Root had cautioned him many times about the effects of using Essence in a large way, and raising a wind large enough to push a boat was…large. "There are always consequences," he had said. "When the dragon flies close to the sun, the world is cast in shadow."

Mek stole furtive peeks in all directions. They were in the middle of the sea, except for the island jutting the horizon. Surely if he brought an Essence wind here, there would be no consequences to the island so far off — and as for the immediate surroundings, it was simply water and air. Consequences were impossible in two elements constantly moving!

How to do it without notice? He knew that, too. He dug his bare heels into the slimy wooden hull and reached down and down, to the sea floor. Making the mightiest effort of his entire life, he pulled Essence up and up, and flung it through his body straight into the sail. Bang! The sail hummed, taut as iron, as from behind a kelp-veined wave swelled and swelled, its crest tearing off to strike the galley horizontally, driving the ship forward with the speed of a swift on the wing. His. Nose stung. Blood? Just a little.

"Ship oars," roared the shipmaster at the back.

Oars lifted as the galley rushed, huge bow waves rising on either side. The gigantic wave forward, the following wind almost gale force.

Had he brought all that water up, too? Seemed so. Mek collapsed forward like an emptied bag, his forehead hitting the oar with a thok!

"What's wrong with the brat?" the shipmaster asked. "That's one of the lord's own culls. You'd better not be playing off your games."

"We did nothing! The demon wave must've flung him forward," the big oarsman protested. "Look. He's rousing," he pointed out as Mek sat up with a muffled groan, smearing his bloody nose on the back of his hand.

The wind persisted for long enough for them to be given water, dried fish and wheat bun wrapped in cabbage. Mek forced his trembling body to sit upright, and to take that needed sustenance. Strength began to trickle back.

They passed a miserable night, with rain coming down intermittently. Mek tried to catch drops in his open mouth — the sips of stale water were never enough. They slept where they sat. If they had to relieve themselves, they did it over the side, no privacy. At least the winds blew, and kept blowing for two and a half days, until they reached the rocky, mountainous north shore of the island.

Here, the slaves were ordered to the shore, their legs shaky, arms and backs throbbing.

There was a stream emptying into the inlet where they docked. All the slaves intended for the mines rushed to the water's edge to slake the horrible thirst. Brackish as that water was, Mek sighed as the water coursed through him, cooling his parched body. He dug his toes in, soaking up revitalizing Essence.

Tai lifted his head, the sight of leafing osmanthus trees a painful reminder of his father's small estate on the Tiger Island, and home. Home! Even his cousins, once dreaded, seemed no more than the whine of a gnat.

The slave guards barked, "March!"

Tai glanced at Mek. When would he remove the slave bindings? But then what? *Patience.* As his old tutor had said, the mulberry leaf, with time and patience, becomes the robe of silk.

Ahead, a mountain loomed.

The march lasted most of a day as they toiled up road alongside a winding stream. A fissure as high as a nine-story pagoda opened in the mountain's side. Carts had dug deep ruts to and from this fissure.

The first person they saw swaggered up, a sash tied under an aggressive paunch. This man had thick bow legs and a broad face dominated by a bristling mustache. A whip had been stuck through the sash, the braided thongs swinging at each step.

"Hai-yoo, you're early, this year," he observed in a loud voice.

"The lord has been summoned by the First Prince," said the older slave guard. "Five to you for the gold mine."

"Looks to me like four and a half," Mustache stated after staring at Mek, his head to one side.

"Those two are Muds," the slave guard pointed out, as if that explained everything.

"I hate Muds," Mustache stated. "Spies? No, he'd fling them in the pit."

"Washed up on shore after a storm."

"Bad luck for you two, eh?" Mustache addressed Mek and

Tai in a loud, distinct tone. "Do you speak Father Dragon's tongue, Mud-Eyes?" He gave a crack of laughter at his own wit.

The slave guard said, "They speak it well enough to take orders."

"Hai-hum, I do hate Muds, demons plague them all. But I need crawlers, now that Toadspit has grown himself to that awkward length." He waved the slave guards off. They tramped across the muddy yard toward a building higher up the slope, and out of Mek's and Tai's lives.

The boys and the other three culls were left facing Mustache, whose genial expression had entirely vanished.

"You are going to spend the rest of your miserable lives finding gold for Bar Gatslan. Whatever you did to be condemned here, I don't know. Don't want to know. Miners are always one step from death. You know it. I know it. Do your job—that means, meet your quota, either in gold or in measure, you live. That's if you don't cross your crew. Or another crew." He spat on the ground midway between Tai and the nearest of the other three. "I've got two crew right now short-handed. "Hangis!"

A voice from a tunnel, "Boss?"

"Take these three to Crew Nine."

A tall, stooped man appeared, gaunt, pale eyes. A whip at his sash, too. He jerked his chin at the other three slaves and grunted. They followed one looking around in fear, another sullen, fists clenched, and the third resigned.

The boss jerked a grimy thumb at Mek and Tai. "I'll deliver you myself to Crew Six." His voice dropped on the word *six*, as if it were an evil omen.

Then commenced a long walk down into the dripping, clammy underground. Tai shivered, his slave tunic still sodden from the rain that had fallen on them during the walk.

Mek breathed in the damp air, strengthened by the sense of earth all around him. Here, he could rip down the inner door in safety—and his awareness spread out and out. He sensed snakes waking from their long sleep, lethargic from cold but driven by hunger. Tree roots extending to drink in the water seeping from melt. Insects innumerable, going about their lives.

He stumbled when the boss stopped abruptly. They stood in a narrow tunnel that smelled of ancient sweat, lit dimly by flickering lamps as five figures of various sizes stopped their work and lowered their tools to the ground before straightening up, empty-handed.

"Very prompt, very prompt," the boss grated with approval, and to Tai and Mek, "If I see you with anything but gold in hand, it's ten lashes. And we go from there."

To the miners, "Here's two Muds the lord sent us. Put them to work." He scowled at Mek and Tai, and jerked a thumb toward a scrawny young teen. "That's Toadspit. Crawler. Which you'll be doing now, runt." The thumb then indicated a glowering middle-aged man. "Badger is assistant crew boss when Diggy isn't bossing."

Then, in quick succession, a globular-faced fellow who could have been any age from sixteen to sixty, a lean young man of maybe twenty-five years with curling hair even wilder than Mek's, and a spider-limbed, long-nosed individual who coughed into his elbow: "Mo Thi, pickman; Waha, pickman; Thief, the only carter in Six, but you'll be doing that, Mud." He pointed at Tai. "Meal once a day, if you meet quota. You work, you eat. You eat, you live. Unless you cross Diggy. Then you don't live, ha ha ha!"

He stepped aside, and Mek and Tai made out a sixth figure, hereto hidden in the shadows. A huge young man sat against the wall, the weak lamplight throwing exaggerated shadows over his narrow, craggy face, no light at all reaching his eyes.

The boss said in that ill-omen growl, "And *that* is Diggy."

SEVENTEEN

NO ONE GLOWED WITH Essence, Mek noticed as soon as the boss tramped back down the tunnel. He could investigate his surroundings without worrying about discovery.

There was enough danger enough right before his eyes.

Badger, the glum middle-aged man said in a loud, slow voice, "You speak our tongue?"

"Yes," Tai said, and Mek nodded.

"Then you can understand our rules. The rules of Crew Six." He nodded at Diggy, still silent and unmoving, then struck his broad chest. "You do what you're told. You don't talk. No one wants to hear it, and it uses up all the air, once we get in the narrower wormholes. That's enough yap. Waha, show them how to use the tools."

That commenced a period of arduous toil, Badger, Mo Thi, and Waha at the farthest reach of the tunnel. Mek and Tai had to pick up the rubble the pickmen had prised and chiseled out of that solid wall of stone, adding it to what was already piled in the cart. This lasted a weary eternity until the sudden crash of a gong reverberated through the tunnels.

Thief pulled and Tai pushed the heavy, wooden-wheeled cart down the tunnel. Mek and Waha carried the lamps, which threw jiggling spears of light about, making shadows jump and jitter. Diggy was a huge, threatening shadow staggering drunkenly behind them, one big hand shading his eyes.

A sharp turn brought them to a crevasse with a ledge. Here water sheeted down the stone in a continual, rushing hiss into a drop far below. This ledge was where they slept. They relieved themselves over the edge and drank from the shockingly cold water.

Thief and Tai took the cart away.

Diggy dropped heavily to the ledge, long legs stretched before him. His clothes were rags, once a thick, long-sleeved garment cut up the sides over trousers. He wore a greasy rag as a headband. His hair was a thick topknot, skewered with wood.

The miners sat with their backs against the stone, making occasional low-voiced mutters largely inaudible because of the water. Mek didn't try to listen. Instead, he did some more exploring with his inner senses.

There was little gold in the vicinity. More silver and even more copper. Why should he tell anyone? He didn't care if that demon-cursed lord got more gold or not. He didn't care if these glowering, filthy, stinking men toiled futilely at nothing but solid stone.

He stayed still, hands pressed against the stone at his back, until the rumble of the empty cart brought Thief and Tai back.

In silence, Thief set out a bucket of oil for refilling the lamps, and with his grimy hands, passed out the food. He began with Diggy, laying the biggest of what turned out to be a thick, doughy pancake next to Diggy's loose hand on the stone floor.

Mek and Tai were last. Mek's had been torn in half. He looked around to see who got his other half. No one was holding an extra piece—but was Diggy's thicker than the others? Mek brushed the worst of Thief's oily thumbprint off his half, noting that the bread had been slit in the middle. Two desiccated pieces of dried fish had been put inside, along with some very limp greens.

Tai sat down next to Mek. "Want a chunk of mine?" he murmured softly.

Mek waved it off. He was used to short rations by now, and he really didn't mind. Much.

"Did you learn anything?" Mek asked in imperial.

"Yes. 'Measure' is what we take away. Evidence of our labor. We don't get anything to eat if there isn't a full cart. But if there is no gold, we're last to get food. Those who find gold get first choice of food, and if you earn enough, and the boss likes you, you can get your pick among the clothes of dead men."

"Probably unwashed," Mek muttered.

Tai had taken to breathing through his mouth. "There was fruit, but we—"

Diggy slowly lifted his head. "Shut. Up." His deep voice grated with menace.

"The gold is going in the other direction," Mek had wanted to tell Tai.

He could feel it there, a couple man-lengths deep in the stone, but the vein twisted away from the direction they were excavating, and down. They would miss it completely. Aish! What a dilemma! If they got the worst food for not finding gold, that meant Mek and Tai would suffer along with these other rats. Yet he dared not say anything, because surely they'd ask how he knew where the gold was — and the danger of revealing Essence skill would shadow him all over again.

Quiet fell, and the sound of long breathing, broken intermittently by coughs, made it clear that it was sleep time. No blankets. Mek curled up, longing for Yellow-dog's comforting warmth, built his inner wall, and slid into sleep.

When Mek woke, Diggy was up and waiting. He didn't speak, but the way he simply stood, like a warrior poised for action, got both Mek and Tai scrambling to rise. Tai longed to wash, even in the horribly cold water, but the others were already grabbing their tools, so he contented himself with a drink, and they tramped up the long tunnel.

Every so often, Mek saw Diggy take an awkward step and brace against the rough stone wall. Was he still drunk? And where could he have got any liquor?

Those questions faded when they reached their destination. Diggy picked up a pickaxe much larger than those wielded by the others, and attacked the stone with shocking strength. Huge cracks appeared in the stone, and rocks bounced on the ground, rubble spinning in all directions. Tai and Mek chased this rubble, stooping and lifting through a tiring day as the cart slowly filled. At least, Mek thought grimly, it was better than manning an oar on a galley. Though not by much.

With Diggy leading the pickmen, the cart was piled nearly to overflowing.

For three days, measured by the cart going away and coming back with dry, stale pancakes, they toiled away at the new tunnel. On the fourth day, they broke through to a wormhole.

Toadspit grinned at Mek. "Your turn." He thrust a lamp at Mek. "Go as far as you can. Look at everything that glitters. If you see anything that might be gold, you dig a bit out with this." He thrust a chisel at Mek. "Bring it to…" He paused to cough thickly. "To us. We'll tell you if it's gold or not," he finished hoarsely. That much talk made him breathless, and he began hacking.

Mek climbed into the hole. He already knew there was no gold anywhere near it, though a very thin layer of copper crossed it, thin as a butterfly's wing.

He'd thought climbing tunnels would be easy, and it was, but he soon discovered the problem: no air. He turned his face back toward the opening into the larger tunnel, where he could see a couple of the others peering at him.

"Go on," Badger ordered.

"No air," Mek called back.

"Go on!" Badger commanded more forcefully, glancing back at Diggy, who remained silent.

Mek could feel the dust clogging the thick, fetid air. He crawled a little way forward, then paused again, and this time he shut his eyes and brought air from behind the others. It caused the dust to swirl, then settle, and he took a cautious breath.

Now he understood why Toadspit and Thief coughed all the time, Thief most likely being the tunnel crawler before Toadspit. The tunnel narrowed and flattened. He sensed the weight of stone overhead, and paused to explore it, finding an immense slab of stone resting against another monumental slab. The horizontal one, riddled with fractures, poised to slide against the other—which would crush him, and anything beneath. Several tunnels beneath. He turned his awareness downward. Two tunnels, one above the other, going in different directions, glowed with human life forms.

No wonder there were no burrows nearby. The underground creatures must sense the instability of that stone, large as it was.

What ought he to tell the others? Beyond the fissure there was gold, probably cushioning the huge slab. But getting there might be deadly, especially with the strength of Diggy's blows.

When the gong reverberated, sending dust sifting down from between nearly invisible cracks, he wriggled back out, coughed the dust from his lungs, and he lied. "The wormhole flattens to nothing. There isn't any glitter at all."

Everyone turned to Diggy. Even though he wasn't the oldest. But he was the strongest.

"Dead end?" he asked Mo Thi.

Mo Thi mumbled, "Saw what I saw. More like a shadow. But there."

"You know the rule," Badger added unnecessarily. "Dead end means we'll work on the opposite wall." He pointed away from the wormhole. "Take the cart in," he added — though Thief and Tai were already putting their muscle into getting the thing moving.

Mo Thi's globular face turned downward and he scurried after the cart, rubbing his arms over the holes worn into his sleeves. Waha sauntered after, Toadspit at his heels, coughing absently. Diggy leaned both palms against the mold-covered stone, head dropped between his powerful shoulders.

"Are you —" Mek began.

"Get!" Diggy snapped with such ferocity Mek skipped away.

Thief and Tai returned with the cart and even more dismal rations; though it was difficult to see in the lamplight, the smear on the side of Mek's share seemed to be mold, not just grime from Thief's unwashed fingers.

No one spoke as they stretched out to sleep.

Mek settled back, and let his mind sink into the stone.

And while he did that, several day's storm-sea sailing and three weeks of treacherous mountain travel southward, Ardal sat in the aerie, head in her hands.

Odval still refused to speak to her.

Each day had dragged by since Uncle Gatslan's departure, Ardal trying to fill it with work. She dared, and failed, three more experiments with Grandmother's secret herbal. If only Mek were here. If only Grandmother were still alive!

If only Mother could return!

She locked the herbal away again, renewed the Essence seal, and walked across to her sister's room. At least Odval wasn't still lolling in bed. She sat at the window, looking northward into the storm. Thunder, in spring!

"Are you ill?" Ardal asked.

Odval turned a distraught, exhausted face her way. "I'm *concentrating*. If you can Hear, I can too, if I work hard. I keep trying."

"You look as if you've given yourself a headache," Ardal said, striving to keep accusation or even protest out of her voice. She had come in here to make peace, not to drive a wider wedge between them. "Shall I fetch you some calming tea? Or a willow twig, as Mek suggested?"

"No. It doesn't *work*, trying to Hear," Odval wailed. "I'm stupid, is that it? You're the smart one and I'm just stupid."

"If it's true that I'm smart, then you must be, too, because you understand me quicker than anybody. 'Hearing' seems to be like writing with one hand or the other, something inherited. I can Hear. You got the gentian blue eyes and the handsome countenance that Grandmother did not have, but Mother has. And I don't have."

Odval's lip twitched; Ardal knew she liked being pretty. She liked being admired. Odval sighed, and some of the rigidity went out of her frame. Ardal noticed then that Odval's braids were bare, not a dangle anywhere, and discovered she missed that golden sparkle, the sweet chime. Twinkle-tinkles, her northern cousins called them.

Ardal sat down in the carved window embrasure next to Odval. "What can I do to make you feel better?" She leaned forward to stroke her sister's hot forehead.

Odval leaned into her touch. "Bring Jetai back. Both of them. They shouldn't be in the mines," she added.

"You know I can't do that, not without Uncle finding out. And I don't know what the consequences would be. He might even have them killed. Steward Hathi hinted that he took notice of them because of…hum, your notice," she finished gently.

"Then it's my fault?" Odval pulled away, her voice rising.

"Not fault. Don't think that."

"It's someone's fault," Odval retorted.

"It's Uncle's fault for putting him there, supposedly out of our way."

"But why? It's just malicious! We never did anything to deserve that! And neither did they," Odval amended in afterthought.

"Grandmother says in her secret herbal that no one *deserves* slavery. But there they all are." Ardal lifted a hand to indicate the entire fortress.

Odval's gaze slid away. "That's different. Our slaves are born to it. They expect it, and *someone* has to give the orders, so why not us? Grandmother even said that we must be benevolent masters. I *remember* her saying that."

"She did say that. However, in the secret herbal, she says she has come to believe that our ancestors lived better lives without slavery."

"But most slaves are perfectly content, as long as we're benevolent," Odval protested, though she felt this argument sliding far away from what mattered most.

"We don't actually know what's going on behind obedient faces and soft voices," Ardal said. "I find that thought unsettling. She said to read the history of Empress Zirmas, whom mother was named for, and the Battle at Three Heroes' Bridge, and others. In every one of those histories, there's someone powerless, a slave, or a despised younger brother, or in Empress Zirmas a wife, professing loyalty until they had a position of trust. Of power. Then turning on the one in power, fast as a viper."

Odval crossed her arms. "And Uncle thinks that Jetai would be one of those, just because he's a Mud?"

"Because he has no reason to be loyal to the treaty, or to the obsidian throne, even if he decides to be loyal to one of us personally. I think I can see that. I don't agree with what Uncle did, *at all*. But I think he wasn't just being malicious for no reason."

Thunder rumbled across the sky.

Ardal went on, "In the secret herbal, Grandmother says that the Thousand Island Imperials and our Dragon Empire aren't all that different in that both teach their young to respect elders, in what they call filial obedience. We're taught to respect skill and strength. There is the same ladder of rank. They used to have slaves, too, by the way—and they had some terrible slave rebellions. Their Sage Empress said that slaves are not *permitted* to choose loyalty, so how can loyalty forced on people be true?"

"It would be nice to free them," Odval said wistfully. "Except who will do the slave work? Nobody would choose to…to scrub dirty clothes, or clean floors. I know *I* wouldn't. Did Grandmother explain *that*?"

"She said it has to do with forms of trade, that is, in trade for the work, you get things."

"Things like?"

"Food. Clothes. A place to live—yes, I can see you're going to say that they get those now, but these trade things were theirs, and they chose them. The way we might buy things if we go to the capital and visit shops."

Odval's eyes widened. "I would love to do that! Do you mean, slaves would be buying things?"

"I don't really understand it. I mean to find out," Ardal added. "But before then—"

"If you can't free Jetai, can you at least find out if they are still alive?" Odval demanded. "You've always hated the obsidian throne's poison creeping over us, taking away what our ancestors had. Grandmother would have found a way."

Ardal smiled. That, right there, would be her excuse to try to reach Kimek through the inner door. She would do it for her sister's sake. Or try. Kimek might be too angry and never open the door again.

"I will try to find a way," she promised, and returned to the aerie. There, she settled down, shut away her vision, and consciously opened the inner door. When she did not sense Kimek, she *reached*—

And he was there, but the distance was an enormous …weight, exactly as distance strained her Hearing. No words came, only an onslaught of truly horrible perceptions—dirty darkness, choking dust, stench, cold, brief glimpses of angry-eyed miners. Above all, hunger.

Hunger? She knew she had increased the outlay for the mines after Grandmother died. The mine boss had sent a long list of expenses: tools, equipment such as wood for carts, clothing for the miners, herbs to counter the scrapes and contusions expected in mining, and of course food. It had been one of the first orders she had passed.

She tried to shape words, but the connection was so tenuous! She gave up when an idea occurred, and she ran back to Odval's chamber. "I know what we can do, if you're willing," she said.

Odval was eating, at least. She looked up.

"This is perfectly within the treaty. I think. That is, we shall go north and inspect the mine."

Odval's eyes widened, all listlessness gone. "Let's leave tomorrow!"

"Not into a storm! As soon as the weather clears, I will arrange things," Ardal promised. "I want to see how the mines are using that double share of gold. You can see that Jetai is still alive." And if he was as dirty and greasy and smelly as those images from Kimek, maybe that would put out the fire.

EIGHTEEN

MEK WAS TAKEN BY surprise when Ardal's awareness appeared outside the mental door, which he had let lapse. He didn't try to reach her. He was far too tired, his head panging from all the dust he'd breathed, and what was the use of talking to her anyway? She wasn't going to share that mysterious herbal with the Essence lessons. She'd made that clear.

He renewed the inner door and slid into sleep, waking at Toadspit's morning cough, which always preceded the crashing gong that meant *get to work!*

They tramped back up the long, winding tunnel to their former work spot.

Badger turned to Mo Thi, who stood there, rocking back and forth, then mumbled, "I still say it's somewhere here."

Mek looked at him in surprise. He'd paid little attention to any of Crew Six, except to avoid Diggy, and to wish he could fix Toadspit's horrible cough—and Thief's, not quite as bad. Mo Thi's affinities were very mild, less even than Tai's, but akin. Tai's affinity was pure metal, but Mo Thi's was a blend of metal and earth. That might be why he didn't have that horrible dust cough—his affinity might strengthen his meridians without Mo Thi even knowing.

As the crew began on the opposite wall, Mek considered the stone beyond. It seemed to have been near the surface once. At least, those long fingery things felt like tree roots that had turned to something like iron long ago. Somewhere beyond them the land sloped into a deep valley. He could sense light and air beyond. Oh, how he wanted to reach them!

And deep under that vast slab, a cushion of pure gold.

Diggy attacked the wall, Waha at one side and Mo Thi at the other. Toadspit hovered, coughing and spitting as he threw his chisel from hand to hand. It was his job to break down big chunks of stone for the cart. He reminded Mek of those fingery tree roots, he was so skinny and spidery and nervous. A fire affinity? Very small affinity—just enough to torture Toadspit with all this mold and darkness and dank, heavy stone, for he needed sunlight. The only fire in him now was the ugly rash all around his neck where his grimy collar rubbed the flesh.

Mek looked away. He knew how to cure both rash and cough! But he longer had access to that splendid healer's garden—

Badger kicked Mek, sending him sprawling in the sharp-edged rubble. "Stop lazing and get to work!"

Mek began scraping together the small rocks, piling them into his dank, flapping tunic, and dumping them into the cart.

This went on until Diggy's pickaxe caught on the first of those iron root-fingers, the sudden halt to the force of his blow jerking his head back. He uttered a crashing curse and sat abruptly on the stone ground, fingers spread over his face with such intensity that the tendons stood out.

Badger picked up Diggy's pickaxe—using both hands—and began hacking and tugging at the root, as Waha and Mo Thi widened the gap around it. Mek did his best to scavenge rocks around Diggy without touching him. A single blow from one of those powerful fists, and no amount of training in how to fall would save him.

Diggy remained there, a huge obstruction in the middle of the area they were working in, but everyone carefully stepped around him, Thief going so far as to shield him from stones tumbling out of the rock face as the others continued hacking their way in.

No one spoke until the gong rang, and then Waha sighed, working his right shoulder in slow, painful circles as Tai and Mek finished loading the cart with the last of the rubble. Mek was scraping the smallest bits from the shallow cave the others had carved into the stone when Diggy at last got to his knees, rose, then staggered and fell back, his big body flattening Mek against the stone wall. Jagged stones gouged into Mek. He yelped, instinctively opening the door to Diggy's mind.

The resulting waves of nauseating, world-rocking dizziness knocked Mek flat. He was dimly aware of Diggy sliding to sit against the stone wall, clutching his head again. Mek struggled up on his elbows and shook away the reverberations, staring in shock. Diggy wasn't drunk. He was suffering from dizziness of demon-devouring intensity.

Instinctively Mek scrambled up and peered into Diggy's ugly, pain-wracked face. "You've got Loose-Eye. Ayah, that's what? Eye…Loose? In Dragon tongue?" The term in imperial got its name from the way sufferers' eyes jittered, as if the strings to their eyeballs had been cut, according to the herbal Mek had read so many times.

Diggy squinted at him. "So?" It sounded like a threat.

Mek said, "I can fix it. I think I can, that is," he added humbly. "But I *can* take away the…" He rubbed his stomach and made a puking noise. "I use *acupoints*." He reverted to imperial. Then, remembering too late that healers were forbidden, "Common cures in my family."

Diggy ignored that, squinting against the pain. "Do it."

Ayah! Here was yet another Westerner who didn't scorn the idea of healing. "I'll need your hands."

Diggy held one out. The hand of a swordsman. Or did a pickaxe cause the same calluses? Mek found the tendon, which was like a steel band. He knew he had the right acupoint when Diggy's muscle jumped. Yes, so much blockage there…Mek close his eyes, pinched the nails of thumb and forefinger together, and pressed into the acupoint, flooding it with Essence. The nasty red surge fought him, then broke, burning out, and Mek sent cooling Essence through that acupoint. Diggy's breath hissed in, expressive of profound relief.

Mek performed the same on the other wrist, and then strengthened the effect by clearing the six main acupoints around Diggy's head.

Diggy breathed slowly. Warrior breathing. Then he opened his bloodshot blue eyes. "They said there's no cure."

It depends on the cause," Mek said carefully.

Diggy seemed to consider this, as they remained alone there at the work site, with one lamp between them. "Can you find it?"

"I can try," Mek said—wondering how far he dared to go.

Diggy grunted, and got to his feet once more. He staggered—the nausea was for the moment abated, but the vertigo was not cured—then tramped down the tunnel, leaving Mek to patter after, the lamp held out in front of him with both hands, in a mostly futile attempt to keep the shadows from jumping.

Back in their ledge beneath the cascade of pure, cold snowmelt, Diggy sank down. "How?" he said to Mek

Mek crouched down, knees under his chin, grimy toes digging into the slimy stone as he braced himself. Diggy's inner door was wide open. Once again, Mek met that terrible, fractured, swimming perception, and discovered so deep a well of anguish, of despair, that he recoiled from that abyss of absolute desolation.

Mek sat back, pressing the palms of his hands into his eyes. Diggy's human misery was a silent reproof, a reminder that these miners were people. Each one different. Like Tai. Like Ardal.

Like him.

Mek reached once more for Diggy's wrist. As he dealt with the tendon acupoint, he launched his awareness into Diggy's meridians, following the red surges up and up to one side of Diggy's head…ah, *there*, the inside part of his ear. Tiny bits of crystal, so tiny, but when they knocked about within that inner part, they disturbed the equilibrium of the waters there. A tiny bone seemed to be out of place, affecting those crystals.

He looked up. "Red clover and nettle leaf in ginger tea, and every day pressure on this acupoint might take it away," he said, pointing to Diggy's thick wrists. "These are all very common herbs. Root of purple thistle, too. Not a *cure*, but it would help." He named the herbs in imperial, but the others did not react, and Mek wondered if they'd even know the names in their own language.

"We've got to get it for him," Toadspit muttered, rubbing his dirty hands. "We got to get it. I'll ghost down to—"

"No. You won't," Diggy said. "They'll hear that snorting a field away."

Ginseng, longevity root. Vasaka, and turmeric for Toadspit and Thief as well, Mek thought. Licorice and mullein. In peppermint to soothe the breath meridians. "They have herbs, here? Healer herbs?" he asked. "I thought healers forbidden."

"Too many accidents in mines," Waha said softly, lounging against a jut of stone. "Too many of us die. They try to patch us up in order to send us back in, just as you patch up tools."

"There are always exceptions that no one talks about," Mo Thi observed mildly. "Favorite ring fighters do somehow find their ways to any healer they want, so I hear," he added wryly.

"Their patron does," Diggy corrected. He then cut through to what mattered: "Boss Tangat has herbs. A book that says how to use them. But only his favored crew gets them. Unless there's a find."

The rumble of the cartwheels announced the reappearance of Tai and Thief with their day's rations, even more meager than before.

They ate in a silence whose quality seemed to Mek different than previous. More thoughtful, less like a wall between Muds and Westerners, new and old.

Presently Diggy spoke. "Let's see what you know."

Everyone turned his way. Tai puzzled.

Diggy said, "I won't be beholden to no man. Let's see what you know, squirt."

Mek said, "You mean…cures?"

"Martial skills. I know nothing of cures," Diggy said slowly. "You had training. I see it when you move. Show your forms."

Mek would not have chosen to practice right there in front of enemy Westerners, especially on a mossy ledge with a sudden drop of who knows what depth scarcely two arms' lengths away, but he got up, clasped his hands from long habit—though he hadn't done so for two years—and let body take over mind as he began the familiar warmup forms. One, two, three. Four…he kept having to stop and check how close he was to the edge, because four and five broadened to a square.

Diggy held up a hand. "You." He pointed at Tai.

Tai was going to protest, glanced at Mek, then rose more slowly. He moved equally slowly through his three forms. Diggy frowned, then got to his feet. "Spar." He gestured to Tai, and took a swing at him.

The blow was straight from the forms—at least Tai knew that much. And he knew how to block! They exchanged ten or twelve light blows, then Diggy put his hands up and said, "Hai-yoo, I get it now. You spar downward, for short partner. He taught you?" With a thumb at Mek.

"Yes," Tai said.

"Good form. Very good form. But no power. Yet. Squirt, I teach you and…"

"Je Tai," Tai said.

"And I'm Ki Mek," Mek added, hoping to smother Squirt

before it could get attached to him.

As usual, Diggy didn't hear two names. "Jetai. Kimek."

Better than Squirt, Mek thought with a resigned sigh. He had enjoyed the sparring, once he understood that Diggy was not going to smash them into rubble, but it left him sweaty — and then cold.

As everyone settled down to escape for a time through sleep, he winnowed himself up the ledge as far as he could, near to where he sensed a snake winter burrow. Oh, how he missed Yellow-dog, and Three-Leg, and also Master Root's snake friends, who liked to curl up inside clothing when it was cold, soaking in human warmth and then sharing it back, like a little scarf…or blanket…so smooth to the touch….

He was deep in a dream of a summer's day when, from a distance, a hoarse scream ripped through the air. His head jerked up as he peered into three bulge-eyed faces, lamps held high. Mek wriggled out of his warm blanket—oh. It wasn't a blanket.

Snakes heaved and wriggled around him. Diggy appeared, shoving Toadspit and Waha to either side, his mighty pickaxe held high.

"Don't hurt them, don't hurt them!" Mek shrilled as the snakes slithered in all directions, vanishing through unseen holes. "They didn't hurt me," Mek explained to the ring of faces crowding around. "I invited them. I think. I was so cold. They like warmth, too…"

The pickaxe lowered, and Diggy pointed a finger the size of a cucumber at Mek. "You." He stopped there, and shook his head slowly. "I never yet forced any man to tell his secrets. But I never met a…a *one*—" (stumbling past the word *man*, Mek thought with an inward tremble of laughter) " —like you."

Nineteen

Mo Thi muttered, unheard — or unheeded — by anyone but Mek, "I thought he had a ghost glow."

Mek said indignantly, "I'm not a ghost. Not a demon, either." He used the imperial word for *demon*.

Diggy turned to Tai for the expected translation, which Tai supplied, then grunted. "No kin of the Antlered One is a healer. Poison, yes." He shot an accusing look at Mo Thi.

Mo Thi remained unmoved. "My ma said, never admit if you see ghost glow. The snakes'll take you away."

Diggy swept a look around at the others. "No one's blabbing to the Cobras, if they come around. Agreed?"

"Agreed," Toadspit exclaimed, then fell into a fit of coughing.

"I hate the Cobras," Mo Thi said — having now spoken more than Mek and Tai had heard from him since their arrival. "Told you what I was told."

"Your ma told you that so you wouldn't get snatched," Badger admonished. "Doesn't mean anyone's tainted by the Antlered One."

"Know that," Mo Thi said, struggling to express himself. "It's a *glow*. You don't see it? Like…like a new moon behind cloud. Dimmer."

Diggy turned his head Mek's way. "Do you see glows?"

Mek hesitated, already hating how many lies he'd had to tell so far. "I see glows for all living things. Essence glows be bigger. Mo Thi's is like he said. New moon, behind clouds."

"You're brighter now," Mo Thi observed.

Three sets of eyes shifted between Mek and Mo Thi.

Toadspit was coughing too hard to pay attention, and Thief stared uneasily at a hole where he'd seen a snake slither.

"Can you see where gold lies, too?" Badger asked Mek cautiously.

"Mo Thi is right some of the time," Waha offered.

"He's right this time." Mek pointed downward. "It's there."

"How far?" Badger asked, the rest listening in arrested silence. No one wanted to dig downward, the most dangerous direction to mine in.

Mek shook his head. "I don't know. I mean, it's *there*. Lots….like a pond. And that way is open air."

"Which is closer to us now?" Badger asked.

"The valley. But I don't know how to measure."

Badger and Diggy exchanged looks, and Badger said warily, "We'll test you by going for the valley first."

Diggy grunted. "What he did to me was real."

Mek turned to Thief and Toadspit. "If I had the herb garden, I could fix you two. It's easy enough."

They stared back, one in total in disbelief, the other in resignation. Then Mek said, "Sit down. I can maybe clear your meridians. A little. Also, you've got to drink more water—as much as you can." There was no way to translate *meridians*, as well as any other healer terms. Mek decided to use them anyway.

Toadspit scowled. "But it's the water in my lungs I want rid of. I drink as little as I can."

"And the dust makes the coughing worse," Mek said. "My…teacher says, how clean is dishes washed in one cup water?"

"But—"

"Drink," Diggy said.

"Then I just gotta piss more," Toadspit protested.

"Wash the dust out," Mek said, reaching for a skinny wrist.

Toadspit pulled back, eyed Diggy, then slowly extended his hand, and braced as if for a beating. But a clogged breath or two later, he said cautiously, "It doesn't hurt as much. Here." He tapped his breast bone.

"Drink," Diggy added, jerking his head toward the waterfall, and Toadspit drank. Thief after him.

The next day, they started on the new tunnel with fierce attention—and after their meal, it was time for martial arts practice. It was immediately clear that they had been doing it as a regular thing before Mek and Tai appeared. Maybe they had their own escape plans…

Grandmother had warned Ardal that gossip sprang up like weeds, so pervasive it often carried more conviction than mere fact.

If you decide you have to inspect — and your reason had better be sound — your best pretext is to let it be known that you're making a progress in order to reward everyone for their diligence in obedience to the obsidian throne. And provide said rewards! Few questions will go beyond "What will we get?"

"You'll be in charge of the gifts," Ardal said to Odval.

"Such as?" Odval asked. She knew what girls her age liked, but adults?

"Come," Ardal said brisky.

They went below into the vast storage chambers. One entire cavern was filled with "family treasures" — which turned out to be cabinets and shelves of beautifully made, crushingly expensive lamps, bowls, utensils, hairpins and clasps, braid beads, embroidered shoes, tables, musical instruments, and of course weapons.

"Gifts. Bribes," Ardal said as she picked up an inkwell carved of jade, with a lotus blossom cap luminous in the lamplight. "Most are bribes, but some are ancestral wedding gifts, years' worth of Grandmother's birthday gifts, and visitation gifts." Ardal waved toward one half of the vast cavern

"After the treaty, gifts had to be in the style favored by the obsidian throne, which means relating to the Three Blessings: horse, bow, and sword." She nodded behind them. "Gifts before the treaty, during the days of the Golden Islands, were always pretty things one used in the household, or wore. Each one is labeled with the date and the giver."

"What can I give Jetai?" Odval asked, putting down a gold-inlaid lute. The strings, long untuned, rang discordantly. "I can't give him music, or poetry."

Ardal had hoped that Odval's fire for the handsome Mud slave would damp down. She'd been careful to say nothing, for she knew that any hint of opposition was more likely to spark more flames in her stubborn sister. "He's a slave, and the obsidian throne's law states that slaves can't own anything. Therefore an appropriate gift for them is usually food."

"Food!" Odval exclaimed. "What I want to give him is his freedom," Odval said mutinously.

"Then he'd promptly go home," Ardal stated.

"I don't care," Odval retorted, though she did—but if it were to happen, he would always know she had given him his freedom, and maybe…

"We'll prepare a nice basket of food. And Kimek can have a basket of herbs," Ardal said, breaking into Odval's daydream.

Mek watched Toadspit anxiously over the following stretch of days, not seeing much improvement, though he did his best with clearing his and Thief's clogged meridians every morning and evening. Thief seemed to be improving somewhat, but Toadspit remained the same.

But that kept no one from sparring.

This style of Diggy's reminded Mek of Brothers of the Fist, an aggressive martial sect that depended more on power than on speed. Speed was therefore Mek's primary defense. When he slipped under a blow and eeled away, sometimes Diggy's white teeth flashed in his grime-dark face.

They reached another thin, broken vein of gold feeding down to the great pool the day before everything changed.

That morning, they had just fallen into the rhythm of daily toil when he sensed Ardal outside his inner door. Not at a distance, either. Bright and clear, as if she were somewhere in the mountain—"We are at the harbor."

"You're *here*," he asked, nearly dropping a stone on his foot. "Why?"

"Kimek!" Badger bawled, aiming a cuff at Mek for disturbing the rhythm—though the blow never landed. Not on the one who assuaged the cruel giddiness that cursed Diggy's life, and made Thief breathe easier in the mornings. "Why are you standing there?"

"Wait," Diggy commanded.

They waited, staring at Mek's oblivious form as Ardal said in the mental realm, "Kimek, I have come to find you because there is no one else in this island who can Hear. The Cobra Sages take anyone born with the talent—you know that."

"Yes."

"I need your help." She caught a rapid series of images full of what seemed to be wounded snakes and birds and dogs, and strange herbs she had never seen.

Encouraged, she reminded herself that he was a boy of twelve, who had never shown the least interest in matters of power. To turn to him in secret was not any kind of treachery. She would only share what he was interested in—and learn through him.

She said, "We've almost reached you. I have a basket of food the ship's cook put up. We will give you that, but I have a hemp bag full of the herbs that Grandmother listed as necessary in the healers' time, medicines that they all carried. I am going to try to hand this to you."

"There is no way they won't see."

"Except now, for I learned a charm to keep things from being seen. As long as no one looks hard."

Mek went silent. Listening to others? She waited, though she could see by the increase of cartwheel ruts that they were very near the mine.

Mek's awareness appeared at her inner door again. "They say, no one is let into the mine."

"Leave that to me." It was her turn to close the inner door.

Mek blinked, and found everyone staring at him. "She's coming on inspection," he blurted, then smacked his hand over his face.

"Who?" four voices demanded. Toadspit coughed, and spat into the darkness, a sound no one ever noticed anymore.

Tai said, "The Heir?"

Mek sighed. "Yes."

Gazes shifted back and forth at each exchange.

"How do you know that?" Badger demanded.

"That's easy enough," Waha drawled, leaning on his pickaxe. "Everyone says she's like old Bar Thranis, spots a seagull flying two days away. No raiders can ever take this island by surprise. I don't know how she'd talk to anybody that way, though. Is it the same way you sniff out the stone?"

Diggy swung his head toward Mek. "That true?"

"Yes," Mek said, and tapped his forehead.

"If she talks to you," Toadspit croaked hoarsely, "why are you *here?*"

"Bar Gatslan," Tai said tightly.

The others fell silent as Mek closed his eyes. When he opened his eyes again, he said, "If they send a basket of food. Will we get to keep it?"

"No," six voices stated emphatically.

Mek shut his eyes again, and they got back to work around him.

Outside the mine, Boss Tangat himself came down the road to welcome her, bowing and smiling, full of compliments.

Slave assistants scurried about a canopied area well outside the opening to the mine, complete with delectable refreshments, as Boss Tangat smoothly offered his ledger for her inspection. "I take it upon myself to assume that you will be carrying a report to Bar Gatslan, may Dragon Father watch over him. Showing what we've brought out so far this year. He has been very clear in his orders, and we strive to obey…"

Ardal sat on the prepared cushion, turning over pages in a ledger that she suspected was prepared exactly for these occasions. "This looks very fine, Boss Tangat," she said, then, turning to Odval's painfully expectant face. "If we may tour the mine to see the general state of the miners, I can assure my uncle that his orders are being obeyed."

Boss Tangat bowed. "Alas, the tunnels are dangerous, strictly forbidden to any visitors, on the lord's specific orders. We cannot risk your precious life — he would have me flayed."

In the face of self-justified resistance, oil your tongue, Grandmother had written. *The more the better, even if you have to wring it out in buckets afterward.* Ardal ignored the heavy scent of fermented goat's milk and reached for the peeled lychee nuts and plump dates on a golden plate as she exerted herself to speak in her oiliest voice. "I strive to remove as much burden from my uncle as I can, so that he can put all his skills to work for the glory of Angja. And I learn so much from the superlative example set by highly esteemed chief such as yourself. One of his precepts is that we always carry out promises, even to those who serve, to preserve our honor in the all-seeing eyes of Father Dragon. For example, before he sent the latest consignment of miners, one of them — a Mud — tall, thin — had translated a necessary text for us. I'd promised a small reward to be put directly into his hands, which was overlooked in our haste — for you must have noticed how early these miners arrived?"

"Just so, just so."

"Caused by the First Prince himself requiring my uncle's

attendance up north. Of course he must set sail at once!"

"Yes, yes."

"You will, of course, be rewarded for your trouble, I need hardly add," she added, indicating the heavy chest hauled up by slaves. And at the widening of that toothy grin of greed, she said, "I understand that my sister and I must not tread into that dirty, dangerous mine. Therefore, would you summon out the two Muds we sent you, so that I can keep my promise and hand off this simple basket?"

The boss's eyes narrowed as Ardal extended her hand to Odval, who held the basket in her lap. This plump, covered basket gave off strong and delicious fragrances of fresh grilled fish, spring vegetables grilled as well, and very rare saffron rice from the southern islands.

"It is merely some foods left over from our early meal this morning. It would be a shame for it to go to waste, and I'm sure the slaves will be grateful, and work harder," Ardal said and added a false yawn. "But I must think of my reputation and keep family promises."

The mine boss bowed, then turned to his assistant and uttered a low-voiced order. As the man pelted straight into the dark hole leading into the mine, he turned back, bowing. "I have dispatched my assistant, as you see. However, finding them in the many tunnels might take time..."

"Thank you for your concern," Ardal said with her most oily smile. Sweet oil, the very sweetest! "You have thoughtfully made us so comfortable here, with these exquisite offerings! And the spring weather is so pleasant. It is a relief to take a little time away from the press of affairs, is it not?"

She then rambled on about her journey, not permitting the boss a chance to find an excuse to thwart her wishes. As she talked, she got up and wandered about the tent, as she held the hempen net full of herbs alongside the folds in her dark blue riding robe; the chief's attention kept straying toward that chest.

It seemed an eternal wait until two figures appeared as if thrust through the mine's opening. Two faces still reddened from what had to have been a rude scrubbing, wearing ill-matched but clean slave tunics of undyed cloth and loose trousers over straw shoes: Kimek and Jetai.

The two Muds advanced, performed the slave bow, and stood, eyes downcast. "Jetai, here is your reward for completing your task, as promised," Ardal said.

Jetai came forward. Odval advanced, her gorgeous gentian-blue eyes wide, but Ardal noticed he avoided looking as her as he always had, his expression closed and wary as he stiffly took the basket. Odval described the treats, determined to coax an answer out of Jetai. Ardal stepped near Kimek, who looked so small and twig thin. But his grip was surprisingly firm as he took the hemp handle from her.

She backed away, and then began oiling the mine boss with gratitude, as she tugged Odval's sleeve.

Odval obediently backed away, still staring at Jetai, who also was far too thin, but in the time between his leaving the fortress and coming to this mine, he'd become lean, long muscles cleanly defined. Aware of male attraction, though far too duty-bound to permit herself to be attracted, Ardal wondered how Jetai managed to look even better after toiling in a mine, underneath the ill-fitting slave garb.

The boss jerked his head to one of his slave guards, who said, "Back to work," to the two.

Mek and Jetai trotted back to the mine, as Ardal and Odval spoke their farewells to the mine boss, whose attention was already on the box full of expensive treasures. They parted with amicable good wishes, and the girls returned to where the slave held the horses in readiness.

"Odval? I'm sorry Jetai did not speak to you," Ardal said gently, once they reached the road.

Odval turned to look at Ardal, her expression odd. Thoughtful. Stubborn, yes, but not mutinous. "What do you expect, when he's treated like that? Did you see how thin he is, how red and rough his hands? Both of them. No, I expected nothing less." She was silent the remainder of the ride.

And later, when they were in the boat, Odval said, "I think I would like to go to the capital, to see Mother, before the cold weather comes." There was an odd note in her voice, too. Of decision. But she refused to say more.

TWENTY

As it happened, Boss Tangat was so pleased with his bribe, and with his success in keeping the young Bar from nosing into the warehouse supposedly full of supplies for miners, that he let the basket of food go.

And so, unmolested by the mine guards, Tai set the plump, promising, fragrant basket down, but before Crew Six could dive at it, Mek held up a hand. "You all know I've had some healer lessons. Yes?"

Thief looked impatient, but Diggy cut him a glance, and everyone fell back, mouths watering.

Mek said, "Our usual ration is so dry I don't think anything could make it worse, but this here is fresh food. That means you have to eat it with clean hands. Otherwise, your guts won't keep it in. Also, you must eat very slowly, or it will come up as fast as you eat it."

No one thought much about dirt anymore. You could get used to anything that wasn't actually eating you. But now there was indeed a startling contrast between the two Muds—who as Ardal had correctly surmised, had been seized and forcibly scrubbed down—and the rest of them. It was easy to imagine how much of that black grime got inside them when they ate.

"What's the use of clean hands when everything else is mud?" Toadspit protested in a whine.

"For that," Mek said happily, "I now have the cure for that cough. But it won't stick unless you start wearing a bandage tied over your face. To strain out the dust. Thief, you too." He held up a strip of clean bandage, pulled from a net bag that seemed to come out of nowhere.

Diggy was the first to move to the cascade. He thrust both his huge, strong hands into the cold water, which blasted the grime away within a couple of short breaths. He even cupped his hands, gathered water in them, and scrubbed it over his face. He turned, dripping. "Do it."

The others complied, as Tai meticulously divided the food into fair shares.

"Slow," Diggy growled, pinching a tiny bit from the grilled fish.

Slow it was. Perhaps they enjoyed it the more for taking time to enjoy each bite. Then Mek took bandage-wrapped packages from the net bag, sniffed each, nodding at familiar scents.

To the row of faces, he said, "I can made medicine from these. But soon I'm going to need a bowl of some sort, to heat into tea."

Toadspit said, "I can chisel you a bowl, nice and smooth, until we can find some copper. And a shelf to put the medicines in." He patted the stone wall behind him.

"Good. Until then, you will have to drink the medicine cold. It will be bitter."

Toadspit vowed, "I will drink *anything* if it takes away this rheum."

They slept well that night—Mek having reminded himself to open the door within his dreams. Ardal floated in a wildness of images: distortions of the fortress, mostly, dominated by the wrinkled face of an old woman whose deep-set, narrow eyes resembled Ardal's. That had to be the grandmother.

Mek isolated Ardal's image in the half-dream. "The miners say, thanks for the food."

"That was for the two of you," Ardal protested.

"We share. They are too hungry. I must sleep soon. We mine early. Herbal? The one you try to learn—healing bone?"

She recited the herbal, but it was her almost-understanding that reached him more than the words, not all of which he comprehended. Their separate methods for reaching and shaping Essence flowed between them, the quicker for not being bound by the limits of spoken language. All the senses contributed in this half-waking world of dream, perceivable to each.

He—trained in the fundamentals of healing—grasped the process first, and then she—shaped by a lifetime of precise and sustained concentration — saw how to apply it. Wordlessly he promised to try it on Diggy, and wordlessly she rejoiced in the success of her plan, anticipating the morrow.

When Diggy woke, sitting up very slowly as he had ever since he'd recovered from the head wound that had devastated his life, Mek was sitting cross-legged before him, a somewhat comical little figure half-lost in clothes meant for a man, his curls a wild, uncombed halo. But his eyes reflected the lamplight, dominating his round, snub-nosed face as he chirped, "I have the medicines to settle stomach. Better, can we try the true healing?"

Diggy would have submitted to a knife if it would remove the constant claw of nausea and unsteadiness, but he did not have to. Mek's small hands pressed lightly on either side of Diggy's face, and Diggy shut his eyes in anticipation of pain, an old, familiar comrade. There was only a sense of heat between the back of his eye and his jaw — and then an inner, steadying sense of a lock snicking.

And the world righted.

Dazed — light-headed — he looked around cautiously. Mek's face was covered in sweat, and he was breathing fast, but he whispered, "It worked. It holds." He drew another hissing breath, then uttered a stream of imperial to Tai, who turned to Diggy.

"He says that there is a, a binding to set the bone chip where it belongs. It is not completely healed. He says to try not to jar it until it can reattach."

"We'll wield the pickaxes today," Badger said, indicating himself, Mo Thi, and Waha.

Mek had already turned to the medicines; he scrupulously cleaned his fingers before carefully pinching ginseng, licorice root, and mullein as well as a tiny bit of precious longevity root together. They had no bowl, yet. He mixed it in the palm of his hand as he infused the medicine with Essence.

Toadspit cleaned his own fingers, dipped two in the greenish sludge, and licked the mixture. Then he shuddered and gasped. He kept at it, choking down the rest until he'd scraped his finger over Mek's palm and brought it up clean.

"You might cough out a lot more," Mek said. "I think. But that's good. We want your body to not make more green spit. Drink a lot of water! It will clean it out faster." He turned to Thief. "Now you."

When that was done, Toadspit making faces and drinking more water to get rid of the horrible aftertaste, Badger said, "The gong rang. We've got to fill that cart."

"Bandages," Mek reminded the two.

Toadspit and Thief tied bandages around their faces to filter the dust, and off they went.

The next night, when Mek remembered to reach for the inner door within his dreams, he found Ardal waiting. She flinched at the sensory residue of his dreams: lingering memory of reek, the gritty, slimy feel of mold-covered rock, the relentless toil of chipping away at rock for someone else's gain.

She taught him the fog-making spell.

"Easy," he said. "I can raise a wind—I've always been able to do that. In fact I brought a good wind out to push that galley along when we got sent to this mine."

To his surprise, her emotions rippled through change like clouds covering the sun. "Is *that* the cause of the terrible storms in those days after you left?"

"How can it be? We were out on the water! There's always wind on the water."

"But winds reach across islands," she responded. "There is writing for that: my grandmother said, *Have you ever struck a stick through water, then watched the swirls and ripples? They cross the entire pond before settling. Air is much the same.*

This was more of what Master Root had said about consequences, Mek thought, abashed.

"I cannot say those storms were caused by you for certain," was her scrupulous addition, "but there is another saying that I think might apply. This was something my mother said before she had to leave us, that the worst evil is action that cannot be unmade. We both must reflect on that, before we use these spells."

That, too, sounded like something Master Root might have said.

Toadspit's skepticism about the efficacy of wearing cloth tied over his face ended that first evening when he untied the bandage that had irritated him all day, and he saw the gray-green grime in the middle, shading to two black holes over where his nose had been. He put on the new one without complaining, and washed out the old one, hanging it over a lamp to dry.

Days passed.

Washing bandages was necessary, but they did not dry completely clean. Even so, moral pressure from everyone kept Toadspit diligent.

Thief was enthusiastic about the bandages. "If wearing this thing keeps me from having to choke down that vile medicine, and stop coughing, I'll wear it forever," he said.

A clean bandage only worked on a clean face, and so — gradually—Tai was able to heed his own hatred of dirt, especially on himself, and for his next gold share, asked for another piece of clothing so he could wash dirty ones and wear (relatively) clean.

That and the disappearance of Toadspit's disgusting rash, as well as the abatement of the wretched coughing they had had to live with, inspired the others to begin washing in the icy water.

Far to the south, Ardal and Odval drew nearer home — and finally landed.

The dahlias were blooming now, harvest beginning. Odval began to prepare for going to the capital, and Ardal studied. She now had a goal; she must finish learning from Kimek.

That happened sooner than she expected.

Mek met her as usual that night, but with his appearance waves of exhaustion so intense she struggled not to lose focus and waken just to yawn. He said, "I have the herbal recipes in memory now. The rest is all your wards that don't use blood. For your borders. I'm never going to need to put wards on borders. Nor will I be reducing gunpowder to its elements. I do need to sleep." There was an air of expectation.

Ardal reminded herself that he was just twelve. But she'd made a promise. "I know I said I would see to it that you and Jetai get freed. This I cannot do until my uncle comes next spring, and I will have to find a reason that he will accept. I might have to convince him to put a limit on your sentence, commuting it from life."

Mek scarcely listened to the words. He already knew how much she wrestled with feelings of powerlessness, and here was yet another proof of it. "We are finished?" In his mind, he made the slave bow to her in farewell, and he sensed her relief.

They were indeed finished.

It was odd, he thought as he curled up to sleep, how much he'd been inside of another person's mind, and then to have it end. He couldn't fix her Heir problems, and she couldn't free him or Tai. It was good to end it; as Tai had always said, they were on their own.

As for Ardal, she waited two more nights as she caught up with all her tasks. Kimek did not reappear in her dreams.

Now, at last, she at last could attain her longest-desired goal.

The third night after their arrival home, she shut herself into her bedchamber, then hung talismans around the four corners of her bed to create a ward, like an inner house instead of just an inner door. This so that any diamond-level Cobra Sage who might be scouting in this strange realm without material boundaries could not Hear past the walls.

Then, fingering the precious letters that her mother had touched with her own hands, Ardal dropped into the familiar half-sleep and as a dream comprised of memories rose around her, she reached…and there she was!

"Mother?"

"*Ardal?*" Mother exclaimed within the dream.

"Don't waken, Mother! I am in your dream, but I am real. I can explain everything…"

TWENTY-ONE

WINTER GAVE WAY TO spring, and the dragon-prowed raiders appeared on the horizon, black dragon banners streaming in the wind: the lord had returned. Bar Gatslan's stay was barely two days, long enough to collect his gold.

Deep in the mine, the lord's visit went completely unnoticed. Mek had no communication with the Heir, which meant that she had failed with her uncle to free them. As Master Root used to say, don't be like the thousand foolish monks who toiled across a single log bridge without thinking to build a wider or a second one. Mek was going to find an escape another way, and kept busy with his experiments.

His first was to begin adding Essence to all his efforts. Not much, in the beginning. Especially after he discovered that adding Essence force to a punch hurt his hand at least as much as it impacted Diggy's palm when invited to "punch harder."

Whenever he wasn't scraping up rocks, he took to practicing by tossing a pebble and kicking it out of the air. He got good enough at his aim that he tried using all the power he could reach, and his stone imbedded itself in rock.

The next discovery was inadvertent. During a sparring session his bare heel slipped on a patch of mold, and he began to fall backward toward the jagged stones below the cascade. Essence surged. He flung himself upward—on another ledge. This one was so narrow there was barely room to stand with his back against wet stone.

He stared across the cascade at the others, who gazed back in shock. Waha, against whom he'd been scrapping, called hoarsely, "I'm sorry, I'm sorry!"

"Wasn't you. I slipped," Mek called back.

"Can you get back?" Diggy stood poised, as he was going to try to spring across the twenty paces between them to rescue him.

Mek closed his eyes, remembering the sickening sense of losing his balance, the startled breath, drawing in Essence. Yes, this was just like throwing Essence, only he was throwing *himself* with Essence.

He tried deliberately—and sprang, his arms windmilling wildly. He tumbled onto their ledge, and fetched up against Badger's sturdy legs. He grinned up at Badger. "I did it."

"Teach me to jump like that," Toadspit demanded, dropping down on his haunches beside Mek. "You were practically flying!"

He had been. Mek flinched. Hurtling through the air like that brought up the still-disturbing memory of being thrown across the sky on that ruined door, then the world spinning as he tried to right himself. "You pull Essence to you, and up you go," Mek said slowly. "But I'd rather have solid ground under my feet."

Toadspit sighed. "More of that *Essence*."

Life was easier, now.

Tai had gotten better at sensing metal in the rock, though he preferred to let Mo Thi point out thin, broken veins of copper and gold. Tai did not want this ability to sense the presence of metal in rock to be a talent.

Mek sensed copper, gold, silver, and tiny chips of other odder metals, as easily as sight. Twice, always in dream, his mind cut free and sank down and down and down to where the island was glowing fire, and below that to where the dragons slumbered, dreaming of distant suns.

Mek felt oddly heavy after waking from those dreams, so he stopped them. They were not good. Or maybe they would be if his affinity was pure earth, but he needed free air, and the living quiet of wood. Getting pulled deep into the earth was dangerous.

It was wood that drew him toward the fold in the land that made a steep valley. That summer, they reached dirt and live roots, presaged by clumps of soil. Badger exclaimed, "The boy was right. If we dig much farther, we're going to find air."

There ensued a frenzy of burrowing until at last, Diggy's pickaxe broke into air. A cascade of dirt showered on them, and they gazed out at the infinite summer sky as warm, sweet air flowed in. Silence wholly possessed them, once the hiss and clatter of debris halted. Gradually their awareness shifted to tiny sounds not heard for so long: the rustle of leaves, the chirr of insects, the cry of distant birds. And far above, silhouetted against the sun, wings outspread, they spied a heron. Or a crane. It was impossible to tell, staring against a sun so bright.

"Oh, I want to run," Waha breathed.

"And they'll drop you dead," Diggy muttered, touching the headband hiding his tattoo. "They won't even bother searching for your body, which means you'll be there for the ghosts to harvest."

Badger rubbed at his forehead around the slave tattoo, the skin corrugated from years of squinting into the darkness. "This was right where the boy said it would be. That means he's right about the gold," he said.

Toadspit grinned. "Let's get at it!"

"I think we need to talk it out," Badger said slowly. "But first, fill the cart. And make sure none of this soil goes in, or they'll know we breached the surface, and be demanding the site."

Toadspit bobbed in emphatic agreement. "It's *ours*." He jerked a dirt-encrusted thumb. "I want to run for it," he breathed. "See how far I get. You won't tell them I ran, will you?" He looked in appeal from one set face to the next.

"And die of some invisible fire or poison after ten steps? What if the lord had the snakes blood-bind the mountain?" Mo Thi wiped his sweat-gleaming, glabrous face against his filthy sleeve.

"Blood-binding fence," Thief muttered, and spat into the grass. "You think they might have done one here?"

"It is a gold mine," Mo Thi said slowly.

"There isn't—" Mek began, then caught himself.

Six sets of eyes snapped to him, and he sighed. Once again, he'd tripped over the things he could say and the things he probably shouldn't. Only he wasn't *sure*. Because how could he truly know the consequences when people didn't always know themselves how they'd react?

"Of course *you'd* find it first." Waha studied Mek. And then came the question Mek had been dreading. "Can you break the blood-binding on this cursed snake-mark?" He flicked his tattoo.

Everyone stared, except Tai, who had closed his eyes, his lips a thin line. For him, that invisible division between Westerner and imperial, enemy and target, never truly went away.

Mek couldn't get the words right, to explain that Westerner and imperial didn't matter. Except that it did, in the sense that he knew Tai didn't want things to suddenly turn into enemy sides.

Mek said, "I can." He added in haste, "That means I can break the binding. I can't make the tattoo go away."

The others scarcely heard these last words. It was that *I can* that changed everything.

"Let's get back down to our den, where we know we can't be overheard above the water," Badger said, low.

They trod back to the cart and filled it the rest of the way with rubble.

Once Thief and Tai returned with their dry, stale rations — no gold flakes today — they sat in a circle, and when the worst of their hunger had been assuaged, they slowed down to make the scant ration last.

Badger turned to Mek. "How big is the gold you sniffed out?"

"It's like a pond," Mek said, gesturing wildly but uselessly with his hands. "A deep one."

Toadspit and Waha grinned. Mo Thi shook his head, his shoulders hunched. "If it's even a tiny vein, they'll take it from us. Might even kill for it."

"They can try," Diggy uttered, smacking a fist into his palm. "Don't think defeat. If you think defeat here." He tapped his forehead. "Then you're down before the first strike."

Badger raised his hand before the talk could devolve into combat philosophy. "We can't take *any* of it," he reminded them. "Merely the possession of gold is an instant death sentence."

"I want to run," Mek said with such longing that his voice cracked for the first time.

Tai closed his eyes again, braced for threat, for betrayal. He still heard that casual reference to castration in his dreams; he was never going to trust these Westerners. And here was Mek, blabbing right out, like...like...like the boy he was!

Tai's inward turmoil was so intense he missed the low tone of conviction, of a spoken vow, when Diggy addressed Mek:

"I'll see you safe to wherever you go."

That was met with thoughtful silence. Then Badger said slowly, "I always thought to finish my life out here."

Waha lifted a shoulder. "We were condemned for life," and Mo Thi nodded soberly as Diggy looked grim.

Badger said, "I sold myself to keep my boy out of the pits. No, don't say anything. I never told you because there's no use in whatever you'll say. That was fifteen years ago, near as I can guess. Might be more. I could never go back—I'd be reported faster than a snake strike. Not sure I'd want to go back. My wife probably moved someone else into our bed, and who'd blame her? Not I. Fifteen years, my boy is no longer a boy. Wouldn't know me by sight, I don't doubt." He looked over at the cascade. "Fifteen years. It seems an eternity in here. Most don't make it five years. I can still name those who came before all of you."

Toadspit snickered. "I thought, all of us were condemned as thieves, except for Thief, here."

"Shut up," Thief mumbled, punching Toadspit in the arm.

From long habit most braced for Toadspit to fall over, coughing up disgusting green spit, but he just grinned at Thief.

"You're...not a thief?" Waha said, looking incredulous.

Thief punched Toadspit again, muttering, "Now see what you done?" But he wasn't angry. Mek could feel it, and the others saw it. His eyes stayed on his palms as he said, "My dad named me Thief after my ma died, not long after I was born. He blamed me. Said I stole her life. But before I got sold off, my aunt told me it wasn't true, that he nagged my ma into getting up too soon, and she didn't eat to look skinny again, dancing for dad's company. When she got the same lung rot I did, or similar, she sickened fast and died. But he blamed me."

He fell silent, but Toadspit—who was the cart pusher before Tai—said, "His pa moved a new woman in, who didn't want him, so she said he'd go to a relative for training but she sold him, and his rat of a dad never came to find out."

"She sold me to the ring, but they said I was going to be too small, and they sent me here to crawl tunnels, and." He shrugged, hands outspread.

"I was no thief," Diggy said slowly. "I was bred for the ring. I was good. The best. Until I took on four scrappers who wanted me out of the competition. One saw to it I took a fall on a brick." He smacked the side of his head. "Didn't kill me. For a time I wanted it to. Because I couldn't get up. Not without the world spinning. Couldn't fight. Sold here."

"And you taught us," Toadspit crowed, spinning into a side kick, and landing while holding his breath. But no cough came.

Diggy lifted massive shoulders. "What else was there to do, except fight? It's all I know. I thought, train us all so we could take out Crew One. Maybe even challenge the boss. *He'd* work for *us*." He shrugged. "Kept me alive, that plan."

"I can't go back to my old crew. It was my second who turned on me," Waha said ruefully. "When his woman came after me. I'd run today, but I won't go back to the capital. Badger?"

"I'll run," Badger said. "Go back to cooking. Galleys can always use a cook, any age."

Waha crossed his arms, jerking his chin toward Badger. "You're thinking, use the gold as a diversion?"

"That's right," Badger said. "If Kimek here really can break the blood curse on us, we run, and they don't trouble with us while Crews One and Eight fight over the gold. Maybe even take on the boss. All fighting each other."

"Then…they won't search for us at all?" Mo Thi mumbled.

"Exactly!" Badger clapped him on the shoulder. "If we're careful not to leave any sign behind us. And we go out in the world not looking like we just crawled out of the mine. We'll crash our breakout tunnel behind us. They'll assume we're under all the rock. They won't dig for our corpses as long as there's no sign of gold. Never dug anybody out from collapses long as I've been here. It's death if we're caught," he reminded them.

"Then let's not be caught," Waha drawled.

TWENTY-TWO

Badger, who once had planned complicated banquets for wealthy merchants trying to rise to the notice of Father Dragon's Chosen, was systematic in organizing Crew Six's break for freedom.

"Let's locate the gold first," he suggested. "Kimek still can't tell us how long it will take to reach it. If it's down deep and requires shoring, that might put us all the way to winter."

Behind Mek's ribs pulsed the urge to reach through the stone for the gold. But the idea frightened him. Like that almost-flying. Or sinking down to where the dragons slept. It wasn't so much that he might get stuck, if the gold was very far off, but he might become…not Mek anymore. If he closed his eyes and explored through that inner sense, it was so easy to imagine finding a long-hibernating seed there in the stone, giving it a bit of Essence spark, then helping it to reach up and up through rock and soil, branches stretching to the sky…

He blinked, and was himself again, warm blood coursing, heart beating, breath going and coming. It was actually a mild jolt. He needed to be in the sun again. They all did!

They began digging before the morning *get to work* gong, and kept at it feverishly; Mek and Tai sensed the proximity of the gold first, then Mo Thi emerged from the narrow tunnel, coughing black grit, and gasped, "It's *right there*."

And, the next day, there it was.

They broke through to an enormous cavern, their lamps throwing light on layers of stone slanting at an angle overhead. Gold lay in a deep bank against smoothed rock among pebbles of a variety of colors. Badger studied the piles and piles of rich, sun-colored gleams and, veteran of fifteen years of crawling in the deeps of mountains, said, "There must have been a river here, long ago. Maybe even part of the valley we found. Dropped all this gold here, piled against the rock there."

"Now we plan," Waha said finally, rubbing his long, clever hands.

That broke the gold-fixed reverie the others had been caught in.

Badger said, "We need to think about after we get out. We'll need clothes that won't mark us as miners as soon as anyone gets a look at us."

"But that would take weeks to earn it," Toadspit protested.

"Not," Waha drawled, "if we take it." He spread his long-fingered hands. "I never get caught."

"But you did get caught," Toadspit protested. "Or you wouldn't be here!"

"I was *never* caught," Waha retorted, his sharp-cut chin raised. "Betrayed, yes. There was no evidence, or the snakes would have been gathering up my blood in the pit to use in their wicked deeds years ago. Everyone knew I was the leader of the best crew in Baris Tharan."

"It's risky, even for you," Badger warned. "If there's even a suspicion of someone thieving, you know they'll do a search through all the tunnels, then we're lost before we can get away."

"If I go with him?" Mek offered. "I don't know the tunnels, but I remember the place where they keep the clothes. And I can put that distraction Essence over us. The one that kept you from seeing my net bag."

"Can you make us *all* invisible?" Toadspit asked. "Then we don't need clothes."

"Not invisible," Mek said. "I can make us unnoticed. As long as they don't look hard. There's a difference."

Waha turned to Mek. "Just to be clear. You could put that spell on our tattoos, but the first thing suspicious guards look for is a slave tattoo. In which case, they look, they see it?"

"Yes," Mek said.

Waha shrugged. "That spell is part of the protection traps in the great roundhouses of the Dragon's Chosen. At most it distracts the eye. It doesn't make anything vanish. We do not want to depend on that spell once we are outside."

Badger thumped his fists on his knees. "In that case, you

must see if there are headbands or head-scarfs. You two should shadow Thief and Tai, and when they turn in the cart with the gold nuggets, and all attention is on them, you get the clothes. And shoes. Very important, shoes. And as soon as you get back, we leave, because there will be parties to scrag us for our find not long after everyone's down to sleep."

They loaded the cart with chunks of gold, then Mek carefully formed the distraction charm over himself and Waha, saying, "I don't know how long it will last. But I put as much Essence in as I could."

Thief and Tai took off, conscientiously never looking behind them.

Mek and Waha, now trained to move in a martial catwalk, drifted soundlessly behind the two. They waited until everyone crowded around Crew Six's cart—even the slave guards.

When Boss Tangat sauntered up, bawling, "What is this? What is this? A find?", his attention solely on the cart's contents, Mek and Waha ghosted behind him, and down into forbidden territory.

Mek had trouble seeing Waha clearly. The distraction charm rendered light smeary, a disagreeable sensation as Waha led them unerringly along seldom-used tunnels. He'd said as they'd started out, "Luckily everyone stinks, or they'd nose us out in a heartbeat. But let's not pass directly by anyone."

They didn't, having to press against walls twice as guards sauntered by.

The storeroom was unlocked, and unguarded. They slipped in, and Waha went for the clothes, careful to choose those of laborers. The same with scarfs, headbands, and hair ties. He then meticulously shifted about all the piles so as to conceal what was missing and how much.

It was Mek's job to gather the straw shoes, which he stuffed under his enormous tunic, then he tied the flapping hem around his hips to keep them from dropping out.

When he was done, Waha was already waiting, a bundle tied in a cloak hitched over his shoulder. Mek performed the distraction charm over this bundle, then Waha gave a short nod: let's go.

They catfooted back the way they had come, passing Tai and Thief, who were being loaded with good food and even a pot of wine, ha ha, you've all earned it! And then Thief's voice rising in the words Badger had coaxed him to memorize, "We think we've even found another site, not far off! If we're right, it'll be even bigger! But that's tomorrow's discovery, ha ha ha!"

Once the two were safely up the tunnel, Waha muttered, "Did you see Hengis there, licking his lips? I don't think Crew One is half the danger he is. Get us drunk, slit our throats. And the boss standing by."

As soon as they reached their dank, dark ledge, Badger didn't wait for their report. He took Waha's bundle then said, "Strip and scrub. Kimek, you first, so you can remove the curse-binding on each of us after we're scrubbed clean."

Mek gleefully shucked those scratchy, dirty oversized clothes that had been tripping him up since Ardal's visit. Over the edge they went.

When Tai and Thief returned with the cart and enough food for a feast, they were startled to discover a clean, dripping crew almost unrecognizable in shabby but regular clothing, their straw shoes stuffed through sashes or in pockets, to be put on as soon as they got outside.

"We'll find a stream to wash our feet in before we put on the shoes," Badger said. "There can be no telltale mine grime if we're seen by anyone."

Tai and Thief cleaned themselves up, pulled on new clothes, then stood still for Mek to break the binding, slow at first.

"I didn't feel anything," Thief said worriedly, rubbing the skin of his forehead. "Should I?"

"No," Mek assured him.

"I felt a burn, kind of," Tai murmured to Mek as Badger began passing the food to each of them to store in their clothes.

Mek put all his precious herbs in his new tunic. "Mo Thi jumped when I did it. I definitely felt a burn. I think those who have a bit of Essence talent might have felt it."

"Do we take the pickaxes?" Toadspit asked. "If we have to defend ourselves?"

"Can't. They'd mark us as miners at first sight," Diggy said.

Badger raised a hand. "We'll take them, so it looks like we wanted to get ahead on the supposed second site. We can't leave them here, or it'll look strange, us gone without our tools, and that might cause an outside search. The tools have to be left in the tunnel collapse with the cart, as Diggy said."

They threw the tools into the cart, distributed their food, then sped up the tunnels to their exit. There they stopped, as Diggy pointed upward, and picked up his pickaxe. "I'll bring it down. If it catches me, I'm the strongest. Best chance of pushing me way out."

No one argued—no one wanted to risk being under a collapse.

"Wait," Mek said. "Let me try punching it."

One by one they dropped their tools in the cart and eased out the hole into the clear air of twilight, as Mek turned back to the tunnel. He eyed the unstable soil overhead, and beyond, the narrow tunnel of stone. He sought an unstable spot where the stone gave way to soil. "There," he said to himself, aiming at the withered roots of a date tree long dead.

Pulling up an immense amount of Essence, he drew back his fist to give the Essence focus, and threw it directly toward that spot. Then backed rapidly away.

At first nothing happened. He was about to go back inside to try again when dirt began to trickle, hiss, and quite suddenly the ground beneath their feet jolted as WHAM! Dust spewed from their tunnel, knocking Mek rolling. Then the entire hole disappeared entirely.

Mek sat up, spitting dirt, as the others began brushing dust and grass from themselves. They began to walk up the side of the mountain, at first tentatively. Badger—and Mo Thi—braced to be caught by a vicious ward.

But there was none.

"We're free," Thief observed quietly, relishing the words as they paused on the shoulder of a slope to get their bearings.

"Then I'm not Toadspit anymore. I'm Toad," declared that youth.

No one commented.

Toad turned to Diggy. "You could have a new name."

"Diggy *is* a new name," said he, mildly. "In the training yards, we were all numbered in birth order. I like Diggy," he added, and Toad—about to protest—closed his mouth.

"Let's go," Badger said, and for the first time in memory, he smiled.

TWENTY-THREE

As THEY PROGRESSED SINGLE-FILE to obscure their number, and no bells reverberated from the slopes, nor did lines of armed slave guards or hunting dogs emerge on trails below, the former Crew Six began to believe that no alarm would be raised. Boss Tangat—and his greedy assistant—were surely busy dealing with equally grabby crews determined to claim credit for that gold cache in the cavern, once they'd discovered both it and the fresh collapse.

That first night they slept under the stars, relishing the softness and sweet scent of grass under their tired bodies, and the sough of pure air through the trees. Tai studied the stars, for once not upset by the skewed celestial architecture, evidence of how far he was from home.

They had breakfast on waking, rationing out the food likeliest to spoil, and supplemented it with wild fruit and berries gleaned along their climb. After eating, when Diggy got up and began warming his muscles, they fell into practice without complaint. Then they set out again.

They'd decided to hike over the lower hills to the northern extremity of the island, where the largest harbor lay, expanded and fortified by the Dragon's Chosen after the treaty was made. The seventh day, they reached the heights of the tallest hill, from which they could glimpse the ocean in the late summer haze. Around them, osmanthus trees filled the air with scents of apricot and peach, and when they paused beside a rilling stream to drink and to pluck wild berries and tubers, Mo Thi sat with his back against the bark of a young tree, shut his eyes, and said, "I'm staying here."

They assumed he meant for a rest, though he was not known for uttering unnecessary words. But when they got up, intending to reach a lower slope by nightfall— "I think we might make it to the harbor in a fist of days if we push hard," Badger said—Mo Thi replied, tranquilly, "Not I."

They stood around him in a half-circle. Puzzled, uncertain. Wary (Tai) and angry (Toad).

Finally Badger said slowly, "We were forced together, but we never swore to stay together."

"But..." Toad looked from one to another. Then he slumped. "I don't know what I thought."

"For a time we were a real crew," Waha said mildly as he pulled off his headband to wipe his sweaty face. As he retied it, once more hiding the slave tattoo, his brief smile flickered Mek's way. "The boy here did that. By making anything possible. However, even real crews come to an end. As does everything."

Some began to protest, but Diggy said, "Possible." The others fell silent. He jerked a huge thumb Mo Thi's way. "Possible means free to choose. He wants to stay, he stays."

Toad dropped down on his skinny haunches beside Mo Thi. "What're you gonna do?"

"Can breathe here." Mo Thi looked up at the white flowers spangling the long, finger-slim leaves. "Breathe. When I get enough of this air, maybe go back to working clay."

These cryptic words raised a lot of questions, but even if he answered, that wouldn't change anything.

Badger said, "Leave him a couple of pancakes."

Thief silently laid two pancakes on the grass beside Mo Thi, and they started off, traveling single file again. Toad kept glancing back, as if he expected Mo Thi to change his mind and come running, but presently he was out of sight, and later, when they camped under some sheltering willows, he was present by his absence.

"What do you think he'll do?" Toad asked.

"He said something about clay. I don't know anything about where he came from. Or why he was caught stealing," Badger said. "But I remember how thin he was. He was probably trying theft because of hunger."

"D'you think he'll sell us out?" Toad asked, nervously scratching at his neck, though the rash was long healed.

"Won't," Diggy said.

"He knows the reward would be a garrote," Waha murmured wryly.

"You don't think he'll…give up?" Toad asked, his pale gray eyes wide.

"Kill himself?" Badger squinted skyward. "Hai, hum, mum, mum. I think more like, be a hermit for a time. Until the cold weather comes. We've had good days, so far. He's probably forgotten weather."

Mo Thi's absence continued to be felt in the gradual reformation of the group, with Toad and Thief walking together more often than not.

When Badger signaled a halt at night, it was these two who hunted for food in the lengthening shadows as autumn began to breathe cold air on northern slopes, while Mek ranged about alone, spotting wild vegetables and fruits, and now and then overgrown vegetable patches behind ruins long abandoned.

Six days after they left Mo Thi in the osmanthus grove, they glimpsed the sea between slopes.

They began washing up in the mornings, and finger-combing their hair before retying headbands. They left the trail, moving northwards, and mid-morning they reached the top of the last hill, hugging the slope of a higher conical mountain. Here they paused to stare down into the harbor.

Back when Angja was the capital of the Golden Island archipelago, this harbor had been purely for trade, a community built along the bay in a warren of houses on stilts for the flood season. After the treaty brought the obsidian throne's protection, the conical hill's wormholes had been dug out and fortified with cannon that could reach the harbor below.

The footsore hikers gazed reflectively up at that imposing fort, then down again at the array of ships in the harbor, galleys all. Tai sustained a visceral hatred at the sight of those banked oars, but he knew that taking ship was the only way to get home.

Mek wondered if there were Cobra Sages up in that castellated aerie atop the fort, and once again built up a firm bank to block his inner door.

The general reverie broke when Toad nudged Thief, who side-eyed the others furtively, then mumbled, "We talked. Don't want to go on no ship. We're going to try wrangling horses. Toad used to, before he got caught."

"I love horses," Toad said, scratching again.

"Might be tough, when you've got no family to speak for you," Badger said.

"That's why we're going to offer ourselves as guards first," Toad said eagerly. "We'll be brothers. Thief, here, wants to try a new name, Salamander." He pushed up his headband to expose the slave tattoo. "Mo Thi could read. Did you know that? He said once, if we were to add two slashes more, and the roof character over the circle, the slave mark looks like 'salamander'. That could be a guard sect name from some other island. And we got here after a shipwreck."

"That could work," Badger said slowly. "You two are young enough not to raise suspicions, if you're careful and respectful."

Toad ignored that. "We'll cut each other, soon's we can find a knife. When it heals over, we'll find a stable."

"You've thought it all out, it seems. Father Dragon's fire go with you," Badger said.

A brief silence followed, everyone looking at one another.

"You trained us," Thief-now-Salamander said finally to Diggy. "We'll get on fine."

"You healed us," Toad said to Mek.

Then, as if tempted to remain, he whirled about and walked off, Salamander sending a brief smile over his thin shoulder before he followed.

"I hope those two don't turn to theft," Badger said tiredly, as the two vanished beyond a tangle of white and green fringe-flower shrubs.

"Toad knows the streets," Waha observed, then crossed his arms. "I don't know this harbor—I was condemned in the capital, and transported here when the lord purchased fresh bodies for the gold mine. I expect the local garrison will operate the same way they do in the capital."

Seeing that the other four were listening, he went on, "If a group of strangers walks into town, especially you." He lifted his chin at Diggy. "They'll be on the watch. If they're bored, interrogation. And if they need bodies for grunt work they don't want to do, they'll find a law we're breaking. But one at a time does not draw so much attention. I make out a fountain there, midway, before that road up to the fort. I'll be at the fountain by noon."

He loped down the road, his run awkward because of the

straw sandals that were falling apart after that long hike.

Badger turned to Diggy, and eyed his ugly face, which could have been any age. "If you walk with the boy, they might take you for a young father going about his business, whereas alone..." He gestured largely.

Diggy was fine with that suggestion, as it fit with his determination to protect Mek. "Come along."

He and Mek moved in Waha's wake down the goat trail toward a road on which traffic moved along in the dust, carters, porters, and a miscellany of others.

At Badger's insistence, Diggy had that morning taken down his fighting topknot—the sure mark of the ring warrior—and Badger and Waha helped him plait it up in three braids, tied off with modestly beaded strings Waha had taken from the mine supplies. Nothing would change Diggy's height or his martial cat walk, but he did try to shuffle as he bowed his head.

Tai followed behind Mek some twenty paces, utterly unaware that he, too, appeared to the casual eye to move like a young warrior, only there was something different in his bearing, the remains of his early training, even if he had not worn silk and long sleeves for nearly four years. His alertness had heightened, now that they were in the center of the enemy, and he felt those stares—but, with his slight short-sightedness, mistook admiration for suspicion. He kept his gaze straight ahead.

Only Badger stumped along like the weary middle-aged man he was, though one with plenty of muscle. No one looked at this dull-looking, shabbily dressed man with an unkempt, small beard, whereas Diggy caught the eye immediately.

He felt the impact of gazes without seeing how they slid from his unattractive face—jaw too big, making his lower teeth protrude in a manner that called to mind a wild boar, and the sparse beard that had begun to sprout in the last year only emphasized it. He had misshapen ears from so many cuts, and a scar from his hairline across one cheek. He looked like a warrior, but one who had a boy skipping at his side, squirming and twisting as he tried to see everything. Mek had hung his trail-worn sandals from his sash in favor of bare feet, making him look even more like a common laborer's urchin, with his delighted grin below his wild fluff of hair escaping its binding, as he whistled and coaxed and petted every street hound he saw.

Mek spotted the fountain first—then forgot all about everything but the pitiful sight of a small, thin, rib-stark dog of an unsightly mud color with an infected hind leg. The animal's hindquarters quivered as it tried to balance on the lip of the fountain in order to assuage its thirst.

Mek left Diggy's side, dodged people and carts, then leaped over a children's game scratched into the dirt, as a group of dirty, ragged children played with sticks and pebbles. He slowed when he reached the fountain, advancing slowly and talking to the dog in a soft, coaxing voice as he dared a quick reach with his inner mind, sending wordless promise of safety. Of healing.

The dog stilled, tail still tight between those back legs, small upright ears canted, as Mek slowly approached, then lightly ran his fingers along the sharply delineated spine, scratching lightly. The dog, still trembling, closed its eyes in a kind of anxious bliss. Mek slipped his hand around that thin ribcage, then, taking a gentle but firm grip, tipped the dog toward the water.

At first it panicked, but Mek kept coaxing until thirst gave the dog enough courage to permit Mek to hold it steady so that it could lap up water. Then he sat on the edge of the fountain with the dog lying across his lap. His herb packets crackled in the bosom of his tunic as he tried to gentle the dog enough for it to permit him to check that leg.

"Now you've done it." This derisive comment came from the leader of the street urchins playing nearby. "That's Donkey Turd. He's the color of—"

Mek cut through the sharp, caustically shrill voice, which was causing the dog to tremble again. "Everyone deserves a friend," he said, recognizing the anger beaten beneath every scar. Master Root had said every bruise might heal on the body but left a scar on the soul. "Loyalty is better than a cart of gold."

"You talk funny," the urchin said surlily.

"Everyone does when they lose a tooth," Tai cut in, speaking pure, accent-free Dragon tongue. He sat down next to Mek, assiduously avoiding looking at the two armed guards not ten paces away.

The boy studied Tai's erect posture, the curve of muscle beneath the sleeves of his faded tunic of green and yellow, and turned back to his game. The guards walked on, their attention on Diggy until he said, "Come on, boy, we've much to do."

Mek heard the urgency in Diggy's low rumble, but he was not going to let go of that little dog until he'd healed it. He gave a nod, carefully picking up the dog, and following. As they walked, he scanned the signs outside the shops, each with objects depicted for the illiterate.

The biggest building appeared to be a gambling den, right next to another big, brightly colored building from whose open doors music streamed out. Mek's heart pulsed with longing for his flute, but he squashed it.

"I want to get medicine," he said to Diggy.

"We have no coin," Diggy reminded him.

"I know. But maybe I can trade one of my herbs for salve."

Diggy fell silent, and they walked this street then the one behind it.

Mek turned his back on the shops catering to wealthy shipowners. "We've seen all the shops," he said, hitching the dog more securely under his arm. Mek could feel its heartbeat pattering beneath his forearm, and he stroked the filthy head, then rubbed behind the ears. The dog leaned into his touch as he looked more slowly. "I can't believe there's only that place, with the sign for herbs with a horse head beneath. They don't allow healers, but they cure horses?"

Diggy had nothing to say; this was his first experience with open streets.

Mek headed for the horse apothecary. As soon as he entered, he recognized a great many of scents layered within the complexity of that atmosphere. He approached the counter. "Do you have wild marjoram and honey-garlic salve?"

"How much do you need?"

"A very little," Mek said humbly, and indicated the dog. "I have some very fine herbs to trade. Already powdered."

The counter man's upper lip crimped at this; the boy was clearly not a real customer. Then Diggy stepped up right behind Mek, and the horse apothecary's breath stuttered slightly.

With a false attempt at a smile, he said, "What do you have?" And when Mek began to take his somewhat crumpled, grubby packets out of his clothes, the man raised both palms. "Tell you what. I've the last scrapings of a jar. You just need it for that hound, yes? Take it, take it, and..." He made shooing motions.

"Thank you!"

They returned to the fountain, to discover that Tai was gone. While Mek sought his medicine, Tai had given in to desire and walked down to look out at the sea, just to find that the old comfort he'd had from it as a boy was gone.

He retreated, arriving before Waha sauntered up. The sun burned down from straight overhead. Mek had done his Essence repair of the fractured bone, then washed and smeared the ointment on the injured dog's leg, murmuring endearments the entire time. When Tai and Waha arrived, the dog stared into Mek's face with that trusting intensity peculiar to dogs.

Mek didn't even notice Waha, whose appearance had changed startlingly. His clever, attractive face was scrubbed clean, emphasizing his thin mustache and the scruff at his sharp chin. He now wore a fine pair of high boots that showed off shapely calves, and though he had on the same clothes he'd been wearing, over it he wore a dashing long vest of dark blue edged with crimson, his slim waist sashed with green. He jingled something in his pockets and said, "How about a hot meal that we didn't have to grub ourselves while we wait for—"

Badger emerged from behind a string of carts loaded with barrels just taken off a ship, and fixed Waha with an appalled gaze. "You didn't steal those, did you?" he whispered fiercely.

"And have everyone on the street howling about theft? Come on, Father," he emphasized the word with a roll of the eyes. "I'll tell you while we eat."

TWENTY-FOUR

"YOU'RE A THIEF," BADGER said, clearly stung. "Of course I'd think you'd been stealing, endangering us all."

"I'm a thief, but a *good* one," Waha murmured. "It's not just a skill but an art. That means certain, hum, call them limits. No one's interested in us." He laughed. "Are you all as hungry as I am? Here." He pointed to the open doors of the pleasure house. "I'm told that the food is the best."

The building was painted in bright contrasting colors, dominated by blue, red, and green, with yellow trim. Sweet incense drifted out, carried by music.

They entered. Mek settled the little dog on his lap as he studied the instruments as all four of the others' intense gazes fixed on the women dancing beguilingly on the raised stage in the middle of the hexagonal room. None of the four had seen a woman in a very long time.

Tai as well had definitely reached the age of interest, and though he had determined he would have nothing to do with Westerners, the diaphanous fabrics fluttering about those rounded forms, the lithe expertise of the dance, enhanced by little bells at the dancers' ankles, arrested his attention so fixedly that he shut his eyes, struggling to get that set of emotions shoved into their box and locked into the cabinet.

Male or female mattered less to Waha than that they were reasonably attractive and knew how to laugh as well as to play. And that central dancer…she wore a mask, but wasn't there something familiar there? Or was that a condition of beauty, a shared quality?

Mek gentled the dog's ears, which had relaxed, and scanned

the hexagonal room decorated with patterned hangings in bright, contrasting colors, and above, a balcony painted in green with red, yellow, rose, and blue flowers. Most of the other patrons were men, and older at that—Badger's age and above, with some graybeards in the far corner, bent over some game. No guards or soldiers in sight.

Mek turned to Waha. "How did you get boots?"

"Gambling." Waha tipped of his head toward the building next door. When a waiter came up to the table they'd settled around, Waha ordered several dishes, along with spiced fermented goat's milk and the dark, sweetened tea favored by the Westerners. Then he laid down a handful of coins.

The waiter took these up and scurried away.

"Won't winning large amounts draw attention?" Badger asked.

"Yes, which is why I played small games. When I'd made enough to rid myself of those demon-cursed sandals, I went out to the street booths down at the far end, to haggle over used clothes and boots."

He stretched out his legs, turning the squared toes from side to side, then, after admiring the fit, "I went back to the gambling house again, to the higher stakes tables. I only played two games, and I was careful to lose at first. The sun was still a finger off midday, so I went to the wharf to see if any of my old signs are still in use."

"Signs?" Mek repeated.

"Private signals, you might say. Shared among certain of us in the craft. That might lead me to someone I know, or connected to those I know. I began at the small craft, and worked my way up to the grand boats."

"And?" Diggy said.

"All I can say is, the Fox God is with me—you Muds acknowledge him as well, eh?"

"Gallant wanderers do," Mek said, slowly stroking his dog's grimy, sparsely-furred head. "Some."

Waha leaned in, lowering his voice "Wasn't going to go near the military ships or the pleasure boats of the Chosen, but a decoration in the biggest one's banner caught my eye—"

"Biggest military or pleasure boat?" Badger asked uneasily.

"The pleasure boat. Why would I pay any heed to a military boat?"

"How can you be sure it's not a trap," Badger asked.

"Honey lures flies—"

A sudden ruffle of drums, and clash! The sweet ring of cymbals as the dancers leaped off the stage and began to dance among the tables. The central dancer seemed to hang in the air a heartbeat too long, or maybe that was just the belling of her gauzy fabrics. Essence light skill? Mek squashed the impulse to check outside his inner door.

The dancer shimmered close to their table, rounded the table once, dancing with gauze fluttering close, then the waiter appeared, hefting a tray full of aromatic dishes, and she whirled off in a tinkling of bells, leaving behind a trace of ambergris and pepper fragrance.

They dug in with the focused appetites born of years of scanted rations. The spicy dishes were dominated by picked mussels, vegetables grilled with saffron, and hazelnut-flour dough discs fried and drenched with hot honey.

Mek fed the dog tiny bits, one bite for him, until every bit of sauce was scraped up.

The dancers had returned to their platform by that time.

Badger leaned forward. "Let's try to hire out. What skill do we offer?"

"Whatever you can do. I expect they all want oarsmen."

"I'll do that," Diggy said stolidly.

Tai looked down at his hands, not seeing the healed nail beds—the bitter mine grime had defeated that habit. Oars again? But they weren't slaves anymore, he reminded himself, and how else were they to take ship for home? If only another wind would rise, and blow Mek and him back!

"They might need a scribe," Mek said to him.

"That's entirely possible," Waha conceded. "Literacy is not a requirement for galley or sail."

They strode purposefully out into the hot sun, and Tai lingered until Diggy, Waha, and Badger had departed in different directions. Then he took hold of Mek's shoulder, saying in an urgent undertone, "I'm going to try to find a ship for you and me."

"You want to desert the others?" Mek asked.

"We're not *deserting* anyone," Tai retorted. "They're Dragon's Chosen. This is their empire. They will be fine, which I cannot promise for us. We have no baggage, so we can just...go." The last word was husky with longing. He took a few steps, then glanced back. "Are you coming?"

"I want to make sure this dog has somewhere to go."

Tai knew how much Mek cared for animals. "Where will I find you?"

"I'll be right here in the square somewhere," Mek said.

Tai loped off in an easy run that would have been impossible for him a couple of years ago, leaving Mek — still holding the dog — to take a slow walk around the central square. He soon spotted the pack of strays that this dog must have been part of, and sat down to watch. The leader had a tendency to snap and snarl as the dogs ran about.

The dog shivered, pressing against Mek's ribs, looked into his face and then away, his head low. "I won't leave you."

The dog looked longer into his face, ears forward as it sorted his tone — and then, apparently reassured, uttered a small sigh, and lay down right next to Mek, muzzle on Mek's knee.

Tai set off in high expectation, but with each successive conversation, his expectations lowered. When he reached the end of the wharf and saw only scruffy fishing boats that surely stuck close to shore, he ran back — and found Mek just after Diggy's arrival.

"Bad luck?" Mek asked Diggy.

"Went only to hired boats for cargo. All wanted to hire me, but none going east," Diggy said. "They would take more men as oarsmen, but none wanted a cook or a boy."

Mek turned expectantly to Tai, who shook his head, his expression utterly shuttered, but the tension in his shoulders and hands answered before he even spoke.

Avoiding Diggy's eyes, Tai said, "I kept hearing the capital mentioned. That's north. Not east."

Badger joined them. "Nothing," he puffed. "Hai! It's hot. Everyone told me that the military is always hiring cooks." He added without much conviction, "New craft must sail in all the time. We must —"

"There you are." Waha sauntered up. He gave Diggy a wry look. "If anyone was looking for you three, they would not have had to exert themselves. I heard gossip along the wharves specifically about a big oarsman who wanted to go east, and they were speculating why."

Badger's face grayed, and Waha patted his shoulder. "Worry not, Grandpa, they seemed to be assuming he had a lover out there somewhere, and they were trying to guess which island." Essentially good-hearted, he did not add how they had laughed at the idea of such an ugly man having a lover.

Back to Diggy and Tai, "We probably ought to have talked about this before, but when finding out information, you don't give away anything if you can help it. The way to find out is to chat generally, like asking how long their usual trip is, which harbor has the best drink, and so on, until you get a general idea of their intended route."

Diggy jerked his chin down minutely. "I will remember that."

Tai flushed, saying nothing.

"You're too honest, that's the problem." Waha grinned at Diggy, then squinted at the sky. "I see a few high clouds, but nothing threatening, meanwhile we need to consider tomorrow. My suggestion is, we sleep out under the stars again, and wash in a river, as we've been doing. Eat once a day, until we either find a hire, or have to hire ourselves along the strand. If I keep going back to the gambling den, they're sure to peg me sooner than later —"

It was then that Waha noticed the loose ring of young, tough-looking martial artists closing gently in from all sides.

TWENTY-FIVE

A SLENDER, HANDSOME YOUTH strolled toward them with a martial air, hair as blue-black and shiny as Tai's pulled severely up into a topknot. An assessing sweep from familiar black eyes — Mek was sure he'd seen them before — then, in a husky voice, higher than expected, as if it had not broken yet, "Let's move to a quieter place."

And the circle advanced purposefully.

Waha and Diggy both stilled into ready stances, then both marked the armed guards strolling past the fountain toward the gambling house. No fighting, then.

Waha's lips curved in a challenging smile. "Lead on."

Badger bunched his fists, looking sullen and worried, as the entire group drifted past a row of sea-related business and then warehouses toward the far end of the wharf, where a cloud of seabirds cawed, circled, and skimmed, looking for the bits left by the fishermen.

This was the poor end of the harbor, where laborers and trusted slaves lived among the fisherfolk in dilapidated houses built on platforms to accommodate the occasional flood tide. These houses were built in a rough circle around a central area where the street vendors sold mostly used items from blankets and makeshift bamboo shelves. As the sun began to rim the rooftops to the west, outlining sky-tipped eaves, these vendors were busy packing up their flimsy shelves and rolling their blankets for the night.

When Crew Six and their escort reached the dusty circle, Waha turned. "What do you want from us?"

Mek had recognized those black eyes by now — they

belonged to the dancer who had come so close to their table in the pleasure house. This was not a teenage boy but a young woman, dressed for fighting in a belted, long blue shirt over loose trousers, and a dark red vest over all. Her boots were worn and supple, and the only visible weapon was a long knife at her belt.

She stopped, crossed her arms, and regarded Waha for a heartbeat or two, her chin high. "Recruitment—perhaps," she said. "But you're awfully sloppy."

Waha recoiled slightly, stung. "What?"

The young woman turned her head. "Zan?"

One of the circle stepped forward, a thin girl about the age of Mek's sister Zar, whose name sounded similar—but there the similarities ended. This girl was smaller and thinner, with prominent front teeth. She gazed at Waha from wide-set eyes so narrow that their color was impossible to discern as she piped, "You used the Gather the Lilies trick three times, Tap the Jug twice, and Spider Hand at least six times. And you never noticed me counting."

Waha's belligerence gave way to a flush, and an unwilling laugh. "Right. I was sloppy. But what's that to do with recruitment? And for what?"

"That," the young woman said, "is a matter for later. First we need to know where you learned the sheep sigil, how, and why are your fingers so out of practice? Does it have anything to do with that prison pallor underneath your recent sun dusting? And the fact you did not risk calling out to the guards when we flanked you?"

Mek's gaze flicked to the hem of Waha's sleeves, and the neckline of Tai's clothes, and only then became aware of the revealing edge of paler skin. Sharp eyes indeed.

"Not prison," Waha said, almost inaudible. "Mine."

"For?"

"Theft, me. Sold, those two. Lord consigned these two." Waha's long hand waved from himself to Diggy and Badger and then to Mek and Tai.

"For?" The woman's gaze caught briefly on Mek's and landed on Tai.

"We don't know," he said tightly.

"Capital crime would have got you beheaded," she commented. "Being thrown in the mine is usually for talking back, or getting caught at love-play with the wrong person, but that one's far too young for that, eh?" A tip of the head Mek's way.

"Thieves," exclaimed one of the hitherto silent watchers. "Brethren!"

The young woman went on, ignoring this outburst, "All except the boy were noising up and down the wharf about ships going eastward. Left a wake of speculation. Where east?"

Tai said, "Ki Mek and I were blown westward. We ended up here, made prisoners and slaves. Against our will. We want to go home."

"Released from the mine or escaped?"

A hesitation, Waha looking at the others. He was quite ready to lie, but Diggy said stolidly, "Escaped."

"All of you? That's impressive! The most we ever hear of it the occasional one, maybe two. And they're inevitably brought down between the searchers and the slave bindings. But there's been no sign of a search," she mused. "A lot is missing here that I very much would like to hear. But it can wait."

A tall young man commented, "Are you any good with your hands?"

"Try us," Waha, said, his posture insolent.

And, to Mek's surprise, the young woman glanced at the tall young man, then waved a mocking invitation.

The tall young man charged Waha, who uttered a laugh and met his attack with a flurry of feints and deflecting blows, then an open-handed smack on his back.

Diggy stood like an oak, his stance promising death, but at that slap, and the retaliatory chortle from Waha's assailant, he understood that this was a test. There was no intent to maim, much less to kill.

Then a crowd charged him.

The unknowns were very good, clearly experienced, but Waha was just that much faster, as difficult to catch as an eel. That had been his strategy for years for evading the heft of Diggy's instructive blows; as for Diggy, though there were now some fifteen or eighteen of the unknowns gathered, he began disabling them one after the other until the young woman with the topknot drifted in, light as a leaf, tapped behind his head with a fan she'd pulled from her sash, and Diggy froze, eyes wide.

Mek knew that meridian, and the expertise of the blow made it clear that she was an Essence master of some form. Mek gently set the dog down—-free to go or stay—and added himself to the general melee. The first two assailants, both taller and older, made to swat him out of the way, but he sidestepped their blows and began to freeze elbows, knees, and then two spines to match the one that took Diggy out of the fight before the young woman noticed him.

"Hai-yoo," she exclaimed on a long, appreciative note of surprise. "This I did not expect!"

And she attacked him.

Aish! Whereas he was earth and wood with metal and a bit of fire, she was air and metal with a lot of fire, a rare and very dangerous combination, because it tended to be as stable as lightning, Master Root had said.

He was glad now of all that practice with Essence and pebbles as he barely escaped her darting strikes with just a fingertip. Air whooshed past him—and when he tried to strike, she was always just out of reach.

The others halted to watch. It felt like an eternity but it was merely an exchange of ten or twelve combinations before she gave a slight nod, her smile twitched—and in a whirl of moves, and a tap behind his ear jolted him into stumbling. She pinned him down at once.

Immediately she held out a hand to pull him to his feet. "Hai, ho, a Talent, I see! It's very few of any age or size who can engage me this long. This was what you were hiding," she said past Mek to Waha. "And well you might."

Mek picked up the dog again, and, holding him close, said with heartfelt sincerity, "Tai and I really want to return home."

She brought her chin down as she tapped her fingers over her heart and said, "To the Mud Empire? That can be arranged. Come! The lot of you. Where are you lodging?"

"On the grass under the willows," Waha said.

She gave a crack of laughter. Mek tested cautiously, to discover that she had now had a solid mental wall.

"Come along," she invited again. "You must be hungry. But…no dogs on this mission."

Mek stopped. "Then I'll stay here."

Diggy, fighting the fading nerve-binding, tried to say, "I'm staying as well." It came out a garbled whuff, but his intent was clear.

Black eyes met brown, neither giving way, then she flashed a smile. "But for you, little mystery Mud, we shall make an exception. Let's go."

Mek thought, she sees my Essence aura. But that was not necessarily a bad thing. He picked up the little dog, and the entire company trooped down to the wharf, and then back to the back yard of the enormous pleasure house. A narrow staircase led up to where the staff had their own gathering chamber, with various tiny cubbies leading off.

They gathered in the center, pulling cushions into a kind of circle, before the young woman said, "I am Snowhawk. We were preparing to set sail tomorrow, for we've a full complement, but then you came along." She turned to Waha. "The pretty boy there is Tai, I gather. The rest?"

Waha named everyone, then said, "That can be arranged? What does that mean?"

"It means, you join us for—" She lifted her head sharply, raising a hand.

A heartbeat later they all heard the patter of quick footsteps, then a sturdy youth burst in, panting. "The snakes are out."

Everyone stirred, looking apprehensive, grim, and afraid.

Snowhawk turned to one of her people. "They will surround the building before they enter. Zan, make Kimek up as a dancer. Jetai, you're going to have to be one of our pretty boys—with a customer." And at Tai's blank shock, "They'll only stick a head in if it looks like you're busy." She laughed, sent Badger to the kitchen, and Diggy out to the yard to haul a wagon full of steaming dishes to the pleasure boat.

Then she crooked a finger at Waha, giving him a challenging smile. "You," she said, "are with me."

The girl Zan, giggling to herself, hauled Mek into one of the cubbies, and thrust him on a stool and opened a cupboard stuffed with gauzy fabrics. "Your little dog can go on a cushion in back. They won't pay any heed to him there—but they might be looking for a boy with a dog. If Snowhawk is right about you. And she's always right."

She ordered him to strip to his drawers. When he began to refuse, she said impatiently, "I've two brothers. Skin is just skin. Hurry! They usually start at the gambling house…"

Mek' pulled up his tunic and all his packets of herbs fell out.

Zan stared open-mouthed. "That's what made you so stout? What's in those?"

"Healing herbs."

She gathered them up and thrust them into a box among

many other boxes. She began dressing him in layers, then pushed him onto a footstool as she opened a box that contained makeup, a comb, and various decorations, including silken headbands with tiny chains dangling down.

She dragged a comb through his flyaway hair. It stuck straight up, crackling with tiny sparks in the dry air. "When did you last comb this rat's nest?"

"When I was ten," Mek mumbled.

She shook her head. "Never mind. At least it's thin as down…"

Her fingers flashed over his head, and he watched his own reflection in a very poor polished bronze mirror as Zan scraped his soft, feathery dark brown curls into a kind of elaborate headdress, then fitted a veil over it.

She replaced his headband with one of her embroidered silken strips with golden dangles, swiped his lips with a winsome shade of rose, smeared color onto his eyelids, then she stripped off her own clothes.

Mek was embarrassed, and closed his eyes until the rustles of cloth and the impatient snorting breaths halted. He opened his eyes to a veiled dancer more or less like him.

"Let's go."

She thrust a paper talisman at him. He took it, looking away from the symbols that seemed to crawl and wriggle, and he felt the buzz of Essence in the paper. He fumbled with the unfamiliar clothes and tucked the talisman into his skirt's waistband.

The dog was carried to the yard, and left on a cushion. Zan tugged Mek to the door to the great chamber, where six other dancers waited.

"I don't know what to do," Mek whispered.

"Sure you do. Copy me."

The male dancers followed them out, and Zan began swaying her hips from side to side, doing a quick two-step, then added arms in a slow circle, one then the other in a martial form the Ki clan called Dispelling the Smoke.

Mek was beginning to feel that he could do this when the door opened and two guards walked in, followed by a pair of Cobra Sages, one young and one old. Mek gritted his teeth, making his inner door into a banked wall of close-packed dirt strong enough for a fortress as the two scanned the people at the tables.

They barely looked at the dancers, then separated, a guard with each, as they went from room to room.

Upstairs, Tai lay beside one of the young men he'd been scrapping with earlier. He was mortified and terror-stricken both. They'd stripped him and gave him only a pair of billowy trousers, then doused him with spiced goat's milk.

Someone yanked his hair loose so it tumbled over his shoulders. "Hai-yoo, you're muscled like a panther," a male voice muttered with a laugh, causing a furious blush, and then they tumbled onto cushions with scattered dishes about, and a couple of empty jugs.

"Now," his partner whispered as footsteps clomped outside the chamber, and the door was abruptly yanked open.

Tai was pinned down by a hard body and vigorously kissed. Shock ran through him at the utterly unwanted intimacy—and he barely had a moment to find it thoroughly unsettling before the door slammed shut again and his partner freed him.

"Never been kissed, hum?" A pair of merry gray eyes crinkled knowingly, and the fellow laughed at his red-faced, appalled expression. Tai kept wanting to spit the taste of this person from his mouth but suspected it would be taken as rude, so he grabbed up one of the cups, hoping it wasn't truly dirtied by someone else's lips, and gulped down the contents.

The unfamiliar fermented, spiced milk hit his stomach and burned as he sat up.

"My name is Siu, by the way. Did I hear the boy call you Tai? We probably ought to exchange names if we're to pretend to be lovers."

Tai was too stunned to speak, looking away from those weirdly light eyes, a contrast to skin the same shade of dark bronze as his own.

"Here, have some more," whispered Siu. "They might be back—we need to look like lovers who've been at it all day."

Tai drank. This time the liquid burned all the way to his head, and suddenly the situation—himself in these absurd clothes—being kissed like that—struck him as infinitely funny, and he began laughing.

"Good, good." Siu patted his bare shoulder. "Just like that."

By the time Tai got control of himself, finding his limbs oddly heavy and shaky at the same time, someone else burst in, saying, "They're gone. We're off to the boat."

"Come, Tai, to the boat." Siu yanked him easily to his feet—and though Tai was conscientiously trying not to stare, he noticed that Siu was muscled like a tiger.

Tai could only stumble after, the wine still burning in his belly, his carefully constructed cabinet forgotten. He caught a glimpse of Mek hurrying along in a flurry of pink, orange, and yellow, clutching a silk bag close. Zan was with him, in similar garments, carrying Mek's dog as she crooned softly to it.

Three of the crew dashed out and came back with musical instruments, which they began playing as loudly as they could, so that the sound drifted to the wharf. Along the brightly painted gangway, figures in silk lounged, laughing loudly, fermented spiced milk dishes in hand.

Dusk had gathered the shadows as someone passed along, lighting boat lamps. They bustled aboard the huge pleasure boat, and settled in a room unlike anything Tai had ever seen, covered with bright, patterned hangings on all walls, the deck covered with soft woven rugs and furs, and on those embroidered cushions and tiny tables with gold-edged bright blue dishes.

Tai thought the space lurid and vulgar, as his childhood had been spent among rich but sparely furnished spaces, designed to elevate the mind. But Mek liked the bright colors, and the spicy scent of the incense clinging to everything. He settled his dog onto his lap, looking around with interest.

Snowhawk was everywhere at once, moving smoothly assuredly, calmly, but Mek sensed tension radiating off her. That did not ease until the ramp had been pulled in, the crew shouted *Cast off the bow, hai, bow cast off,* and *Cast off astern, hai, stern cast off,* then *Raise oars! Full forward!*

Crew Six looked at one another, no one certain whether to celebrate or commiserate as the mighty craft began to move out into the bay. Diggy had been completely bewildered ever since the fierce bee-buzzing had finally cleared from his meridians. After that, everything seemed to be moving too fast, except for one urgent directive: he must not be caught by the Cobra Sages.

The lights of the harbor began to dwindle to strings of fire, reflected in the slow wake as they gathered speed. They could feel each tiny tug beneath them as the oars dipped and lifted, dipped and lifted. Midway into the bay, well beyond the headland, the sails caught the wind at last, and the boat began to pick up speed, a sense of coming alive as the wind aided the oars.

They passed one, two, four military scout boats, skimming along the water at an impressive rate, archers sitting in platforms above the battened sails.

When the isle of Angja was no more than a hump on the horizon, barely discernable against the night sky, Snowhawk and her crew came in from all directions, divesting themselves very carefully of their silken finery, and placing it all in a waiting trunk.

A few began systematically removing the hangings, revealing thin but sturdy flats cleverly joined. Some of these came down, opening up a larger space to the air, so that the tops of the heads of the oarsmen could be seen.

The baskets that Diggy had brought aboard were unpacked, and food distributed with practiced speed.

Waha lifted his head. "Where are we going?"

"To the Forgotten Islands. Hai! You are looking blank. These are somewhat to the northeast, the significance of which can wait upon the morning. Eat! Drink! Get to know my crew."

All were full of questions, but the food was superlative, the drink strong, and no one seemed to mind when they stretched out on the welter of soft cushions and cloths, and dropped to sleep. Mek's dog lay pressed against his side all night, a warm if smelly comfort.

And when they woke in the morning light under a cloud-streaked sky, it was to find themselves alone in the middle of bare deck. Surrounding them—to their astonishment—was not the trappings of a flimsy pleasure boat, but a powerful ship of war.

TWENTY-SIX

"RISE, RISE, RISE!" ZAN fluted, lugging a huge basket. "The sun is coming up, and the demons will drink your dreams." She set out covered bowls of a congee made of wheat simmered in goat's milk. It smelled of honey and a little spice.

"Where is my dog?" Mek asked.

"Sniffing the entire ship," Zan said cheerfully. "Father Dragon knows what he makes of it, as he seems to sniff longest at spots in the deck where nothing is to be seen."

Mek said absently, as he ran his finger inside his empty bowl lest he miss a crumb, "The world is different to a dog. What happened here?" He waved at the open air around them, which had been walls when he shut his eyes.

"The inner bulkheads are all joined," Zan said, hugging her knees to her chest. "It's something our carpenter learned in the southeast of your empire, before he was shipwrecked and took by pirates. Their houses are said to be made up of flimsy boards that slide, so doors might be walls and walls doors. Our *Dachi* appears to be a pleasure boat that would sink in a storm, and no faster than a snail on the seas. But when all the false sides and walls are dismantled, we get this." She threw her arms wide, her entire countenance a-beam with pride. "It's stowed below, where they used to carry horses for invasions."

"Then this *is* a warship?" Waha asked,

"Yes." Zan grinned. "Finish up there. We need to clear the deck for pattern work."

At that Diggy raised his head as if summoned by drums. He'd used that word "pattern" for what Mek had called morning warmups, formations, and sparring.

"But this is not a military ship?" Badger asked cautiously, sending a fearful look around, as if armed guards were hiding behind various structures. "Is that a *cannon*, at the front?"

Zan snickered. "Would *I* be on a true warship? Hai-yoo, you don't know me, you wouldn't know I was once a gamble-sharp before Snowhawk found me. And she found this ship, our *Dachi*." Zan wiggled her fingers, her lips quirked as she spoke the word *found*. "That gun is our forward bow chaser."

"Found as in took?" honest Badger asked, his lined forehead puckered.

"Yes. We raid the raiders." Still chuckling, Zan began loading the empty bowls into the basket to be taken away for washing, as the others rolled up the blankets and quilts and furs. "That reminds me. Kimek, you must either teach your dog to use the head, or clean up after him."

"I will," Mek promised. "Show me where the cleaning things are kept?"

"I'll show you all where you can wash, and we have plenty of clothing to spare."

They even had a shallow basket of willow sticks for cleaning one's teeth. Daily cleanliness was so new again that the sense of freedom — of having truly escaped slavery began at that time.

Shipboard adherence to strict rule was dictated by space. The sizable crew must fit together in this limited wooden world, like the clever joins in those false walls. Tai was reluctantly intrigued, finding tightly executed, sensible patterns appealed to his orderly soul.

The ship ran on three watches. The day's oarsmen were on the lower deck level, though at present "riding easy," a command everyone liked, as the wind was abaft the beam, moving the ship in a northerly direction.

Siu was waiting when they came up from below, clean and in clean clothes. Crew Six joined the other new hires on the deck. "Listen, now. First, everyone serves at the oars," he said.

Some recoiled. "No one said we'd be galley slaves," one muttered.

"You're *not* slaves. But galley *rowers*, yes. We all are, by turns." Siu grinned. "For now, let's find out what weapons you know, and how you handle yourself on deck." He held out his hand. "This is Battle Master Yarth."

A bald, scarred man turned away from sorting through a

weapons locker. He was about Waha's height, broad through the chest, with long, thick arms.

He went straight to Diggy, the tallest and toughest-looking. "You've got the lines of the ring all over you," he said in a voice like a tumble of rocks.

"It is so," Diggy said, dipping his head.

Yarth tossed him a heavy, long sword. Its sheen, and its dark reddish-purple hue identified it to Mek as red sandalwood—a heavy wood that, unlike most woods, would instantly sink in water.

Battle Master Yarth hefted a wooden sword twin to Diggy's. "We're not warmed, so this will be short. I need to see what you know." And he charged.

Diggy stamped forward and met his swing with a crack that echoed off the masts. The watchers exclaimed as the two covered the deck in six fast combinations, then Yarth lifted his blade, and Diggy instantly took up a ready stance. "As I thought," Yarth said.

He went through the rest of the new people. Only one other could manage well with the heavy sword, though he was slow. Waha gritted his teeth, fighting to keep his usual speed, but when that blade was knocked out of his hand, he said, "I'm better with knives. Or my hands."

Yarth gave a short nod. "So I figured. You. Boy?"

Mek took the heavy sword from Waha. The point promptly dropped to the deck. The watchers laughed. A few hooted. Mek shut them out as he brought up Essence into the willing wood, coming from the entire ship. The sword was still too long, but he could lift it as the battle master made a couple of slow, testing blows. When Mek evaded those, his feet keeping him in a small square as trained, he reached twice with his other hand to try for meridians—but Yarth was ready for that, and deflected him.

One slightly faster blow, and Mek knew that he was about to lose, so why not try a last push? He gathered all his Essence, turned smoothly *inside* the blow, and pushed Essence through his first two fingers toward the battle master's elbow meridian.

"Ouch," the man said, grimacing. "Nicely done," he added appraisingly—the only favorable comment he'd made that session. "You've been trained to ship fighting."

Mek said, "Yes."

"The rest of you are all over the deck. This is not a field.

You're going to have to concentrate on footwork before we get to the north." He nodded to a gray-haired woman. "Except for this boy."

"He will be working on other things," Siu stated from where he lounged against a barrel. "Though today, with the rest."

"Footwork it is," the gray-haired woman. "I'm Cedar, and will be instructing you. Move out to arm's length, novices."

Mek smothered a laugh at the affront some of the new hirelings expressed at being called novices. But by the time the next bell rang, they were all drenched in sweat after the vigorous workout she put them through. Then came a break for water, tea, and honey-cakes full of chopped nuts while one of the watches came to the deck to work through their formations.

Mek observed avidly. Halfway through there was the tick of nails on the deck and his dog appeared, eyes bright, tongue lolling, and for the first time, his scraggly tail was up, curved to one side. In spite of his limp, he was clearly a happy dog. Mek checked his leg, finding a cleanly healing scab.

They then had to learn the parts of the ship, and how to load and fire cannon. When a gong rang, it was their turn at the oars.

Mek reluctantly went where he was pointed. Five or even six could fit on this bench. He remembered what he'd discovered about the possible consequences of raising winds, even at sea, and mentally prepared for misery.

A thump beside him, and Snowhawk sat at his left. "Flat wrists," she said, demonstrating. "Don't bend them until your hands pull back level with your ribs."

"Do *you* row?" Mek asked.

"Everyone does. Pay attention to the row master. You must learn the commands and the motions, for all our lives depend on instant obedience to commands. One oar clashing into another can cause a fatal snarl when we're in action."

Mek turned his attention to the row master, who sat high, where captain, signals, and sea could be seen.

They were well out to sea, no islands in sight, sailing under light airs. "This part of our journey is to train you newcomers to our ways," Snowhawk said, rowing easily. "The oars take the place of strengthening exercise. You novices will only serve half a watch at first, until you build some strength."

Mek said, "I'm about as strong as a noodle if I don't use Essence."

"Who said you don't use Essence?" she retorted. She even used the imperial word for Essence. "That's why I'm here with you right now. You must learn how to draw from the air."

"Air?" He looked askance.

Snowhawk turned her head so that he got the full impact of her black gaze. "You're going to tell me your affinities limit you. Yes?"

"Isn't it the truth? Ay, I can push air, but my true strength comes from the earth."

"You can't learn?"

"Right fill," the row master bawled.

Mek hesitated, then remembered what that meant, and shifted his grip.

"It'll come," Snowhawk said. "Kimek, you're a Talent. But you seem to have fixed it in mind that you will trust mainly to soil and wood, eh? And metal?"

"Isn't that right?"

"Not for a Talent like you. What happened to cause you not to trust air? Hai-yoo! You need not answer but to yourself. I will say only: once you make peace with your air potential, I believe you will find better balance. How are your light skills?"

Mek made a terrible face, remembering that terrifying journey through the dragon winds. "I *really* hate being in the air."

"I need leapers. While the others learn footwork, you're going to work on air and fire. Did you not play with fire when you were small?"

Mek hesitated.

Snowhawk smiled. "It's in you. You just never let it come. Probably to protect yourself. Fire is terrible when you're small. So dangerous. And my guess is, your training did not include any light skills."

"None. Very few Kis have Essence abilities," Mek admitted.

"And so, someone saw to it you worked on the affinities safest for you."

Mek was not certain how much that was true and how much she wanted it to be true. He knew that reaching deep into the earth felt natural in a way that sensing metal, or causing a little flame, or pushing air did not. Wood caressed him as he caressed it, but he was no wood-worker.

But he loved to learn. Why not? Master Root had always said to learn whatever you could.

That first session at the oars was not long, as promised. They had plenty of cold, clear water waiting when they finished, and then it was time for the evening meal, shared with all—for it was the breakfast time for the night watch.

After that, the evening practice, and then the night watch took over, the newcomers went below to where they had hammocks waiting, and their cubbies. Mek had been assigned a low hammock with a trunk below, so that his dog could jump up, turn around experimentally, then settle across his knees. His herbs were in the trunk, along with the second outfit he'd been encouraged to choose.

He was asleep before he drew a second breath.

Tai was not.

Tired as he was, he had to see the night stars and calculate the heavenly stem. It made him feel less unmoored in the world.

He was now terribly behind in learning the intricacies of divination. He had once been proud of having reached level five, but the truth was that this was barely half of the necessary rules and relationships governing the connections between the Three Transmission, Four Classes, the Heaven and Earth plates, and the Twelve Houses, He'd even forgotten some of the more complicated formulations, for he'd stopped reviewing these when he and Mek were tossed into the mines, and he no long knew what day or night was.

It didn't matter as much now. He had given up guessing his future, once (he thought) as fixed as those stars above. At least he could see the stars. He could even watch marine life again, during breaks. He did not feel *un*safe, for the first time since he and Mek realized they had been captured rather than rescued. But safety—a true sense of safety—was still a retreating mirage.

Once Tai saw that all questions were referred to Snowhawk, he kept quiet. But they never went away.

One afternoon, after martial arts patterns, she sat beside him for oar duty. "Question—or problem? Why not ask? If it's not time for an answer, nothing will happen."

"Why do you need us?"

"For a raid. Did we not say?"

"What sort of raid?"

"We're going to raid a trader full of silk."

Tai pulled hard. "If you are stealing from our Jade Island silk traders, then you're pirates."

"Who said," she replied coolly, matching him strength for strength, "we're taking the silk from you easterners?"

"You're robbing your own people? That's still piracy."

"Pirates? Hai-ho, that is not so easy to define," Snowhawk retorted without any heat. She studied him as water plashed against the side, and the deck master called the time. "Do all you easterners think exactly alike, with exactly the same allegiances?"

He could have responded that when it came to treason, or traitors, loyalty was of first importance, but he thought of his eldest Ji cousin and hesitated. Rank was Venshai's primary importance. Physical prowess Cousin Lekshai's.

Snowhawk dipped her head minutely. "In this moment I'll say only: I have good reasons. Of course everyone says that." She uttered a mocking laugh. "It's up to you to judge my reasons. I know you will. I see judgment in your face all through the day. Even of the food."

When their watch was over, she leaped up onto the rail, seemingly tireless. She launched out into the air, turned a tight somersault, and landed lightly on the foredeck of a scout craft alongside. She never looked back.

TWENTY-SEVEN

MEK HAD FIGURED OUT the fundamentals of light skills when leaping around the old herb garden on the slope behind Ardal's fortress. The next time the "novices" did footwork with Cedar, two of Snowhawk's crew came for Mek, bearing wooden swords.

"We'll teach you flying," the elder of the two stated, a tall fellow about Tai's age, named Red. He always wore a red kerchief bound around his brow, and long, shiny black, beaded braids of which he was proud.

The younger, a teen, handed Mek a sword, and the two waited expectantly.

Mek knew each aspect of this skill, he was just reluctant to use them together. But with those two looking expectantly at him, he had to try. He discovered that he *did* have a sense of balance on the sword, that drawing up Essence and rising into the air on the sword was utterly unlike being spun against his will through the middle of a storm.

The three practiced flying above the deck, then ventured out over the water, and Mek rose in the air to the highest reach of the masts, fascinated by the subtle differences in Essence perception: the wooden world sustained him when he stood, whereas air and water were filled with swimming…life-essences. Everything, even time, seemed different in the air.

"You can really fly?" Tai said later, when Mek joined him at the rail, where Tai was watching the ocean in the last rays of the sun.

"I can."

"I wish you could teach me."

"Why? I don't see any use for it in fighting, if that's what you're thinking. It would be a fast way to get about, but any enemy would easily be able to shoot you out of the sky, because there's no hiding. What would you do from the sky?"

"See what's coming," Tai said in a low, fervent voice. Then, unsettled at the rawness of his own voice, he added in a more controlled tone, "At least until we get safely back within imperial governance. And also, I imagine it might be like watching the deeps. I could see all the lives invisible to me."

Mek could see Tai's longing, though he didn't understand it. A little later, as he fell with a sigh into his hammock, the little dog wriggling up against his side, he murmured into the fuzzy ear, "I'd rather play with you than watch you." But then watching pups play was fun, especially when it was hot out, or he was tired. Maybe that was it: Tai liked to see creatures under the sea going about their lives without any human interference. He could understand that.

"I still like to play best." Mek hugged the dog.

The tail thumped his side.

Two storms, one right after the other, overtook them, and the *Dachi* folded in on itself like a beetle, riding fast on the waves, just enough sail on the foremast to take the strain off the rudder with its ten or fifteen strong hands keeping it steady, prow pointed up into the wind as water sluiced down the deck and washed away into the sea.

The day after the last storm, the lookout called out, "Sail on the horizon, straight astern!"

A short time later, "It's *Yufi!*"

Yufi it was—another Jaguar-class warship, consort to the *Dachi*. Captained by Snowhawk's half-sister, Owlfrost.

Snowhawk drew her sword, leaped onto its blade, and raced over the water to the *Yufi*, which labored along with a fished foremast, and considerable damage. The crew was busy working at repairs, but all ceased when she landed and grasped her sword in a quick gesture. With becks of greeting in response to respectful hands laid to hearts all around, she went aft seeking her sister.

To the casual eye, the two might be mistaken for twins, though Snowhawk was taller.

"There's been no scout," she said the moment they saw one another.

"Not good," Owlfrost answered; though their eyes were

shaped similarly, Owlfrost had inherited her mother's changeable blue gaze, troubled now. "There was a bad demon storm south of Angja. Bar Ganis destroyed the silk convoy under cover of the storm. They've reached Icecrown Island by now—"

"Spawn of the Antlered One! Then we've lost it, is that what you tell me?"

"Not quite. The Ganis paddlefish also took considerable damage at the height of the storm. I considered giving chase, but Ganis had Angja as well as Haxu riding convoy, so I kept below the horizon, relying on our eels. Right now that paddlefish is barely afloat. It will not sail for a moon."

"We need to know if the silk is still in the hold… It's gunfire that penetrates below the waterline, not wind." Snowhawk was talking fast. "Yes. An attack in harbor was our backup plan, but I think it's now our only chance."

Owlfrost thumbed her lips. "Raid the silk under their noses? Then, on top of the fighting, there is still the possibility of ruin in heavy weather."

Snowhawk grinned fiercely. "Take the paddlefish with the silk safely inside."

Owlfrost dropped her hand, her eyes closed. "Assuming you can pull it off…"

"I can." Snowhawk spoke confidently,

A paddlefish! Ideal for carrying either warriors or goods, fast, and quiet—unlike the jaguar, lion, and tiger class ships—named after loud-roaring land animals, as these ships were built to carry cannon.

No one would be expecting a raid, as long as the Mud navy was distant, for Icecrown Island was near the islands considered the border between the west and the Thousand Isles Empire.

Owlfrost sipped from a fresh dish of spiced, fermented goat's milk. "You'd scarcely think it, after all the rain we've been having, but remember, Three Games is nigh. This is a terrible time for a raid. Everyone in the island will be in that harbor for the festival."

"I count upon that," Snowhawk said, pacing around the cabin. "They'll be at the ring to watch the fights. Or at the field to see the archery and the horse races. Or drunk in the pleasure houses. It's the *perfect* time. As long as we take them completely by surprise."

Owlfrost left strategic planning largely to Snowhawk, as all matters of the unseen world were (equally largely) her own concerns, though they were in the habit of talking out their ventures.

She tried once more. "I am fully confident that if anyone can cut out the paddlefish from under their noses, it is you. But there will likely be a chase. And that brings the possibility of discovery. Our best defense so far has been our complete invisibility, you said so yourself. Do you want to lose that? First Prince will surely declare a blood hunt against us."

"*If* he identifies us," Snowhawk said, chuckling under her breath.

"Then you have a plan to avoid that?"

"Yes. Among the hires is a Talent. Such a Talent! I really think he might be the broom-star you saw in that storm the Red Horse year."

"Hai-yoo!"

"He's just a boy—his voice is barely changing—but with some work, I think it possible that he could master all the elements. Of course you'll know better."

Owlfrost looked puzzled. "That broom-star came out of the east."

"Just so. He's a Mud—there are two of them, actually. The other is a very pretty boy—*very* pretty. Half the ship flirts with him. Would stand on their heads for his smile, though he looks at them as if they were rocks, perhaps, or trees, ha ha! That aside, he's coming on well with his hands, but it's a shame he wasn't trained from a young age, the way Kimek was. His fundamentals are too new. Though he's furiously determined to learn—a metal, though no Talent. In any case, the two came right along once I promised to take them back to Mud territory, once we succeed in this raid."

"You said, with some work," Owlfrost repeated, studying her sister. "Surely you will keep your promise." Owlfrost trusted no one as much as Snowhawk, but she never overlooked the fact that Snowhawk, who had endured much before the sisters had reunited after their father sold them off, sometimes had a…flexible view of such things as inconvenient promises.

"Naturally I will! And I'll definitely hand the pretty boy off to one of our eastern friends when we chance to meet next. But between now and then, if I cannot convince a squeak-voiced urchin to join our battle—"

"It is *our* battle, after all. If they are Muds, they will care nothing."

Snowhawk's smile vanished. "It will become the Muds' battle if the First Prince seizes the obsidian throne. Then nothing will stop the snakes from riding every raider that goes east, so that they may prey on all the Talent there."

Owlfrost said, "Send your Talent over. Let me evaluate him."

"Done."

Snowhawk returned to the *Dachi*, and passed the word for Mek to take himself to the other ship.

Mek received this order in surprise. "I'll be back," Mek said to the dog, who waved a tentative tail. He comforted himself with the reminder that everyone had apparently adopted his dog—which is why he still didn't have a name. Or rather, had ten or fifteen names, all of them affectionate. Even better proof: by the time Mek had collected cleaning things, he'd discover someone had already seen to removing the dog's leavings. And there were nights when the dog ended up in someone else's hammock—most often Zan's.

He took a practice sword, drew in a deep breath, then threw himself into the air. It was getting a bit easier.

He looked down at the two vessels, long oars moving in "slow pull" in a way that called to mind the legs of many-legged insects. The ships looked to him like beetles, not at all like land animals.

He landed on *Yufi*, a short, slight figure half-obscured in clothing far too large for him, his fly-away dark brown curls barely contained in a topknot and headband.

Owlfrost observed him. Where was this tremendous potential? This boy was utterly blank in the realm of the ineffable. Too blank. She invited him in, asked his name, and how he came to join Snowhawk.

His accent was strong, his tone friendly but cautious, almost wary. She remained noncommittal, watching his gaze take in the cabin, and what could be seen beyond; more than once his attention returned to her musical instruments, kept in an open-sided cabinet against the far bulkhead.

She sent him out to spar with the night watch. Despite his size he was swift, sure, and had the potential to be formidable. Especially when he began using a little Essence.

The night watch began by treating him carelessly, as a child and beginner, but by the end of several bouts, after some stings to very tender nerve clusters that rendered his opponents numb for a few breaths, they were regarding him with more respect.

By the time the sun was coming down and the evening meal had been served out she had decided on her approach.

The watch bell clanged, and Mek turned her way, hoping she was going to send him back. He couldn't quite tell why he'd been sent to this ship, unless everyone was going to be sent over to meet this woman who reminded him of Snowhawk. Only with blue eyes.

Owlfrost beckoned to him, and said, "I noticed your attention to my music instruments. Do you play?"

"I haven't for a long time," he said, his gaze straying longingly to the flute.

"Why not now? I, too, haven't played for a time—we were caught up in a demon storm, then repairs, and before that, a long chase. Try my flute there. I'll play the pipa to you."

"I only know a few of your songs," he said apologetically. "Ones slaves are permitted to play."

"Play anything you like," she invited. "It will be a challenge to me to find a complementary melody."

He was very out of practice. It had been longer than a few months, judging by the way he flexed and wrung his fingers as he warmed up with scales, but she waited patiently, and presently he began, tentatively, at first playing only for himself.

When she recognized a melody, she played the accompaniment. He faltered, caught on quickly, and then they began a duet, he with his eyes closed, she listening in that space above hearing.

She imbued her music with a promise of safe boundaries, of understanding. As the music began to soar, melody following melody, his wall dissolved, and there was conversation without words, emotion driven by Essence. He was still very much a boy—there was no strategic awareness whatsoever—but so much talent, oh, so very much potential!

Snowhawk was right: someone very early in his life had bound his natural affinity for air. To keep him earthbound for safety? Or to guide him to develop the potential in his lesser affinities? She sensed no malice in the traces of that long-ago talisman. Far from it.

She hesitated, then thought: *it is your life. You are ready to choose what to do with it.*

Sensing his surprise and enthusiasm, she cut the binding. Then she handed Mek the flute. "Take it for now. You can give it back after you make your own," she said. "I think you will enjoy making your own: you will know the wood and the wood will know you. What music you shall make then! The simplest flute will sound better than one cast in silver."

Mek bowed—the gallant wander bow, which was a true bow for him. The slave bow was only play-acting.

He retrieved the wooden sword from where he'd left it leaning outside the door, put the tip down and his foot against it.

This time, the rush of Essence lifting him into the air was very nearly effortless. He swept up into the night air, watched by all the crew on deck and at the oars, for they still had that heart-wrenching music echoing in their ears. Snatches of it had even reached across the sea to the *Dachi*.

Mek soared up and up, testing himself. Waiting for the brief pull in his stomach that would roil into imbalance. But that was gone.

He drifted slowly in the subtly altering currents as memory welled up. He'd completely forgotten how, before he slept that first night, Master Root gently traced a character on his forehead. "The Ki clan will never trust your practicing air affinities. And there is danger in doing so. Kanda wrote: *When one cultivates on the principle of harmonic balance, this not far from the path to wisdom.* We shall bind it except for music, and leave the rest to fate. You will remember this, I trust, when you are better able to comprehend."

Rain began splattering him from a clouding sky, cold and wet. He descended, to find Snowhawk waiting. "What happened?"

"She gave me this!" Mek pulled the flute from inside his tunic. "Not gave," he corrected conscientiously. "I'm to make my own."

"She prizes that one very much. I'm surprised she let it go out of her cabin. What else?"

Mek gave a jumbled account of the binding Owlfrost had discovered, and severed for him, after which Snowhawk said, "You ought to feel more in balance now. Air and wood and earth, a very powerful, stable triangle. And you have trained yourself to strengthen the counterbalancing triangle: fire, water, and metal. Many suppress those affinities without thinking. As self-preservation. Put together—which is very, very rare—the six are not only stable but strong."

"What does that mean?" Mek asked doubtfully.

"It means, right now, that you don't need talismans to summon Essence. It's there, around you, yes?"

Mek shut his eyes. Yes, it was. Through his toes, the familiar, steadying earth. Around him, the infinite promise of air. And the beauty and strength and patience of living wood... He opened his eyes. "Yes," he breathed.

"I suspected as much, the moment I saw you." Snowhawk grinned. "You must keep practicing to integrate them—and to shield yourself from roaming demons. That aside, we have a more immediate goal. Let's get to work. You'll learn while you practice your part in the raid."

Within a couple of days, the general practice became more specific as teams were made up, each person to a specific job.

Mek and Tai usually ate together. After the division into teams, Tai said, "What are you assigned to?"

"Looks like I'm going to be watching from the air, so I can raise fog from the water, which will hide everyone as the boats come in."

"Fog? You can make fog?"

"It's easy. Then, if I see something wrong, I go help. How about you?"

"I'm with Siu, in the boats." Every time Tai mentioned Siu, he remembered that kiss. He did not want to explore the matter with Siu—not at all—but the subject had wakened...questions in his mind.

Questions he refused to define until they reached the empire again. Locking the matter into that mental cabinet, he said to Mek, "We have to sneak up on the patrol eels and tamper with the tillers, so when the alarm goes up, they lose steerage." He turned to Diggy, an enormous shadow nearby. "Can you tell me what Three Games is to the Westerners? They didn't hold any Three Games at our end of Angja Island."

"That's because Angja had its own ways, before the treaty that brought them under the obsidian throne. Three Games is the midsummer festival out of our Junsa past," Diggy said seriously. "To celebrate the Three Blessings: the Horse, the Bow, and the Sword. Though the obsidian knife has for the nobles replaced the sword in the rituals, and in ring duels."

"I remember seeing obsidian knives at the fortress," Mek said. "Though only two people had ones made of obsidian: Bar Gatslan and his son Jathyam."

Tai managed to catch himself from making a spitting motion at Bar Gatslan's name. But he must have made some reaction, as a couple of people gave him puzzled looks. To avoid questions, he said quickly, "Junsa?"

"Jun-sssa," Zan said slowly.

Siu slanted her an amused glance. "Jun Suai, you ignorant whelp," he said affectionately, and she grinned. "Way, way back, when we lived mostly on the big, flat ice islands. Us and our horses. We even expanded east to two vast islands in the heart of your Muds' northern empire for a time, ruled by the greatest of our clans—this was when we had clans. Before we got our own empire. This was the Manta banner. Did you know that they married right into your eastern ruling clan, and their descendant sat on your throne?"

Dynasty, not clan, Tai wanted to say, but he kept that to himself. Siu had treated them well, despite being an ignorant western barbarian.

"Enough, enough, enough," someone bawled. "Up and get your weapons—we're going to attack *Yufi*, and tomorrow they attack us! Let's not shame ourselves…"

Tai was just as happy to let the matter drop. He'd thought that escaping the mine was the worst he'd ever face, but now that seemed nothing in comparison with the pitch of emotion knowing you were preparing to risk your life in a complex raid. That he might not survive this raid. He listened intently when Snowhawk, the battle master, and Cedar talked about the capabilities and limits of the warships. He experienced these as the two ships ran endless exercises, trying to cover every eventuality.

"Remember!" Snowhawk said to the crew of the *Dachi* the night before they expected to come within patrol range of Icecrown. "The moment we lose surprise, it *will* turn deadly. Gatslan of Angja and Haxu will most likely be perimeter guards. We can use fog if we must escape them. It's Ganis who will be holding the island and guarding those ships. Ganis has never lost a duel, ever. He lives for bloodlust. You've all heard how severe the punishments are for even small infractions on Ganis Island. Bar Ganis flogs with his own hand, often to the death. His clan *brags* about it."

Here, a kind of bitter laugh rumbled through the listeners.

"Once we're discovered, they will fight harder. Remember also: this silk means the pinnacle of glory and honor to First Prince Toshan."

With that warning, she left them to liberty for the rest of the evening and night, save split watches so that all might be ready come the morrow.

She and Mek then took to the air for *Yufi*, visible by its swinging lanterns across the water. Occasional snatches of music reached them, strengthening as they neared, until Mek could identify all the instruments.

Yufi was a more musical ship—crew going from one to the other to join or get away from it. Many sang and danced on the broad aft deck as musicians played stirring Three Blessings airs.

Owlfrost, seeing the arrivals, nodded a greeting and led the way to the cabin. They went over the signals one more time, which the three flyers were to convey to various teams.

Snowhawk then said firmly. "Kimek: you and Owlfrost dream-speak only in need. Very fast. Because there is sure to be at least one Cobra Sage serving Ganis—and watching him for their own plans."

These words were like an icy pail of water in the face.

When Mek and Snowhawk returned to the *Dachi*, Tai paced the deck, trying to calm his churning stomach. One more effort, he kept reminding himself. Survive this, and he and Mek could leave the Westerners forever. Last year it had seemed he would never see the sun again. They had come this far! One more effort!

He was still reminding himself *One more effort* when he followed his boat team down into the long, narrow rowboat early the next morning. They set out on a gray sea under a cloud-streaked sky, once the Angja outer patrol ship had passed hull down on the horizon—now *Yufi* would shadow that patrol, as *Dachi* followed the Haxu ship.

Tai shivered in the chilly air; this far north, the sun came up very early. He put his back into his oar. He'd soon be warm from the effort.

Their narrow boat sliced through the waves. When the wind strengthened, they stepped their single mast, and sped over the water. When they spotted the highest point of Icecrown, they halted in a line, shipped their oars, and silently passed out their meal and water. Now, to wait for the sun to set, and paddle the rest of the way in under cover of darkness. And Mek's fog. Mek had been practicing off and until he could raise vapors with a gesture.

Snowhawk was in the leading rowboat. When she raised her left fist and pointed upward, that gesture was swiftly passed down the line of boats until it reached the three flyers. The two teen flyers affixed their paper talismans with the obscuring charm into their sashes, flew into the air, and headed for the row of docked ships.

Mek did not need a talisman anymore. He headed for the wharf.

The rowboats below were mere shadows on the night-black sea. On shore, the rain had lifted, though clouds sailed silently overhead. Light trails glimmered in puddles and pools, reflecting the glow from the many lanterns overhead and swinging from sticks as people strolled about.

He hung in the air above them, riding the air currents. It looked like fun down there. Especially the martial arts contests in a firelit ring, where children and youths competed with wooden swords, arms and legs and bodies padded. The adults had the serious ring with rows of benches, at the end of the road — which was where Bar Ganis would be.

"No padding," Siu had explained when Tai asked. "Part of the ritual is to shed blood, and win glory. The weapons will be obsidian knives, mostly. Ganis will be there, slaking his bloodlust — and his snake will be there where the wounded are taken, with the other snakes, taking up the blood for their secret purposes, though they are there as medics. We want to be swift, in and out, so he is never disturbed."

Occasional roars from the spectators rose from that direction, and Mek wished Tai had not asked. He tried not to imagine what the Cobra Sages' secret purposes might be.

Mek couldn't see the rowboats. Good. They had to be utterly silent now, the oars dipping without any splash, moving in perfect synchrony. One clack of oar into another could prove fatal.

Mek's fog began to drift like ghost-fingers along the water, swirling slowly in the air currents. In his rowboat, Tai shivered once, his clothes damp.

The signal came for the rowboats to separate, each to a ship. Tai's attention narrowed to the labored breathing of his boat mates as they strove to pull without splashing until Waha, chosen to be leader of this rowboat in spite of his newness to the crew, vehemently waved his hand and pointed.

They eased up on their ship's lee—fended off so there would be no betraying thump—and while stern and bow oars held the boat, the others moved to execute their task. Tai found his hands trembling. His nerves sang. One last task, he thought over and over. One last task, and soon home.

The cold, wet, barnacled pintles scraped at his hands. But he knew his part. The tiller disabled and left in a precarious state, they pushed off, and away, to converge on the silk paddleship. Now, the most dangerous part, boarding and carrying the paddleship.

One more and home…

TWENTY-EIGHT

MEK PEERED DOWN TOWARD the paddleship. He could barely make out the masts in his fog. Chilly, damp fog. A little light-headed now, he was aware that he'd been in the air longer than ever before. He needed to get to earth. Feel soil beneath his feet, and draw up more Essence before taking to the air again.

He began to hunt for an uncrowded space to set himself down.

A cacophony of angry, frustrated shouts internal and external—

"Ganis is coming!"

Did he hear that inside or outside? Suspended in the air at head height, he heard a clamor of shouts, and swept in a dizzying circle to discover bodyguards crashing through the throng, stirring up panic and confusion. Behind them ran a nobleman, the obsidian knife in his golden belt glinting in the lantern light. He stumped alongside a stretcher on which an anguished youth lay, teeth gritted, his pain a howling shriek in the mental realm.

That man was Bar Ganis! Mek had to stop them from reaching the ships!

He bumped to the ground, the wooden word clattering on stone. Luckily, no one in the vicinity noticed, as the gathering crowd exclaimed, trying to see.

Guards strode forth, forcing people back with halberds. When the people saw the noble, they dropped to one knee, fist to heart. Mek stared—until a guard scowled directly into his face. He'd been seen! And he wasn't bowing!

The guard raised his weapon to knock him to his knees.

Mek's gaze shifted to the writhing figure on the stretcher, and he stumbled forward before the guard could strike. "Apprentice!" he yelped. "Let me by!"

Ganis was alternately cursing and shouting, "Where is the demon-souled snake?"

"Bar Ganis, lord, Cobra Sage Kian is in the wounded lazaretto—"

"I want her *here!* Now!"

Mek took one glance at the slim youth—a boy his own age—on the stretcher, his gashed, horribly misshapen leg swelling alarmingly, and croaked, "Stop! Set him down."

The guards in front raised their weapons, but Ganis cried, "Who are you?"

"Apprentice—" Mek remembered in time that they didn't have healers here, and gabbled, "Farrier. But they send me to injuries..." Where? What was he *doing?*

But he had to halt Ganis, and that boy's pain hammered at the inner door so loudly and forcefully that Mek's own meridians began to echo his pain, splintering his attention.

"Let him look," Ganis snapped hoarsely. "Until that foul snake gets here." To Mek, with raw ferocity, "If you hurt him, by the Antlered One himself, I'll..."

Mek shut him out, too, and dropped to his shaky knees beside the stretcher. He met the anguished gaze of the boy lying there, his teeth bared against the need to scream his pain. *I'm ruined. Just kill me.*

The thoughts were as clear as speech.

He's another of us Essence talents, Mek realized. Must have figured out the door instinctively, but the severity of that shattered leg had blasted down his inner door.

Shattered leg, Mek replied, mind to mind. Hadn't he gone over the charms and talismans for repairing bone, over and over, with Ardal? He'd repaired the dog's fractured leg! He shaped a thought: *I know the charm to fix it.*

The sudden hope and pleading in that boy's mind, heart, and eyes transcended language. Enmity. They were just two people, one in terrible pain, and the other with a remedy.

Mek touched a finger to the boy's shin below the gash, and reached mentally inside... one bone shard was sawing at muscle—

A sudden flash in his mind, and there was Owlfrost: "Trouble."

A heartbeat later he heard cries and clashes off to the right.

Mek hesitated, a little dizzy. Then he was himself again, with all these people staring at him, and the angry lord *right there*. Mek laid his hands to the leg, and focused inside. Essence. Drawing in; fit pieces together... The big break, separated... "Hold on," Mek whispered. He gave a quick, hard pull—the boy screamed—the pieces locked together.

Bar Ganis raised a weapon, but halted when the boy gave a sob of relief. "Hai-yoh-h-h-h, that's *so* much better," he whispered.

"What. Did. You. Do," Ganis snarled, standing over Mek.

The boy lifted a shaking hand. "Better. So. Much. Better." The hand dropped, and he fainted.

"Bind the gash," Mek said—and as one of the stretcher-bearers did so, "don't move him," he managed to bleat. "Until it gets splinted. The bones are back together. But only time can knit them true. Splint first. *Don't* move him."

Black sports whirled around the edges of his vision. No, he couldn't faint—

Owlfrost's mental command jerked him alert: "Get out, get out."

Mek's hands dropped to his knees. Then to the ground. The blessed ground. He drew Essence from the earth. It poured through him in a cool, clear stream, banishing the black specks as on the stretcher the boy roused again.

He reached to grasp Mek's sleeve. "Don't go."

"I have to," whispered Mek, as the lord barked orders, and somewhere clashes rang, then the boom! of cannon—

Again, mind to mind: *Don't tell them about me.*

Mek understood the context at once: this boy had been hiding his talent. *I won't*, he promised, conveying wordlessly his determination never to tell the Cobra Sages anything!

The boy struggled to sit, but Mek pressed him flat. "You need a splint. Don't move." Just as a guard ran up, brandishing two pieces of wood.

"She's coming! The Cobra Sage is coming," a guard cried hoarsely.

Mek scarcely noticed. His awareness recoiled from a sense of red, glowing eyes. Inimical eyes, lusting for blood. No, not for the thing itself, but the anguish and anger of fresh—

Go then, the boy urged him, mind to mind. Images were swifter than words: a sinister Cobra Sage with a diamond tattoo on her forehead, her mind shared with an entity that gave her power in trade for blood. *Blood demon! Go!*

The lord glanced away, and all eyes turned. Mek sketched the not-seeing charm over himself, scooted a step back, another step—

The lord spoke to the Cobra Mage, who said sharply, "Stop that boy!"

A quick glance—she pointed right at him!

Mek saw his sword—bent to grab it, but he couldn't fly—they'd shoot him—

Two of the guards reached him. Mek's eyes, hands, and reacted before his mind could catch up. He grabbed up the sword, used it to block the closest reaching hand, twisted it to tap that acupoint beside the elbow bone, and shot Essence into it. The man staggered, gasping. Mek swept the wood blade toward the other, who half-stepped back, then altered his approach and Mek threw Essence to his breastbone acupoint, which jolted the man to a stop as behind them, another arrival shouted, "Lord! Haxu is taking the silk paddleship!"

"Take it back!" Bar Ganis roared. "All of you! NOW!"

Mek's assailants whirled then staggered, still fighting the effects of Mek's Essence attacks on their meridians, and stumbled after the guards racing toward the wharf.

Mek dropped the sword, leaped on, threw another obscuring charm over himself, and rose as fast as he could into the air—forming a deflection.

And there it was, frighteningly fast, some kind of weird charm from the Cobra Sage. The edges of it brushed him, raking him with invisible dragon claws of ice through his extremities.

He dodged and zigzagged, putting a building between himself and the Cobra Sage. Then he raced straight up and out as fast as he could, pulling vapor behind him until he was out of her reach.

"Retreat, retreat!" that was Owlfrost, mind to mind.

Mek flew higher, aware that it was taking more effort now. It felt as if he'd plunged into water wearing a lot of clothes. Everything was chaotic, obscured by his fog. Fear seared Mek's nerves, driving him higher into the air. The fog lay below him, a soft cloud. Where was the *Dachi*? It had vanished! No. He forced himself to search, though by now his head throbbed— and there it was, its outline shimmering and shifting in a nauseating way: talismans obscuring it.

As he flew toward it, he saw the scout rowboats emerging from the vapors. In some, only two rowers, or four, plied oars, still figures sprawled in the boats. Some inert, with swiftly dimming glows of life: the wounded, and the dying.

He dropped on the deck of the *Dachi* as the first of the scout rowboats reached the ship. "I need a rope chair for the wounded!" a cry from below.

Snowhawk appeared at a run, the force of her fury like a fire. "You! Help," she snapped at Mek.

The other healers pounded up, and then began a new nightmare. Again and again Mek pulled Essence from the air. He knew so *little!* How could he put a binding on an internal organ that had no bone? Two people died while he and another healer fought desperately to stanch terrible wounds, and then suddenly there was Diggy, Badger sobbing over him, "His back, his back!"

"He fought a rearguard action. To let us get into our boat," Waha said tightly. "Save him."

Mek was already caught by Diggy's steady gaze. A trusting gaze. Before they turned him over, revealing a morass of dark blood, his clothes soaked through.

"Ignore the slashes," the older header said. "The punctures…"

Mek's head ached so badly he had trouble seeing. He laid his hands in the gory wreck of Diggy's back, and threw his awareness inside. Shock crashed through him at the damage, but he forced himself to sort, to fit. *If I can put a bone together, I can put a blood vessel…* Careful, careful, slow… There. Bind!

He was subliminally aware of the ship heeling as they worked, then he worked as the other healers were pulled to Cedar—

Frantic, frantic, I'm losing . . . no . . . four more bad ones . . . two . . .

One.

Gasping, Mek collapsed to the deck, his mind still sensitive to Diggy's internal being. Living being.

"…can we move him?"

Someone shook Mek insistently, and repeated the question.

"No," Mek croaked. "Not yet." Those bindings were far too tenuous, but the words of explanation failed him.

Then there was Owlfrost, saying. "Leave him be, while all Kimek's repairs take hold. He cannot be moved until then, so we must make him comfortable and warm as he is."

Then Owlfrost moved away, and Mek tried to rise, but now his body failed him. Then Tai was there. "Mek? Can you…"

"We'll put him in his bunk." That was Waha.

And here was Badger. "He saved Diggy. He saved Diggy." Then darkness.

Mek woke to Tai sitting by his hammock. "Here. You're to drink this."

Mek tried to sit, wincing against the headache. His limbs were so heavy.

He slurped a hot, bitter concoction whose components were familiar, and the pain began to recede to a low murmur.

"What happened?" he asked.

"The raid was a failure," Tai said in imperial, his voice soft. "It seems that Haxu turned against Ganis They were right behind us, in their own scout boats, and we ended up caught between the Haxu attackers and the Ganis defenders. The Haxus got the paddleship. Now Ganis and Bar Gatslan are chasing them west toward the capital."

Mek said, "Us?"

Tai's mouth curved in a slight smile. "Running toward home."

Mek lay back, sighing.

Tai said, "You're going to have to rise soon. Everyone has to be there, I'm told, as they bury the dead at sea. They are writing memorials now."

"Anyone we know?"

"Cedar. Four others. A lot of wounded. Zan and Diggy are the worst. Your dog has not moved from Zan's side."

Mek's hand groped beside him for a dog that was not there. For a short time, he'd forgotten his little companion, whose loving heart seemed to have gone to Zan now. Zan's heart had gone to the dog the first day. *Find them a good home*, Master Root had taught him, *until you have a home to give them.*

"Want help?" Tai said. "You're covered in dried gore."

"No. I'm just a little tired. Not hurt," Mek said.

He got cleaned up, put his clothes in a bucket to soak, and rummaged for new things in the baskets. There was congee waiting for him, and even spiced goat's milk tasted good, mostly because of the warmth.

He went to see Diggy, who was deeply asleep. Someone had cleaned him up as best they could, and he had blankets piled over him. Others came around; Mek saw concern in *Dachi*'s crew, even awe.

At noon, they gathered on the decks of both ships, the dead wrapped with stones at head and feet, and an altar set up. One by one the crew members put their memorials on the altar fire, and watched the smoke rise, carrying their words to the spirits in heaven. The others chanted an old verse exhorting the dead to carry their glorious deeds to the Antlered One as their toll for passage, so that they would not be cast back to the world to wander as ghosts.

When that was done, the different watches got a meal in turn, while Snowhawk was over at their sister ship in consultation. Her mood was so vile that Mek sensed it like a bruise on the spirit.

Red, the lead flyer, said to Mek, "She was disappointed in us all for not seeing or sensing the Haxu."

"But they used the fog against us as well as Ganis," said Shan, the second flyer. "No one saw them slipping up."

"They were far better practiced then we were," Siu said. His lip curled. "Doesn't take a shaman to predict harder and longer practice ahead."

Mek decided not to mention that most of his attention had gone to healing Bar Ganis's son Jhax.

After the meal, when the call came for their watch to row, Tai found Mek at his hammock, turning Owlfrost's flute over and over in his hands. "Sandcrab says that if we continue another day seeing no sail on the horizon, we'll stop for supplies at Albatross Island."

"Where's that?" Mek asked.

Tai's lips thinned in an almost-smile, his tilted black eyes wide enough to reflect the dancing beams of sunlight through the scuttle. "I don't know nor care, except for this: it's a neutral port."

Mek's heart banged his ribs. "Does that mean…"

"It's like Anchor Island in the south. Anyone can trade there, as long as they don't make trouble. West, east, raiders, traders, any cause trouble and get their ships burned." Tai tipped his head toward the flute. "Get your things ready. Be prepared."

Mek did his usual jobs, including playing his flute for the wounded. He sensed that the music pleased them. Even the wounded deep in sleep, or coma, seemed to breathe easier. The dog burrowed closer to Zan, ears pricked, tail stirring.

Diggy listened with his eyes closed, until Mek left.

Two days later, after the lookout announced an island on the horizon, he sent Badger to summon Waha. "Go with them." It took all his strength to speak. "You. See them safe."

Though other wounded lay close by, Badger feeding soup to some, Diggy's bloodshot gaze stayed on Waha, and Waha returned that gaze, chin up, as if they were alone.

Waha was now free to do what he liked. Diggy could not move to reinforce his order. Both knew it.

But Diggy knew Waha the way one knows another who has suffered side by side day after bleak, hopeless day; Diggy had never been taught the vocabulary, but he recognized in Waha one who craves purpose. A hero. Though Waha would be the first to scorn the word.

Diggy tried to think past the pain for more words. Both those boys had potential, though in different ways. They could easily make it on their own, but let Waha think himself a guide, a protector…

But after all, no more words were needed.

Waha bent to flick an insect away from Diggy's face. "It's an idea," he said.

TWENTY-NINE

TAI WAS IN AN agony of worry. He remembered Snowhawk's promises about how she had planned to train Mek to be her weapon.

Mek didn't think past his relief at escaping before that Cobra Sage with the demon could catch him.

Siu drifted up to Tai and Mek as they stood at the rail watching the ship approach this new island. Both looked puzzled when they saw the two wooden blades beneath his arm.

"Owlfrost said to pass these to the two of you," he said. "You might need them. The border is where pirates lurk the most."

They thanked him, Tai stiffly, as he was afraid something would keep them from leaving. Mek held out the flute. "Could you return that to Owlfrost?"

Siu took it. "I will."

No one spoke except in response to orders as the *Dachi* slid into a long, narrow harbor, the galley watch back-oaring expertly to ease the ship up snug against a pier.

Out slid the ramp. Wham! It landed on the pier.

Siu kept watch, signaling with a glance to Waha when Snowhawk was the first down the ramp, her mind right now bent on negotiating for supplies before she had to return to Angja and the *Dachi*'s role as a pleasure ship. Behind her tramped the first watch to get liberty.

Waha hefted his bag over his shoulder, and walked with Tai and Mek, who joined them.

From her deck, Owlfrost watched them, the two tall, lean

young men and the short boy trotting to keep up, his topknot of brown fluff bobbing. She was deeply convinced that Mek was the rarest of Talents, and she hated to see him go. It was that strong desire to keep and mold him that she did not trust. Nor had she said anything to Snowhawk, who would be stung at their disappearance, but she had promised.

I will see you again, Kimek of the east, I believe, Owlfrost though silently—careful not to let the words escape the confines of her own skull. Meeting him surely was Purpose, though it might seem chance, as the rain might seem to the ant laboring on the ground, who cannot perceive the great patterns of cloud and beyond them the stars.

Unaware of any of these matters, Mek skipped after Tai, whose long-legged stride was just short of a run, his breath visible in the frigid northern air. He wanted only to get as far from the *Dachi* as possible.

Waha's alert, wary gaze swept constantly, taking everything in. He, a thief trained to prey on the Dragon's Chosen, was about to enter the intriguing world of the Muds. Would he survive their first sight of his pale eyes? It was worth the risk!

None of the three spoke as they walked down the muddy streets, dodging puddles from a recent rain. They passed various shops, Tai letting Waha lead, as most of the writing below hanging boards was western. Presumably he'd know what to look for. Finally they came to a corner building whose board over a south-facing door had words in both languages, saying only TRADE.

"This is what we want," Waha said.

"We don't have anything to trade," Mek said, wondering if he'd get laughed at for carrying a wooden practice sword.

"You do. Your ship skills," Waha said. "This is where hiring goes on, going both ways."

Tai's indrawn breath of relief and pleasure caused Mek to swallow down his questions. They eased inside the door, to find a sizable crowd. On all sides they heard sing-song, clipped consonants, and the nasal twang of various dialects, along with more familiar cadences and tones of westerners—and over there, the rise and fall of voices that evoked their childhood homes.

There were two counters, one for western ship captains and one for easterners. They got into the second line, which was some twenty people deep.

"Hai, it seems I'd better learn some of your language, squirt," Waha said with an odd smile that managed to be both rueful and ironic.

Tai met his gaze, something he rarely did. Waha sustained it, hiding the flash of nerves. He knew how innocent Jetai was. No, strip the sentiment: how oblivious he was.

Tai said, "You kept your promise to Diggy. We're in home waters. Or very close. Do not think me ungrateful for your help. But why are you with us now?"

"Because Siu and the other old timers believe that Snowhawk is going to tie herself tighter to the fight circling around the First Prince. She wanted badly to see him take a defeat in our raid on that silk. But instead, he'll not only have it, he'll have the Haxu raider fleet. You saw how trained they were."

Tai acknowledged that.

"I don't want anything to do with obsidian crown matters. I don't give a spit who sits on that throne. If I set foot in the capital again, someone in my old crew is bound to see me, which is a death sentence."

As if aware that he had been serious for far too long, he snorted a laugh. "Besides, I kind of like what I've heard of the gallant wanderers of the east. Thieves, but *popular* thieves. Sounds like fun! Certainly easy work."

Mek shrugged, accepting this reasoning. He was too busy listening outside his mental door. Was there anyone with a strong glow — or worse, a Cobra Sage lurking about? He still shuddered at the memory of that demon-entity looking out of the Ganis Cobra Sage.

Tai glanced ahead. Nineteen people. This was going to be a long, wearying wait. "My understanding was, the obsidian throne's next emperor is chosen by election. Why all this maneuvering?"

"To influence the election, of course," Waha said, low, but on an escaping laugh soft as a breath. "One might even say, to be in so strong a position that one can command the outcome."

"Then what is the use of an election at all?"

Waha shrugged. "What's the use of any process when it comes to power? In the old days, it was the headman, or head woman, of each clan who came to the great tent to elect the chief of the Junsa, who then presided over clan disputes, and consulted the shamans for the good of all. Some say that in the earliest days the shamans spoke directly from the gods, and the chiefs listened, but whether or not that is true, we're told the elections were purer. But I ask you, how pure is anything mankind does?"

Tai felt the words forming, *How pure is anything you Westerners do*, but he thought of his Ji cousins, and kept his tongue between his teeth.

"Snowhawk and Owlfrost hate the First Prince. I don't know why. But it has something to do with their family."

Tai had no interest in the sisters beyond staying out of Snowhawk's reach, for he'd seen how she looked at Mek. His insides gnawed. They were so close. It would kill him to be snatched back now …

Three people. Two. One, who apparently needed to talk until the world ended. But at last it was their turn. Most of the eastern captains had already left, their requirements filled. Left was a very weary, grizzled captain who said, "I carry ice island ironwood south, and ebony-teak north. I had to rebuild my entire stern as well as replace the masts lost in that last dragon storm. Half my crew left."

Tai sensed Waha stirring at his side, and spoke quickly, before Waha could ask why they left: "We can handle tiller and batten-sail. And also defend."

At that the captain's beetle brows slowly drew together over his nose.

"I'm a *Ki* defender," Mek stated.

The captain put his head to one side as he regarded the smallest of them, then he said slowly, "I trade regular at Great Ran. Will they speak for you there?"

"Yes," Mek said stoutly.

"What are you doing this far west, is what I'm wondering."

"We were blown by a storm," Tai said. "We just want to go home."

The captain's brow cleared. "I guess I can see that. And it's been a long, wearying day. I want to catch the last trade fleet before winter, and they've already begun sailing. You're hired…" He went on to describe parsimonious pay and arduous labor with too few hands, but once Tai had heard "Great Ran" he would have volunteered to row in a galley.

They set sail that night, to Tai's immense relief, in order to labor up to the tail end of the trade fleet.

They were on their way home at last.

The trader was a fractious old tub, requiring constant attention to the sails and tiller in order to keep up with the rest of the miscellany of traders. But Tai complied willingly with every order, grateful even when the clouds flung sleet down: at least this was not a galley.

It did not have a series of watertight holds, but a single one extending the length of the ship, with slings and buffers to carry tall ironwood spars. These had to be examined every day for wear, and during storms those on duty had to stay down in the hold with a spare, dour man as grizzled as the captain—his brother—who, though blind, knew exactly how to balance against ship and the swinging of the heavy spars, pushing and coaxing them with cloth-wrapped spears to keep them from smashing their way through the hull.

During the long days, each shorter and colder as the year slid toward winter, it was Tai's and Mek's turn to teach their language to Waha. Tai was more methodical, giving Waha categories of verbs and going from there. Mek was far less organized, but probably more fun. He jabbered much as Old Daldi had, switching between languages. He and Tai scrupulously kept those sessions on deck, where the sound of their voices was blown away by the wind, in case the captain might distrust Westerners.

Meanwhile, Tai watched the traders maneuver against wind and water. He entertained himself during the long, lonely watches by comparing the difference between eastern and western ships, strengths and weaknesses.

Mek discovered lengths of broken wood in the hull. Once the captain grunted permission to do what he wanted with them, he began experimenting with carving his own flute. One, two, three failures, until he got it right. Sometimes he obscured himself, and practiced his flying; he had begun to relish it so much that he wanted to try flying and playing music to the wind.

That finally happened during a lull in the weather. The air was murky, rather than clean, and one morning old Mun (who hadn't said a single word to the newcomers) fixed his sightless gaze in his brother's direction and croaked, "Storm."

The three happened to be together that watch, eating the plain pancakes that formed the basis of all meals, when this happened. None of the three reacted until the captain jerked his head upward, mouth half open. "Mun?"

"Storm," the grizzled old man barked emphatically, tapping his nose with a half-eaten pancake. "Smell it. Bad one."

By noon, the hazy light had taken on a greenish tint, which gave the whitecaps a restless appearance. When the sun began to set, the clouds overhead coalesced into a towering form whose aspect began to resemble a dragonish face: darkness for eyes, behind which lightning flickered, and from the snout long streamers extended, sending slants of hard rain.

"Do you see a dragon in that cloud?" Mek asked Tai as the rising wind whipped at them.

Tai squinted skyward. Violet-hued lightning flared from horizon to horizon, and he turned his face into his armpit, his eyes watering. "No. Keep your attention on this rope—the storm is bad enough without imagining worse."

Mek peered up again, expecting to see the clouds forming some other shape. But no, that face was clearer, though more reptilian…and from it, descending like snakes questing, thin red lines. He knew that red binding.

"Cobra Sage," he whispered—his words snatched away by the wind.

He let go his rope, not hearing the protest of the others holding the sail taut, ran to fetch flute and wooden sword, and hurled himself into the sky. He had to dissolve that line before it multiplied and tangled the entire fleet.

The wind smacked him away, nearly tumbling him end over end, but he had learned enough by now to ward the imps playing about in the gale. They were there. Hundreds of them. He sensed their curiosity, an avidity that wasn't good or evil as he understood such things, and he played to them—

Above, high above, demons roiled. Ah, they were bound! He played an Essence charm that drew all the imps, then he drew the character he had learned on Angja Island: there! The imps dispersed, breaking the binding into thousands of pieces that withered to ash.

The dragon face smeared, rolling slowly. The storm still had plenty of power, but it wasn't cruelly focused by the hand of an evil demon-guided human with malicious intent.

He flew back down, and discovered he was shivering. He stomped and swung his arms, doing his warrior breathing to force warmth to his extremities, and took his place on the rope again.

For a time they remained, until the captain was satisfied that the storm was not going to worsen, and he dismissed the day watch to their rest. Tai took Mek aside. "What did you do?"

"There was a Cobra Sage binding in it."

"Why would they do that?"

To find me? But it seemed preposterous to think that, unless he was being chased out of revenge. Mek shrugged. "Whatever reason, it's broken."

They got their tea and evening pancake, for dinner stuffed with two kinds of onion, pan-fried fish left over from the midday meal, and greens. The captain stamped in, shedding water in all directions (including on his crew sitting at the table, though no one said anything), and gave a satisfied grunt. "I did not want to have to shelter in Persimmon Bay. Poison Bay, we call it. Seized by pirates or Ghost-Eyes, as often as not. We've enough stores to bypass it entirely. Those who stop, I hope their gods protect them." He made a spitting motion in the direction of that unloved island. "We'll thread the Red Reefs with the others. Much safer, much."

He got his food and stamped to his cabin.

Tai murmured to Mek, "Do you think that storm and this Persimmon Bay might be related?"

Mek opened his hands. "Don't know."

"I've heard of Persimmon Bay," Waha put in, setting his dishes down next to Mek and across from Tai. "Siu said the sisters always avoided it, even if they took damage."

Tai regarded Mek thoughtfully as the boy thumbed up every tiny crumb from his dish. He looked so ordinary, but in truth, he was truly becoming a qilin in a parasol tree.

If so, and if they'd just escaped some kind of plot, it seemed the Cobra Sages knew it, too.

THIRTY

A DAY LATER, AS the fleet compressed into a long line snaking through the deceptively calm waters known as the Red Reefs, Tai and Waha shared a watch. "Do you know how far the Cobra Sages can reach into the Empire of the Thousand Islands?" Tai asked—in imperial.

Waha shifted his grip on the rope as they waited for orders to swing the sail about. He squinted at sky and water as he mentally arranged his sentence, then said, "Here is what I is told. They reach as far as they can. But the Mud—hum, the imperials, have ways to detect them if they act. So says Owlfrost."

"Then they are active on the border."

"No one knows their plans. You get at least one, sometimes two, for each lord. They act as healers. Relay messages from the Sun beside the obsidian throne." He tapped his head.

"You mean, they're spies," Tai said.

"And assassins." Waha lifted his hands. "They are borrow knives, as they say, but whose?"

Tai tried to suppress an impatience that threatened to intensify to anxiety. First it had been to escape slavery. Then to escape the mine. After that, to escape the Westerners entirely. Now, it was to get himself well inside the empire, so that he could find someone who might be able to remove that vile tattoo from his flesh. After which he could do his best to shut away the Westerners' vile language and his vile experiences entirely from his memory.

Once they reached Great Ran, Tai reminded himself endlessly, he and Mek would be able to find a ship going east to Mountain Peony, the empire's capital. And then, if they couldn't find some kind of a boat, they could sail one themselves...

He was mentally reviewing the Three Transmissions and the Four Classes when the ship approached the first of the prospective two halts before achieving Great Ran at last. This was a small island with a narrow passage into its harbor, which was protected by three bluffs. They sailed up the long passage, constantly sounding the depths, until the rocky coast widened into a neat little bay in which three capital ships of various sizes lay anchored, luck talismans and banners limp in the light breeze.

"Mighty quiet," a crewman remarked.

"Usually more lively," commented the tough middle-aged woman who handled the tiller during tricky passages. Cousin to the captain, she traded off navigation tasks with him.

The captain stomped out of the cabin, squinted around, and grunted. "We need more greens." He stumped back in.

Once Tai assured himself that there were no galleys in the harbor, he lost interest. Mek sensed no Cobra Sages' distinctive bindings, and looked forward to getting his toes on land again.

Waha made certain his weapons were loose as he noted knots of men: loungers near the single wharf, at which a capital ship was tied fore and aft. A group of three playing Large/Small in the dust outside an inn or tea house. Another group over by some market stalls, though sellers seemed to be absent. All the signs of an ambush.

The captain and his crew did not seem unduly alarmed. Maybe that was expected here. Waha was hesitant to betray his heavy accent, so he joined Tai and Mek, murmuring in his home tongue, "The sun is warm, when you would expect to see everyone outside who can be. But I see no children. No oldsters enjoying the sun. No sellers at those booths. Unless there's a funeral, and I see no shaman or funeral platform, I am made uneasy."

Mek's eyes widened. "What ought we to do? Tell the captain?"

Waha considered. "He might listen to Jetai, but not to me. Or to you. Why don't you take to the air? Come around back way."

Mek waited until they neared the shore, then took out his sword, covered himself with the obscuring spell, and lifted into the air, and flew around to the back of teahouse. When he landed, he closed his eyes, relishing Essence surging up from the soil.

He tucked the sword under his arm and eased up to one of the oiled-paper windows that had been propped open to the length of the stick.

Coming from the sunlight, at first he thought the main room was empty, so still everything was. But as his eyes accustomed themselves to the gloom inside, he made out silhouettes. Mostly male. Very still.

Central, a man at a table, with a single candle burning. His hands lay flat on the table, his head turned to regard another man standing over him with a naked sword held at his neck.

Shock burned through Mek. He scanned the rest of the room. Standing with their backs to the walls, more armed men, menacing what appeared to be customers and innkeepers alike. A young man lay very still on the floor.

He opened his inner door, sweeping the glows of human focus. No Cobra Sage bindings…

Then more shock, this time icing his veins: more of those blood demons. Not within anyone, but hovering close, especially to the swordsman threatening the one sitting. What to do now? He had been wrong to assume that blood demons were confined to the Cobra Sages. He considered the charms he knew. Fog would be useless inside that building. He wasn't certain he could obscure any of the threatened people at this distance—and would it even work when those holding the weapons glared steadily at the unarmed ones?

Mek slunk back and flew to the trader, as the day crew was busy lowering the boat. Mek landed next to Waha, who started, hand coming up with a knife. He relaxed and Mek gave Tai and him a fast report. Tai remained silent as Mek finished, "What should I do?"

Waha lifted an expressive shoulder. "Nothing? It isn't your problem."

"It's exactly what gallant wanderers would solve," Mek mumbled.

Tai said slowly, "If I were one, I'd use the same type of plan that we attempted at Icecrown."

Waha turned to him, an arrested expression in his face. "Ah?"

Mek said, "You mean, somebody distracts the ones with the

swords, and while they turn that way, someone comes in behind." He grinned. "Someone like me?" He mimed poking acupoints. "Let's do it! We can do it without hurting anyone, if you make a good distraction."

Waha read Tai's austere expression as a challenge. He grinned at Mek. "I can distract them, but you'd better act quickly since there are only two of us." That in oblique challenge to Tai.

Mek looked from one to the other, puzzled by currents he did not understand. He shrugged, and flew back.

While the captain and the crew with liberty rowed the short distance to shore, watched with fixed intensity by those in view, Waha and Tai dived overboard on the far side of the ship, and began to swim.

Mek landed behind the inn, and eased up to the window. He peeked in to find a vehement argument going on between three of the armed men.

Unseen by Mek, Waha and Tai swam mostly underwater to the other side of the horseshoe arc of the village, and sloshed ashore. Tai shook the stinging brine from his eyes and face. He and Waha silently assaulted the outer guard, who had been peering toward the teahouse without troubling to look behind them.

From there it was a matter of fast steps, taking up some drying laundry here, dipping an end of the cloth into the fire under an outdoor stove, and then touching fire here and there while shouting, "Help, help, fire!"

Aided by quick-minded locals, the preternaturally silent scene became a riot in the space of two heartbeats.

Inside the teahouse, the heads of the armed men turned sharply toward the noise — and that was when Mek tumbled in through the window, crossed the room in two light bounds, and tapped the acupoint at the back of the swordsman's skull, freezing him in place.

The gray-haired man who had been sitting with his hands flat whirled up and in a flow of martial skills that instantly won Mek's admiration, disabled three of the other swordsmen who had rushed up. Disabled — they lay groaning and cursing.

The rest of those who had been held hostage either ran with purpose, or darted around screeching in panic. Mek dodged a couple of small children and ran out the door. There were Tai and Waha, safe on the other side of the square as they helped put out the fires they had started.

The gray-haired man looked about, gave a slight nod, and turned to regard Mek, who was at that moment crouched beside an aproned man lying on the floor, hands pressed against his side.

Mek touched him, then said, "It's a scrape. But your ribs are fine."

"Doesn't feel that way," the tea master said between his teeth. And, as Mek moved to a prone swordsman nearby, he added bitterly, "Don't trouble yourself over that trash. Threatening my family, and for what? I told him we mostly deal in trade. I scarcely have ten boaters to call my own." He pointed a trembling finger at the frozen swordsman whose eyes flicked back and forth.

Mek extended his senses into the young man lying so still on the floor. Still alive, but his shuddering breaths alarmed him. Someone had kept beating him after he was knocked unconscious from behind.

"He'll live?" the gray-haired man said to Mek, kneeling beside him. "I'm Bian Ze. Most call me Uncle Ze. You are?"

"Ki Mek."

"A Ki defender? Which Kis?"

"From Mountain Peony," Mek exclaimed so joyfully that his voice broke in a squeak. He reddened, but his grin was undiminished. "You know us?"

"I know Ki Yuek slightly. We traveled together once." He indicated the prone young man. "I gather the Kis have changed their attitude toward Essence skills?"

"No," Mek said, reddening even more.

"Ah, I see there is a story here. I would like to hear it, perhaps when things are more orderly."

Mek turned his attention back to the young man, found blood seeping under a bruise at the side of his head, and dissolved it. The young man began to rouse, groaning.

Bian Ze murmured to the dizzy young man, "If you must be a thief, you might at least consider not following someone who cares nothing for your survival." He made a dismissive gesture toward the swordsman still frozen.

The young man husked, "...said there's a thousand gold...for a charmed sword..."

"You ought to know by now that stories about charmed swords that kill on command and suchlike are all tales told by the puppeteers and tale writers."

"Said he saw it," the young man mumbled. "Ten years ago. Bronze, overlapping scales. Like yours."

"My sword is fine-looking, indeed, but this style used to be common in the west, before they adopted obsidian."

Common, Waha was thinking as he stared down at the sword in considerable surprise. That sword was not common. It was the sword of a king—from the old Jun Suai days. He'd seen another like it in a victory parade once. Half his band swore they were going to steal it until their chief said sardonically, "And where would you sell it? You can wager your life the imperial throne recognizes them all."

Not this one, Waha thought, laughing to himself as the gray-haired man put his fists on his knees and bent over the wounded pirate. "What would you do if you had a charmed sword, assuming it existed? Kill everyone in sight?"

"Sell it," the young man stated with the firmness born of many days of hunger. "Said a duke wants it. Promised a thousand gold."

"Dukes can be foolish, too, when it comes to stories about charmed swords," Bian Ze said. "They also have a habit of handing you a stiff reward and then making sure you never live to spend it. Take yourself off."

The young man managed to sit up, then struggled to his feet, shooting an glower toward his former chief.

Bian Ze said to the frozen swordsman, "You, we will leave to local justice, whatever form it takes. You did send two defenseless people before their time to the King of the Underworld." He walked out of the tea house, leaving Mek to follow or not.

Mek followed, but his attention went to the wounded, who lay scattered about. A quick glance made it clear who was a local, for neighbors or family members clustered around them. Those who lay untended were the ones he moved to. When he'd repaired what he could, he discovered Bian Ze talking to their captain.

Whose scowl and pinched mouth indicated extreme displeasure as he addressed Tai and Waha. "I don't pay you to mix up with pirate trash. You surely ought to have the wit to leave such matters to the village headman. I will dock your pay—"

Bian Ze cut in smoothly, "You could be rid of these

troublesome sailors altogether. I have here some likely replacements," he added quickly as the captain flushed, mouth open to protest losing crew at this juncture.

He waved the battered, somewhat sheepish former thieves toward the captain, and then said to Tai, Waha, and Mek, "I would like to invite you to winter over at Eagle Island."

"I want to return home to the capital," Tai said, his angry flush at the captain's flagrant unfairness beginning to fade.

Bian Ze looked at that splendid air of righteous reserve, suppressing a smile. "I might remind you that the capital is all the way on the other side of the empire. No one will be going that way at this time of year. Some of the passages are already beginning to ice over. Spring will bring plenty of opportunities for travel, but in the meantime, why not hone your skills?" He turned to Mek. "That goes for contacting the Kis—if we don't encounter some of your kin on our way."

Gallant wanderers! Training! His family, soon to discover he was alive! Mek tried not to hop from foot to foot in his elation.

Last, Bian Ze turned expectantly to Waha, who had followed most of the quick-spoken, accented words. He pointed toward Tai, saying, "I go where he goes."

"Then let us get ourselves to our craft, and set sail before the snow I smell in the air has a chance to fall."

THIRTY-ONE

BIAN ZE'S SHIP WAS a small, fast scout. He took the tiller himself, and on Mek's behalf, hailed any boat willing to slacken sail enough to listen. They met no Kis, nor anyone willing to halt long enough to carry a message: everyone wanted to reach a safe harbor before winter storms set in. They finally caught up with another scout, and after exchanging greetings and news of pirates (none) and krakens (also none), Bian Ze called, "Any Kis of Mountain Peony among you?"

By now Mek's hopes had dimmed to resignation. At least he was back in the empire now. He'd find someone in the family in spring—

But then a familiar balding head (now very much balder) appeared, as a husky gallant wanderer boomed at his shoulder, "Kis there are, though no longer from Mountain Peony. Who wants them?"

Bian Ze turned toward Mek, hand extended, a broad smile on his face.

"Fourth Uncle," Mek yelled—and his voice cracked again. "It's me! Mek! Twelve!"

"Is that—Little Twelve?" Fourth Uncle boomed even louder than his companion. "You're alive?"

"I am," Mek shouted—and so great and sudden was his joy that he darted a few steps toward the hatch to fetch his wooden sword to fly over there, then he remembered that his family had not wanted him to do Essence studies.

He'd completely forgotten! Was it unfilial to have disobeyed? It might be taken as impertinent to fly over to that boat! He stared, feeling odd, as if he'd put on a piece of clothing he had known forever, and it fit all wrong.

But while he hesitated, the two scout craft neared until a pancake could be tossed from one to the other. "Where were you?" Fourth Uncle cried. "What happened? That end of the *Blue Albatross* was entirely stove in. Your cousin Hu took the blame upon himself for not having watched over you properly. It grieved him for—ayah, the important thing is, I will take great pleasure in letting him, and your father, know that you are among us still, Little Twelve. Is the other boy with you, I hope?"

Tai had come to stand nearby.

"Yes! This is Je Tai. We were prisoners of the westerners," Mek cried back. "We were turned into slaves."

At this, Tai turned away, ashamed to hear those words spoken before strangers.

"But we got away, and we're coming home. I was going to look for some way to get to Mountain Peony as soon as I could."

Fourth Uncle's expression turned somber. "As well you did not," he called. "Grandmother's soul passed over the moons' bridge the year after you disappeared. It was not your doing," he added quickly. "She said the King of the Underworld had been stalking her dreams for years. She also said she was sure you were alive somewhere, I think because old Master Root came by and claimed he saw you alive in his dreams."

Mek gulped, his emotions swooping.

"It's perhaps as well that she is now reborn somewhere else, because we had to give up the home she had always known. There's evil doings among those imperial court families," he added, making a sign to ward demons. "We found ourselves threatened by a young duke who said his family owned our land—he said we had to swear to become his personal guard, or pay a fine we could not possibly afford."

Mek's voice cracked again as he protested, "But surely they know the Kis are trade ship defenders! Not land warriors."

Fourth Uncle spread his hands. "No one argues with a duke and wins. We took whatever ships we could find, so we're scattered, but we've begun to meet at Fox Point for the spring competition." At this, he saluted the banner flapping over Mek's head, a brown eagle against a green background. "I expect to see your father by New Year's Two Moons. He'll be as happy to hear that you're training with Eagle Island Sect as he will be to find out that you're alive."

The rising wind began to make the waves fractious, and Fourth Uncle's last words had to be bellowed. "I'd take you now, but I'm a mere hireling on this run." Here he clasped his hands briefly in salute to the yacht some distance away. "There's scant space on this scout, too many of us already. There's been word of a pirate gone ashore, to set up as a local king in one of the western harbors…"

"That would-be king has been given over for justice," Bian Ze called.

At that, all the faces along the scout turned into beaming smiles. "We will pass the good word! Twelve, I think you're better off where you are, just now. You must have luck in your stars, to fall in with the Eagle Islanders."

Mek's next question, *Will you take me home?* died in his throat as he made his deepest gallant wanderer bow. He was not to go with Fourth Uncle—because there was no home.

But he discovered he really didn't mind so much. For one thing, it didn't look as if there was anyone his own age over there on Fourth Uncle's scout, whereas Bian Ze had promised that there were plenty of youngsters training at Eagle Island. And more importantly, he knew his family still lived, except for Grandmother.

Fourth Uncle and Bian Ze traded respectful bows—Fourth Uncle's the deeper as he suspected who had dealt with the pirate-king—as the ships pulled apart. Flakes of snow whirled down from the white sky, soon hiding the ships from the other.

Mek turned away, so delighted with this news about his family that it was a shock to see the bleak expression hardening Tai's face. "Tai?" he asked.

Tai's face smoothed to blankness.

Mek had begun to understand that blankness a little. "Your family is surely safe from being threatened."

Tai's bent head jerked up. He seemed about to speak, then, in the flat voice Mek knew meant he disliked the subject, "That is so."

Tai was quite certain that he knew that troublesome duke. If his First Cousin had inherited his father's ducal title, that meant that Venshai's grandfather, the commandery prince, had died. Grandfather Ji had been cautious and prudent. Too much so, the younger Jis had often said in Tai's hearing. The Ji family would no doubt be maneuvering now to find a way to raise that rank.

Without seeing Mek's curious, sympathetic gaze, or Waha's interested, amused smile, Tai turned to face the cloud-streaked sky to the south, his mind reaching over the endless green waters.

Just as well he was going to spend a winter up north. He owed it to his parents to return home, and be ready to resume his studies. That meant he had all the winter months to gain strength, comb for what news he could glean, and study what he could to try to catch up.

I will pass quickly over the journey to Eagle Island, which was the principal training ground for the sect.

Once Mek understood that the spring competition was entirely friendly, that is, the expectation was to compare skills and learn thereby, not to claw one's way to fame over the bodies of competitors, he was euphoric. By the time the island's dragon teeth appeared on the horizon, he knew all the gallant wanderers on Bian Ze's craft. Not just their names, but their special skills, and their histories—for they valued storytelling as much as they valued music—and he was already striving to learn from each. Especially from Old Barnacle, who was a miracle with a hulusi. Mek proudly showed them the bamboo flute he'd made with wood he'd scavenged two harbors ago. Ugly as it was, its sound was true.

He did worry a little about Tai, whose mood remained unchanged as Bian Ze's ship nosed slowly north and east under slackened sail. However, he was there for every practice, no matter how bitter the cold. Bian Ze heartily approved of Tai's zeal.

The weather cleared briefly when tea-terraced Eagle Island appeared on the horizon.

The scout joined two other equally small boats inside a secluded inlet. Everyone helped to tie everything down for the winter, and then they trudged up a narrow defile to a village overlooking the bay—a lookout post. Here, they were given two covered carts pulled by fat horses shaggy with winter coats.

Waha, used to bitter winters, offered to drive one, and hopped blithely up. Tai crowded inside the bare cart, suppressing his revulsion at the rough plank benches, and the press of huge, unwashed bodies around him—for there was no bathing in winter on a crowded scout.

I have endured worse and lived, he was thinking, when Waha leaned around and beckoned. "Learn to drive?" he asked, as always careful to mimic the Mud accent. Tai climbed up beside him.

Mek looked around, then gave a laugh. "I think I'll ride on the roof. Otherwise I might get squashed!"

"That's where all the young ones want to go," Old Barnacle cackled. "G'wan with you, pup."

The thump of Mek squatting on the cart's roof preceded a jerk and a rumble over ruts, and the cart was in motion, the men joining in singing a song about coming home.

The sun rose in its low southerly arc as the carts climbed steadily into the hills. The singing had abated and the night watch had dozed off when they entered a narrow canyon, carved by waters long ago. The narrow cart path, with its two deep ruts, bumped them upward until a sudden sound, sweeter than the liquid trill of a lark or nightingale descended in a waterfall of melody.

Waha squinted upward, looking first for threat. Tai caught a brief glimpse of color, then nothing. Inside the cart, a few of the sleepers woke. The others fell silent, including their chief, who knew the players, and how rare this greeting was.

Then from the roof of the cart rose a single melodic answer from Mek's flute. He repeated the melody, once, haltingly, then a second time with more skill. Bian Ze waited—the elders among them waited—then from above the wind instruments answered in wordless welcome, a joyful sound. Mek brazenly joined in.

The duet continued for a short time, and even the horses lifted their muzzles, snorting as they picked up their pace a little. Then, as suddenly as they had come, the unseen musicians vanished, and Mek put away his flute.

Inside the cart, Gingko Nan said to his chief, "Old Uncle seems to have come across."

The cart crested a sudden hill, opening into a gallant wanderer village in a gentle valley, plain buildings mostly of one story, their only ornament heaven-tilted eaves. The largest group lay terraced around a flat square that Mek recognized as a practice field; a trail, edged with ornamental rocks and bamboo stands, led up to what had to be a hot spring.

They all itched to get into that spring and wash the salt out of their skin, followed by a hot meal.

"I'm Mo. You'll bunk with us," a cheerful boy said briskly. "What style have you been studying?"

Mek wondered how much to say about Diggy and the miners, and about Snowhawk's style, which was different from Diggy's. Then he thought about his father's frequently repeated maxim that eagles don't catch flies—if Ki defenders are busy blabbing, that means they aren't listening. "I'm a Ki," he said only.

Mo's thick eyebrows rose, and he grinned wider. "A Ki! I heard they don't usually let you go on the trade roads until you're grown."

"I went with my uncle, cousin, and sister. Then things happened," Mek said evasively.

The "things" became clear in the baths, when their grimy headbands came off at last—Tai's very reluctantly. But the most reaction they got was mild surprise, no shock. Mek then noticed a couple others with marked foreheads, and Old Barnacle said, "Auntie Nua is good with a needle."

"Is there a way to get rid of it altogether?" Tai asked, without much hope.

"Only digging it out, then you get a big blotch of a scar, like a third eye," he was told by someone else—he tried to catch all the names and faces, but there were too many.

But the idea remained, and after a thorough scrub, when Bian Ze said, "Auntie Nua has her needles ready if any of you three want to be rid of your tattoos—"

"Yes," Tai said, longing bursting past his old habit of courtesy.

Bian Ze seemed unperturbed at being interrupted. "Why don't you run along to Heaven's Ease? Young Hok will show you the way. There will be a meal when you're done."

Young Hok, a thin teen whose prominent front teeth called Zan to mind, looked at Tai, who loathed having that noisome tattoo bare to the world. Then Hok scrupulously looked away, though he was wildly interested, having heard about how the Ghost Eyes marked their slaves with dangerous charms. He sensed that this was not the person to ask. The girls were going to go wild over him; *they* might be able to tease his story out. Hok chuckled to himself as he took Tai back down the path, pointing out and explaining the layout of the village.

Every building had a name, but the general layout was the familiar one that bespoke order. The main building had a south-facing door, and everything to west, east, and north belonged to the understood divisions: men, women, elders, youngsters. No ranking otherwise, but he relished the return to proper order, instead of the repellent chaos of Angja's fortress.

Heaven's Ease was a clean, spare space with plenty of windows. On some walls a hand with adequate calligraphy had inscribed famous poems by Lu the Wanderer, and by Ar Laq, along with some of Kanda's most frequently found sayings. All these signs of normality were unspeakably soothing to his spirit.

Auntie Nua was one of those strongly built, square-faced women who are ageless even when their hair turns white. She studied Tai as Hok said, "I was to bring him for getting rid of the Ghost Eye slave mark." And with that, Hok flitted away.

"Most people have no idea what it signifies," she began, after Tai clasped his hands in polite greeting to an elder. "But this is your face, so you ought to decide what is on it besides what your parents gave to you. And the enemy forced on you."

"I know what I want," Tai said steadily. "A tiger's eye."

"A tiger's eye?" Auntie Nua repeated. "It's simple enough—very simple." She sketched the shapes in the air. "Yet some might regard a tiger's eye as a challenge."

"If they see it," Tai replied flatly, and flushed. In a more polite voice, he added, "My ancestors come from the Tiger Islands, so I see it as less a martial challenge than as respect for my forebears."

"Ayah, that is a different matter indeed! Very well. You sound quite decided, as if you have thought deeply about it. This is good, because, like that slave mark, it is permanent."

"I'm certain," Tai said, with utter conviction.

"Sit on that stool there. So simple a thing will not take long, and the light is perfect just now."

She was quick, and skilled. Tai relished every prick and sting; to him, each jab of the needle was a vigorous, and permanent, rejection of the Westerners' violation.

At last, his skin raw and a little bloody around the marks, Tai went where he was pointed, as a gong rang from a nearby building. Children rushed from somewhere, leaping and skipping on either side of him. From another direction young people swarmed, and as Hok had predicted, he was soon surrounded by the older girls, who cheerfully competed in offering him tidbits (after they fixed a plate for him) and telling him about the island.

Waha looked on with considerable amusement, while obliquely eluding that sharp-eyed Auntie Nua. He was not at all ready for any intensive conversation that might reveal his accent, and he suspected that these Muds would regard a western-born convict slave differently than one of their own taken into slavery against his will.

Auntie Nua bore down on Mek next. He, too, was surrounded by a gaggle of youngsters, but they were trying to outtalk each other to impress the newcomer. All fell silent at Auntie Nua's approach, and after she asked if he wanted to be rid of his tattoo, he blinked, rubbing at it, then said, "Won't it fade? I was told by the Westerners that children have to have theirs redone a few times while their heads grow."

"That's true," Auntie Nua said. "It will fade, but not vanish completely."

Mek shrugged. "I always wear a headband anyway. Thank you for offering," he hastened to add, remembering his manners.

Auntie Nua chuckled, turning away with a brisk step. Waha cursed to himself, sliding away to take a stroll outside. If anyone asked, he'd say he was exploring.

But when he rounded a building, there she was. Alone. Waiting for him. She said in slightly accented, but quite good Dragon tongue, "Why are you here?"

Waha stared, completely taken aback. She'd said nothing about the tattoo, yet she uttered no threat. She was unarmed, her tone merely curious. But her choice of language made it clear that she was aware of his origin. Even though he'd seen two sets of greenish eyes in the hot spring pool. Which meant that at least one of the gallant wanderers on that scout had figured out what he thought he had successfully hidden.

When not actually challenged, his usual recourse was to deflect with flippancy. "I'm following Bing Tai, of course."

Auntie Nua tipped her head back, looking up over the eave toward a row of redbark trees planted by a long-ago hand on the hill overlooking the hot spring, their branches silvery in the moonslight. Then she regarded him with mild curiosity. "I don't know him, but I recognize his affinities. And I strongly suspect that Je Tai will never choose you."

"As well, for I'm not the kind to mate for life. I promised someone I'd look after him and Kimek, and he's interesting. He's a fire mountain. I want to be there if he explodes."

"Mmmm." Auntie Nua's skeptical glance was as mild as her curiosity. "That tattoo. Do you want it gone?"

"What character is it that he got?"

"The eye of the tiger."

"Hai-yo! I'll have that. Tiger's eye. Very fierce. Good one for a martial wanderer."

It was gnarl-handed Old Barnacle, the unlikely expert with the hulusi, who introduced Mek to Old Uncle, the expert who played the seven-hole side-flute. This was a wispy-eyebrowed, wire-muscled oldster with a wizened, wrinkled face and a benign smile. His usual winter garment was a threadbare long tunic-coat embroidered over with osmanthus, lotus, and begonia blossoms, clearly by hands long departed to their next lives.

Old Uncle's music was filled with Essence. Mek saw that this elderly master's chief attribute was air. When he played he taught, wordlessly. Mek blissfully followed those melodic airs as they untangled occasional taut, knotted emotions around them, and combed them into silken strands. It was a kind of healing that instantly appealed to Mek, and during the following days, he practiced until his throat dried to a husk and his nose numbed after hours of vibration. That was after a strenuous day of forms and sparring, which he loved.

They had arrived too late for mid-autumn festival; Sky Wishes Day came and went, lanterns sent to the skies with wishes frivolous and profound. Mek and Tai stood side by side, soothed by the reappearance of the festival days of childhood.

Not a week later it snowed again, this time for four days straight. And the snow stuck: winter had arrived. Tai asked if there might be any books on Divination.

He braced to be laughed at, or worse, interrogated, but the three who heard turned to Mo, who said. "What we have of books is kept by Uncle Tuen, the scribe, and by my mother. Go across to the Main House. My mother is always trying to get us interested in squinting at the stars. You can have my place!"

Tai shrugged into the coat that someone had grown out of

and bent into the wind, trudging through the fast-filling canyon that had been dug out earlier in the day.

Mo's mother, Auntie Mim, was found in the village scriptorium, with her single student laboriously copying out a chart of the Heavenly Stems and Earthly Branches. The student, a girl, looked far too old to be laboring over something Tai had mastered at half her age.

He shifted his attention to Auntie Mim and bowed. "This ignorant student once was training in augury, but it's been a long time since then, and I know I am far behind my peers."

Auntie Mim studied him. "From your accent, it seems you're from the far east. The school at the Silk Islands, perchance?"

Tai bowed again, aware of a conflict of reactions: he was proud that she'd so quickly guessed, but ashamed of his ignorance.

She gave him a paper, an inkstone, ink, and brush, and said, "Let's see how much of the Heavenly Stems and Earthly branches you remember."

Tai sat down and wrote out the great chart as elegantly as he could, rejoicing in putting brush to paper in his own language once again. He brought his finished paper to Auntie Mim, who studied it carefully. For a heartbeat he wondered if she even knew the chart, but then he saw that she was examining his handwriting, and his pride dissolved: what blemishes unknown to him did she see there?

Then she began a series of briskly spoken questions that made it clear she was not at all ignorant, regardless of how far away from the center of the empire she had come.

At the end, she gave a slight nod. "With some review, I believe you could begin study in the *Book of Wisdom*."

That was reserved to the class above his! He could not prevent a smile as he bowed to hide it. "Might this ignorant student request teaching?"

"We'll begin right now. You may review by testing Anise on the Five Elements in both the generating and the overcoming cycles. Anise, you may lay down your brush. I think a review might be of aid in getting the north forms securely into your head."

Tai itched to get at the books, but obeyed his new instructor, and sat down on the mat across the low table from the girl, who looked up. He regarded a plain face above a short, round body.

Though she seemed somewhere between his own age and Mek's, he didn't remember her among those girls who always crowded around him at meals, trying to touch him, which he hated.

Her long braid looked hastily made, with hairs escaping. Below her blob of a nose her mouth curved in a welcoming smile without a shadow of resentment at thus being summarily superseded.

She carefully set aside a clumsy-looking inkstone that might be found in the carryall of a dirt-poor student hoping to better a meager life by studying for the Imperial Examination, and said in a soft voice, "Welcome! My name is Han Anise." And when he glanced at the paper she had been laboring over, she blushed to the ears and confessed, "I was taught a form of augury that has come down through our village—based on shells. Auntie Mim says that our form of augury is really more akin to shamanism, as the shells are cast to speak to the ancestors, rather than the proper study of the stars."

Tai was thrown back to memory the Angja Island shamans, but he shook that off. "Shells?"

"Hundreds of them," Han Anise said candidly. "Many beside the 144 traditional ones. I had to begin all over again. Please be patient with me, if you can." She bowed humbly.

THIRTY-TWO

I MUST TAKE YOU back in time and place.

The children of Crimson Lychee village did not get much schooling. Now and then a wandering storyteller or a monk or nun on their Ul-journey might stop for a week or for a winter, and as often as not traded teaching for room and meals.

It was one of these who cautioned the children by repeating the wisdom of the ancients, such as the sutra about impulsive actions being like seeds: most take to the air, landing in water, or road, or in the eye. There they rot, or wither, or get flung away. But some land and take root. If the seed — or impulse — is one of kindness, or generosity, or insight, it can flower up to fruit tree or medicinal herb or fragrant blossom. If the impulse is born out of mischief, anger, or spite, it becomes a weed to choke gardens or poison the unwary.

Like those seeds, these words mostly vanished into the air, except for one pair of ears that took them in. Young Han Anise, daughter of Midwife Han and niece of Augur Han, heard and heeded, athirst for beauty in a bleak life.

Not just beauty. Though she rarely saw her father, she had inherited his sense of humor. A young monk's lively story illustrating "A crooked beam makes a crooked roof," as he drew with a stick a higgledy-piggledy drawing of a tumbledown cottage in the dust of the small village square, had made the children laugh aloud. Many remembered the story. She remembered the saying.

And though her aunt once exclaimed, "Aish! The Sage Empress was likely as smart as a rock, but had some nameless scribe scribble all those tiresome sayings in order to better her name," Anise cherished those sayings anyway. She had little reason to believe her aunt's derisive comments, instead pondering how the Sage Empress — and other ancients — might have once had lives similar to hers, for why else would they speak so wisely about avoiding strife and evil?

Before her soul even entered the world, her story began with a pair of sisters, the eldest of whom had defended her right to inherit the family post as village augur. Her younger sister, realizing at a young age that she was being shut out, chucked her studies and walked across Crimson Lychee to the home of the midwife — who loathed the augur — begging with forehead to the floor to learn a skill that owed nothing to augury.

Each had a daughter. Those cousins grew up much like their mothers, with such quarrelsome vitality that the village showed signs of dividing between the two, for the new augur was wont, purely out of spite, to pass nuggets of midwifery wisdom couched in terms of augury, and as for her cousin, she learned to slyly offer to save her patients their hard-earned coins by consulting the ancestors on behalf of infants before and after birth.

This feud rose to such a pitch the village headman was forced to intervene. He could not deprive the villagers of the services of these important figures, so he declared that the two cousins must trade their firstborn infants until there was sufficient peace in the village. Only then could the children be returned to their rightful home.

All the village agreed that it was just, and so it happened. Anise was raised by her aunt, the augur — and when she was just shy of ten years, the village headman was prevailed upon to return the girls to their rightful mothers.

Anise crossed the village to her unfamiliar home with her very meager belongings (for her aunt had always said there was no use wasting clothing on her when it would just be stolen by That Woman) as well as a loud pronouncement before interested neighbors that Augur Han had done her best for a child born under cursed stars. And the augur's daughter returned to her mother, woefully ignorant about midwifery, for Anise's mother had kept her hated cousin's brat scrubbing laundry, sewing, and cooking lest she spy out midwifery secrets. That girl returned to the augur bitter and angry enough to assure the continued feud, but we are not following that story.

Everything that went wrong in Midwife Han's life was attributed to Anise and her unlucky stars. Midwife Han had since Anise's forced removal had a second daughter raised entirely by herself, who at six knew more about her mother's skills than newly-restored Anise, and who jealously protected her position lest her elder sister displace her.

There was also a little brother of five, but as he was destined for the fields or the fishers, he was of scant interest to mother or the favored sister. However he was everything to love-starved Anise, who cuddled him, protected him, and even taught him to read and write, despite their mother scolding repeatedly that this was as useless as teaching the harp to a bull.

So matters went on until Little Brother Tek turned ten, and his father came to claim him for his apprenticeship, leaving Anise bereft.

Later that spring a group of gallant wanderers arrived in Crimson Lychee, after having driven off some raiders from the west. They were full of exciting stories, many related by the youngest of them, a girl only two seasons older than Anise — and when the gallant wanderers left, Han Anise packed up her winter shoes, her winter clothes that she had made herself, and her old inkstone with *Han Anise* etched on it by her once-met grandfather, and left to follow them.

The gallant wanderers discovered her hiding on their craft shortly after they put out to sea. She was miserably sick, and they were going to return her to Crimson Lychee, but she was deadly serious when she threatened to clasp a rock and hurl herself into the sea. After hearing her story, and finding her ever cheerful and willing to work and above all to learn, in spite of her seasick complexion and inability to eat much more than a bite, they brought her to Eagle Island.

This was the year before the arrival of Mek, Tai, and Waha. When they arrived, Anise was almost sixteen, and striving to unlearn the tangle of imperfectly passed-on sigils, mixed with trickery, that she had gleaned from Augur Han. She was also striving to catch up in forms and sparring; it helped that she had spent a great deal of her childhood running errands and carrying out work that strengthened her.

Tai, tasked to help her (as Eagle Sect was firm in their belief that the young learned best not only while being taught but while teaching) at first was wary. Slow to trust, and reserved even though he was at last returned among imperials, he soon came to realize that Anise was quick and eager to learn. She made his task easy—unlike some of the tumble of young cubs for whom forms and fundamentals was the most boring part of the day, and therefore to be augmented by as many pranks and jokes as possible.

He was also fascinated by what she'd been taught. "I watched my aunt through a fingerhole in the window paper. Which I did not dare to make! There were things she did not teach me, but taught her daughter, who sometimes sneaked over to see her mother."

"Such as?"

"Such as how people might think they are being absolutely still, but no one can truly control the black of the eye. Unless maybe they are Uncle Ze, or Old Uncle," Anise corrected with a smile and a quick gesture that draggled her braid through her ink. "Aish! I swear there are imps in the ink, and they leap up," she muttered as she tried to mop the ink gall from her hair much the same color. "But as I was saying, she told her daughter—I never think of her as a cousin, ever—that when the black of the eye changes size, that means a change in emotion, and to regard that as a sign."

Tai had never seen the blacks of people's eyes change—he was too shortsighted to see the difference between pupil and iris—but he was impressed with such acute observation. "What kind of sign? That the ancestors speak through that person?"

"Maybe..." Anise drew the word out, her head tipped consideringly, one hand with the smudged cloth frozen in the air. Then a flashing, merry smile. "I think the truth is, she didn't hear the ancestors at all. Though she always claimed to. It was the way she'd say, 'You then tell them that the ancestors heard their plea, and though they are difficult to understand, with proper respect paid them through sutras, prayers, and return visits...'" A quick gesture—and the smudged cloth left her equally smudged fingers, and landed with a splat straight in Tai's lap.

"Ayah," Anise exclaimed, jumping up and scrabbling for a fresh cloth. Having seen to the tidiness of a beloved younger brother, she made to dive toward Tai's lap to mop the smear.

Tai fended her off, but not unkindly. He could see that her intent was to repair her error, and not an excuse to press closer to him, the way certain among the other girls did when they tried to flirt.

"I'm already dusty from grappling practice. I will wash it out later," Tai said. "Then, your aunt passed down fraudulent lessons? But you said she taught the basic signs."

"I think she might have been a mix," Anise said, her high, round brow wrinkled thoughtfully. "I know that many think no one can actually speak to the ancestors. I heard Uncle Ze once say that if the ancestors are still sitting around us as ghosts, then how could they go over the bridge to be reborn? Would that not mean that the ancestors are villains, if bound here as ghosts? And I know that Aunt used to use the most flattering words in her auguries for the headman and his family, and for others who paid well."

"Then she did not believe she spoke to the ancestors?"

"I think she put words in their mouths, yes, but she was always very, very careful never to cut a long noodle. She refused to accept coins in an unlucky number. And once, when her daughter was about to leave, and it was raining, and she opened her umbrella before going outside, Auntie smacked her right down to the floor, then bawled for me to sweep the entire house before bad luck could get inside. Then she made her daughter kneel and recite five sutras to propitiate the ancestors, and the only one there to see it was me, yet I was of no account. Yes, she might not *hear* the ancestors, but she was deathly afraid of them seeing or hearing *her*."

The brass gong rang then, and as there had been a recent thaw, she flashed a quick bow to an elder sibling and flitted out to join the youngsters standing ankle-deep in mud.

Mek greeted her absently. He was one of those tasked to teach the lowest ranks, which were mostly children, except for Anise and one boy who never seemed able to tell right from left, though he was regarded as a qilin with the horses.

Mek got them lined up to begin the forms as they warmed up their muscles. There was nothing said about Essence in these drills.

"Part of Essence training is knowing without having to think about it how much power to use, or how little," Mek had been told by Uncle Ze. There were times when he must use none—for teaching fundamentals, and for competitions to test skill only—but other times he was expected to use full power, because it was surely going to be used against him. And so Essence was a part of his martial training with certain among the elders.

The youngsters worked until the welcome gong announcing the midday meal.

Mek was always hungry. The youngsters often called him Ki Pig, though this was merely teasing, and not at all a warrior name, which was a different matter. Mek accepted the teasing along with second and third helpings, for he was *finally* growing.

The thaws gradually began to last longer, and familiar holidays arrived and passed one by one. Everyone began talking about Spring Festival, which meant the yearly competition down on the peninsula at Fox Point.

Mek was sparring with Tai one warm morning, the air filled with the scents of budding trees and plants, when he said, "Were you going to leave for Mountain Peony soon?"

Tai blocked a punch. "I thought once I would, but I realized it's already too late to get to the augury school for this year. I think I'd arrive just as everyone is being sent home. That's assuming I can get across the empire quickly. If I have to earn my way, it might take a year. Aunties Nua and Mim have plenty more to teach me, and I'm learning fast in Eagle Island style." He nicked his chin toward the rest of the field.

Mek grinned. "Then you'll come to the competition?"

"Yes," Tai said. "Why do you ask?"

"Because of the bets," Mek said.

"What bets?"

Mek's eyes rounded. He bit back an exclamation, *Don't you listen?* But Tai never heard anything when he got that blind look that meant ferocious focus, especially when he practiced with bow and arrow.

Mek hadn't handled a bow since he was ten, and Tai never — his Ji cousins had seen to that — and so Tai was always out practicing when he had free time; though the targets were fuzzy, he was learning how to shoot in spite of that.

"The others — some of the others," Mek corrected conscientiously, "make bets on who will win among the masters. They bet chores they hate. I overheard someone saying they'll have to repair most of the roofs next year, and I want to get out of that if I can win enough wagers. You know they'll do it in summer, when there's scant rain, and I hate toiling in the hot sun. Picking tea sounds easier. At least it wasn't hot in the mines —"

Tai scowled, looking around quickly, but no one seemed to

be listening. How he hated any reminder of that time! "Foolishness," he said shortly, and walked away when the bout ended.

Mek sighed. What had caused that mood? Mention of the mines, of course. Tai was so odd about that—ashamed. It wasn't as if they'd chosen to be slaves!

A couple of other boys approached to ask if he wanted to get in extra sword work. He agreed, though keeping an eye out for the appearance of Old Uncle in his flower coat, for he would not willingly miss a moment of music if he could help it.

When sword practice ended, Mek spotted Old Uncle out on the porch, sitting in the sun with his eyes mostly closed, his flute on his lap as he listened to Squirrel, one of the big boys, practicing the harp.

Mek ran to fetch his flute, then approached quietly and sat cross-legged beside Old Uncle's stool, content to listen. The delight Squirrel took in that harp brightened each note, even the false ones.

At the end, Old Uncle let out a contented sigh. "Truly, young Mek, music prospers the spirit of all things."

"All things?" Mek asked.

"All things," Old Uncle repeated. "I know you are thinking of living things, but who is to say that stone and soil and fire do not live, in their own way? Stone as slow as the centuries, and fire… How to explain fire's Essence? We can't explain it, but we know it *is*. Come. Let us take to the air."

Mek had had plenty of practice with the few who could ride the winds, but never with Old Uncle. "Shall I fetch my sword?"

"Why, when we have our flutes?" And at Mek's blink of surprise, Old Uncle said with a hint of impatience, "The sword is merely to trick the mind into balance. A flute will work just as well."

Old Uncle leaped nimbly into the air, one hand fitting the flute to his front foot as a guide. Mek did the same. He still had residual memory of tumbling end over end in that terrible storm that had thrown him and Tai west, but he knew that there was no more binding on his air affinity, and he knew balance.

Mek watched the old man swoop high, leaning effortlessly as he rounded rocky spires, and he found his flight as assured as when he used his old, battered wooden sword. Below them the island spread, its contours gracefully outlined in terraced tea plantations, the low, spreading trees now fuzzing green.

Old Uncle glanced back, the wind toying with his beard and hair, then gave a nod and reached with one hand as if cutting the air as his speed increased. Mek copied him, wildly exhilarated as they shot skyward toward wispy clouds, wind imps tumbling about them. Old Uncle dodged wind-carved pillars of stone, and through rocky arches. Together they soared, racing side by side ever higher, where only the little goats leaped.

"We must first pay our respects to my old master," Old Uncle shouted.

There, on a square chunk of mountain that had split ages ago from those surrounding, grew grass and a pair of sky-touching firs leaning eastward, bent by the relentless west wind. They spiraled around this mountaintop so astonishingly like a meadow, and came to rest before the group of trees. Mek saw something whitish, thin and curved: bone.

They stopped before a skeleton that leaned against the trunk of the middle fir, hands resting on a staff that crossed long thigh bones. Man or woman, Mek couldn't tell; wind and weather had scoured away all signs of the living person once inhabiting that set of bones.

Old Uncle made a low bow, and Mek hastily copied it. Old Uncle's expression was difficult to interpret, other than a rueful sadness. "My master found infinite peace here, but so lofty and lonely a pinnacle is not for me. I want to breathe my last among those I love," he said, and to the bones, "I am the last of us; you are all gone on. Do you know one another in your new lives?"

Old Uncle turned to Mek. "We are remembered through our deeds, when everything else is gone." He sighed, stroking his beard, and for a time stood lost in memory, then bowed again. Mek did, too, as Old Uncle said, "Come. It will be dark when we return—there is not enough moonlight to guide by unless you know the spires well. We have lost wind racers in the past who got careless."

"Wind racers?"

"Oh yes, cannot you imagine it? The fastest of the young generation is Mim. Auntie Mim to you children."

Mek was thinking: young? Auntie Mim was almost Grandmother's age! Once again they took to the air, knifing the lengthening shadows. Mek could see the entire island now, obscured partly by its much-broken fire mountain; to the north and east lay many more small islands. Not all were terraced for tea; other trees added their colors, and here and there were mere rocky spires.

Old Uncle drew near, pointing, as the wind rippled his sleeve. "There is Sky Mirror, where you will come to train. It's my family's ancestral island, where our tomb lies. That is where we do Essence studies in earnest. Your Master Root was one of our number, once."

Mek understood then that he had passed some kind of test, or perhaps only a level. His heart sang, and still sang when at last he landed, fingers and toes numb from the flight, and Anise and Hok were there waiting. "There you are, Mek! We saved your dinner for you," Anise said.

THIRTY-THREE

A GALLANT WANDERER'S FIRST spring competition is often the most exciting of all, because everything is new—and so it was for Tai and Mek.

It was fascinating to Waha. There was none of the blood and death of the ring. Also, no Cobra Sages drifting around like ghosts in silver, "ministering" to the wounded and dying.

The Eagle Island Sect descended the mountain, often singing, to find a sizable gathering busy setting up camp in a huge ring around the various competition spaces. Numerous sail craft anchored in the bay leeward of the peninsula. Newcomers approached the insouciant statue of the nine-tailed fox god who stood poised as if to leap into the air, one hand holding a mask. They made their bows and laid down gifts of flowers and food before coming to greet old friends and relations.

When Waha saw that statue, he was stunned; if ever he was to feel a sense of home, it would be at the foot of the Fox God.

Mek bounced eagerly along, scanning for his family. Names resounded all around him as people greeted one another, or called to point out famous figures. Bian Ze was one of these: Mek discovered that Uncle Ze was known as Bian of the Pearl Sword, or even just Pearl Sword, a name never used on Eagle Island. Uncle Ze only smiled when it was shouted at him during the subsequent competitions, as if he had received a greeting meant for someone else. Or by the wrong name.

Mek was eager to compete, but far more invested in finding his family. He helped the other Eagle Island Sect youth set up the tent, then to chop and mix for the first meal. After he gobbled down his share, he raced off, moving from tent to tent.

No Kis in any.

But when he went out to warm up with his friends on the second day, a man bawled out, "That's Twelve, right over there, see?"

Mek turned—and his breath whooshed out as a pair of strong arms encircled him, squeezing until his ribs creaked. "Mek!"

Mek stared up at Cousin Hu, who was a young man now, a mustache growing on his upper lip. Cousin Hu's eyes were mere slits, glittering with tears. "It really is you! I was so sure you'd died when that trader crashed into us. And I was the one shoving you down there—I thought you'd be safe—what happened?"

"Mek!" That was Father, grayer now, his face lined. Another hard hug, and when Mek regained his feet, Father said, "You'll be asking after your mother—right over there, came on the *Virtue* from the Silk Islands—went to fetch your little sister."

"Where's Zar?" Mek asked., thinking his older sister must be grown now!

"She's Zar Moon Blades now—fighting pirates off the Great Sea," Father said with pride.

Elder Brother put in, "Little Sister wants to be a navigator, and those Silk Island clans always hire women first, if they can get them." It was his turn for a hug, and a head-tousle, which completely undid Mek's thin topknot entirely, and everyone laughed.

"There! He still looks like a duck's butt, all fuzz!" Father said fondly as Mek scraped his hair back up properly, blushing. "Now, tell us your story. I can see by those fiendish Ghost Eye marks on your face that you've faced your share of wolves and tigers..."

Mek was used to telling the story by now. He'd discovered that fast was best, as no one had much interest in people he still dreamed about—Odval and Diggy were interchangeable to those who did not know them.

When he was done, it was time for their own stories. Mother arrived with Little Sister in the middle of the competing voices. Little Sister was now a stringy colt of a girl with Mother's face, and the same flyaway hair Mek had. Only hers was much thicker. He sensed a considerable water affinity in her—no wonder she chose the sea. "You're going to be as bald as

Seventh Uncle," Little Sister remarked after he finished tying up his hair.

"Then it won't tickle as much," Mek replied, and she snorted a laugh.

"Let's see that Ghost Eye slave mark," Fourth Cousin burst in, elbowing her way among the crowd of cousins. And then, when Mek took off his headband, she crowed a gratifying, "Ooo-ooo!"

Little Sister then began to enthuse about navigation—and learning the stars, interrupted constantly by the others, who found that tedious beyond bearing, and did they think that Ma the Quickstaff or Lim Ko of the Iron Fists would win staff defense over Second Uncle?

It was both strange and familiar to be with his family again. Everyone had jumped so suddenly in age! The competitions began and he ran back and forth between his family and the Eagle Islanders in order to see and to cheer. Though Ki training in many respects was as good as that of Eagle Islands— especially the knife forms, to be expected of those who mostly defend on the crowded decks of ships—there was no place for Essence among the Kis. They didn't say anything against it; it was more that it did not exist.

They came to watch him, and their attitudes changed, their shouts and cheers louder when he blew through those his age and size, and began competing against adults. But here, it got harder, and Mek began to realize that his relatives (as well as most of the other gallant wanderers) didn't see Essence when used in fighting. But then Essence did not do the fighting. It was a tool, and required control.

After he beat Cousin Hu with the wooden knives, they still called him Fuzz Butt, but with a different tone, and even though he was eventually knocked out in archery, then sword, then staff, then grappling, and finally by double knives by more skilled Essence fighters, his father clapped him on the shoulder, saying, "A loss against Li Hyacinth is a win against anyone else. She commands pure gold, and gets it, when she goes out with the trade fleets. You were lucky indeed to land among the Eagle Island Sect, my boy. Very lucky."

And with that—and Little Sister's stories about the navigational school in the south—Mek realized that the family truly did not expect to take him away. To what? They no longer had a home.

How did he feel about that? He was not certain; he stood around, barely noticing Li Hyacinth beat huge, hairy Ma Quickstaff as he searched his feelings. It wasn't that they didn't love him. He saw it, and heard it in voices, and felt it in those hugs and topknot-tousles and shoulder-claps. They were being practical. Grandmother would approve of that! They had no home, and so they all came here to compete, for that kept their skills honed, but also to see each other.

Mek blinked and looked up when red-haired Bian Tian-Tian and Anise appeared, arm in arm. "Good match," Anise said softly.

"It was! Next year you'll make her sweat for that win," Tian-Tian said. "Come on with us—there's wild garlic still unscavenged over on that slope. And Anise here just finished making up the loquat cakes."

"I don't want to miss watching Tai's next match."

"Why?" Tian-Tian asked, rolling her eyes. "You can't see past all those girls with their tongues hanging out, when he doesn't so much as give them a glance!"

"I still want to cheer for him," Mek said. "He was right there for me."

Anise gave a nod. "He's fifth down the list. We could get to the slope and back if we hurry."

Tian-Tian agreed to run, but shot a skeptical look Anise's way. "Don't tell me *you're* all clouds and flowers over him, *too*."

"Not at all," Anise said comfortably. "He reminds me of my little brother. Not in age, of course, but Little Tek was quiet the way Tai is. He appreciates things the same way. Not in words, so much as the way he talks, and remembers little things."

"Aish! You're the one who studies with him," Tian-Tian said with an airy dismissal. "I just can't get over how Fei-Fei and her gang cawed like crows every time he rode a horse to shoot, and his arrows didn't hit the middle once!"

"He will," Anise said equably. "You know how hard he works."

"I think he will, too," Mek said. "He's much better than I am, and he'd never been allowed to ride a horse before, or to put arrow to bow."

"Enough," Tian-Tian said, and began to run. "I already hear too much about him in the dorm! Waha Fast Hands is *far* more interesting." she called back over her shoulder. "*He* smiles back!"

Mek had not been surprised to overhear some of his older cousins talking about Waha, as he was now in the top five for knife fighting, which the Kis considered their specialty. However, later that afternoon, he'd been considerably surprised to overhear in a drift of speculation that Waha was referred to as an escaped galley slave.

When he heard that, he slipped away before his relatives could think to question him, and found Waha after a while at one of the tents for gambling. He was just as popular with gallant wanderers as he was among the Eagle Islanders.

Waha spotted him hopping anxiously, and when the current game finished, wandered his way. "Why are you disturbed, young Kimek?" he murmured softly in his own tongue, smiling around to make certain no one listening.

Mek also looked around, then reported what he'd overheard. "Did you tell them that?"

"I did not. That very deft and very agreeable woman with the double dagger-axe yonder seems to have come up with it on her own, and I never disagreed." And at Mek's puzzled look, "It puts me far from the capital, do you see? And from the mines. I doubt very much that word of someone as insignificant as I might travel west, but if it does, better that it lead away from me and Snowhawk's people. The First Prince's spies are many."

Mek said, "But he lost the election, didn't he? Someone said that your — that is, the old emperor on the obsidian throne died right before the new year, and his brother is now the emperor."

Waha looked around once more before responding. "You might not realize that the First Prince's ambition breaks knives and sinks boats. Or as you easterners put it, his ambition is a thunder of dragons." Still smiling, he tapped his eyes and then swept his arms around. "And the West's new emperor is even older than the previous."

"Waha!" a voice called. "I'll have that rice wine you owe me. It's fresh and hot!"

Waha returned jovially, "Coming, coming!"

Mek shrugged. The First Prince was now far away, his matters of no interest, unlike bald Seventh Uncle, called Tuft for his tiny beard, just now stamping out of the Eagle Island tent, apron around his middle and a stirring spoon in his hand.

Anise popped out right behind him, grinning in triumph. That meant that the loquat cakes had come out well! She, Mek had discovered, was a very fine cook, having learned young that if she did not want to always get cold leavings, she should learn cooking. Tian-Tian was with her, looking virtuous—which meant that Mek would be dunking dishes.

And so it proved. Bian Ze listened to their cheerful voices as he walked out to squint up at the two moons, one rising and one sinking.

Moon and starlight caught in silver hair and touched the lotus embroidery on a worn coat as Old Uncle descended softly from the air and landed beside his grand-nephew.

"Ah, my boy. How are we this year?"

"Respectable," Bian Ze responded mildly, not mentioning his own win. He competed because the Eagle Islanders, indeed all the others, expected him to win. He did. His skills guaranteed that his rules for the Eagle Island competition remained firm: those who desired duels to the death might fight them elsewhere.

"And our qilin?"

Bian Ze said, "Ki Mek's fundamentals were always good, and he seems to have integrated whatever styles he was taught in the west, putting him quite far up the competition. Where he struggles still is in gauging Essence with the precision needed to stun but not harm. Then he invariably slips out to ask his opponents if they need healing—not always welcome. A few see it as officious. Others are indifferent."

Old Uncle hummed to himself.

"There's more. It's in the music. He seems to be using the music in the same manner. He doesn't have a remarkable voice, and his flute is not brilliant, yet there's such joy in his playing. It's infectious. Is it related to the dream-walking that is not given to me to comprehend?"

"It's the healer in him, I think. That's what brought me; he seems to be striving to draw anger and malice when he perceives them, nullifying them with his music. It is a rare form of healing, and he is groping toward it on his own. Perhaps I ought to have expected it from a student of Master Root."

It was Bian Ze's turn to hum. His grand-uncle, and his master, had his own way of testing, usually by waiting for possible knots to smooth themselves. He seldom acted on his own; thus that sudden mental order when Bian Ze had just wrapped up that pirate the year before, and was about to settle the matter. *A comet comes,* Old Uncle had said, directly into his mind. *I need to see how it resolves.*

The easiest way was to let the pirate captain get his blade at Ze Bian's neck and thereby regain control of the situation. His band, suspecting a ruse after such a clumsy fumble, had resigned themselves, ready to act if necessary. The surprise had been that Old Uncle's comet was neither of the strong, trained young men who crashed in to the rescue, but their third, a mere boy.

"It's time for me to take him to Sky Mirror," Old Uncle said.

Bian Ze touched the pearl in the handle of the sword Old Uncle had placed in his hands twenty years ago — and with the bronze, scaled sword, responsibility for Eagle Island Sect. He thought with mild regret of his own son, an excellent man and a careful father. Formidable against pirates. Bian had thought that the sword would pass through his family. "Is the sword…choosing Mek, then?"

Old Uncle had said that the sword did not speak the way he could through dreams, but she certainly had intent. And volition. He knew that well.

"Yes," Old Uncle said, gently.

To no one else would Bian Ze speak from the heart. "Why? Is my son unfit in some way I don't see?"

"No. Never. You know that. But the sword does what she will. I can only guess that whatever…entity…dwells within sees somehow that Ki Mek is to wield this blade."

They both considered the boy with the sunny disposition, whose intent, most often expressed through music, charmed the heart — and who right now seldom thought past his next meal. He'd had to get new shoes twice since his arrival, not quite a year ago.

They both considered the implied burden.

"But let us give him as long as we can, shall we?"

Thirty-Four

Descending from low, thin clouds over Sky Mirror Island, Mek saw the double rooftops with flying eaves of an ancient temple. It was built around a rocky shrine, and surrounded by outer buildings in a circle.

"This was a Phoenix God temple back in the Sage Empress's time," Old Uncle explained. "They moved southward after two very hard winters, and the Bian clan became custodians of the shrine."

Mek soon discovered that the sense of sanctity imbued in ancient rock and the sound of falling water, whispering on a soughing wind, seemed far older than the long-ago Yslan Dynasty. Perhaps even older than the Golden Dragon Dynasty, whose origins were lost in the mists of unwritten history. A few people were able to perceive at times an immanence, sometimes in a shimmering incandescence in the cascade, and others the impression of some vast entity.

"Who *is* that?" whispered Mek, when he and Old Uncle left. "Or, what?"

"I cannot answer that," Old Uncle murmured, further down the path, lest they disturb those cultivating on the grassy cliffs and rocks in that shrine. "Many do not perceive anything."

"There's…something, or somebody, there," Mek insisted — though with an air of question.

"How can you tell?"

"It's…" Mek wriggled his shoulders. "I don't know."

"The aura is there," Old Uncle said, laughing a little. "You yourself don't see auras in colors, or smell then in fragrances, or hear them as wordless voices or the hum of bees, as many do. In some ways your perception might be the purest form, and yet it's the most difficult to grasp. Like trying to shape air, or water."

Mek said, "What do you perceive?"

"I, like you, sense a presence."

"Is it what makes this shrine sacred? Or was it drawn to what it found?"

"I do not know. As for what it does, that, too, I cannot begin to fathom! It might be cultivating. It might live as trees do, in a time much slower than ours. It is certainly peaceful. All I can do is try to protect the harmony of this valley."

Mek bowed acceptance, wondering when lessons would begin, not yet aware that those had commenced when he first set foot on the island.

Kanda wrote many maxims about education. The one that Old Uncle lived by stated: *By three methods we may learn knowledge: First, by learning from the ancients; second, by imitation; and third by experience, which is the bitterest path, and yet the surest way for knowledge to flower into wisdom.*

His style of teaching was to interfere as little as possible with his student, preferring to demonstrate when needed, otherwise leaving the student to find his own path. Wisdom, to Old Uncle, did not come in molding his students into replicas of himself.

Mek was therefore left to explore, and to work.

Mek one day found that a group of Suanek's nuns had arrived; he heard some of them singing as they wove at hand looms. Their prioress was also a skilled maker of medicine, and an expert in the health and growth of the tea trees that produced the leaves that were the island's chief trade product. She taught any who wished to ramble with her over the hills and meadows, Mek was one of these. They came back after each excursion with baskets of pungent herbs, which were then dried, minced, and made either into cakes or unguents. Mek's knowledge thus expanded.

When the first lotus and peony flowers began to bloom there appeared a set of folk who followed the old sun god, their only ritual (that he saw) the touching of a finger to whatever they drank, before it was raised in salute to the sun. He learned quite a bit about the ways of animals from them before midsummer; one day they were there, the next, gone.

There were jovial phoenix god monks on their Ul-wanders,

and devotees of the Snow Crane, and silent, sinewy Ghost Moon monks. Not just human seekers came and went, but creatures of fur and feather, four footed and two, or none, in the case of the snakes who warmed on the shrine rocks in summer.

Mek and Old Uncle, sometimes in company with other players with their favorite instruments, wandered up the paths to one or another of the small shrines, and there practiced their music, conversing through Essence-infused melody. Sometimes, when those conversations reached a height of emotion, or discovery, or mutual understanding, the music resounded over the entire valley, causing those working in the vegetable gardens, or repairing wood, or making brick, to pause, and look up, and then go back to work with thoughtful or renewed vigor.

Mek's studies did not always take up his entire day. There was the work of maintaining the dwellings, the mending of clothes, and the preparation of meals—and of course the picking of tea leaves when summoned: they did grow their own, but gallant wanderers were expected to volunteer at the various farms at harvest time, a sharing of labor as well as sharing the island. Everyone turned a hand, and then were free to study, paint, or cultivate in silence. Mek roamed on foot and in the air, exploring the peaceful lake, the waterfall, the bamboo forest that gave way to interwoven redbark families and soughing cedar conveyed an aura of peace.

Mek's only daily pattern, a result of lifetime habit, was to begin each morning with the Ghost Moon monks who practiced the staff arts, and led the martial drills.

It was late in the eighth month, after Suanek's followers had propitiated the water gods to ward floods from the late summer storms, when the gaunt prior of the Ghost Moon monks stayed Mek when he would have gone off to the midday meal.

The old monk, an unprepossessing figure with one nicked ear and a nasty scar down that side of his face, plunging over his collar bone into his robe, squinted at Mek, then said, "Why do you come, when you could kill any two of us? Any four, I'm thinking, with your speed, and that Essence I see around you like lightning?"

"I don't want to kill anyone," Mek said.

"I see that, yes. All you do is chill the acupoints."

"That's what I come to practice," Mek said earnestly. "Getting the control to do that. Maybe freeze a limb for a breath or two."

"Ayah," said the monk encouragingly.

Mek's face heated. "When I first met the Eagle Island chief, it was on an island some pirates had taken. I stunned the chief, I assumed for a watch or so. I did not find out until Uncle Ze admitted to me that he had to heal the pirate—once the rest of them were rounded up—or the man would have died of thirst, still frozen. And I thought myself so cultivated!"

"I think you have surpassed that blunder, eh, young Mek?"

"I want to be sure. And..." Mek hesitated, then said, low, "What I really try to do is find a way to cure the anger in attackers."

The monk's gnarled hands smoothed his staff. "By fighting? Ay, there are times when a good bout cleanses the spirit. But that's only of petty irritations. Just as real fights seldom resolve conflict, merely alter it, or even increase it, you cannot *cure* anger."

"I can try," Mek said.

"You can. I believe it worth the effort. You must first remember that anger can be righteous. Were you not angry when you discovered that pirates had attacked that island, and held the helpless at sword's edge?"

"Yes," Mek exclaimed. "That anger is like a burst of Essence. It went away as soon as the danger did. I'm talking about the kind of anger that some hold onto. And turn it toward malice and destruction, though they call it righteous."

"They might believe it's righteous," the monk said. "Can you judge wisely?"

Mek flinched inwardly at that. He remembered his and Tai's anger toward Bar Ardal, who never wanted to hurt them, but slavery was a part of her life. Yet their anger was not *un*righteous in being forced into slavery.

"I can't," he admitted.

The monk chuckled. "But we all do judge. Especially when we are young. Not that you are entirely wrong. There are those for whom malice is everyday life. It's rarely demons at cause," he added. "Though they feed on the pain that results."

"So I'm told," Mek said.

The monk tapped the end of his staff lightly on Mek's shoulder. "You might join us for an island or two on our wander. See more of the world for yourself. Not now," the monk said. "We go nowhere with winter nearly here. If you decide, find us next spring."

He turned away, not expecting an answer, and Mek bowed to his back.

The final tea harvest was gathered, as well as general harvest, before a series of storms. Harvest Moon rose and waned, yearning toward Ghost Moon as the year wound toward its end. That far north, winter arrived early, and stayed, everyone's breath smoking, and steps squeaking or crunching the ever-present snow sometimes lit gold by the evanescent sun, until buds began fuzzing the trees. The beginning of spring sent everyone up to pick the first flush from the tea trees on the south-facing mountain, always first to bloom, while the north-side trees were still waking from winter.

Mek had worked hard, and he deeply appreciated the island, but he was by a large margin the youngest one there, and as the sap began to run in the northside trees, and the soil warmed and moistened, ready to be seeded, his thoughts bent southward toward Eagle Island. And the young people there. He was sure he'd grown taller—a thing that had begun to matter, even though he laughed at himself, because he knew that he was not, nor would be, what others regarded as handsome. He was too much like Elder Brother, and Father, and no one ever called *them* handsome. His desire was more modest in wanting to see the girls eye to eye, at least, so they wouldn't see him as a little boy. And he was now eye to eye with many.

"Time to go," Old Uncle said simply, one morning. "You should arrive in time to help set up the Bian tent for the competition."

Mek clasped his hands, paid a last visit to the shrine, and this time, he flew south alone.

He arrived on the peninsula in the midst of the hubbub of camp setup, assuming he'd blend in as always. And for the most part, he did, though there were those among the young people who blinked for a few moments at this slim young man of medium height. He had neat, capable hands, and below a topknot loose with fine, flyaway dark hair, a smile of singular sweetness.

"It's Fuzz Butt," Little Sister shouted, from near the great gathering, where she was helping sweep away the detritus of winter. "And you said he wasn't here!"

"He wasn't," Tian-Tian retorted, dropping her broom and crossing freckled arms. "But now I guess he is."

Behind Tian-Tian, Anise put down the basket of brush she was carrying away and stared, her nerves tingling with snow. Mek had *changed* so much! Though she couldn't quite characterize how. Except he was taller, of course. His face was still round, but not baby round, as one might say. Was the change in the way he carried himself? He was so *quiet*.

Over the rest of the day, she couldn't quite stop watching him, trying to figure out what had altered. He was welcomed by Kis and Bians and Eagle Islanders alike as he helped pound tent pegs, and steady poles, and fetch buckets of water.

By the next day, she was the only one who noticed that between last year and this he had stopped eating meat. He said nothing—in fact he talked little. Instead he was constantly looking at this or that person as he listened, his eating sticks sometimes poised in the air.

Mek finished in the top ten of all skills except archery—he was still only middling in that—then joined the spectators to cheer Tai on, whose horseback archery practice this past year now put him also in the top ten.

Tai was edged out of fifth place, which, he told Mek as they walked away, had been his goal. "It's not the top five," he said to Mek. "But sixth place means that I can hit what I'm shooting at."

"Which is something I can't always do," Mek admitted.

"Was there no practice on your island up north?"

"Not shooting practice. But I made up for it with staff work," Mek said. "Ghost Moon monks only carry staffs. But even pirates keep their distance from them."

"I know," Tai said. "I admire them for that."

Mek grinned. "They protect the weak, but they don't get involved in governing affairs. I admire that most of all!"

And he was about to pass on the invitation from the Ghost Moon monk when Tai spoke. "Someone must govern, though," Tai pointed out with conviction. "If all the good people go to the mountains to paint scenery or become scholars, that leaves governing to the rascals."

Mek remembered that Tai's father was a magistrate, and decided against repeating the monk's invitation. "You're right."

"What else did you learn?" Tai suspected he'd been too peremptory in what was after all only chat following a bout. After a year of not seeing one another at all.

"A lot about medicine. And tea. It's surprising how close medicine and poison is. When I was small, I always thought they were different entirely, like whales and birds. Enough about me. How go your own studies?"

Tai might have returned a noncommittal answer, as he usually did. He knew that most gallant wanderers found divination and matters of augury puzzling at best. Most were bored, except of course for Anise, whose partnership had gradually fused study with zeal. But he felt he owed Mek in somewise for his condemnatory words, and so he said, "In a sense, delving into the Book especially seems more like a mirage. The more I study, the more mysteries I become aware of." And, in a quick rush of words, "The masters keep warning that true divination — that is, the clear truth — only emerges after many years."

To his surprise, Mek pursed his lips and gave a nod. "Old Uncle said something about it, that we study to perceive the advance and retreat of the stars, the circles wheeling within and without larger circles. It's order — but then there are the comets of surprise. Perfect order might be impossible, as is perfect harmony. And yet they are worth striving for. Is that it?" Mek asked.

"It is, and yet the study brings us no closer to predicting the future. Its place in the order can only be seen in hindsight. And so comes the…" Tai was going to say *trickery*, for that was the term both he and Anise used for the little signs, like the enlarging of the pupils, that revealed emotions. But that could be misconstrued as implying that the grand study was based on falsity. "…and so come the methods by which augurs find ways to express what they see."

"Even geomancers?" Mek said.

"Geomancy," Tai repeated, casting Mek a surprised glance. "That is a different study. Though related. What did you learn about that in your secluded island?"

Mek hummed to himself, then said slowly, "I didn't learn much. I listened a lot. A passing scholar told us that geomancers are taught that the talismans that bind the earth are called natural, as they destroy nothing. They fit within the vast harmony of the circles." He frowned, reaching for the right words. "She told us that augurs are different from geomancers in that they look for elements of fortune and interpret signs for each item in a query. So, for example, a seeker is born on a day when earth was prevalent."

"Yes. And so?"

"Something in their query is under the influence of earth, and so the seeker's fortune depends on, ay, now I've forgotten the rest, except that fire can produce earth through ash mixing with water, as earth can multiply wood." He lifted his face in question. "The augur has to interpret that for the seeker, isn't that right? Who asked about the probable success of investing in a load of silk, or whether to plant hemp this year or next. Have I got it right? Whereas the geomancer has to find a way to ease the ground when the firedragons stir. We talked about them, too."

The only other person Tai talked to about such matters at any length was Anise. "I take it your year meant a lot of scholarly discussion?"

Mek reddened to the ears. "Did I just turn boring? Yes. Winter was very hard up there. Almost nothing to do but talk. And make things."

"I'm not bored," Tai assured him. "I'm unused to anyone outside of divination study wanting to know how or why I might try to divine an answer. Sometimes they've asked, but they don't listen to the process behind the answer. If there is an answer."

The next day, the celebrations began.

The winners were feted at a banquet, and then the spring festival became a different sort of celebration entirely. The children had helped with the dishes, then been chased off to bed, or to their own pursuits, which was usually storytelling; out came musical instruments, and there was even a huge drum brought by one of the more wealthy sects.

Mek, of course, was with the musicians. Tai hadn't seen him all day, nor had he thought about him, but on catching sight of him again as he tootled away on his flute along with four flutists, and a jumble of other instruments, the conversation the previous day returned. Mek seemed to be studying in a different way, but their aims ran parallel, just as they had when they first landed on Angja and struggled to get the little turtles to the water after their arrival brought them out too early.

Mek, like Anise, seemed to believe, as Tai did, that Purpose was to make life better for all. Only they seemed to have different ways of doing it.

Tai looked around for Anise, a habit now. He spotted her in the midst of a group of laughing young women. Between the end of the matches and the dinner most of these (and a good many of the young men) had contrived to rid themselves of the dust of the field, and to put on their festival clothes. Anise, he discovered to his surprise, had added ribbons to her braids — as had many of the others.

Pushed by Tian-Tian, Anise leaped barefoot up onto the big drum. There, with sweetly ringing bells tied round her ankles, she began one of the popular dances.

Thrrrump-a tump! The drum rumbled, hand drums rapping in a galloping counterpoint as the hulusi trilled the melody, and a pipa and all the flutes sang back. Anise twirled and leaped, posed and stepped, her sleeves whipping from side to side.

When she stopped, breathing hard, out came her rare grin, as she looked back at…Mek.

Tai had never seen that expression in her eyes, and he thought he knew all her faces.

His gaze shifted to Mek — who didn't even seem to see her. That is, he finished the song, his attention on the other players, before they turned as a group to applaud Anise.

Anise bowed, leaped down, and then began coaxing one of the others to dance, leaving question to linger in Tai's mind. Mek? Tai was so used to thinking of him as a boy. And Anise?

"Don't make a palace out of two bamboo poles," Tai muttered under his breath, but even so, he found himself watching them both as the evening progressed, and gradually people strolled off toward the tents, or the balmy darkness — in pairs.

He saw that look from Anise again, a quick, unblinking look of question, aimed at Mek. She was in a passing group of young women, as Mek spoke earnestly with his cousin Ki Hu. "No, wood — ay, paper, actually — charms easiest. That's why talismans are made of it. Air and fire are the hardest to charm…"

"What puzzles you, Jetai?"

Tai stilled, to find Waha at his elbow, holding out a jug of warm rice wine. A woman Waha had been seen with earlier was making her unsteady way toward the Cloud Mountain Sect's tent. Waha himself was flushed with drink, eyes glittering in the firelight.

"Nothing puzzles me," Tai responded.

Waha, of course, wouldn't take that for an answer. "Your Anise jumping ship?"

"She's not my Anise," Tai said shortly. "We study together."

Waha bowed, almost lost his balance, corrected with a quick gesture, and said, "Forgive me if I've misread the situation. Though it seems to me that, hai! You're the one who tells the world, *If only we...!* Whereas she's seeing our Mek as one who asks, *What if we...?*"

Tai's long, slanted brows quirked at a steeper angle. "What do you mean by that?"

"Clumsy." Waha shook the jug, which sloshed. "Different, is what I mean. Might be looking about for a different..." He was caught by a yawn. "Hummm, I don't know what I mean. Except, why hang ono a dead branch when surrounded by a forest of trees?"

He saluted Tai with the jug and sauntered off, only slightly unsteady.

Tai retreated to consider. Waha was drunk. But even muddled by too much rice wine he must have seen something, or he would not have spoken at all.

Anise was Tai's study partner, but what did that mean? 'Study partner' had changed materially in the year and a half since they'd met, or why was there this sudden hook in his heart?

They studied together—and that meant they practiced together, which included the disciplines of internal alchemy. They were together some part of every day, studying the highly esoteric doctrines that guided the discipline of the dedicated augur. How natural it was to go from sitting side by side with knees touching, to checking for fever on raw days, to the unselfconscious, gentle affection that she gave to every living thing! And he, scrupulously raised to firm self-discipline, felt that affection with all the intensity of a seed's first warmth of sun.

He was not unfamiliar with passion. That door had been opened by Sui's laughing kiss, before they escaped Angja Island at last. But Tai had shut that door and locked it while still among the Westerners.

Eagle Island was at least in the empire, but here were gallant wanderers. For most, Waha especially, passion appeared to be ephemeral. Waha dolphinned through currents of it as limitless as the waters of the sea and the winds of the skies. Tai longed for something more…stable?

What? The question gnawed at him that night, causing fitful sleep, and then again the next day, when—in that great tent, everybody gathered—he saw Anise herself bringing Mek a dish. That in itself was normal. She was an expert cook always willing to come forth with something delicious exactly the way he liked it best. But the way she handed the dish to Mek, and smiled into his face, that was… *different*.

Aish!

He must be honest with himself in the bright, uncompromising light of day. As he helped to dismantle the great tent, he perceived that in that year and a half Anise had gone from being his study partner to being…his.

His what?

He pondered that as they rolled and packed up the tent. Not his future wife—not long after his hundred-day celebration following his birth, his parents had betrothed him to someone agreed on between the families. He'd always known that, even though he'd never met the girl. And even if that betrothal had been broken by now, everyone assuming he was dead, he had always meant to return home to his parents. That was filial duty. And to the proper studies. That, too, was duty. He had begun reading with Auntie Nua to catch up, but she had told him before the New Year that she had little more to teach him, and that he could practice. Which he had.

They both had.

Then Anise smiled at Mek in a way that was solely for him.

It hurt. Quite sharply. But Tai's habitual self-discipline forced him to face the situation straight on: Anise was no dolphin playing through the easy passions of the gallant wanderers. But she'd picked Mek. Who deserved to be picked.

As for him… what was he doing here, really? He should have gone home at the first sign of spring.

He moved through the rest of the day, half-aware of people

gathering in twos and fours and fives to exchange farewells. He had nothing in Eagle Island—he'd brought all his scant collection of clothes.

It was foolish to make sudden decisions after a sleepless night, but guilt prodded him when he realized he had not thought about his family for weeks. Months. Not since he'd lit incense and prayed for their well-being at New Year's Two Moons.

He prowled around the area where the cooking had been done—now all in pieces waiting to be packed up. He was unsure why he stood there, or what he'd say, when Anise emerged out of the group discussing how to fit it all onto the cart.

"Tai," she said, with that brisk smile he was used to seeing every day. A warm, brisk smile, but so unlike that expression in her eyes when she'd looked Mek's way.

"I'm going home," he said abruptly, then stopped, a little bewildered, as if someone else had used his voice.

"Home?" she repeated, glancing toward the path leading up the mountain.

"To Mountain Peony." And at her surprise, "I ought to have gone half a year ago. Maybe longer."

"Aish! This is so sudden!"

"Will you come with me?"

And there was the shock he'd expected. Perhaps wanted? If only he wasn't quite this tired—except his mind raced, his heart thundered, and he comprehended from her reaction that her shock was at the idea of her leaving more than at the notion of his leaving.

Her brow puckered, and she began, "I—I never thought to—"

He flung up a hand. "It was a foolish question." And it *was* a foolish question. Even if he had no betrothal left, he knew what would happen if he brought home a young woman from a fisher village, with no family to speak of, no wealth or rank. They would both be punished, maybe not by family law, but in all the cruel ways his cousins had tormented him when he was small. And his father would disapprove of his making such a decision without consulting his parents, unless Tai relegated Anise to a mere consort. Marriage would be regarded as an unfilial act.

"A passing thought. I'll return one day."

Her smile brightened. "Of course you will!"

But he knew he wouldn't, because she gave him that ready, generous smile, without a hint of regret.

He walked away, and almost blundered into Bian Ze, come to see how the last of the packing progressed. "I think I ought to return to my family," Tai said. "I ought not to neglect them."

Bian Ze said, "I would never keep anyone from their duty, especially to elders. This is sudden, but certainly a good time to find passage. Where did you say you came from? Let's see if we can get you a berth. I know many will welcome a deft hand with defense, and I can vouch for your ship skills..." Bian Ze motioned him to stay.

Tai remained where he was, suspecting that Bian Ze did not want to risk anyone losing face if they could not take an extra passenger.

Word passed with its usual speed—and many crowded around to fire questions like arrows, "Why so suddenly? Where to? Had something happened to your family?" A few of the young women who had not given up hope of drawing his attention began some loud lamenting, but it was Mek's startled gaze that brought him out of the morass of inner questions.

"Tai?"

"I ought to have gone back last year," Tai said.

Mek clasped his hands. "I hope you will be able to send word of your safe arrival once you reach Mountain Peony," he said—conscientiously not offering to check in the dream realm. He knew how much Tai hated the very idea.

"I'll try," Tai said, and Mek faded before the others crowding in.

Bian Ze soon returned with word that a ship going southeast could definitely use another hand, as one of their tiller handlers had decided to stay in Eagle Island.

Tai began to thank everyone, then halted when Waha turned up, gear over one shoulder, his eyes bloodshot but his gaze aware. "Make that two of us."

"Why?" Tai said, meeting his gaze.

Waha sustained that straightforward, utterly honest gaze, afire with...he thought of it as possibility. Not sex. He already knew Tai's gaze strayed toward women—if it strayed at all. Possibility. "I'm going that way," he said with a shrug. "We can keep working on your fundamentals. You do need that."

"I do," Tai said on an exhaling breath, for here was Anise,

running up, something clasped in her arms. His emotions swooped, undefined except for painful expectation and then a shot of hard doubt, at what his family was sure to say when she showed up at his side—

But then he saw that the item clasped in her arms was far too small to be her travel gear, as she held it out with both hands. "You ought to take something back to your family," she said.

He had not thought about gifts; when he left, he was a boy, and adults saw to the matter of gift giving. Of course he must take a gift.

"This is fresh spring flush," she said. "It's wrapped in three covers, which should get where you are going nicely dry." She continued to hold it out, her smile the generous one he had taken for granted—had come to depend on. But there was nothing beyond ready friendship in her countenance.

He took the package of tea, muttering a word of thanks.

And consciously took the first step.

THIRTY-FIVE

TAI AND WAHA HAD scarcely stepped onto the scout that was to take them south when Mek's father clapped Mek on the shoulder, startling him. "We will be departing soon, but first, the family has all agreed: you have earned your knives."

It took Mek a heartbeat or two to wrench his mind from Tai's sudden departure, and he exclaimed, "But I was only in the top ten in all my weapons forms."

"You could have won in knives and staff," Second Uncle stated, almost accusingly, as the rest of the family joined Father. "Grappling, too, I suspect—"

Father coughed rather loudly, then proffered a fine pair of knives. "These belonged to Great-Aunt Fan, known as Fan the Swift for her speed and precision. Like you."

"Looking back, I suspect she had those Essence talents of a sort," Fourth Uncle put in.

Father continued, "Wear them with honor."

Mek dropped to his knees, and held up both hands to receive the knives in their newly-worked sheaths. He took the unfamiliar weight, and as his father raised him by the elbows, Second Uncle said, "There's a place for you on the east-road tea trade fleet. If you get your gear, you can join us."

Mek clasped his hands respectfully—the knives tucked under his arm—and said, "Perhaps next year? I promised to wander the northern islands with some Ghost Moon monks."

"Monks!" Second Uncle yipped the word, then his brows met over his generous nose. "You're *not* thinking of turning monk?"

"No, no, no," Mek said, and blushed as he thought of his

previous night's tryst with a very willing gallant wanderer his own age. She'd had lots of experience, which she'd shared with enthusiasm.

But Second Uncle was going on. "…if you had any ambition, you would have won those bouts! And now going off with a lot of shave-heads? I always said it would be a mistake to bring that old monk in."

Father said quietly, "Master Root was not a monk."

"He might as well have been," stated Eight, who Mek could see had grown up looking just like Second Uncle.

Fourth Uncle said hastily, "We ought to remember that Grandmother brought him in, and it is not filial to tarnish her memory."

"True, true, true," Second Uncle said, harrumphing. "But all I am saying to young Twelve is that he has very fine skills, that we could put to use. Especially with that Essence. Why would you want to go off with monks instead of us?"

"I do want to join the family, but there's something I'm working to learn—it has to do with music, and…and…healing a conflict, so I might say, before it begins. I can't really do it on shipboard," Mek began, stumbling over his words. "Where I'd know everybody, and there aren't new faces. I need to learn how to… how to…" There was so much he didn't have the terms for!

"But—" Second Uncle began.

"Next year, then," Fourth Uncle cut in firmly. "The Eagle Islanders have their own ways, remember, Second Brother. And he's still young. It could be that we are going to have to consider better training, if more of us turn up with the talent."

Mek gazed in surprise, then Father finished with, "Heaven has its own plans—and here we are, about to depart, all our vessels at the ready. And no trade fleet will wait on us."

After a last round of hugs, back pats, and exhortations of luck and avoiding evil, the Kis began to depart toward their various vessels.

Mek stayed on shore, waving to everyone, one hand clasping his new weapons against his side.

New knives. New place in the family. Tai gone. It was strange to think of Tai gone, though they hadn't seen one another this past year. But whenever Mek's thoughts had returned to Eagle Island, that had included Tai. Would he come back? The impulse to listen outside Tai's inner door was there, but he curtailed it with ease; he knew Tai would not welcome that.

His thoughts turned back to his family. Might the Kis now accept Essence training? Things could change!

He sought Uncle Ze to say his farewell. "The monks will have finished building their raft about now. They go from island to island on rafts, which they take apart, and give to locals every time. I won't have to search for them."

"Go," Bian Ze said, clapping Mek on the shoulder. "Go. Learn. Come back next spring, eh?"

About the time Mek and the Ghost Moon monks had reached their third island, after having settled a bitter feud that had begun over a pig rooting in the wrong garden, and helping a small trade town restore a bridge, Tai and Waha found themselves in sight of Mountain Peony Island, with the Tiger Islands stretching eastward like jade beads on a string.

Though the family estate lay on Tiger Island, Tai's father was a magistrate in Dawn's Placid Sea, Mountain Peony's eastmost harbor, where much of the empire's eastern trade came and went. That's where their house was.

Tai and Waha worked with the rest of the day watch to bring the heavily-laden ship in safely. As they did, Tai reflected that this journey would not have been nearly as easy without Waha's ability to make easy conversation with strangers, something he hated doing.

He might not even have survived; two ships ago, they'd had to hire onto a slovenly trader bringing second-rate rice north — the kind usually consigned to the making of rice wine — whose stingy owner had insisted on a supply stop at a harbor with a problematical reputation. But one in which there was no guild fees, cheating the empire of its due, at the risk of anchoring alongside smugglers or even pirates.

It had been a hot summer night, the sort that tended to ignite tempers, and the two had gone to an eatery offering pepper-spiced fish broiled skewers when a fight broke out between two equally drunken parties of smugglers who accused each other of being pirates.

Tai hadn't taken two bites of his dinner before a heavy body crashed into his and Waha's table — whereupon both sides went for them. Waha backed Tai with smiling efficiency, and the two together had cut through the wild, untrained brawlers like a knife through noodles.

Alone, Tai was not at all sure he would have walked out of there alive.

The ship docked, and the two fetched their carryalls. "Deep this far into the empire, they seem to take me for a northerner," Waha observed as they disembarked. "You're looking at me as though I stole your stockings while your feet were still in your boots. Will my presence be a detriment?"

Tai knew Waha was curious about Easterner homes. He was about to see one. "No. But they might assume you are a servant."

"I can play the role," Waha said. "Isn't life a series of roles?"

Once, Tai would have argued, and thought himself justified. But he'd been enacting roles ever since that ship disaster. "Better to be a bodyguard," Tai said, sidestepping the question. "Otherwise you will be sent to the outer yard to fetch and haul."

"Bodyguard it is."

Tai briefly described his family as they climbed toward the finer homes, then finished, "The pavilions are terraced up this hill."

"I'm looking forward to entering one of those famous south-facing doors with the stone guardians at either side—"

"—and you'll continue to," Tai cut in. "For we will go through the side entrance."

Tai's heart drummed when they drew near to the modest door in the high wall. Two house men stood on guard, both scraping their gazes in silent contempt from Tai's and Waha's salt-stiff hair down their threadbare laborers' tunics to the straw shoes sailors worn on land in the warm months. But one's eyes flicked back to Tai's face, lingering on those long phoenix eyes below blue-black hair, salt notwithstanding.

Tai was going to order, "Let me through," but all those early years of careful training caused him to still. He could not be certain of his welcome until he knew who lived and who had died. And what the primary family might have done.

"I am Je Tai, returned home," he stated.

The second, unknown guard was going to protest, but the first one—familiar—bowed, his face shocked. The second hastily opened the door.

Waha stepped behind Tai's shoulder as they entered.

A paved path zigzagged over a modest garden—suitable for the lower ranks of a great house. They started on this, both aware of swift steps heading onto another modest path screened by decorative bamboo: the second door servant, sent ahead. Tai stepped firmly onto the zigzagging path, which led to two little arched bridges over rushing water. Before they reached any of these fine buildings with fitted pillars holding up heaven-tilted roofs, and painted walls, a servant in gray emerged and approached.

Tai drew on the old ritual: when in doubt, you can never be too humble. "Convey to my respected and esteemed father that this unworthy and unfilial son will be kneeling outside the Hall of Ancestors."

The servant's startled gaze flicked between them, then the man sped off, and Tai led the way through a moon gate into a fine rock garden. Waha suppressed a whistle when Tai entered a courtyard before a building surrounded by redbark and parasol trees, from which a drift of incense emerged. He muttered, "The kneeling is not for bodyguards, right?"

"Wrong," Tai stated with wintry almost-humor.

But they were not left to kneel on the hard tiles much past these words, for the rustle of silk and the soft wisp-wisp-wisp of tiny steps preceded the arrival of a gray-haired woman and a girl, both tall and slender—the woman almost gaunt. Her long phoenix eyes widened even more, and she uttered a soft sob, instantly suppressed as she descended in a cloud of floral scent. "It is you, my dear son! Returned, and safe at last!"

Waha's fascinated gaze shifted from this woman, to the girl behind her, who was as handsome as Tai. Her eyes dominated her face, a mirror to her mother's and her brother's. Waha realized he was staring when that gaze met his, utterly indifferent. As affront began to contract her up-tilted brows— staring was considered rude among imperials—he looked away. But not before he noticed the revealing worn spots along the seams of her silk over robe with its long floating sleeves, and an ink stain not quite rubbed out on one.

Tai's mother kept up a stream of questions too quick for him to answer as she drew him to his feet. Waha rose, too, as Madam Je—Han Chui before her marriage to the magistrate—said, "I sent the little wood boy to your father, but he might be in the middle of a hearing. In any case it would distress him to see you like this. You must go and bathe, and I'll send over some of your father's old clothes, until we can get something made… Ayah! My head's in the wind and my heart full of singing cranes — I cannot decide what to do first — a meal! You must be hungry! I will see to it myself…"

Tai found himself overwhelmed by his mother's reaction as he pressed Anise's gift of tea into her hands. He scarcely had time to notice his sister Lei, and to exchange a quick and awkward greeting — for the last time he'd seen her, she'd been a child learning how to grip a brush — before a crowd of servants appeared.

At the prospect of a bath, the itch of brine and inadequately cleaned clothing could no longer be suppressed. Very soon he plunged into the welcome heat of the bath-pool. He waved off hovering bath attendants, and scrubbed fiercely until his skin stung. Then he floated in a blissful torpor as he watched a pair of servants warm pure white undergarments between hot stones, and another servant swing a censer of oh-so-well-remembered Celestial Pool incense so that the vapors brushed the silk of a dull red robe. All familiar sights and smells, once taken for granted, and now deeply soothing.

When he emerged and submitted to being toweled off, his hair bound up, he shivered as the cloud-soft linen underclothes slid over his clean, scoured flesh. Then another summer-weight robe in pale rose, and over that, the robe of deep, dull rust-red modestly embroidered with bamboo leaves; Tai's father scorned to ornament anything with tigers, much less two-clawed dragons, though the primary family did.

Recognizing this brought back the weight of old resentment, but Tai no longer cared what his cousins would say to him, or think of him. He was home again.

He submitted to having his hair combed out — at least it had grown out sufficiently — and he recognized the rosewood clasp as one he'd been given on a long-ago birthday. His things had been preserved, then.

He gave a thought to Waha as he left his room — how large and commodious this room seemed after years of cramped quarters! — and two heartbeats later, there was Waha himself, outside the door. He, too, was clean, dressed in family gray, but he wore all his weapons.

Tai went to the dining room, and beckoned for Waha to follow.

Waha found everything around him an absorbing mix of the familiar and the strange. He had been astonished to discover, during idle talk during their journey south, that Tai and Mek had seen the cherished palaces of the west as chaotic in organization. Though both were sharply observant in their own way, he had discovered that they did not, or could not, perceive how the most prized palaces were reserved for those volcanic remnants whose lava tubes were most circular. Emulating the ancient circular tent of the old Junsa times.

In contrast, this palace contained no circular or round shapes. Everything was angled, if not square, every entrance with a raised threshold to be stepped over — the easterners' way of confusing evil. Junsa believed that round structures led demons in dizzying circles forever, and the easterners that breaking straight lines thwarted evil demons.

Waha's bath had been summary, in cold water, leaving him time to explore; the servants had eyed his weapons, and faded out of his way.

Inside that south-facing door, there had been a room which seemed to have no purpose beyond a spirit screen — here splendidly painted with a scene of cranes rising from a pool surrounded by bamboo — and a door to the left.

That sharp angle gave onto a square courtyard surrounded by buildings, behind which was another pair of courtyards. Tai's rooms, as befitting a first son (so Waha expected), lay in a line with the first spirit screen with the cranes. It had been guarded by its own screen, depicting ducks, frogs, and butterflies around their own pool. The master's rooms had to be even grander.

Beyond that, a garden, bordered with gingko trees. Little pathways twisted among flowers and stands of picturesque, pocked stones. The windows were wooden lattices covered with oiled paper, some painted, others plain. Everywhere sculpted or painted birds — herons, cranes, nightingales, swallows, but no hawks or eagles, and above all, no dragons. He'd always heard that the easterner nobles and royalty decorated everything with dragons.

They were taken to a pavilion built in the middle of a still pool, reached by zigzags over the water, in which golden fish could be seen darting about. Here, Madam Je and her daughter waited at a table on which servants set many dishes. Waha tried not to let his mouth water: though until today he and Tai had eaten together, he strongly suspected he was only going to be watching this meal.

Tai greeted his mother, and she clasped his hand in her trembling fingers. "I will keep my questions until your father is able to—"

But a noise at the far door heralded the appearance of Magistrate Je himself, still in his robe and hat of office as he hurried anxiously forward. Tai leaped to his feet as he father clasped him tightly. "It is you," the magistrate said, his voice husky.

Who among those silent servants waiting so composedly would be reporting to the primary house over on Tiger Island? "I must beg your forgiveness, Father, for I did not return immediately, but took time to catch up on my studies." A flash of memory—plain and yet somehow beautiful Anise—the shape of her neat hands, her voice as fluid as falling water, and softer than a lark's trill—and he suppressed it, and began a report of his experiences.

THIRTY-SIX

TAI DID NOT GET much past, "Then Ki Mek and I were flung into the air, and carried by the storm, or by wind demons, all the way west until we landed on a westerner island, where we were made into slaves—" before his mother let out a cry, and before anyone could move, she whirled up, and ran to a cabinet of lacquered green and gold.

Tai had half-forgotten this cabinet, which had rarely been opened in his presence when he was small. His mother brought out a flat piece of wood, and a very old wooden shoe painted with talismans. She then drew quick characters with her finger on the wood—Tai recognized "west"—and then began to belabor the wood with the shoe.

Nine times she performed the ritual while banging away, and then another nine for emphasis, beating the villain. That is, this ritual aimed to chastise wrongdoers by hammering out the bad luck they caused, and then send it right back to the perpetrator.

If merely hearing the word "slave" was to provoke such a response, Tai decided to shorten his history. Magistrate Je sat in silence until Tai finished, then said with a slight frown, "I understand that the outlaws who call themselves 'gallant wanderers' effected your rescue, and if I ever meet the individuals who were so generous toward you, I will not withhold my gratitude. But I must confess it disturbs me to see you mimicking their habits." Here the magistrate touched his forehead.

In silence, Tai removed his headband.

His mother gasped, and his father leaned slightly back.

"Our ancestral tiger eye," he murmured on an indrawn breath. "I...feel obliged to point out that while venerating our ancestors is praiseworthy, it might be better had you done so with a painting, or commissioned the tiger eye in embroidery. And then..."

He stopped short of pointing out that should the primary family hear of it, they might consider his tattoo presumptuous, but the thought was clear to all.

"It suits you," Tai's sister Lei observed softly, her first words to him since her greeting much earlier.

The magistrate's brows contracted, but Madam Je laid her hand on her daughter's wrist. She did not approve of tattoos. "Your opinion was not sought, Daughter."

To his father's questioning expression, Tai said, "The Westerners mark their slaves with the word 'slave' in their language." He drew in the air. "If I added..." He stroked again, "it became 'tiger eye' in the old script."

"Ayah! Ayah! Now I understand. And I find I cannot disagree. Hum," Tai's magisterial father harrumphed. "And I also understand why you wear a headband to hide it. Hmmm...wearing headbands also a fashion among some of the more flamboyant students, especially in the imperial city. Only they favor flower symbols. Perhaps you might consider adopting such, for now. Until you earn your badge of office..." Here he gestured toward his head. "Your loaf, even at a modest ninth rank, will cover the tiger eye mark, which does appear a trifle...martial."

"Or he'll start a new fashion," Lei commented.

Tai bowed to his father, mindful of his long sleeves lest they draggle across his plate. How troublesome these things were! "Father, Mother, I know it is late in the year for being sent south to White Jade to continue my studies. Surely the divination students are on their way north and home for New Year's Two Moons. But if you desire me to return to my studies in spring—"

"When we just received him safely back?" Madam Je protested.

Tai's father stroked his sparse beard slowly. "We shall see," he said. "He is only just returned. Such discussions can wait."

After that, the conversation was about recent activities of their relations, until they parted for the night. Tai's mother lingered. "I will go make you some blood-strengthening medicine myself," she promised.

And early the following morning, his mother burst into his room bearing a hot dish of bitter-smelling brew. It tasted worse than it smelled. But his reward was a splendid breakfast after he dutifully forced it down—his mother must have been up half the night supervising its preparation.

Nothing was too good for Tai, as far as his mother was concerned. She had ordered all his once-favorite foods, and on seeing that he displayed no interest in a dish of candied haws, nor sweetened sticky-rice cakes, she had the servants bear those away as she begged to know what he would prefer. She also prepared his tea, insisting on the full tea ritual. "That tea you brought is the most perfect silver-leaf green, worthy of the imperial house. I have only bought so precious a tea once, to celebrate your hundredth day! I even bade the kitchen to bring out my hoarded dew gathered when Phoenix Moon was full, after being blessed with a hundred sutras..."

He decided against pointing out that this was the everyday tea he had been drinking for a year. Even so, every bite was watched from dish to mouth—and when he was done, she swept him off to the Hall of Ancestors to light incense, bow, and give thanks for having been restored to his family.

When that was done, he discovered that his mother had the cart waiting. Off they must go to the temple to thank the Phoenix God, with a stop at the morning market to purchase the finest fruits and vegetables as offerings. Every person Madam Je recognized was greeted effusively, followed, by, "My son has returned to us at last! We shall be giving a banquet to celebrate."

Tai had to stand under the scrutiny of eager eyes, and a bombardment of questions that his mother deflected with practiced flattery.

After they made their offerings and obeisance at the Phoenix God temple, they must make the pilgrimage to Suanek's temple, climbing on foot up the steep steps to the pagoda on the mountain, which housed the huge golden prayer wheel. Here, they walked out their prayers in nine times nine circles.

It was late afternoon when they returned—to find tailors waiting with bolts of fabric. By the time clothing, embroidery, length of sleeves, tassels, and accoutrements suitable to his rank as heir to a magisterial house had been discussed and chosen, it was time for dinner.

Afterward he retired, feeling very much as if it was he who no longer fit, not the clothing. His mother's attentions pulled him between the remembered customs of boyhood and what was expected of a young man—expected, but never practiced.

Waha came in shortly after.

"You've got two snakes in the hole," Waha said. "I spotted them before dawn releasing messenger birds. I followed them as best I could through the rest of the day, and I believe they are known to at least some of the servants. Your father's steward, certainly. I could do nothing about those birds, but do you want me to capture any future ones?" He mimed bow and arrow.

"No. My father has been living with these spies for years. Surely he knows who they are. His defense is..." Tai stretched out his hand. "To live openly. But I don't want the primary family to find out about my martial skills. Is there somewhere we can move without drawing notice?"

"There's a good place in the farthest yard, beyond the old lumber," Waha said.

"Then let's go out there before the house rouses in the morning." He hoped if his mother found him awake and gone, he would not have to endure another bout of medicine, as if he were midway between infancy and illness.

They woke to rain, but ignored it from habit. Tai knew that only the first forms would be cold and uncomfortable. He would soon warm from within, and so it was. They sparred until sunrise grayed the clouds, then went in to bathe and change. Tai discovered that his mother had again come, but finding him not there, had gone away again, leaving strict orders for the servants to prepare whatever he wished as soon as he wished it.

He went to the dining room, where he found his sister Lei alone, her eating sticks suspended over a dish of rice and egg with spiced vegetables as she perused a scroll.

At his appearance, she looked up. "That was a clever idea, giving her that precious tea. Mother will be using it to effect."

Tai found her calm manner comfortable; her nature was a lot like his own. "I was living on a tea island." He sustained a vivid image of Anise—and a pang of hurt. "What effect do you speak of?"

Lei laid down her eating sticks. "Have you forgotten everything? No, I have to remember that you were in the south studying with the augurs, and before that, you were small. I expect she's already begun a campaign to find you a suitable marriage."

"Marriage?" he repeated. Surely not yet!

"You're of age. And your betrothal was rescinded a year after you vanished. Ti Fan married last year. And though we're not as high a rank as the Ti family—as Fan never failed to remind me whenever we had to meet—we're far too high a rank for them to try to bring you in as a second consort."

"What about you? Is there maneuvering to marry you off?"

"The primary family has tried, twice," Lei said. "Dolts and brutes, rich and powerful enough to bring them prestige, but no one they want for Cousin Qishai. Anyway, Great-Aunt Dowager Princess Ji promised the both of us that if we tested in the top ten at the Imperial Examination, we could choose whom to marry, and when. And I mean to test well, not for marriage, but because I'd like an interesting position. Cousin QiQi as well."

She was…surely only sixteen? Very young to be talking about the Imperial Examination, but some took it merely to learn what to study for the next time.

She went on, "Mother knows that Great-Aunt Dowager Princess Ji watches out for us, though she approves of First Cousin Venshai's other ambitions to forward the Ji family."

First Cousin Venshai. Tai had not heard that name spoken aloud for years. It had once caused a flood of fear to pool inside him. "Cousin Venshai," he repeated, and regarded his fast-cooling congee without seeing it. "He's now the duke, the heir?"

"Yes. His highness Uncle Ji Houduo inherited the title, and also the position as Left Chancellor, when Great-Uncle Prince Ji died right before Phoenix sixth month of the Dog Year."

"Did Cousin Venshai drive the Ki Defenders out of the island?"

"The who?"

Tai realized then that she was unlikely to know. But his father would.

Lei then said, "I was going to tell you, Mother says that she is going to do everything she can to bring you to the notice of the governor's wife, and to the high council. She has her eye on getting you invited to act as Hero this year, which would surely bring plenty of the highest-ranking families to send matchmakers to propose their daughters. This will circumvent First Cousin Venshai maneuvering to match you for an alliance to benefit the primary family, the way he's done for two of the third house cousins. He gets our uncle to agree to most everything he wants. So don't go refusing Mother's plans."

"Thank you for your care," he said to Lei, and she returned to studying Mana Ta's *The Perfect Word*.

Waha, coming in toward the end of this conversation, saw her perfect profile abruptly shift focus from Tai to the scroll as Tai's perfect profile shifted to his breakfast, and—highly amused—wondered if either of the siblings really understood the effect of their stunning looks.

When next he was alone with Tai, Waha said, "I overheard part of your talk with Young Miss. What is this Hero she mentioned?"

"It's part of the Fire Wishes Festival. You remember that, surely?"

Waha said, "Lanterns everywhere. A few people painted wishes or prayers on lanterns with bamboo wicks at the bottom, set these aflame, and the lanterns rose in the air. I saw couples light and release them together." He wiggled his brows suggestively—of course to be utterly ignored by Tai.

"But here, in this city, there is a firedragon made of lamps, and carried by volunteers. This dragon battles heroes all down the main street and to the waterfront, as the entire city follows, cheering and setting off firecrackers or banging on drums and gongs."

"How did this come about? Is it an interesting story, with a real firedragon, I hope?"

"I don't know if it's interesting or not. It's certainly an old tradition, from the Tiger Islands," Tai explained. "We—the islands—are at the border of the Great Sea. Occasionally pirates preyed along its edges. Found these islands. Once a lookout spotted pirates, between banks of fog. Someone got the idea of dragging out a costume dragon head and putting lanterns in the eyes, and then forming a long body made of lanterns held by villagers wearing dark colors. From the water it looked like a firedragon stalking the shore. The pirates hauled their wind and fled."

"Clever!"

"They made the firedragon dance in celebration, and again the next year on the anniversary. All the Tiger Islands eventually adopted it. Then, a few generations back — it was a couple of generations after the Tan Emperor brought the imperial capital here to Mountain Peony Island — there was an Easterner hostage named Prince Noh. He was very popular, or so the story goes. The emperor thought he was too popular. Prince Noh heard about this tradition and wanted to see it. The emperor did not trust him going away, even as close to the capital as the Tiger Islands, so he ordered the provincial governor to see to it that the firedragon danced here in Dawn's Placid Sea."

"How does the hero come into it?"

"The emperor wanted the prince surrounded by warriors to protect him — or keep him from leading a rebellion. The governor here at this end of the island got the idea of combining a tradition from some of the northeastern islands — gallant wanderer islands — that celebrate gallant Jong Siang's triumph over the corrupt court in the Hero Dance. The governor removed all references to gallant wanderers and introduced the idea of changing the Hero Dance to a mock fight with the dragon, with guards as mock fighters. It was so successful that we've had it here in this city ever since. The imperial guard provides some of the dancers, and a few city youths who are very well trained. But it's always someone from the noble ranks who plays the Hero."

It was very clear from Tai's flat affect that he disliked the prospect of being put forward for any such display. Waha kept his own countenance strictly bland, but he went away chuckling inwardly.

That evening, his father summoned Tai to his study.

Magistrate Je sat, a thick calligraphy brush in hand as he slowly drew the ancient character for patience. He studied it, frowned over the tail of a stroke that he deemed unsightly, and set aside the paper to be pulped as he dipped his brush to try again. "Son," he said as his brush glided smoothly over the paper, his free hand keeping his silken sleeve from touching the desk. "Let us see how your calligraphy has survived your ordeal."

Tai demonstrated. His father nodded acceptance, then gestured toward the Circle board, and they commenced a game as they discoursed on the classics. Tai pleased his father with his knowledge, but the sight of the board elicited one of Magistrate Je's rare comical expressions.

"I began losing at the second move," Tai said.

"Do the Westerners even play Circle?"

"Slaves don't."

And so, beginning the next day, the Je family fell into a pattern: mornings early, Tai and Waha went off to do martial arts. Then Tai returned to study, as Waha wandered the city, listening and learning. In the evenings, Tai played Circle with his father as they discussed their reading. Sometimes this included Lei.

While in the west, Tai had longed for the home he thought he would never again see, and an orderly life of scholarship and of appreciation of beauty in nature as well as in art, like a bolt of the smoothest, finest brocade. And now he was home.

But, like a single thread pulled, marring the brocade into rumples, there was the effort of getting used to moving in silk with long sleeves, and the social gatherings to find a suitably rich and well-born bride, beginning with the banquet to celebrate his return. It would be unfilial to complain. He had been raised to expect his parents to choose his future wife, and his mother showed her love by making his future family her chief concern.

But that brief glimpse of the possibility of happiness with a specific person had seeded in him a wish he scarcely acknowledged: not for Anise herself. But for the miracle of an Anise who would choose *him*.

Outwardly, nothing could be more peaceful or exemplary than those family evenings of study and Circle with Father and Lei, as mother saw to tea, and embellished with her exquisite stitchwork their much-used clothing. Tai expressed his inward turmoil in his secret writings, then locked them away.

Outside, the weather steadily cooled until it was time to pack up and make their duty visit to the Ji family in the capital, to celebrate the new year.

THIRTY-SEVEN

MOST PEOPLE GATHERED AT their ancestral homes to celebrate the turn of the year. But the Ji family—along with all the families most prominent in the imperial court—remained in what once had been called Cloud Terrace Harbor, and since the arrival of the first Tan emperor and his imperial court, the Celestial City.

The Celestial City was terraced into the sides of a steep ridge, dominated by the enormous imperial palace all along the top, a great gleaming crown set among smaller gems. From the sea as one entered the bay, the eye was immediately drawn toward Heaven and the proud golden-edged eaves in triple layers, and the tall pagodas and towers of the palace.

Lei came to join Tai at the rail. "Imperial Princess Lam told us that the palace is older than the Tan dynasty," she commented. "It was rebuilt during the time of the Sage Empress, by a prince who had aspired to marry her."

"The imperial princess likes such tales?" Tai remembered having caught from his cousins' snide references to the imperial princess—the single imperial heir—being "difficult." He'd thought at the time, who could be more difficult than them?

Lei took a moment before answering, a pause very like their father's considered pauses. Tai had heard from his mother that when Lei was brought to the capital, she had been twice invited to join Cousin Qishai in waiting on the princess. "She seems to like plays and stories," Lei said finally, and wandered off again.

He was more interested in observing the expert handling of the naval escort to the three-decker they sailed on. Tai saw faces his own age on the closest escort scouts. This was probably how they trained those hoping to be promoted to naval command.

The rising tide floated the three-decker to a pier. Then all passengers of lesser rank had to trudge through the slushy snow to their destinations, while two carts with Ji banners awaited the Je family.

The journey was short. Tai could have run it. He had to suppress the impulse. This was not a gallant wanderer island. He knew his parents would consider it a terrible breach of manners.

The sole cart sent for the family was warm and close. The other cart was for their baggage. He suspected a silent reminder of their secondary importance in the fact that there had not been a cart for his mother and sister, and one for his father and himself. Instead, they were all four crowded on the two short benches more comfortable for one.

He soon found himself wishing he was out of this stuffy cart, even though the wind was icy; he glanced through a crack in the tightly shuttered window to catch Waha pacing beside the cart, chatting with one of the Je servants. Their faces glowed red with wind and walking uphill.

"Dear son," his mother murmured, burrowing into her furred coat. "Please. The air is full of wicked wind imps. I can feel their bite."

He twitched the curtain closed.

The Ji mansion was grander than Tai remembered, fronted by much larger guardian statues, which now bore the insignia of imperial chancellors for three generations. Above the south-facing doors, a proud sign proclaiming FAITHFUL AND FAR-SIGHTED JI in golden lettering. Golden lettering meant the hand of the emperor himself had been scrupulously reproduced. Fear and dread, Tai was certain, had caused this place to seem darker and more sinister in memory. But then the back areas would be dark, dug into the mountain; he distinctly remembered a guest chamber hung with old screens to hide that it had no windows. The servant rooms would no doubt be even smaller and closer.

The great nine-paneled silkscreen titled "Cygnet and the Swans" that had seemed so vast when Tai was young had apparently shrunk to the size of most fine nine-fold screens. He glanced at the graceful figure in white, who (he'd been told in insufferable detail when small) was the second wife of the first prince of Mountain Peony, whose daughter had married into the Jis; he was completely unaware of how many of her features had re-emerged in his own face.

First Uncle Ji—now prince and Left Chancellor to the imperial court—was much grayer now, resembling his departed father as he welcomed the Je family from just within the outer gate. He would only come all the way out to the street for royalty above the third rank.

There behind him were all the cousins, lined up with a respectful distance behind First Cousin Venshai—who, Tai was startled to discover—was half a head shorter than he was. He couldn't be any taller than Ki Mek! Though he looked imposing enough in his ducal scarlet (proclaiming him as a fourth ranker) imperial court robe with the insignia of the Censorate. His brothers wore green, and that had to be Lekshai—as a paternal first cousin to the prince's sons—in blue. He was the tallest, though lowest of the nine ranks.

The brothers were all moon-faced, still difficult to tell apart. Tai hoped he would not see enough of them to discern the differences. No one from the third and fourth houses was there; that was a blessing, as those cousins all did what Venshai told them.

Cousin Venshai advanced with words of welcome echoing his father's, followed by his second and third brothers: Kandashai, who shared his mother with Venshai; and Torshai, whose mother was the Prince's second consort. At Torshai's shoulder, Lekshai. These four, once the menacing gang that had made Tai's life a painful misery whenever they got him alone. Tai's muscles unconsciously tightened to readiness; he did not at all want a brawl, especially in the middle of the greeting hall, but he was ready for it if it came.

Waha, walking correctly behind Tai, noticed with mounting interest how the duke, heir to a princedom, gazed in round-eyed, jaw-dropped shock at Tai. It was only a heartbeat's naked expression, then his moon-shaped, pleasant-featured face smoothed to welcome. Waha's interest sharpened at the speed of that smothered expression, as the elders carried on with mutual compliments and self-deprecations, a ritual dance complete with stately bows and gestures with long, silken sleeves.

Hot, fragrant rice wine was brought out, consumed after many mutual toasts, and refreshments offered and refused—everyone knew that they would be momentarily sitting down to an enormous meal.

Finally the prince said to Magistrate Je, "Sadly, these gray hairs on my head only multiply with each passing year, and it must be an early night."

Thus reminding everyone that the imperial courtiers of the first five ranks must be kneeling outside the Tan Dynasty's ancestral hall when the emperor returned from his night's vigil at the imperial graves.

The prince indicated Venshai, who of course, as duke and heir, would be accompanying him. "On our return we shall make up for our neglect. I believe my son has arranged many delights for the younger generation, while you and I, dear cousin, try one another at Circle, and amuse ourselves with our brushes in a more sedate manner. I always learn from you."

"Too kind, too kind, your highness, but I fear my skills have never gone beyond the mediocre," said Tai's father.

"No, no, you must continue to address me as Cousin. After all, we are still family, and our respective merits reflect on us all." Their exchanges had been much the same when Tai was young, the prince pretending modesty and deference in a genial way, and Tai's father filial in actual deference, too slow and reflective to be seen as obsequious.

Then, a variation in the old pattern: "My grandfather, may he look down on us in blessing, would be so pleased to see all his progeny gathered under his poor roof, including your son returned to us, healthy and happy!"

Here the cups were raised in toast to Tai, who bowed his thanks as Waha took in how those male cousins in their beautifully embroidered layers of silk shouted in agreement, and dashed off their cups, led by the young duke in scarlet.

The household steward glided in to whisper to the prince, who smiled broadly and pointed the way toward the dining chamber, his long sleeve nearly brushing the tops of his embroidered shoes.

"I trust you will grace our poor meal with your esteemed presence, and forgive any lapses..."

Much later, after the sumptuous meal that boasted five times the dishes and decorations that Madam Je had offered at her banquet in honor of her son's safe return—golden dishes bearing expensive delicacies named after the Heavenly Houses—and a short play often seen at this time of year, everyone retired so that the prince and his son could catch a few brief hours of rest before shivering their way to await the emperor at his ancestral hall.

Waha, as servant-bodyguard, was alone with Tai. Once he'd thoroughly examined the chamber for peepholes or hidden doors, he said, "The play was interesting, but the best entertainment of the night was the looks on the faces of your high-born cousins when they first laid eyes on you."

By habit, Tai was reluctant to admit to any of his dread. Then he considered Waha, who was so very observant, and said with some hesitancy, "When I was small, they used to torment me for their own amusement. To remind me of my subordinate position."

Waha was neither pitying nor scornful. He said mildly, "Probably to be expected from a litter of cubs raised to think too highly of themselves, at the age of what, ten or twelve? How old were you?"

"It began when I was six, and first allowed out of the nursery. Venshai was ten, yes."

Waha uttered a laugh. "It's the same sort of thing in the West. Perhaps more so, as it's strongly encouraged. The idea being to make them tough enough to survive the dueling ring. Though I must say, these young hounds' welcome was friendly enough."

"I don't trust them," Tai stated—which was for him loquacious.

"You made that very clear. Hai-hum, not in words, no, I don't want to imply that. It was your stance." Waha's appreciative smile widened. "I think you startled them. Made them wary, anyway, if only instinctively. Though I must admit it would be fun to see them try such tricks now."

However, there was no more lurking outside the dark guest wing in order to pounce on the hapless visitor.

In Venshai's view, those long ago attentions had been entirely for Cousin Tai's benefit, for he'd been maddeningly stubborn, refusing to defer, flatter, and follow. That was simply fate—he'd been born to the secondary family, so it was his place to serve.

Venshai had let his temper go in trying to kick and thump the lesson into Tai, but since the latter's disappearance, he had long since abandoned such tactics. That sort of thing could be left to the rabble. It was unbecoming to his rank. Only Lekshai had a taste for bruises and bloodshed, but the elders had curbed that tendency with many, many hours of kneeling at the ancestral shrine—after beatings more vigorous than any Lekshai had dealt out. Ji Family Law was strict. Now Lekshai was an official in the Court of Justice, where he could put his passions to use for the good of the empire.

On hearing the news of Je Tai's survival after all these years, Venshai had arranged a week of far more subtle plans to convince Tai (should he prove to be as stubborn as he'd been as a boy) of the wisdom of bowing to the necessities of natural hierarchy.

He experienced the first setback on the arrival of the Je family, and he looked up at a Cousin Tai grown surprisingly tall. Tai was still slim, but no longer the weedy Little Lamb stumbling over his own feet. He was also startlingly handsome, though dressed modestly. Except for that headband. But even that was modest, and Venshai remembered what it had to cover: the Ghost-Eyes' slave tattoo.

Tai was silent, apparently content to sit a little behind his father all during the banqueting, and through the following day of New Year's rituals sweeping out the bad luck lingering from a Pig Year and lighting fresh fires to welcome a Rat Year. Venshai's brothers and cousin, his chief support, reported no sign of him while the prince and his son were waiting upon the emperor. Apparently he sat in his guest chamber and read.

"Father," Venshai said smoothly, on the third day of the Je family's visit. Now that official duties were over for the festival week, he appeared splendid in black brocade with patterns of three-clawed firedragons climbing like flickering flames over the sleeves and up front and back. His hair clasp was dotted with rubies. "Shall we entertain our newly returned cousin today by taking a little exercise?"

"Excellent idea, my son," the prince said genially. "Young men needn't sit here watching us old men linger over the Circle table. You must always remember that, should dire circumstances rise and there is a call to defend the empire, the emperor—" Here a pious clasp of the hand in the direction of the imperial palace. "—will turn to you young men of rank first."

Thus, brimming with gratification (and anticipation), Venshai led the way out to the stable yard, which was kept lower down, below the residence wings, to avoid the smell.

Magistrate Je was known for his refusal to adopt

extravagant ways, such as keeping horses, which were of little utility in the mountains. Horses, in the imperial capital, were entirely a noble extravagance. Ten years ago, Venshai and his brothers and cousin had relished taking Tai out to "teach him riding." How he had bleated before the inevitable fall! That had resulted in his name among them: Little Lamb.

When they arrived, Venshai stole a look Cousin Tai's way, just to confront that same stolid, stubborn stone face the exasperating demon-spawn had worn as a boy. "Here, Cousin Tai," he said. "Try Plum. She's the gentlest of the mares."

Plum truly was gentle — to riders she knew. And when there was no distraction. Tai swung up into the saddle with such ease that Venshai blinked. Gone was the lamb, not so little. More like a buck, ready to charge; when on signal Lekshai sneezed suddenly, then flapped his sleeves, Plum tossed her head and sidled, but Tai kept her well in hand as they proceeded up a winding trail between the high walls of courtly mansions. One they reached the back ridge, with diminishing hope Venshai suggested a gallop, to discover that Tai had in the intervening years learned to ride well on difficult terrain.

Did the Ghost Eyes teach slaves how to ride? Venshai knew that in the long-ago past they'd brought to the empire a lot of barbarian customs, while roaming around far in the north, living in tents.

He was going to have to find out — though he'd promised his father not to raise the humiliating issue of slavery, lest it discommode Magistrate Je.

Now expecting another setback, Lekshai suggested they do some riding and shooting. During childhood, archery had been a sure cause for laughter. Once Tai even snapped the string in his face, when trying to string a bow. But now, as with the riding, he handled a bow with a familiarity that foretold what was going to happen. He wasn't a perfect shot — from his squint he was short-sighted, like both Lekshai and Torshai — but he was better than any of them — who'd had scant practice ever since they'd assumed imperial court dress.

They rode back, the talk determinedly light, on every subject but riding.

When they retired to change, Venshai caught his sister outside the conservatory, and said, "When we entertain the maternal cousins tomorrow, I want you to bring up Cousin Tai's slavery — "

"I won't," she said bluntly.

"Why not?"

"Because Father told us not to, which is why you are trying to push it off onto me," she stated.

She was getting to be as blunt as Cousin Lei, he thought impatiently.

"So? Grandmother won't let Father even scold you. Either of you," he added, still thinking of Cousin Lei, who at sixteen, and the image of the famous, scholarly Princess Cygnet, could be the beauty of the imperial court, except she stubbornly spent all her time with tutors, preparing for the imperial examination, without demonstrating a vestige of the ambition to marry high, which would bring credit to the primary family whose forebears had graced her with that face. What a maddening family!

Qishai said, "I think it might be interesting to find out what life was like among the Westerners, but I won't ask. Cousin LeiLei says that her brother hates talking about it. And who *would* want to talk about being made a slave?" She turned away, leaving Venshai annoyed—she'd been a lot more biddable when she was small. But she was the only girl of rank Venshai could get to speak well of him before the princess, so he let it go.

There was always Lekshai—and a way that wasn't as direct.

The next day—the day before they were all supposed to go to the imperial palace to make their bows to the imperial princess—an opera company had been summoned to entertain the younger generation, which included all the cousins from the minor houses, and maternal cousins whom Venshai rarely troubled himself with. Still, he graced the gathering in silvery-mauve brocade decorated with long-tailed swallows and white fringe-flower.

The opera was a traditional one often brought out for New Year's Two Moons. They all had seen it, and Venshai knew there was a ponderous joke coming up that made a play on words at the expense of the barbarians to the west.

After the scene ended, Venshai signaled Lekshai with a glance.

Obediently, Lekshai leaned toward Tai to say loudly, "Did you know that?"

Tai—who had read the play the opera was based on when he was small—said, "Doesn't everyone know this play?"

"I meant the joke about the Ghost-Eyes' word for hair sounding like mare."

"Yes. I understood it when my tutor explained it to me," Tai said flatly.

At a sharp nudge from Venshai, Lekshai said, "Can you speak the Westerners' demon tongue?"

"Yes."

And then the maternal cousin Venshai had bribed said, "Were you really a slave to the Westerners?"

Tai turned his way. "Yes."

Lekshai scoffed. "Prove it. Say something barbaric."

"They have their own slang for four-eyed rats," Tai said in the Western tongue, which elicited a muffled snort from Waha, which he turned into a cough as he stared woodenly straight before him.

No one noticed because Second Brother Kandashai spoke at that moment, his brow perplexed. "I almost understood that. Sounds northern, doesn't it? Related, yes?"

"The languages are related long ago," Tai said. "Or so I was told."

Torshai caught Venshai's glance, and said awkwardly, "Did you really get a slave tattoo? Isn't that for life?"

"But…I was told that there are terrible Essence charms in their tattoos," protested a girl cousin. "Something about poisoning the blood."

"Is that why you wear a headband?" Three of the maternal cousins were part of the playboy poetry circles, sporting headbands extravagantly embroidered with flowers associated with romance, but Tai's was modestly embroidered with small peace knots.

"He's hiding it!"

"Let's see it!"

A clamor of voices rose. Tai was furious, but decided that to refuse would be to hand Venshai (because he was surely behind this interrogation) a weapon.

Tai slipped off his headband. There was the tiger eye for all to see, the central character dominated by a wicked, slashing curve resembling a fierce feline eye.

"That…can't be a slave tattoo."

"It isn't. Or, it's there, but beneath. I had it changed."

He most certainly had! As they stared at that tattoo above those long phoenix eyes that glittered like obsidian, suddenly everyone…wanted one.

Tai stated in that emotionless voice, "And, yes there was a charm. But Ki Mek, the boy I was imprisoned with, secretly figured out how to remove it before we escaped."

Escaped! This was no menial groveling, humiliating to admit to. "Escape"—and from a death-curse tattoo—suggested courage and dash! Yet Tai could not be lying. For one thing, he'd never been known to lie, and for another, he was here, not there. No one just let slaves go.

Venshai suppressed a groan at the way Kandashai—even Lekshai looked impressed. Fascinated.

He raised his voice. "I promised his highness my father that we would not harass Cousin Je Tai about that terrible occurrence. Look, the scene's been changed. Let's resume the opera." And he waved at the musicians, who along with the players, were quietly waiting for the nobles to finish their conversation.

The opera proceeded without further interruption, the dancers following them performed beautifully as an unending stream of delicacies appeared and disappeared, and then the minor cousins climbed into waiting carts under lazily drifting snowflakes and trundled home, dazzled by the Ji family largesse—but full of tales of the phoenix-eyed cousin who had escaped slavery in the West.

Late that night, Venshai was summoned to his father's inner chamber. Rarely a good omen.

Venshai bowed low, and remained bent as his father dipped his brush and carefully inscribed a few words. Yes, definitely displeased.

Finally he said with a soft sigh, "Sit down. And enlighten me with an explanation for why you not only acted counter to my orders, but today, when every pair of ears in court was present—no doubt carrying tales at this moment."

"*I* was not the one who brought up slavery," Venshai began.

His father shot him a weary glance that choked off the excuse. "My third brother's boy doesn't piss without your permission." The prince was rarely rude, unless seriously irate.

Venshai quickly amended his excuse. "It was oblique. Meant to—"

"Meant to humiliate Cousin Je's boy, which I specifically instructed you *not* to do. With the result that he is no doubt lighting incense at this moment, cursing your name. Thereby undoing all my hard word at propitiating his father."

Venshai stared at this; the prince, ordinarily reluctant to utter anything but courtly pleasantry and flattery, was moved enough to say, "You may laugh at Magistrate Je Pan for his threadbare robes and his slow, maundering speech even when asked what the weather is like, but what you don't seem to have grasped yet is that that reputation for frugality comes of his living strictly on the meager pay of a magistrate. He has never taken the smallest bribe. And I've tested him. So have the imperial ferrets, I imagine."

This reminder of those secretive figures around the emperor sent chill through Venshai's meridians. As near as he and his father were to the imperial family, through constant striving, they still had absolutely no access to the ferrets. The only time they saw their chief was in rare imperial interviews when punishment was in the offing. Never a good time to be staring.

"That reputation for probity," the prince went on, "is in its way a stronger foundation for our family than all our wealth combined. It is exactly this that I trust will ease the House of Ji onto the throne without causing a ripple. I don't want rebellion within the family, Venshai," the prince stated, his voice rasping. "We can't afford it, for so many reasons. You are to court Je Tai, and undo as much of the damage you young idiots caused as you can."

And here he glanced at the window. The precious window. A common enough item of architecture over on Tiger Island, where their estate spread over their land, bisected by charming gardens, but here in the capital a very rare commodity.

Venshai began picking at the exquisite embroidery on his robe, plucking the threads until they shed stray strands that would take days to repair. "That was Lekshai," he muttered, head bowed. "I never did anything more than light slaps. My kicks barely—"

"Son." The prince put thumb and forefinger to his brow. "Please do me the honor to respect what brains the interminable stresses of government leave me. Lekshai is a cudgel, but yours has been the hand wielding it. Lekshai is not to go near Je Tai. Make that clear. I want to see Je Tai smiling when the Jes depart."

"I will do my best, Father," Venshai promised, bowing low again. "But Father, I was just speaking to QiQi, and the way she talked about him—just a mention—anyway, what I feel certain is, the way Je Tai looks now, I don't think we ought to introduce him to the imperial princess tomorrow. You know her penchant for handsome players."

"I already thought of that," the prince said, waving his brush. "But I'm glad to see you thinking ahead for once. No, the imperial princess need not meet that boy, who takes after his grandfather on his mother's side. Ayah! Just today the governor of eastern province sent a pigeon to the Imperial Guard, naming Je Tai as this year's Hero for the Fire Wishes dragon battle."

Venshai suppressed a scowl. There had been a time when he had wanted to be picked, but despite some hints, and some stiff bribes, it had never happened.

"Just as well that though he looks like the dashing Flying Tiger General Han Zeg of your grandfather's day, that boy's character is exactly like his father's. Our eyes at the Je house say that he studies all his free time, except when he runs off somewhere with that bodyguard he brought back, apparently a disgraced soldier connected to the Ryus. The two come back disheveled, leading to the conclusion they are trysting."

Relief surged through Venshai. If Cousin Tai liked the boys, he would not look twice at the imperial princess, whose beauty resembled the gorgeous Sixth Imperial Consort, her mother. He said, "Should we make certain he goes back to the augurs at White Jade for more study? That would get him away until next year. People will forget about him."

"I thought of that," said the prince. "But then he would come back to test next year, and he'd surely win the kingfisher feather, as his father did in his day. Those Jes have formidable memories. If he were to win first place, that would put him directly before the imperial family, and open too many doors I intend remain closed until we can trust him to follow orders obediently, for the family's greater good. Do. Not. Lose sight of our plans."

Venshai bowed.

"Therefore. I want you to see to a special appointment in the archives for your Cousin Tai. Take this as an assignment, to make up for your blunders today. As well he likes augury. We'll bury him safely there until we need him. Full flattery—a special title—make it sound good to his father. I will endorse the appointment, and get them an imperial pardon from the requirement to take the imperial examination. The excuse will be an acknowledgment of all those years the boy lost."

"Which archive, Father? Surely not the imperial archives."

"Of course not. He studies augury, does he not? The divination archives down at White Jade are vast, what with daily observations going back every day since the beginning of the dynasty. Let him wallow happily there. But that's later. As for tomorrow, the imperial call will not be postponed. We cannot afford that. But I will send the Je family to visit their Han relations early. A compliment to the Hans. The Jes will be sent by us in the good carts, *both* of them. With hot wine and snacks. You see to it."

THIRTY-EIGHT

CUSTOMARILY, MAGISTRATE JE FINISHED out the family's duty visit to the Jis by calling on his wife's family before sailing for home. But the prince himself came to bow humbly and report that to his vast regret, an imperial command had circumvented their domestic plans, and as a chancellor, the prince must put the emperor's requirements above his own. And would his esteemed cousin care to make an immediate to the esteemed Hans?

To underscore the prince's deepest shame at being denied a day of enlightenment from his cousin's wise company by cutting their visit short, his son had offered to make it his personal business to arrange transport as comfortable as possible from their meager resources, aboard his own vessel…

There was much more, and Magistrate Je bowed his thanks, not saying that he would have accepted at once, saving so *very* many words.

The Han family's rank was beneath the notice of the lofty Jis, so Magistrate Je was charged to carry greetings and wishes for peace and abundance in the new year. Madam Je, Han Chui at birth, was delighted to see her maiden family. Tai and Lei were welcomed among their Han cousins, crowded into a modest home with only a single bank of west-facing windows. Their chief treasure was the fading painting of Kang Cygnet, whose eldest daughter had inherited her famous school for both boys and girls after her mother married Mountain Peony's first prince and was elevated to princess. Kang Cygnet looked down with a smile, one hand holding a scroll, and the other a willow wand, symbol of Suanek.

Madam Han presided over a banquet in honor of her esteemed Je in-laws, and she gave her Je grandchildren a great deal of advice that Tai and Lei knew was well meant.

In short, there was much good cheer among these Han relations, but late in the afternoon, Lei appeared at Tai's side, where he was idly watching some cousins playing pitch pot. "Great-Aunt Han wants to see us."

Great-Aunt Han had been a geomancer connected to the Departments of Rites and of Works, this latter requiring geomancers to do their divination and charms before any building project was put in motion. She was the one whose influence had put Tai in the studies of augury, so he owed her a debt of gratitude.

Great-aunt and great-nephew and niece greeted one another with interest as well as genuine affection. "I was very sorry to hear what had happened, but Suanek blessed us in guiding you safely back!" After he bowed his thanks, she said briskly, "Now, how much do you remember of your studies?"

This question sparked a lengthy discussion of all Tai had been reviewing and pondering.

At the end, she clasped her hands. "Ayah, my dear boy, you truly have the memory of a qilin. Like your father. If you wish, I could write to the third secretary over at Rites, who is connected to us. She would be able to get you an interview if you wish to sit down to the departmental test this spring. Or do you intend to sit to the imperial examination, and try for a position elsewhere in court?"

Tai bowed his thanks once again, then said, "This ignorant student wishes to observe that he is not ungrateful..."

Great-Aunt Han pressed Tai's hand between her warm palms. "Dear boy, speak your mind. Have you settled on following the divination path?"

"I have not. It's...the *Book of Wisdom*," he admitted. "That is, I have no quarrel with the mechanics of divination. We look for elements of fortune and interpret like signs for each item in a query: this pattern in the sticks points to earth, your possible wife's birth is under the influence of earth. Fire can produce earth, as earth can multiply wood, and as you each carry signs of fire and wood, the whole means the heavens see this union, in this life, as auspicious. That is straightforward. Yet..." He was not quite certain how to express his still-amorphous doubts.

"Straightforward, yes, but still only a part of the whole, for we cannot truly see past today, is it this that causes your hesitation? There are the auspicious signs, but that does not *necessitate* a harmonious union?"

"In a sense..."

"That question, I assure you, is very common. Or is there more?"

Tai bowed. "I know that all order is sublime; as Kanda said, it is we who are imperfect. But when the last portion of the book—the part for the student who is approaching the final test—talks of training us how to speak, and describes how to convey the reading, ay-yah! I know it is my own shortcoming, but it reminds me of something my fellow student said earlier this winter."

"Fellow student? I thought you had not been able to study."

"I did, but informally. With one other student. Han Anise—no, no relation to us, her Han is said in the Cloud Above tone." His finger sketched in the air.

"Not our Earth-root tone." Their venerable great-aunt tranquilly made the familiar character for her own Han family. "No connection. Very well. Go on."

"Her mother was an island augur, and she'd begun to teach Anise outright falsities as well as the fundamentals, and a lot of trickery meant to uncover what the seeker wants to hear..." He fumbled a description of Anise's mother's deceit, and how in the course of teaching Anise the proper fundamentals he had occasion to review all his knowledge quite thoroughly, then he said in a low voice, "I realize that what the *Book of Wisdom* teaches is to enlighten the ignorant, but there were, are, aspects that keep reminding me of what this distant Madam Han does. Which sounds like telling the wealthy what they want to hear, but enough to keep them coming back. The warnings..."

To his surprise, his great-aunt—so very respected—rocked back and forth, her face wrinkled in smile lines of mirth. Then she said, "In short, the *Book of Wisdom* teaches augurs how to divine for kings and emperors and not get themselves executed while expressing divinations that royal ears might not like hearing."

"Is that it?" Tai said. "The aim is diplomacy, not falsity?"

"Indeed. But. Make no doubt. There *is* room for falsity, if you are looking for it. You've only to review your history. I'm certain you learned all about Ban Erno the Traitor and his miserable end when the first Kun Dynasty was coming to its own end. No doubt hastened by him and his greed."

"I remember."

"You want divination to be pure. So do we all," she said. "Purity is virtue, mirroring the Jade Emperor's own world in the vast realm above. But that is a world of divine beings, who *can* be pure. We humans aren't, as you said before. The best we can do is strive for virtue. Once I would have said that of all the branches of the Departments of Rites, ours in geomancy was the purest, as we geomancers only acted in nature..." She paused then, looking away for a very long time, long enough for Lei and Tai to exchange glances. Was she suffering a syncope?

No, she sat unmoving, gazing into the distance, then straightened up, and her tone altered, her words brisk. "Our Essence studies are steeped in the truth found in nature, beginning with the fact that wood — paper — charms are easiest, air and fire hardest, but you know all that, even if you don't work with Essence. Forgive the ramblings of the old, my dears. We talk too much about ourselves, for we want to be remembered as we were in work and life, and not dwindle to mere names to those who come after! I haven't even asked you where lies *your* interest, if you are apprehensive about working with the imperial augurs."

"I'm not certain," Tai said, bewildered by that sudden alteration, but one did not interrogate one's elders. "However, first I must concentrate on doing well at the imperial examination."

"Indeed so!"

The interview came to a close a short time later, after their great-aunt inquired into Lei's studies, then pronounced herself very satisfied with them both.

They returned to a final day of music, opera, and constant streams of delectable food at the Ji mansion, during which the male cousins seemed to be vying with one another to flatter and please Tai, as if he were the duke and Venshai the lowly cousin. Venshai even troubled himself to arrange for handsome male dancers as well as the usual band of female dancers the Jis were used to hiring for their entertainments.

The result?

"Did *you* see him looking at the Gray Crane boys dancing?" Venshai asked later.

His brothers both shook their heads, and Lekshai muttered, "He gave them the same face he gave the Lotus Bud girls. Our favorites! It's like he's made of bamboo."

"At least he'll be gone tomorrow," Kandashai offered.

"For now," Venshai muttered, turning to Torshai, as Lekshai—as usual—completely missed the import of his remark, and began scheming for a sure way to have some fun, and win merit.

As for Tai, at first he saw mockery in the flattery and deference. Surely he was being set up for some elaborate ruse. He never relaxed his vigilance until at last it was time for their departure—not crowding onto another crowded three-decker with the many other festival travelers going home, but a gorgeously appointed yacht.

Delightful as that journey was, they all were relieved to arrive home again, to simple food, and quiet rooms, except when Tai and Waha slipped out for their martial arts sparring—until Magistrate Je, having cogitated through a couple of days, called the family together, and informed his son in his ponderous way that if Tai was to perform creditably at this unwanted honor, he must begin preparing for the Hero dance.

His mother took it upon herself to oversee the making of the traditional Hero costume, though it would only be worn the once, for there was a different Hero every year.

Waha later said, "I think I'd better run with your heroes. There must be some way to arrange it."

"You believe there's a need?" Tai asked in surprise. "I'm supposed to have a company of selected imperial guards."

Waha, far more experienced in assessing potential danger in complicated situations, had over New Year's Week assumed the blank face of stolid stupidity that had been his armor back in his mining days whenever he encountered Boss Tangat and his corrupt, greedy assistant. This worked with the Jis, who were accustomed to ignoring their servants as long as they stayed silent and out of the way. He'd thus been able to observe the Ji family without them paying him any heed.

To Waha, gangs invariably took on a gang personality as well as individual characteristics. He had learned that under Diggy's leadership, Crew Six was very different from Crew One. But they could have been a lot like Crew One, if Diggy had been like Crew One's leader.

"I think that the one cousin who likes blood is not done with you, even if the rest of them have backed off. He asked too many questions about that festival. Doesn't he have connections through the Court of Justice?"

Tai considered that. "Yes. I guess that would enable him to tamper with the imperial guards in some way. I'll insist you go with me, then."

After that, they ran together each day, and Madam Je — who very much approved of a bodyguard at her precious son's side — directed one of her maids to make a costume resembling the ones the imperial guardsmen would wear.

Hard winter had settled in, making the month seem endless, especially when Tai and Waha toiled through ice, slush, and mud, though knowing that the day of the festival there would be an army of laborers under the governor's command sweeping the streets. But Tai thought the extra toil would make him hardier.

A handful of days before Fire Wishes Day, there was a brief thaw. Tai was obligated to accompany his family to a wedding of another magistrate's son, so Waha used the opportunity to pace the firedragon's course. The firedragon parade always began at the governor's palace, rounded through the two main streets — one above the other — and ended up back at the governor's, where all would be rewarded with a fine banquet and endless hot rice wine.

When Tai returned from the wedding, Waha reported what he'd done, ending, "There are two places I'd look for an attack. The first is that sharp curve where the upper street bends to lead to the lower. There are no houses, and the cedars grow very close to the road. Anything could be hidden there."

Tai shook his head. "It looks that way now, but by the time of the festival, there will be lanterns on poles, and guards every few paces. At least, they were always there when I was a boy."

"We'll assume no change, then." Waha dipped his head. "The other place has the opposite problem: the crowd. That big, three-story inn directly off the quay seems to be a popular entertainment house. The crowd was thick in front of it today, in spite of the falling snow. Lots of foot traffic to and from the ships in harbor. It would be easy to dart out of that crowd, attack, and vanish among the people."

Tai nodded soberly. "We might be winded from the run by then, too. That seems a good time to attack, doesn't it? Yes, let's be vigilant." And he decided, late as it was, to go out for another practice run.

The day before the festival day dawned. Magistrate Je and his family accompanied Tai to the governor's palace, where he was expected to rehearse with the dragon-players, and then to spend the night as the governor's guest.

After many bows and mutual compliments exchanged with the governor's wife, Magistrate and Madam Je withdrew to await the morrow. Tai and Waha were escorted to the back court, where Tai was introduced to the two men who had been playing the dragon head for the past few years, one guiding the head, and the other, behind him, manipulating the claws, which were bamboo poles which protruded from inside the head on pulleys.

"It's very simple," the older man explained. "You're running back and forth in front of us, see, then we stop and do up a mock fight at the stations."

"Stations?" Tai asked.

"The musicians. They can't run *and* play, so we've got musicians in threes—drum, gong, and suona—posted along the route, some on the upper street, and some below. When we reach the next three, that's when we stop and the Hero fights off the dragon's claws with his bamboo spear. Then we run on."

By now the imperial guards had arrived from the capital. To them this festival was a lark.

The entire company gathered in their lines, and did a sort of rehearsal around the governor's forecourt. Tai found he was expected to run back and forth before the dragon, which undulated behind. The dragon head tossed and swayed, hundreds of streamers of crimson and yellow fluttering in the air. The dragon forearms and talons clawed the air, and Tai learned how to swing his bamboo spear at each arm and smite it lightly, twirl around as if he'd been struck away, then smite again. A few exchanges like this, then they ran on again.

"That's it, that's it," came the muffled voice of one of the dragon head players. "Big movements, so that everyone at the back of the crowd can see. The gong players will strike every time the spear touches the dragon's arm, the drum pounds, the suona screeches, and we sound like a thunder of dragons!"

They practiced until everyone was summoned to a meal.

They ate, drank, toasted one another and then everyone but Tai retired to a space made for them in the governor's barracks, where further drink appeared. Tai was given a guest chamber above. He refused any more drink, choosing to sit out on the balcony with his cloak wrapped around him as he studied the winter stars. Oh, how he loved the familiar winter-night sky in its proper place!

The next day, they gathered early, this time wearing their costumes. Tai was glad he'd had all that rehearsal time when he had to put on his painted Hero mask, which severely limited his vision, sometimes by the wind playing with his crimson-dyed feather headdress and blowing the feathers in his face.

Waha vanished among the imperial guards, all wearing costumes of black garments under green-and-scarlet tunics.

Another careful run-through in the courtyard preceded a fine banquet, then the governor came down to wish them good luck, and before they knew it, the sun had vanished behind the mountain at the estate's back.

The moons, playing hide and seek behind ghostly clouds, were near the full, a finger's breadth between them, one sliding up and one sliding down. The air had gotten much colder, so that breathing out seemed like smoke. The slush had turned to ice, diligently crushed and swept, the tiled street spread with a thin layer of sand by the city patrol.

Everyone was laughing and calling until a gong crashed. The dragon men formed up, hidden under the long, bright crimson dragon back, and the imperial guardsmen jogged up in a disciplined line on either side of the dragon. Tai looked searchingly at these, wondering who and how many might be Ji Lekshai's hirelings, until Waha slipped up to his side. "I've sounded them last night. None of these are suspect, unless they are really adept at hiding intent—they all look down on the Court of Justice guards."

Tai barely had time to feel relieved, then it was time to go.

He was very glad of all his practice as he raced back and forth in front of the dragon's head. The first stop and battle were jerky and awkward, but by the second he caught the rhythm, and excitement rose as their feet pounded the ground, the suonas screeled, the drums and gongs crashed. Loud as they were, the sound was nearly drowned by the crowd lining both sides of the upper street. Little children ran alongside in spurts, falling away as the dragon and the heroes rounded the steep curve toward the lower street.

The trouble, when it came, nearly caught Tai by surprise. He was so focused on the rhythm that at first he didn't understand why the guards shrouded entirely in black loomed up at him, waving…real weapons?

Waha appeared out of the imperial guards, laughter soft and anticipatory. Here at last was the challenge that would ignite Tai's slumbering dragon! Together the two of them whirled into long-practiced defense, each guarding the other's back.

The imperial guards, caught at first utterly by surprise, had milled about as they tried to figure out whether this was a part of the parade's mock-fight, until an eager attacker managed to rip Tai's mask entirely free before Tai dropped the useless bamboo spear and leaped up in a whirling kick, sending the attacker sprawling on the sandy, icy ground.

A bellow of authority roared from the back of the imperial guards, who obeyed instantly, converging—or trying—on the attackers. These latter began to scuttle in all directions, as some of the spectators rushed forward either to help or just to see better, getting into everyone's way. Most of the assailants dove into the crowd, bundling their black cloaks and masks under their arms. Several of the assailants lost their heads entirely and ran in the wrong direction until the imperial guards rounded them up and then vanished with them back up toward the governor's mansion.

That left Tai standing alone in the street, his mask crushed by many feet.

"Keep going," a voice urged in a hoarse whisper from the dragon.

Tai began to run again, the icy air cooling his sweaty cheeks. The dragon, which had hitched to an awkward stop, immediately began to move. The dragon's back swiftly caught their rhythm again, and the parade—cheered ever more loudly—picked up its pace, resuming the dance until they reached the end of the street. One last, quick dragon fight, then they and filed up the guarded road to the governor's palace again, where everyone began shouting at once, "What happened?" "Are you hurt?" "Who were those people in black?"

"I don't know," Tai said, when faces turned his way.

That was all they had time for. The governor then appeared,

with a swarm of his own guards. His anxious face cleared when he saw Tai. Once again, that strange, strained sense of underlying tension gripped Tai as the man—so calm and dignified yesterday—barked questions, repeating them as if he could not yet grasp the spoken answers.

Then the guards escorted the players off toward their promised feast, and Tai was accompanied—by more guards—to the palace, the governor at his side.

The next morning, he was smilingly dismissed, accompanied to the front door by the governor's wife. He bowed himself out.

At the same time, up in the interview chamber, the governor listened to a report from his guard captain, "...we kept them separately locked up, no food or water. They were ready enough to talk by this morning. All told the same story, it was meant to be a jest, a test for fast entry to the Court of Justice guards." And as the governor's face flushed with fury, the captain lowered his voice, adding, "As to who sent them, they spoke the same name: Ji Lekshai."

The governor paled at that. No one willingly caused trouble for the powerful Ji family. After a long moment's thought, he said, "Any other names mentioned?"

"None, sir," the captain replied, with an air of question.

That question was not answered. The governor gave orders to send the miserable miscreants off to the capital to be dealt with there, and he retired to his own wing, where his wife said, "Who *was* that you were guarding so closely?"

She pointed toward the main street.

The governor turned strained eyes to his wife. "If you want our heads to remain on our necks, don't ask. Don't say anything at all."

THIRTY-NINE

As COURIER PIGEONS WHIRRED through the air in all directions, Tai and Waha took back alleys down to Je House. "You were right," he said to Waha. "That had to be Ji Lekshai behind that scuffle."

"Did you notice that the imperials caught a handful of them?" Waha chuckled. "Hai-yoo, we ought to send thanks after them for giving us a bit of brisk exercise." He chuckled again.

Tai responded absently, "There's a different Hero every year. At least it's done. "His tone firmed. "Now, nothing is going to get in the way of my studies."

Tai was welcomed home, and went to his chamber, where he stood looking at his table, his brushes, papers, scrolls and inks. He unlocked his lacquered cabinet, and became so absorbed in expressing his disgust with the Ji family that he failed to note Waha's soundless entrance with the baggage.

When he'd stowed things, Waha stood silently, looking at that glossy bent head with a sense of weary disappointment. Ever since that splendid dust-up in the street, he'd been assuming that it would be the first of many encounters to come. Waha had envisioned the two of them setting out in the gallant wanderer world, leaving legends behind them. And if their partnership became intimate, even better!

But that was mere dream. The reality was that Tai had finally found the life he wanted. There was no changing him, any more than one changed a diamond to obsidian, as they said in the West. Or, as he'd heard here in the east, wisdom was learning when to stop trying to cook with a cold cauldron.

Though Je Tai was young, strong, handsome as the Cloud Horse King, he just wanted to close himself up with that pile of old scrolls.

Waha saw himself extraneous in this resolutely unheroic family; though he'd begun to teach the beautiful daughter some martial fundamentals when Je Tai was at social events, it was an idle pursuit, for she was even less martial than her brother — and as impervious to flirtation.

Waha decided ruefully that Je Tai's fire mountain was not likely to explode in this lifetime. It was time to think about a new road.

The imperial guard company returned to the capital bearing their morose captives.

Because these were emphatic that they had been hired by a Ji, the matter had to be handed off to a higher-up. No one wanted to interfere with anything having to do with the Left Chancellor. The hirelings were given ten strokes apiece and kicked out of the capital, with warnings never to be seen again echoing in their ears.

Ji Lekshai didn't fare much better in his interview with the prince, despite his protest that his orders to his hirelings had been strict: not to *harm* Je Tai, just to humiliate him a little. And maybe to cut up his face a bit, to solve the problem of Je Tai being too handsome for his own good.

The prince narrowed his eyes, which made Lekshai drop forehead to the floor, and his own father — standing in the background — had to lock his knees at the rigidity in his elder brother's countenance.

"The only reason," the prince said precisely, "that you are not in prison now is because of the respect that is held for our name. A respect that you have now tarnished." And he held out his hand for the rod kept for administering the Ji Family Rules.

A short, painful time later, Ji Lekshai slumped toward the ancestral hall to begin his latest vigil — not knowing (yet) that his career in the capital was at an end, and he would soon be posted far to the northwest to guard against Western incursions until his tarnish on the Ji name had been rubbed off.

"I trust that's the last of this foolishness," the prince said to Venshai afterward, when they were alone. "My question to you is, what have you learned about Je Tai's experiences when he escaped from the Ghost-Eyes?"

"Nothing," Venshai had to admit.

"Nothing," the prince repeated in dissatisfaction. "It seems that he got *some* kind of training. Serious training. He and that bodyguard succeeded in fighting off all Lekshai's rats before the imperial guards figured out that Lekshai's idiocy was not part of the festivities."

"Serious training," Venshai repeated gloomily. Did the Westerners really train their slaves in martial defense? But the reports all agreed, Je Tai had alone fought off several of the hirelings. That was all of a piece with Je Tai's ease with riding and shooting.

The prince went on, "When asked about it by the imperial guard captain, young Tai apparently told him that during his escape from slavery, he'd been caught in galley battles, and had to fight his way to freedom. *We ought to have known that! You ought to have known that! What did I tell you about family unity? Especially now? He should have confided in you! I blame you for that! How can this family attain the glory of imperial dynasty if we are not all united?"*

Venshai shrank under his father's terrible frown.

Then the prince sighed and pinched his brow. "At least there is no permanent harm done. There is something else that disturbs me far more: a report that the governor's own guards were not on hand. The governor had put most of his own guards 'elsewhere'."

"What does that mean?" Venshai asked. "What, or who, else were they guarding?"

"Near as my eyes there can discover, until Lekshai's fumblers appeared to mar the firedragon dance, nothing out of the ordinary had been reported. Other than areas of the palace and some inn being closed off by the governor's own guards. I find it difficult to believe that more than half of his guards were necessary to preserve his family from having to bump shoulders with carters and fish sellers. It's never been the case before. He likes to be seen—part of his effectiveness is accomplished by the esteem he is held in by his people."

Venshai whispered, "You don't think it was..." *Her?* He didn't dare give voice to the word even in this sanctuary.

They both considered the imperial princess, who had shown a tendency in the last year to like going out anonymously. But the protocol for imperial heirs was iron-rigid even when there weren't inexplicable...moods, whispered about third- and fourth-hand. If during one of these excursions her eye lit on a handsome man of rank—such as Je Tai—it was always possible that she—as the only child of the emperor, and the treasure of his eye—could influence her marriage negotiations. Especially as the Left Chancellor had managed to circumvent all likely candidates, so far.

Finally the prince turned a warning gaze on Venshai. "Je Tai *cannot* be in the imperial city taking the imperial examination. I gave you orders, I believe?"

Venshai had put off the trouble and expense of arranging a position for his irritating cousin. "Yes, Father."

Venshai left, his mood sour. He headed for Kandashai's chamber, where QiQi and Torshai were playing Circle, with Kandashai alternatively giving unwanted advice and painting the winter-bare branches outside the propped-open window.

Venshai walked unseeing around the perimeter of the chamber, then gave vent to his emotions by picking up Torshai's golden dish of carved Circle markers and flinging it violently at the wall.

He watched them scatter, then muttered with heartfelt venom, "If she did run off all the way to the other side of the island without leave, the emperor will just pat her on the head. As always. And the maddening thing is, we don't even know if she's actually his daughter."

The younger Jis looked around quickly, though Kandashai had waved out his servants the moment his brother turned up with that face full of dust and demons.

QiQi didn't like the Sixth Imperial Consort any more than her father did. Yimu Lily was notoriously rapacious, jealous, capricious, and greedy, insisting on her family being appointed to high positions without the least vestige of talent. But QiQi knew her brothers—though her elders by a year, Torshai and Kandashai believed any random thing Venshai might throw out in a temper. And speculation about the parentage of an imperial heir could get an entire family wiped out, all generations.

She said firmly, "The emperor believes Imperial Princess Lam is his daughter."

That sobered everyone.

Torshai began picking up the Circle pieces, as they all

contemplated the beautiful Imperial Crown Princess Lam.

So far, the emperor—whenever the subject of his daughter's marriage was brought up—insisted that imperial blood required royal blood. As Venshai's father had remarked wryly just last year, "Our one protection until our suit is favored is that the emperor appears to be in no hurry to arrange for a young and vigorous man to be stepping on his heels."

At that same time, high in the mountains traveling back toward the imperial palace, Imperial Princess Lam sat quietly in her sleigh as it hissed over the icy paths. The only person permitted to sit with her was Nanny Alk, who kept a copper bowl of coals within a ceramic pot on her lap, ready to warm one of her potions should it become necessary.

So far—though figuratively the entourage held its collective breath as they ran beside the sleigh—they weren't necessary. The princess sat peaceably enough, gloating at having slipped away and back again without her mother knowing and interfering. And oh, her secret journey had turned out better than she could have ever imagined. She'd been so sure that Je Lei's brother had to be as beautiful as she was, and she'd been very suspicious when the Ji family did not bring the Jes when summoned to the palace after the Near Year's Two Moons ritual.

She dwelt happily on that vivid image from the lamplit square below her inn window, the tall, martial figure fighting off the shadow demons, then—his mask gone—turning, his handsome face bared to the wind that blew back his long black hair. And in the center of his forehead, a tiger's eye.

That was a suitable prince consort, she thought.

If only he could somehow be made a prince.

Days passed in the monotony of study, martial arts, and Madam Je's determined search for a suitable wife for Tai, until change happened.

It occurred midway between the Season of Awakening of Insects and Phoenix Moon's Third Full. To the vast surprise of the Je family, no less a personage than a graywing, complete to the famous gray hat with the long, stiff wings spreading to either side, appeared at their gate with an imperial message for Je Tai.

The graywing was young, and the tassels hanging down from either end of the scroll he bore were not gold, which meant that the message had not been decreed by the emperor himself. It had been issued under the seal of the Bureau of Personnel.

That meant the entire household did not have to fall to their knees, only the person concerned.

Tai knelt and listened in growing astonishment to the flow of compliments to his father, to his family, and finally to him. It seemed that the Bureau of Personnel was waiving the necessity for Tai to take the imperial examination, as, through no fault of his own, he had been denied the years of training that the youth of the empire got.

"…word of his exemplary discipline in studies, and his filial piety, having reached the attention of the Bureau of Personnel, under the benevolent gaze of his imperial majesty, Je Tai is hereby informed that he has been deemed worthy of promotion to the ninth rank, and a position as an officer in the Bureau of Divination. His first appointment shall be as Third Secretary to the Archive at the White Jade Island Academy of Augury and Divination, where he is to assume his duties. You will take my place on the courier that brought me," finished the graywing — who would be going uphill to serve at the governor's palace. "The ship leaves at first tide tomorrow morning."

His future had been settled.

Tai bowed to the floor, uttering the ritual gratitude and promise to obey, and the graywing smiled and handed him his new papers that officially — and inexorably — catapulted him into the world of adulthood.

Magistrate Je indicated for his steward to reward the graywing with a clinking pouch, and Madam Je offered refreshment, which was turned down graciously. As soon as the graywing took his leave, Tai gazed blankly down at the papers in his hands.

"I must sail *tomorrow*," he said to his parents.

"There is scarcely time to order a properly fitted robe and hat," Madam exclaimed, midway between pride at her son's career thus beginning, and her profound dislike of his being swept off to the southern border of the empire. And not just for a year, but maybe forever!

Magistrate Je said, "There is my ninth rank robe laid in silk. I believe I have my old loaf as well…"

"I'll get his new clothes packed properly," Tai's mother

declared. "He'll only need the one official robe, being that far away from court," and whisked herself off, her voice echoing back in orders as she sent servants running.

Magistrate Je said to Tai, "You must go to the Hall of Ancestors to light incense and give thanks. Your mother would probably like it if you were to go to the temple as well, and pray for auspicious weather."

Tai wandered in the direction of his bedchamber — soon to be left once more, perhaps forever.

Servants scurried about, but he scarcely noticed them when his gaze lit on Waha, dressed to travel, with his gear bag over one shoulder.

"The courier ship sails tomorrow," Tai said, in question.

Waha smiled, a wanderer again—no playing the role of bowing servant as he said, "I know. Are you content?"

"Yes! I think. That is, it's the sort of post that I'm certain I'll enjoy. But…"

"Jetai," Waha said, evoking old memories by using the Western pronunciation of his name, "martial skills are a duty for you. You don't need further training. I'm going back to Eagle Island for the spring competition."

It was surprising, but reasonable; a short, awkward pause ensued, Tai not knowing how to take farewell of someone with whom he'd shared so much experience. It never occurred to him to suggest they go out for a meal, for instance, or even to offer to see him to the road. He said when the painful pause had become a silence, "If you see Mek, give him my greetings."

Waha had expected no more. Je Tai was a king's sword, like that pearl-handled bronze belonging to Ze Bian, but a king's sword who chose to remain sheathed. "I will." He broke the moment by turning to busy himself tidying the room.

"Incense," Tai exclaimed, and went to obey his father; when he returned from the temple, Waha was gone.

FORTY

TAI'S ENTIRE FAMILY ACCOMPANIED him down to the wharf the next morning. Here, after he bowed to both parents, Tai handed to his sister a luck talisman he'd contrived to get at the temple the day previous. "For the imperial examination," he said. "Do well for us both!"

He was then waved on board the sleek courier poised to take wing.

Take wing, he thought as he was shown to the tiny, stuffy cubby that he was expected to live in for the long journey south. In the empire, that meant sails ready to drop down. Ships took wing in so many poems written all across the centuries. But in the west, taking wing had meant the oars of the galleys lifting and dipping in unison.

By the time he had stowed his belongings satisfactorily, he came to the deck to discover the ship already well out in the bay.

As he watched the long wake lead back to Mountain Peony, he was aware that once again he was alone, heading south by southwest to avoid the drifting smoke off the former imperial island. But he was no longer ten, his only companions the creatures of the sea who came to him mainly looking for easy food.

He was alone, but not lonely. The crew of the courier was small, everyone soon acquainted. Tai was one of three passengers, all with a respectable though not high rank, and all going south to new appointments. He was the youngest. The meals were plain, though plentiful. When the captain—no older than Tai, the courier his first command—noticed Tai early in the morning dutifully doing his fundamentals, he invited him to spar with the crew later in the day.

Tai was quite willing—there was nothing else to do—and so the days passed swiftly. It being far too early in the year for demon storms, they made excellent time with favorable winds and currents, catching the outermost drifts of the smoke from Mt. Lir far to the east, over the horizon.

One day, before the wind took the last of the smoke away, Tai asked, "Have any of you ever seen the old imperial island?"

A general *no!* rose at that, someone adding, "Nor would I want to. It would be just my luck to have the dragon rise right after I landed."

Everyone agreed, and the captain added, "From all I hear, the only luckless souls who set foot there are the Rites inspectors, or some such."

"Geomancers," someone else said. "Though obviously their charms and plinths aren't strong enough to hold the dragon down. I don't envy them! They must all have been thieves and liars in their past lives."

Everyone made signs warding bad luck, and the subject passed on to other matters, leaving Tai wondering idly if his Great-Aunt Han might have been sent to that dangerous place at least once.

After an uneventful journey, they spotted the Jade Islands on the horizon. Also called the Silk Islands—for that was their chief trade—the islands were home to the Imperial Southern Fleet.

The naval installation at Gold Island was the largest. The courier had been ordered to report there, so Tai had to catch one of the many local boats to take him to White Jade. Before they parted, the young captain told Tai the name of one of his naval friends who was serving at White Jade, with a recommendation to spar with them if he liked.

It was so strange to be back again, after so long! He avoided the school buildings, going to the wing adjacent to the temple below the observatory on its conical mountain. Nothing had changed. It was as if all those years and terrible experiences had never occurred.

He was passed along to the fat, jovial Chief Archivist, Su Laq, who greeted him with a laugh, glanced carelessly at his papers, and said, "Ayah, and none too soon? Ay, ay, ay, we've plenty for you to do, young man. Find one of the grays or better, go to the dining area where you're sure to find Senior Student

Inke. He will show you about. We'll put you to work tomorrow, soon enough."

At the outer office, Tai discovered that his trunk had already been carried to the secretarial wing. No more dormitories for him—as a duly appointed official, albeit at the bottom rank, he was entitled to a room of his own.

A student emerged from the dining area and said with curiosity, Welcome! You're new?" And after Tai introduced himself, the student, a tall, thin fellow who appeared to be seventeen or eighteen, said, "I am one Su Inke. I'll be glad to show you around."

"Su, as in..."

Su Inke grinned briefly. "Yes, you already met Grandfather, I take it. And of course he sent you to find me. He thinks because I'm family that I'm at everyone's disposal. Ayah, at least I find out the news ahead of everyone! Where shall we begin?"

Tai felt obliged to admit that he was familiar with the school side, having attended when he was younger. Su Inke's bushy brows rose, but he asked no direct questions, only said, "Then how about half a tour? That leaves more time for a meal, if you're hungry. It's fish, cabbage, and plain rice on those navy scouts unless you're at least a red robe—and only then if they are sent stores ahead of time."

Student Inke was talking fast as they crossed a courtyard garden to the men's wing, and down nearly to the end. Inke found a door standing open, and waved Tai to look inside a narrow room with bedding neatly folded on a shelf above his trunk. Other than a desk and an empty rack for scrolls or whatever he wanted to store, the room was bare. It would take less than a tenth of an incense stick to organize his things.

"Do you want to settle in, or shall I show you where you'll be working?"

"Please."

They passed behind one of the school wings. Tai heard chanting of the Heavenly Stem and Earthly Branches for Ghost Moon, throwing him back in memory to those classrooms. Overlying that, a poignantly sharp memory of Han Anise's laughing voice as they roamed about in the sunshine, or did their fundamentals, chanting lower-level calculations in unison on each move.

They climbed up stone steps to the archive wing—which had been forbidden territory when he was a boy. "Grandfather says this was a prince's palace, back when the Silk Islands had its own king," Su Inke told Tai, his nasal honk lifting in youthful pride at his being able to instruct an elder. "Then it was a fortress, then merely an observation post, until the imperial island was under threat of Mt. Lir exploding."

Most of that history Tai remembered from boyhood, but he said nothing as they passed rooms in which secretaries or scribes sat writing, and gray-clad servants whisked around soundlessly in soft slippers, carrying papers, scrolls, grinding ink, and so forth.

"Aish! At first, you will be collecting and carrying, until you get used to how the reports are summarized and written," Inke said easily — as if he'd said it many times before. "My guess is, they'll put you over here, probably at Miss Bing's old desk, as she was promoted over to Gold Island's scribes last week. You'll be between Third Secretary Yao Swan of Rituals and Sixth Secretary Zik Hemu of Procurement. Make friends with Secretary Zik if you can, he gets extras of all the best stuff!"

They walked past the desks. This was where all the reports of daily observations were compiled, not just heavenly readings from the observation platform, but reports from all over the Silk Isles as pigeons or boats brought them. These had to be organized by date, copied out neatly, then stored in racks, all dated by year. Weather. Starless nights, clear nights. How many comets, where, angle, when. Records pertaining to the silk season. There was a room solely dedicated to the diligent reports from all over the empire of the numbers and flights of birds.

And once all those were compiled to build a picture of the heavens' revelations, then sent by regular courier, along with military reports from the naval bases, to the capital to be correlated with reports from all over the empire.

For the first time, Tai contemplated the vast scope of these steady reports that the imperial augurs must master continuously. When leaves appeared, then fell; good crops and bad. Fires, floods, famine, unrest, tremors requiring the geomancers to ease the ground as dragons turned beneath — only then could the imperial augurs divine warnings, and celestial guidance be better understood.

Tai followed Su Inke past room after room. He had always understood this work on a theoretical level, at least, but his focus had been solely on the complexities of Heaven's workings.

"I expect that you'll probably be assigned to collecting the silk numbers," Inke finished. "And soon, copying them into the archival scrolls. No under-secretaries or scribes are let near the archival books, which require summary skills as well as perfect calligraphy." He stopped. "We've reached the end. By the time we get back, they should be ringing for dinner!"

"What's down there?" Tai asked, pointing to the far door, which remained closed.

Inke waved a dismissive hand. "Oh, that's the crypt—where they used to store the ice, and the cold storage, before the palace was rebuilt larger. It's large enough down there, I think, but no one has ever gone to see that I know."

"Is it empty, then?"

"Oh, no. It holds the *old* records," Inke said. "You don't want to see that."

"Why not?"

"Because…ay-yah! You may as well see why, and then forget it, lest you find yourself assigned down there. Grandfather sometimes threatens to stick someone there. But trust me, he'd never actually do it."

Inke opened the doors with a key on his chain, and they entered a cool corridor of bare stone, smelling mainly of dust. A lamp waited at a side table. He lit this and led the way along the corridor.

Another door unlocked, and they started down steep steps as Inke said, "When our ancestors had to flee the imperial island, the bureaus did their best to preserve records, but of course they couldn't take everything. There was too much of a hurry, with smoke boiling everywhere, and Mt. Lir belching fire, but also, there is only so much space on even the biggest tower ships. Grandfather says that the sailors wouldn't know how to read, much less understand the markings of the various bureaus, and everyone was in a hurry, so Augury and Divination got their records mixed with Personnel, and Finance with Justice, and so on. There was some sorting afterward, but when Golden Celestial Chariot General Tan became Emperor, almost his first decree was that since Heaven was clearly dissatisfied with the old ways, everyone must begin anew, and so organizing this tangle of dragons without a head was always pushed off to the future."

At that he unlocked another door, lifted the lamp, and Tai gazed into a vast columned chamber filled with trunks and baskets and racks of scrolls in heaps and piles. At the near end, someone at some time had made an attempt to sort and stack neatly, but it was a mere scratch on the surface of chaos.

"I see," Tai said, aware of his fingers itching to tug this trunk straight, and right that fallen rack with its spilled scrolls still tightly sealed in their silken bags. It was exactly the sort of puzzle that called to him for ordering.

But he was new, and there was no doubt much to learn of his duties, he reminded himself as Su Inke closed and locked the door again.

While Tai was settling into his new work there in the northwestern reaches of the empire, various ships converged on Eagle Island bringing gallant wanderers from all directions.

Tents went up, swiftly filling the accustomed space around the pavilion adjacent the forest with its tumbling stream, but still the boats came.

One morning, Bian Ze and a couple of the seniors of the sect woke to discover four ships on the horizon. "At this rate," Uncle Tuen said, sticking his brush absently behind his ear, "we'll have tents extending clear down to the Fox God."

"He'll be glad of the company," declared Auntie Mim, fists on her hips. "We're going to have to clear more ground for more competition circles."

"True, true," Auntie Nua commented. "Word seems to be spreading."

No surprise. Many gallant wanderers welcomed a competition that emphasized training and talk and shared meals rather than death duels—though there were those out there who craved being known for their kills. But most of those seemed to be going west, where they were sure to find a good fight against the Ghost-Eye raiders.

Old Barnacle cackled. "I'll get Hok to put the youngsters to work." He shuffled off, chuckling in anticipation, for new arrivals meant the possibility of new musicians to join in with his hulusi.

By nightfall there were so many offerings around the Fox God that Auntie Mim sent the younger children to fetch all the baskets up to the kitchen area, the virtue surely having gone to the heavens with the sun. At least they would have plenty to offer refugees from the demon storms who arrived with only the clothes on their backs. And there were many of those.

Han Anise had offered to take charge of the cooking, as long as Auntie Mim could use her authority as an elder to provide labor, especially with pot-scrubbing, fetching, and carrying. Anise felt that keeping busy through the entire day was a good way to keep herself from watching the horizon for the Ki clan.

The fifth day after their arrival, the familiar voices of the Ki clan mixed with a new batch of arrivals. Anise heard the shriek of girl Ki cousins greeting friends, and set down the dough she had been kneading. She ran out—and there was Ki Mek in the middle of the laughing, talking Kis, topknot askew as flyaway strands escaped it, his face a beam of smiles, as three exceedingly scruffy dogs limped and lolloped at his heels.

"Where are we to set up?" one of the Kis called, squinting skyward.

Anise was astonished to see low clouds moving in fast—until that moment, it had seemed midsummer morn for brightness.

"Is it aa demon storm?"

"They usually don't come this far north."

"Hai! We need a hand here!"

The popularity of the Kis was manifest in how many people turned up willing to get their two tents—a large one for the adults and a smaller one for the youngsters—set up quickly, and all their gear stowed inside before the first big spats of a spring shower began to fall.

"Now, how can we help?" Mek's Fourth Uncle asked, rubbing his palms together.

Anise knew his name—Ki Yisin. She knew all the names of the Ki family, numerous as they were, the names carelessly furnished by Mek's Fourth Cousin, Spring Snow, a girl on the verge of adulthood who tended to have five questions for every one you asked. But Anise dared not presume by addressing any of them by name, only by the generic Grandpa, Grandma, Auntie, Uncle, Brother, or Sister, that everyone used toward everyone else.

Auntie Nua, who was in charge of this year's camp, swiftly divided them up, sending most of the elders to help clear fields of weeds and to rake the ground and place rocks to create new circles. To Anise's delight, Mek along with his tall, quiet Seventh Brother Tusa and Spring Snow were sent to the kitchen area to help lug baskets of vegetables to the stream to be washed, then chopped.

"Go play," Mek told his dog companions, who gazed at him, tongues lolling, tails waving. They trotted off to sniff at the other dogs chasing after some thrown sticks.

Auntie Mim thrust a basket of yams into Spring Snow's arms. "Go wash those. If you chop as fast as your tongue flaps, we'll have dinner ready before sunset."

Spring Snow only laughed and headed out toward the trees.

Ki Tusa was given cabbage, carrots, and turnips to scrub. He followed his cousin.

"And you can get started on chopping those mushrooms," Auntie Mim said to Mek, indicating a basket of freshly-washed mushrooms picked that morning. Then she turned away to resume preparing the fish she'd caught.

That left Anise standing alone with Mek. "How…was it a good year?" she asked.

"Great," Mek answered, going to the cutting board near the one where she was rubbing yams with garlic. Then he halted, his entire face flooding with color, as he shot Anise an apologetic look. "I guess I ought to, uh…" He stopped as Anise blinked at a bright green snake head that poked out of his sleeve. "Sorry," he mumbled, backing up.

"Why ought you to be sorry?" Anise asked, holding out her palm to the snake, who slithered from Mek to her. "This little friend will like a dry spot, well away from flashing knives," she said. "Have you another?"

"Just the one," Mek said, and Anise carried Little Green over to the rocks piled up for the cooking area, which would be warm. There were plenty of nooks for the snake to crawl into, and it vanished to find a cozy spot.

When she came back, Mek had begun chopping mush-rooms, but paused to say, "You don't mind snakes?"

"Not *that* girl," Auntie Mim stated from a few paces away. "I've seen her rescue frogs left high and dry after rains dry up. I expect she'd share her meals with rats and wolves if they turned up, never mind it's said that they were all murderers and poisoners before being reborn four-footed." She chuckled as she hefted a tray to be carried out.

Anise saw Mek blink, and she suspected that he had shared at least something with a rat or a wolf.

"I don't know many snakes. But the ones I've met are so pretty and so quiet, like the water snakes when I used to go to collect seaweed. As long as I moved slowly, and let them nose my fingers, they never troubled me—and I never troubled them." And at Mek's obvious interest, she added, "Sometimes they slithered over my hand. I loved the way they felt."

Mek said approvingly, "Most are perfectly willing to share the world. I don't know any that attack to be attacking, as humans do. They defend themselves, sure."

He paused, thought with regret of a dancer he'd befriended on an island during summer, who had been fun and lively until she saw him with a snake—she'd actually screamed, and then wouldn't even talk to him, as if *he* had turned into a snake.

But Han Anise was like Little Sister Fi, he discovered with approval as they talked about the odder creatures they'd encountered. Right after Uncle Tuft bellowed, "The cakes are all done! Let's ring the gong," he said, "You should come with us when we take off. You'll get to see them, too!"

Anise stared after him, her expression a mix of yearning and regret—while Mek was reluctant to leave. They'd barely begun talking! But family was family.

Music followed the dinner. By then the rain had cleared away, so people moved out from crowding under the pavilion, built a couple of bonfires, and the evening began with music, but ended with stories shared about their year's travels.

Hok called out, "What about you, Mek? You took off with those Ghost Moon monks on a raft. But here you are back with the Kis. Were the monks too slow?"

After some general ribbing, Mek said, "A lot you know. Those monks were too fast for me! Turns out their favorite game is tossing their staffs through tiny rings, and they can drum in circle all night, then go straight out to spar for half a day before getting into the fields to weed, or plant, or harvest, or to help build. And when Throwing-Water Festival came around, they were lifting half-barrels! I slept for two days after I parted from them. I found Elder Brother on board the next boat, and we ended up helping rebuild two villages that got flooded out by snowmelt, so we traveled together..."

As Mek described their wanderings, he mentally sorted his experiences. Some were fun, some tense—when he'd helped break the hold some bandits had on an estate mostly run by elders while their younger generations were away on various pursuits. He knew these stories would entertain, but he kept back the few instances when he'd had to call upon his Essence.

A lot of gallant wanderers were uncomfortable with Essence skills—but even when they weren't, it felt…prideful, somehow. Whereas a tough fight against bandits or thieves or the like was something everyone could do.

He also kept back that odd sense that a lot of demons—the dangerous kind—seemed to be drifting west.

The next day the competitions began.

Mek's staff work had improved the most, and he came in third. In all his other skills he held his own in the top ten or so, knowing that if he called on Essence he could win, but what use would that be? He had sensed before he even landed that except for Old Uncle, his Essence was the strongest of anyone's there. Most of his attention strayed toward Han Anise, who liked animals as much as he did, and could catch him up on all their doings. No one else seemed to care about the personalities of green snakes, chickens, and the messenger eagles, but the two of them found the stories intriguing. How different and how marvelous were animal and bird minds!

Mek became aware that Anise seemed to be leaning toward the healing side of divination, and away from prediction; they often chopped vegetables side by side, comparing the tastes and efficacy of different herbs.

But Essence was never far from his mind. Including the fact that Old Uncle's had diminished a little. It sorrowed Mek, though he'd known it was coming. He was relieved to find Old Uncle as sharp as before, his many-colored coat neatly mended, though he moved little, and not without wheezing.

Mek also sensed that Old Uncle and Uncle Ze were watching him, to some purpose.

After the big celebration at the end of the competition, Mek helped haul a stack of cook pots downstream to be washed. He'd nearly finished when he became aware of Uncle Ze at his shoulder. Mek began to clasp his hands—and promptly dropped a pot.

"Young Mek, I believe that while we have calm winds and quiet waves it is time to give you a gift that might also be seen as a duty. I hope not as a yoke."

Mek noticed then that Uncle Ze was carrying his fine sword, the one with the white stone in the hilt that sometimes gleamed with iridescent color. "It was after a competition that Old Uncle gave her to me, as it happens," Uncle Ze said with a quiet laugh as he held the sword out to Mek.

Mek's hands came forward, but he was so astonished he just stood there as Uncle Ze laid the sword on his palms, saying, "I'd just been defeated in a final bout—"

"You lost it with intent," Old Uncle said, coming up on Mek's other side, breathing heavily. "Bai the Red Spear was quite old. It was his last competition. Your loss permitted him to end where he had always longed to be, but had never quite attained. Good man," Old Uncle sighed. "Good man, wise in his way, and still much loved among the Bai Sect, though he's been gone since the Water Ox Year."

His words gave Mek a moment to recollect himself.

"It—you said gave *her* to me...*she*...thinks?" Mek asked, eyeing with suspicion the sword lying heavily on his flat palms.

"There are a lot of mysteries about this sword," Uncle Ze said. "She seems to be different for every wielder she chooses. Old Uncle gets messages, in a sense, in dreams. Though I don't. She's always been quiet for me—except she has always come to my hand when I've needed her."

"But I..."

"Rather than argue, I'll prove you were chosen. Go beyond those trees and reach for the sword. In your mind," Uncle Ze said.

Mek was already so practiced with mental exercises that he ran past the three of trees he'd pointed at, turned, reached— and the sword smacked into his hand so firmly he rocked back a step.

That's when his mind filled with voices. Deep, high, cracked, soft, in accents so ancient he barely understood—and he staggered back, flinging the sword away as he landed hard on his butt.

Old Uncle promptly began to wheeze with laughter.

"It's haunted," Mek squawked, his voice breaking.

"No, no, this is no demon blade," Bian Ze said—though with a question to Old Uncle.

Who wiped his eyes, sobering. "Quite right. A demon blade with captured souls is a vastly different thing. Terrifying. These are merely memories of trainings, of a sort, willingly furnished by some of those who once held this blade. I don't quite know how that was managed, except I believe a demon must have been involved, binding these trainings into the sword with Essence. A benevolent demon. You will see when you have a chance to work with her."

Old Uncle had perched on a rock. He nodded soberly. "Perhaps you are what will be needed."

That definitely made it sound like someone—or some...*thing*—was living inside the sword in some way. Mek cautiously picked up the sword again. It—she—was light in his hand, as if she had always been there. Mek looked up, his brow puckered. "Thank you?"

Old Uncle rose with a grunt. "Thank you, young Mek. Now I can go back to Sky Mirror and start on my carving. I want to leave something behind for people to remember me by."

Mek's gaze slid to Bian Ze, who said, "I always regarded that sword as a temporary visitor. I'm back to my knives. Speaking of which, let's get in some work before you take off again. You ought to have placed higher."

Bian Ze squatted down and helped Mek finish scrubbing the pots as they discussed the intricacies of speed and balance with double-knife fighting, promising a morning session.

By then all three dogs had adopted themselves to willing hearts, and half the Kis had departed. Little Sister Fi, the navigator, had unsentimentally taken leave of everyone, saying that beginning next year she'd be on board some ship, so this was her last gallant wanderer competition.

Remaining behind was Fourth Uncle, who had a job waiting aboard a tea convoy scout owned by the woman he was courting. She needed five hands who could crew as well as defend, and Mek had agreed to travel with his brother Tusa, who had a modest but steady Essence gift that the family had been unaware of. Tusa wanted to learn to use it, as it was a water affinity—always useful for convoy duty, he hoped. Fourth Cousin Spring Snow was to be their fourth.

Mek trotted back, exhausted and sweaty after his session with Uncle Ze. The pavilion was mostly packed up, but there was Han Anise, who had tea waiting, and a plate of onion pancakes.

"Some extras," she said, greeting Mek. "Would you like some?"

Hungry and thirsty, Mek accepted gratefully, aware then that he would miss their conversations quite sharply. Did he have to? "Why don't you come with us, if you haven't made other plans?" he asked.

Han Anise's face flooded with color—then paled as Spring Snow gave a laugh. "And have the poor thing spewing all over us? Didn't you know she gets seasick?"

Han Anise looked down, frozen with humiliation.

Until Mek said, "But that's easy to fix. I know a recipe mixing ginger with longevity root, and with a very easy charm, it goes away unless there's a bad storm. And a lot of us get the heaves in a storm."

"It's not a cure," Auntie Mim observed, looking speculatively from one to the other. "That's to be taken every day, yes?"

Mek agreed, his gaze going to Anise, who turned to him in question. He was very adept at not opening the door between minds, but her door was so very thin, it was nearly transparent as she waited for him to despise her for such a weakness.

What could he say? "You'd be welcome." He must not be selfish! "But if you like to stay on Eagle Island, aish! Someone has to!"

Han Anise's tense shoulders came down from around her ears.

"Anyway, Tian-Tian already agreed to go with us," Spring Snow declared, throwing her arm around the shoulders of the girl with dark red hair frizzing out of stiff braids. "Her knife work was good this year, and she's so fast and agile at hand-to-hand. And she cooks, too. Though not as good as Anise!"

Mek left the others talking, and came up to Anise. "Would you like me to try to find a true cure?" he asked. "Do you want to join us one day?"

Anise raised her eyes, her gaze searching. Her heart was there, generous and big enough for snakes and frogs and little birds and turtles as well as everyone in the Eagle Sect. Mek smiled, and she smiled back to see that smile. "I actually like holding house," she whispered. "I'm so happy in one place."

Did she say that or think it? Her spoken voice and her inner voice were exactly the same. Most people's weren't. Mek knew his wasn't. He stared at someone so transparent, so good of heart as if it was the most natural habit, and he said, "I think knowing that there would be someone to come back to, someone happy, would be..." He began to grope in the air, trying to find the words, and his fingers thumped painfully against the still-unaccustomed sword sticking up beyond his shoulder.

"Mek!" Fourth Uncle called.

"Wonderful," Mek finished.

"Go," Anise said. "And come back."

Mek grinned and loped away, wringing his fingers.

FORTY-ONE

THE AUSPICIOUS DAYS FOR the imperial examination were announced.

The plan was to send Lei to stay with her Han relations in the capital city for the duration, but when a letter arrived inviting her to stay with her Ji family and ride with QiQi to the examination hall, Magistrate Je told her she could not possibly refuse.

At least she could look forward to staying with Cousin QiQi.

So it was.

The morning dawned when Lei and QiQi joined the short women's line to have their satchels, and then their clothes, inspected for cheats. She had her ink, her brushes, a jug of water and one of tea, plus two pancakes baked crisp so that they would not quickly go stale or moldy. QiQi had more to eat — her mother had insisted — and finer brushes as well as a golden case for her ink, but the important matter was in their heads, not in their satchels.

They were assigned cubicles with nothing but a bare table that faced forward so that the roaming inspectors could see you writing, and a thin army bedroll behind in case you needed a short rest.

One moment Lei's stomach roiled, then the graywings came around with paper and questions. The world narrowed to paper, ink, brush, and the flow of her thoughts.

She was startled by the brassy gong ringing the examination was at an end. She had actually finished before, but was desperately rereading — or trying to reread — lest she had omitted an important quotation or logical progression. Her wrist ached as her paper was taken away, and suddenly she was desperately tired. QiQi and she feverishly compared notes on the short journey back, laughing somewhat giddily when it seemed they had used most of the same poems and quotations.

There followed the agony of waiting for the results to be posted. Madam Ji signaled her dislike of the entire matter — she would have preferred to be planning a splendid wedding for QiQi — by remaining home as if nothing were occurring. Dowager Princess Ji was very interested indeed, but she was too frail for the journey, so the girls went together with only their maids and two burly Ji guards.

They clutched each other's hands when at last the imperial guards came out to force the waiting crowd back, and graywings began posting the notices.

Neither name was in the bottom thirty.

"That's terrible," Lei said, sharply disappointed. "I failed."

QiQi sighed. "Lei, you must remember that your esteemed father won the first rank. It's possible we're in the middle ranks..."

They waited as the next ranking up was posted, meaning those who had done well enough to find positions somewhere in the imperial capital, if not in the court.

But neither name was there.

That left only the top rankers. All around them young men leaped and crowed or went off laughing. Two high women's voices joined them. Everyone else waited painfully.

The last poster was hung, and....

QiQi grabbed Lei's hand so hard her knuckles cracked painfully. "LeiLei, you are *Number Five!*"

Lei's heart filled with joy, but she forced herself to remain silent, and to read the names more carefully. But there was no Ji Qishai. Firmly squashing her elation, she turned to QiQi. "I'm sorry," she breathed.

QiQi's chin rose. "Ayah, what matter? I'll take it again. And at least I can postpone Mama trying to force me into marriage with some horrid man whose only quality is his wealth, probably with ten consorts — and a string of unmanageable children. Grandmama will see to *that*." But her eyes gleamed as she spoke, and when Lei reached for her arm to comfort her, she discovered that QiQi was trembling.

They made it to the cart. QiQi slammed the side windows

shut and burst out, "It's Father's fault. But it's unfilial to say it. To *think* it. But it's true! If Venshai had not made me go up to the palace to wait on Imperial Princess Lam so often and court her for him, I would have had far more time to study. I told him, even Father told him, it would never work." And she wept bitterly.

It was only to get worse.

Upon their arrival back, his highness the Left Chancellor summoned both girls. It was clear that he had his own method of ascertaining the results, for he frowned before speaking. "I want you both here as I congratulate Je Lei for her success, which is the result of true diligence. As for you, Daughter, you should be rightly shamed in comparison."

QiQi dropped to her knees, tears running down her cheeks, though she made no sound.

"Fifth," the prince said, turning his pouchy, alert eyes back to Lei. "Out of who knows how many candidates, most of them men who have studied with imperial tutors. I wish it could have been third, for then you would be in parade behind first and second, bringing credit to the family. Even so, fifth is superlative, an achievement worthy of your father, who was first in his day. But he was older than you, was he not?"

Lei didn't trust herself to speak, so she only curtseyed, avoiding looking at poor QiQi, still kneeling.

The prince sighed. "It will be a pleasure to consider which of the many offers for positions to accept. You will of course want to be placed in a position that will aid—"

A hasty knock at the door presaged the steward putting his head inside.

"Why have you interrupted me?" the prince said curtly.

"Your highness Left Chancellor, there is an imperial graywing here—"

The prince cut him off: "I will come at once."

"Your highness, the summons is for…Miss Je."

All eyes turned to Lei, including QiQi's tear-drenched ones.

"Me?" she said weakly.

"Come along, child," the prince said briskly. "It is never a good thing to keep them waiting." He scowled at QiQi. "All of you."

He strode out, long silken sleeves fluttering. The girls followed in his wake, QiQi hastily drying her eyes.

In the grand main hall, with the great screens depicting

cranes flying with a phoenix on one side, and a pod of whales leaping from ocean waters on the other, a graywing waited with a scroll with silver tassels depending from it.

They all went to their knees, and to Lei's witless astonishment, amid all the flowery compliments about her grace, diligence, and talent, was a summons to report as personal secretary to her imperial highness Crown Princess Lam.

She was to report to the Imperial Household Bureau at first gong on the morrow.

For a few desperate heartbeats Lei could not hear anything. Her thoughts froze, her meridians thunderstruck. Then QiQi prodded her, hissing softly, "Forehead. Thanks."

Bang! Lei's forehead hit the cool tiles and she whispered the ritual words of gratitude learned in early childhood.

Then she rose on watery legs, her trembling hands received a heavy scroll made of brocade, with words painted on it that her eyes refused to parse, and she blinked rapidly as around her people spoke, bowed, thanks, a clink of coins, and then QiQi tugged her gently.

She found herself back in the prince's fine inner chamber. Her legs collapsed under her on a waiting cushion, and then a dish of fragrant rice wine was pressed into her fingers. "Drink this."

She seldom had rice wine, as her mother did not approve of unmarried girls drinking anything but tea and boiled water. She choked, her eyes burning.

"All of it," the prince ordered.

The rice wine burned its way down, but recalled her wits from wherever they had gone. She carefully set down the dish, and the prince said, "Better?"

"Yes—"

But before she could utter the proper self-deprecating words of gratitude, the prince cut across her. "This is a signal honor for the family," he said. "It is surely to honor our Ji house—which includes the subsidiary branches, including my esteemed Cousin Je—that you have been raised to so exalted a position at so young an age."

He paused, and Lei realized that while she had been in a daze, QiQi had been sent out, and Cousin Venshai had come in. He stood silently at his father's shoulder as the prince sat behind his beautiful desk carved with running tigers.

"But the fact that this appointment came directly from the imperial palace, rather than through the Secretariat or even the Household Bureau, puzzles me a little," the prince stated. "Perhaps it is only the imperial princess's impatience to find someone suitable who is also her age. How old are you again?"

"Sixteen, your highness—"

"You may address me as Uncle Ji, Niece, now that you are to be counted among the adults. Marriageable age—I will come to that. But first, I must emphasize that once you enter the imperial palace, you cannot leave freely, only when permitted. And so there is a great deal of preparation to be done today."

Lei bowed, not knowing what else to say or do.

"Of course you will stay here when released from duty. Your first instruction, your duty to your family, is to pay attention to everything. *Everything*," he repeated, laying his hand on his desk, a jade ring glinting on his finger. "You are now lofted to the highest level of the imperial court, where mistakes mean death. But the rewards for conscientiousness and obedience are unlimited."

Another bow, for that seemed unanswerable.

"In specific, you must remember everything the princess says. Every word. You are too young as yet, too full of scholarship, to understand the intricacies of imperial court, therefore you are too ignorant to determine what is useful and what not. That will come, especially as we educate you during your free time away from duty."

Lei bowed a third time.

"The most important matter for you to concern yourself with is the imperial princess's marriage. Negotiations are ongoing, and as an adult, you will be in a position to hear everything discussed in the imperial heir's household before we can. You must not write anything down, ever. Even if they permit you to write letters, except for your duties to your parents, do not write to anyone else, because you do not know how many sets of eyes will see what you write before it is ever delivered. The simplest words can be misconstrued—or twisted to say what an inimical mind wants them to say."

He said this with so much conviction that Lei shivered. How did he know that, unless he had done so himself? Or had the family been so slandered?

"...I will be instructing one of my sets of palace eyes to contact you—you've only to wait until I've safely set it up."

Once again the steward interrupted; two messengers awaited him.

"Venshai, escort your cousin and begin instructing her, until I can see to these court matters."

Venshai walked her out. "I wish it had been QiQi, for she'd know what to do," he said in a low, heavy voice as they walked. "But fate had other plans, it seems. Still, you're a smart girl," he added with genial condescension. "Remember what my father said, and also this: there is no privacy in the imperial palace. *Everyone* is reporting to someone. Their lives may even depend on it. And last, try to say good things about me to the princess."

He led her to his own study, which was nearly as fine as his father's. Here, three-toed dragons were the main motif. Three-toed dragons were permitted to princes, or ducal heirs to princes. But still they were daring. Ambition in the form of art, who was it who said that? Mek Mak? No, On Lu—

"Cousin Lei, look here. I will draw out a diagram of the court," Venshai said, waving a hand for a servant to lay a cushion down for her.

Lei knew the generality of the imperial court's organization, of course: the Three Departments under the emperor, the Secretariat, the Chancellery, and State Affairs. The Censorate was somewhere in there, as well. The Bureau of Justice came under State Affairs—her father talked occasionally of them. Archives came under the Secretariat, and Ritual and Rites (which included Divination) worked in conjunction with Archives—that was where her brother Tai was beginning his service.

Venshai listed the various bureaus under each of the three departments, naming not only bureau chiefs but secretaries and even agents and under-secretaries. The names streamed by; at first she tried to memorize them, but there were too many. Instead, as she'd been taught by her father, she listened for patterns. This was easier, for Venshai had something disagreeable to point out about every one of them, in particular his fellow Censors, but especially Right Chancellor Yimu, uncle to the emperor's Sixth Imperial Consort.

Venshai's condescension altered from forced friendliness to a kind of weariness as he caught himself. "I can see you're lost. I went too fast. Listen, Cousin Lei, the important thing is, nearly all these I just named owe something to us." Here, he leaned forward, his voice clear with conviction. "Don't *ever* let yourself get into a position of owing anything to anybody."

"But what about filial duty?" she asked, her head throbbing.

His mouth tightened, then he said hastily, "Of course, that. Always. I'm glad you remembered our first duty is to our parents, to our family. I'm talking about others. The easiest are controlled by bribes, but the troublesome ones will expect service. You want to *be* owed, not owing..."

He went on to name more names, and there was more about who was watching and reporting on whom. He seemed to mean well, that is, he was diligently carrying out his father's orders to instruct her. But she longed for her father's slow, careful manner, always measured, rarely contemptuous, and never condescending.

The prince was also measured, but that contempt was there in his tone, reflected in Cousin Venshai. Lei had largely been indifferent to the boy cousins, who had ignored her until last year, when she'd turned fifteen, and on leaving the main hall after making her bows at New Year's Two Moons, she'd overheard Venshai saying to his father, "Did you *see* her? That little stick has turned into a phoenix! Why can't we auction her off?" And the prince's short, "My mother will not hear of it..."

She'd lost the rest of the words, not that it mattered. But the way Cousin Venshai had referred to her—and that word *auction*—had made her feel like a marker on the Circle board. And after that, she'd noticed that he treated QiQi the same way. And had secretly rejoiced when QiQi stoutly answered him back, protected by her grandmother's benevolence.

The prince summoned them, and there was a repetition of names until Lei could recite them. She endured the rest of the long evening, ostensibly a banquet in her own honor, with no attention paid to woeful QiQi, except for Dowager Princess Great-Aunt Ji patting her hand reassuringly.

At last Lei was able to retire, her head still aching a little, until QiQi came in. "Dear and patient LeiLei," she murmured. "I can see you are tired past bearing. No, no, don't stir, and don't try to comfort me. I'll do very well. Grandmother will make sure of that, and I'll be first next time!" She sighed, patting Lei's hand. "There's one comfort I take now, and that's that Father and Venshai will now expect you to take over praising Venshai before the princess." Her smile was wan.

She went out soon after, and Lei tried to sleep, tossing and turning until Ji servants came in before dawn. She hastily bathed and dressed, swallowed some tea and a single small bun, before she was escorted to an actual imperial palace cart—though a plain one—and conducted up to the palace, through a back way.

She had never seen any of the Household wing. It was a bewildering maze of narrow corridors and rooms. While she was being measured and fitted for her secretarial garment, a protocol servant read to her from a list of palace rules. There was a different set for the emperor, the empress, and the consorts as well as for the imperial heir. Because of her visits accompanying QiQi, a good many of the rules were already familiar, in particular the bows, and how many paces before and after each.

As soon as the measuring was done, maids whisked the fabric away and a new steward conducted her to an exquisitely decorated little antechamber which she understood was to be her room when the princess did not demand her presence.

It was while she stood there, her eyes burning with exhaustion but her heart beating too fast for tiredness to register, when the maid at the door bowed and withdrew, and a woman entered, wearing silk-edged soft gray over a brown under robe: the garb of the highest-ranking servants.

She recognized Nanny Alk, the imperial princess's chief nanny, whom QiQi had pointed out in whispers just last year. "Everyone says she's the only one who knows what to do during the princess's *moods*."

Lei hastily bowed, and after a searching gaze, the woman said calmly, "Welcome to the imperial crown princess's service, Secretary Je Lei. I've come to show you over her imperial highness's chambers, so that you will be familiar with them."

Lei willingly followed her. There were several maids in soft gray akin to Lei's own new garments, except theirs were plain, without the gray silk facing that would mark her off.

The nanny's voice was soothing as the softest merino. Lei's tightened muscles gradually loosened as they walked from exquisite room to exquisite room and the nanny explained what the imperial crown princess liked and didn't like. Lei noted that there were fewer silver phoenixes—a princess's right—in the decorations than Cousin Venshai had dragons in what she'd seen of his chambers.

When they returned to the outer chamber, Nanny Alk opened the doors to the balcony, which overlooked the bay far below, a view blocked only by the emperor's tower to one side. Here, a cold wind toyed with their clothes and hair. Lei was glad she'd paid attention to securing her own hair with two wooden hairpins, and she tried not to shiver.

Nanny Alk turned to her. "Maybe I offer you advice?" she asked.

"This ignorant one would be grateful for instruction," Lei said, her soft voice ringing with sincerity.

Nanny Alk's lips twitched. "If the princess likes you, she might put questions to you," she said, and paused.

Lei looked back in question.

"You have not spent a lot of time with your Ji primary family?"

"Only New Year's Two Moons," Lei said, wonder in her tone—this question appeared to her to open a completely different subject. "But now I'm told that I will see them when I am granted liberty. As my home is at the east end of the island."

"I see," Nanny Alk said. "You know that every word spoken, every action, has consequences."

Lei bowed.

"Some of those consequences are brief. Some long-lasting, and perhaps not intended. If you do not intend influence, it can be safest to claim the ignorance of your young age, and then beg for enlightenment. Few object to being asked for counsel," Nanny Alk finished with a smile. "Most, even princesses, are used to being told what to do and to think. They quite naturally like to regard themselves as persons capable of instruction."

"Thank you," Lei said with real gratitude. She might be ignorant—well, she was—but she was very aware that she had just received the gentlest of warnings.

"I've decided to trust you, a little," Nanny Alk said suddenly. "My motive is the princess's safety, comfort, and well-being. I have no interest in imperial politics—to me it's the grunts and tweets of a thousand birds. And about as lasting, in the great circles of years."

Lei bowed, her expression still perplexed, but not the least resentful, or secretive.

"You might have been told that there are times when the princess suffers…maladies." Here Nanny Alk touched her head and then her heart.

Lei, greatly daring, whispered, "Moods, is what I was told."

"Moods will do. It is the general term used. Fate decreed

that she should be burdened with what can only be called a double nature. And no, she is not infested with a demon. The imperial physicians as well as two shamans have examined her."

Lei gasped — *that* had never occurred to her.

"Most of the time she is a princess of great talent and many interests. But if you are in her proximity and she suddenly becomes deeply morose, or wildly angry, whatever happens, you must send for me," Nanny Alk said. "The only remedy we have is a medicinal tea. It helps her." After a moment, Nanny Alk said, "I can see your doubt. You're thinking perhaps of irritation felt in the days before one's moons-blood, or a justifiable temper if one breaks a dish or a nail. But these moods are more like storms than breezes, and she can no more halt them than she can the thunder overhead. She had gone a long time without a mood, until this past winter, she suddenly ordered the entire imperial court boarded up and set on fire."

Lei's hands flew to her mouth.

Nanny Alk's expression had not changed. "She does not have the power to order the deaths of the imperial court. Do not worry over such things. Further, once the mood passed, she would have been very sorry if that order had been obeyed. Do you understand me now, how important it is to send for me, if I am not by?"

Lei dropped to her knees, and would have pressed her forehead to the floor, but Nanny Alk's chilled fingers raised Lei very firmly. "We do not discuss these matters outside of these chambers. With anyone. At all. Do you comprehend? Those who must know do know. It does only harm to whisper beyond these walls. It has happened. And persons have had to suffer the consequences." Nanny Alk sounded grieved.

Thoroughly unsettled, Lei bowed.

"I think that is enough, then. You will do your best for her, call for me when needed, and keep your own counsel, yes, Secretary Je?"

"Yes, Nanny Alk."

The doors opened suddenly — and without warning, there was the princess herself. Tall — taller than Lei — with a perfect oval of a face, expressive eyes the color of cedar, with a bud of a mouth above a softly dimpled chin. She was dressed in layers of gorgeously embroidered gauzy silk of peach, green, and silver, with celestial blue accents for contrast. Long ribbons flowed from her headdress all the way to her heels. Her hair was nearly as long.

"She is here," declared the princess.

Lei had dropped to the floor, and beside her, Nanny Alk bowed deeply. "Your imperial highness, I was just now finishing instructions pertaining to your chambers."

Imperial Crown Princess Lam snapped her tasseled fan open and fluttered it, saying, "There is no need to burden her with a lot of rules. Secretary Lei, I know we've met before, but I don't think we ever got to speak, not with the Left Chancellor's girl putting herself forward all the time."

This was not at all how Lei would have expressed those tense, seemingly interminable visits during which poor QiQi had tried to do her duty, but Lei remembered her instructions, and only bowed.

"Did you see my desk? Come, let me show you my drawings. I draw much better than I write. You wouldn't think it was one or the other. Both ought to go together, ought they not? But my calligraphy is horrid…"

The imperial princess turned and swept back inside. Lei was careful to keep five paces behind her train, without getting in the way of Nanny Alk, who smoothly glided to walk beside the imperial crown princess.

The fan dismissed hovering maids with a flick. Imperial Crown Princess Lam never stopped talking as she displayed drawings of animals and flowers around a pool—very conventional subjects, but done with care, and a meticulous eye to detail by someone, Lei was soon to realize, who had far too much time on her hands, and few ways to fill it.

Pausing her sprightly speech, the imperial princess said, "Nanny Alk, did you get anything to eat while I called upon Mother? Of course you didn't. Go ahead. Get something. There is no need to stay here and starve. Secretary Je and I will be fine, looking at my drawings, and I might ask her to show me her calligraphy, though I'm very sure it's better than mine."

Nanny Alk perforce bowed herself out, after a last brief glance at Lei.

The imperial crown princess laid out two more drawings, and after Lei admired them with properly spoken gratitude and praise, Lam dropped the rest and threw herself on a pile of silken cushions, skirts, sleeves, and ribbons billowing around her. "Come. You may sit. How clever you were, to write so excellent an examination. As soon as I saw the list, I knew how I could finally get you up here without that tiresome girl's company, always talking honey and flowers about Ji Venshai. *She* will never pass the imperial examination," Crown Princess Lam's tone didn't alter a whit, though her eyes narrowed. "Ever. No matter how clever she is, at least I can see to *that*. But you are not their spy, are you? Do you have a speech ready about how wonderful Ji Venshai is, hmmm?"

Lei thought about the prince's instructions. And Venshai's. And poor QiQi, who had never wanted that duty, but all she said was, "I scarcely know him."

"That's what I found out," the imperial princess said. "The almighty Jis have little time for the secondary or tertiary families, they are so busy fighting my uncles in court. In spite of two of their girls married to my cousins." She snapped her fan again, waved it dismissively, then leaned forward. "Now, tell me *all* about your brother."

FORTY-TWO

"MY BROTHER?" LEI REPEATED, then hastily added the proper honorific and bobbed a bow from her cushion.

The crown princess studied her intently. "Is not Je Tai your brother, sent away last winter to toil in the augury school archive?"

Lei stared, unsure what to do or say. Among all those instructions she'd been receiving, some repeated direfully, there had been nothing said about her brother.

"Why do you not speak?"

"This…this ignorant wretch knows not what to say, your imperial highness. He is so newly returned to us—he vanished when this your servant was still in the nursery. There was a tablet for Tai in the Hall of Ancestors, and the family always prayed for rebirth within the clan. But he came home last fall."

"And?"

"He and this ignorant one studied together, until he was sent away again."

The imperial princess's brow contracted. "Yes. I imagine I know who was responsible for *that*. Sent him off before he could even sit for the examination. You were fifth, but I would wager anything he would have won the kingfisher feather instead of that dullard from the Lan Island." The princess snapped her fan open. "*He* will be just as happy over at the Treasury, totting up coins once his parade is over. Which I will *not* go to see. He's at least thirty, and he has a face like a potato. Whereas your brother would have been a perfect Imperial Tutor, wouldn't he?"

Lei saw that the princess actually expected an answer. "The brother of this your servant was an excellent study partner, your imperial highness," Lei said cautiously. "But if this foolish one may trouble your imperial highness with a question—"

"Speak, speak, speak."

"This ignorant seeker of knowledge assumed that imperial tutors were aged and venerable persons, and Tai's not yet twenty-four."

"Father Emperor's first tutor was no older than I," the princess replied. "He ranked first at only fourteen—which no one had done for a hundred years. But I want to hear about what happened to him in the west, when he was a slave. See, I know that much. And I know that he managed to get martial training. How did that happen?"

"This ill-informed one is desolated to report ignorance, your imperial highness. He said so little about what happened to him there. He might have told our father, but if he did, it was when they were alone."

The princess lifted a shoulder, smiling. "Then we shall both hear, when he comes back. Now, let's see your writing…"

Nanny Alk, listening from another room, held her breath. The entire household held its collective breath, but the interview was successful. Je Lei was quiet, tidy, had excellent calligraphy, and listened seriously to everything the princess said.

The rest of the day passed with equal success, and on the morrow the princess casually forbade the formal third person deprecations when they were alone: Lei was strictly ordered to assume the pronoun "I." By the following day, Crown Princess Lam began to treat her new secretary like something between a little sister and a toy.

At the end of the week, she said to her steward after dismissing Lei for the night, "I don't want those Jis getting their hands on her and ruining her. See to it."

The steward, a ferret, bowed expressionlessly.

Far to the south, on White Jade Island, Tai found his duties to be easy.

On Eagle Island, most idle talk besides martial skills had been about tea. But here so far in the south, it was silk—and storms. He was back in the part of the world that suffered the demon storms that had flung Mek and him west.

Two struck within a month after his arrival. At the advent

of the first, when he smelled that metallic singe on the still air and looked eastward at that lurid green sky, he was astounded—and frustrated—to discover a kind of instinctive fear drying his mouth and shivering in his belly. He had not been this sick with dread on the eve of prospective battle; at least then, he had his weapon. But there was no fighting the shrieking horror of demon winds fighting to claw apart the world.

However, the palace walls were thick, and for the most part, the shape of the island was such that the worst of the shredding winds struck the far side's steep rock, which left the sloping land full of low, tough mulberry trees mostly in the lee of the storm, barely beginning to bud.

Once the storm passed, leaving every surface scoured, life returned to normal. After a few days he had mastered summarizing and recording the daily reports from the silk farms. He bent his attention to learning more about the sericulture seasons from his desk neighbor.

Third Secretary Yao Swan of Rituals was a precise person some years older than Tai, regarded as odd by their fellow secretaries. Her work was overseeing and recording completion of the proper rituals related to sericulture.

Su Inke, who often ran errands at that end of the secretaries' corridor, noted that Je Tai never laughed at her bat-squeak of a voice, and further, when the secretaries had occasion to share a meal, Je Tai waited for her to help herself from the dishes before she arranged her tidbits on the curiously flat dish she'd brought from her home island. He'd noticed that she wouldn't take food from any dish that someone else's eating sticks had touched, nor did she permit foods on her own plate to touch. Tai had shared the same inclination before those early days of near starvation in Angja's prison had broken him of the habit. Waiting for someone with that habit seemed merely sensible, as there was always plenty for everyone.

His kindness functioned as oblique reproof to the youngsters, who regarded her as a hilarious figure. Yao Swan was grateful, more so when she understood that Tai would never disturb her painfully orderly desk by borrowing ink or brushes. His things were always tidy and ready for use. She willingly enlightened him about the intricacies of silkworm growing, feeding, warming, the Three Sleeps, spinning, then the centuries-old secret art of coaxing the moths from the cocoons to find mates in order to lay next year's eggs.

They began talking during fourth month's Water Wishes Festival, when the blessing dances were carried out before last year's silk was bailed and sent north to be sold, once the sky was clear. At sixth month, he accompanied her, tally brush and scroll in hand, for the ritual of bringing silkworm eggs out and warming them for hatching, and later on, he volunteered to go when everyone who had two free hands was sent up into the lush green hills to strip the mulberry leaves from the trees and haul them down in baskets to feed the hungry worms.

Those rituals merely occupied a day or so out of a given month. For the rest of his free time, he went up several times a week to the garrison on the next hill in order to spar—and finally, got Chief Su's permission to try organizing "the crypt."

The jolly old chief laughed when Tai first brought it up. This was nothing new. It was always the studious ones. Usually the request came during the winter, when everyone was shut in by terrible weather, and they'd always given up after a few days of cold and dusty toil down there, for the studious ones were seldom strong enough to do much beside lift their brushes.

"I've never had a single order about those trunks," the chief said to Tai. "And I doubt one will come. But someone or other might turn up to inspect someday. Who knows? If so, progress down there might be considered a merit."

Tai expected to face this challenge alone, completely un-aware that Su Inke and his friends were fast making him their latest fashion. He was kind, he was excellent at his work, and he wore those handsome headbands because he was modestly hiding (as they discovered in the baths) an even more amazing tiger eye tattoo, which surely he'd won in some bloody duel when he was living among the criminal wanderers, after (it was said) he escaped from slavery by fighting single-handedly against a galley. Because he was also a martial artist, while the only exercise they got was walking between buildings.

Who could possibly be more of a hero?

Therefore he was considerably surprised when a good portion of the idle seniors and gangling, donkey-voiced young messengers turned up as volunteers when he tackled the crypt.

The demon storms rent the heavens, eventually spinning themselves out far beyond the Golden Isles of the western seas.

Fierce storms had been common enough in the past, but these had steadily worsened, especially over the past five years. Refugees were swarming northwards in both empires.

At midsummer, Anchor Island—named that for the two small but excellent harbors on either side of a ridge, as if bites had been taken out of each side of a plank—had lain directly in the path of the latest storm. The harbor was full of the sound of hammers when the Owlfrost's privateer *Yufi* listed in on the tide. Flotsam all around the shattered ship evidenced the strength of the storm.

"Looks like it was as bad here as it was on the water," croaked First Oar—who could see most of the harbor through the huge gash in the hull where a massive tree had crashed against the ship on the top of a wave.

"There won't be a free laborer to be had for six months," muttered someone else.

Owlfrost wanted to shout, "Quiet fore and aft," but they were only saying what everyone was thinking. Very gloomy thoughts. What had she done in her last lifetime to deserve—

The complaint had scarcely begun forming when out of the wrack heaving on the rollers a rowboat appeared, heading straight for them.

Owlfrost squinted against the glare of the sun—and recognized that face below a headband of shipwright blue. Not one of their own; one of Snowhawk's rescues taken off Angja. What was his name… *"Waha?"*

Waha's dashing grin flashed, then he called, "*Yufi* hoy! Need a hand?"

"I need about a hundred," Owlfrost called down.

They were permitted to anchor within the relative shelter of the inner harbor—at a swingeing fee, as every other ship coming in listed and wallowed with damage.

"I'm making a half a gold piece a day at labor that used to gain me maybe a hand of bronze bits," Waha said after he joined her in the cabin, his handsome face even handsomer when he laughed. "I never thought I'd be grateful for Snowhawk making us learn repair."

"How much? I can't afford gold. Or even silver."

Waha raised a hand. "If you let me sail with you once you're repaired, I'll do it for nothing. I might even have some hands for you. I've been here for almost two months, hoping one or both of you would turn up. Siu had said this was one of your safe harbors."

She nodded; Anchor Island was considered midway between the two empires. Westerners used the western harbor and imperials the east. As long as no one caused any trouble, they could do business and then leave. "Doing business" had sometimes involved selling silk or rice that had been taken off raiders who'd stolen the goods themselves.

"Done." And, that settled, Owlfrost poured the dregs of her tea—it tasted like brine—and said, "Are the storms as bad for the Muds as they are here?"

"In the south, yes," Waha said. "Getting worse."

"And lasting longer into the season," Owlfrost said, a line between her brows.

Waha remembered that she did something or other with Essence—though that had been Kimek's concern. "Is there some reason?" he asked.

She thumbed her eye sockets. "The shamans don't agree. Some blame the Muds. Other warn that the rot around the obsidian throne is causing celestial retribution. My abilities don't reach that far; I suspect even your young friend Kimek would not be able to determine cause. Speaking of him. Have you been among the imperials since we saw you last?"

"I have." Waha gave a brief, light-hearted description of his time masquerading as a gallant wanderer, then as Je Tai's body-guard, and finished, "I made it to Eagle Island ten days after the competition had ended. Kimek had already left, and so I work-ed my way west. I don't see Diggy or Badger. Are they still with Snowhawk?"

"Diggy is Snowhawk's battle master. Badger still cooks. I haven't seen *Dachi* since winter," she added, her gaze sliding in a troubled way to the next ship over, an old trader that had been completely dismasted. She lowered her voice to barely a whisper. "My sister seems to have been caught up in a Cause, fighting against those surrounding the obsidian throne under the secret leadership of, hai-hum, call her a visionary—not only against the snakes, but against slavery."

Waha snorted in disbelief. "It's a cause that will only end in grief."

"Which makes it the more glorious for Snowhawk. No." Owlfrost raised a hand, palm out. "I don't want your opinion. I see enough of it in your eyes. We will not discuss it." Her voice returned to normal. "Tell me about Kimek. When did you see him last?"

Waha's brows rose. "When I left Eagle Island with Jetai. Why do you ask?"

"After the last storm, we picked up some survivors of a shipwreck, three players. Result of our kindness, we have entertainment every night that only the Dragon Knives can afford. They brought the latest gossip out of the far north."

"Let's see...more trouble between First Prince and his allies?"

"You could be an augur!"

They laughed, and Owlfrost went on, "Sidax, that's one of the players, heard that there's a Cobra Sage hunt for him."

Waha shuddered through the rest of the brackish tea to be polite, and sat back. "Why?"

"It's Jhax of Ganis Island, son of Bar Ganis. Kimek saved his life, or his leg. Maybe both. It was during our failed mission."

"And he wants revenge?"

"No! Jhax wants to reward him, according to rumor. Ganis will do anything his son wants. But that Cobra Sage they have, Kimek had told Snowhawk that she was possessed by a blood demon, and she's the one hunting Kimek."

Waha slapped his knees. "Tell you what. I'll still work on this ship. I said I would. And winter will be here before long. But when spring comes around, I'll work my way back up north. Because I know where Kimek will—"

They looked up as a shadow fell across the door. Waha sat up straighter at the sight of a slender man roughly his own age. Instead of shirt or tunic he wore only a ring-worked vest, his bare arms from shoulder to the back of his hands tattooed with climbing roses. More vines visible from the hollow of his collarbones down, disappearing below the waistband of his trousers. A pair of black eyes met Waha's, crinkled briefly in a smile, then the man said to Owlfrost, "There's someone out here wants to discuss berth fees."

Owlfrost snorted. "The harbor is a wreck, but they're right on time with their palm out. Waha, this is Sidax, one of the entertainers I mentioned. Barhal and Kerkam are somewhere about—she sings, and he can play any instrument with strings. Sidax is their face painter, but he sometimes does tattoos."

"Only occasionally," Sidax said, smiling as his gaze roamed Waha. "For works of art."

Black eyes and black hair had always been Waha's weakness. Sidax didn't have Je Tai's pure black hair and his skin was the pale of the west, but those arms, that chest, shaped the vines nicely. "Works of art," he repeated slowly, and Sidax laughed.

Within a day the ship repair commenced. And it was hard labor. But at night, they relaxed—and as Owlfrost had said, Barhal and Kerkam were quite willing to share their talents with all, for only the price of a meal.

As for Sidax, he was willing to share more. He enjoyed Waha's tales of his adventures so far, and told some of his own—not that players got into many off the stage. But when they were done talking, there were other pleasures to be shared.

Right before Owlfrost was ready to sail, they took a night to celebrate, enhanced by jugs of excellent rice wine. Come morning, Waha woke up with his head throbbing, as well as the inside of his right forearm from wrist to elbow. He sat up in a tangle of sheets, ignoring the bite of icy air, and stared down at the still-seeping tattoo of an obsidian dagger with a climbing rose twined around it, and a single crimson blossom. Because of the healing seepage, the rose was especially realistic.

When he went out in search of something to drink, one of the crew let out a low whistle. "Wicked," he said, eyes wide.

"Seduction without a word said," Berhal the singer commented. "But insanely dangerous if you ever go back. The Junsa would kill you for it."

Waha looked at his arm, torn between intense admiration of the artistry, and a sense of *What have I done?*

Hai! It was there. It was done—there was no erasing tattoos. "Easy," he said. "Since I'm never going back." He spotted Sidax helping to bring fresh produce on board.

Sidax smiled his way, and Waha wondered what he'd said to inspire what must have taken all night to do. In the sane light of day, he was aware that he never would have asked for that tattoo.

He forced himself to say, "What do I owe you?" After all, the man was a skilled artist.

"Nothing. Yet," Sidax said, smiling broadly as the other idlers laughed or called out mocking exclamations. "We'll see one another again."

Owlfrost appeared then, looked around at hungover faces, and pointed at the hot water warmer steaming away. "Looks like everyone needs two dishes of strong-brewed dandelion tea before getting ready to sail."

FORTY-THREE

As THE DAYS TURNED into months and the moons revolved inexorably away from one another, Lei's life fell into patterns. The crown princess taught Lei embroidery, and delighted in her precision of eye. She taught her to use a fan, and to dance — all things the modest, scholarly girl had only received rudimentary training in, her time being devoted to her studies.

When the crown princess suffered headaches, it was Lei's soft, soothing voice she wanted reading her favorite romantic wanderer stories — books that had been forbidden to them both, except of course princesses eventually got their way if they were persistent enough. And it was Lei with whom the imperial crown princess went out anonymously one evening (as anonymously as one can be with an entourage of serving maids and a company of hidden guards moving silently from shadow to shadow as an invisible shield) to watch the players and dancers perform one of On Lu's rare operas. But this was not repeated, as Imperial Crown Princess Lam discovered that none of her former favorites was half as beguiling as the remembered sight of her tiger's-eye Hero fighting off a lot of wicked assassins.

Lei enjoyed her days. But there was always that sense of…waiting for a storm. Whenever the imperial princess gave a sudden laugh, or a yell, all the visible household stilled. Waiting.

The first Mood that struck seemed to have been caused by a thunderstorm. Lei did not see what happened. She was trying to sleep when she heard shattering glass followed by shrieking. She ran to her door, peeking out in terror — and caught the silhouette of Nanny Alk gliding into the crown princess's chambers, the smell of medicine drifting after her. Corydalis root, and clematis. Stephania and white peony, those scents Lei recognized. Though the fragrances were mitigated by several other rare herbs. And even a faint whiff of poppy.

The next time occurred after the imperial crown princess returned from making her bow to her mother, to Lei a rarely-glimpsed, gorgeous figure who dressed more like an empress than did the saintly empress, save only for an absence of the golden phoenixes that were the empress's prerogative.

That time, her imperial highness lay on her bed staring up at the ceiling, her eyes open, but she was utterly unresponsive.

Unsure, Lei ran out to find Nanny Alk in the far room. Only a look, and Nanny Alk gestured toward the boiling teapot she always kept nearby, and the maids set out a fine porcelain dish as Nanny Alk brought out her precious herbs. Lei saw her gesture charms over the tea, the air glittering.

When she came out of the imperial heir's bedchamber, she whispered only, "You did right, child."

For a week the princess's wing was redolent of medicine, then a day dawned when the princess sent for Lei, her manner bright, as if nothing had happened.

Lei rated herself far too low to ever expect communication from home, though she missed her parents. Of course she did not dare to write. Her world had shrunk to these rooms high up in the palace, with windows all around. Festival days arrived and passed, always on duty, which meant she did not have to go to the Ji Mansion.

The imperial princess's eighteenth birthday arrived, amid celebration and fireworks over the entire city. The air carried incense from all the temples as people went to pray for her health and longevity, and Lei stood in the background during the interminable banquet, and the new play afterward, taking note of everyone who came forward to congratulate Imperial Crown Princess Lam. Each gift was recorded, and its sender, to receive a personal letter (penned by Lei) on the morrow.

A month later, Lei's birthday came and went unremarked; it never occurred to her to tell anyone. She received a fine new hairpin from her mother, with a loving note, to which she only responded with a single line of thanks.

There were no more letters.

She was not the only one with no communication from

home. Tai had written to his father on his arrival, though there had been little to report. Too little, probably. Though he was careful to keep the letter short, and to send it with the courier carrying everyone else's mail to the capital — they were permitted to do that, at the captain's discretion — he received no answer, not even to report how Lei had done at the imperial examination.

He assumed his frugal father would only write if something was necessary to convey, otherwise trivial matters could wait for Tai's journey home for New Year's Two Moons. But as harvest time cooled toward Sky Wishes Day, Tai began to wonder if he should arrange his own journey back to Mountain Peony for New Year's Two Moons, or if his father would send instructions.

Then he received his first letter from his father.

After a curt though proper salutation, his father wrote:

Your Uncle Ji points out that a winter spent diligently at your new post would gain you considerable merit when it comes time to consider those worthy of promotion. Though your mother and I would very much like to see you here, we both agreed that we must lay aside our selfish desire to reunite in favor of your future promotion.

Tai put the letter down, finding that though he was a little disappointed, he was not as much as perhaps he ought to feel at the prospect of avoiding another visit to Ji Mansion. That was unfilial! He would make up for it with useful work. Beginning with reading through all of those old trunks, and tagging each with its contents, which would speed reorganization once his helpers returned from home.

A month later, he watched a troop ship carry off the naval people who were rotating home for liberty as well as the students, then trudged back, bent against a wet, wintry wind, to commence his new project.

Toward the end of the year, while he was deep into the puzzle of day-to-day records of the last dynasty, in the capital, Lei was summoned to the imperial princess's graywing-steward, who handed her the tiniest scroll she had ever seen.

Marveling, she realized she was receiving her first pigeon letter! That, more than anything so far, made her feel very grown up as she took it to her room to carefully unroll. The rice paper was delicate, her mother's handwriting tiny, with many omissions of strokes and particles in order to fit everything in:

Daughter, we've rec'd reg. & fine repts of you. We'll fetch you when we land. Only us. T. stays @ W.J. We've rec'd good repts of him, but he's too busy to write yr father. I know you can be trusted not say anything, as your father feels it deeply.

Lei was sorry not to be seeing Tai, but so many years had passed without him that she accepted it. Far more worrying was the prospect of facing his highness Uncle Ji and Cousin Venshai again. Of course they would interrogate her.

What to say?

Worries about them had receded through the months. Now they were back, as she returned to finish writing out the New Year's Two Moons greetings that the imperial princess must send out along with gifts.

She was copying the eleventh one, and no longer had to refer to the model letter that the imperial princess had dictated, when there was the princess herself. "And so, Little Lei? You received a pigeon note?"

Lei laid down her brush and bowed from her cushion, for she no longer had to go to the floor. "It is from my mother, your imperial highness."

"Of course it is," the imperial princess said brightly. "Unless you have been hiding a flirt or two?" Her wide eyes crinkled with mirth above her smile. "You must bring your family up to meet me. All of them, mind. Don't let those Jis keep your brother too busy to come, or will I have to send an imperial order?" Her tone was still joking.

Lei bowed again, saying, "My brother is to stay at White Jade, your imperial highness. But I will bring my parents." She looked up from her bow, and stilled.

She had never before seen all the mirth go out of a smile, leaving it a rictus. A frightening rictus, below wide, glittering, unblinking eyes.

"...duty," Lei mumbled, scarcely aware of what she said.

The imperial princess said airily, "Oh, duty! Very familiar, duty. We must all do our duty, must we not? Carry on, carry on." She swept out.

Lei did, but her hand shook, and she spoiled one of the beautiful, creamy papers that the imperial chambers were supplied with. And without quite knowing why, she crumpled it and tossed it onto the brazier warming the chamber.

She didn't see the imperial princess for the remainder of that day, as she had gone over to dine with the emperor. Lei hurried to finish her task without defining to herself why the sense of urgency, but some instinct was at work because somewhere between turtle and tigers hours a scream jolted her awake, followed by shouting, and running feet.

She tore out of bed. Grabbing her robe, she ran to the door when she heard the imperial princess's voice rising — only to be shoved unceremoniously back into her room by one of the graywings who guarded the outer doors. As always, lanterns lit the halls, a soft glow.

She stayed where she was, her door still open, and briefly glimpsed a bloody figure being carried quickly toward one of the far doors, followed by a graywing holding up a night maid, who clasped an arm, her gray robe splattered with dark spots.

Lei retreated into her room, her head swimming. The imperial princess was still shouting and screaming. Lei could not quite make out the words, but gone was her impulse to rush to her side and see what she could do to help.

The steadying, medicinal scent, mixed with the weirdly numbing almost-scent of distilled poppy flowers, drifted along the hall. Then a crash of porcelain, more angry shouting, and Nanny Alk's low voice, speaking one of her charms. The screams broke into gasping sobs, then low voices. And, presently, silence.

The next person Lei saw was the graywing-steward again, this time with no smile. "Secretary Je. Where did she get that dagger?"

"What dagger?" Lei bleated. Only then did she realize she had never seen any sharp-edged implement in those chambers. Even embroidery scissors were rather dull, and very tiny. And when embroidery was over as an activity, the golden needles and scissors had been tidied away instantly by the ever-ready maids.

The steward's mouth tightened. "I see." He left.

Nanny Alk then appeared. "Je Lei, you must be more vigilant. If you go to the opera or bookstore and you are alone with her, and she says she must visit the privy, you must say you have to go as well. You can *never* leave her alone for an instant."

Words crowded Lei's throat — she'd always assumed that the guards she knew were around tended to such things. She remembered those screams, that bloody figure, and forced the words of protest, of self-defense back. There was no defense.

She bowed in apology, tears flowing, then said, "Is…is…"

"Wounded. Garnet severely, when he tried to take the dagger from her."

They withdrew, and the household breakfasted in silence that morning, as the imperial princess slept. She remained in her own chamber for the last two days of Lei's stay, then emerged again, a little wan, but acting as if nothing had happened. "Is it not today that you go away, Little Lei?"

Lei forced herself to bow as she normally did, though the instinct was there to go to the floor, protecting her face and back.

"My head hurts a little," the imperial princess said, rubbing her temples. "I know I said I would greet them, but give my excuses to your parents. I told the steward to reward them with presents in my stead. Do bring them to me when you return. Remember that."

"This ignorant…I promise," Lei whispered. "They will count themselves honored."

The princess walked out again, her brocade silk trailing behind her, and Lei heard her murmur, "No, no, I feel I ought to sit by Garnet. Or maybe I ought to send a gift to his family…"

On her way out, Lei caught a narrow glance from Nanny Alk, and knew what it meant: to be circumspect.

Lei would be circumspect. She dared not be anything else. But as she walked the last distance to meet her waiting parents, she thought, *What happens when the emperor dies, and she is crowned?*

FORTY-FOUR

LEI'S PARENTS LOOKED SO…shabby.

The thought smote her in the heart, so unfilial it was! And it was not even true, if shabby meant neglect. She'd always known that they all wore mended clothes; she'd helped Mother with ribbon-stitch to strengthen weakening seams but now she really saw it. She also saw that their robes were made from third grade silk.

As Mother and Father exchanged bows with the graywing-steward and thanked him ponderously for their care of their daughter, she recognized with sorrow that they looked older than she remembered.

They had not been young when they married, she knew: her father had postponed the wedding until he had attained a position worthy of his betrothed. He'd been near fifty. Lines around dear Mother's eyes that had seemed soft had more furrow. Her pure black hair showed the glint of white. Father was definitely grayer, his sparse beard completely so.

As they walked down to the Ji cart, Lei suspected that both parents were coaxing yet another year out of those robes because Mother had been spending generously, probably too generously, to court suitable families to find a wife for Tai.

But now, after a year of hearing careless talk from the imperial princess about the alliances among the imperial court families, Lei knew why there was no potential bride. Tai was admired by everyone, but the Je family situation would not be. No well-born, ambitious family would be likely to marry a daughter into the Je family, in spite of her father's reputation for probity. Though he was close to the Jis in blood relation, he was still a city magistrate. There was no promising future in rank and wealth for Tai, destined for just such a life of dignified, frugal rectitude—but at a lower level, as he had never taken the imperial examination, but had been buried in a faraway archive, unlikely to see promotion.

She became aware of the silence having gone too long when her mother asked if she, too, were unwell?

"I'm healthy, thank you, Mother," Lei said quickly, and bestirred herself to ask about matters at home.

That occupied the short trip to the Ji mansion, and then here they all were, the prince looking expectantly at her

The poem she had recopied so many times as a child repeated in her mind:

> *Rearing its cubs,*
> *The righteous Tiger trains them to bravery,*
> *Its reared head a safe wall,*
> *Its waving tail a banner.*
> *Even the King of Hell*
> *Dreads a tiger after dark!*

Tigers the Ji uncles and male cousins were, but safe walls?

A Tiger Year—especially a Red Tiger Year—was meant to symbolize bravery, aspirations, and no fear of hard work, but Lei could only think about frightening teeth red-stained with blood. Even if the "red" was actually for the element of fire.

She knew that human will affected the coming year more than the names, but she still felt when her gaze lit on Cousin Venshai's long tassel below the Tenacity knot, and his outer robe's embroidered three-toed dragons among lilies and darting swifts, that she would miss the relative quiet of the Water Ox Year. The fact that that robe was made of the highest-grade silk—which could only be worn by the highest ranks—testified to the family's lofty ambition.

As the elders went through the elaborate ritual of mutual toasts and compliments as well as self-deprecation, Lei considered what she ought to say at the expected interrogation. Lie? "Ah-yah, of course I mention Cousin Venshai to her imperial highness every chance I get!"

But when she looked at her mother's profile, her resolve faltered. Mother's silken robes were made up of much-mended third grade fabric, but that silk was still soft and lustrous, it breathed in summer, it floated when Mother walked, emphasizing her grace. Third grade silk was still good silk in all the ways that mattered. Mother never had to lie awake counting up her lies in order to remember them.

Kanda spoke so many warnings about the hard path to virtue, written over and over as Lei mastered her writing. She had not thought about their meaning until now: once you began lying, the act got easier. Eventually you would even lie to yourself, but before then, you would have destroyed trust.

Do I want my uncle to trust me, she wondered as QiQi fought back a yawn. Dear QiQi! She had never scorned Lei's own third-grade silks. Lei glanced down at herself, wearing the deep green robe covered with lilies that Mother had had made for her last year, unworn until now because as Secretary Je she always wore the gray of the imperial heir's household. QiQi, like her brother, dressed in heavier, more lustrous first-grade silk, and her hairpins were gold with jade decorations instead of polished cedarwood, but QiQi had never made any comparison, ever.

I have to be able to trust myself, Lei decided.

That resolve was put to the test that very night. After the long banquet, and before the early parting so that the prince and Cousin Venshai could get their rest in anticipation of the extremely early rising, QiQi invited Lei to her own chamber, but in a way that instantly put Lei on alert.

And sure enough, Cousin Venshai showed up before they'd even poured out the waiting tea, and summoned her to his father's study.

"Niece, you never came to us all year," was the first thing the prince said.

"It was not permitted," Lei replied, bowing.

"Yes, so my eyes in that wing discovered before both were sent away after they tried to communicate with you," Venshai said. Lei had not even been aware of that. "It's going to take time and effort to replace them."

"And expense," the prince murmured on a sigh. Then came the question she had dreaded: "What can you tell us about the imperial crown princess. Specifically these mysterious intervals that get whispered about?"

She regarded her uncle and cousin, wishing that smart words would leap to her tongue.

They looked back, and Venshai's brow drew down. "Is it bribery you w—" A look from his father silenced him, and he struggled to contain his own emotions, then said in an effort to be reasonable, "Cousin Lei, it's good that she seems to have won your loyalty. But your first loyalty must be to your family..."

The prince raised a hand. "Niece, consider the probable future of the imperial court. Of the empire itself. If there is a demon hiding inside the future empress—"

"There is no demon, Uncle Ji," Lei said.

The two sat back, one skeptical, the other wary.

"You seem very sure," Venshai ventured.

The prince said, "It is good to have that corroborated by one so often in her imperial highness's august presence, but then more questions remain, still troubling. But let us shift from the individual to the consequences of that individual's actions. Niece, you are very young, and you were never raised to the intricacies of the imperial court. Yet even you must perceive the need for a watchful tension between court and throne."

He paused, and so she bowed.

"It's a way of limiting...errors on the imperial scale that are easy for one individual—even Heaven's Chosen—to make."

Again a pause, and again she bowed. That much, she had begun to see the truth of.

"Our purpose..." Here he indicated himself and Venshai first, then extended his hand to include the entire household. "Our purpose is to share that burden. The true purpose behind the Three and Six is founded on Mana Ta's sagacious observation that more and wiser heads avoid errors. Think about that, Niece, in the coming year."

Venshai's gaze flicked to his father's face, but the prince laid his hand flat on his fine desk, the jade ring gleaming. Venshai bowed his head.

"That is all," the prince said, smiling. "We must retire, for the turtle hour comes very fast on such bitter nights, and the imperial House of Ancestors is not hospitable to old bones."

He let her go; Venshai accompanied her out, and when they got to the hall, he said, "Does she mention wedding negotiations? Do you talk about me to her? Did she mention me at all?"

Lei had at least an answer for that, and spoke the truth: "She has no desire to marry yet."

Venshai sighed, his gaze rolling upward, but he accepted that, and she was left alone. But not in peace. Because the prince was right about trying to limit errors. Were he and Venshai right after all? She knew she did not want them to be right, because she did not like Venshai's callous ambition. Though maybe you had to be callous and ambitious to be part of the imperial court?

She reminded herself that these decisions were not up to her. She was a secretary, not a decision-maker. Still, as Kanda said, gaining knowledge was a lifetime pursuit—and Suanek said that harmony was a lifetime pursuit.

She had to learn more for her own sake, and from those she trusted for knowledge and harmonious example. Nanny Alk seemed to be one. Mother was another, but she would tell her to do whatever her elders instructed. Which brought her back to Uncle Ji and Cousin Venshai.

There was always Great-Aunt Han, who had once been a part of the imperial court's Bureau of Divination as a high-ranking geomancer…Yes! Surely she would be able to show Lei the right path—and if she said that Lei must trust her uncle and cousin in spite of her dislike, then she would resolve to conquer her own pettiness.

The rest of her stay at the Ji mansion went better than she'd allowed herself to expect, once that initial interrogation was over, thanks to the arrival of Prince Yimu Guan, brother to the Sixth Imperial Consort, to whom QiQi's cousin Meishai from the tertiary Ji House had been married the previous year.

Meishai, once very much a dependent like Lei, wore so many jewels in her headdress that she would have outshone the imperial heir as she gave Lei a sulky, bored greeting in a single word, "Cousin," before she swept by.

"Cousin Meishai doesn't look happy," Lei ventured to QiQi.

"How could she be? That Yimu husband of hers has got so many consorts for her to keep track of that he's rumored to be building yet another palace just to house them. A pleasure garden, he calls it. So vulgar." She flicked her fan in warding. "Just think, Lei. But for my grandmother, that position as his first wife probably would have been yours. "

"Was Cousin Meishai bullied into marrying him?"

"She! No, she drove a hard bargain before agreeing. I guess I respect her for that, though she's always been a snoop and a tattletale. Which is exactly what Father wants! But she got an enormous dowry out of Father first—you know the Third House has next to nothing—and she also got the wish of her heart, marrying a title higher than anything her two sisters can expect."

They watched Venshai take the smirking Prince Yimu Guan off to some male entertainment while Meishai was whisked off to be closeted with the prince, which lasted quite a while, preventing any possibility of Lei being pressed into more "instruction."

Then came the day Lei looked forward to, when she and her parents went to visit the Han family. Twice she tried to speak to her great-aunt alone, to be sent away by her maid the first time, and then by Grandmother Han the second time.

Grandmother Han had always been kindly, making sure everyone had enough to eat, even though she was rather prone to handing out unasked-for advice. But that was typical of elders.

Even so, Lei was taken aback to be scolded, right there at the table before the entire family. "Granddaughter, we are all proud of your attainments, but you must learn not to put yourself forward, presuming on your lofty promotion. My aunt has her good days and her not good days. You were told that earlier. She is in company as much as she can bear, and we haven't forgotten how you and your brother preoccupied her last year, upsetting her."

Lei bit back an exclamation that Great-Aunt Han had summoned *them* last year — that would be arguing with an elder.

Another cousin leaned over to whisper, "Don't be expecting a great inheritance from Great-Aunt Han. Even though she never married or had children, she donates everything to Suanek's temple."

"That's right," a young Han cousin added in a hiss from Lei's other side. "Sometimes I think that the refugees from the demon storms are better off than we are, crowded into this house, three to a bedchamber meant for one." She poked her sister, who poked her back. "Anyway, *you've* done well enough for yourself, secretary to the imperial heir. Leave something for the rest of us!"

Lei had never once thought about inheritances! But she suspected that no one would believe her.

At least her parents had genuinely been glad to see her as the Tiger Year began, and genuinely reluctant to part when it was time to return her to the imperial palace, which inexorably closed around her.

The imperial crown princess was in her sunniest mood. "A tiger year," she exclaimed. "We will look out some stories about tigerish heroes, shall we not? Your esteemed family is well?"

Lei thanked her for asking, and said, "My parents are quite well."

"And your brother? I know he did not leave his current position, but I trust they are delighted by good reports from him?"

Once again Lei thanked her for her kindness in asking, and once again fought the temptation to lie and say all was well. Because she did not actually know that. "He has not written, but we assume he is well," she said carefully.

"No letters to his father, even? So unfilial," the imperial princess said.

Lei could not defend her brother, because there *were* no letters, so she could only bow unhappily.

The imperial princess stared at Lei's lowered face, her expression impossible to interpret. As always, Lei held her breath—they all held their breath when the imperial princess stilled, or paused, or seemed that she might be on the brink of a Mood.

But then she only said, "There is surely a reason. And I trust it will emerge next year. Even the strictest court minister would not keep someone from a home visit two years in a row. And a year passes fast. Aish! A year passes fast."

The imperial court was also on Tai's mind—only that of the previous dynasty, as these endless boxes and baskets were all from that time and place.

His reading had begun as merely a way to catalogue the contents of the trunks strewn about with no order whatsoever. But without any distractions, Tai was able to scan with the rapidity of his schooldays filled with rivers of text. He preferred reading to liberty time over at Gold Island, where there were entertainments—and entertainers—to be enjoyed. He'd had a surfeit of entertainment when his mother insisted he attend every social event.

During his time as a slave scribe on Angja, when he had to master another language, comprehend the gist of old imperial, then recast it to be understood by the Westerners, he had become skilled at summarizing context. The more Tai read, the clearer his perception of that long-ago court.

He spent longer and longer hours shivering in the crypt, with two lanterns set on either side to cast no shadows on those neatly written pages, and a warming pan for his hands. He brought scrolls and sheafs back when he had to eat. Only exercise broke his concentration, but as he sweated through fundamentals and sparred, his mind was far away, considering what he read.

He saw how it all fit together, just as those beams overhead fit together, interlocking into a whole that was far stronger than any single log. Even when great winds made the pillars and ceilings creak, the fittings had enough give to protect the whole. A building, like a court, was only as strong as its weakest beam.

For the first time he looked past the archival language that the dynasty had changed, and tried to tease out *why* it had changed. Two things were missing: one, whatever those long-gone ministers and princes had done behind closed doors.

Second? The geomancers' reports for the imperial island. Ayah, it could be overlooked, for though the geomancers were vitally important, they were completely independent, no part of court. Their mandate was simple. Straightforward: to ease the earth, so that when nature caused it to shake there was no devastation. And yet Mt. Lir had threatened to explode to the extent that the entire capital had had to be evacuated.

Yet there was *nothing* from the geomancers. Conspicuous, possibly only to a tidy mind, by its absence. He had to refrain from making assumptions based on an absence: it might be that, given Mt. Lir's threats, there were far too many records and so there had been another ship entirely, all those records born away elsewhere. Or even kept at the far end of the former imperial island.

The last of the Ox Year faded and the new Tiger Year dawned, unnoticed by Tai. He kept reading, as winter set in, and days passed in which he could not even get to the garrison for the heavy rains. At least snow here was seldom, and never lasted long. Except for the demon storms, the weather here in the south was so much milder than in the north.

He searched the remaining trunks for anything relating to geomancy.

Nothing.

"I brought you back a brick of Celestial Leaf," Inke said one bright day, as the corridors filled with the sound of happy voices and the clatter of divination sticks used in games. "My sister sent it. She says our Cousin Hyacinth over on the east coast saw you as the Hero last year. This year's Hero wasn't nearly as good, I was to say, and if you would like to write to Cousin Hyacinth — or to my sister in the capital…"

Tai didn't even hear the last words of this winsome invitation. He waited until Inke was done, thanked him for the tea, then asked, "I'm sure you were at the chief's office when the courier's bags were brought in. Were there any letters for me?"

"Not that I saw," Inke said — which meant there weren't any, or he'd have known. "Which reminds me. You never mentioned that your sister ranked fifth in the imperial examination! And she was made personal secretary to the imperial heir!"

Tai bit back the impulse to exclaim, *What? That's because I did not know!*

"But that's Secretary Je Tai, never brags, even about his family's merit, much less his own. I hadn't even known you'd run as the Hero over in Dawn's Placid Sea! My Lui grandfather took us brats during the Dolphin Year to see the dragon parade…"

Tai didn't hear the rest of what Inke said. He was too puzzled. As a child studying here, he had received two letters a year, one for his birthday, and another to inform him when and how to return home for the New Year — unless there was great news. He had assumed when he received no birthday letter that his frugal father deemed him too old for such expenses. And he had received that one letter instructing him to remain over the festival season.

Of course letters did get lost. One courier had been swamped and nearly sunk in one of the demon storms, all communications having been ruined in the brine that came through the hull. Another had been driven off course, arriving after two months of beating against current and wind. But it had arrived. Without anything for him.

He briefly considered someone deliberately keeping his letters from him, but why? Tampering with officials' matters, even personal ones such as family letters, was strictly forbidden, with terrible penalties.

At the other end, who would trouble themselves to interfere with Father's letters? The only ones who conceivably had the wherewithal would be the Ji cousins. But would even Lekshai risk his life by tampering with the governmental courier system? What would destroying home letters get him? Nothing but that terrible punishment if caught. Anyway, Venshai had gone to great efforts toward family amity at the end of Tai's stay at the Ji mansion, and Lekshai had been sent north.

Tai slept badly, wondering why he had not heard about his sister's news. Had something changed at home and he was unaware? Perhaps they were so used to him being gone that he no longer came to mind!

Worrying at the matter was like thrusting a stick into a pond and dredging up the old leaves and things mixed into the mud, which made the water turbulent. He woke feeling that he was missing something, but it had nothing to do with those wretched cousins.

It wasn't until he reached the crypt, meaning to clear his mind with more sorting and reading, when the sight of the waiting trunks and that puzzle overlapped with the letters puzzle, and he stopped in the doorway, muttering, "Geomancers."

It was during the conversation that he and Lei had had with Great-Aunt Han. The way she had broken off. He could not recollect her words exactly, only the general context: she'd said something about geomancers, and something about the court—but she hadn't finished the thought. Then, after that lengthy pause, she had changed the subject.

Odd. And probably no matter. But now that he was thinking about it, he might write to her about this archival puzzle. Surely she would know something about where the geomancer records of the last dynasty ended up. Why not ask her? In his experience, elders liked to be asked about their experiences during their young years

That decided, it was back to regular work.

A day or so later, his volunteers reappeared, restless and ready as the weather was far too rainy for outdoor activities during their liberty time. And for the rest of the winter, they shifted trunks and boxes and racks and baskets, now all neatly labeled. With an end in sight, the mood was cheerful with anticipation for the banquet he'd promised to treat them to when they finished.

The next courier arrived on time.

He didn't even go to check. But they were mid-way in dragging trunks to the far wall when one of his volunteers appeared, saying, "I've been summoned home."

"You just got back!"

"Nothing bad, I hope, Yufin?" Inke asked, making a sign of warding.

"No, no, it's just that my first brother got promoted to assistant registrar under the governor at Myrtle Island. They found out the day after we sailed. He's to be married first, and the whole family must be there. Back I go! Ay-eee, no study for me!"

"You'll be making it up," someone else predicted with mock grimness.

"No need to look for red comets for that," another chimed in. "They'll pile extra on. Sure as rain."

"Croak, croak, frogs," Yufin chortled. "It's I who will be lying at my ease on that boat while you are sweating out Purple Star Readings for Old Grump, and I'll be watching the dancing girls at the Magnolia while...." He was buried under a hail of dusty scroll bags and broken baskets.

As Tai helped extricate him, he got an idea. "I'd like to ask a favor, if I might, Yufin."

Yufin, who had returned with a fresh tattoo on his forehead but hadn't dared to bring it out to dazzle his friends yet, brightened. "Anything, Secretary Je!"

"Do you know where the Han Mansion is? No, you probably wouldn't—"

This really was Yufin's lucky day. "But I do! My Second Uncle is steward to Chief Engraver Han! I used to play with the Han boys before I was sent here to study augury."

"I've a letter for my grand-aunt. Would you take it to her? Then I needn't trouble the official couriers at all."

"I'd be happy to," Yufin said, and he brightened further when Tai—who never spent his pay—promised him a string of coins, beseeching him to enjoy a good meal for his trouble.

That night, Tai sat down to finish his letter, and considered writing to his father, too. But he hesitated, for anything he'd say about lack of news from home could be mistaken for unfilial complaint. Instead, he added a carefully worded request that when his great-aunt happened to communicate with Tai's mother next, she might convey Tai's respects to his parents, and his wishes for a prosperous and healthy year. There. Nothing objectionable in that!

Yufin went off the next day aboard the courier vessel, Tai's contribution nicely weighing in his sleeve pocket, and life settled back to normal.

FORTY-FIVE

Winter reluctantly loosened its claws in the north, and gallant wanderers who had been in one spot over the extent of the cold, icy, snowy season hailed pools of melt with relief and began finding their ways toward Eagle Island.

Mek arrived with two other flyers met during a defense against pirates the summer before.

He walked past Eagle Island Sect's Heaven's Ease, pausing only to drop his things in the dorm shared by all the young men. "Empty," he said happily, and chucked his gear into the space he liked best; it never occurred to him that the others pointed out to occasional guests, "No, that's Ki Mek's place." He'd assumed only the Bian family and their relations had permanent places.

He ran down to the kitchen yard, and paused at the flimsy gate, put up to keep the chickens from wandering off. It was a nice day, and it looked as if cooking had already shifted outside. Chickens pecked and clucked about the yard, ignored by and ignoring the cat who advanced on some errand of her own, tail up except for a curl at the end. Under the awning support, two new nests had appeared, cheeping audible from both.

And there was Han Anise at the prep table, kneading dough for noodles, a short-haired black and tan dog sitting at her feet, muzzle upraised. Mek didn't recognize the dog.

As he watched, Han Anise's untidy brown hair stirred, and a pigeon poked out of her jumbled topknot. Delight rushed through Mek.

Anise dusted her hands and reached up to stroke the

pigeon. "Yes, yes, I haven't forgotten you, Daisy. Let's get these noodles on the boil." She brought her hand down — then caught sight of Mek. And her face beamed with delight to match his own. "Mek!"

"I'm back," he said. "Is the pigeon hurt? Or are pigeon hairpins a new fashion?"

Anise chuckled. "Something tangled on one of her toes. She had a torn leg, and I kept her with me while she healed, but now she seems to think a warm nest of hair just the thing. I'm sure she'll flit off when the weather gets warmer." Anise's smile brightened even more, then a thought occurred and she exclaimed in dismay, "Are all the Kis with you? There are so few of us here. I don't have nearly enough dough..."

"There are only two with me, over at Heaven's Ease to see Uncle Bian. I'll go greet him, but I hoped maybe I could snatch a bun — I'm hollow down to my heels."

"He's not here. Few are. They're still helping somewhere in the south. There's a lot of rumor about Western raiders, or pirate fleets, or both." She looked worried. "Why would there be pirate *fleets*?"

Mek considered what to say, and opted for what was easiest. "Most of 'em are desperate fishers or traders or the like. Storm damage has turned a lot of people out. I think they're finding piracy tougher than they thought, and if the imperials ever get to fixing the damage, they'll go home again."

"We've been hearing about you," Anise said then. "Not the Ki family, but you, though it's not as Ki Mek. At least, Sagacious Blade, that is you, isn't it?"

Mek reddened. "That's not really me, it's her." Her jerked his thumb over his shoulder.

"Her?"

He held out his hand, and Anise blinked, startled when a golden gleam flashed and suddenly Mek was holding the beautiful bronze sword with the overlapping scales. "Right after I left last year with Four. We caught up almost immediately with Seven and Ten. I was trying to get used to the sword, see. I was on the deck doing warmups when she spoke to me. Just once. This little voice, like a kitten. There are other voices, but those are...charms, I guess is the way to say it. Past wielders."

"Their souls are caught in the sword?" Anise asked doubtfully.

"No. It really is like a charm." He was aware that he wasn't making sense. "The voices don't speak to *me*. It's more like they're giving instruction. As if a charm caught their words. It's not always martial skills that they talk about. Sometimes it's Essence skills."

He'd learned that the less he said about the sword the better, as most people knew little to nothing about Essence matters. But Anise—who studied divination—accepted his assurance. "Ah. Then the sword is not cursed. That's good. Though I would have been surprised if Old Uncle and Uncle Bian would cherish a demon-cursed sword."

Mek said, cautiously, "There...might be a demon."

She dropped her knife, startled and worried.

He waved his hands. "If there is, it's not evil." He hesitated, groping inwardly for the words to explain that instant's sense of a vast awareness when that suffused him when that tiny voice spoke.

"As for the sword's name—the *sword's*, *not* mine—what happened was this: when it spoke to me, I yelped *Sagacious Blade?* Four started calling me that, and the rest followed, though I've begged them not to. Even threatened—but of course that just made it worse," he admitted. "You know us Kis. Anything for a joke."

Anise suppressed a smile, and returned to her noodles. "You're Mek to me," she said comfortingly. "Did you catch up in time to join the convoy, then?"

"They were waiting for us at Standing Stone Harbor. I thought it would be boring, but it wasn't." He thought of the swarms of rootless survivors of the demon storms everywhere—and the many things he was learning about Sagacious Blade. "We got the tea down to Lan Island, right enough, and once New Year's Two Moons was over, they had rice ready to come north." It was rice many new pirates were after, not silk or even tea. Rice, to avoid starving.

"Isn't it early for the rice convoy? You must have been sailing in winter," Anise protested.

"We were. But the rice convoys are all sailing earlier now, before the demon storms start up this time of year. Though those seem to be coming earlier, and staying later." He frowned—though it was futile to hate nature. Except sometimes it was almost as if something drove the storms, though that wasn't right: if there had been malicious intent in them—like the storm he'd sensed driven by an Essence wielder, when he and Tai were on board the ebony trader—he'd have known.

Anise broke that familiar, useless circle of thoughts: "Here's tea. Drink up! Did you see any krakens?"

"Only one, and way down deep, passing under us."

He sheathed Sagacious Blade, washed his hands, took a last slurp of tea, and picked up a knife in order to chop the waiting vegetables. He knew she would not want to hear about the galleys chasing their rice convoy, or the fight at Kandra Sutra's second harbor, which had been taken by a ship of Western raiders in order to set up an outpost. Anise wanted to hear about the cranes he had seen flying across both moons the night after New Year's, and about the green parrot that had adopted Seven, and the way it delighted in feeding off Seven's shoulder.

In her turn, she told him about the progress of the Eagle Island Sect children, and about all the animals, most of whom she'd named, as they cooked up the evening meal.

Bian Ze and five scouts of Eagle Sect returned two days later, the signal to leave for the competition site, where several crafts of various sizes were on the approach—Waha with them.

He'd zigzagged his way north, working alternately as a night crew hand on various scruffy fishers and the like, and on land as a door guard, a wharf laborer, and for a very interesting week as a palanquin-bearer for an entertainer getting on in years who augmented her visual allure by being carried about by hand-picked comely young men with martial tattoos.

Everyone gossiped. When he heard the name "Sagacious Blade," he shrugged it off as just another faceless, muscle-bound bravo. Until the night he was earning a bed by serving behind the counter at an inn, and overheard a drunken slur, "No, I'm telling you! He told the tea traders to get b'hind the lead vessel, see, then he stands right there on the stern of the last one. Seen with these eyes, right here." A swipe with a huge paw toward his flushed, bleary face, as if to present evidence that he possessed organs of sight. "He hoists this golden sword into the air, and I'll be a viper for my next ten lifetimes if I'm lying, but I saw him cleave those demon winds right into two, and the line of ships sailed right down the wind as slick as oil in a pan."

"A sword made of gold, ha ha ha!"

"Just as well he was cutting air with it—gold wouldn't cut

cabbage, unless it was boiled."

"Shut up, shut up, shut up! I want to hear more about this qilin who can wave a sword and kill storms."

"Not kill," the storyteller insisted, thick brows meeting over a glowing nose. "Did any of you hear me say kill? I didn't say kill. I said cut through the wind. Sagacious Blade even said after he woke up that he can't stop storms. Who can? Outside of a god, of course."

"After he woke up?" Waha asked—pouring the storyteller more freshly warmed rice wine.

The storyteller grunted approvingly at this bribe, and said, "Soon as the winds died down some, and we dared to go up on deck, Sagacious Blade staggered as if he couldn't hold up his arms, and said, *Drink!* And Old Shou thinks first thing of wine, of course, and brings up some fresh white, the strongest the captain had. Sagacious Blade drank it all down in one gulp, gave a hiccough, fell on his butt and keeled over flat, snoring."

Everyone laughed at that, and Waha thought, yes, that *has* to be Kimek.

"When he woke, we gave him hangover soup and bread, and a bucket or two of water. He was better at once, and told us he can't stop storms, only cut them."

After that, Waha listened for the name Sagacious Blade. He heard it once or twice, mostly rumors about the storm, but another one about pirates, before Eagle Island bumped up on the horizon at last.

He hefted his gear over one shoulder and in his free hand carried a bag of dried apricots to lay before the Fox God. Though he followed no god—because no god followed him, and to Waha, any relationship had to be equal—he liked that sly smile. It had real knowing it in, as well as mirth. And the cock of the foxy head with the three tails curling up over it added a hint of mockery that somehow wasn't cruel.

He discovered that the Kis had just arrived, their rising tent as usual a center of noise and talk and people stretching and warming muscles. He was about to go look for Kimek when he heard a familiar cry, "Waha!"

There was Kimek himself—a little taller, a little broader, but still very much himself, flyaway hair escaping from his topknot. "You came back! Weren't you with Tai? Did he get home safely?"

"I did, I was, and he did. Now he's gone off to bury himself in some archive, so I left him at it. I take it you're now calling yourself Sagacious Blade?"

Mek's ears reddened. "Don't *you* start that! My family thinks it's funny," he admitted sourly. "As if I'm still a sprout of ten. I'm *twenty* now! As for getting a sword, all of *them* have had swords since long before they got their first chin hairs!"

Waha didn't see any chin hairs on Mek, and chuckled. "Twenty! Oh no, a venerable graybeard!" And when Mek grimaced, he ceased his mocking tone. "I suspect the distinction is not due to your having acquired a sword. It's what you're doing with it. Like cutting storms in two."

"I didn't know I could do that until I did it," Mek said uncomfortably, and looked down at his scruffy boots, an intriguing mixture of the boy Waha had known in the mine, and the man he was becoming. Apparently a legend already, though that was difficult to believe right now.

Waha said, "Listen. Now that no one's listening, there's another aspect to it you need to consider. One of the other reasons why I came back here this spring. Remember Jhax of Ganis?"

"Who?" Mek blinked, then snapped his fingers. "The boy on the dock. With the badly mauled leg. During our raid."

"He's mounted a search for you. I think he means to recruit you, but the problem—according to Owlfrost—is that the Cobra Sage attached to that family is running the search. Owlfrost was concerned enough to feel it worthwhile to pass it on."

Mek's grin vanished. "Cobra Sages," he said uneasily.

Waha said, "I haven't seen any. They'd have a hard time within the empire, it seems to me. Though they have paid eyes and ears. Here's my point. If you go on letting the world call you Sagacious Blade, it fouls the trail for Kimek."

"I didn't tell him my name."

"Someone somewhere did," Waha said soberly. "Maybe there were survivors of that failed raid who went off bearing grudges. Maybe Bar Ganis nabbed one of Snowhawk's followers and questioned them. It's something to keep in mind if you stay with convoys on the west side of your empire. You might even consider going east for a time. If you vanish, the hunt will inevitably die down. No Cobra Sage stays long away from their blood games."

Mek clasped his hands, bowing his thanks. "I'll remember."

His brows twitched together, and his eyes widened as his gaze fell on Waha's forearm, bared as he'd rolled back his sleeves. "Ayah! Where did you get that? How did you afford it?" He pointed at the long tattoo of the obsidian knife with the climbing rose.

Waha laughed. "From one of Owlfrost's rescues. You don't have face painters in eastern theaters, I discovered here, except for the boring ancient plays. For the daring plays, everyone wears a mask."

"That must be in the empire," Mek said. "Gallant wanderers don't dress up when they do plays." He brandished his flute. "We just…play." He put the flute to his lips and trilled a little flourish.

The competitions began.

Waha was pleased to end those first two days having not been eliminated from any of the contests he'd entered, and he noted from a distance that Mek hadn't either. But they didn't have a chance to speak again until Waha rose early on the day of the prospective final bouts.

He went to wash up, and when he came back, he found himself face to face with Mek, whose expression was odd. "I have a favor to ask," he began. "Tai needs my help…"

FORTY-SIX

BUT FIRST I MUST go back a day, and return to Tai.

The mulberry trees on the hills up behind White Jade's garrison were fuzzing green when the monthly courier arrived early, having been driven on the wind of an incoming storm.

Yufin appeared at the dining room, soaking wet. "Just in time for supper," he panted. "Take this. It's yours," he added, coming directly to Tai. He dug into his carryall, pulled out something wrapped tightly, and handed it over, averting his head.

Everyone at the table reacted, waving hands before their noses or wrinkling faces in disgust. "Phew, what *is* that stink?"

"It's like the ground demon-dirt root my mother made me drink when I was little!"

"Tree tar, too," someone else said, glaring fixedly at the wrapped item in Tai's hands. "My mother was the herb wife in our village. I know that reek."

"I do, too, and now you know why I refused to have anything to do with my father's pharmacy," a gangling youth added.

"I was to inform you that it's a family remedy to cure anyone who's costive," Yufin said, suppressing mirth. "I had to keep it in the hold."

"I'm not costive." Tai peeled back some of the wrapping on a ceramic jar, sealed with the Han character clear. There was no mistake — it seemed to be intended for him.

Yufin handed him a crumpled, slightly damp letter; Great-Aunt Han had written back. "Here's this, too. Sorry about the wet. It rained the entire trip," he said apologetically. "Now that

I'm rid of that stenchiferous medicine, I can put my stuff away and join you, so don't eat all the peach buns!" He ran off.

Tai had been sitting with his student volunteers—who had stuck with the project, though he had not expected them to. As the ranking person there, he could not be chased away, but he successfully interpreted the side-eying and sniffing and little suppressed coughs, and rose. "And away it goes," he informed the others, to their enthusiastic thanks.

He waited till he reached his tiny room to open the letter. It was short, full of good wishes for the new year, exhortations to work hard, and the rest of the letter conveyed greetings from the entire Han family, named one by one. And not a hint of anything about geomancy. That was odd. He laid letter and half-unwrapped package down, and returned to finish his meal.

The evening was spent in cataloguing the now-organized crypt, amid much discussion and speculation about those long-ago events when everyone had had to suddenly evacuate the imperial capital and learn to live somewhere else. Though he was curious about that package, he consciously stuck to his habit of making sure that he noticed each person's labor in some way. It was something he'd seen Bian Ze do on Eagle Island, and how effective it was to be aware of everyone's contribution. How willing they were to work—the opposite of the caustic opprobrium Ji Venshai handed out when he was ordering everyone around.

When he finally entered his room, he was met by the terrible stink again. He was tempted to take the jar out to the compost heap, but the storm was already rising, the winds fierce. He pushed his window out to get rid of the smell. The window shuddered in his hands, wind scouring through the room.

He shut the window, unwrapped the jar—and realized that the stink was actually coming off the wrapping. He opened the window, tossed out the heavy cloth, which was promptly whipped away on the wind, and pulled the window shut.

Then he examined the small ceramic ointment pot. Costiveness? This was very odd! He'd never heard of anyone under the age of fifty who complained of that disorder.

He broke the seal and pried off the stopper, holding his breath—then stared in surprise. Inside was no salve, or even medicinal tea, but a small scroll, tightly rolled.

He pulled his candle close and carefully unrolled the

scroll—to discover that the letter was written in the ancient characters. He hadn't had to look at that script since his days on Angja, and hated the reminder, but there, at the left, was his Great-Aunt's name. Clearly his idle question about geomancy of the past dynasty required this effort toward secrecy.

He bent to translate.

My dear, good child: First and most important, if you are writing to your family, your letters are not reaching them. This New Year's Two Moons past, your mother admitted to disappointment that they had not heard from you at all, though your father faithfully sends a letter off every change of Phoenix Moon. He even troubled to take the latest letters directly to the courier ship himself.

I will not speculate on the reasons. There might be any number, including the increase and severity of the storms.

Second, your questions about the location of the geomancy records of the former dynasty. I cannot answer that question either, for I do not know where these records might be — or even if they exist.

But I do know the reason they might be elsewhere, or burnt, for my own grandfather confessed to me shortly before he died, as I was the only one of his descendants to take up the geomancy arts.

He confessed that his own grandfather was involved, against his will, in a conspiracy instigated by Golden Celestial Chariot General Tan before he ascended the golden throne to become the first emperor of the present dynasty.

You probably know that the previous dynasty was riven by three warring factions, led by three of the seven imperial princes. The empire was on the brink of civil war. Two princes were governors of big islands, and raised significant armies.

You might also have read that, before the change of the fatal year, the augurs of the former dynasty had seen a swarm of inauspicious stars in the sky on a night of a red body showing brightly, when both moons were on the wane. The Chief Augur interpreted these signs as a warning that war was nigh.

But what I am about to confess is not generally known, as the first emperor issued strict orders to annihilate the entire families of anyone who revealed what my grandfather's grandfather confessed to him.

The general either had a shaman who interpreted these signs differently, or caused a shaman to be found who interpreted them differently. This shaman whom no one knew predicted the imminent eruption of the dragon under Mt. Lir, which would destroy the entire island.

The General (so my grandfather was told) captured the Chief Geomancer, and instructed him to cause tremors from the mountain, or his family would pay the forfeit. These tremors, though mild, alarmed everyone, and the last emperor issued his famous final edict that Heaven had rescinded its trust in him, and that the imperial city was to be evacuated, before he took poison.

Every child learned that the last emperor had decreed that the imperial capital was to be moved in order to save lives. Thus, in dying, his last thought had been for his subjects.

How true was that? Mysterious shaman? New prediction? Tai had found no sign of any of this in all those trunks! And now he suspected that he was not going to find any. The General oversaw the great migration in safety, and he was proclaimed by the grateful people the first emperor of a new dynasty.

Tai lowered the paper, contemplating the scale of such an undertaking as evacuating an entire city. He remembered the chaos of that attack at Icecrown, and that had only involved the harbor side of a town. If evacuating an entire city while the ground was shaking and everyone predicting doom was not to be utter chaos, causing endless panic and destruction and wanton death, there had to have been planning for every contingency.

And that took time. Implying considerable organization beforehand. No wonder the records were not lying about here for anyone to stumble across!

Tai stared unseeing at his rattling window as the wind shrieked, then jumped when something slammed against the wall outside. Maybe he ought to block his window? But with what?

He turned his back on it as he considered the time that had elapsed since those long-ago days. Great-Aunt Han was surely not the only person who had heard deathbed confessions. Secrets that large did not entirely die, even under the threat of annihilation of an entire family.

What good would come of revealing the truth now? At least one thing was certain: whatever motive the General had had, he apparently had not only circumvented a deadly civil war, but he had succeeded in uniting everyone in moving the imperial capital.

Then why was this confession written in the old language and tucked inside noisome wrappings?

His candle flickered as the wind howled outside. He bent over the note.

You might be wondering why your old, foolish great-aunt has gone to this much effort to communicate this way.

That is because there is a more urgent dilemma facing the imperial court, which is related. After pondering matters, I am taking the risk to inform you because I believe everyone <u>ought</u> *to know by now, which is: the ground beneath the capital here is unstable. The geomancers have to reinforce the plinths — more plinths here than there are almost anywhere else —* <u>every single day</u>.

These mountain ridges are not strong enough to support so many great dwellings even without all the tunnels that the common folk have delved into the foot of the ridge over time, to find space to live. Having no windows is only the "face" of the problem.

The imperial court is locked in conflict over this and other matters, ignoring the Bureau of Geomancy, which has been implicit in keeping the secret. And which is not able to predict when the ground could give way, or how much ground will be involved. I suspect that many ministers of rank are confident that their fine, strong-walled palaces will survive, and only the tunnel homes of the commons will be crushed. Regrettable, but easier than packing up and moving back to the imperial island.

The imperial island, you are probably saying? Yes. Because my once-independent department, purely dedicated to the good of the world, has been compromised by political suasion: each year, someone has to sail to the old imperial capital to see that the fires on Coral Island are maintained, to preserve the illusion of threat.

There is no threat from the dragon under Mt. Lir. There never was.

Coral Island is just an island of rock, with no life on it. The east wind carries the smoke westward over the sea, causing no damage, or I never would have agreed to it, even if they took my life. Because I never married or had children, until five years ago, that person continuing the fires was me.

I understand my grandfather's desire to confess before

relinquishing this life, in hopes that his sins would not follow him to the next. I have been watching and listening for some years, and I have decided that you are the one to confess to. I nearly told you last year, but I did not want to burden your sister with such a secret.

And there followed her name and seal.

He straightened up, ignoring the leaping shadows in a tiny room he knew very well that he was alone in. The astonishing contents of her letter, combined with the shriek of the wind, combined to squeeze his skull with a sense of threat.

No, not of threat. He knew how to deal with threat, which was straight on. It was the pressure of responsibility. His purely academic question to his great-aunt had brought him a burden that he now felt morally obliged to bear. But what could he do? What should he do?

He read it through again more slowly, and more questions rose. Everyone ought to know. That was true, and yet talking indiscriminately without all facts was no solution. It was too easy for people to catch hold of one fact and begin weaving it into whatever frightened them most, believing it to be true. He could imagine the more ardent divination students turning to the *Book of Wisdom*, ignoring the warnings that too much consultation on personal matters was to risk distorting rather than revealing truth, like relying on a mirror.

But whom would he tell?

He could tell his father—except here was another serious matter. His assumption that his father had forgotten to write, or had decided against it, was false. He had written, according to this letter. But his letters were not arriving here. Further. Though Tai trusted his father absolutely, Great-Aunt Han had not turned to him.

An image of his father's worn, tired face rose before him. His father was over seventy, when many were retiring. He was a magistrate! But one of middling level, far at the other end of the island from the capital. He had no influence over the upper ranks of the ministries of the imperial court. Such as—

The Jis. Were they behind the disappearance of his letters? They had the power. And Tai absolutely believed that the cousins, at least Venshai, had the capability for such petty malice. Except *why?* Tampering with the imperial couriers was not like locking someone in a closet. There was a death sentence awaiting the tamperer.

He read the letter again, then put it in his writing case. He went to bed, but sleep was impossible. What to do? He was a ninth-level secretary, in charge of counting daily silk records for a single island.

As he lay in the dark, the wind buffeting the entire building, his mind ranged back to those terrible days on Angja, which he had thought the worst dilemma he could possibly suffer. How simple those days seemed now!

Even the mines...

The mines. Mek, and his sensing the gold deep beneath the ground. Surely he might be able to sense whether the imperial city was in imminent danger? But if a boy of his age could do it, without any formal schooling by the geomancers, there had to be practicing geomancers in the imperial city who were equally capable—if not more. They all studied Essence matters. Though apparently there were degrees in ability as well as skill. He remembered Snowhawk saying something about Mek being that rarity, two triangles of Essence powers balanced like a star. How rare was that?

Yet another question he couldn't answer. He rolled over, buried his head beneath the covers to try to mute the noise of the storm, and tried to will himself to sleep, but the roar was too great, the shock too strong, and the memories too sharp.

He wasn't aware of his mental door being open until Mek's voice, clear as if he stood beside Tai, spoke inside his head: "Tai? You were calling me in the Essence realm."

"Did I?" Tai sat up in the dark.

"In a sense. You did think of me, in a way that jumped me right out of sleep."

"What hour is it? Where *are* you?"

"I'm at Eagle Island, and it's first or second dragon hour, I think. I retired early because I've been sparring all day. Where are you, and what hour?"

"White Jade, the augury academy. I don't know the hour, but I suspect dawn is near. I've been awake all night—" As he consciously fashioned the words mentally, he was not aware of the flicker and flash of memory until he sensed an intake of breath from Mek.

The letter; the imperial capital; his sense of loss concerning the letters; he didn't have to speak it. Even trying not to think about it was thinking, and he knew Mek got those fleeting images. But he'd forgotten how endlessly sympathetic Mek was, and so he let his mind range, faster than words. It was a relief when it was done.

Mek said, "What do you want me to do?"

"I don't know." But as Tai shaped the words, he did know. "There are two things. First, the danger of the imperial city."

Mek said doubtfully, "If they were in imminent danger, I think the geomancers would know better than I."

"I wondered about that. But then there's the old imperial city and Mt. Lir."

"I can do that," Mek said, after a short pause. "Waha says I ought to disappear for a while. Never mind why right now. This is a way to do it. Let's sleep. I can feel your tiredness and I know I'm stupid with it." He was gone then, like a candle snuffed.

Tai fell back onto his bed — he hadn't even known he'd sat up — and despite the tearing wind, he slumbered until mid-morning, as in Eagle Island Mek decided he had better get some rest before attempting a new experiment with Sagacious Blade.

For Mek the night was early, but in the Jade Islands, a dark, storm-dreary day had begun. During the demon storms, no one was to leave their rooms lest they be swept away and no one know it. Everyone had a jug of water brought each morning; no one was bringing any now, but Tai had half of his left from the day before. He drank that, then opened his writing case to see if that letter was still there, or if he'd dreamed it. Its presence brought back all his questions.

But by noon in the Jade Islands, the howling wind had died away to torrential rain, which slowly began to diminish, so he ventured out, finding several of the other secretaries along his row discussing whether to try for the dining hall.

They went together, to be welcomed with lanterns and hot food and tea. After that, during what daylight remained, they all helped clean up the detritus strewn about by the storm. No one was getting much work done.

By then dawn had brightened Eagle Island's spring competition camp. Mek woke, dressed, slung his travel satchel over one shoulder, then went out to seek Waha.

"I have a favor to ask," he began. "Tai needs my help —"

Waha sensed adventure. "You want some backing? I can be ready in a moment."

"If I were going by ship, or horse, or foot, I would say yes and welcome. But I'm going to try something new. My favor is, will you tell my family I'm doing an experiment, and pass my farewells?"

"You're leaving now? You'll miss the final contests," Waha pointed out what they both knew. "They'll howl."

"Which is why I'm asking you to tell them." Mek grinned.

Waha clasped his hands, gave him auspicious wishes in two languages, then trotted off in search of the nearest Ki.

Mek meant to leave right then—except he really disliked leaving Han Anise without saying anything. He could leave his family, and they might protest, but it would be pretend-affront. They'd been used to comings and goings even before they lost their home. But it was different, with her. She never asked for anything, but that didn't stop him from wanting to give her…things. Even as simple a thing as a farewell.

He was in luck, finding her alone fetching water, without Tian-Tian or the others who liked teasing. Thank you Fox God, Mek thought, and got the words out in a rush, "I've a task. For Tai. So…I'm off."

Her gaze shifted between his eyes, then she smiled. "I hope…"

"I'll be back." That seemed too short, but what else was there to say that didn't sound silly? As if of its own volition his hand rose and cupped her cheek.

Her free hand, chilled from holding the bucket, touched the top of his hand and she kissed his palm. Then he walked away, aware that his wanting to return had changed somehow: he wanted to return to *her*.

He paused beside a tree, closed his eyes, fingers gripped on the hilt of Sagacious Blade, and concentrated on Tai's image…

At that time, Tai had just returned to his room to change out of his wet clothes before dinner. He was in the middle of rummaging through his trunk when there was a sudden blast of dusty air and a heavy thud, followed by a muffled groan.

Mek sat on the floor of his room, the back of his wrist pressed against a bloody nose. At his side lay that bronze sword, gleaming like fire in the candlelight.

"It worked," Mek mumbled. "Thought it might. Sword comes right to my hand. Passed through a wall once. No hole. No mark. I thought she could take *me* along, to you. But oh, it *hurt*. And I don't think I ought to do it unless I know exactly where I'm going. I fixed on you, see."

"How…" Tai began. "No, don't tell me. I expect I won't understand anything beyond the word Essence. But a very short time ago, I was in the middle of a lot of seniors, working. Your sudden appearance would have been difficult to explain."

"Ayah!" Mek exclaimed. "Somehow I pictured you alone in some archival cell somewhere."

Tai couldn't help a smile at that. "Have you ever seen an archival cell?"

"No." Mek dropped his hand, wincing. "I really don't intend to do that again. I'll sail back, when I leave. Or fly." Still wincing, he said, "Tell me where I am, and where I'm to go, and I'll get to it. " He remembered then that he had neglected to get any breakfast. "Though some water and food might be good. Water."

"I can get you that," Tai said. "The main naval base for the southeast is here at the Jade Islands. It's from here that the regular patrol goes up to cruise the coast of the imperial island, keeping people away. I got the impression it's about two weeks of fast sailing, stopping at Azure Tranquility for supplies, before going on."

"At least it's not winter." Mek patted the sword. "If you can make me up a packet of pancakes and maybe some peaches, or whatever is ripe, and fill a water flask, I can take it from here."

Gratitude surged in Tai. "I don't know how to begin—"

Mek waved that off. In spite of the way his body throbbed, his palm still remembered the warm contour of Anise's cheek. "It'll be fun." He considered. "Interesting, if not exactly fun. And I always did want to see Mt. Lir."

FORTY-SEVEN

SPRING HAD RIPENED TO its full strength in Mountain Peony Island, the days warm and full of blossoms in all the pots on the imperial princess's terrace.

The capital's wealthier scholars had gone off to the Journey to the Cloud Empire, along with many lower-ranking imperial courtiers, and a few more impecunious poets whose wit guaranteed their worth.

Lei only knew that they were gone because Imperial Crown Princess Lam sighed one fragrant spring day, saying, "I would so love to see the orchids the poets wrote about. I understand it's nothing but beauty, glorious scents, laughter and music. Do you know, the imperial court used to go, not merely poets?"

Lei thought she'd seen some references in her studies, but she knew the imperial princess loved instructing her, so she bowed and claimed ignorance.

"In the imperial archive, there are some pages they say are written in On Lu's own hand. Plays written for the Sage Empress, specifically to be performed on those great sampans. Except if I were to prevail upon Father Emperor to let me go, it would be just be moving the same rules and constraints from here to there. I might as well sit up here in our aerie." She spread her hands wide and spun around on the terrace outside her private chambers.

It was true that the view from here was absolutely spectacular, looking down over the complexity of upturned roofs of the palace with their guardian animals at each corner, and below those the elegant rooftops of the nobles' mansions, and far below those, the city roofs. Then far out, the bay, the sea, and on the clearest days one could just make out the Dragon's Teeth that protected the capital from the possibility of an invading fleet. The only access being the Miracle Path made (according to legend) by the Sage Empress herself.

Lei doubted whether she would be granted the same view as the imperial princess if they did sail on the luxury sampans to see the legendary Journey to the Cloud Forest; she'd heard one of the maids remarking once that however nice the nobles' barges were, the closets the servants were stuck in where even more like boxes than their rooms in the palace.

That was life. You were born to the rank your soul was deemed to deserve. And there were constant reminders from above not to encroach—and from below not to get above yourself, as Grandmother Han had scolded last winter.

The day passed uneventfully—but late that night there was a Mood.

Lei was readying for bed when she heard an anguished scream. She snatched up lamp and a scroll, then rushed toward the imperial bedchamber, her first thought to offer to read the series of romantic poems that the princess had been enjoying earlier. She hesitated inside the door, staring at the princess, who lay unspeaking on her bed, staring upward.

Nanny Alk was there in her nightrobe. She nodded, and Lei began to read, valiantly attempting to keep her voice from trembling, as the princess lay there unmoving. Perhaps unhearing. She kept on, striving for a soothing tone.

Nanny Alk approached the bed, carrying medicine, then shock burned through Lei when Imperial Crown Princess Lam sat upright and hurled the medicine away. The bowl smashed on the Circle table and exploded into shards that hit Nanny Alk as well as tinkling and clattering through the room. Three nicked her face, which began to bleed.

The imperial princess stared in shock, then flung herself into Nanny Alk's arms, wailing, "I'm a demon! I'm a demon! Just kill me—I won't raise a hand to stop you. I deserve it, I have such terrible thoughts!"

Nanny Alk held her, flicking a look with her eyes toward the graywing at the door, who went with one of the noiseless maids to bring more medicine.

Lei slipped from the room, understanding now why there was always at least three doses made up, ready and waiting, though much of it went to waste unused day after day. She still remembered Graywing Garnet nearly losing his life, and she consciously emulated the maids' silent, unobtrusive walk, as they retreated to the back storeroom and whispered yet again, asking the questions that consumed them all in the aftermath of Moods: what had caused it? What must they avoid to prevent the next?

The following day she was wan, wanting only to be read to. Lei did venture a question, after reading so long her throat was dry, "Would it help you to…talk about what troubles you?"

Crown Princess Lei sat up at that, her great, lustrous dark eyes narrowing. "Why would it help to relive what I'm trying to forget?" she snapped, and Lei blanched — had she just caused another Mood?

But the princess collapsed back, sighing. Almost inaudibly, she murmured, "I have such terrible, terrible thoughts. Be grateful you are so innocent, Little Lei. I want you to stay that way. Pure and innocent. It helps me to remember that there are people like you in the world. Read that poem by Ar Laq about the crane woman and the weaver again…"

Once again they sank into the world of story, and it struck Lei after a time that the only people the princess actually knew were those in stories. Even poor QiQi — who could have been a friend, if QiQi had not been constrained by etiquette and her brother's demands — was no more than a noise to the princess.

The following day it was as if nothing had occurred.

Spring began to slide by without further upset, a series of beautiful days during which rain mostly fell at night, leaving the potted hibiscus, tall, proud oleander, and the drooping, winsome peony and chrysanthemum blossoms fresh with droplets in the mornings. The imperial princess was frequently obliged to attend fabulous entertainments hosted by the Sixth Imperial Consort to please the emperor.

Gifts were frequent at these. Lei was very good by now at noting gifts and givers, then writing a suitable note of gratitude, with the princess's thanks.

"Another birthday," a maid named Brightflower commented when Lei ventured into the lightless back room for a better brush. "Yet another of the emperor's ancient aunts, an excuse for the Sixth Imperial Consort to shower gifts of gold on someone who hasn't needed such things since before we were all born. But try and buy as she might, she'll never get him to set aside the empress." Here a quick clasp of hands toward the emperor's tower—in case he was somehow listening.

"But he gives her everything else," said the cook under his breath as he sorted turnips.

Lei left them to their gossip; she had admired the stunning beauty of the Sixth Imperial Consort, heralded by the evanescence of the agarwood and orchid with which her clothes were aired.

Lei had never actually seen the reclusive empress, who spent most of her time in the temple to the Crane God. Though the empress had never succeeded in giving the emperor an heir, he refused to set her aside—if Lei was to believe servant gossip, she was so good, so saintly, that he was afraid to do so and risk angering the Jade Emperor in heaven. Crown Princess Lam had to call on her once a week, addressing her as Imperial Mother, but she said repeatedly that this duty was merely tiresome because of all that time she had to spend on her knees, bowing and praying. Those visits had never caused Moods.

It was her visits to her actual mother, the Sixth Imperial Consort, that sometimes seemed to bring Moods on, though that might be an accident of frequency, as the princess saw her birth mother far more often than anyone else. Just as frequently after these visits, the imperial princess's face was full of smiles.

"Come, Little Lei," she said cheerfully after the latest. "Duty done, and now we play. Let's go down into town. The rain is light. We can ignore it."

That meant another anonymous venture in a plush but plain cart—surrounded of course by silent, hidden ferrets, instead of the princess riding in a palanquin born by twenty men and walled by a company of imperial guards, banner bearers and musicians tramping before the imperial palanquin. That was the requirement of etiquette, reinforced by the Sixth Imperial Consort, when Crown Princess Lam went out as imperial heir.

Lei preferred these "anonymous" ventures, as she suspected the crown princess did as well, judging by her sunny mood. Of late, the princess had even sent Lei alone to choose books for them to read, while she went to this or that playhouse to watch the dancers. Though none were permitted near enough to speak to her.

Lei began to realize that any young man daring—or foolish—enough to venture near was very swiftly warned off by unsmiling ferrets the moment the crown princess's attention was elsewhere.

"You better not have hurt him," Lei returned to the cart in time to overhear.

The servant only bowed.

The crown princess said on a rising note, "All I did was ask who wrote the new songs. I used to talk to them all the time when I was fourteen!"

The servant bowed again, saying that according to Her Noble Highness the Sixth Imperial Consort's orders, he was to convey any answers to questions her imperial highness raised.

"Then you did have him flogged," the crown princess's voice rose. "I hate that!"

Everyone—including Lei—went to the ground, wet as it was. Lei pressed her forehead to the wet stone and prayed that a Mood was not about to happen here, outside the playhouse, even though the street had been cleared around their cart.

"Take me back," the crown princess said dully. "LeiLei, where are you?"

Lei leaped up, bowed as best she could with the armload of new books that she was trying to protect from splattering raindrops, then clambered into the cart.

"It's so stupid," the sulky princess muttered.

Lei waited, not sure if she was expected to respond or not. She hoped Nanny Alk walked outside the cart. Did she have a hand-warmer of medicine somewhere about her?

"Don't look so green, Little Lei, I'm not furious with *you*. How could I be? You're as helpless to change anything as I am. It's so absurd, thinking that by merely speaking to a winsome man I'd be stupid enough to endanger the precious purity of the imperial bloodline." She spoke the words sourly. "As if I don't know how to avoid *that*. But no, my mother says it's too dangerous, that I can have as many consorts as I want once I'm married, but my first child must be *pure* royal blood. I think it's because she's afraid I'll only have one, like her," she finished pettishly.

Lei dared not give any answer to this.

"I wonder how precious I'll be if she does give Father Emperor a son. She could, you know. She's midway in her thirties—when they instructed me about moon matters, the imperial physicians told me that she could produce another heir for at least another ten years, maybe more. And I know there are half a dozen physicians outside the chamber when she goes to visit

Father Emperor for the night—and at least one shaman praying all night for luck. Forget about her silly orders! I'm going to ask Father Emperor. Let's see what you brought me."

Later on, as rain thudded against the windows, the imperial princess swept off to dine with the emperor, and Lei went to get her dinner. And as sometimes happened, entered on an echo of the imperial princess's utterance, "She said to the Sixth, 'If you're only granted a single child by heaven, as well it is an emperor's,'" Tigermoth was repeating low-voiced to the other maids, with a glance toward the tightly closed windows.

"Shoe-peddlers, the Yimus were, before she caught the emperor's eye on the street one day," the cook said, sitting back, his big hands fisted on his knees. "Now the greediest, graspingest crooks in the empire—and the stupidest."

"They are not stupid," Nanny Alk's dry voice interrupted from the door. "But not raised to a sense of duty. Of course they're dazzled by wealth, without seeing that what can come easily can be taken as easily."

"That lesson could also do for some of these nobly born ministers who can quote Kanda about duty while plunging their fingers into each other's belt pouches," Graywing Opal put in dryly. "In any case, speculation like this is in its way just as stupid. Any of her noble highness's people might walk in at any moment. And we'd all be carried out feet first."

Lei had only met the one of the Yimus, married now to Ji Meishai. He was the Sixth Consort's brother, and though Lei had not liked his smirk, she'd had to admit that he was as handsome as the Sixth Imperial Consort was beautiful.

The princess liked one of her other uncles, and adored a small cousin, though Lei did not see any of these people. The Sixth Imperial Consort seemed to prefer to keep her family visits confined to her own palace wing in the harem, except when the emperor was well enough to be entertained by them.

As Lei went to sleep that night, she wondered if the Yimus' souls had been deemed worthy of street sellers of shoes, until the chance glance of the emperor toward a pretty face. Or was that destined?

The question went unanswered like so many, eventually to be forgotten, as the sun rose higher each day, the warmth ripening toward summer, and at nights the moons drifting ever farther apart. Lei was busy with plays, books, writing, and always watching every flicker of the imperial princess's eyelids, every quirk of her mouth, and listening to the most subtle variations in her voice. Worry about a Mood was never far away.

Summer arrived with a crash and a boom.

The mind might forget the thousands of reflections that go unanswered through a day, but the body never forgets a scent. And it was a scent that saved Lei from execution one night early in summer, during an enormous thunderstorm.

The imperial crown princess was dining with the emperor, the empress, and the Sixth Imperial Consort. As the emperor sometimes fell asleep during these formal meals, at which time the imperial women sat quietly until he wakened, the imperial crown princess had Lei waiting with whatever book they'd been reading that day.

Lei was startled when Tigermoth appeared, having been stationed in summoning distance.

"It's too early for it to be ending," Lei whispered.

Tigermoth's wideset eyes were bright in the lamplight. "News just came, that old aunt of his imperial majesty's died today. The empress is taking our highness to the Hall of Ancestors to light incense and pray. Our highness says, you're to go by the back way up there, so she can get that." Tigermoth pointed to the scroll.

Lei departed, scurrying swiftly—the Imperial Hall of Ancestors was up the stairs and far away via the twisting servant passages that bent around the perimeters of the great rooms.

She had not gone past two halls when thunder crashed directly overhead, a blast so loud that the ground shook, and a cold, wet wind suddenly scoured down the hall, extinguishing every lamp.

Lei had to grope her way now. In the complete darkness, these endless halls were all alike. She could not tell the difference between servant corridors and those belonging to the imperials, where she had no business being. She'd heard hair-raising whispers about what happened to those who displeased the Sixth Imperial Consort, to whom the emperor had granted the keys to the harem—implying stewardship of the entire imperial palace.

She paused beside a wall that turned out to be a pillar when there was a flicker sending wild shadows leaping, and above the noise of drumming rain she caught the rustle of slippers and billowing silks. Servants? But no servants wore silk—

"What's *wrong* with her? They said it's not a demon, but

what else could it be? Not one of *us* goes mad like that. Gainu had a temper, I remember, but not this bad."

"Shut up, shut up, *shut up. Never* dare to say that name!" It was a woman's hiss.

Lei assumed these were servants, as their accent was the same as that of the yard servants and the launderers. But wearing silk? She hesitated, then caught a drift of that distinctive fragrance, soft as a moonbeam. Then it was gone.

Lei pressed tight against that pillar, not daring to breathe, though she was sure her thudding heart could be heard for several floors. No servant could ever afford agarwood and orchid per-fume.

The rustle of clothing, the hiss of indoor slippers, and the two speakers moved on, taking the weak light with them. Lei bit her tongue against whimpering, reminded herself that she had a *reason* to be there — Imperial Crown Princess Lam's direct order — and forced herself to keep going for what seemed an eternity, bumping into unseen furnishings, until a light flickered and here were two graywings, one she recognized.

In the light of the candle they carried, both faces looked stern.

She looked in mute question at Graywing Opal, whose usual pleasant demeanor had harshened. He murmured, "Where did you come from?"

"I was to carry this scroll to the Hall of Ancestors. Then the lamps were blown out, and I got lost. I don't know where I am."

The two exchanged glances, then a little of Graywing Opal's kindliness was back as he took the scroll. "I'll take that. There are new orders from her noble highness the Sixth Imperial Consort to permit Imperial Crown Princess Lam to rest without being disturbed."

His expression, his flat tone — a Mood had happened. Caused by that thunderclap?

He pointed back down the hall she'd come from.

She left them promptly, but moving so slowly in the darkness beyond the ring of light from their lamp that her quick ears caught Graywing Opal's soft undertone, "Do we report her?"

"No. She was here on the heir's orders. Let's not give her noble highness a reason to kill yet another one on some whim."

Lei's meridians flashed painfully at that, and she rushed back as quickly and silently as possible, and shut herself in her room.

FORTY-EIGHT

IT WAS THE BEST time of year for Mek to be traveling on a military scout ship. "On" is literal—he flew to the wharf before dawn, lit on the roof of the cabin structure of his chosen scout ship, and set up camp there.

It had taken Mek some effort to get himself to the Silk Islands' main naval base, at first because he needed to recover from the wrench of his instant shift from Eagle Island to Tai's chamber at the augury school. Then several days of sleep and internal Essence healing, after which he flew in short hops. When he reached the naval base, he got a job waiting tables and listened to the chat. Once he found the right patrol, he used his earnings to buy supplies.

As few people ever look up, and then a mere glance, no one noticed a smear in the sky above the third scout in the next patrol going up to cruise the outer perimeter of the old imperial island.

He'd been told a couple years ago by a white-haired Ghost Moon monk that Essence flyers had been common at various times through history, always in peaceful eras. And when leaders came to power who did not have peace as motivation, shooting flyers out of the sky, and forbidding Essence flight by law, was invariably one of their first actions. That resulted in fewer Essence wielders passing on of the skill. "We were taught that Essence flyers were common during the Sage Empress's Dynasty, but in the short, terrible Five Dynasty Era that followed, none were seen in the skies."

"Why? Essence flying is not useful in war, I'd think. You can't carry heavy things to drop on people, or not very long.

And if you manage, you're there, exposed to all the archers on the ground."

"But Essence flyers see all. And they are above those who crave being set above others. They cannot bear that."

"Heaven is above them," Mek had said. "Birds, and dragons of air and fire."

The old monk had uttered a creaking laugh. "Neither heaven nor birds are other men. And many of those men do not see dragons."

The patrol sailed without incident, Mek lying flat on one's roof. That did mean enduring getting rained on, but that only happened a couple of times, and the weather was warming by the day toward summer.

The patrol stopped briefly at Azure Tranquility for supplies, news, and two pigeons to replace those that had been sent south, then sailed on the next tide. Mek watched the sky, and sometimes followed the minds of passing birds. He listened to the idle chat of the sailors. They didn't talk about much outside of daily concerns, or game playing during their free watches.

When the sailors sparred, that meant they were outside on deck, so he could do his warmups and formations on the roof. The best one for that was the Bian knife fighting formation, which he had been combining with the Ki family's formation, adapted to the limited space of a ship's deck.

He'd wondered how he was going to find Coral Island once they reached the imperial island—but he ought not have worried. They saw the billowing smoke first, gouting honey-brown high into the sky, then stretching slowly westward in a dissipating, dirty-looking smear. That smoke had to be drifting on for days before it faded. Already Mek's air and earth senses clamored with alarm.

That was the place that the patrol turned west to sail along the dimly-perceived length of the imperial island.

Mek picked up his carryall, patted the water flask that he'd recently refilled in the scout's water butt, waved the deflection charm over himself and took to the air on Sagacious Blade.

He kept sailing north, straight into the smoke. When he neared the silhouetted island, he tucked his nose into the crook of his elbow, and though it was years too late to effect a rescue, he scanned for living things. Nothing. This was one of those rocky, straight up and down islands that humans avoided. But what about those whose voices humans did not hear?

He saw no signs of any life. Not even lichens, as he slowed to fly in a great, sweeping circle over ages of stone falling sheer in twisting chasms, a chaos of striated rock and spikes through which milky, churning rivers frothed and plunged with a noise like thunder. Zigzagging down and down the ravines, dizzying if he followed too closely, to mineral-clogged streams among a tumble of boulders before they evaporated in a hiss of steam.

The sun began to set, interleaving the peaks until only the shadows looked solid, and he settled at last on a ledge with a steady supply of easterly wind so that he could breathe. Smoke still singed his nose, and the atmosphere tasted metallic, as if he'd been trying to chew on his sword. He could feel his hair lifting and crackling. The air slowly twisted and writhed unnaturally above the distorted earth.

Mek threw himself flat, keeping Sagacious Blade close beside him. To cure this abyssal earth-wound, he would have to permit himself to take on aspects of earth. No, of stone. So dangerous—it would be so easy to let human concerns diminish to nothing. However he sensed that Sagacious Blade would be vigilant, however long it took in time.

Impatiently he unraveled the charms the geomancers had diligently bound to the earth. Whoever had done this most recently had been far too vigorous, and for a moment or two he followed the twisting wound not downward, but up, up into the heavens' realm, so high that the harm even reached beyond where the condors flew. Here, the air currents distorted into knotted dragons of air and fire—the source of the demon storms!

The thought seemed to come from very far away.

His awareness shot back down to his body on the cliff. He steadied himself, then lowered his awareness down past the surface layers, which had been forced open to permit hot, liquid rock to gout up to feed those fires. Fissures extended from the pressures forced onto the seabed, burrowing deep under in all directions. The instability at that depth had built to sun-hot pressure. If that gave way—*when* that gave way, it was terrifyingly imminent—the resulting eruption would be catastrophic for all living things within days of sail.

It must be eased—*now*.

With infinite patience. He had learned patience, sitting beside Old Uncle. Chanting peace sutras with the monks.

Breathe, listen. Now, tiny shifts, so tiny. A grain of rock here. A glint of mineral there. Shift. Ease. Shift. Ease. Slow…slow…s-l-o-w…s—l—o—w—l—y…

Thunk. Slabs of rock slid. Came to rest. Rumble: more rock shifted, easy, easy. Cracks blended—and vanished. Rock, forced unnaturally rigid for years instead of moving with the gradual breath of earth through lubricating sediment, slid into place. Easy. Easy…

Sometime during the careful, incremental task of reparation, rain began to fall, at first another thunderstorm, but then a torrent of pure, healing water, and great gouts of steam rose into the air, towers reaching skyward to blend with the clouds.

Restoration progressed more rapidly then, as air and water, earth and the diminishing fires sorted themselves into balance again.

Mek began to return to himself, painfully at first. His body was so very heavy. Dense as stone. He grunted in effort to winch his head toward an insistent pain like the whine of an insect's wings, and discovered that he had gripped the sword by the blade so hard that its razor-sharp edge had cut into his hand. There was not much blood, and what there was had formed into misshapen ruby-colored crystal.

Mek concentrated, loosening his fingers one by one. He sat up. His blood began to move again through his body. He could feel its surge and flow, painful at first, like the burn of a thousand hot needles. A tremendous thirst gripped him, and he drained the entire water flask until his belly ached. But the water absorbed into his flesh almost as rapidly as he'd drunk, and he breathed easy again. Now ravenous. He sat there in the warm torrent, bent over as he devoured the stale pancakes he'd hoarded.

With renewed strength, he rose to his feet, turning in a circle as his senses took in the balance ramifying not just through the settling seabed but up into the air currents.

"Time to leave," he said to silent but vigilant Sagacious Blade. "And…if I'm not wrong, that has to be the imperial island, there on the northern horizon."

He flew through the night. Wind dragons danced around him, buoying him up. He knew not to attribute human emotions to them, and yet he felt approval in their gently buffeting play. He could feel the need for sleep gathering around the edges of his awareness. There would be a cost for all that

Essence expended; sleep and water, then food, would restore him.

But as night faded to blue in the east, he flew over the coast of the capital at the base of Mt. Lir, which soared upward, a magnificent silhouette. A wide river wound down from a far distant spine of mountains, emptying into the west side of a broad harbor that was sheltered on the east by a long peninsula.

The sun's fiery rim limned Mt. Lir's snowcapped crown, now gleaming pearlescent in the pure morning light. Golden shafts picked out the tops of trees all down the mountain. As he approached, the shafts strengthened, gleaming in the tripled ranks of upturned eaves.

There was no hint of smoke marring the pure white of that mountaintop. Not that he'd expected there to be any. The geomancers had not dared to tamper with the great fire mountain, having chosen small, uninhabited Coral Island for their deflection.

Mek flew slowly over streets empty of humans. Walls, houses, alleys, and gardens had been boarded up tight and left untouched. Perhaps someone was about, caretaking the buildings. If so, they remained unseen so early.

A pack of dogs trotted up a broad street, plumed tails high. Birds flew everywhere, pecking on the ground, and drifting over the shoreline. Larger animals appeared here and there, briefly: there were deer trotting over an arched bridge in a vast, wild garden surrounding a lake in the center of the palace's grand design. A cat sunned directly below Mek. It glanced up at him, untroubled by his presence once he touched its mind and sent thoughts of amity.

He remembered what Tai had told him about Mountain Peony's capital, and knew that humans would be back. And it was right. This was a human dwelling place, made with talent and skill. Mek liked the carvings, and even the fading paintings caught the eye, inviting his admiration. But he knew that he wanted to always remember it this way.

He found a pavilion in the middle of that vast garden, and landed next to it. Sleep was beginning to press on his eyes, his limbs, his mind. He wandered with heavy step to the lakeside where the water ran clear, drank, then stretched out on a grassy spot, and had barely enough strength left to cast the obscuring charm over himself.

He woke, drank, slept, woke, drank, and slept again as the

sun rose and sank, and the moons performed their slow, stately Dance of Harmony around both earth and sun.

Finally he woke with another dawn, unsure how many days he'd lain there. He vaguely recollected snuffling muzzles sniffing him, then leaving him undisturbed. He sat up, did his breathing, then reached for Tai's mental door.

Tai responded at once: "Mek?"

This time the flow of images ran from Mek to Tai, far easier than words.

Tai's astonishment slowly changed from wonder to severity. "There was imminent danger from that island?"

"I think there would have come a volcano," Mek said. "I think. If I'm right, it would have made Mt. Lir seem a hill by comparison—and it would have killed every living thing from horizon to horizon. Did they know that?"

"I have only my Great-Aunt's confession letter, but judging by the single line she wrote in reference to that, they believed the smoke was harmless."

"It wasn't! The heat was boiling the entire sky! That was the source of the demon storms!"

"Are you certain? Did those storms not rise south of the imperial island?"

Mek tried to find words for the inexorable, mighty vortex so vast it was broader than many of the broadest islands, spinning gradually tighter as it moved.

The image was enough. Tai's question had hardened to conviction.

"Aish, when is it?" Mek asked. "I just realized the morning sun has leaped southward."

"You have been silent for months," Tai said.

"No wonder I've been sleeping for days. I guess there's no spring convoy for me, then." Mek looked around. "On the other hand, I'm going to be able to scavenge a princely breakfast here in what I strongly suspect might have been the old emperor's private garden."

Tai's mental voice was still smooth and tensile as a sword as he said, "Perhaps you had better go straight to Mountain Peony."

"I don't really have the training to assess much beyond something really obvious, such as Coral Island was."

"I don't think you could do harm. It could be they don't have Essence wielders as strong as you. In any case, whatever you find will be more than I could ever learn."

Mek avoided cities for preference. He did not want to go to Mountain Peony, the island his family had been booted out of. And whose capital was sure to be packed with clamoring inner voices usually to be avoided. But what he'd found at Coral Island—the disaster he'd averted—was beginning to disturb the detachment that had been a part of his stone semblance. Human emotion was returning as swiftly as his blood revitalized. "Yes," he sighed on a breath. "Where do I go? And once I get to Mountain Peony, whom do I talk to?"

"There is a naval base on the north side of the imperial island at Peaceable Breezes. You'll find patrol ships there. When you get to Mountain Peony, you can avoid the capital. I won't be going there. We can meet at my parents' home on the east coast, at Dawn's Placid Sea. After what you just told me, I feel the need to speak to my father. In spite of whoever wants us not to correspond—or apparently to meet. I shall get permission from Chief Su to go myself."

FORTY-NINE

IMPERIAL CROWN PRINCESS LAM examined her headdress, a beautiful and elaborate construction of gold and gems in the form of lotus and nightingales supporting a phoenix made of pearls. Sapphires swung at her ears.

"This thing is so heavy I'm sure to get a headache by the end of the wedding banquet," she said to Lei. "But my favorite uncle, getting married! I have to look my best, for as long as I can bear it." She turned her head. "This will be an excuse to take you with me. You can carry my silver phoenix hairpins, and a silk satchel, and if I can't support this thing another moment, we'll switch them quietly."

Lei bowed — there was no question of refusing. Besides, she was curious to see as much of an imperial wedding as possible, though inevitably she'd be off to the side, behind screens or plants.

The imperial crown princess shifted her gaze from her own reflection. "Come here." And when Lei stood beside her so that they were both reflected in the highly polished bronze, Crown Princess Lam waved her hairdresser back and rummaged through her many trays of hairpins and ear dangles, necklaces, bracelets, and pins.

She found a pair of golden butterfly hairpins set with jade inlay, and held them to Lei's glossy blue-black hair. "You are so *pretty*. I think you might be prettier than I am. I'd love to dress you up!" Her tone was odd, a rush of words almost anticipatory, puzzling Lei.

Then the imperial crown princess sighed, and threw the exquisite pins back on the tray with a carelessness that made

Lei suppress a wince. Some jewel artist had bent over those delicate, fragile handiworks for untold days, applying considerable skill.

"What's the use of being pretty, if comely men cannot admire you lest they get ten with a big stick, and then find themselves kicked out of the imperial city?" The princess's voice sharpened.

Lei's heart thundered, and she said quickly, "I think you'll be admired at the wedding, and no one will dare to hit any admirers with a stick."

The imperial crown princess uttered a laugh, and turned back to her reflection, which she studied intently. "This sky-blue silk does suit me, doesn't it? And the end of the year is approaching fast. There will be some changes then." At Lei's inquiring look, she laughed again. "You'll be a year older — and I will be proclaimed heir at my coming of age, and they will have to begin including me in court. No more sitting up here yawning over endless tragic tales of poor but handsome scholars and neglected daughters of evil ministers." And the dangerous moment passed.

The formal imperial palanquin had been waiting, along with an entourage of fifty people: besides the palanquin-bearers, the musicians, the banner-bearers, and the twelve maids who walked directly behind the palanquin, a company of imperial guards awaited them.

Lei, as secretary, was permitted to walk beside the palanquin instead of in the dust with the maids.

The autumnal day was fine, the pistachio trees bright red, considered a very auspicious sign for weddings. Lei enjoyed the walk, her steps unconsciously following the beat of the crashing cymbals and the gongs.

It was not far to the Huin mansion; the wedding was to take place at the bride's home, and afterward the couple would parade to the groom's city mansion, which was so splendid that (as Lei had overheard a servant say) few would remember that the Yimus had never had a family estate or mansion.

Among the more conspicuous guests were Left Chancellor Prince Ji Houduo and his eldest son, Duke Ji Venshai — there as a Censor under the Chief Censor, who was also father of the bride. Both Jis were dressed in their finest robes, jade at their belts, long tassels dancing under Longevity knots. There was no sign in their practiced smiles of the hard bargaining that had taken place among the most powerful court families to get a daughter into the Yimus—but the Jis had given in to the powerful Huins with grace, the prince reflecting that he already had one niece well placed within the enemy camp.

The rest of the Ji family sat with the bride's family inside the ancestral hall, paying court to the Sixth Imperial Consort; father and son wandered about greeting various ministers and high-ranking nobles, so they were able to witness all the arrivals. Such as that of the imperial crown princess. She disembarked from the imperial palanquin, and beckoned Lei to follow her as she swept inside, past low bows.

Both father and son bowed low, eyes meeting eyes: Ji Venshai and the imperial crown princess had been playmates back before either understood the distinctions of rank or ambition. Venshai had been raised by his ambitious and long-sighted father to marry her, and he was very aware that he'd been too complacent in the assumption of her cooperation when they'd reached their early teens.

Crown Princess Lam acknowledged the prince's bow with an elegant nod, and Venshai's to a much lesser degree before she tapped her fan possessively on Lei's shoulder and smiled at Venshai with a hint of malice, as if to say: *Look who gets my favor. It is not you.*

Venshai had to swallow this insult as he had swallowed many others since he'd reached adulthood. She swept by, magnificent in celestial blue, standing out against all the crimson and gold of the wedding decorations. She looked like an empress. But there was no admiration in her gaze for him. He wished QiQi was there to speak for him—but she had turned stubborn, refusing steadfastly to intercede between him and the crown princess ever since the imperial examination.

He began to follow, mentally reaching for complimentary words, but the prince touched his fan to Venshai's wrist before unfurling it. "Bide," he said under his breath. "Watch: the stewards will cull Je Lei. That's where our priority is right now. The princess as events permit."

Venshai watched. As expected, the wedding steward gestured maids forward, and as six of them bowed and guided the princess away, one drew Je Lei over to a side area, as her rank was an anomaly—not quite a servant, but not high enough to be appointed a Noble Companion permitted to sit behind the princess.

The imperial princess turned as if to look for Lei, but at that moment the Sixth Imperial Consort saw her daughter, and sent a summoning glance from the high table, where she had been reigning since her early arrival.

Both Jis saw Lei sit alone with a rather forlorn attempt at dignity. The prince was reminding himself that she was only seventeen or so, and Venshai thought that in that soft silvery gray, which only enhanced her cloud of blue-black hair above slanting phoenix eyes as black as that hair, she was startlingly like the nine-fold screen depicting Princess Kang Cygnet with the swans, which stood in the Ji Mansion front hall.

"How can she look more like our ancestral princess than any of us?" Venshai observed ruefully.

"Because blood is like that. And she inherited a double dose. Do not forget that the lowly Hans are descendants from Kang Cygnet's first daughter, before the princess married Prince Huyun Shandek."

Though that first daughter, who had dedicated her life to running the schools that Kang Cygnet had founded, had never attained any political significance, Prince Ji Houduo at least appreciated that while the Jis' own connection had attained a lofty title, the Huyuns had faded from history just as swiftly as their rise, whereas the Swan Schools had educated boys and girls of high and low degree for generations — which was why this island had so easily supplied the newly-arrived Tan emperor and his imperial court with ledger keepers, scribes, and the like. Cloud Terrace had boasted more playhouses than any other city in the empire *before* the first Tan emperor made it his capital, as there had existed an educated public to support them all.

"Now," the prince said as there was a stir by the door, and a rush of laughing young men accompanied the popular groom up the crimson carpet to await the appearance of the bride.

Lei, standing alone, had had that one entrancing glimpse of elegant guests inside the ancestral hall, winking with jeweled brilliance against the crimson wedding decorations. Then the steward corralled her gently but firmly, a reminder that there was an invisible yet insurmountable divide between her in plain, servant gray and those elegant figures rainbowed in lamp-refracting headdresses.

A surge beyond the crimson banners and hanging screens dividing her off. Between those breeze-swaying bolts of red cloth, she saw the young men turn, profiles riant. In their midst, Yimu Chen, handsome in red edged with gold, and here and there embroideries of green and blue figures of luck.

A cry went up, "The groom! The groom!"

Then Lei was startled by the appearance of her uncle and cousin, who greeted her with compliments as they slipped into her secluded nook.

She bowed to both as the wedding announcer out in the ancestral hall cried, "The bride arrives."

"I know that this is an awkward time to attempt a conversation," the prince said gently to Lei. "I mostly want to find out if you are doing well. Or if there is anything that your old uncle, in his poor way, might do for you."

"I'm fine, thank you, Uncle Ji," Lei said, bowing again.

"Because of the importance of your position, sadly, we have seen nothing of you since the turn of the year. But surely you have witnessed, perhaps experienced, much that would be enlightening," the prince went on.

And though Lei had not felt any trepidation on her own behalf as these two relations approached her, all her alarms for the crown princess rose. They were surely about to begin interrogating her about Crown Princess Lam.

The announcer cried, "The bride and groom step over the saddle!"

Lei would never say or do anything to harm the crown princess, who was so good to her. Who tried to be a good person. Who did not want those Moods any more than anyone else did, and invariably felt wretched after.

But Lei did not feel the same loyalty to the Sixth Consort.

"The bride and groom step over the fire!"

She couldn't see the wedding couple, and barely heard this joyful instruction. Instead, before her eyes, rose Graywing Opal's harsh face that summer night, and his words, *Let's not give her noble highness a reason to kill yet another one on some whim.* Her *noble* highness, not her *imperial* highness: the Sixth Imperial Consort was the only person granted the honorific of 'noble highness.' 'Imperial' was reserved for those of imperial blood — or their equals.

"The bride and groom bow to Heaven and earth!"

Lei was briefly distracted by a glimpse of red silk flowing as the wedding pair bowed toward the Huin family altar. But her uncle and cousin looked intently at her, their backs to the wedding ritual.

"There was something," Lei said, hoping those confusing words she'd overheard from the other side of the pillar would satisfy these two. She still did not know what exactly had precipitated those remarks about madness—they *could* have referred to the princess, whom Lei had not seen again that night, or they could have pertained just as easily to one of their other consorts, or even to the departed imperial aunt, whom no one had seemed to miss. That didn't matter to Lei as much as what the graywing had said.

The prince murmured encouragingly, "Speak plainly, child. You are among family now," as inside the ancestral hall, the announcer called, "The bride and groom bow to the elders!"

Lei obediently forewent the deferential third person and described the situation: having been sent by back ways to the temple for the princess, the thunder, the gust of wind. Getting lost. "I didn't know whether to speak or not. They had the accents of commoners…"

"The bride and groom bow to family and friends!"

"The man said something about madness—which could have been a slander of *anyone*—and then said, 'Gainu had a temper, I remember, but not this bad.' And the woman said, 'Shut up, shut up, *shut up. Never* dare to say that name!' Then I smelled agarwood and orchid, and couldn't move. Though I've never heard the Sixth Imperial Consort speak, I know that scent."

Lei stopped—had that been a hitch of breath from the prince?

The announcer called, "The bride and groom bow to one another!"

"Then two graywings came, and one said, *Let's not give her highness a reason to kill yet another one on some whim.* And so, I'm telling you, because I want to know if she really does kill people on whim? I don't dare put such a question to the princess about her birth mother. Or anyone in the staff, really. Not after hearing that."

"Did these graywings hear her words or the other man's, Niece?"

"I don't think so. I don't think anyone heard but me. But *why* would she get whims to kill people?"

The prince looked at that earnest, honest face, and said carefully, "You were very right to wait to ask us. The Sixth

Imperial Consort is notorious for what might be called overly strict governance of the harem, and that sadly includes having servants put to death for what in other houses might be regarded as minor trespasses. Your instinct to remain silent was laudable. Heed that,. Remain silent on this matter. And you should be safe."

At that moment, bride and groom finished drinking the wedding cup, and the entire company shouted their congratulations, children throwing rice.

"It is now time for us to toast the wedding pair. Enjoy the rest of the festivities, dear Niece," the prince said, smiling. "You did very, very well."

Lei rejoiced. It had worked! She had distracted her inquisitive uncle from interrogating her about the imperial crown princess. They could talk all they wanted about the Sixth Imperial Consort's meanness.

Venshai stared at his father, whose eyes were stark and almost unseeing as they slowly made their way back to their place among the guests.

When those around them were busy toasting and shouting witticisms at the expense of the groom, Venshai leaned over to say to his father, "She tried to hide it, but that was about the princess, right? Do the Yimus think she is *mad?*"

His father looked around before whispering, "It doesn't matter what they think, son. Quiet. Wait."

Venshai had to be patient as the toasts went on and on, then finally all the men got up to join the parade following the bride and groom to their new home a level above the Huins', as the women stayed behind to pay court to the Sixth Imperial Consort.

But once the bride and groom had gone off, the prince located their horse servant among the others lurking outside the Huins' gates, and to Venshai's surprise, sent their carriage home, saying, "The night is fine. We shall walk, and clear the wine fumes from our heads."

That only meant one thing, a subject so private that Venshai's father did not want to risk *any* ears overhearing! He burst out, "Who is Gui Nu?"

"You heard incorrectly, Venshai. Guinu. One word." And, at Venshai's puzzled frown, "Who has only single names?"

"Commoners. Servants—"

"In the imperial palace, the lowest servants have object

names of a noun class," the prince reminded him. "Flowers. Herbs. Minerals. Birds—who has a single name, usually two syllables?"

Venshai said, "Imperial guards…"

"Exactly." And then the exasperated prince saw enlightenment widen Venshai's eyes: madness, inherited madness, the Yimus don't have it…

"*Really?* But…" Venshai was thunderstruck. Oh, he and the boys had joked about the crown princess being fathered by someone else, because the old emperor was so wheezy, with a list an arm long of things he could not eat—and that was in the days when he was well enough to dine with his court. There had been the usual ribald jokes about him not knowing what to do with a fine woman, though everyone knew that he obviously had, once. Presumably still did, for he had nine living consorts.

But only one had produced a baby.

Venshai whistled softly. "If it's true she was already with child when she caught the emperor's eye, that was some risky planning on her part. And she must have been younger than QiQi."

"Who is smart enough to have concocted such a ploy, had she wanted to risk the terrible penalty for Deceiving the Emperor. But getting access is entirely another question. The emperors are surrounded by rings of protectors for more reasons than assassination, though that's primary."

Venshai nodded slowly. "If it wasn't *her* plot, then…"

"Think, boy."

Venshai said, "Any of those uncles of Lam's. Each is greedier than the next. Except maybe Yimu Chen."

"Correct. Yimu Chen is surprisingly effective as Chief of Trade Revenue—except for the occasional salt ship he claims was sunk, while he sells off the profits, but I really believe that's at the orders of the four-eyed rat his uncle in the right-hand chancellery." The prince raised his fan in a negating gesture. "The rest of Sixth Imperial Consort's brothers are obvious in their craving for titles and wealth to fund their search for endless pleasures. Their intent doesn't reach much beyond the next pretty face, or trunk of gems."

Venshai bowed agreement, aware that his father sometimes criticized him for similar short-sightedness.

"Who is the most dangerous of them? Who sits there in Benevolent Winds, controlling the main of the empire's gunpowder—as well as nominal command of half of the navy's East Fleet in order to guard it?"

They contemplated the shadowy figure of the Sixth Imperial Consort's other uncle, Yimu Ban, rarely seen. The uncle who had once been a brawling street-wolf before joining the imperial guard, back when the Yimus were shoe sellers.

"What do we do?"

"Nothing. Yet. Until we have solid facts. And the right moment."

"Shall I…"

"No. You must do nothing—anything you ask will surely be reported. I will put my best man to inquire into Guinu. And if it turns out, as I suspect, that he was a guard, or something similar, and that he suffered a mysterious accident the same year the imperial crown princess was born, then we wait." The prince's voice lowered to a raspy hiss. "We wait."

FIFTY

MEK AND SAGACIOUS BLADE soared up into the lush, hilly country behind the former imperial city. He stopped to rest, at first frequently. Each time he forced himself to his feet he felt heavy, as if he'd plunged into water wearing all his clothing.

Remember how tough this recovery is, he reminded himself. You knew it was dangerous when you tried going down deep at the mine. No more being rock.

The first morning he woke feeling himself again, he lay quietly, listening to the distant honk of geese flying south, his thoughts turning toward Anise. He would never invade her thoughts without asking—but one moment he wondered how she was, then a fulgent burst of joy ignited in his mind, and when the shower of nerve-tingles cleared, he caught shards from her own thoughts as she sat on her bedding in the cozy little room off the kitchen yard at Heart's East, three little snakes in her lap, and a crow exulting behind her. "Mek!" She had been readying for sleep.

"I'm sorry—I didn't mean to—"

"I pray to Suanek every night that you might dream-speak to me, and here you are, and I'm still awake!"

There followed a hasty exchange, as he was not sure how much of what he'd been doing was his to tell. But his own joy reached her, more reassuring than any words could ever be. And he promised that when he woke next, he'd reach for her. She agreed with fervent elation, which lifted his heart for another long day of flight.

The more he flew, the better his air affinity cleared the stone residue from him, and each morning, he and Anise spoke across the distance, both longing for physical proximity, a longing that reached the other even if they were each a little shy of saying the words. But Anise shared every part of her day in fast sensory shards that Mek deeply relished because it was so clear that every bird, snake, wild rabbit, cat and mouse, was vital to Anise.

When the sun appeared, it was time to fly. He discovered a few scattered small villages, and only raided a few fruits and vegetables from gardens—one carrot here, a yam there—one apple, one pear—as he proceeded north.

He felt the city, Peaceful something-or-other?, before he saw it, and avoided that, too, coming around to the naval side of the harbor at night. He used the last of his earnings to buy some pancakes and listen to sailors discussing orders.

Then it was a reverse of his previous journey, camping on a courier carrying messages to the imperial capital at Mountain Peony. Only this time he was not alone. Anise was his companion in the mental realm as the sun lifted the darkness in the east—and far west at Eagle Island, she sat in moonslight, waiting for him before she slept.

He left the scout before they slowed to enter the dragon's teeth reef, and flew high to take in the city laddered into the ridge.

Mek was appalled. He could feel the weight of all that marble hauled up to land that had never produced a stone so dense and weighty. To his eyes—unaccustomed to imperial architecture in all its impressive glory—the rows and rows of great mansions, walls, and the like, seemed destined to collapse today.

He edged Sagacious Blade around the towers of what had to be the imperial palace, noting that not a single sentry ever looked up, and came to land farther along the ridge toward the east.

He kicked off his sandals, buried his toes in the loam, and let his senses sink. Ignoring the familiar lights of human souls, he noted the hundreds of tiny lights belonging to small creatures and green things, overlaid by a complexity of glowing golden threads: the geomancers' bindings.

Though he was not at all impressed by the arrogance of building enormous structures along a ridge never intended to support them, he had to admire the thoroughness of the geomancers' work. The soil itself slumbered, vast and strange.

It existed utterly detached from the frenetic speed of human presences: he sensed the rhythm of sedimentary build from below followed by topple and fall, a natural part of karst ridges. This added weight would eventually be shrugged off, as if a kraken shrugged off a barnacle seeking to attach to its bulk for a ride through the seas.

Slowly he pulled his awareness from the soil, stretched up into the winds for balance—and then reached for Tai's mental door.

Tai was there at once. "Mek. Where are you? They tell us we are a day out of Dawn's Placid Sea."

"I'm behind the capital. I should go east all the way to the coast?"

Wordless assent from Tai; Mek was already on Sagacious Blade and rising into the air, the deflection charm refreshed.

It took two days for Mek to fly the length of the spine of mountains—two or three weeks' journey on foot. The landscape changed, as often happened. The farther east he traveled, the more stable the land, with no fire dragon beneath. He remembered that the old Ki homestead lay in a mountain valley not far from the east coast. But with no Kis there, he had no wish to see it.

A day later, there was the sea, with a string of small islands lying to the north: the Tiger Isles. He landed in the harbor of Dawn's Placid Sea, asked directions, and by midday stood before the austerely grand gates of Je Mansion, looking doubtfully at those massive doors. Two servant-guards stood before those gates.

Mek approached the guards, a scruffy figure in very grimy, salt-stiff gallant wanderer tunic and trousers, sandals on his feet, and a sword at his back with a stone in its hilt that appeared to be worth a king's ransom.

But they had been warned. "Ki Mek?" one asked.

Mek's friendly grin crinkled his eyes.

Despite their instructions, the more rule-bound of the two was tempted to send this beggar around to the servants' entrance, but the other guard said, "I'll inform the Young Master." He slipped inside as Mek looked around, eyes half closed as he spread his senses. This city was far more in harmony with its surroundings.

A short time later here was Tai, almost unrecognizable with his hair up in a silver hair clasp, wearing a sober brown silken robe with long sleeves. "Mek! Come in, come in. You look travelworn."

"I could use a bath," Mek admitted. "And hot food would be welcome."

The two appraised each other as Tai led Mek into the finest place he'd ever entered since Ardal's chambers. To Mek, Tai's home seemed a palace fit for a king.

"My father is sitting in court, but will get here when he can."

Mek lowered his voice. "What happened to your letters?"

"My great-aunt was right. Except for the one, none of his reached me nor mine to him, but he refuses to speculate on who made it happen, or why, without evidence. I would expect nothing more from him. You've plenty of time for a bath. And you can probably wear something of mine from before we were swept to the west."

Mek had grown, but he was still half a head shorter than Tai, neatly compact in shape. The round contours of the boy had planed to a…self-assurance without self-consciousness, as he looked about admiringly without a thought to how he appeared.

Tai went away to give orders.

The bath was an enormous tiled pool, scented with lemongrass. Mek sank into the water with a sigh of bliss. Only hunger brought him out; he felt as if he could have remained soaking for a year.

Neatly folded clothes awaited him, aired with a pleasant peppery scent: underthings as soft and light as the touch of a cloud, then silk over that, slippery to the touch. The under robe and over robe were slightly too short, not that Mek cared for that. Instead of his worn, grimy sandals, Tai's unseen servants had provided house slippers.

He followed his nose to a dining hall that seemed as grand as the rest of the house, where he found Tai waiting for him. "I remembered that you stopped eating meat. Is that still true? Otherwise I can—"

"Still true," Mek said. "Monk fare for me. Though I don't want to be a monk."

Tai thought immediately of Han Anise. She and Mek were two of a kind, not creatures of polished jade, but the opposite — lilies in sunlight, transparently…themselves. He busied himself with preparing the tea and serving it correctly, though he knew Mek was utterly unaware of such niceties.

Mek spooned up a huge helping of rice. Hot, freshly cooked rice! Piled on top, pickled beets, seasoned and crisped yams, and beside, a just-baked pancake of corn, onion, and walnut—a food he'd discovered in the north.

"What did you find?" Tai asked once Mek had taken the edge of his appetite. "Is the capital in imminent danger?"

"Danger, yes," Mek said thickly around the last of his pancake. "If I'm right, that entire mountain will slide into the sea."

"When?"

"That's hard to say," Mek admitted. "I don't have the training to gauge time in…in human terms. Or to know what more those geomancers can do. But I do know that palace up on the ridge should never have been put there."

"You can't hazard an approximation?"

Mek drained a second dish of pear cider spiced with wolfberries, and turned the dish around and around in his hand before saying, "If they don't do something before ten years are up, I think maybe it will be too late to stop it. You've got to tell them."

"Ten years," Tai repeated, rubbing his thumb along his lower lip.

"Ten years," his father repeated later that evening, once introductions had been made, and a formal meal consumed.

Mek was glad that Tai had put him in the way of a delicious meal earlier, so that he did not have to worry about arcane manners before this tall, gaunt elder with the severe expression.

"Ten years, and they clearly know of the danger, or there would not be daily reinforcement of the plinth charms," Tai said, frowning. "Why would the emperor wait?"

"I cannot guess what the emperor is thinking," Magistrate Je said, clasping his hands toward the capital. "Or what he's been told. Though they surely cannot be lying to him outright, as deceiving the emperor is a crime punished most grievously. But my guess is, gold."

"Gold!"

"More precisely, who controls how the treasury is allocated once an imperial edict is handed down—or, where to allocate it first. I am not a part of the imperial court," the magistrate informed Mek with painstaking precision. "But I am very certain that repairing the widespread damage caused by the demon storms had strained the imperial treasury."

"What repairs?" Mek asked sourly. "At least in the islands along the trade routes, there did not seem to be any aid besides what we provided ourselves."

The magistrate gave a nod of acknowledgment, neither approbation nor censure, then said, "This, we must put to my cousin, Left Chancellor Ji, who oversees many of the related bureaus."

Mek said with extreme doubt, "If it's the same Ji as the duke who threw my family off our land for refusing to be part of his private army, I don't know how much trust I'd put in anything he said."

"Your family?" the magistrate repeated.

Mek said, "The Kis—ay! My branch—come from this island. Not far up the mountains west of here. I was told that a young duke booted us out after his father inherited a prince's title."

The magistrate then wanted to know if Mek had been there to hear the exact words, or to personally witness the result of them, and Mek remembered that this man was a magistrate. Also related to the Jis, but there was no censure in his voice or face as he asked, "Did your family report their grievance to the local court?"

Mek had to admit that they had not. The magistrate asked if the Kis owned that land, or had settled there with or without consent, and when Mek did not know, he said, "Very well. It is a side issue, and I could put some questions, but first I want to understand exactly what you found off the former imperial island. In your own witness."

Mek began slowly, striving to get physical impressions into language. It was always difficult when he attempted to translate Essence matters into words for those who could not intuit Essence skills.

Respecting others' mental doors had long become habit by now, except when he consciously reached, but occasionally—in situations of sufficient intensity—some of what he'd survived conveyed itself.

The magistrate considered himself oblivious to Essence affinities, but like his son, he had a trace affinity, in his case of stone. It took an effort to focus on words and not extraordinarily vivid images, and he was not entirely successful, except that when Mek neared the end of his recital, Magistrate Je was convinced that Ki Mek was expressing what he believed to be truth.

And then Mek finished, "When I was in the air currents above, I discovered that the geomancers' forcing the liquid fires to continue their deception was the cause of those storms."

That took the magistrate aback.

"Can you prove that?" I asked.

"I might be able to do so to a geomancer who understands Essence," Mek said. "But I think to everyone else I can prove…*around* it, so to speak. That is, those patrols should have reported back a month or two ago that the fires have been doused. If the storms cease, or even lessen this next year, won't that be convincing?"

Indeed yes—proving also that this young man, who lived outside of governmental constraints, was at ease with immense Essence power. Magistrate Je said slowly, "I believe that these matters touch on imperial concerns. And as such, it is my duty to at least consult my cousin, Left Chancellor Prince Ji."

Mek recoiled—no more than a tightening of shoulders, and his brows drawing down, but his mistrust was plain. "And now we're back to the Ji duke who drove my family away because they wouldn't join his private army."

"Private army," the magistrate repeated. "Private armies are strictly forbidden. Forming them is a capital crime, extending to entire families. Are you certain of your facts?"

Mek said scrupulously, "I wasn't there, as I said. This happened while Tai and I were still in the west. But I believe my uncle, my cousins, and my father believe that that was the cause of our being turned out into the world."

"I am grieved to hear it," the magistrate said slowly, again reserving judgment. "Still, I believe that the import of the subject at hand…"

Mek, in looking at memory, had reached mentally for his Fourth Uncle—but before he could close off that uninvited reach, he caught a familiar voice reaching for *him*.

Physical distance was nothing to him. The other voice was faint until he opened his mental door—and there was Ardal—but this was not the voice of a teenager. It was the fast, clipped inner voice of a young woman, though highly agitated. "Kimek! There you are! I feared I had lost the ability to Hear you."

Mek had to concentrate to think in the Westerners' tongue again. "Bar Ardal? Why you need me?"

"To warn you." With the carefully shaped words flooded sensory perception, as always, plus memory; though an adult now, Bar Ardal still did not perceive how much memory and sensory impressions she shared with her words.

"The First Prince has promised rice to the obsidian throne: come spring he leads an alliance to attack your empire. My sister Odval hears a little of the proposed plans to invade the northwest of Mud empire and take rice ships."

Mek had not thought about them for years; in his mind they were still two teenage girls. But he learned by sifting those swift impressions that far more had changed for them than for him — while hedged round with danger.

Especially for Odval, now a young woman living with their mother as they fought in secret against the Cobra Sages. Not just against them, but against the laws binding people to slavery — and Ardal thought it madness, and feared for them both. Tumbling among these worries, vivid images of islands devastated by the strengthening demon storms. Including Angja, desperately rebuilding outside their mountain.

Struggling to comprehend so many changes, he asked, "The bluenecks?"

A little humor brightened her turmoil of emotions, "The birds do better than we humans. They hide among the redbarks during storms. Water passes without harm over them. Wind cannot hurt them as branches take the brunt." The humor was gone. "People are starving."

Mek wanted to promise that the storms would end, except that he could not guarantee that. He had cured the cause. But the damage to air currents had been so vast, and unperceived except in effect, that it might take time to settle again to the accustomed shift from east winds to west as the seasons changed.

"But that is only part of my warning. I have also, through Mother, heard from Brother." And again, elusive memories. Nothing physical. Ardal apparently still had not met her brother, taken away by the Cobra Sages around the time that she was born. But he had remained in secret contact with the Grandmother, a formidable Essence expert. Her brother did not even have a name, except an image of sun-touched dandelion fluff drifting in a breeze: Windseed. "The Cobra Sages seek Kimek."

He already knew that, thanks to Waha. However, she was

risking detection by lurking Cobra Sage experts to pass on these warnings. This much he could give her, in trade: "The source of the demon storms is now mended—"

"…Mek? MEK?"

To Tai and his father, Mek had gone silent, his gaze blank. The magistrate stared in mounting concern, but Tai knew that look. "Mek!"

Mek blinked, rose, and said, "I have to go. Right away. I…got a warning. Remember Bar Ardal?" He tapped his head as he glanced at Tai. "The First Prince's galleys are invading the northwest. I have to warn Eagle Island. They can spread the word." He bowed awkwardly.

Then Mek extended a hand, and both Jes jumped when a beautiful bronze sword appeared with a wink of light and the hilt smacked into his palm. The magistrate stared in astonishment.

"Tai? May I take these clothes? I 'll have to fetch my others from the laundry. I guess they can dry…" He pointed into the air.

Tai nodded, and Mek bowed again then hastened from the room.

"Could that be a way to avoid speaking to Prince Ji?" the magistrate asked.

"His leaving this moment might be. The Kis were very incensed about being forced to abandon their home of generations. But Bar Ardal was always truthful with us, though an enemy. Did you wish to speak further with Mek? Ought I to go find him?"

"No, no, do not press him. Whether there really is trouble on the far side of the empire or it's merely a, we will call it a polite deflection, I take his point about his family. Judging by his rather astonishing revelation, it occurs to me that putting your Ki Mek within the grasp of my ambitious relations might be like putting wings on a tiger. I still believe we must consult my cousin, but let us not put further temptation into his path."

Tai bowed, and wondered if Mek had flown off still wearing house slippers.

His father said, after silent cogitation, "This cannot wait. I believe you and I must leave for the capital."

FIFTY-ONE

"WE MUST BRING JE Tai into the family plans," his highness Prince Ji Houduo remarked to his eldest son on a cold morning as the year drew toward its end. A sliver of Ghost Moon hung off the rooftops through the window, the morning sky still dark around it.

Venshai pulled his robes closer, knelt on a warm cushion that had been placed near the brazier, and gratefully warmed his hands with the tea dish before drinking.

When the subtly flavored Three Clouds tea was warming him inside, he looked down at the strip of paper his father pushed across the low table. "My Uncle Je is coming…and Tai, too? I thought we were going to keep him down south," Venshai began.

"Apparently he left before I was able to convince my cousin that it would be best for his future career to remain another year," the prince said dryly. "Which I'm beginning to believe might have been an error. Je Tai left White Jade with highest approbation from that lazy old bear Chief Su, who bestirred himself from his winter cave long enough to report that. He also reported that your cousin seems to have employed his free time in organizing and cataloguing a vast sub-archive no one uses, left from the previous dynasty. What's more, Je Tai recruited a host of students to labor at it for an entire year, knowing that there was no more reward than a banquet at the end of it. I need not point out that such initiative and leadership is invaluable!"

Venshai protested, "But what about Lam?"

"What about her, my son?"

"She sneaked across the entire island to go watch him play

the Hero in the dragon dance—"

"What was she at that time, seventeen?" the prince observed. "I foretold she would forget about him in a year or so, like every other youth that age. Did she attempt to write to him, especially after she prevailed on his sister to be appointed to her household? She did not. Moreover, she even ceased flirting with male dancers and the boys at the playhouse. Though perhaps we can attribute that to the Sixth Imperial Consort's vigilance." His voice had gone very dry indeed.

Though the prince required decorum at all times, even in private, ever since they had ascertained that there had indeed been a handsome, if temperamental, imperial guard named Guinu who died in a field accident six moons before Crown Princess Lam's birth, Ji Houduo had gradually ceased being scrupulous about appending all her imperial honorifics when referring to her. In his mind, Lam was a masquerader, a product of common blood—nevertheless, nothing in their plans had changed.

The prince tapped the strip of paper, brought by a pigeon that morning. "We have a few days to prepare. Remember, everyone has a price. Your task is to find Je Tai's. We need his allegiance—or at least his cooperation."

Venshai bowed uneasily. He still could not accustom himself to the change in Tai between the days of Little Lamb and the phoenix-eyed qilin of that last visit. Aish! A qilin? More of a tiger.

His uneasiness boiled up into a kind of anxious envy when Tai himself appeared some days later, taller even than his tall father, and looking more like a young tiger, whereas old Uncle Je Pan was just gaunt.

It was like swallowing a fly to force welcome into his voice and flattery to his words, the worse as Tai was merely polite in return, those black eyes about as expressive as the glittery obsidian the Ghost Eyes out west valued so much.

The prince didn't have much better success in overwhelming his abstemious cousin the magistrate with all the luxuries of a princely home. While remaining scrupulously polite, Magistrate Je made it clear he had serious matters on his mind, and presently the four were ensconced in the prince's study.

After a short, polite nod from the prince, Magistrate Je said with ponderous care, "I must admit outright that I am deeply conflicted. I cannot find the correct path between duty to my family and to the emperor." He turned then to Tai. "Please explain, son."

Tai was looking straight at Venshai as he said, "As none of my letters home were reaching my father, I had occasion to correspond with other persons. In the course of which I discovered an anomaly related to geomancy and the former imperial island. A friend with related affinities offered to investigate..."

Ah, there was a hint of telltale color in Cousin Venshai's face, and his gaze shifted, but then all his attention returned as Tai gave a swift outline of Mek's subsequent actions.

Both the Jis sat there with eyes widening; if either Tai or his father had had the temperament for bursts of laughter, they probably would have been convulsed by the similarity of those owl-like gazes.

Tai spoke, again looking straight at Venshai, "When he finished his task, my friend returned to the northwest, where his family has no home—after apparently being driven from this island by a duke—"

"That was recruitment," Venshai burst out.

"Son," the prince said with quiet reproof.

Venshai drew in a deep breath, but could not prevent himself from reddening. "First, that land belongs to *us*. It always has. After Grandfather died, we promised that land to the navy for training, remember, Father? I thought those trespassers up there, next thing to criminal wanderers, would *want* to give up scrabbling after convoys, and train with the navy, then the best of them could join our own Ji defenders at Tiger Island, and—"

"And misapprehensions ensued, I gather," the prince cut in smoothly. "As will happen when youth are too impetuous. That is a side matter at present. I gather this Essence-wielder of yours will not be easily summoned to speak before an investigative tribunal?" At Tai's bow, the prince turned to Magistrate Je. "You have relations by marriage connected to the geomancers, as I recall. Have you discussed this with them?"

"I have not," the magistrate said in his precise way. "There are two, my wife's cousin, who is on duty somewhere far in the south, and my great-aunt, whose health is uncertain, and the physicians advise no undue excitement. I was going to attempt to approach her next."

The prince frowned in a way that made Venshai uneasy; it was not often that he wore that expression of narrow-eyed detachment, but it was never a good sign. At least the subject of his recruitment attempt seemed to have been entirely overwhelmed by all these other things.

Venshai's own mind felt too much like a swift caught in a cage, flitting desperately without lighting anywhere long enough to see the way out. Geomancers! The imperial island! Coral Island! This was something the Jis ought to have known about. Everything Tai said revealed holes in the Ji family's influence.

The prince spoke at last, his voice as slow as his cousin's, "I regret to admit that I've no influence with the geomancy bureau chief. I have two nephews in the Department of Scrutiny, but one is an assistant of an agent overseeing the Ministry of War, and the other at Personnel." A vein beat below the prince's hairline.

He shifted slightly, then said, "You've endured a long journey, Cousin. Nephew. I invite you to refresh yourselves and rest while I make some inquiries. I will strive to discover the best person for each of these respective matters."

"I would think the emperor must be informed," Magistrate Je began slowly. "But I don't know the correct channels of approach for matters outside of my own branch of the Justice Ministry. Thus I thought to consult you, Cousin."

The prince gave a grave nod. "I can arrange that. Those of us who deal with his imperial majesty often — sometimes almost daily — know the best time of day, and the best manner of approach that both enlighten his imperial awareness and yet protect his health." All saluted the imperial palace at the mention of Heaven's Chosen.

"Thank you for your wisdom and forbearance." Magistrate Je bowed his thanks, and the prince summoned servants to lead them to the guest wing.

Once the prince and his son were alone, the prince's hand shook as he pressed fingertips to his eyelids. "Venshai, I cannot overstate the severity of…"

"Tai's stories about Mt. Lir being completely cold, and the fires being on another island altogether?"

The prince dropped his hand. "I've known that for years," he said wearily.

"Father!"

"You know there are matters I cannot yet disclose until you are safely on the golden throne. Few, but they exist. This is one, and you must see why."

Venshai could only bow.

"But the truth is in the chancellery records, and not to be shared until the best manner of revealing it has been decided. We cannot know what is in the emperor's mind until he shares his thoughts. In the meantime, every ministry has unshakeable reasons why it must take the lead in this or that aspect, and we are all very aware that revealing the truth will undermine the dynasty. Frankly, I was waiting until you were safely married to Lam—and the emperor joined with his imperial forebears at the Imperial Tomb—so that you could begin your reign much as the Tan emperor did, by revealing the truth and have that be counted a virtue."

Venshai understood the sense of that!

"As for the city, I thought we had at least half a century. More. I believe the geomancers did, too, but *I don't actually know that* because I just realized they only tell me what they want me to know. Not what *I* want to know."

Venshai blinked, then understood. "The geomancers probably have some way of finding out. We can't be the only ones aware."

"I'm certain the navy is as well, but they will be under orders. They won't talk. But *I* didn't know." The prince's voice was hoarse with fury, his pallid forehead gleaming with moisture. He drew a shaky breath. "Lam's matter has occupied my mind entirely of late, I admit. I should have been more vigilant. I wish we could lay hands on Tai's Essence wielder, who sounds—if even half of what Tai says is true—entirely too powerful to be running around without supervision by wiser heads."

"He did do something meritorious," Venshai began, wondering what price would attract someone that powerful, once they found him. Venshai let himself imagine what kind of influence he'd have with someone like that under his orders!

"But what will he do next?" the prince murmured.

"Do you want us to try to find him?" Venshai asked, shifting thoughts to whom to send.

The prince rolled a bloodshot eye in his direction. "A youth who flies on a sword? Let it go. If there are Western raiders pestering those northwest islands, he is better off there. Really, these Essence-wielding criminals ought to have been eradicated generations ago, but never mind: that's for you to handle once you are seated on the dragon throne. Right now I am wondering what other matters of vital import I have been kept in the dark about."

"I don't see that it can be much, Esteemed Father. Because there is the whole to consider, as you have taught me. What Tai says—*if* it's true, and we don't know that yet—doesn't change the fact that the Tan Dynasty is finished. And you're the one who did all the hard work finding out that they did it to themselves, with their secret elixir of immortality." Venshai's tone was admiring, coaxing. Anything to get that sick look out of his father's face.

The flattery didn't go unheard, and the prince permitted himself to be distracted for a moment. "You would think, with the best education possible, they would understand that that was how the first Kun Dynasty destroyed themselves."

He fell silent, and they both brooded on the unsettling truth that with medicine, no one knew until it was too late if slow cures were reparative or actually slow poison. There could be very unpleasant effects before cures were effected. The former emperor had apparently doubled his dose of a secret and costly elixir, plus putting his elder two sons on it—slowly killing all three of them, and severely harming the current emperor, who had been just a babe in arms.

Venshai said with more confidence, "The fact doesn't change that *you* are the one who discovered that the imperial blood really is barren."

When—and how—to reveal that without throwing the entire empire into turmoil and war was now consuming Prince Ji Houduo's concentration. Carefully, step by step, he had moved the Ji family into positions of influence before this confirmation of a guess—all while waiting for news that an imperial heir (male) had been born. He knew now that there would never be a male heir. The plan was the same: a smooth transition to of a new dynasty, the Ji Dynasty—by marriage with the imperial crown princess.

"That will not matter if those Yimu wolves act before we can. They certainly have known Lam's parentage all along." The prince drew another, less shaky breath, blinked, and set his jaw. "We have inadvertently discovered a new path that has hitherto been closed to us. But we shall amend that. Venshai, put on your Censor's robe, and go over to Tuoba Niu."

"Tonight?"

"Now. It's early enough—barely. But this cannot wait. Don't let anyone deflect you: say 'Coral Island' if they attempt to forestall you. That ought to bring the old snake Tuoba slithering..."

The prince's hand still trembled as he pinched it to his forehead. "No," he husked. "I'll have to go to him or he'll never consent even if the entire city starts sliding into the sea beneath our very feet. Now I know why he's so stiff-necked a stickler for the rules: it's inherited guilt. We must rouse the Jes; this is too urgent to wait."

Somewhat to the prince's surprise—and Venshai's astonishment—Magistrate Je put down a scroll he had brought with him and said tranquilly, "I believe I've done my duty in bringing Tai's discoveries to your notice. The consequences are not within my realm of expertise. Tai will inform me if there is anything I ought to know." Then he picked up the scroll.

And so Tai found himself bundled into the Ji carriage, a handwarmer on his lap, for the short journey down a terraced layer to a modest mansion the size of his own home.

And here, Tai was introduced to the elaborate ritual of a meeting between members of the imperial court. Nothing could appear more cordial on the surface, as everyone bowed constantly, offered and refused everything except tea, then toasted one another with the tea, all the while establishing the boundaries of the conversation.

It was as unlike Mek's transparency as could be, yet Tai remembered being taught the civilities that preserved everyone's face, especially in situations of mutual distrust. Perhaps even mutual dislike, he realized belatedly, after the Jis were repeatedly complimented and thanked for their wisdom in all matters, and their perspicacity in this one by bringing forward this young man who apparently had stumbled into imperial concerns far outside of his department.

Tai had not spoken a word so far.

The gongs had rung the second turtle hour when at last the generalities became specific: guilt or no, Bureau Chief Tuoba refused—in the most polite, flattery-laden way possible, framed between two Kanda quotations—to permit another ministry to trespass into his bureau's matters without imperial edict, and the bureau chief would not speak to Tai at all unless they were to have their interview alone.

The Jis departed after the tea was drunk amid another round of mutual compliments and self-deprecation. Tai knew that the moment he returned to Ji Mansion he would be interrogated, but the thought did not disturb him unduly: if Venshai cornered him for questions, Tai had a few of his own. Beginning with his missing letters.

Once they were alone, Chief Tuoba's sphere of a face relaxed into twinkling affability. "Now, young Secretary Je, let's open the door and see Mt. Lir. In present case, almost literally, ha ha! His highness the Left Chancellor mentioned that you learned Coral Island's secret through someone you corresponded with. My guess is, your venerable…ayah! Is she your grandmother? No, great-grandmother…"

"Great-Aunt," Tai said, since it was clear this man would be familiar with all those concerned with Coral Island.

Chief Tuoba rocked back and forth, plump fingers patting his knees. "Very good woman. Worked for us well into her eighties. And so, a confession. Yes, I said 'a' confession. It has happened — the most common confessions being made shortly before the King of the Underworld comes calling. Our predecessors, like us, have labored under the burden of our forebears' decisions — but it is not for us to question. Let me hear precisely what you found."

This time Tai did not hold anything back. Gradually the humor in the jolly little man's face diminished, and when Tai got to the revelation about the cause of the demon storms, Chief Tuoba was actually weeping quietly. "Ay, ay, ay," he whispered huskily, then his voice strengthened. "We had no idea. How could we know? We thought we did right, opening the earth to free the fires. No cutting down forests of trees to haul out there to burn…it was an imperial edict. We must obey. The imperial island must be perceived to be uninhabitable until imperial decree." He shook his head, mopped his eyes, and sighed, shoulders bowed.

Tai waited, keeping to himself his opinion of that long-ago general who lied his way to a throne.

Chief Tuoba sighed. "Your friend has earned a merit inestimable, and yet it could be perceived as trespassing into imperial matters. We shall have to proceed carefully, very carefully: you know the saying that when the clam and the snipe fight, it's the fisherman who wins?"

Tai bowed. Every child had to write that old saying numerous times in practicing characters.

"It has sometimes been recast: when the kraken and the whales battle, it's the fisherman who drowns. We have to consider the emperor, who has so many pressing matters before him. The sudden addition of a new problem out of the past is going to be far from welcome. And yet, ten years…It is clear that *something* must be done, and soon. The emperor is the kraken, but the whale pod would be his subjects if rumors were to get out. Who would blame them for coming in a mass to demand the truth?"

"Please excuse this insignificant ninth level secretary's ignorance…"

"Speak, my boy. Considering what you have brought me, I would be honored to hear your thought, however uninformed."

"Thank you, Chief Tuoba, for your forbearance. Perhaps there is potential good news. Mek did not say he thought the imperial city of old uninhabitable, though it was uninhabited," Tai ventured.

Chief Tuoba smiled again. "Uninhabitable! Uninhabited! No, he probably could not see the Caretakers, especially if he was viewing the city from on high early in the morning. Who would see a few grains on a vast shore of sand?"

"Caretakers, if this one might inquire?"

"It's only a handful of us, but we've been there as guardians of the city from the beginning. At first mainly to sweep out and tend the imperial ancestral hall. Unimaginable to let so sacred a place languish until it became a home for rats and spiders! And I believe our predecessors believed that the first emperor would bring everyone back after a few years."

Tai tried to imagine the scope of that!

"The city is there, the soil is good, and many of us are recluses by nature. There has never been a dearth of volunteers to live there, gather each spring to unlock and sweep out the imperial buildings, then reseal them. I myself spent five years there, until promotion required me to return," the bureau chief said, then laughed. "The competition is most vigorous for the libraries and archives. Aish! The ancient imperial city is there, and ready once a little work is done, but there remains the matter of forcing everyone here to upend lives and the affairs of the empire to go there and begin again. Could the dynasty survive that? Even thinking about it is a trespass on imperial concerns." Here, the chief clasped his hands and bowed toward the imperial palace.

Tai said, "It was no surprise to the Bureau of Geomancy that the fires on Coral Island were put out?"

Chief Tuoba shook all over in rueful laughter. "We knew. There has always been a craft left for emergencies unnamed. On seeing the skies completely clear in the south, a party of geomancers took this craft to Coral Island, inspected, discovered what had been done, and that the ground had so reformed that it would require at least fifty of us, and a great deal of time, to renew the fires. Until your appearance, my young secretary, the debate has been how to inform the emperor when we could not tell him how it happened. But now we must reconsider *everything*. Of course I will dispatch our most experienced Essence-masters to investigate, but...can you not convince your invaluable friend to return and speak to us in more detail?"

Tai tried to imagine Mek instructing geomancers. "He might come, but he says himself that he has no geomancer training." Tai remembered those halting words about nearly turning into stone. None of that was taught in any class! "Much of what he does he has trouble expressing in words. And in any case, he would never reopen what he called a wound in the earth."

"Yes, the storms...I do not see the connection, but perhaps wiser minds will. Ayah! I have learned so much tonight that my head is swimming, and yet I know we must proceed with care and caution...other ministries... fishing in muddy waters... ay, ay, I am rambling unmercifully! Forgive me, Secretary Je. I will send you back in my most comfortable conveyance. Though you bring a fresh set of daunting troubles, it was with virtuous intent. I want you to go with my most earnest gratitude..." The bureau chief paused and added shrewdly, "And I suspect there is another interrogation awaiting you elsewhere, but as this is a matter under imperial edict, I must forbid you to discuss our interview until his imperial majesty has been informed. That ought to keep the temple sealed and the wolves at bay, eh?"

Tai bowed, returned the correct compliments, said that he would walk—no need to disturb his carters so late, he really preferred the open air—and he left, relieved that the matter was now in the proper hands.

FIFTY-TWO

T HERE WAS NO WARNING.

One moment Lei was admiring the robe embroidered with silver phoenixes that Imperial Crown Princess Lam was to wear for her first appearance before court to be officially appointed the heir, and the next the Sixth Imperial Consort swept into the dressing chamber, trailing maids and graywings, her eldest brother, Prince Yimu Bo, at her side.

"There's some new rumor burning through court since yesterday, and it has to do with that four-eyed rat Ji Houduo," she said to the imperial crown princess—and then turned on Lei, who had retreated to the back wall with the maids, as the Sixth Imperial Consort blocked the door with her train.

"You," the Sixth Imperial Consort said in her wispy, lispy voice. "Aren't you related to the Jis in some way?"

Lei promptly dropped forehead to the floor, her heart hammering. Her soft tones were barely audible as she murmured something about primary family and secondary.

"Then it's your brother who arrived a few days ago, and set them all in an uproar? What is it about? No one is talking." The Sixth Imperial Consort glared down at Lei, whose forehead remained pressed to the floor tiles, so neither saw the flash of surprise and intensity in the crown princess's face. But Yimu Bo saw it, and his interest sharpened.

Lei mumbled something disjointed and totally inaudible.

The exasperated Sixth Imperial Consort was going to kick her, but the princess said, "Mother. Why don't I go to Left Chancellor Ji's with Secretary Je to ask? There will be no possibility of denying *me* an interview."

The Sixth Imperial Consort turned to her, and smiled. "A very fine idea. You must go in the heir's chariot, mind. Wear that robe you've got on, and order that boy to come here. The Jis won't dare to oppose *you*—"

At this, Prince Yimu Bo interjected, "She can wear the heir's robe but until next week, she cannot issue orders as heir. That white-eyed wolf Prince Ji would demand to see the heir's tally, and we all lose face."

The Sixth Imperial Consort, thus reminded that she herself could not issue orders that pertained to court matters, turned a pout his way, then lifted a shoulder. "This is practice, Lam. When you sit on the throne, you will be dealing daily with these rats and wolves, so it's time to begin using your wits."

"I'll tell Venshai to send him. He won't say no to *me*," the princess said acidly.

"Then bring the boy here, since he can't enter the harem. I want to talk to him, and without Prince Ji interfering."

"Then I had better accompany you," Yimu Bo said on a weary sigh. "Unless you're actually considering his suit, Lam?"

"No!" The imperial princess exclaimed.

"Well thought, Bo," the Sixth Imperial Consort said. "If I were empress, I could do something about the ridiculous rules of imperial court etiquette—" She saw that her brother was impatient with a subject too often mentioned over years, and her daughter wasn't listening at all. She hastened on. "After next week Lam can call on anyone as acknowledged heir, but as yet she is still an unmarried princess. You must go with her." She swept out, her entourage following her long train.

That left Lei still on the floor, trying to control her shuddering breathing.

"Come, come, Lei," the imperial princess said, a note of glee in her voice that Lei had rarely heard. "We're under strict command, did you hear? The Emperor of Heaven himself dare not stop us. We must obey!"

Lei rose, whispering, "I did not even know my brother is here in the capital."

"A sublime surprise for you, is it not, Little Lei? We shall shortly find out why he's here so early—we've half a month before the moons kiss. Garnet! Oh, he's gone—probably to get that monstrous chariot of Mother's out. They can barely get it around Kanda's Eternal Wisdom Switchback, but that's not our worry. Tigermoth! Gossamer! Swallowtail! Get the phoenix headdress on me. Nothing else will do, with this robe…"

When they settled in the capacious chariot, handwarmers in their laps, the imperial crown princess rubbed the back of her neck. "If only Imperial Mother were not quite so austere, I would ask her if one ever got used to this heavy weight on the head."

Lei thought of the empress and her sword-straight back, glimpsed from afar.

"But she'd lecture me on duty, and recommend I copy out some sutras on self-discipline…Distract me, Lei. We can talk about something else."

"May this…may I ask a question, your imperial highness?"

"Ask, ask, ask. Did I not command you to distract me?" The princess groaned softly. "I thought I was done for the day."

Lei flushed, but said resolutely, "I know that your imperial highness has referred to my Ji cousins, and I never wished to trespass asking why they have displeased your imperial highness, but just now, you mentioned my Cousin Venshai…"

"Ay, Venshai," the imperial princess broke in to exclaim disparagingly. "And his pack of wolfish brothers. Or, I think at least one might have been a cousin. I don't dislike Qishai, not at all. Except when she would bring up Venshai's manifold excellences, when she knows that I know that there aren't any. As a husband, I mean. He is probably a fine censor, for all I know—and I'll find out as soon as I'm permitted to attend court," she added, scowling.

"He is very filial," Lei said, and the imperial princess noted her dutiful tone.

"A wolf and his cub." The imperial princess gave a jade hairpin an impatient poke, sending the tiny golden ornaments dangling wildly. "He was always a rough cub. We were all cubs when we were small," she admitted with a half-smile, rubbing the back of her neck again. "But as soon as he reached fourteen, he turned horrid. Ordering everyone in sight, as if *he* were the imperial heir. He kicked those he didn't like, or who didn't follow him. I saw him do it."

"He didn't dare to kick your imperial highness?" Lei looked aghast.

"No. In a way it was worse. He smirked at me. And treated me as if…as if the augurs had already set the wedding date. He's got better since, but I don't believe a word of his flattery. Here we are, Ji Mansion, and look at the size of those stone guardians, as if this was the imperial palace. Very good, Lei, very good, you distracted me perfectly."

A graywing approached the door sentinels, who were already bowing, having seen the banners with the imperial Tan character. One opened the door, and the other sprang to help get the stepladder down for the imperial princess's descent. Then Prince Yimu Bo joined her from the second carriage.

By then Imperial Princess Lam's heart was crowding her throat. She had waited so patiently until now. Had Je Tai turned ugly? Or worse, would he smirk at her the way Venshai did?

The call was unexpected, and at any other level it would be considered rude not to have sent a warning on ahead, but imperial calls were blessings by tradition, almost by law.

His highness the Left Chancellor was first to lead the bowing. He had a look of someone who had assumed his court robe in some haste; the imperial princess barely gave him a glance, affording a brief nod to Princess Ji, and nothing at all to Venshai. Her gaze searched, then found Tai standing correctly in the background at his father's shoulder.

There was no smirk. No smile at all as he bowed. His glance met hers—such eyes he had, just like Lei's only far, far more compelling, in that handsome face! Then he quickly averted his gaze most properly, as they were both unmarried.

She knew she ought not to stare but just a moment longer, just one moment…and she saw the sudden, transforming smile he turned on Lei when he recognized her. That unguarded, kindly smile for his little sister confirmed him in the status of a hero prince from the ancient tales. Had that rat Venshai ever smiled at Qishai that way? No, he hadn't, not in all the years Imperial Crown Princess Lam had known them…

Uncle Bo cleared his throat slightly, and the imperial princess became aware of the silent chamber. Everyone was waiting for her to speak! Think! She had been reminded to use her wits by her mother but she had lost them completely.

Uncle Bo then stepped forward to accept the Left Chancellor's greetings, and—smooth as oil poured onto a pool—uttered a series of compliments while informing the Jis that her imperial highness had just learned that the brother of her loyal and dedicated Secretary Je had arrived in anticipation of Two Moons' New Year—and because said loyal and dedicated secretary had been too vital to be away for liberty visits this past year, her imperial highness wished to make up for it by inviting Archival Secretary Je Tai to the imperial palace for a visit with his sister.

"Laudable, if this humble servant of their imperial majesties may be permitted to offer his poor and insignificant opinion, most laudable and kind," the Left Chancellor said, pouring his own jug of oil. "Exactly the sort of kindness her imperial highness's subjects have come to expect, *but…*"

While this elaborate ritual was carried out, Lei was horrified to discover herself the center of it.

Venshai was horrified to see the imperial princess staring at Je Tai in that fixed way.

And Tai was horrified at the prospect of being carted off to the imperial palace, without a doubt for interrogation about the same subjects that Chief Tuoba had given him a direct order not to discuss. Whose will prevailed in such situations?

His highness Yimu Bo had seen that hungry gaze toward Je Tai. He mentally shrugged. Je Tai looked like the Morningstar God come again, as the poets warbled, but his rank was negligible. If the infatuation lasted, Je Tai might make a consort—once Lam was married to a suitable (and obedient) prince.

His highness Yimu Bo had no real interest in any matter save those that impinged on his own prerogatives, but he very much liked the excuse to sting the Jis in their own house, and slinging another barrel of oil, addressed Tai in pressing the invitation. Leaving the Jis out.

But the Left Chancellor was far too experienced a duelist. In an even longer speech, while regretting deeply that Bureau Chief Tuoba might be sending a summons at any time—as was his right in matters of geomancy—he managed to intimate that the Sixth Imperial Consort (and her daughter, not yet heir) could not issue imperial edicts. Much as Je Tai would be flattered by so august an attention, pending the expected, imminent summons by Chief Tuoba, he must remain in the home of his family relations.

A check. Prince Yimu Bo had to accept that, smiling and bowing while mentally acknowledging a win for the old wolf, a winning move but not a win of the game. Much amused, he decided to make a try from another direction, but before he could get much past initial compliments, the imperial princess had recovered her wits at last, and stepped forward.

As she held the highest rank there, everyone fell silent. "I completely understand the necessity for the demands of departmental precedence. But I am so regretful over having neglected to permit my secretary to visit her relations that I wish to make up for that now. Secretary Je Lei, why don't you remain here with your father and brother, and once the moons have been properly celebrated, return to your duties?"

Whence she would be able to interrogate Lei as much as she wanted about whatever she heard in the Ji household. Everyone there knew it. But as Venshai and his father were about to assure the imperial princess they would never dream of depriving her of her secretary, Magistrate Je bowed and said, "This insignificant subject dares to offer his sincere gratitude."

Kanda's first rule about filial respect had been evoked: a father and a long-unseen child took precedence in a very complex situation. And so, after mutual insincerities of empyrean poesy, the imperial princess and her uncle took their leave, and Lei stayed, the princess giving her a fond farewell and promising to send her belongings over at once.

The prince took over. The Jes were left alone in the kindest way, and offered a sumptuous chamber for their reunion. All three thought immediately of peepholes, but Magistrate Je was unperturbed, having decided in youth—once the existence of such things had been introduced to him—to live his life so that anyone could hear his words at any time.

Lei smiled at Tai, delighted to see him again, and said, "I'm to understand there is some imperial affair about which you cannot speak? My only question is, can we expect war coming to the city, or an imminent pirate attack?"

"No, nothing like that," Tai said. And as Venshai and his father's best investigator behind two separate walls pressed closer to hear, he said, "Fifth place in the imperial examination! I don't believe I could have done half as well, especially given all those years of no study. I wish I had been home to celebrate with you. Can you tell me all you can recollect of the questions?"

The two Je offspring and their father contentedly debated the strengths and weaknesses of various scholarly works, and Magistrate Je retold the story of his own achievement so long ago—discussed at length by his children—until a servant knocked to announce dinner.

During the meal, Venshai pressed Lei to talk about her position. QiQi unconsciously supported him, saying eagerly,

"Her imperial highness is always so poised when I make duty calls. Never any sign of temper tantrums, which makes me think it's all just the sort of mean gossip mean people like to make up about other people. But what is it *like?* Are you surrounded by luxuries? Can you order anything you want?"

"Luxuries there are, though scarcely less beautiful than I see here this fine home," Lei said with a bow toward Princess Ji, who smiled broadly at the compliment. "As for ordering things, it is not I who gives the orders. I merely pass them along."

"But you've been seen at the two best bookstores. Lu Suanek says that they chase everyone else out just for you — the imperial crown princess isn't even there!"

"I tried to get them not to do that. But they seem to see me as her imperial highness's representative, so I always try to be quick. She lets me read anything I wish — in fact we usually read together. Though lately she has been reading more of the historical writings and fewer storybooks, for you know she is shortly to be proclaimed heir, which means she will be taking her place in court..."

While QiQi pestered Lei for titles of the historic works that the imperial crown princess was reading and what she thought of them, Venshai was watching Tai, regretting again those demon-cursed letters. Who would have thought Tai would bring the matter up again, when he was reunited with his father now? Tai had brought that up the moment he'd returned from Chief Tuoba's, and of course Venshai and his father had maintained they were not connected to the ministers who oversaw the imperial couriers, but Tai stubbornly made it clear he was going to pursue the matter.

Venshai had to get Tai to forget about all that foolishness when they were boys. They were just boys!

Tai didn't spare a thought to the imperial princess, so briefly seen. She was handsome, certainly, at least as handsome as current popular poems and plays intimated, but he had met that kind of unblinking, almost devouring glance many times, and didn't like it.

His primary speculation was bent toward what the geomancers would have to say to him next, and so he returned the briefest responses to Venshai's leading questions about his impressions of the imperial crown princess.

No one really believed that Chief Tuoba was going to find himself in urgent need of Je Tai, so when a graywing showed up first thing the next morning, summoning him to the imperial presence, they were all shocked.

"I must dress properly," Tai began, his voice clashing with Prince Ji's insistence that he accompany his nephew, a guest under his roof.

No, the graywing stated, he must come as he is; Bureau Chief Tuoba was also in the cart. The two impassive imperial guards bearing halberds flanking the graywing reinforced the immediacy, and the gravity, of the summons by their presence.

Tai squared his shoulders and marched out into a sleeting rain, then up into the waiting cart.

"Good morning, Secretary Je," the chief greeted him.

Then to Tai's surprise, slid his considerable bulk from the opposite bench to that next to Tai, and whispered a finger's breadth from his ear, "It is well that you organized that archive from the previous dynasty, because I am going to intimate that you put together your clues from papers you found there. Once the emperor decides there is no living target, I believe he'll shift his attention to more vital matters."

He hauled himself back to his bench, nodding significantly.

Tai realized then that he was being invited to corroborate a lie. He despised lies. He also hated death threats, and his great-aunt had gone to great trouble to confess the way she had because even at her great age, she could be executed. Therefore he had two choices: lie, or risk her life.

Fury ignited in him. *How* he hated lies! But if the truth would lead to an old woman, whose entire life had been dedicated to her work and her family, to an ignominious and painful execution, then…he would lie. Then never again.

And the rest of the ride was spent in mentally reviewing what he might say.

The previous emperor, knowing that he would not survive to see his single remaining son reach manhood, had written a letter to him, sealed with an edict that the letter must not be opened by any but his successor at fifteen.

Each day you face the court [the letter said] you will hear them exhort you to live ten thousand years. My father actually believed it was possible, swayed by a rascal who claimed to be a student of Kan Da. I believed, as he did, that the precious elixir he found at the end of his life was just taken too late, and I not only began ingesting it when I was young and healthy, but I insisted that it be added to the diet of my three sons. The cost of my greed for time beyond what we are allotted was our lives — you are spared because your dose was the smallest, taken only during your first year.

He had then outlined the imperial issues of his day — one of them being the Coral Island deception — and had finished:

You will often read, and hear, people referring to their court rivals as wolves, sharks, rats, snakes, poison-eels, spiders, and tigers, but the truth is that no living creature is as greedy, as wicked, as full of deceit as our fellow humans. I include myself among them — my craving for eternal youth. Deceit in the animals is confined to defense, the getting of food or mates, and none that I know of value rocks in the form of gold and jade as a means of gaining power over others.

Learn to cherish truth. Even if it hurts. It was a physician who dared to tell the truth that preserved your life, even though it was too late for mine. All the others told me what they thought I wanted to hear, to save their own lives, an instinct so strong it has the force of natural law.

The present emperor — once he had wrested power away from the regents who had tried to rule through him — began his rule by ruthless enforcement of the punishment for Deception of the Emperor. Eventually he had to admit that executions did not guarantee truth, it merely made people desperate: there were four attempts at poison during those early years. As well he had chosen to make condemned murderers his tasters, rather than young serving maids, or worse, his innocent dogs whose unquestioning trust he would never betray. *They* were always fed from his hand after his food proved to be untainted.

He came to make a reluctant peace with a certain amount of peculation and misdirection, as long as the intricate apparatus of governance proceeded. Weary and disillusioned, he trudged through his days, determined to live long enough to give his daughter — his one Heaven-granted miracle — a less desperate coming-of-age than he'd endured, and safely wed to a man of noble blood who understood the preservation of the apparatus.

His chief graywing announced the newcomers.

Geomancy Bureau Chief Tuoba, he knew well. The Je boy did not resemble his Ji relations in the least. Now to see if he resembled them in manner, or intent.

Tai, in entering the imperial presence, gained a swift impression of a vast chamber filled with art, but his attention arrowed to the thin, straight-backed figure in gold seated on the throne. The golden embroidery of a great five-clawed dragon glittered with each imperial breath.

Tai and Bureau Chief Tuoba dropped to their knees and pressed their foreheads to the floor as Bureau Chief Tuoba told his carefully prepared story.

Then: "Look up, Secretary Je."

Tai raised his head, but kept his gaze on the floor.

Bureau Chief Tuoba had gauged his emperor correctly. "Whom did you tell about your discovery?"

"Only my father, my uncle Prince Ji, my cousin Duke Ji Venshai, Chief Tuoba here, and the Essence wielder who healed the island and the sky above it."

"This Essence wielder's name?"

Je Tai hesitated, then said resolutely, "Ki Mek."

"No one else involved?"

"No one else, your imperial majesty," Tai ended, belatedly adding the honorific.

The emperor's sickly complexion paled a bit more, if that was possible, and he rasped, "What inspired you to meddle in imperial affairs?"

Tai stiffened. *No lies.* "Your imperial majesty, this insignificant subject is slow of wit and lacking in experience. Not apprehending that this was an imperial matter. It appeared to be a...a geomancy problem, related to the Archive." He touched the wooden tally at his belt, with its character for an archival official of the ninth rank. "When I discussed it with a person whose skills seemed to fit him best for resolving what might be a grave...irregularity between earth and sky, and it was revealed to be a serious threat—" His firm conviction lent his words an air of truth.

"Yes, yes." The emperor winced. "I understand about that. Archivists and geomancers both appear to be solitary individuals, whose intent is on the solving of the problem before them. Bureau Chief Tuoba, perhaps educational methods stressing the desirability of first reporting 'irregularities' to those appointed to oversee such matters?"

"It shall be done, your imperial majesty," Tuoba murmured, forehead (and generously proportioned nose) still pressed to the floor.

The emperor shifted his gaze back to Tai, who was as unlike that slithering flatterer Ji Houduo as was possible. After years of assessing men, he was convinced that this Je Tai was like the Magister Je Pan reported in Judiciary assessment records: straightforward and scrupulous. But Heaven seemed to have granted this Je a talent for organization.

He would make use of that talent now. "Pending emendation by your investigators, Bureau Chief Tuoba, it seems we have ten years to prepare for something that no one in the empire is going to want or to like. Ten years, when we'd counted on having at least fifty." He eyed Tai. "All things considered, I believe that the best person to draw up and oversee a complete plan for removal to the ancestral capital iso you, Archivist Secretary Je Tai."

Tai's face jerked up, his startlement plain.

The emperor said, "You will discuss this interview with no one, beyond the fact that you are now serving under imperial edict. There will be lodgings over in the Secretariat wing provided for your use, to keep distractions to a minimum."

Distractions — and listening ears.

"I am not entirely without mercy. You may recruit a staff, but these people will locked in for the duration. I want a plan that will ensure as little trouble as is possible. My ancestor contrived the evacuation without bloodshed or untenable disruption to imperial function. You will duplicate it. Do you have any questions?"

That was usually merely a signal that the interview was over, but Je Tai braced himself as best he could, kneeling there on the hard marble floor, and murmured, "One only, your imperial majesty."

"State it."

"May this slow-witted subject be permitted access to the archival records of the time?"

It was effrontery — but it was also a very good question.

"You may. In fact, it occurs to me that your inquiries might involve archives outside of Rites and Divination. Nothing is to leave any archive, but you will be granted complete access within each premises. Do well — present me with a workable plan by this time next year at the latest — and there will be promotion and commensurate rewards, Secretary Je. Graywing Chief Emerald, see to it."

A graywing glided in and led the two out, leaving the

emperor to yet another pot of tea brewed with ginger root, coriander, fennel, and peppermint, the only concoction that seemed to keep his meals down once he'd managed to ingest them.

When he'd drunk the cup, he said, "Chief Ar."

A nondescript man of about fifty years appeared from an unmarked side door.

"I want your ferrets to find this Ki Mek, and bring him here to me."

FIFTY-THREE

BACK IN THE CART, Tai breathed away the trembling in his limbs, composed himself, and thought hard about Ki Mek.

Then there he was, as if Mek sat beside him. "Tai?"

"I just came from an interview with the emperor. Who now knows your name." As always, during the time it took for Tai to consciously form the words mentally, vivid sensory impressions carried context to Mek.

At the end Mek asked: "Am I in trouble?"

"He did not say so, but he asked specifically," Tai said apologetically. "I couldn't not tell him."

Mek knew that Tai was very firmly an imperial subject. Mek was not against the empire. But gallant wanderers thought themselves just as firmly as people living alongside it. "Thank you for warning me."

"I hope it's not a warning." Now Tai was truly grieved. "He might want to reward you?"

They both felt the question there, for who could penetrate the ways of emperors?

Mek thought it would be as well not to express that he'd as soon avoid whatever obligations came with imperial rewards. "I'm going back to the other end of the empire from Mountain Peony, and I'll stay there." He sensed the stress that Tai himself was only subliminally aware of, and closed the mental door again.

Tai sat in silence, still mentally reeling.

Bureau Chief Tuoba said soberly as the cart neared Ji Mansion, "Send word if there is any aid I can give you, I or any of our people."

Tai said softly, barely audible over the rumble of the cart wheels and the clop of horse hooves, "Reassure my great-aunt?"

The chief clasped his hands, bowing assent.

The cart stopped, Tai climbed down, and entered the mansion.

Tai discovered the consequences of any contact with imperial power by the way an invisible wall seemed to form around him as soon as he got inside. Before sending him off to pack up his things (for the cart was going to wait), the graywing had given Tai a tally of gold in the form of an owl, which confirmed that he was now under a very short chain of command.

Tai bowed to Uncle Ji, then held out the golden owl. "I've been forbidden to speak about my interview. Also, I'm to remove to new lodgings."

"New lodgings?" Venshai repeated. "Where?"

"At the imperial palace."

"The imperial palace!" That was Kandashai, who exclaimed, "And the owl tally. Aish! That gets you into *any* of the archives. You lucky soul! How did you manage that?"

Prince Ji sent a frown his younger son's way, and turned to Tai. "I will give orders to have your belongings packed at once."

Tai bowed to Magistrate Je. "I apologize, Father, for being unfilial. It seems that once again, I will not be able to celebrate with the family. Will you convey the apologies of this unfilial son to Mother when she arrives?"

Magistrate Je said, "Yes, yes. It is easy enough to surmise what your new orders concern, but perhaps the least said the better. I am silent on the subject. Your mother will understand."

Tai spoke his farewell to Lei.

"I wish I could help you," she said.

Venshai followed him to the guest wing. "I take it you're now going to be living in the palace?"

"It seems so, Cousin," Tai said as he began to assemble the few scrolls he'd brought, and to pack his writing case himself. Clothing could be left to the servants, who did a neater job than he ever managed.

"Then you'll probably be seeing a lot of the imperial crown princess," Venshai stated — his thoughts still churning over that look she had given Tai.

"I cannot guess who I will see," Tai said, having ascertained with his fingers that his private code writings had not been disturbed. He began arranging his writing brushes.

Venshai struggled against resentment—even jealousy—and lost the battle the moment he refused to recognize the emotion for what it was. "If you're going to be having interviews with the imperial—family," Venshai corrected himself. "You should probably know that Lam—Imperial Crown Princess Lam—is not actually the emperor's blood."

Tai glanced up at him, surprised by a subject that had come out of nowhere. "Why would you say that?"

"My father has been investigating for years. Eventually it will come out— Yimu Lily was selling shoes on the street before she caught the emperor's eye. That's well known, though no one dares talk openly about it, except in playhouses islands away, in mask. My father found out only recently that she was already with child by an imperial guard, a lengthy investigation concluded mostly by the trail of suspiciously dead persons, beginning with the guard, named Guinu."

Tai lifted a shoulder. It had absolutely nothing to do with him—even if it was true. And he doubted that. It sounded exactly like the sort of tales that Venshai and Lekshai had concocted ten years ago, then scorned him when he believed them.

Venshai got no reaction, and added quickly, "Crown Princess Lam doesn't seem to know. But the Yimus certainly do, which might be why they're grabbing up every title they can, as well as much of the treasury as possible, before the truth inevitably is revealed…" Venshai sensed he was on uneven ground, and strove for the virtuous-sounding motivation. "My father's goal is to make sure there won't be civil war when it does come out."

The writing case lock clicked, and Tai straightened up. "Is that all?"

"Keep it to yourself, I need hardly say," Venshai murmured. "It might help you to maintain a proper view when dealing with them personally. Mind! I'm trusting you with a secret that would get us all executed, with no hope of proper burial."

"I wish," Tai said in that detached voice that Venshai loathed, "you had not told me anything. But fear not. I won't speak about it to anyone."

He walked out, leaving Venshai unsure whether the revelation had had the effect he wanted.

Tai spared a brief thought for that princess. In a few words she had gone from a staring figure in grand silks to a piece on the Circle board of imperial politics. Apparently an unwitting one. But as he made his last bow to his father, and spoke polite words of thanks to his uncle for his hospitality, the matter faded before the sight of two imperial carts, and the servant lugging his trunk of belongings out as two other servants brought Lei's things in.

Mek's first day had been a long, high, fast flight over endless waters, pushed by an east wind veering northward. It had indeed dried his clothes, but he had forgotten his old, much-repaired straw sandals. He hoped Tai wouldn't think he was a thief, but he was going to have to sell these fine embroidered house slippers as well as the silk robe, because the air was getting colder the father north he went.

He spent a chilly night huddled in all his clothes on a tiny island uninhabited by humans, his only relief his usual dream-speaking with Anise, though he did his best to hide how miserable he was.

The second day, when Ji Mansion was invaded by the imperial crown princess and her uncle, Mek was flying low over lashing treetops as a rainstorm turned into snow, muffling vision.

He caught sight a group of men galloping along a muddy path. He circled around overhead as the snow thickened. Through the thick flurries he made out the pursuit: eight mounted men wearing tattered uniforms of some sort. The pursued, two women. As Mek neared, he saw that they were not running fast. They seemed to be arguing. One gestured back toward the pursuit with a short staff — the other flung her hands wide — then they stopped to face the pursuers, who quickly caught up.

The men galloped around them in a circle. The women waited, the one holding her staff, the other pulling from her belt...a fan.

As Mek tried to decide whether to join the two in the center or to attack from behind, half the men dismounted and began advancing on the women. "I'll take those packs," one said, opening negotiations.

Mek dropped down in front of them, swept up Sagacious Blade and knocked the leader's spear spinning. Two more dismounted, roaring as they ran toward him.

The woman with the fan took on the next two, the fan flickering with blurred speed, blocking and feinting, then snapping closed to prod acupoints with agonizing precision. The other woman's short staff shot leafy tendrils out, which tangled around weapons and limbs as the assailants yelped in fear.

The horses all began to panic at the weird sight of that writhing wood, and stampeded—including the two still with riders.

Mek tapped knee and elbow joints with firm zaps of Essence. He and the two women left the assailants groaning in the slushy mud as the one with the fan went efficiently through what little the men carried on their persons, and the other ran off whistling on a curiously coaxing note.

The one with the fan straightened up. She was short, barely reaching his eyebrows, a brisk, shapely person maybe five years older than he, wearing gallant wanderer blue and brown. A pair of merry eyes the color of amber met his gaze as she said, "Thank you. Though we could have taken care of those bumblers ourselves."

"I see that now," Mek said.

"Call me Butterfly. You are?"

"Ki Mek." The strength of her air affinity crackled in that weird realm.

"My partner busy robbing the robbers is Tanglewood. Which we will shortly be discussing, but any relationship is a carving never finished, ay?"

Mek turned to discover that all eight horses had come running, several nosing curiously over Tanglewood, who was tall and sapling-slim, her long curly dark brown hair hanging in a horsetail down below the base of her spine. She cooed and clucked to the animals as she moved about swiftly undoing horse tack. Travel bags slumped to the mud, and each horse galloped off, manes flying.

When Mek and Butterfly reached Tanglewood, the latter had begun looting the saddlebags.

"What did we *just* agree?" Butterfly demanded, fists on hips.

"Coin will go to the needy," Tanglewood fluted. "But these rats need a lesson in consequences. I'm going to toss all their underclothes into the sea. A noisome job, but won't the chafing be a better reminder than any scolding?"

Butterfly tipped her head. "True." Then, "But you shall collect the noisome garments, and I will take charge of the coinage."

"Aish, it hurts when you distrust me, Butterfly darling, it *hurts*." Then she looked at Mek. "You are wearing house slippers," she observed.

"I know."

"House slippers fit for a king, if those pearls on the tops are real. Where did you thieve those?"

"I didn't," Mek said, then amended, "Aish! I sort of did. But I don't think he'll mind. It was accidental theft."

She turned back to her looting. Greatly intrigued, Mek paused to watch. Butterfly collected clinking bags and emptied them efficiently into one as Tanglewood strewed the men's belongings over the slushy landscape. Her unappealing gleanings lay crumpled on a cloak. "Overdue for a wash anyway. Phew!" She bumbled up the cloak. "Let's move. The snow seems to be passing. And they ought to be stirring about now."

"It'll be a long walk," Butterfly chortled, and reached behind her for the sword that Mek hadn't noticed until now. She knew the deflection charm! "Want to come along?" she added. "I can see you're good in a scuffle. Alas, far too many deserters from the local governor's rats rampaging over the countryside while the imperials try to sort out the good from the rotten."

Mek didn't even know which island this was, other than its relative smallness compared to Mountain Peony behind him.

As he hesitated, Tanglewood hefted her bundle of cloth over her shoulder, dropped her staff into the mud — the tendril tangles had withered and dropped off by then — and stepped on it.

Butterfly laid a thin-bladed sword down, positioned herself on its blade, and Mek discovered that they were flyers, forced down by that oncoming snowstorm. Butterfly was even faster than Mek at the deflection charm, and all three rose into the air. Mek glanced back once, seeing a string of disconsolate robbers limping in a slow line along the snowy path.

As they slanted skyward over the green ocean, Tanglewood dropped her bundle, and immediately her flight became brisker. "Ayah-h-h what a relief," she yelled over the wind. "Why is it that nothing you wear makes you heavier but anything you carry is like a boulder on your back?"

Butterfly shrugged, and off they soared as the clouds broke overhead, cold wind driving them northward.

Mek and his two new companions flew with exhilarating speed until sunset, the women squabbling in a comfortable, habitual sort of way, reminding Mek of his siblings, cousins, and their various lovers. It was utterly without acrimony: Tanglewood wanted to keep some of the loot for an inn with a hot bath and a good meal, and Butterfly insisted that if they wanted luxury, they had to earn it.

When at last they landed in a harbor whose scruffy old boats, buildings, and denizens clearly belonged to gallant wanderers, Butterfly marched determinedly to the small temple to the Crane God she'd spotted from the air. Tanglewood uttered a single groaning whimper, then Mek said, "This silk robe is already spoilt by rain and wind, but we can try to sell these slippers. I'll have to get shoes to replace them, but the pearls ought to guarantee a good meal and maybe beds."

Tanglewood brightened, and they looked for a likely place to sell the house slippers. As they walked, Mek discovered that Tanglewood had an affinity for wood—obviously—but the laughing slyness of her tilted eye, the insouciant slouch of her walk breathed fox. Mek looked instinctively for plumed tails, but of course saw nothing. Whether she was part fox by inheritance, or a fox wearing human form, he could not discern. But she definitely had fox traits.

They found a shop that sold belts, shoes, and bags. "Ten silver for these fabulous house slippers, esteemed proprietor of fine things. See the pearls?" Tanglewood said, waving at Mek's feet.

"Why would you try to cozen a poor trader, trying to scrape a meager living? I see mud. And feet inside the shoes," the merchant said with a weary, put-upon act. But her gaze lingered.

"O venerable, honest and kindly proprietor who reputation is sung throughout ten islands, permit us to observe that a brush takes care of the mud," Butterfly coaxed.

"And the feet will leave. Notice the socks are clean."

They were clean, too, because Mek had changed them at Butterfly's insistence moments before they entered the shop.

"My dear young women, no one will pay two for them, with all that mud."

"Five, please, good, generous proprietor. And a pair of straw shoes?"

"Two—without the shoes..." After some haggling—both women were vigorous hagglers—they left with a new pair of straw sandals on Mek's feet, and three strings of small coins.

One string bought them a sumptuous meal and space in an attic with a number of other travelers. In the evening they met a pair of brothers who played the pipa and hulusi, who welcomed Mek with his flute. They made music until late, and everyone retired.

They were sharing breakfast with the brothers next morning when Tai's anxious thought appeared outside Mek's mental door, as we have seen.

At the end of the exchange, Mek opened his eyes, and the thick, pungent atmosphere of the travel house closed about him, the chief odor one of wet wool, with an overlay of hot plum wine and braised meats.

Mek said nothing as he finished up his noodles with egg and sesame past; the brothers went off on their own pursuits, leaving Mek alone with the women. Butterfly gazed at Mek out of those tawny eyes, which were lighter than her skin. "You went away," she said, tapping a finger to her brow.

"Away?"

"Here." Another tap. "What my grandmother used to call dream-talking. I can't do it, but I saw her when she was doing it."

Mek said, "It was a friend. I...did something. Essence work. And, uh, I think I might have gotten in trouble of a sort with..." He lowered his voice to a whisper, sidling a look around the busy eatery. "The emperor."

"The emperor?" Tanglewood yelped, then hunched down when some other customers turned to stare. "Which emperor?" she whispered

Butterfly rolled her eyes. "How many emperors are there?"

"I don't know...I thought the Ghost Eyes had one, and—"

"Never mind that." Butterfly turned back to Mek. "Is an army on the way to drag you back?"

"I don't think an army...But if an emperor asked your name, they want it for a reason, don't they?"

"Depends what you did," Butterfly retorted with foreboding. "Out with it."

And he found himself going into detail purely from the

Essence perspective.

But at the end, Butterfly said, "And?"

"And," Mek said, lowering his voice, "the imperials might think it was meddling. Because I just did it."

"Imperial politics," Butterfly said, one side of her lip curling as if she'd just encountered a spectacularly nasty odor. "And so you have to avoid imperials. Ayah! What was your family name again?"

"Ki."

Tanglewood looked more startled than she had at the mention of emperors. "My sister is married to a Ki. The Kis of Hundred Day Tree Island."

"My family was from Mountain Peony—"

"Never mind that," Butterfly said. "There are Kis all over. I've met them—and none were related to Tanglewood's sister's Kis. If anyone is going to search for you, they'll have a tough time, as Mek is a popular name." She eyed him. "You're experienced, but you haven't a name yet?"

"You just heard my—oh." Mek reddened. "Gallant Wanderer name."

"Like us." Tanglewood patted her chest, then tapped Butterfly's shoulder. "You didn't think I was named Tanglewood at birth? It's a name I *earned*, fighting with my trusty Tangle, here." She stroked her staff, which was leaning against the table.

"Uh, Sagacious Blade," Mek said, low.

Both pairs of eyes arrowed straight for the winking pearlescent stone in the hilt of the blade sticking up over his shoulder.

Butterfly grinned. "Your solution is obvious, isn't it? From now on, you are Sagacious Blade. It's the best disguise in the world, because it isn't a disguise. And if that emperor sends sinister black-masks out to find Ki Mek, well, they'll waste their days with a lot of innocent Ki Meks who know nothing of Essence matters, won't they?"

Mek's expression eased. "It's true."

"We were on our way to Dogleg to fend off the galley-slavers anyway…"

Tanglewood said gleefully, "Let's get the world talking about Sagacious Blade while we go."

FIFTY-FOUR

TAI HAD DECIDED TO begin with his trusted archive volunteers. First Su Inke, who had just this autumn finished his studies, and would be looking toward taking the imperial examination.

Tai sent cautiously worded notes to his team of archivists, who had all sailed home for the celebration. Most of those homes being right there in the capital. While he waited for answers, he began immersing himself in various archives.

As expected, the geomancers had all the trunks that he had never found down at White Jade. Since he could not remove or copy them, he sat on the floor, lamps at his side, brought scrolls to his nose, and began reading.

When he returned from Geomancy Archives for the last time, numbers in his head to be copied down before he forgot, it was to discover that Su Inke's little brother brought a short note saying basically, when and where you do need me, once the moons kiss?

Days passed.

Tai, left alone, paid no attention to New Year's Two Moons. Replies began to trickle in a week after the Rabbit Year began. Two had earned the promotions they had longed for, and one was to marry in summer. A few more were uneasy at the idea of a complicated archival project that required being shut up for maybe as long as a year.

Six accepted outright. Su Inke had a sister, Holke, over in the scribes, who he knew would volunteer, as she had expressed bitter envy at having missed out on the fun of organizing an entire archive. Puzzles were her passion. And once she arrived, and learned what was afoot, both she and Inke vouched for another Su cousin they were sure would fit in nicely.

As they came in, Tai put each to work.

Department of Revenue. Works. Personnel. Divination and Rites. Even the Ministry of War, which was mostly concerned with affairs of budget, had records going back to the Relocation. These he read, and brought back to dictate to his staff, one department at a time.

"They ought to have been doing this long before now," the last to arrive complained, eyeing the trunks.

"They thought they had years," Su Holke stated, giving him an impatient look.

Su Inke, working next to his sister, chuckled, glanced around, and although they were alone, he whispered, "We don't have the tough part. Whoever is going to be knocking on doors and telling people they have to move, and where, has the job I wouldn't volunteer for even if they made me a prince."

"That," Tai said, "is not our task. Be grateful! Sooner we get our part done, the sooner the Ministries of Works and Personnel begin theirs. Here are Works' present records," he said to the new arrival. "Those trunks are last year's Personnel and Tax totals. Adapt what they did before to what we need to do. Once we've got a sense of the requirements, we'll build a timetable."

They got to work, and braziers burned aromatic woods, and ink and paper arrived each day, along with excellent meals from the palace kitchens, eaten not at proper tables, with tea prepared correctly, but haphazardly, tea dishes sitting everywhere. Inke finally took up his old schoolday task of picking up after the others, and putting dirty dishes outside the door on trays, which vanished most gratifyingly. Adulthood at last—he wasn't washing dishes!

Not that he could waste time crowing. The crypt had been fun for puzzle-solvers. This new project had the added excitement of being real. Necessary. With a time deadline, and even a death threat!

"We solved the crypt in a year, but that was in free time, most of it spent dragging and stacking. Can we do this by spring?" Inke asked—and dived back into the trunks, ink-stains on his fingers, the cuffs of his clothes, and all over the side of his head where he'd absently stuck his brush a few times.

Tai was confident about having a preliminary timetable by

spring, though what all those ministers would do to it to preserve their own importance—and their access to the treasury—he couldn't guess. And he didn't care. What he wanted to understand was how the Celestial General had avoided civil war by perpetrating his enormous lie. Surely it was not merely an excuse for gaining golden robes and a throne? That didn't fit at all with the traces of the general that turned up in the various records, characters even and neat, emphasizing detail.

The last department to be researched was the navy, who would carry them from Mountain Peony to the imperial island.

Naval Command Headquarters was all the way out on the peninsula, where a massive tower troop ship had been anchored permanently. By this time, well into winter, Tai had left the palace thrice to visit archives not kept in the endless warren of dark corridors that made up the back areas of the various ministries' records. Each time he'd had to send a petition to the emperor for permission, and each time he had received permission in the form of a plainly dressed individual whose movements betrayed excellent martial arts training, though no weapons were visible, accompanied by a driver and a cart, anonymous except for a golden stripe under the roof, indicating imperial business.

Nu Lim, the Minister of the Imperial High Seas, had been an admiral until she was promoted to this mostly desk position. She was near Tai's mother's age, or a bit younger—sixties at least, but vigorous in spite of her gray hair, a short, solid woman with graying eyebrows more tilted even than Tai's. Flying Tiger brows.

If she resented having to dismiss everyone in what was obviously a very busy command center, she showed no sign of it; the tower of the ship had been expanded, and the desks were still crowded side by side, each loaded with papers and other paraphernalia when an ensign led Tai in. On the walls, maps of every kind, including one of types of clouds, and sailing times, with symbols for current and wind.

The vast chamber's windows had all been pushed out wide, letting in the icy air; Tai's breath smoked from running up three flights of stairs after the ensign who'd brought him. The only acknowledgment of winter was a brazier burning near the command desk, probably for thawing fingers enough for writing on the tiny strips of pigeon-leg paper that lay ready.

"I have a note here from the emperor himself." Here she clasped her hands toward the great towers far above them atop the ridge, gleaming in the wintry light. "What do you need?"

"Records of how many ships were used in the Relocation, and if possible the order of departure, and who and what was on each."

Minister Nu smiled broadly. "I expected such a question, and I copied out numbers myself, plus lists of craft used for convoy protection, and for communication when the weather made it unsafe to trust to the pigeons."

"Thank you," Tai said, bowing gratefully. That was exactly what he'd come for—and he wouldn't have to memorize the paper on the spot.

He glanced out the nearest window, distracted by the glide of a seahawk, a warship built for speed—that much he'd learned aboard the courier scout. Its swivel guns fore and aft gleamed as sailors polished them, and others swept the deck. Banners streamed in the wind: the empire's banner, signal flags, and above, the thin streamers of talismans to ward demons of sky and sea. Two scouts sailed alongside the seahawk, like cygnets alongside a battle swan.

He turned to the Minister, whose time he was wasting. "This ignorant slow-wit is grateful for the help," he said, clasping his hands.

"But?" Minister Nu prompted, a brief quirk to her lips.

"This—"

"Speak plainly, young archivist. We sailors actually prefer plain speaking. It's quicker when arrows are flying about your head."

"Thank you. It is probably unnecessary. Certainly brazen. Maybe even forbidden. I know the general belief is that he was avoiding civil war, but I keep trying to discern what the Celestial General was really after, with so great a deception. It seems to me that averting civil war is an emperor's task. And if this general did covet the dragon throne, he could more easily have taken the imperial city, rather than forcing everyone to leave it," Tai finished quickly. "He controlled the army. It would not be the first time."

"Not at all," Minister Nu agreed. "I expect that if his imperial majesty the first Tan emperor disclosed his secret thoughts, it was solely for his heirs. However, I believe though you cannot read anything he might have left to his successors, you can fathom some of what was in his mind—what was important—by what he did then and after."

"How is that?" Tai asked.

"Come. Look at the military map." She indicated the inner wall, opposite the windows, where another seahawk was slowly gliding in on the swelling tide.

Tai had never seen a military map before. As expected, it depicted all the great islands, but only in outline except for military establishments, with supply lines in green, and patrol lines in red. Then there were the army training fortresses—the equivalent of his own school of augury. And finally, the great garrisons, where army waited to be deployed, and naval ships were stationed to patrol, and if needed, to deploy that army.

Seeing Tai's gaze shift from Whale's Haven up in the northeastern reach of the empire over to Ice Fortress farthest to the north, watching the west, Minister Nu said, "He completely reorganized the empire-wide standard of communication as well as of training. So that, for the first time, a captain trained here." She tapped a northern academy. "Could be sent all the way to Lan, down here in the southwest, and would be immediately understood. Also, shifting army captains and commanders around guaranteed that no particular garrison's loyalties went to one commander. This was a standard established in the navy centuries ago, and I believe he used our model."

"I see."

"I think not quite yet. Do you see a central command outside the capital?"

"N-no..." Tai murmured, taking in the scattering of purely naval harbors, then of garrisons where the army was stationed, to be deployed in various directions at need. "No," he said more strongly, as the pieces began to coalesce into a whole. "Generals are confined to single garrisons?"

"Exactly. They are little kings in their own command, but their rank is equal with each other, because the emperor." Clasp of hands. "Is their commander. What does that tell you?"

"That the first emperor knew how to bring all these into a single command under himself. But that just supports my point."

"Except he already had that position. What else?"

Tai considered. That general had, in earning his rank, driven the Westerners off at least twice—that was after clearing pirates out of the islands far to the south as a young commander.

Tai said carefully, "And so he understood the, ah, danger of a very powerful commander who might come into conflict with imperial will?"

"You have the dragon's tail. But you want to understand his motivation—the dragon's head. So look again. Remember what you know of history."

"There was threatened civil war, and auguries of danger, which were interpreted as heaven turning from the old dynasty," Tai said. Which was what all school children learned.

But as soon as he spoke he remembered his great-aunt's letter: ...*the previous dynasty was riven by three warring factions...led by three of the seven imperial princes... empire was on the brink of civil war ... significant armies...*

Tai said, "I see that he already effectively held imperial power. But I still don't see how he prevented civil war by evacuating of the imperial capital."

"Consider imperial law, then. Capturing those rival princes would have meant executions, not just of them, but of their supporters, and imperial law requires their families to nine generations to also die, as a warning. The higher the rank, the more severe the punishments for treason. You know the law. Do you know what happened to those princes during the Relocation?"

"I do not."

"Two of the warring princes were military-trained, and under his command. He put them each in charge of part of the evacuation, one to the outer perimeter on the Great Sea to protect the government in transit, the other to monitor the west in joint command with the Prince of Great Ran, who had his own army. Soon disbanded—one of the emperor's first acts was to strip Great Ran of that enormous army, as that prince had been ready and waiting to take the throne once the imperial princes destroyed one another, and whoever was in their paths. Do you see?"

"They had to lay aside their feuds in the face of imminent disaster that threatened to destroy everyone if Mt. Lir exploded."

"Not if. *When*. Faction fighting was overwhelmed by entirely human fear. In that deception, the Celestial General saved untold numbers of lives of subjects, the lives that rarely get reported except as numbers to bolster outrage."

"Then it wasn't merely a desire for a throne..." Tai murmured.

The minister smothered a small laugh. "I do not pretend to penetrate the minds of those chosen by the Jade Emperor—or guided by divine will. But how many times can anyone's motivation for monumental effort be reduced to a 'merely'? Anyone sane, that is. I cannot speak for the mad. But he, by all accounts, was not mad. Does that help you, Secretary Je?"

Tai understood then that he had taken up enough of her time—and that their conversation had probably veered close to treason, though treason against an emperor long dead.

He bowed, uttered his thanks, and departed, his mind so full of maps and numbers and the minister's revelations about that long-ago general turned emperor, that he was not aware of a figure following at a discreet distance (unlike his impassive driver, who was also a ferret).

That figure followed them all the way up to the side-gate of the palace letting in functionaries, then flitted back down to Ji Mansion, where he was soon closeted with his grace, Duke Ji Venshai.

Venshai listened closely. He'd spent a great deal having that gate of the palace watched, his only reward the rare times Je Tai ventured out, always alone except for a driver. Cousin Tai had always gone to some dusty old building housing archives, never to anyone in power. Until now.

"Naval command?" he repeated.

"He was in there a long time. Long enough for me to get to the pier where they sometimes let fishermen unload their catch in winter, and I used my glass. He and Minister Nu were standing before a military map, talking away. I couldn't see which map."

"It doesn't matter," Venshai muttered. "Military maps. I didn't know he knew anything about the military." He dismissed the spy, brooding. Only two cousins in the military — one from the third house in his last year at one of the academies. And there was also Lekshai, but he was far away in the north. Who knew if they'd ever see him before they were old and gray. Neither of them anywhere near command level, therefore useless for winnowing out information.

Should he tell his father? No...Father had been looking ill ever since the arrival of Magistrate Je and Tai that cursed day.

"Though the emperor was surely as shocked as we were about that prediction of ten years, I believe he is also getting exactly what he wanted," Father had said after Cousin Tai was taken away to the imperial palace.

"Je Tai belonging to no faction," Venshai had exclaimed.

"Precisely. Je Tai is very like his father, so blunt that the emperor must have discerned within two exchanges that Tai is *not* ours, though he's part of our family. We erred badly. We're going to have to amend that. At least we have family blood on our side."

Venshai had been forced to agree, though it made him wild with anger. How unjust! Little Lamb gets snatched away for years, and on his return leaps effortlessly to a private interview and position directly under the emperor? Venshai had never had a private interview! And when they saw Tai next, they were going to have to bang forehead to the ground and speak only honey and flowers.

FIFTY-FIVE

SHORTLY AFTER TAI'S VISIT to the Naval Command Center, Mek, Butterfly, and Tanglewood reached Eagle Island—just ahead of a massive blizzard.

He stamped his way into Heaven's Ease, where most of the Bian clan had gathered for warmth. He shed snow at every step. Butterfly and Tanglewood flanked him.

"Kimek!" Waha exclaimed. "We meet again!"

Greetings and introductions were followed by Butterfly and Tanglewood trading off retailing some of their escapades over the past months, interspersed with demonstrations of skills—most notably Butterfly's fan form.

"I was told it originated with nuns who protected princesses, but who knows?" she said—then Tanglewood, recognizing a new and appreciative audience, offered the details of their adventures with Mek while traveling north.

Mek said nothing. The moment they entered, his heart had galloped in his chest as he searched the firelit faces.

There she was. In two quick strides he reached her and sank down beside her. Neither spoke. After the intimate rhythm of mind to mind, words were insufficient. And had fled anyway, before the overwhelming felicity of touch, and feel, and sound. They sat shoulder to shoulder and hip to hip, and Mek did not hear a word because he could not concentrate on anything but the spice-salt scent of her, the ruddy light on the cedar-hued curve of her cheek, the soft hiss of her breathing.

Her smile brightened like those flames, and he knew where he would be that night.

After a shared meal, and music, Tian-Tian offered to show

Tanglewood and Butterfly to the guest quarters. Then Bian Ze sent Mek a glance, stopping him mid-step. "Old Uncle?"

"He's at Sky Island. No longer flies."

"He's lost his Essence?"

"Not that I know of. He says he doesn't trust his head at heights anymore. He sleeps a lot. Mim says it's likely this is his last winter."

A wash of grief sobered Mek, though Old Uncle had said he felt the end of this life coming. *I'm ready for the next, when everything will be new*, he'd said to Mek last year.

"You vanished so suddenly," Uncle Ze said.

Mek gave a fast explanation, then ended by explaining Ardal's message. "She would not have done that if there hadn't been a reason. Have the Westerners have been seen?"

"Raids only. The weather has been so foul that we can't tell if there were scouts or a vanguard, before most of the harbors north of us froze over."

"Then there's time to plan a kind of defense?" Mek asked.

"You have something in mind?"

"We talked about it while journeying. It's Tanglewood's idea, actually, to deceive them with fogs. Butterfly can make fogs as fast as I can."

"Fogs." Uncle Ze rubbed his ear. "But then the raiders're still there."

"Very true," Mek admitted. "We can't keep up fogs forever, and what happens when it lifts? You've got a fleet of angry enemies, and they're in galleys, which means they don't need wind. But there might be an answer."

"Eh?"

"Butterfly can also create illusions. When she and Tanglewood join together. These wouldn't fool anyone long up close. There's no shadow, and in strong sun you can see right through them. We played around with them a lot when we were grounded by bad weather. The important thing is, from a distance they can make it look like there's a mountaintop above the fog, or an image of forestland if the vapor thins."

"So even if the Westerners have charts, they might assume they're wrong. Do they have charts? How much do they know about these islands, and what little defense we have? What are their capabilities?"

"I don't know. I wish Tai was here," Mek said. He could open the mental door, and he was fairly certain that Tai would be willing to answer, now, but it had sounded like he was in the middle of the difficulty consequent to Mek's healing Coral Island, then leaving. "I never paid much attention when Snowhawk's people talked about Westerner ships and raids. I was too busy learning to fly. But Tai listened to Siu and Yarth and Diggy. Waha might have listened," he added doubtfully, remembering that Waha had been a street thief in the Western capital before being stuck in the mines.

"He's already told us everything he remembers about the ships you were on, but he said he was too busy with martial skills to pay attention to how the ships were conned," Uncle Ze said, going to one of the storage cabinets. He took out a map and spread it carefully. "Here's Eagle Island." He pointed.

Mek glanced at the map, then recollected seeing the island from the air. Old Uncle had taken him high enough to make out the rippling shadows of leviathans below the water, following currents through the two main passages leading eastward into the Empire of the Thousand Islands...

"How does this sound?" Mek said slowly, his gaze back on the map. "They want to attack the rice convoy, which comes up through here, past the east side of Great Ran." His finger trace upward, then eastward.

"Deep into the heart of the western portion of the realm," Bian Ze agreed.

"But if we were to create a wall of fog and illusory islands along here, and over here," Mek tapped the map. "Causing them to go north to get around it..." He swept his hand over the countless little islands surrounding Sky Mirror Isle. "The farther north they go, the narrower the passages. If they push far enough east, they emerge at Ice Fortress. Then they become the imperials' problem."

Bian Ze said, smiling broadly. "That looks like a good plan to me. However, unless you plan to sustain your fog continuously, you'll need lookouts posted well south of here, so that there is time to get the illusion in place before they arrive. That means someone up along the ridge, here, at Ten Leopards, where the passages fork."

"Ten Leopards?"

"It's—it was—an ancient fortress, back when this whole section of island chains was a kingdom. I was at Ten Leopards once as a youth. High island plateau, around a beautiful lake. At that time it belonged to a sect of Ghost Moon monks. They were all Essence wielders. Flew on staffs. Mim's grandfather joined them late in life. They went...somewhere, my point being, it's empty now. But it's a perfect place to watch that entire sea. If the enemies are seen below, and your fogs block the right-hand passage and coax them to go north instead of east, then they'll definitely find themselves mired up there in the Ice Rocks—maybe even as far as Ice Fortress." He patted the northmost part of the map. "They'll either find Tiger Claw Army there—not a prospect any pirate or raider would welcome—or else they work their way back west and home again."

Mek said, "Soon as the snow lifts, how about I go take a look at Ten Leopards? A mountain plateau sounds like fun."

A week later the sky cleared, leaving a world of sparking white below. The air was frigid, but Mek, Tanglewood, and Butterfly took that as a challenge. As Ten Leopards was approximately a two-day sail, they knew they could fly the distance in less than a day, as long as the wind wasn't against them.

Nevertheless, Auntie Mim insisted on going. She knew that plateau.

It took a morning and a part of the afternoon to reach Ten Leopards, as the wind was with them. There was a tiny village off an equally tiny harbor, like a bite nipped out of the steep, rocky cliffs of a once-vast fire mountain whose top had long ago vanished. In its wind-smoothed center lay a deep lake of pure water, now frozen to glistening ice. A crust of rocky ridge surrounded the circular plateau; from the harbor up to the plateau, long-ago hands had widened a goat path, surmounted by a crumbling gate of massive size with guardian gods gazing out at the southern seas.

Mek sailed close to one of those age-softened, serene faces, liking the idea of these sentinels. Perhaps they existed from even before the garrison, whose remains seemed a different style, centuries newer.

Most of what remained of the garrison was longhouse buildings, patched and added to over the years, with an expansive garden behind, now overgrown in rich soil. This garden was bordered by a sizeable orchard dominated by pear and apple trees—and wild pears grew along the foot of the ridge, all spiky and winter-bare. So much space! One could put in the finest healing herb garden...

"There are the lookout towers," Auntie Mim called, pointing to the ridge along the south. "From the eastmost one, you can see Eagle Island on a clear summer day. The south tower is here…"

"Do we have to put someone in the west or north?" Mek pointed to the ridges far in the distance.

"No, because the sea beyond's a vast, treacherous reef. My grandfather told us that when the king firedragon burst up, that's where all the rock from the top of the mountain landed. Reefs all the way to Icecrown. No one sails between Icecrown and Ten Leopards, in winter not even fishers, with ice floes everywhere."

The south tower looked like a day's walk from the buildings along the lakeside, not a long distance at all for flyers. The tower was made of the local stone, three rooms one on top of the next, with a round room under the roof.

"This would be comfortable, fitted up," Mek said as they landed and entered the tower. The lower room was big enough for storage and cooking if one couldn't cook outside. A narrow stair led up to the middle room would be snug for sleeping. The top was accessible by ladder. This was the smallest chamber, with windows all around. Wide windows, so they could as easily get to that top chamber by flying.

"It's getting dark," Auntie Mim warned. "We should find a place to bed down for the night."

Dark, and far colder. They flew back to the empty buildings, and looked around the silent central square. At the north end, someone had built a temple, surrounded by pears, magnolia, and redbark; the altar was there, with a statue to the ancient sun god. Serenity in the vague features echoed that in the stone guardians at the ancient gate. Or maybe it had never been a gate, but an archway? Mysteries!

There was a big central building with three huge rooms in a row, kitchen in the center. Above, an attic with sleeping platforms down both sides. The monks had probably slept there. Outbuildings had small single rooms, either for crafts or storage or sleeping. Sturdy barns at the southern end, doors open.

Mim pointed, saying, "The monks must have let the horses go free when they flew or sailed away. There's a wild herd of them scattered across the plain. Though some live in the village below. I suspect they were brought here to haul things up that path we saw."

"The kitchen has some old stores, still good," Tanglewood called.

"If there's dry firewood, we can cook up what we brought," Butterfly said. Mek, can you melt the ice and fill these buckets of water? I don't want to have to chop ice—it looked so thick!"

By the time Mek had dragged enough water up to fill a barrel, the pale winter sun touched the western ridge above that mighty gate. He brought out Sagacious Blade and took to the air again, flying low over the lake—so low that he could have reached down to touch the ice.

The lake nearly reached the ridge at the north end, which proved to be a mountainous area, thick with forest. Mek sensed animal life amid the winter-slumbering trees, and overall that sense of Essence-drawn warmth woven into the soil long, long ago. Patient and slow. He wished he could explore. Later! The idea filled him with anticipation as he swooped up and then sped back, shivering in the icy air.

When he landed, he discovered that the others had lit lamps, and from the promising smells, they were cooking. Hot water steamed on a warmer, and a cannister of Eagle Island tea waited for steeping in a plain but good ceramic pot found in a cupboard.

A short time later, they sat on the floor around a brazier in a bare room that Tanglewood and Mek had swept out, as Auntie Mim and Butterfly served up the meal.

"We were talking while you were out exploring," Butterfly said to Mek. "The three of us could start keeping watch at that south tower, since we're the ones who'll have to do the Essence illusions. But someone's going to have to bring us supplies. Oil, for one thing—though I saw lots of olive trees along that southern ridge, where the sun would be strongest."

"Olives! This far north?"

Mek shut his eyes. "There is warmth beneath the surface."

"A hot fire mountain?" Tanglewood, brave when faced by most dangers, looked uneasy.

"No. It's…Essence warmth, but slow. A part of the soil now. Those olives must have become accustomed to this island ages ago."

"But that won't help us now. All that's here are those dried chickpeas, beans, and rice. Though it should be all right to eat since there's no mold or bugs in the barrels, which were beautifully fitted, airtight."

Tanglewood leaned back on her elbows. "Also, we'll need some others to take a turn."

"Yes. And a pair of our eagles for messages," Auntie Mim said—referring to the trained eagles from which Eagle Island got its name many generations ago. "Mek, I know you can dream-talk, but that's a burden, expecting you to be our only conduit between here and Eagle Island. I know who'd bring a perch over—our eagle master says one of his apprentices is ready to ship her first convoy this spring, but she could start her first assignment up here."

Mek agreed. It was a practical suggestion, even important. If Ardal was right, the danger was real, and imminent, and he needed to be here. But his first thought went to Anise. Wistfully he thought about their night together, far too short after so much time away.

Auntie Mim held her hands over the brazier. "All right, I'll go back in the morning, if the weather permits."

Mek forced himself to agree. It would be selfish to ask Anise to suffer seasickness just because he was happier with her by his side. He'd go back as soon as this Western threat was resolved—and they could continue their nightly conversations in the mental realm, to which she slowly agreed.

Auntie Mim took to the air as soon as it was light the next morning, under a sky slowly clouding over.

And for that first week, he, Butterfly, and Tanglewood figured out a watch schedule to divide the daylight hours. While Tanglewood was up in the tower, Mek and Butterfly went out when the weather permitted, so that she could continue drilling him in the fan form. He loved using the fan to tap acupoints—so much better than a sword, or jabbing his finger and risking jamming the joint.

At night, the three of them flew out over the lake, and in the dim starlight, practiced creating their illusions. They had to be quick, and create vapors that appeared natural when seen from a distance. And now that Mek and Anise were relatively close, they could visit in the mental realm before going to sleep.

Two days of snow kept them inside, then the weather cleared to a white world. This world of blues, silvers and white shades was so beautiful. He liked it here. If only by some miracle...

"If only's" miracle turned real when a familiar scout pulled into the tiny harbor. Mek, with morning duty, noticed from the tower, and pulled on gloves and a hat in order to fly down to see if there was something he could help with. The first person he saw was Hok's rabbit-toothed sister with an eagle perched on her shoulder, and behind her, a couple of husky Bian cousins who leaped down and began dickering with the villagers for a sleigh with a pair of the big horses to pull it.

Up from below the deck, carrying boxes and barrels, came Seventh Brother, Fifth Cousin — and last, Anise, looking wan as she climbed down the ramp, picked her way along the pier, and stood on the shoreline breathing deeply.

"Anise?" Mek landed beside her, sheathing Sagacious Blade.

She opened her eyes, and there was her wonderful smile. "It was so very hard to hide from you! But I wanted to surprise you."

"You did," he exclaimed so joyfully that she drew strength from his response. You'll need a cook," she murmured into his ear as they hugged.

They helped to load supplies into the sleigh, Anise moving slowly and wearily. It was a long, slow journey up that steep path, but the big horses seemed used to it. Mek flew, so as not to add extra burden.

At last they topped the rise, then the sleigh began to race over the snow as the horses picked up their pace. They knew their way across the snow and ice to the barns — and Auntie Mim, familiar with the island, had seen to it that the supplies had included coinage to pay for plenty of fodder, which filled the back of the sleigh.

Everyone worked to unload the baskets and trunks into the enclave's central building. "There's more on the ship, but we can go down there tomorrow to get them," Seven said, smacking their cousin in the chest.

"I'll get the kitchen fires going," Anise said, her voice a lot stronger.

"I'll help," Mek said. "I know where the firewood is stacked."

When his brother and cousin had gone off to explore, and Mek and Anise were alone, she said, "I came because I can't bear to hear you here." She touched her forehead. "But not have you beside me. Also, I discovered a thing in myself that is small and mean and you might find it disgraceful. I do up here," she added candidly, touching her forehead again. "Though not here." She patted her heavy woolen over-tunic.

"You could never be disgraceful," Mek said.

"But it is. I am. There's no grace in discovering I can't bear the idea of sharing you," Anise said, taking his hand in both hers. "You are so giving! If you need other lovers, we will be friends?" Her voice turned wistful, but her gaze was steady.

Mek blinked. He'd enjoyed his experiences with other women, but those experiences were like the poets said, moonbeams and clouds, orchids and blossoms. Everyone parting with a fond farewell the next day. He looked into her face. "You're the sun. I can live without all those other things. I can't live without the sun."

Anise beamed. "Then we should marry."

"Marry?" Me repeated, aware that Anise had become so strong a part of his heart that he had never defined it. The word "marry" caught him by surprise, for that belonged to the future Mek, a man his father's age. But Father had been his age once. "Marry," he said more firmly. It felt new. And right.

Mek and Anise lit incense in the temple, but she insisted on the two of them making their bows before the kitchen god, her favorite, until such time as they could be properly married before his family. (The first thing she had done when leaving her own home was cutting off a slice of her old robe and leaving it on the shore, which meant she was quit of her mother and aunt.)

They waited until they were alone, then lit incense, bowed to the god, to each other, then shared a cup of rice wine.

"Now we are husband and wife, in good conscience, even if we haven't spoken to your elders. What I have is yours," Anise said, giving him that transcendent smile he loved.

He looked at the wealth she brought—steaming baskets, a fine wok, crockery that she had carefully made herself, a star chart that she had also made, and divining sticks, plus her personal belongings.

"And what I have is yours," he said, looking a little sheepish. "Though it isn't much beyond dirty laundry. Because with only the three of us on watch I haven't had time to do it. Then there's my flute. And Sagacious Blade—but I don't think of her as mine. I think of her as herself, and someday she will go to someone else, just as she came to me."

Anise nodded seriously.

They went through the house looking for a room they could make theirs, scrupulously leaving the larger rooms to Uncle Ze, or any of the elders who might appear. They chose a corner room that overlooked the orchard. The room was small enough that though they barely had enough belongings to fill a shared trunk, it didn't look too empty once they had a bright quilt on the bed, the star chart on one wall, and their shoes put before the door.

And so began married life.

They'd scarcely had two weeks of happiness before a dawn brought banging on their door, and Tanglewood's urgent voice, "Mek! The raiders are *here*."

Mek scrambled into his clothes, grabbed Sagacious Blade, and stumbled out into a blue dawn. He had to remind himself to concentrate on the deflection charm; not quite a month and already he'd fallen out of the habit.

Tanglewood waited, no sign of the insouciant fox smile. The three sped high over the green-gray ocean. Butterfly was already raising wisps of vapor below them as Mek looked southward into the weak glare of morning sun. Ten…twenty ships? More. He couldn't count them in the morning haze.

He and Tanglewood arrowed after Butterfly, whose vapors were beginning a slow swirl at ocean level in the weak breeze. Tanglewood flew above Butterfly, the two talking in a quick, brief exchange almost like code. To the east, where the passage led toward Eagle Island, and beyond that to the northwest trade route, the fog began to form in a thick line, here and there a brownish-gray shadow jutting above the line of mist. It really did look like mountains.

Mek began to bring his own fog up, so that the entire ocean began to blur.

Then he lanced skyward, noticing in dismay that the vanguard of the enemy was still coming on, galley oars steadily dipping and lowering in perfect rhythm. Scouts and larger ships, with archer platforms. Tai would remember what kind of ships, Mek thought bleakly. To Mek, they all meant danger, black dragon banners flying, marked with unfamiliar clan signs.

They were heading east by north, as if the false island was invisible…

But at the same time the sickening conviction gripped him that they'd miscalculated, and the Westerners had some way of discerning illusion without banishing it, the vanguard's galley scouts' oars lifted, like wings of a soaring raptor, then banked.

"They're trying to figure it out." That was Tanglewood.

"You haven't blocked the north…good. Nice job! Vapor thinner there, clear sea beyond…come on, blue-eyes, your charts are wrong. Come north, that's it, north north north…yes!"

The oars began to dip again, the helms adjusting, so that the ships began to describe a gentle curve, correcting course—for the north.

The three soared in steady circles high above the Western fleet through the rest of that day, ignoring numb fingers and toes as they kept the east full of impenetrable vapor and artistically forbidding mountain tops here and there. Tanglewood even added snowy crests.

They were all drawing fiercely on Essence by the time the sun finally rolled westward. Without even discussing it, Mek and Butterfly combined their flagging strength to befog the enemy fleet so that they were forced to anchor for the night lest they drift onto a dangerous lee shore.

Once the enemy oars were banked, with darkness closing in, the three flew back, tired and cold, to find hot soup waiting, and rice wine that Anise warmed.

"We can't drink much," Butterfly warned Tanglewood, who was already gulping down her second dish. "We have to be there when the sun comes up to make sure they keep going until they're well into the ice rocks."

Tanglewood let fly some vivid curses, but agreed. Mek ate, crawled into bed and shivered in Anise's warm arms, then slept like a rock until Butterfly banged on the door.

That day passed much like the previous, but the plan worked. The enemy fleet kept trying to push eastward, now encountering little island after little island, barely visible in the drifts of fog.

When the three left the black dragon banner fleet, it was well within the maze of small islands, dodging ice floes. Their choice now, risk the east—they had to know about Ice Fortress—or the south again, which Mek kept a solid bank of fog, or westward back home.

He and Butterfly and Tanglewood left the Westerners to their dilemma—and to the Icecrown patrols to find them—and flew back, barely reaching the tower before collapsing.

"What now?" Tanglewood asked.

Butterfly shrugged, exchanging glances with Mek. "We wait for the next."

FIFTY-SIX

A SMALLER FLEET FOLLOWED a few days later, and about the time that they spotted the next on the horizon, a muffled figure in a threadbare military cloak and sodden hat splashed up to Ji Mansion.

The servant-guards half-pulled their weapons, until the figure lifted his head, and they recognized that red-nosed, blotched face as Ji Lekshai in the uniform of an army courier.

It was late on a miserable afternoon. Imperial court had been dismissed early. Both the prince and Venshai were there, in the prince's study.

Lekshai was right on the steward's heels as the man announced him. He thrust the steward out of the way with numb hands, and gasped out, "It's war."

"What?" Venshai barked, as the prince drew in a painful breath.

"Tiger Claw…Ice Fortress…commander…made me a courier and a lookout. Sent south as fast as…too cold, bad blizzards for the birds…I have to report to imperial guards…but I stopped here first." He gulped stale tea. "Now you know… First. Must go." Lekshai wiped a snow-dotted sleeve over his face.

"S-slow dmmm," the prince began to say, oddly slurred. He winced—and slowly slumped sideways, stiffly upright as if unwilling to lose his dignity even in physical distress.

"Uncle?"

"Father?" Venshai ran to the door, shouted for the just-departed steward, then yelled in the astonished man's face, "Physicians! Now!" Then, to Lekshai, "Sit down. Give us a coherent report, if you can."

Lekshai shook his head. "I daren't stay — I'm sure to catch a beating if they know I stopped here first. Westerners sailing in fleet. Ice Fortress patrol found them. Heavy fighting. More were spotted before the commander sent me." He lifted the cloak, revealing a pouch that he had to deliver. Both knew that touching sealed letters would bring more trouble than it was worth to get the details.

"Go," Venshai said.

Lekshai scrambled to the door and fled, leaving pools of water on the fine floor.

Venshai bent over his father, who was in enough pain to groan, and try to sit. The prince scrabbled with trembling fingers at his other side, which seemed oddly loose, as if one side of him slept.

"Lie flat, Father," Venshai murmured. "The physician is coming. Did you hear Lekshai? It's war."

"Paw...paw-wuh," the prince whispered, his trembling fingers touching Venshai then sliding from his arm. "Guh."

At that moment, most of the rest of the household arrived at a run, and Princess Ji pushed her way in.

"He'll be all right, won't he, Mother?" Venshai asked. "What kind of illness is it? Or is this a demon attack?"

"It looks as if he was taken by a syncope," Princess Ji said. "My father had several of them before..."

"But he can't," Venshai said. "Esteemed Grandfather was in his nineties before he had such an attack."

Princess Ji bit her lip. "My good first son, your father is not your grandfather. I hope and trust that if he has quiet, and if the physicians bleed him well, he will recover."

She turned to the faces crowded at the door and issued orders for his highness to be carried gently to his bedchamber. "The rest of you, go on with your work."

Servants fled. Venshai lingered. He could do nothing here.

He saw his father's tally on the table, hesitated, then picked it up. Those hoarse words, what was Father trying to say? Was it *palace, go*?

He knew what his father wanted. The imperial court would be assembling as word went out, but if he got there first — to represent his father — he might be permitted into the interview chamber at last. He had to be a witness to whatever was going on at the palace. He shouldn't throw away the slight advantage

Lekshai had brought with so much trouble and effort.

Venshai caught up the tally, ran to his bedroom, shoved aside his servants and whirled his court robe from its clothes tree. It wasn't even aired with incense, but that would have to wait.

"Fetch the cart!" he shouted as he began pulling the loose part of his hair up into a knot, then fixing it in place with his best hair clasp. He snatched up his court shoes, his official loaf, and his jade belt, kicked off the house slippers, then ran in his socks through the house to the front door, where he was relieved to see the horse-drawn cart being led up.

"Palace," he yelled, flung himself inside, then pulled on the shoes as the cart lurched into motion. He jammed the loaf onto his head, wrestled the belt on, tried to yank the robe straight as the cart rumbled and bumped over slushy snow, and was hanging his father's tally from the belt when the cart pulled up before the court entrance.

The tally got him past the outer guards, but he was hesitating outside the side-entrance to the Hall of Governance, his heart hammering, when he caught sight of the Imperial Guard chief hurrying toward that door.

Venshai ran to follow him—and when the guards at the door gripped their spears to stop him once their chief passed inside, Venshai yanked the silver Chancellery tally from his belt and brandished it.

The guards fell back. Venshai pelted after the chief, then slowed as the hated Yimu uncle currently infesting the Right Chancellery swaggered up, jowls jiggling, embroidered sleeves in silver-thread brocade reaching all the way to the floor.

"It appears you're lost," the older man said in his attempt at a pure court accent, but he'd never gotten rid of the streets in either pronunciation or expression.

Venshai forced a polite bow. "My father, his highness Prince Ji Houduo the Left Chancellor, was taken indisposed and sent me in his place."

Venshai wasn't sure he'd get away with it, but apparently the emergency was new enough that court ritual was somewhat relaxed. Or, there might be a different ritual for the sudden onset of war? He didn't remember being taught one. Not even by his father, he reflected as he followed the massive, bowed shoulders of his highness Right Chancellor Prince Yimu toward the closed doors of the inner chamber. From the other direction, the ministers of Revenue and Personnel bustled up, one righting his loaf, which was pressing on one ear.

Then the tall door carved with fire dragons opened, and out came… *Je Tai?*

"What are *you* doing here?" Venshai exclaimed, then added nastily, "What could a *slave* tell the emperor about—"

The word *war* froze in his throat when right behind Je Tai the emperor himself appeared, framed in the door, as he leaned on a walking stick.

Everyone froze. Then went to the floor, face down.

"Slave?" the emperor repeated.

By then Venshai's brain had caught up with his mouth. Je Tai wouldn't be there about the declaration of war! He'd probably *been* there, to deliver a report on his progress with the… He did not even dare let the words form in his head. He clacked his teeth shut, longing to somehow grab those words and stuff them back down his throat.

"Slave," the emperor repeated, his voice lowering. "Duke Ji?"

Venshai had really stepped in it. But Father always said, the only way out was forward—remember rank and dignity. From his bow, Venshai said, "Je Tai was a slave in the Western empire for years. This inexperienced one assumed he must be summoned to provide information. About the enemy."

The emperor turned to Tai, who knelt almost at his feet. "Is this true, Secretary Je? Get up. Come back inside. All of you." The emperor was already rough-voiced with the effort to stand, though it was said he forced himself to walk the length of the palace daily. When he was able to get out of bed at all.

They filed in silently, the ministers ranging along the back. Venshai tried to get behind them, but the emperor's eye singled him out, and the others moved away from him as though proximity would drag them into whatever was to come next. "What is this about slavery?" the emperor prompted, looking from one to the other

Venshai swallowed in a very dry throat as Tai said, "If it pleases your imperial majesty, this lowly one was swept overboard in a demon storm when a youth, and made a slave by the Westerners for a time."

"Oh? And they sent you back?"

There was a stir at the door, as Yimu Bo entered, handsome and imposing in rich silk. But it was a fleshy sort of good looks,

Venshai thought, disparaging even in a sticky situation. Je Tai might be a wolf dropping, but he had the refinement of good blood.

"No, your imperial majesty," Tai said, his back now to Venshai. "Your insignificant subject was made to learn their tongue and to translate a number of our books—mostly old texts by Mana Ta, and Liad Il's *The Way of the Blade*, before being put in the mines. After escaping that, this subject was on a ship of independent raiders, and sailed in an attack on a stronghold held by two allied clans, before effecting escape from the west."

The emperor had settled behind his desk. "I see. I was told only that you had been thought lost in a shipwreck before returning home, where your studies were deemed complete enough for a promotion to the archives. I see there was much missing."

Tai bowed, trying to deal with the sudden whiplash: his mind had been full of lists and numbers, a messenger had insisted on entrance, and the emperor had changed from interested to angry, dismissing Tai and following him to the door, as if to get whoever waited there in faster.

Then Venshai appeared out of nowhere, blabbing about slaves.

The emperor glanced down at the somewhat waterlogged report carried all the way from Ice Fortress. He tapped it two or three times, as everyone in that room breathed as silently as possible. "Then you are familiar with their language, Secretary Je? Written as well as spoken?"

"Yes, your imperial majesty."

"You were in a battle? Not as an observer, but you wielded a weapon? In combat?"

"This subject had to fight or die, your imperial majesty," Tai said.

"What did you learn of their military organization?"

Tai had no time to organize his thoughts. He began to describe what Snowhawk's battle master had taught them, usually in conversation with Diggy, who had been raised to be a kind of combination gladiator and palace guard. He remembered what he'd learned from Owlfrost about Cobra Sages aboard raiders, and about the ambitious, bloodthirsty First Prince.

Midway through this stream, there was another stir at the door, and Minister Nu entered. Tai was vaguely aware of her listening as intently as the emperor.

At the end, the emperor said, "It seems that you absorbed a surprising amount of valuable information. But I ought not to be surprised, Secretary Je, for you have just given me a preliminary pattern for an endeavor that I had assumed would require at least a year to prepare."

"This lowly subject cannot claim merit earned by a hard-working staff—"

"A hard-working staff chosen and led by you. No, we have not the time for the luxury of excessive modesty. The truth is, my illustrious forefather the first emperor would have known exactly what to do next. It was his enlightened efforts that granted us generations of peace. So much peace that I know nothing of military command, and I do not have the equivalent of Celestial General Tan, my forefather. Thus my summons, that we might all put our best thoughts together for a solution. Minister Nu?"

"Your imperial majesty?" She bowed.

"Have you a suggestion for how to proceed from here?"

The minister gazed in thought, but before she could speak, Yimu Bo bowed then blustered, "Your imperial majesty. This dedicated subject seeks to prove his loyalty by volunteering to command forces of sea and land to smite the enemy until they plead for mercy."

Right Chancellor Prince Yimu gave a nod of approval, his heavy jowl wriggling. The Minister of Works stroked his beard, smiling; everyone else remained silent and still, as if no one had spoken.

"That sounds very fine, Second Brother-in-law," the emperor said. "How would you proceed?"

"I would request the golden tally from your imperial majesty's august hands," Yimu Bo said, bowing again, more deeply, hands clasped and raised so that the rings on his fingers glinted in the lamplight. "Then I'd raise every garrison in the empire, get them onto ships, and sail to the north, surround the enemy and attack until there's nothing left of their raiders but firewood—"

Tai recollected then something Ki Mek had said, which dislodged more memories: Snowhawk's plan to feint at the supply ships, as the main attack went for her target. Battle Master Yarth, saying the night before the action, "Hai, hoom, more often than not it comes down to what our Jun ancestors liked most: strike with noise and banners in the west, with stealthy teams from the east…"

He must have frowned, or reacted, for the emperor's voice broke into these thoughts. "You disagree, Secretary Je?"

Startled, Tai glanced up. He bowed, then said carefully, "This person of slow wit was told once by an experienced Western warrior that the oldest and most-used strategy is one written by our own Liad II, called 'blow the horn in the east while the knife strikes in the west.'"

Minister Nu smiled a little, those flying tiger brows lifting.

Tai said, "While no one is more ignorant about what is in their minds now, your slow-witted subject recalls that the damage from the demon storms had worsened not only for many of our southern islands, but for theirs as well. If they are raiding for food, then it seems that the horn would be blowing in the north, which doesn't have much that they'd want. If our ships and armies were to go rushing north, would that not leave rice islands like Lan all but unguarded? The Westerners could enslave the people there and send all the rice they grow back to their islands."

Soft murmurs, then the emperor raised his hand for silence, and turned to Minister Nu.

She said, "Our reports from the southwest have mentioned raiders, pirates, and the like all targeting the rice convoys."

The emperor regarded her—his same age. Perhaps they knew one another as children? "You have not commanded a fleet action since…"

"It's been thirty years, your imperial majesty. And my knowledge has been confined to searching and seizing pirate outposts along the southeast."

"You have seen more warfare than our generals," the emperor observed. "Until this day I was proud of our having not undergone invasion attempts larger than the occasional raid for many generations." He looked up, decision hardening his features. "I want you to take command, Minister Nu, with Secretary Je here as your liaison with both land and sea. He is to have a command office tally, which permits him to be present at all war conferences. His information is to be heard before decisions are made."

Minister Nu bowed to the ground, accepting the command. Belatedly Tai also performed the full formal bow, his mind catching up with the realization that he'd just been ejected from a task that he thoroughly enjoyed, among people he was comfortable with. To be hurled into a situation he never would have wanted, among a set of strangers who probably would resent his interference.

Ayah, had not that been his life so far?

"You will sail at dawn," the emperor decreed. "You must be in the west and ready at the first lift of winter. Historically, that's always been the war season has it not?"

No one was going to deny that.

As soon as they got outside the interview chamber, Minister Nu said to Tai, "Can you clear your affairs and join me this evening, while I get our fleet into readiness?"

He bowed in assent, and hurried off to explain to his staff that they were on their own now. At least the emperor had accepted the provisional draft, and the rest was mostly negotiating with the various ministries who would no doubt all believe that their matters were the most urgent...

He, and Minister Nu, did not notice Yimu Bo glowering at this chance for glory (and gold, and a promotion to princedom) snatched from under his nose. Nor did they notice Ji Venshai, who followed the other ministers out.

It had happened *again!* Je Tai swept to prominence—without the emperor, or anyone else, reacting to the stigma of slavery, as any normal person would, under any other circumstances. They hadn't even demanded to see the slave tattoo—though if they had, Venshai thought bitterly as he shuffled out into the slush, Je Tai would have revealed that tiger eye and no doubt they would have hailed it as the mark of a hero, a qilin, the Morningstar God come again...

As he slumped past the other ministers' carts in search of his own, he remembered with bitter clarity that it was he who had brought up the slavery. If he hadn't spoken, Je Tai would have scurried off, back to his burrow, and no one would have thought of him again.

In the cart, Venshai kicked the opposite bench over and over, relishing the sting to his foot. What was Father going to say to *that?* Maybe it was better not to report it. No, he couldn't pretend it hadn't happened, not with that snake from Personnel right there, ears stretched out. He was sure to be making remarks to Father over at the Chancellery, first chance he got.

What would be the best way to make it sound reasonable? Of course, come at it from the angle of family. Promoting the family, yes — Je Tai's glory is Ji glory — Father would like that…

The cart pulled up at the front gate, and Venshai jumped out, head bent to avoid the slushy, slopping snow falling. Spring seemed a thousand years away, and yet the days were longer, the snow mushier, pools of melt here and there. Spring, warfare…

He ignored the bowing guards, mere shadows on the periphery of his vision, and trod heavily inside, reviewing his wording, when he became aware of a different quality to the silence.

He looked up, his cloak half-off, and it was then that he saw the undyed cloth tied around the steward's arm. And the two physicians coming toward him, their faces bent in the way of men who had —

"Father?"

The steward bowed low, as one physician said, "Your grace, you must comfort yourself with knowing that the end was swift, and painless."

Father was *dead?*

"Painless?" Venshai repeated, his voice rising. "How do you know that? He looked like he was in pain to me!" And then an angry shout, "And it's *your highness.*"

The physicians both bowed, making no response. Long experience with nobles had taught them that of the many ways that grief expressed itself, those used to giving commands often sounded outraged at the presumption of fate.

He glared as they passed, but then he saw them from the back, two old men, stoop-shouldered. *Old.* His father *wasn't* old. Seventy-eight wasn't old, Grandfather had been old.

But there was no one to argue with.

Those muffled words, wuh, guh, the touch on his arm. Living fingers, was Father trying to keep him at his side? *He should have been there.*

From outside came the loud, mournful cry of the steward standing on the roof and waving the prince's official robe. "Come back, your highness! Come back!"

The sound ripped through Venshai, and he gripped his fists tight lest he run up there and howl along with the steward, demanding his father's soul to return. He had to get away from that ritual call, because each howl drove the truth deeper into his skull: no one had ever answered that call, not that he'd heard.

He wandered about the house, grief-gripped and furious by turns, as the mansion was draped from ceiling to doors with undyed, white linens. His brothers appeared, their silks gone. Kandashai held out a rough-sewn robe to Venshai, the edges already fraying. His man removed his loaf, his outer robe, the court shoes as he stood there. He gripped his father's tally, which he knew would have to be surrendered. Venshai was now a prince, but the emperor would put someone else in Father's place as Left Chancellor. Venshai wanted to smash in that man's face for presumption.

I should have been there. The remorseless though beat with the drum in his temple, and memories flitted and fled through a night of broken sleep, then somehow there was the casket before the family altar, and a brazier with Mother and QiQi kneeling at either side, casting spirit money into the fire to smooth Father's way in the afterlife. Would the King of the Underworld acknowledge a prince and send him straight to a new life? If so Venshai must burn more to ensure it would be a good one. Or would he be kept waiting through the year until next Two Moons? Did the King of the Underworld keep princes waiting?

Was Father still a prince in the Underworld?

It's your highness now, he'd shouted at those useless physicians. He was the prince. He was unfilial—he ought to have been there—but he also knew what Father wanted. What he had worked for all his life.

On the tenth day, the rooftop calls ceased. The robe was burned.

Venshai sat with his brothers before the altar, bowing to those who came to pay their respects: tomorrow would be the funeral parade and burial.

All the ministers came, and Father's own chancellery staff. Friend, ally, enemy. So many enemies. Was there triumph in any of those faces? No, whatever they thought, everyone appeared in sober clothing, their expressions suitable. Death, on display, was a reminder that they could be next.

Venshai's grief, sharp as a knife, simmered with rage beneath it. He should have been there, watching those old dodderers with their useless medicines. He should have listened for his father's last instructions.

It wasn't until the Yimu brothers turned up, with that old wolf the Right Chancellor—given that position not through study and work, but because his shoe seller daughter had managed to deceive the emperor into thinking he could carry on the imperial blood — that Venshai's thoughts crystallized.

He bent to light another incense stick, saying mentally, "I know what to do, Father."

He told his mother to go rest — she'd been up all night — and his sister to accompany her and see that she ate.

Then, with his brothers sitting silently at the side, he waited until the Yimu hypocrites had each bowed and lit incense and put it in the sand with the forest of other aromatic sticks. He said, "We need to talk."

The Right Chancellor merely looked down his nose, as if he'd been born to noble blood. Chen, the imperial princess's favorite, smiled benignly. Guan, relative by marriage, looked bored. Bo, the rat, looked like he was about to leave, until Venshai said, distinctly, "About Guinu."

FIFTY-SEVEN

The landscapes are inspired
And the talents celestial.
Five-colored clouds crown the jade-bright sky
Unveiling frost in wintry lacework
As this humble scholar breathes tranquility
in the pearl-gloss palace
And never heeds the cold.

VENSHAI HAD IT CARVED on his father's memorial tablet. The prince's tastes might well have changed over the years, but he'd told his sons once that it had been his favorite poem when he was a student. Kandashai, whose calligraphy was the best, had copied it out for Father's birthday ten years ago, and it had hung in the study ever since. They burned it to send its essence to accompany Father's soul on its journey.

The funeral procession was over, with thirty-nine days of mourning still to be endured. But life must go on. Father would have it so. And Venshai wanted everything put in train for the future they had worked so hard for. He would see it secured well before that bleating lamb turned white-eyed wolf came back from the west, no doubt covered with glory, to be showered with wealth and promotions.

Je Tai could become a prince, but that wasn't going to get him anywhere near Lam and a throne.

The morning after the burial, Venshai met with the Yimus at Chen's mansion, as the Sixth Imperial Consort could only visit her family without an entourage of protectors. Spies. The Yimus who lived in the capital were all there, except for the princess. Though this meeting would decide her future.

Venshai wore the pure white of mourning. He had no idea if street sellers of common blood had any sense of filial piety, but he felt stronger, clad in the gravitas of bereavement.

The Yimus faced him, a row of handsome but wary, sullen figures. Venshai fingered the tea dish before him—the best porcelain, so thin he could see the candle glow through the sides, below the pure gold of the rim—and said, "Before we begin, you should probably know that there are fifteen copies of the whole truth, including how many bodies you buried alongside Guinu in order to Deceive the Emperor."

Chen and Guan flinched, but Bo and his uncle were tougher. Venshai had heard that the missing two—the eldest brother and younger uncle, both at Benevolent Winds, stockpiling gunpowder and building palaces for themselves— were even tougher, street gangsters before a couple of them got the idea of joining the imperial guard, where the meals and clothes were free, and you beat people up for a living.

"If I drop dead of poison, those fifteen testaments will be turned over to every minister, as well as the emperor. So if you want to send for fresh tea before we begin, I'll wait." His gaze rested last on Lily, the Sixth Consort, whose favorite method of controlling the harem, so rumor had it, was poison.

"I don't want to release that testament," he said, after Bo downed his own tea with a challenging, ironic gesture. "Especially while we're fighting a war. It will cause civil war here—but of course none of you would be seeing it, because you'd be dying slowly of the Thousand Cuts over in the Peace and Justice Courtyard." He sipped; the tea was the best Dragon Silver Leaf.

Bo sighed. "We've got it, we've got it. Spit it out, Ji. What do you want?" he did not even try to hide his street vernacular.

Fine. Venshai could be blunt. But *his* imperial would always be pure. "Marriage. As soon as my fifty days of mourning are up. Because of the war, we've decided against the full three years for a parent. My father, whose every thought was of the empire, would want it that way."

The Sixth Imperial Consort lifted her chin, her lispy whisper sharp. "The emperor adores Lam. He'll do whatever she wants."

"Yes," Venshai said, and here he brazened a guess that had been much discussed in Father's study. "You know him best of anyone. Just think how angry he will be when he finds out she is not really his daughter."

Neither Venshai nor his father had actually known what the emperor was like in private—Father had said that because of his health, he'd been raised among carefully selected tutors. Venshai had ventured a guess, based on Father's report of how many of the elders who'd clung to regency had been summarily exiled, or had died before the emperor finally secured the throne.

Yes, judging by the subtle recoils in the older Yimus, it was clear that Father had been right. They said nothing, but the younger brothers stirred, and Bo flicked a glance his uncle's way.

"I'm now a prince," Venshai continued. "You're about to say that I'm merely a fifth rank commandery prince, but the emperor stipulated a prince for a bridegroom. And the easterners shied off."

"Because of you Jis," Bo said truculently. "You also drove off the Ran heir."

Venshai countered with more of Father's words. "Who wants the dragon throne. And what would the easterner alliance bring that we don't already have? They do their part in protecting the silk tribute that goes to them—they know that if it sinks, they get nothing at all."

No one argued. Father was right again.

"As for marriage with us, you will have the Ji family as allies in court. Our resources will be available. The empire is preserved for our lifetimes, no fighting over the throne. And you know who'd be claiming it if Lam's birth is proved to be..." Venshai twirled his fan toward the throne. "Not imperial."

The Sixth Imperial Consort's eyes flickered at that. Then she lifted her chin. "I'll see that you cannot get anywhere near his imperial majesty to make your claims."

When dealing with her, think of her as Yimu Lily the shoe-seller, Father had said. Venshai retorted, "Then the entire court will kneel outside his windows and chant for justice. You know they will, the day they find out. That's why I copied out the truth, in my own hand, fifteen times."

The Right Chancellor had been thinking. The Jis had so much influence even without the wily snake who had stood opposite him in court. Why make permanent enemies of them? There was plenty to go around. "I can see advantages here," he said to his niece and nephews.

And she gave in. But no grace—she hated to lose. "We'll do it," she said sullenly.

Bo rolled his eyes and got to his feet. "No interference with my interests," he warned.

"Interests such as siphoning off disaster relief funds for the smaller islands, to go into that new palace alongside your brother's at Benevolent Winds? And you, Guan. The salt ships reported as sunk, so there's no tax, while there's new salt sellers popping up in the north? Yes, we know about all that. If you had read any history, you'd discover that this kind of corruption is nothing new. You'd also find out what happens to those who get too greedy with their embezzlements. But no, I won't interfere as long as you don't interfere with me. If the emperor discovers on his own, it's your matter."

Three of them fell silence, but Bo brazened it out: "And I get a title."

"When I get the throne," Venshai said, adding with smooth haste, "Shared with Lam, of course. I'm sure she'll agree. I know she favors you all. You'll have your title—and a governorship to go with it." *As far away as possible.*

He got up to leave. "Let me know. My agents are in place," he added. "If anything happens to me."

He walked out, leaving the Yimus facing one another. "Who is going to tell Lam?" asked Chen.

"You," Bo said, pointing a finger at him. "You're her favorite."

Chen said mildly, "I won't be after I tell her why she has to marry that snake. Do I have to tell her why?"

"Yes," Bo said. "Because she hates snakes. Especially that one."

"We'd better get it over with," the Sixth Imperial Consort said, sighing. "While his imperial majesty is sequestered with this latest ailment. We can't let her see the emperor until she agrees—and convinces *him*. We don't want him asking questions."

"I feel terrible about this," Chen said, wincing. "It's going to hurt Lam."

"You can dry your tears, baby brother," Bo snapped. "You've been enjoying your silks and your pretty pipa boys just fine. We always knew she was going to have to marry someone chosen for maintaining the court. *She* knew."

"But not him."

Guan agreed. "These Jis are like rats, burrowing into every ministry. Every time you turn around, there's another one, prying and spying. Including my wife." He was still stung over that sarcasm about the salt ships—which he'd thought a neat ruse, no one gets hurt.

Their uncle snorted. "Venshai's no worse than that sniveler over in Great Ran, and all his blather about his family being older than anyone's in the imperial court. He might even turn out to be useful—those Jis have a fine eye for gold, whatever their talk about noble blood. Go, Chen. Get it done."

The imperial crown princess was unaware of this meeting, but she was not unaware of an alteration in the demeanors of her maternal relations over the past few days. Or maybe it was the general atmosphere that had changed.

Lei had been sent down to walk in the Ji prince's funeral parade, but as she was a mere cousin, she had returned afterward to the princess's wing. Her only gesture toward mourning was wearing a white armband until the fifty days were complete. At least Lei was not unduly grief-stricken; the imperial princess suspected she'd been more afraid of the Left Chancellor than fond of an uncle. Now, Lei was just a little more solemn, and she refused hot rice wine until the mourning was over.

In the warmest room in her tower, the imperial princess and Lei had been comparing some historical records, and how the same event could be written about differently.

"I wonder how the scribes wrote up that debate about the brocade tax," the princess said. "If it would be different from what I'd write up…"

Nanny Alk appeared at the door, bowing. "Her noble highness is here," she murmured. "With his grace Duke Chen."

"Uncle Chen," the princess exclaimed. At the sound of voices in the hall, the imperial crown princess flickered her fingers at Lei. "Go," she whispered, recognizing a shrill note in her mother's voice. That tone always terrified servants. Even Lei, especially since summer, though the imperial princess had no idea why. "I'll tell you about it later."

Lei bobbed a curtsey and hastened away. The door closed behind her a moment before the Sixth Imperial Consort swept in, Yimu Chen behind her.

They sat down, exchanging glances in a way that prompted

the imperial crown princess to scowl at them. "What is it? Everyone in the family has been…odd, these past few days." A sudden, horrifying thought occurred to her. "The imperial physicians—they didn't say anything terrible about Imperial Father, did they?"

"No, no, no," the Sixth Imperial Consort assured her. "He's getting better. Truly. In fact he was in the study again for a little while today. It's just that he sat up too long the day we found out about the Ghost-Eyes invasion. We told you that. He got chilled, and you know he mustn't get chilled."

The imperial princess relaxed with a sigh. "Then what is it?"

"The fact is…" the Sixth Imperial Consort began.

Yimu Chen gave her an exasperated glance and said as mildly as possible, "The time has come, as you always knew would happen, for your marriage alliance to be decided."

"Did Prince Shang of Ran approach Imperial Father again? Is that why Imperial Father was in the study?"

"No, that was about war reports from the northwest," Uncle Chen said. "As for these wedding plans, he doesn't know yet. Because you will have to help convince him that you are willing to marry Ji Venshai."

"Venshai? No! He's not even…well, he's a prince, now, I suppose, but merely a commandery prince. Fifth level. And I hate him!"

"We need the Ji family alliance," the Sixth Imperial Consort said coaxingly. The princess hated that voice much more than the shrill one. It was the voice her mother used when she got around Imperial Father, begging for more gold, for more jewels, more titles and positions for her uncles. "What with this war in the west…" The Six Imperial Consort stopped there, not really sure how that would affect court, since she was kept out of foreign affairs—and mostly she didn't care, as they did not affect her dominion over the harem.

"We need unity in the court," Uncle Chen said.

"We can get that other ways," the imperial crown princess stated. "I'm learning fast. Imperial Father says so. Though he doesn't want me to speak up in court yet, I can listen, and I can begin to help Imperial Father in other ways…"

"We agreed to the marriage," Sixth Imperial Consort cut in, to get this done.

"No," retorted the princess. "I could bear Prince Shang. He respects rank. Venshai is just a rat."

"A rat you have to marry," the Sixth Imperial Consort stated, her patience shredding.

Yimu Chen raised his palm to her, and took the princess's hands. "It's just a state marriage," he said soothingly. "You don't ever have live in the same part of the palace. And after the marriage, you'll be able to have as many consorts as you want."

"But Imperial Father will want an heir of pure blood first," the princess said.

"Peh, peh, peh!" The Sixth Imperial Consort spat. "Don't pretend to faint at the weight of a petal. No one is impressed. He's not a toad," she snapped with all the pent-up frustration of someone who'd caught the eye of a sickly man over thirty years her elder, and who had spent all the years since cajoling and charming only him, constantly surrounded by those who watched everything she did, day and night, in hopes of a second, male heir.

"He's not *repulsive*," the imperial crown princess hedged. "Until he opens his mouth. But his birth is barely—"

The Sixth Imperial Consort leaned down and slapped her daughter. "That for your 'pure blood' and your hints that mine isn't pure. Here's the truth, *imperial daughter*, yours isn't either. So shut up and do what you're told."

"What?" the imperial princess gave them a puzzled look that turned wary. "What did you say?"

"Your *ears* aren't cabbages, though your head is." The Sixth Imperial Consort crossed her silk-covered arms and looked away. "You heard me."

Uncle Chen took the princess's hand again. "Lam, good Lam, the important thing to remember here is that *we* are your true family. And we love you. We have always loved you, and always will. But Ji Venshai, or his father, winnowed out the truth…Your mother was actually pregnant before she and his imperial majesty fell in love."

The princess stared at him as her mind worked slowly past shock, and the truth burned through her nerves to boil sickeningly in her stomach. "Does Imperial Father know?" she whispered.

"Of course not, or we'd be dead, not even left a whole corpse," the Sixth Imperial Consort said, a tremor in her voice. "I was *seventeen!* I did what I was told by Da and my uncle—" She saw that this was the wrong approach, and fell silent.

Yimu Chen kept holding the princess's hands, which lay like dead things in his grip until she yanked them away. "I hate you," she stated. "Get out. I hate you all. And I will *never* forgive you. *Ever.*"

"Here it comes," the Sixth Imperial Consort said, shrill and hard under that sticky-sweet voice. "The Guinu temper. Did you ever wonder where it came from? Your real father was a brawler from the alleys until they took him into the imperial guard. And if you don't want to die the death of a thousand cuts, then you'll shut up about this, and *keep* your mouth shut, and at the end of Ji's mourning, you'll marry him, and *smile.*" She stalked out, her train billowing and catching on a table. With a vicious yank, she freed it, knocking table and lamp over.

As the two older uncles followed her out, Yimu Chen bent to right the lamp and the table. "Lam, he's still your father, in all the ways that matter."

"*Blood* matters. To him," she stated numbly.

"He loves you. You love him. Don't break his heart over something that cannot be fixed. Hold steady, let him believe, and when the time comes, you will take his place on the throne. He wants that very much. And we do need the court behind us," he added. "Think of all those who would try to depose you and claim the throne for themselves, if the truth gets out."

She sat there, still numb, so he came to her and bent to kiss her forehead. "Think it over, Lam. You're smart, and you've got a good grasp of what's important. It's you who will lead in that marriage."

"But I'll still be *married*," she cried in anguish.

"Which means you get to choose your consorts," Chen said, patting her hand.

"But not the one I want," she whispered as he left. Because she was sure that Je Tai would not marry her as a mere consort, subordinate to Ji Venshai. He would not be willing to sit around being decorative until she required him. Not that straightforward, heroic figure who had escaped slavery, and fought off attackers at the Dragon Parade, and who had helped Imperial Father avert a disaster not of his making. Consorts were lapdogs. Unless they were Mother.

The irony of that made her want to howl, and she knew she was going to howl, but could tell no one why. And when Lei entered softly with her sweet, concerned face that was so like his, yet so unlike, the princess couldn't bear it anymore, and she covered her eyes with her hands. "Go, Lei. Go home. No, no, you did nothing wrong. Nothing. I'll send a trunk of gold, and testaments — I'll find you a better position...just *go*."

Lei did not dare to remind the distraught princess that her home was not in the capital, but on the east coast. And Ji Mansion was deep in mourning.

She ran to her room, tears dripping down her face. She'd packed her trunk when the screams of rage began. Lei, weeping soundlessly, hid until the screams softened to moaning, then slumber.

At last Nanny Alk came in. "What happened?" she whispered.

"I don't *know*," Lei whispered back. "I didn't say a word. I came out when her visitors went away, just as she told me to, and..." In a broken voice, Lei repeated exactly what the princess had said.

Nanny Alk frowned into space, then murmured, "I know her. If she remembers her promise, she will keep it. But if she doesn't, would you like to go teach at one of the Swan schools? I have mine in the one over behind the old temple. I'm sure they would be proud to take in a fifth-ranking scholar in the imperial examination."

"I just want to go home," Lei whispered, tears dripping.

"Wait here a moment." Nanny Alk whisked herself noiselessly out, then was back as Lei checked the latch on her trunk. Nanny Alk pressed a heavy, clinking pouch into her hand, and whispered, "The steward is sending Tigermoth with you. She knows how to arrange for a berth on a ship."

Neither maid nor former imperial secretary to the crown princess spoke until after they reached the civilian side of the wharf, and Lei was left to shiver in the cart as Tigermoth ran to an office.

She was back soon. "You've a berth to yourself. They're sending a wharf rat to fetch your trunk. Farewell, Je Lei," she added slowly. "May the Crane God look out for you."

The Crane — God of the Abandoned. Lei's eyes stung more, but she thanked Tigermoth, handing back a handful of those coins. And then, as the maid turned away, "Nanny Alk. Mentioned the Swan schools. She has *children*?"

Tigermoth looked around, though they were alone — the driver was talking to the man who hefted Lei's trunk. "She has two," she whispered. "They were small when she was widowed, and had to earn her living at a pharmacy, where she became known for Essence cures. The imperial physicians found her there, and her medicine worked. But she did not want her little ones growing up in the palace, and sent them to her friend at the Swan School. And they let her, because she's the only one who…you know."

Lei nodded, pressing her lips tight, bade Tigermoth another farewell, and stepped onto the wet, icy pier to head for the ship.

She soon found herself on her way home, bewildered and grieved—but she was aware of a small sense of relief, too, that somehow made it all worse.

FIFTY-EIGHT

THE WEAKENING WINTER STORMS sped the defense fleet through choppy green waters. Whenever Minister Nu—now Supreme Commander Nu—was free, she summoned Tai to teach him as much as she could about naval capabilities and thinking. When she wasn't free, he exercised with the young sailors, and listened to captains who had seen action.

They did not discuss the subject that had first brought them together—they were both enjoined by imperial degree to silence—but she was not surprised to discover that he brought the same arrow-sharp focus to learning that he apparently brought to archival diving.

The fastest couriers, all equipped with pigeons, were sent on ahead to summon army and naval commanders to meet at Great Ran. Though this enormous island had under the first Tan emperor ceased to be a military presence, its eastern harbor was broad and accommodating.

Captains and commanders, some newly-arrived, were assembled when Supreme Commander Nu arrived in her flagship. All wore tassels on their hats and on their swords; some were in armor.

Neither she nor Tai were surprised when Tai's tally was regarded with suspicion. He was easily the youngest there, dressed soberly in the blue robe of a ninth-level archivist. Worse, his name suggested to some that he was only there due to blood privilege.

"We will, of course, honor his imperial majesty's wishes," one of the sun-seamed commanders said, eyeing Tai skeptically even as he raised clasped hands to salute in the direction of the golden throne on the other side of the empire. "But you will forgive me for asking what expertise you have in strategic planning?"

"Very little beyond brief experience," Tai said.

"What kind of experience? What do you know about Western war raiders and their capabilities?"

Don't hide what you know, Supreme Commander Nu had said. *Command centers are utterly unlike court, where the elaborate ritual of humility not only preserves face, but is meant to assure the emperor that talent and skill are no threat to the throne.*

"Their scouts are equivalent to ours, and there are some similarities with our warships," Tai said. "All ships armed with guns are classed under land animal names that roar as they attack. Jaguar class ships are the fastest—something like our seahawk. Guns fore and aft, but the deck is open, with one row of oars each side, two to three, even four men to each oar. One sail to each mast, square fore, lateen aft, but these are small, so as not to interfere with the archer towers."

"Correct—"

"Tiger class ships have double decks with two rows of oars and a broad beam for carrying marine warriors. Two sails to each mast. Lion class ships are equivalent to our tower ships, with three decks and three banks of oars. They use them as troop ships, and they have heavier guns with larger crews to serve them, but also are trained to board and fight if ord—"

"We know that much," a heavily armored army commander broke in. Thanks to instruction from Supreme Commander Nu, Tai recognized the bronze snarling tigers on his black armor's shoulders, and the great, stylized red enameled claw on the chest, as belonging to the Tiger Claw army, the front-line warriors in the imperial army—the toughest. "Tell us something we don't know."

"My experience was small, but I was an escaped slave a galley during internal conflict, and so was carried into battle."

Escaped slave. A slight stir among those who had been fighting off marauding raiders, and some glances at Tai's forehead—to meet the rim of his plain loaf as he went on, "I learned this: that all depends on the galleys. The sails can be regarded as fixed—very difficult to angle to the wind, unless an independent that has adapted the ship for sail. So speed and maneuverability comes from the oars, and not the wind."

The Tiger Claw commander stirred impatiently, and Tai

said, "If the oars are manned by chained slaves, the galley has fewer crew, which requires fewer supplies. These ships are faster on the water. The slower, heavier ships will be stiff with warriors—"

"Common knowledge," someone interrupted, sounding irritated.

"—but if you are able to board, the oarsmen will not be able to rise and fight even if they want to. The Westerners won't let the slaves free even if the ship is foundering because it's far more likely they'll rise against their slavers than against any distant enemy. But on some ships, oarsmen are hires, or working off a penalty, and looking for promotion once their time is up. These are likely to fight if asked, because if successful, their penalty is shortened, or dismissed outright. If they survive."

A stir among some of the captains. "That's useful," one said mildly. "We're told they are all fiercely dedicated, especially if there's one of their Cobra Sages doing blood charms on them. But how can we tell a ship whose galley slaves will turn on their masters from the others?"

"By the stink," Tai said flatly. "Galleys run by cooperative effort means oarsmen can get up to go to the head when their watch is over."

It took a moment to work that out, then crimps of disgust and shuffled feet and sideways gazes made it clear they had.

Supreme Commander Nu noted the gradual shift toward cautious approval, and she smiled internally. She liked Je Tai, who was earnest, honest, and not afraid of hard work. She respected hard work. It had taken hard work for her to rise above navigator, which was the highest rank most women attained in the navy. Even when they'd commanded in all ways but name.

"What can you tell us about the Cobra Sages and their weaknesses and strengths?"

"I don't know much about them, or how to find out. But I know who can."

"Oh? Shall we send for this expert?"

Tai tapped the side of his head. He'd learned to avoid mentioning Mek's name if he didn't have to. "He's an Essence dream speaker. If you give me your questions, I can put them to him."

"How?"

"He will hear me," Tai stated, still in that detached calm.

"Can you get this Essence expert to dream-talk to me?"

"I could ask him. But you might not be able to hear him. Some can't," Tai said. "And also, if you try too much, my understanding is, the Cobra Sages will hear you. And invade your dreams."

Everyone looked uneasy at that.

"Until then," Supreme Commander Nu put in smoothly, "The emperor wants Lan Island protected, as we believe that is the true goal of this stage of the invasion. We're to prevent Lan's rice from being taken. So let's begin with everyone's situation report…"

While Tai was sailing west, Mek, Butterfly, and Tanglewood successfully deflected a second fleet and two scouts northward.

They failed with the third. This one dissipated the foggy illusions almost as soon as they were made. They flew down a little closer, and began their charms when an iridescent shimmer grew slowly over the ships.

"What's that?" Tanglewood cried, her voice carried away on the wind.

"I don't—" *know*, Mek lost the last word when a dark cloud of arrows hummed up from the ships toward them.

All three soared skyward, Tanglewood gritting her teeth as she sent wild tendrils from her staff to deflect the few arrows that hissed near. Tendrils and arrows—now sprouting—tumbled to the sea below.

Someone down on those ships was searching the skies and, seeing them, pointed where to shoot.

Instinctively they began to fly toward Ten Leopards and safety, but Butterfly shouted, "Fly north, fly north! Away from Ten Leopards."

Mek understood. Ten Leopards had been deserted for many years, and was probably listed that way on the Westerners' charts. If the enemy suspected that they were being watched and lured away from Ten Leopards, that would no doubt be the target of the next fleet.

They soared north until the enemy fleet was fully hull down beyond the horizon, then circled the long way back, keeping the mountains of Ten Leopards between themselves and the ships passing.

When they reached the enclave, cold and tired, they

reported their failure.

Waha, who'd brought the latest supplies, said, "You might have fooled them, but it's best to keep watch from now on."

Mek's Seventh Brother agreed. "We'll handle the watch, so you three can keep flying."

Everyone agreed, and Butterfly, who had grown up within sight of a naval harbor and thus had the most experience with the military, sighed. "I think we're going to have to start seeking them before they get this far."

Tanglewood grinned, that hint of fox mischief strong as she said, "Let's find where they're sailing from. And have some fun."

Mek said nothing.

Anise watched him poke at his dumplings, which she had made specifically for him, and after everyone had eaten supper and gone on to evening chores or liberty, she said, "You are unhappy."

"Something..." He shrugged. As usual, words failing him. "Feels wrong. Very wrong."

"Surely it was that rain of arrows. So very close! You're safe. It's dark. They must be anchored somewhere in the sea."

"It's not them. Yes, it is." Mek got up and paced around their room as he tried to put a shape to that instinctive warning. "Cobra Sage," he said at last. "I think..."

He sat down and shut his eyes, easing the door open while putting a deflection charm over his questing mind. Something he'd figured out how to do the previous year. He did not repose full trust in it, as he suspected that the truly powerful and inimical seekers could see past it, just as someone who really searched in the real world saw easily past the deflection charm. He poked tentatively, but he'd never been good with shifting between that realm and this one.

Then a distinct rumble startled them both.

"Thunder? In winter?" Anise wondered.

But it was too regular, a deep boom repeated in pattern, dulled by distance from the sea.

"Gunfire," Butterfly shouted from the other room.

Everyone came running. "That has to be the imperials from Ice Fortress," Seventh Brother suggested. "They must be coming down after finding the ones you sent up north before."

"At night? Do they do battles at night?"

Butterfly spread her hands. "My guess is, if they sighted on the enemy anchored for the night, and sailed up with lights doused before firing the cannon, they could blast the galleys without having to risk maneuvering in the darkness. We used to sit on the cliffs watching them practice such things in Whale's Haven Harbor when I was little."

The gunfire noise increased — the Westerners firing back — and went on for a while before silence closed in once more.

The next morning, as soon as there was light, the three flyers ventured out to see the damage. From the broken splinters floating on the water off the eastern shore of Ten Leopards, the battle had indeed occurred. But no sign of any ships.

"They were either captured, burnt and sunk, or the enemy retreated southward out to sea," Butterfly shouted.

They flew back to the enclave, since Seventh Brother was now in charge of the watch at the tower, along with a pair of pigeons from the new roost off the barns. Mek sat down, opened the mental door, and put a deflection over his mind. Less tired now, facing southward, he let his mind drift.

There. That same horrible ice-burn sensation he'd felt after he'd healed Bar Ganis's son's shattered leg. *Blood demon*, the boy had said in his own language. Mek still remembered the weary despair in that boy's mind. The fear that Mek would reveal the talent that the boy had managed to hide so far. A talent commensurate with his own, but utterly untrained, because it always had to be hidden.

"Blood demon," he said aloud. How was he supposed to ward *that?*

But when he laid his hand to Sagacious Blade, he sensed a hum in that cool metal. Once again he intuited a presence. Vast, shapeless to his weak human senses. Benign to him, but its steady focus on that faraway ice-burn was like a sword made of lightning: blue-white, crackling and deadly.

Instinctively, Mek gave that lightning sword direction, and it carried him along as it sped, faster than the fastest bird, over the water. Mek's mind reeled with shards of perception not his own, a detonation felt, not heard, then a mind he did not know released suddenly, falling. Not dead. But unconscious, severed from that inimical source of hungry power.

He opened his eyes, struggling to define what it was he'd seen. He stroked his fingers along Sagacious Blade, and sensed muted satisfaction. *You ate the blood demon? Is that it? You took it away from the Cobra Sage and ate it?* he asked.

And felt the sword entity's tranquil assent.

Feeling very small, as if he were an insect trying to comprehend a leviathan, Mek blinked himself back to his physical self, and went in search of Auntie Mim. He found her discussing the layout of the kitchen garden, once the ground had unfrozen enough to turn over the soil.

"My nephew Xing said he'd pack up the seeds…what is it, Mek?" She eyed the bright, polished sword in his hand.

"I think I need to talk to you. About blood demons."

"About what?"

He wandered out, still a little dazed.

Auntie Mim caught up with him. "Mek, what was that about blood demons?"

He explained. She listened all the way through, her gaze going several times to Sagacious Blade. At the end, she expelled an unsteady breath. "My studies are mostly Essence healing. You know that. It's Nua you ought to speak with; though I don't think she knows much more about such things than I. Old Uncle did teach us about some Essence matters, saying that demons could be a very inexact term for ghosts, gods, and cultivating spirits of all the elements."

"But…"

She shook her head. "Ayah! It sounds very like Sagacious Blade wants to hunt these blood demons. Which seem to be *inside* the Cobra Sages. They call them Riders, in their language. What you don't know is if the Cobra Sages were invaded against their will, or wanted it. Or if they know what it means to take the blood demons away."

"It means you're ending the blood demon's ability to kill *us*," said Butterfly from the doorway to the dining room. "By devouring our life Essence, our souls, very much without our will." She turned to Mek. "Tanglewood wants to carry our fight to the harbors. Not to go on a killing spree," she said quickly. "But we could do all kinds of damage to slow up the invasion. I don't think you've seen what Tanglewood can to do the timbers of a ship—"

Ki Mek, Ki Mek, Ki Mek. It was Tai again!

Mek closed his eyes.

And far to the south, in a quiet room at the back of Great Ran's garrison, Tai sensed Mek's presence.

"I'm sorry I fled," Mek shaped the words for Tai. "I hope I didn't leave you with more problems than I solved."

"You did not," Tai returned, and as always, sensory memory flashed: emperor, Supreme Commander Nu, ship. "I am a liaison in Great Ran now. The commanders have decided that protecting Lan Island takes priority."

Mek recalled Ardal's hasty, fearful conversation that day, when he was also tired and worried, with Je Tai's father sitting there like a nine-level pagoda, determined that Mek's duty was to go to the capital to confess to those Jis. "South," he repeated—and because Tai's words leaked the images, sights, sounds, and scents of his immediate situation, along with the stresses, he said, "Ardal said they were attacking north, and then south, I believe it was. I was preoccupied by the warning about the northwest," he confessed.

Tai recollected that this was a favored tactic of the Western raiders. "Can you make sure that is still true?" Tai asked.

"I could try." Mek's words conveyed an aura of doubt. "But you remember how far Angja Island was from the obsidian throne. How they considered themselves different. I don't believe she's in the midst of the war planning, and I have to be careful about too much listening beyond my mental door because those Cobra Sage blood demons might be lurking in this realm."

Tai's unspoken horror echoed as a shiver to Mek. An odd sensation.

Mek continued, "Some Ice Fortress ships were here to attack the Westerners coming up past Ten Leopards."

"They have orders to defend the northwest," came Tai's sure conviction. "I saw the chart not two incense sticks ago. They call that area something else, but they now have ordered someone to defend the fork, which is a major conduit to the empire's western trade route. But no one else is going to reinforce them."

"Then I guess we must go south to try to harass them. Winter! I hate flying in winter. I must have dreamed I whiffed spring on the wind…"

He knew he was grumbling, but he caught a glimmer of humor from Tai. It always felt to Mek like a triumph if he could make Tai smile.

"Mek. They are doing spring planting, here in Great Ran. The snow is gone."

"That's it. We've got a scout ship that we flyers can use to go out from. I'll tell Ze Eight to sail for the south."

FIFTY-NINE

THE EMPEROR DECLARED A day of amnesty for all cases but capital ones, in honor of the imperial crown princess's wedding.

She was back in the capital now. She'd been home for a couple of weeks when the astonishing announcement reached the east coast that the imperial crown princess was to be married. A day later, Lei discovered that the princess had kept her promise: she was appointed to the Scribes as a fact checker, with access to Archives. This meant traveling back to the capital.

Life in the capital was exciting now that she was not in the imperial palace. Her predecessor (a young man) had been promoted to court scribe. Though the evidence of his handwriting, and his ledger, made it clear that his handwriting was adequate at best, and his log not always neat, he was a young man. Most of those in the dark warren where she labored were women. Many quite old; it was clear that this was as far as promotion went for women: responsibility for carrying out orders, but never ministers giving the orders.

She liked her fellow scribes, and she loved the work—the checking of facts for the ministers. The courtiers who introduced new memorials to the emperor by giving a prefatory speech were not to be caught out by someone with a better memory, and lose face. She spent her days tracking down the exact line of an ancient poem, or who had written a commentary in the margin on Ar Laq's own copy of Mana Ta's *Conversations with His Students*—that copy scrupulously recopied, complete with marginalia, after Ar Laq's death.

Also, because she had access to all these historical writings and records, she could begin reading something about those Westerners her brother was risking his life to battle against.

Thus, the job was different every day, and her quarters, housed with three of the other scribes her age, were comfortable enough. They not only had a window in their shared main room, but it had a tiny balcony overlooking the main street, which—Lei was assured—was lovely in summer.

Best of all, she was able to turn down QiQi's offer of lodgings at Ji Mansion, at first claiming that she would be too much trouble during their mourning, and after, that they would be far too busy preparing for Cousin Venshai's grand wedding.

Once in a while Lei wondered if that grand wedding would really happen. She remembered the imperial crown princess's opinion of her cousin Venshai. But the days passed swiftly, and then the morning arrived.

Though QiQi had invited Lei to the wedding, Lei had claimed that as the newest appointee, she had to work; she could not forget how the princess had sent her away for no discernible reason, and dreaded being seen by her.

Much better to lean here, shoulder to shoulder with her roommates, commenting freely on the enormous parade passing by, rather than have to sit stiffly up in Ji Mansion, trying to hide.

Cousin Venshai was almost unrecognizable in his red and gold robes as he rode a horse so decorated it was difficult to make out what color it was. His hair, usually seen in braids, was all pulled up now, as befitted a prince. During his mourning he had not shaved, and because he was marrying immediately after, he left the resulting tiny goatee, which gave length to those round cheeks, making him look changed. Older. Ayah, he was older! Nearly *thirty*, now!

He smiled broadly, as servants walking to either side of his horse tossed real silver pieces to the crowd in the streets. They cheered him and threw flowers and seeds back. Even the weather had cooperated, being clear, though cool for early spring.

The bridal carriage then passed by, a beautiful cart decorated with a profusion of crimson silk flowers, interspersed with aromatic plum and late apricot blossoms. The imperial crown princess wore a fabulous phoenix headdress as elaborate as the empress's, with golden chains dangling at each side, a contrast to the complicated loops of her dark hair. Her red and gold brocade robe was even more gorgeous, embroidered in greens and blues with flowers and birds symbolizing peace, plenty, longevity, and joy, studded with pearls.

What was she thinking?

Lei had assumed she'd gotten to know the crown princess well, but she obviously had not, or she would not have been turned out of her position so suddenly — or at least she might have understood why. Lei leaned on the balcony looking into that cart as she thought back for signs she might have missed. They were easy enough to find — now.

At Fire Wishes Day, for example, they had sat together on the balcony painting lanterns to launch into the sky along with wishes and prayers. Lei, of course, had painted her brother Tai's name on hers. She had no lovers, and her brother was off in the west amid unknown, terrible dangers. She had willingly showed the princess her lantern when it was done.

The princess in turn had showed her a painting she'd done of two swans flying together, but then the princess had written something on the lantern's other side and launched it without showing it to Lei. Secrets, though Lei hadn't thought about it then — she was too humble, the princess too exalted.

How well could you know anyone, if all you can do is agree and obey?

Lei was ready to duck if that elaborate headdress began to turn, but the princess looked straight ahead.

Bang! Clash! Tweedlee-yee-yee! Musicians played loudly, and acrobats tumbled and danced as little palace maids competed with each other in tossing silk flowers.

When the last of the parade had passed by, roommate Diu Bi said, "Let's go down to the Five Lilies and see what everyone is saying."

The others clapped, and Lei agreed; she'd salved her conscience for her lie by getting up early and clearing her desk, though she knew that QiQi would have understood — if she could have explained the truth.

Lei could not know that the imperial crown princess missed her bitterly. She had missed Lei ever since she'd sent her away; she didn't even remember sending her away, but everyone assured her she had. Nanny Alk had even said that Lei wept in sorrow to be parted.

The imperial princess tried not to find that gratifying,

especially as she sensed the warning that Nanny Alk would never speak outright: that she had to try to get control of that temper, or it would truly control her. Lei was afraid of that—afraid of what she might do. Could do.

Wanted to do, when the inevitable happened, and they reached the palace at the end of this torturously long wedding parade. The rest was a merciful blur until the bows had been made. She never looked at Ji Venshai. Reality reasserted itself when they had to twine their arms and drink the wedding cups. There he was, close enough to kiss.

Venshai's breathing sounded as labored as hers, and he looked tired. She remembered that he'd lost his father not long ago. At least he'd had one, a true one, came the thought, and the wedding wine turned to ash in her mouth.

But now the old Left Chancellor was gone. Whereas she still had Imperial Father, and though they were not related by blood, they were related by love.

Imperial Father's eyes glistened with unshed tears as he smiled at her, and he said in a tremulous voice, "Give me a grandchild, Daughter."

His smile was not as tender when he looked Venshai's way. She'd begun to wonder if any prince would have been good enough, really. Because Imperial Father *did* love her. And believed she was his true daughter.

She kept that thought close as the toasts commenced, and the interminable banquet commenced another excruciatingly long parade of dishes and dishes of delectable foods. Those tasted of ash, too.

She tried to watch the dancers, but the phoenix wedding crown pressed mercilessly on her head, and she was sweating in the nine layers of her wedding clothes, and she longed for it all to be over.

Finally it was, and they were escorted to the wedding suite, her uncles and Venshai's brothers competing in ribald wishes, their laughter sharp to her ears.

At last the maids took away the hated headdress, then shut the door behind them, and Venshai and she looked at one another, neither certain of the next move.

Then he said, "Does your head hurt as much as mine does? I'll sleep in that room off there."

She did not hide her relief as he left for the dressing room. And finally she was alone.

They had to get used to going to court together. She, as heir, stood to the left at the front, directly in front of her grand-uncle, the Right Chancellor, facing Imperial Father's right hand. Venshai had been promoted to the first rank now, and stood directly behind the Right Chancellor, wearing the purple robe of the highest three ranks. When court was over they parted, each to their duties. His were new, and he was silent those first couple of days.

Both knew what the emperor wanted. He had plenty of experience, but that was with willing, even eager entertainers who understood the arts of allurement—and expected excellent payment for those trained arts.

The princess…was still a princess, whatever her blood. He knew what she looked like when she wanted someone. He'd seen that look of hers for Je Tai. A look he knew he was never going to see.

So he waited. When they finally slept together, it was at her insistence, with Imperial Father's words about grandchildren and dynastic heirs ringing in her ears. This was yet another aspect of "the scholar on the ice"—the duty that comes with rank. Father had said it in the context of accepting a marriage with the Ji family, and he spoke the old saying to her implying that now she must do her duty.

She'd been dreaming about blood the color of dirt, knowing that hers was as common as that of her mother's and uncles'. Ji Venshai had noble blood, at least, and she would see to it that their children were raised to believe themselves of imperial blood: after all, she'd realized one day on reading Mana Ta, no first emperor of any dynasty save the Sage Empress had been born with imperial blood.

That was what gave her courage—that and plenty of rice wine. She noticed Venshai drank a lot, too, so wine fumes surrounded them both when the time came to climb into the bed. At least he knew what he was doing, whereas she had never been permitted to experiment, so worried everyone had been about possible children not of the right blood.

If only the world knew the truth of *that!*

But she had to make sure they never would know.

The awkwardness eventually eased with familiarity. They hadn't much to say to the other for the remainder of their days;

every third, they dined with Imperial Father and the empress, if his health permitted. Venshai was mostly silent during these dinners, his formal manners subdued, obsequious. The crown princess found him the most bearable then—she could even address him with a semblance of cordiality, which was as close as she could come to the feelings she'd had to profess for him when she'd convinced Imperial Father to accept his marriage suit.

The worst dinners were those with the Sixth Imperial Consort and her older uncles and grand-uncle; though on the surface Venshai was polite, elaborately so, it was an ostentatious, even deliberate politeness that contrasted with their far less polished manners, and the resulting crossfire of innuendo made it clear how much they all hated each other. She invariably left those meals with her head panging.

The first trouble happened after the princess made her every-tenth-day visit to the temple, and the nuns pleaded with her to speak to Imperial Father about the dearth of supplies for refugees—not only those still struggling to survive in villages flattened by the demon storms, but new waves of people who'd fled from the border islands, terrified of the Westerners and their slavers.

"This unworthy subject begs your imperial highness." The abbess knocked her forehead to the floor. "Ask his imperial majesty, who is our Heaven-appointed father, why his children are still going hungry, though we were told that the Department of Granary was to double the distribution?"

The sense of satisfaction the princess had always reveled in from helping to tabulate and pack up donations had vanished. She demanded the back ledgers, and because she was the crown princess, she got them. The numbers were steadily diminishing, a bit at a time. And yet she distinctly recollected hearing Imperial Father issue an edict about easing the suffering of those fleeing the invasions.

She did not want to add yet another worry to the burden borne by Imperial Father, who was not eating well at all, worn down as he worried about war news. Besides, wasn't Ji Venshai now promoted to Investigating Censor of the Court of Surveillance?

She found him on his side of the heir's wing of the palace that evening, in the midst of changing out of his court robe. Without preliminaries, she explained.

He listened as he sat there, while his personal man redid his hair. Finally, he said, "Why are you pestering *me*? You should be pestering your dear Uncle Bo. You know that he's the Granary Superintendent now, crowding right on the heels of the Minister of Revenue at court. And while you're at it, ask him who paid for that fine new palace up on the hill in Flame-in-Ice, the gunpowder island's capital."

"Why don't you ask him? Did you forget that this is our night to dine with my mother?"

Venshai eyed his fine new robe in the polished bronze mirror, embroidered with silver wind dragons, each with four claws. "Convey my respects to your noble mother, and plead my excuses for missing dinner. I have to sit in on an investigation at the Office of Scrutiny tonight."

She doubted that would take more than an hour, this late, but maybe dinner with her family would be less tense without him exchanging glares with her uncles — and Mother glaring at everybody.

She almost collided with Uncle Bo as he was entering the outer chamber of the harem, where Mother entertained her family.

"Uncle Bo, now that you're Superintendent of the Imperial Granaries, when can we expect to see the relief for the refugees? I had to pry the ledgers out of those underlings over at Revenue. We're receiving fewer deliveries, not more. It isn't true that the gold for that went into building your palace on Benevolent Winds?"

Uncle Bo looked down at her. "Ji told you that, did he? Did he tell you that the two of you get two taels out of every ten?"

"Two taels for every ten? What does that mean? You're taking ten taels out of how many...for yourself?"

Uncle Bo uttered a bark of a laugh. "My very dear Lam, who has never gone without whatever she wanted when she wanted it, what do you think the stipend is for Superintendent of the Granary? Nothing. That's right. The hours I spend arguing with Revenue's four-eyed rats, Personnel, Trade, even the navy, are supposed to be an 'honor.' I've got enough honors! You can't build with honors, or eat them." He saw the shock in her face, and relented a little. "It's time you learned what is understood through court: everyone takes their part. How else will these jobs get done?"

"Ten out of how much?"

"Twenty-five," he admitted with a put-upon sigh. "But your grabby Ji husband takes two of that ten, so why he sent you after me when he knows very well is just another evidence of his…penchant for giving us trouble just to be doing it."

What is understood. How much was "understood" by everyone but her?

She was silent during the dinner. Silent after. Silent until Venshai returned to the palace, smelling of wine from whatever party he'd gone to after his hour's meeting.

She confronted him inside his outer chamber. "We get two taels out of ten. 'We?' Who is this we?"

Venshai snapped his fingers, and his servants bowed themselves out.

"You. And I. Have you ever asked where all your wealth comes from, Lam?" His derisive voice was a whiplash — gone was all the respect that imperial blood demanded, now that they were alone.

"I know exactly where it comes from. And I have always stayed within my allowance," she stated.

"Well, we need more. We've got to begin entertaining in court, if we're to 'unite' them, as his imperial majesty desires." He said that, retreated to the inner room, and slammed his door.

And her mood exploded.

To Venshai, it was as if the imperial crown princess he knew had been snatched away and in its place a demon appeared, one with wild eyes and snarling teeth as she kicked his door in, paying no attention to the splinters that ripped through her soft silk house slippers and scored across her foot.

Smearing blood at every step, she began hurling whatever was to hand at him, growling in a guttural voice that scared him more than the porcelain and fine wood and candle sticks flying at his head, "*You* are going to fix it."

"I'll do what I can," he yelped. "I promise. But you have to get that grasping rat of an uncle to stop first, or he'll just take it all!"

She whirled and ran for the door to the hall that led to the visitors' chambers of the harem, leaving bloody footprints at every step. Venshai followed, appalled. What should he do?

He didn't have to do anything. Big, quiet graywings appeared from doors he'd never noticed. It took three of them to catch the shouting, writhing princess, and to hold her until

Nanny Alk, with whom Venshai had yet to speak a word, appeared with some sort of mixture that smelled of medicine.

It took two tries, and Nanny Alk had to pinch the princess's nose—while those strong hands held the princess's head still—before she gulped and gasped the elixir down.

Then the princess was borne off to her rooms, her voice beginning to slur. After a time, silence.

Venshai wandered about his room, shaken, until Nanny Alk appeared, neat in gray, her manner respectful, but her voice firm. "What did you say to set her off, your noble highness?"

"You—how dare you pry into my private life," he snarled, finding her a handy target for his roiling emotions. "You can be beaten for presumption—"

"What did she say?" Nanny Alk pursued, still patient. "What did you say? We keep an exact record of these sparks, to try to prevent them."

His fury turned to astonishment. "Then...it happens... often?"

"Not as often as it could, if we're careful to avoid the causes," the woman said, still standing there with her hands folded respectfully. Venshai saw scratch marks swelling on the top of one of her hands.

He said, "We disagreed about a court matter. I told her to go to her oldest uncle, who is the source of the problem. Is it always like this?"

"No, your noble highness. Sometimes it's weeping. Some- times she lies in bed without seeing or hearing anyone. Not eating or drinking, unless we coax it into her, a spoonful at a time. But it always comes on suddenly. We used to get by with just the medicine, and only use the poppy and Essence-imbued sleep elixir in very bad cases, but the Sixth Imperial Consort insisted three years ago that we go straight to the poppy and elixir at the start of a mood. Generally she wakens as herself again."

"She's possessed by a demon," he stated.

"No, your noble highness. She's been examined. There is no demon. There are others with the malady, the imperial physi- cians say. She should waken back to her true self. Just a little ill. Tincture of poppy is...hard to recover from."

Venshai accepted that explanation—ignoring the addend- um about the poppy without noticing that those words were an indirect plea for an order that would supersede the Sixth

Imperial Consort's command. He summoned the steward later, and said, "Is there anyone else who can cure her imperial highness?" He still resented the way that nanny had come in and demanded to know what he'd said.

"There is no one, your highness. Nanny Alk has an Essence skill. And though there are others with Essence skills, her imperial highness the crown princess does not trust them. Trust seems to be a vital element in Essence matters of this kind."

Venshai went back to his rooms, thinking, no wonder his little cousin Je Lei had looked owl-eyed when Father had asked questions about the princess.

Well, now Venshai knew the real cost of the golden throne.

Aish! He was no coward. He'd pay it, and whatever else it demanded, because that was his life's purpose, and Father would never rest in the Underworld until it was fulfilled.

SIXTY

"THIS WILL BE FUN," Butterfly chortled.

Tanglewood had flitted down to Anchor Harbor's eastside wharf, where a row of galleys was being repaired by the Westerners after the recent battle to be sent out again.

"No one will get hurt?" Mek asked.

"No," Butterfly said. "Though I don't know why you're worried about people who came over here to slaughter and grab galley slaves."

"I hate that. I hate all of it," Mek said. "The Westerners aren't *evil*. Raised to harsh notions about honor and bloodshed, certainly. I know some relish fighting, but also, some want escape. Or at least, they question," he added. "You know Waha by now. There are more like him."

"Outsiders." Butterfly grinned. "Like us." She smacked her chest, then hit his shoulder — gallant wanderers.

He'd learned on that first journey with Butterfly and Tanglewood that she'd been raised in the empire, but when her family had gone traveling up above the Dogleg, a raider had come out of nowhere, killed some of the people on the ship and took others as slaves, claiming that since the locals' forefathers were Jun, they belonged by rights to the Jun. *I was left to live or die, with two other children,* she'd said. *We were rescued by some wanderers from the Eel Sect, who raised us to defend ourselves as well as the weak. Because there would never be justice for the poor unless the gods favor you. Better to help the gods by helping yourselves.*

Butterfly lifted a shoulder. "Watch, now. It takes a bit of time."

They sat on the roof pole of a dilapidated warehouse,

reveling in the spring airs as Tanglewood flitted about. It was hard to see her even watching for her, with the deflection charm blurring her silhouette.

The Westerners, toiling away in the aftermath of winning a hard battle, did not notice her. The ships bobbed quietly as laborers rolled barrels up the ramps to the deck. Farther away, prisoners from the conquered imperials were being herded aboard a troop ship, to be dispersed to galleys needing fresh slaves.

Creak! Cra-a-a-ck!

Here and there the curve of a hull seemed to distort slightly. Heave, even. Then came the groan of wood, amid more creaks and cracks.

Then one mast burst out a tendril, curling and groping.

"Hai-yai, what is that!" a Westerner bellowed.

"Fetch the Sage!"

"He's still in a faint!" Mek and his companions had been too late to help in the actual fighting, but Mek and Sagacious Blade had separated the fleet's Cobra Sage from his blood demon Rider, one that had apparently ridden him so long that the Cobra Sage fell down in a faint after Sagacious Blade devoured the thing.

"Those aren't living trees, are they?" Mek asked suddenly, pointing to the curling vine on the mast.

"No. The tendrils are Essence things. They don't take root and become true trees unless the shoots reach soil. If Tanglewood doesn't bring them back inside her cypress, they'll wither and turn to ash—but the ship timbers are left warped where they were, and nothing keeps out water. The ships still float because wood floats, but they'll soon be useless for sailing."

She was right. The ships began to sag, then wallow, awash in seawater as sailors boiled all over like maddened ants, desperately trying to hack off the mysterious tendrils, plug fissures between planks, and block up gaps where knotholes had widened.

A short time later, Tanglewood joined them on the rooftop as Mek considered what he was learning about battling blood demons in the mental realm. Sagacious Blade, so powerful, actually needed him to limit Sagacious Blade's attack to the demons riding their respective Cobra Sages. Mek had begun to perceive how very powerful his silent companion was; she could, if she wanted, crush a human like humans stepped on an insect.

Crack! A Westerner fell overboard while gripping half a rail, vines waving wildly then disintegrating before the man splashed into the sea. Then emerged, howling for a ladder as he cursed.

Laughing, Butterfly nudged Mek, to see that he was oblivious.

She gave up. Useless to scorn Mek for hating war, not after she and Tanglewood had seen him drop to the deck of the scout, his arms curled uselessly over his head, when they'd arrived far too late to help with the battle; the empire ships already had prize crews aboard, and prisoners were being herded aboard the tiger-class ship, to be dispersed among galleys needing fresh slaves...

Hah! A tiger ship began wallowing helplessly. The Westerners shifted to lightening the holds to keep it afloat. The prisoners were now being haphazardly offloaded, along with stores, into lifeboats.

It seemed the stronger Mek's reach with Essence dream-talking, the more he felt victims' pain when the Western raiders cut up their opponents before killing the weak ones.

Though Butterfly had no problem with sending Ghost Eyes on to the next life, Mek wanted to disable all those raiders, keeping the Westerners from being able to venture on the attack into the empire. So here they were, watching their ships turn into driftwood.

And sure enough...

Mek leaned over. "Let's rescue those prisoners."

"I'm for it, but Mek, it's three against a couple thousand. And how will we rescue several hundred prisoners?"

"Look at them, being put in the boats." Tanglewood chuckled, catching up her staff. "You make fog. I'll see what I can do about their weapons. C'mon, Butterfly. It'll be fun."

With the blood demon gone from the Cobra Sage, who was still unconscious, Mek was able to bring up a massive fog, separating out the boats full of prisoners while the Westerners struggled to keep their ships from falling into warped timbers. Butterfly flew from boat to boat, urging them to flee! Now!

The prisoners used chains as their weapons to overcome then toss overboard the few guards, before vanishing into the mist. Mek reflected that those stores might be trade goods seized, not all water or food, but he hoped they would sort themselves out. At any rate, their fate was now up to them.

It was late tiger hour when the three crept into an attic to sleep. The sun was lightening the eastern sky, Mek's fogs drifting away on a wind, when they woke. No sign of the prisoner boats. The galleys were slowly falling apart.

They flew back to the Eagle Island scout, which still lay at anchor beyond the horizon. "There you are," Waha greeted them from the galley, where he sat chopping vegetables. He looked tired, as if he'd been sleepless, watching for them. "We've got a pepper soup simmering. What news?"

"Wait till you hear." Tanglewood flung herself down on the galley bench. And proceeded to entertain the crew with a vivid brag session.

This was now their new pattern.

Using Ze Eight's scout as a floating base, the three flew out to find and waterlog raiders so that the Westerners would have to limp back to wherever they'd sailed from—while Mek and Sagacious Blade conducted a silent war in the mental realm, hunting blood demons. But Tanglewood could only do so much before she had to rest, and let her staff absorb sunlight and rainwater. The more wood she disrupted, the longer her staff required sun and water.

"We have to leave fleets this size to the empire," Mek shouted, and they returned to the scout.

Tanglewood hated these defeats, or what she regarded as defeats. Mek also hated them, because he knew that battle would follow. Nights before sleeping belonged to Anise, but each morning, Mek gave Tai a brief contact when he had something to report. A quick, wordless check to see that all was well with Tai when he had nothing. Tai was beginning to descry how glad Mek was when he had nothing to report—which he did not share with the imperial command, who would never understand Mek. Tai barely understood him himself.

Today, a fleet to report.

Tai walked into Great Ran's command center, and went to the sand table where artists had built simulacra of the islands considered the western boundary of the Empire of the Thousand Islands.

Two captains with kingfisher feathers in their hats attended Supreme Commander Nu. All the others had been dispatched on defensive assignments.

Tai said to her, "My Essence expert reports that there is a fleet of forty raiders, ten lions, ten tigers, the rest jaguars and scouts, heading toward Dancing Cicada Island, here."

Tai stooped to get a closer, clearer view and put a marker down on the little porcelain representation of a small island midway along the long chain of tiny islands off Lan Island's northwest corner.

The first time he'd reported one of Mek's fleet predictions, he was regarded with lingering skepticism. After Supreme Commander Nu sent the newly-arrived fleet from the Silk Islands to the northwest of Great Ran and they found the enemy exactly where Tai had predicted, that ended the distrust.

One of the waiting captains was ordered to set sail at once for Dancing Cicada Island.

Outside, the sky brightened to a warning glare, and bells rang for businesses to close and board up. Gongs crashed. Ships moved to the lee side of the harbor, battened down as tight as possible.

The storm came on fast, the wind rising to a shriek. Though everyone told one another that it wasn't as bad as last year's demon storms, it was bad enough. The next day the moan of the wind came down steadily, and the following morning the sky cleared.

Pigeons began fluttering in.

By now the pigeons had been trained to go from ships stationed along the route to harbor roosts in a long string between Great Ran and the capital at Mountain Peony. Supreme Commander Nu sent daily reports to the emperor, aware that they sometimes appeared in clumps after a day or two of silence. She knew him of old, how silences gnawed at him. Better to send too many pigeons than not enough.

As spring slowly ripened, she mainly had to report losses, until half of the empire's East Fleet was able to arrive as reinforcement. The naval ensign assigned to report to the imperial palace brought good news at last: they'd driven Westerners into retreat from Dancing Cicada Harbor, after the third try. Anchor Island was in the process of being retaken. Lan Island's outer defense was holding.

"Your imperial majesty," the ensign repeated, eyes wide, "according to Supreme Commander Nu, there is an unknown Essence-expert helping us. A hermit, according to Relay Captain Hou. The hermit finds fleets... somehow... Captain

Ryu thinks by divination. He tells the Liaison Officer Je Tai, who reports them to the Supreme Commander."

The emperor, remembering what he'd been told about Coral Island, thought he knew who this hermit was—though the ferrets had not been able to locate him. Though they had managed to produce three surprised and terrified Ki Meks, whom he'd restored to their blameless lives, with gold to ease the way.

Since this mysterious Ki Mek seemed to be aiding in the war, the emperor issued a quiet order to abandon the summons he'd issued last autumn. "I will direct Je Tai to bring him," he told the ferret chief. "But that will be after the danger from the West is resolved. I must think of a suitable reward, in order to keep such a talent serving the empire."

Altogether the latest news was more hopeful, he understood that battles on the sea could be as ephemeral in consequence as they appeared to be once they were over: nothing in sight, except maybe flotsam. There would be no real resolution until the Western commander surrendered. Or died.

Or he did.

But he no longer worried at that in the long hours of the night, because of a piece of news that delighted him more than anything else in recent years, and infused him with a sense of renewal: the imperial physicians' firm assertion that an imperial grandchild was well on the way.

The news was a relief to the Sixth Imperial Consort, for at last the imperial court's sideways looks at her, the whispered songs and plays about her barrenness after only one child, might fade away. The new generation would resolve *that!*

Venshai was the last of the imperial circle to find out. He'd seen the imperial physicians come up to the tower once or twice, but always assumed it had to do with the crown princess's demon temperament. Her servants did not talk to his at all, and he'd become so wary of her that he'd begun avoiding her altogether unless she sought him.

He learned the news at one of those dinners with the Sixth Imperial Consort and her wolf brothers, when the princess paled as a pungent dish of peppered fish was brought in.

The princess pressed her fingers to her lips, her eyes closed, and the Sixth Imperial Consort patted her on the shoulder. "I'll ring for ginger tea, my dear girl. Remember, the sickness is temporary. Nearly every woman gets it. But it won't last. Soon you'll be waking halfway through the night and demanding breakfast before turtle hour turns to tiger."

Venshai understood then, and managed not to exclaim his surprise. No one needed to know how little he and the crown princess had to say to the other. He'd completely lose face before these accursed Yimus.

But the very next day, he kept his promise to his favorite down at the Perfumed Fan, went to her family, and married her as a consort on the spot. And scarcely fifteen days later, he added another consort, one he'd just met and liked—mostly because he could.

No one said a word about it. He'd done his part. The emperor had his longed-for grandchild on the way. And Father wasn't even there to have some reason for caution, for prudence, for a need to think ahead for the next twenty years, instead of getting his reward for the labor and pain he was going through, *now*.

The turtle never talks to the hawk, as the saying goes. The imperial crown princess had no idea about these consorts until her mother complained about them one day during a visit. "Two consorts within one month. I hope that Ji rat of yours doesn't intend to start adding them on a regular basis, or *he* can find room for them."

"Consorts?" the crown princess repeated.

The Sixth Imperial Consort lifted her finely drawn brows. "Did you not know? Pah! If you don't talk to him, I don't find I blame you, now that the child is safely on the way. But don't go adding your own consorts until well after the birth," she scolded. "We cannot have any snide songs or mask-play whispers about impure blood. The world has to see the next heir from the imperial crown princess and the Ji prince born, named, and passed the Hundred Days, before you can start snapping up pretty boys from the playhouses."

"I don't want any strange men around anyway," the imperial crown princess muttered.

"Just as well. Just as well." The Sixth Imperial Consort shrugged.

Summer brightened, then began to wane, marked by fleet actions off the southern end of the empire. Late in summer, a raider fleet attacked the Ice Fortress defenders at the fork east of Ten Leopards — but the Dragon Claw army fought them off in a bitter, bloody engagement that decided nothing, other than ending many lives, and causing Mek to fly off for a couple of days to one of the towering heights that Old Uncle had shown him, where no one could find him. Tai got a brief contact: wordless, somehow more in need of reassurance that all was as before, than reassuring. Anise, whom Mek reached for every night before he slept, she sensed the pain he could not hide from her, and thought over and over, *I love you, I love you.*

At least he and Sagacious Blade won their private battle, eliminating two blood demon Riders from a pair of Cobra Sages as both fleets retreated with heavy damage, outcome undecided after cannon fire through a day and night.

Mek said nothing before he left, and nothing when he returned to the scout ship, which sailed southward again on its long patrol back and forth between the two empires.

Except for Anise's unswerving support whenever he reached across the mental realm for her, he was alone in this battle in the mental realm. And those reached were more brief by the day. He sensed the blood demons searching, and he could not bear the thought of one surreptitiously sneaking up to surprise them, and attacking Anise, who had no defense. But she stubbornly refused to accept his silence as long as he needed her. And he lived for those brief scintillations of joy, of limitless love.

His training with Sagacious Blade — if it could be called training in the usual sense, as there was no talk involved, and no practice — had taken him beyond the reach of Butterfly and Tanglewood, much less any of the other flyers who had gradually gathered at Eagle Island, when word went out that the spring competition had been postponed because of the war.

Mek discovered that he had gone beyond the other flyers both figuratively and literally. He was used to soaring impossibly high now. At first his travels were only in the mental realm, but Sagacious Blade infused him with the fire of Essence, keeping him warm at those great heights. The constantly weaving, tumbling wind dragons — barely visible, no more than a coruscation in the air on scale and streaming whiskers — brought him enough air. He could spy on Cobra Sages from the cover of those wind dragons; though they were nearly invisible to Mek, they were completely impenetrable to blood demons.

After Sagacious Blade devoured the two blood demons, Mek sensed an intensifying awareness reaching westward, and discovered that he could now differentiate Cobra Sages from their demon riders. Not just that. He descried differences in the demons. There seemed to be some more like Sagacious Blade. There was one, very far off, that appeared to be more like a true healer, delighting in repairing—could that possibly be Odval and Ardal's brother, the mysterious Windseed? He dared not probe. There was far too much vigilant threat from the prowling blood demons; the Cobra Sages seemed to select for the enormous appetites, yawning for life Essence. These blood demons lent their hosts most power. Though demanding an escalating cost in blood—

Sitting on the deck of the scout, he did his breathing, and *reached*. He was scanning at such a distance that Ardal sensed him, opened her mental door, and they found one another. "Kimek!"

It was still strange to have to port his mind over into that other language; he could not stem her flood of stress-driven images, unknown faces, idioms he didn't know, and above all helpless worry before they both sensed a change in the atmosphere and in effect slammed their mental doors.

Mek fell back on his elbows. Vertigo swerved sickeningly, then the world righted itself, his body immediately adapting to the chop and slap of brine against the hull. It was dark, the noises comfortingly familiar: the creak of wood, a quiet step elsewhere on the deck as the single person on night duty prowled around to keep awake. His senses were painfully heightened. He could hear the slumber of the crew, specifically Waha's harsh breathing as he slept below. A nightmare? But he had no permission to open that door uninvited.

And he was so very tired. He lay back on the deck in the warm summer air, closed his eyes, and sorted the jumble of worries and warnings he'd retrieved from Ardal, beginning with the worst: *they're coming*.

The night sky had shifted while he'd been scanning. It was somewhere near tiger hour, the last before dawn.

He rose, and went to grab Sagacious Blade from the tiny cubby he shared with Waha. He barely made out Waha's form on the bed, twisting as if in pain, and smelled the sharp scent of sweat. Fear sweat.

He ventured a step, and stretched out a hand, not quite touching Waha, and tried to draw off the pain and fear, but Waha groaned audibly.

Mek recoiled as if he'd been slapped away. He took hold of the sword and launched into the air, soaring fast and high until a knot of wind dragons absorbed him into their midst, dancing and playful. They sped with him high over the clouds, until he saw the vast expanse of Great Ran below, discernible in the darkness by ruddy, glimmering dragons made by curving street lamps, as no street in the empire was straight.

When he reached what had to be the command garrison — it looked like a palace, and probably was one — he landed, sheathed Sagacious Blade, put a deflection over himself, and walked inside. If he was too early, he could always write a note, he decided as he evaded alert patrols.

But then he found Je Tai sitting at an early breakfast with an older woman. She had to be the supreme commander whom Tai had mentioned.

"I'm here," Mek said to Tai. He spoke softly, but the two both jumped, the woman's gaze going to the door, her brow furrowed. "It's all right," Mek assured her. "Nobody is lax. They can't see me. It's an Essence matter."

"Ayeee!" one exclaimed, backing away as if they might catch it.

Tai slewed around, laying aside a dispatch. "Mek, you're *here*. There must be something very wrong."

"Yes. No. Yes. That's why I came. It's so much easier to come than trying to explain this way." Mek tapped his forehead. "The First Prince is launching everything straight toward you here." And he recited precise numbers.

"That sounds like everything," Tai murmured.

"Ardal seems to think he has to, though she did not say why. I doubt she'd be able to tell me. You remember how far away Angja was from their capital. Her sister is in the capital, covertly working against the Cobra Sages under the leadership of their mother, and that's part of Ardal's worry."

"Really," Tai said, and he, too, had to struggle with that frozen memory of a teenage girl who used to bring unwanted sweet things. His interest spiked.

"Anyway," Mek continued, "Ardal is using all her Essence power to shroud Angja in case we come to retaliate, or look for vengeance — because that's what they'd do. Or something.

Which means she'll be keeping her mental door shut very tight. I thought you should know."

Tai said, "Coming straight for Great Ran?"

"Yes."

"Does that mean they're bringing all their Cobra Sages?"

Mek shifted on his feet. "It's really the Cobra Sages' blood demons that are the biggest threat, because they don't care who wins or loses..."

"They crave blood," Tai said. "I remember. Ours or theirs, it matters little. Is there anything we can do militarily to prepare for these blood demons? Or is it all an Essence matter?"

"Ay. But I'm fighting them." Mek ran a finger along Sagacious Blade.

Tai studied Mek, his concern looking like doubt. "You *alone?*"

"Yes...and no." Mek didn't like to mention Sagacious Blade before others, and endure all the misapprehensions about demons. Yet implying he was alone sounded arrogant.

Tai said, "We will heed your words."

Supreme Commander Nu, wondering how to report this conversation to the emperor, broke in. "Do get further reports to us as you can."

Mek bowed to her, hands clasped gallant wanderer-style, and conscientiously left through the door.

She watched him go, then got up to ask if the two sentries—still quite alert—had spoken to the young man who'd just left, to hear, "What young man, Supreme Commander?" She went back inside. "Very...*unusual* encounter. Is that young man playing the pig to eat the tiger?"

How to explain Mek? He might seem simple, oblivious to protocol and ritual, but... Tai said finally, "I expect that the Cobra Sages would claim that *he* is the tiger."

She looked a little surprised, then glanced thoughtfully at the markers on the strategic map. Markers recommended by Mek had been tagged with green, to separate them from reports along regular command chains. Each had been tagged with a blue Circle marker to indicate that the intelligence had led to successful rout of the enemy, or in three cases, defeat of smaller raider fleets.

"It seems we had better pull in everyone we can," the supreme commander said, bending over the map.

While she spoke, Mek was already soaring back to the

scout. The galley shone with welcome lamplight. It was as quiet as he had left it. He found Waha standing with a small knife, with an array of vegetables before him. Stressed he'd been for days, but now he looked wan, even sweaty, though the air was cool. Mek set Sagacious Blade down outside the door, and entered. "Waha? You were having a nightmare when I left. What can I do?" His gaze strayed to the vegetables. He could at least help with that task, but where was the knife?

He heard a quick, indrawn breath and Waha's step, then pain burned along the side of his neck, flashing to ice-burn before his surprised body could react. He tried to move, but his limbs had turned to stone. Stone! His weakness—he tried to protest, then his mind registered poison and faster than thought he sealed the mental door shut between him and the physical world, dimly aware of Waha catching him as he fell.

Then darkness.

Sixty-One

WAHA KNELT IN THE center of the enclave's biggest gathering hall, surrounded by everyone at Ten Leopards.

He wanted to die. By his hand of theirs, no longer mattered. Get it done.

A circle of closed faces surrounded him, the flushed, angry ones mostly belonging to the Ki family, who on discovering that the spring competition had been cancelled, had sailed over to help defend the island.

Waha knelt head bowed, his right forearm still bleeding beneath an awkwardly tied bandage. He welcomed the throb, but the ache did not lessen his awareness of the Kis glaring at him, some with hands gripping the handles of their knives. They were very ready to kill him. As had been the crew of the scout ship once they combined together and got him flat to the deck after his unsuccessful attempt to cut the demon-cursed tattoo out of his arm.

But Ze Eighth Cousin, the captain of the scout, had said, "I smell the stink of poison. There's more going on here than it looks. Anyway, Eagle Island doesn't kill without evidence. We'll take him back to Ten Leopards and turn him over to the elders."

From then on until their arrival he was invisible to the others, except for grim side-eye now and then that would have made him laugh if it had been aimed at anyone else. He had been equally shunned after their landing. But on seeing him after their arrival, Auntie Mim had stated, "There will be no judgment until all evidence has been presented."

And she said it now that everyone had been assembled in

this circle. "We will listen to all the evidence before deciding together what is to be done. That is Eagle Island's way. If you do not agree, there's the door." She looked around, and in a milder voice, "Where is Anise?"

"We put her to bed," Tian-Tian said. And with an ugly look Waha's way that he felt as a whiplash on the spirit, "She hasn't slept for days. Ever since Mek stopped visiting her dreams—"

"Enough," Auntie Mim said, and looked at everyone but Waha. "Since we don't know when Ze Bian can get here, will you accept my presiding as elder?"

Everyone except Waha shouted *aye!*

Auntie Mim said, "Ze Eight? We'll begin with you."

The scout ship captain made a warding motion. "I was asleep the entire time. Woke to Tanglewood fighting for the knife in Waha's hand. When she got him snarled with her staff, he dropped the weapon. We tied him up—"

Here, Tanglewood called out, "He was trying to kill himself. Not me."

"One at a time," Auntie Mim said as others began shouting questions and comments, and when it was quiet, "Where is the weapon?"

"Here," Butterfly said, pointing to tray holding a small paring knife with a black handle, the sheath beside it. Waha looked away, sick with nausea, as Auntie Mim picked up the tray and moved around the circle to display it.

Eight went on, "I believe the knife was poisoned. Besides Mek's blood—*quiet!*—there was the smell of venom on the blade and in its sheath. Nua?"

Auntie Nua said, "I sensed Essence in the poison, a rare and very dangerous charm that took me two days to track down. In an ancient scroll Old Uncle left me from his master, translated from a Jun Suai shaman. I don't know what they used it for. But I doubt the purpose was healing."

Hisses and angry murmurs rose, then died as Auntie Mim turned to Butterfly. "I think that covers the weapon. Now for direct witness."

It was clear to Waha that Butterfly had had plenty of time to think out what to say during the three days as the scout sailed back to Ten Leopards. "When I woke before dawn, Mek was gone. I thought it strange that he'd gone alone, so I woke Tanglewood, and we went to find him. He was tired. We knew that. He'd been looking bad ever since that battle on the water."

She pointed east. "He hears it when they're dying." She tapped her head.

Several stirred as if to speak, and she raised her voice. "We did a wide circle, seeing nothing. We must have missed him. We were coming back when we saw light in the galley. No lamps had been lit when we left. The fires were still cold. We started down when we saw Waha out on deck. He was staggering like a drunk. He fell to his knees as if someone had hit him. Then—before we could fly down to help him—we saw him pick up Sagacious Blade, and throw the sword into the ocean."

Another hiss of comments. Butterfly said, louder, "We knew something had to be wrong. We stayed in the air, circling—and then saw a huge shadow."

"It was like an absence of light," Tanglewood said, arms wide.

"Then it rippled, kind of, and we realized there was a ship-sized deflection charm. We saw a man rowing a small boat from the shadow. Which was a scout galley, the oars still. Bare arms, with tattoos up them. We started down to confront him but then there was the hiss of arrows—they could see us from the shadow-ship, and we'd just got in range. We had to fly up, while that man got on our deck. Raised a hand toward Waha. His fingers glowed green."

"Green," Tanglewood repeated. "But orangish, too. Essence charm."

Butterfly went on. "We separated and flew up and around to come at the ship from different directions, but Waha got Mek, who was limp. They kept shooting at us he dropped Mek into the boat. Then he yelped, clutching his head. Tanglewood tried to blink away the deflection charm but it was strong."

"It was like trying to see underwater. And when I got close, they began shooting again. Only my staff saved me," Tanglewood said.

"That's when a storm broke. It wasn't natural," Butterfly added. "Lightning stabbing near us. *At* us. We flew away, meaning to follow that ship, but by the time the storm dispersed, we couldn't find it. We fought against the winds and sleet, found the scout, and found Waha trying to cut the tattoo out of his forearm. Tanglewood stopped him."

"That's what must have stirred up these storms the past few days," Ki Zar exclaimed, and everyone had an opinion to offer, until once again Auntie Mim raised her hand.

Then she pointed at Waha. "Now it's your turn." She sat on a stool nearby, her fists on her knees as she looked narrow-eyed at the two young Ki cousins holding knives.

Waha sighed heavily. "Just kill me. It'll be faster. All this talk is nothing more than mending the pen after the sheep are dead."

"Don't say that!" a Ki cousin spoke up, spat to the side three times, and waved to ward off bad luck.

Auntie Mim glared.

When it was quiet, Waha said to the floor, "I first met Sidax on Owlfrost's ship *Yufi*. At Anchor Island. After a demon storm. He and two others were shipwrecked refugees. Or so they said. I'm sure two of them were," he amended. "It was Sidax who I suspect now was a Cobra Sage. At the time he said there was gossip that a search on for Kimek. I think now that *he* was the search. We made friends—more than friends. We'd get drink. He liked hearing my adventures."

He gazed down at the furrows he'd carved in his arm, but despite the gashes, the tattoo was still crisp, clear, and wickedly beautiful. The charm on it still unbroken.

"In time I told him about meeting Kimek. Though I never mentioned the names of this island or Eagle Island—I was afraid he might innocently tell some spy for the snakes. Isn't that ironic?" He uttered a bitter sound that no one took as laughter. "Anyway. One morning I woke up after a lot of drink, to find this tattoo. Don't remember asking for it. Thought it was a gift. Everyone admired it."

He glanced up briefly as Mek's eldest brother admitted, "I thought so, too. Everybody did."

Waha shook his head. "I don't know anything about Essence. And—you can kill me now and I won't raise a hand in defense, but I have to say, none of you who do noticed anything wrong, either. Kimek noticed nothing wrong."

"He'd have to touch it," Auntie Nua spoke up. "Only Old Uncle might have been able to suspect something."

Everyone who had known Old Uncle made the sign of peace to placate any possible wandering ghost.

"What I'm saying is, no one knew there was some charm put in the tattoo. Then we sailed in search of the raiders. I began having nightmares. I couldn't talk about them. If I tried, I'd get nauseous. Hadn't slept for days. Until that night, when I had night duty. I'd dozed, then woke up with my arm on fire. Or so I thought. When I plunged my arm in the rain barrel, there was Sidax's voice. In my head. Told me to use the knife at the bottom of my travel bag. I dumped out my bag, and there it was. I had never felt it there!"

"A deflection charm aimed at touch," Auntie Nua said. "You would not notice it except as another thing, until you sought for it."

"I said no. He set my arm on fire, so badly I nearly blacked out. I think I did. I tried, twice, to tell Ze Eight. The crew. Both times, he used pain to drive me to the deck. Said if I didn't obey, I'd be burned from inside until I begged for death. All I had to do is mark Kimek. He wouldn't even be hurt."

"And you believed that?" Mek's father snarled, wiping his eyes.

Waha turned on him. "Of course I didn't believe it. But I did not understand until it happened that every time I fought Sidax, he…he learned my body from the inside. Until the end there, he took control. He could see through my eyes." He poked his fingers at his eyes, now wide with pain and horror. "Though I fought him even then, but lost. And *how* he relished my losing. It was more intimate than…" Once again the pain, but this was self-inflicted, utter betrayal and humiliation.

Waha sighed. Get it over, he told himself. "Their ship was *right there*. Lightning struck. Mek was gone. So was his sword. I went into the galley determined to cut out the tattoo and if I couldn't, to chop off my arm. You heard the rest."

For a long breath, no one spoke.

Mek's elder brother spoke up in a low voice as he stared at Waha in horror. "You mean that Cobra Sage is looking out of his eyes at us right now?"

Waha gave his head a weary shake. "I'd know. At the end. When he was possessing me, I think I heard some of his own thoughts. He was debating whether to turn Mek over to the Ganis Cobra Sage Kian as he'd been ordered. He might be going straight to the Sun. In Baris Tharan, the capital."

"Sun?" someone asked.

"They have levels of rank. Power. You know their rank by their tattoo, because Cobra Sages don't wear merit necklaces." Waha brushed fingers over his collarbones, then touched his forehead with its headband-covered tattoo. "The Cobra Sages work charms into tattoos through blood. Like slave tattoos. Like

Sidax did to this." He slapped his forearm. "Anyway, Sun is the supreme sage. *He with the red eyes,* as we—as it's said in the west."

"The red eyes are literal, Mek told us. That's the blood demon looking out," Butterfly murmured, fists clenched.

Everyone began whispering, and Auntie Mim raised her hand.

Butterfly's temper was beginning to cool. She'd believed until this meeting that Waha would end up dead. She had wanted it. Mek! Who couldn't bear to squash a stinging bug! She'd told Tanglewood that if the rest were squeamish, she'd have no problem slitting Waha's throat.

But the horror of having your mind subsumed by someone else's will and your body taken over, even if for moments, had shaken that conviction—while not entirely eradicating it. "This is really evil," she began, and when the others agreed, she went on more firmly, "Here's my suggestion. Waha either dies here, or he shows us the way to wherever the Ghost Eye capital is, if that's where they're taking Mek."

Then everybody began talking, some shouting to be heard. It took Auntie Mim longer to get control. Then she said, "First of all, Mek would be the first to say no executions. If we do mount a rescue attempt, it must be entirely voluntary."

"That's right," Ze Eight said.

Auntie Mim went on, "And while my heart yearns to set sail now, my head shies like a donkey at the gate. From everything I've ever heard, you would never get near their capital, even if you were showed the way."

"It's true," Waha said dully. "I was born there. Every second person is in the military in some wise. Cobra Sages everywhere. If you look even slightly suspicious, they're on you fast enough."

Butterfly exchanged glances with Tanglewood, who nodded. "I believe it. But there is a way. Mek told us the entire story of his slave days. He told us about the mines. He told us about the blueneck birds. And he told us about a barge full of performers who go to the capital fairly often."

Waha's eyes narrowed. "Siu. Snowhawk… It's true…"

Tanglewood chuckled, and one or two sensed the playful lashing of nine tails. "Seems to me, if Sidax can pretend to be an entertainer, so can we."

Waha's eyes closed. He had sworn never to return. There

was nothing in the West but trouble waiting if he were to be identified. But in agonizing conflict, those vivid memories of Mek, a scrap of a boy healing Diggy, without even thinking of bargaining first, as any sensible person would. Same with his offer to break all their slave tattoos. Waha knew that he'd been a fool, following Tai when the true fire mountain was right here all along. Mek was more than a fire mountain, he was like a comet. And dour old Diggy of all people had seen it. *Stay with him.*

He opened his eyes. "I'll do it." Ah, there was the singing blood of risk. What better stake than his own life? "Except, what if my presence leads us to a trap? Because any time he wants, Sidax can look through my eyes. What if he tries right now, while we're planning? I'd know he's there, but I can't stop him."

Auntie Nua looked with pity into his haggard face, guessing what the cost of such a violation of soul had been. "No. He can't. Mim and I put up charms at all twelve points around this room. As for that tattoo, I don't think I can completely break the charm. I know nothing of using blood for such matters. But believe I can cobble together a deflection into that tattoo, so any time he might chance to test it, he would always think you are deeply asleep, too deep to invade your dreams. It's a bit like putting a picture in place of a mirror. He'd know at once if he troubled to press the matter, but would he, now that you've fulfilled your use to him?"

"I'm willing to try," Waha said, and turned his dark-circled eyes to Ze Eight, then to Butterfly.

Butterfly gave him a small nod. "I'm willing, too. Though with this warning: Waha, if you start acting the way we saw you, I *will* slit your throat."

Waha's voice husked, "Agreed."

Tanglewood clapped her hands and rubbed them. "We've already lost five days. Let's get sailing."

Five days had passed since Mek's surprise visit. Six. Then seven, and Tai found himself waking earlier and earlier lest he miss one of those brief contacts through the mental door. But there was no door, just him inside his own head. It was if Mek had completely vanished.

Each day had to be bringing the Westerners' invasion fleet closer. The military people debated the best defenses, conversations Tai stayed out of. He'd shared what little experience he had—now, he suspected, his interpolations, even questions, would just be adding to the noise.

On the eighth day, he rose after another sleepless night, and decided that this was a useless way to proceed. When he reached the command center, he caught a few tight-browed glances his way, and suspected that his presence was mere distraction, now that he was not relaying Mek's words.

He went to the supreme commander, who alone remained calm, attentive, serious. "May I requisition a vessel to do some scouting?"

"Still no work from your hermit?" she asked.

"None."

"Do you think sailing out into the ocean will produce him?" She made a gesture toward the sand table, indicating the vastness of the ocean beyond the empire's western border.

He said, "I'd like to explore around Anchor Island."

He'd told her far more about his days with Mek than he'd told anyone else—even his father. She remembered very well his description of the privateer sisters. She understood his reluctance to mention them now—oh, the storm of questions that would arise! "Treating with the enemy." Sometimes, "the enemy" was not at all easy to define.

"I think that might be a good idea," she stated. And issued the orders.

Tai bowed, grateful for her understanding. And for her lack of question; though he had no plan, he had a goal: to find Mek. If he had to chase all the way to Angja, he would do that.

Or even farther.

SIXTY-TWO

THE EMPEROR WAS AWARE of the dearth of news, though distracted as the tenth month arrived. The physicians had predicted that the imperial grandchild would appear toward the waning of Phoenix moon.

Sky Wishes Day passed. The emperor remembered how enormous the Sixth Imperial Consort had been in those last days. Even her celestial beauty had given way to a red face and a graceless effort in rising and sitting, though he had cherished her the more for these signs of the event to come. He felt the same way now, if possible even more intensely. It was even possible that much of his own internal discomfort was sympathetic pains. "These are a known phenomenon," the physicians assured him — hoping they spoke the truth.

When the emperor looked back, it seemed to him that he'd been so vigorous in those days, nearly fifty. He had made it past seventy, though he had not believed it would be possible. Once the empire was safe, and his dynasty was assured of progeny, he'd have accomplished everything he wanted most…

He rose to a cold day, reaching first for the handwarmer to ease the shivering, when one of his personal graywings rushed noiselessly in, eyes wide.

"Is it happening?" he asked, chills — long familiar, though he didn't remember a fall quite so cold — forgotten.

It was happening.

He'd been warned that first babies could take a long time, and he forced his mind to the never-ending flow of imperial demands, but it took only a day after all. The empress appeared that night, bearing a tiny bundle wrapped in the softest cloths, the Sixth Imperial Consort walking at her shoulder. "Our blessed grandson," the empress whispered, her eyes moist. And bent to show off the wizened little face.

"And our blessed daughter?"

"Sleeping, your imperial majesty. She's very tired, but quite well," the Sixth Imperial Consort said proudly, with a sly glance at the empress.

"That is excellent news."

He smiled down at the infant's tiny face. Spidery fingers reaching, as if testing the air. "I shall think of you as my little dragon," he murmured. "My dragon of peace." Though it didn't do to name future emperors 'Dragon'. He'd think of a suitable name, one that would look good in future records.

The little face puckered, and a thin cry issued forth.

The empress looked startled, then worried, and a hovering nursemaid was beckoned to take charge of the infant.

"I want reports every watch," the emperor stated, before a fit of coughing.

The others, knowing that these fits could last a long time, bowed themselves out. He fought for breath, then wiped his lips without looking at the cloth. He knew what he'd see. "Gold for every servant in the imperial heir's household," he rasped. "For his noble highness Prince Venshai, ten horses of pure white, ten bolts of the best lily and acanthus brocade, and for my dear daughter, twenty pieces of the finest jade, to be made into rings or hairpins or necklaces, she is to choose. Twenty bolts of lily and acanthus brocade."

A hovering graywing bowed and scurried off to see these done, and the empress said, "I will leave first, and pray for child and mother to flourish."

The gracious "I will leave first" was a politeness that also carried an implied meaning, when leaving a group that included someone of superior rank: it in effect meant leaving the others to private converse with that superior. This was the empress's single acknowledgment of the years that the Sixth Imperial Consort had tried to oust her, one of those ways being to linger longest with the emperor — with his full cooperation in the earlier days, when he was besotted.

She could leave first, and tranquilly, too: he would never set her aside, though she had failed at the single most important requirement of an empress.

The Sixth Imperial Consort begged her to enjoy good health

until they saw one another again, all part of the ritual, and about as meaningful as the used air it took to speak the words.

The Sixth Imperial Consort was left in possession of the field, though she knew by now that nothing was going to change. Still, she began to fuss about the emperor until he caught her wrist and said, "Lily, beloved, you might encourage your esteemed brothers to permit these eager young students to gain from their wisdom. I speak in particular of the Ji scholars your hard-working noble son-in-law is bringing to the benefit of court and empire; reassure your venerable relations that they can trust to the insight that caused them to favor his noble highness Ji Venshai's suit initially."

The words were praise on the surface, the tone mild, the hand fond, but though she had not been raised to court, and still lacked the precision in court speech that the nobles had been drilled in since infancy, she knew she'd received a slap. And she was now required to convey that slap to her brothers.

The emperor, it seemed, was aware of the intensifying duel for power between Ji and Yimu. And for whatever reason, he was favoring the Ji.

She fussed a bit more, making sure he was warm, and that his ginger tea was fresh, then she bowed herself out, teeth gritted. It was so unjust!

She had no real control over any of them, but here *she* had to eat the north wind, while the men responsible for those excesses carried on just as they liked, all this right after she had seen to it that the emperor had his precious grandchild at last. Was anyone ever as wronged as she?

The days got progressively colder, a clean wind—no longer fouled by the unnatural heat rising skyward from the southeast—blowing straight west.

The wind that favors one is a curse to those coming from the other direction. The First Prince's dragon-prowed war galleys sailed in the teeth of this wind-driven current, until a storm whirled down from the icy reaches of the north, joined the wind, and tore across the sea, driving his fleet southward, scattering them like strewn seeds. It took time to regroup and set forth again, oars dipping and pulling as they once again fought their way eastward toward riches and glory.

The same wind sped Sidax toward his own expected riches and glory. He reached the capital in far better time than he'd believed possible, and bore his captive in triumph to the Cobra Sages' impenetrable fortress.

He then sauntered to the outer chamber to petition for an interview with the Sun, confident that when they found out who he'd captured, there would be a leap in rank over Diamond Sage Kian. But when he arrived at the outer chamber desk, he had to hide his shock. Diamond Sage Kian waited there, along with a pair of hunters in black and the masks of the Cobra Sage hunt.

She gave him a malicious smile—but before she could speak, a runner appeared, bowed to everyone in sight, and piped in the hieratic voice of someone who knows he's merely a mouthpiece for the Words of Rank: "The Sun has issued a summons to Sage Sidax on behalf of the obsidian throne."

Kian's smile widened, though not reaching her unblinking eyes. "You should have reported straight to me," she gloated with all the affront of one whose underling had tried a tiger's leap over their head. "You are really in trouble now."

We shall leave the both of them to this jurisdictional dispute, and return to Mek, who lay where he'd been dropped in a lightless cell.

He had managed to close his awareness inside his mental citadel before the poison could freeze his mind to stone. He was thus able to crack the mental door now and then in order to gauge the danger. He sensed movement for a long time—he lost count of those brief checks—figuring he had been put on a ship. Ship, cart, stretcher…and at last, firm ground. Stone outside as well as in.

He had no fear of stone. But this was not real stone, it was a poison that emulated stone. The instinct to escape by sinking to the center of the world to dream along with the dragons had to be resisted. It was an escape that could only end with his death.

As soon as his body lay unmoved for two, then three checks, he widened the tiny crack in the door long enough to send a sliver of awareness along his meridians to assess the poison. Then he formed a tiny, tiny glint of Essence light, and pushed it out to float to the Elemental Fire Phase acupoint in the notch between his brows, to counterbalance Stone Phase. He waited for his tiny blob of Essence light to settle, sink in—and to refill with the green of poison, leaving only clear water behind in the acupoint.

Then the light, fueled by the Essence it had converted, moved to the next acupoint. And the next.

He sensed a tendril of question—and snap! Withdrew, though leaving the tiny light stealthily doing its job. As soon as the Essence charm wore off, he would need to eat and drink again, or his body would not survive. So his next check had to be much sooner.

This time, he caught a rhythm, as if something had been chanting in a temple, over and over: *…Angja… Ardal… Odval.*

Startled, he paused, listening. *Kimek, here is aid. Remember Angja? Ardal? Odval?* Those were the only words, but there came a sense of kinship.

Ready to withdraw, he responded: *You?*

"No name. It was taken when I was small. I am chaff, floating on a breeze…think of me as Windseed." This time the thought came in words—the words of Father Dragon's Chosen. Mek had been brought West.

"I know you," Mek thought tentatively, and there was the briefest glimpse of Odval, acknowledged by the other.

"You have been brought to the capital. But we saw to it that Jhax of Ganis knows. Cobra Sage Kian also found out, by her own conduits. She is no ally of yours. Be wary of Kian."

With the "we" came an image of a constellation of stars set against a night sky. No obsidian blades, or blood, but the context was an ongoing struggle.

"Windseed," Mek acknowledged, cautiously grateful.

"I will return when I can. Rest. Concentrate on recovery. We cannot get to you yet. You may have to go to the ring. But if so, it will be on the military side. Not hidden in the depths here, where you can be bled and devoured. Hide your strength if you can! Do not become interesting to Sun!"

He had never heard 'Sun' before, but an image flickered: the red-eyed human whose blood demon strove to *eat* the sun and all light below it. A title of the most terrible irony, then.

Once again wordless gratitude from Mek, then Windseed withdrew.

Mek shut himself in, and worked the stealthy counteraction of the poison.

The wind also favored Tai's scout. As soon as the captain said they ought to be nearing Anchor Island, Tai settled himself, shut his eyes, and began shouting mentally, *Mek, Mek, Mek.* And when that produced only silence, as if he shouted at a stone wall, he tried *Owlfrost, Owlfrost, Owlfrost.* He still had no answer, but the inward sensation was subtly different, as if the wind carried his words away.

When he was too tired to keep it up, he roused, discovered he'd lost a day, and forced himself to eat, drink, exercise by moving vigorously around the tiny deck, then compose himself for rest before resuming the shout.

Then quite suddenly, there she was. "Jetai?"

The distinct aura of intense guilt reached him with the words, "If you can get away from your Mud minders, you'll find Zan and Siu on the west harbor. I'll send them now."

He contained his impatience as the scout worked its way around the island to the west-side harbor, recently recaptured by the imperials. The sound of sawing and hammering met his ears.

He debarked, reported to headquarters, then he set out to stroll about. He soon spotted Siu. Next to him, Zan, no longer a teen, but still slim and wiry. The dog Mek had adopted from Angja sat at her feet, tongue lolling, his coat a shining chestnut color.

Siu, Zan, and Tai recognized one another at once.

"I'm looking for Mek—Kimek," Tai said, low, in the Western tongue.

Siu's smile vanished. "He was taken by the Cobra Sages. That's why Owlfrost is risking this meeting. She's below the horizon there." He tipped his head backward. "We were all deceived by that nightcrawler Sidax, pretending to be a theater player."

"Where would they take Mek?" Tai asked, his nerves chilling.

"To the capital," Zan whispered. "Either the snakes will want to use poison to take away his mind, or else they'll put him in the ring to bleed out his life for them to do…whatever it is they do with blood."

Fury burned through Tai. He stared down at the warped wharf boards as the other two waited. First Prince Toshan was on the way—with all those Essence-wielding Cobra Sages. Tai could do absolutely nothing about that.

But Mek could.

He lifted his head. "Would Owlfrost take me there, to try to rescue him?"

Two faces eased into somewhat bleak smiles. "That's why we are here," Siu said. "We've a boat waiting."

"Give me one incense stick," Tai said.

"We'll be here," Zan said, and the dog barked, wagging his tail.

Tai raced back to fetch his things. Urgency gripped him. The Cobra Sages had Mek? How long could he survive their cruelties?

He left a note on the bunk where he had been invited to rest: *I go to rescue my hermit.* He dropped the brush neatly on the inkstone and ran out. At the end of the street, a small temple to the Crane God stood. Tai hesitated. Mek was not abandoned. But he was a prisoner, of enemies Tai could not fight on his own.

He laid the last of his imperial coins in the offering tray, reached for a plain strip of worn cloth, and wrote only the one word, *Mek*. If the gods truly listened, then they would surely know Ki Mek, and what Tai wanted.

He flung the talisman up into the young redbark tree growing behind the shrine, then sped away to where Siu and Zan waited.

Sixty-three

Snowhawk's Dachi and Owlfrost's *Yufi* met up within a complex coral reef around a ring of ridges, as if a fire mountain had nearly submerged itself long ago. Any ship within that ring was effectively invisible to the outside seas, and the coral reefs just below the surface bore the remains of many a ship that tried to chase those who knew this secret retreat. Its treacherous entrance, only navigable at high tide, had never been noted on any chart, but had to be taught.

Diggy was the first person Tai saw, tall and strong as an oak and grim of demeanor. But his ugly face eased a little when he saw Tai, and he gave a slow nod, as if Tai's arrival was not merely expected, but went some way toward reestablishing a sense of rightness, though he said very little, as always.

Tai was surprised to discover Waha and some Eagle Island gallant wanderers on *Dachi*. During the greetings and introductions, Waha lacked the lazy smile that had seemed a vital part of his personality.

Waha accepted with bitter irony that his assumption Tai had buried himself in his archive for the rest of his life had been as wrong as all his other decisions of late. He said abruptly, "Mek was taken because of me."

Tai said only, "I heard from Owlfrost. You didn't intend it."

"I was the sword in Sidax's hand," Waha said bluntly, as if inviting censure, but when Tai did not give it, he turned away as he spoke. "We sailed for Angja first. Toad and Salamander started a cart crew for Snowhawk's pleasure boats, and expanded. Toad runs half the gang on Angja, and Salamander the other half in the capital. They're to get us into the city."

Tai wondered how Snowhawk's secret connections and Odval's had met. But if Waha knew, he did not say. How had Odval turned from a silly girl to a covert fighter against the Cobra Sages? Perhaps better not to bring it up unless someone else did. "Hard to imagine Toad running a gang," Tai said.

"Successful, too. It's the martial skills. They defend cargos." Waha's tight expression eased somewhat. "Toad's married. Has two little ones. He did always want a family. As well as horses—which he probably rides in secret."

Tai remembered then that only the nobles were permitted to ride. "Any news of Mo Thi?"

Waha's old grin flashed, briefly. "He's become some kind of mountain hermit-healer. There are people hiding up in the heights. They found him wandering around the mountain where we left him. Taught him herbs, and helped him build a treehouse. Toad says when he goes up to look for wild horses every spring, Mo Thi sometimes comes down and gives him herbs specifically for horse colic."

Snowhawk called everyone together then. "We still have a long way to go. Tide is high, so we are on our way. Our chief in the capital doesn't know how long Kimek can last."

Or even if he's still alive, was implied.

Tai had volunteered for the long watches at the oars, as the exercise eased the restless urgency that gripped him. He discovered that Waha had done the same, though he did not know if for the same reasons. Waha was no longer the center of chatter as he'd always been. As the days passed, Tai perceived that though the gallant wanderers understood that Waha had not chosen to betray Mek, he had lost their trust. And he knew it.

The two ships cut through the wintry waters. Up this far north winter had already arrived, but at least it was still early for ice floes, so they were able to push on through the night instead of having to anchor.

Though Owlfrost, and to an even more limited extent, Snowhawk, and one or two others, had some sort of Essence ability with communicating through the mental door—dream-speaking, they called it—none of them could reach Mek any more than Tai could.

When *Yufi's* chart aligned with island profiles and the stars above, Owlfrost gave the order to convert the raider to a pleasure boat. In a reverse of his and Mek's escape from Angja, the crew brought out the screens and hangings and rich cushions and decorations from the hold that would convince the world that this pleasure craft was exclusive to rich nobles.

On the last day, when the capital was a notch on the northern horizon, Snowhawk said, "Before we part, let's disguise our Muds."

Zan drew Butterfly off, but Tanglewood hung back. "Don't need it."

Butterfly paused, and glanced at her. "You're certain?"

Tanglewood flashed her sly smile, and instead of answering, she unfastened the tie at her right hip, and right there on deck, shucked her tunic. Raised to equate modesty with respect, Tai looked away quickly, but not before he caught the briefest glimpse of ruddy brown fur rippling into existence over warm clay-brown flesh.

Several gasped, and when he looked back, he was in time to see Tanglewood on all fours, a slender, graceful fox with uplifted narrow snout and several plumed tails waving. But before he could count them, she kept blurring until she was just a skinny wood-hued dog that no one would look at twice.

Butterfly said, "Tanglewood will be able to sniff Mek out no matter where he is." She bent to pick up Tanglewood's clothes, then followed Zan off, leaving Tanglewood to leap about, sniffing and play-bowing with Zan's dog.

A particularly unprepossessing member of Toad's crew had offered to partner with Ze Eight to volunteer for the Baris Khasha, the Westerner version of the imperial guards. This scrawny youth had been delighted when he discovered that the crew's stores included player disguises, specifically fake hair and warts.

Brawny Ze Eight was going to go as a deaf man—which, with his size and training, would guarantee him a place, as servants who couldn't hear conversations were prized. Ze Eight practiced during the entire journey to not respond as people tried to catch him out by talking to him or creeping up and screaming at him.

"It's hardest not to react when I understand," he said. "But that won't be a problem once they're all blabbing Ghost—er, their tongue."

Tai had not expected to find any part of this quest enjoyable. Just necessary. He was unprepared for how much of his old antipathy rushed back when he had to speak the Dragon tongue, taste the hot spices the Westerners liked, and smell fermented goat's milk. But he remained silent as he traded his clothing for the thick, rough long overtunic and loose trousers of a lowest-level house servant, and wound his braids up under a patched, stained cap.

Dachi was now a pleasure boat, and *Yufi* a typical junk: barrels along the rails, common passengers carrying cargos for important people—the Western version of traders. *Yufi*—with Diggy leading the defense—would sail back and forth beyond the patrol perimeter, there if needed, sole reinforcement for a ruse in which a handful of people were going to infiltrate the most watched, well-guarded harbor in all the islands under the black dragon banners to steal a prisoner. And hope to get out alive.

The outer raider patrol ships recognized *Dachi* in its pleasure boat disguise, and let it through the tight cordon surrounding the capital's island. Less tight than usual, Snowhawk assured them with a grim smile, as First Prince Toshan had taken most of the capital's fastest and best-crewed patrol ships.

They were also passed through the even thinner inner patrol guarding Baris Tharan's harbor, and they floated up to the dock designated for entertainment craft and personal ships.

Some of the rescuers' tension eased when they saw Salamander at the dock, the big, bright salamander tattoo in the middle of his forehead marking him as part of a respected wharf gang. Nobody, Toad had assured Waha—and Waha informed Tai as they pulled galley oars—had ever noticed the similar strokes to the slave mark because everyone knew that slaves couldn't run and survive.

As soon as the ramp touched the dock, Tanglewood leaped down and vanished in the crowd.

Snowhawk, extravagantly dressed, with little chains dangling from her braids and more bangles on both arms, walked daintily down the ramp, her cloak swinging behind her. She was the image of a wealthy entertainer. Snowhawk pressed fist to chest to greet a slender figure coming through the crowd of wharf rats, goat traders, patrols, hawkers of hot food, embarking and debarking people.

Was she familiar? Tai squinted, trying to bring fuzzy details into focus, then he heard a familiar voice: "There you are, Boat Chief."

It was Odval, now a grown woman. A graceful one, too, despite that garish Western garb. Tai stared until a glance of indifference brushed over Waha and him, and he remembered to lower his head.

Amusement flared in Tai, heightened by awareness of how his sense of his proper place in the world had become mutable: ritual and protocol were the ideal, but reality all too frequently fell far short.

Here, certainly, he had found no pretense to civilization as he defined it; for written forms of wisdom and poetry, Angja had raided ancient scrolls from his own culture. Yet recently he'd been forced to consider how fractured the imperial court was, the evidence inescapable while he was negotiating the labyrinthine corridors in search of records from the old dynasty —

"Get to work," Salamander bawled.

Tai started, jolted from spectator to participant. He bent to pick up a basket from the deck, and trod down the ramp,

Odval, resplendent in a furred cloak over brightly embroidered clothing, walked with Snowhawk. Courting charms chimed sweetly in her elaborately dressed hair as she trod with noble assurance in her fine embroidered boots. The two "wharf rats" followed with their loads.

Odval had almost not recognized the former, scrawny Tai in this tall, pantherish figure whose trained grace was not quite masked by the ragged clothes, but those long, tilted phoenix eyes were exactly the same. Including that remote, severe expression she'd once found so intriguing.

She laughed at her younger self, and how all-consuming her passion had been. Sixteen! And who else had there been for sixteen-year-old passions? He'd been marked as a slave, but he had not thought of himself as a slave, had not carried himself as a slave even when bowing and deferring, and had not spoken like a slave in spite of required pronouns and titles: he'd suffered himself to play a role in order to survive. Would all slaves feel that way if they could?

Of course they would, she had discovered, when truly watching the lowered faces, the tense hands of those who served in silence. She had overcome that teenage passion in discovering a cause — her mother's cause — ending slavery.

She led them to the servants' alley behind the Angja estate — a route that utterly confused Tai. Everything signified barbarian to his eyes, from the long curved walls along the meandering tangle of streets to the conical roofs poking up above those walls in apparently random order, each cone with another tinier cone absurdly poised above it.

When finally they entered a plain gate off a narrow alley with dirty snow heaped where the sun did not shine, Tai discovered that the illusory randomness was actually a circle: round houses arranged in a larger circle, with the largest roundhouse at the north end.

Odval led them to a roundhouse nearby — farthest from the grand one, surrounded by goat and pig pens, and the clutter of a back yard. Clearly for servants. She stood on the threshold to let Waha and Tai poke their heads inside. It smelled of smoke and oil lamps and spice. Tai got an impression of lattice-work along the walls, with woolen weavings attached. To keep the heat in? At the north end was a very plain, small altar, at the opposite end, a platform under which were hot stones with embers beneath, keeping the platform warm.

"This is the serving men's place," Odval said in a quick, low voice, though no one was in sight. "If you sleep here, you'll find bedding up there above the sleeping platform. Spread bedding with heads toward the altar. When you sit, don't point your feet toward the fire." She indicated a banked fire in the center of the room, directly under the roof openings crowned by the small upper roof. The fire had a swinging pot set adjacent.

"Women sleep there," Odval said, pointing to the round-house next over. "Come into the barn."

That was on the other side of the women's roundhouse. There were several horses, either munching or sleeping, heads drooping. No people, but she still checked everywhere before drawing them into an empty, clean-swept stall. She indicated for them to sit, and everyone did, setting aside their burdens.

In the lamplight, Odval's eyes gleamed that unsettling blue. "Here is our situation. Kimek is alive, though held by the snakes. The empress still holds the speaking stick, but that will not be true if the First Prince succeeds in his war. We do not know how much he is controlled by demons — the Cobra Sages of course deny it."

"Are all Cobra Sage dream-speakers possessed by demons?"

"No. But they believe that they have all our dream-speakers, for they examine every child within its first few years, and take away any with talent. The important thing for us right now is that the Cobra Sages will know before the empress if the First Prince wins or loses. They jealously guard their power to know distant news instantly, while we must either wait weeks, or rely on what they choose to give out, unless someone in the east can dream-speak."

"Except you also have Jhax of Ganis," Tai said, finding his eye drawn to the taut skin of her forehead, the quick intelligence he discerned there. "Or is he not able to reach people at that distance? I remember Mek telling me that your sister couldn't."

Odval glanced up, the impact of her blue gaze startling. "You knew about Jhax? Ah! Kimek must have told you when he healed Bar Than Jhax's leg," Odval whispered, recovering from her surprise. "Bar Than Jhax cannot reach such distances. He is very untrained, for reasons I think you understand."

"He had to hide his talent."

"Yes. Militarily, Ganis has drawn all the banners dissatisfied with the princes, and the empress favors him for…reasons. Jhax of Ganis will inherit Ganis, but because of his crippled leg, can never sit on the obsidian throne."

Tai remembered the Westerners' notions of honor tied up in horse, bow, and sword—and a whole, strong body to wield them.

Waha spoke for the first time; he was aware of a thread of the old amusement in noticing that these other two had momentarily forgotten him. "Back to the snakes. If the First Prince carries his banner into the Mud empire successfully, that means on a tide of blood from both sides. No one wins but the snakes."

"Yes," Odval hissed. "Sage Sun will gain tremendous power—and we won't know when it happens until his demon returns here, in the blink of an eye."

"Details?" Tai asked.

Odval glanced up, brow slightly puckered. In that wavering light, Tai was aware of stirring, and squashed it. She said, "The only way we can force the snakes to relinquish Kimek is for Bar Ganis—and the empress—to agree to the military side's wish to put him in the dueling ring. The Cobra Sages might accept that because they can wring Essence from him as he dies, even if they can't…do whatever it is they do when they catch Essence wielders who escaped them in childhood."

She leaned toward them, her whisper so low that she was nearly inaudible. "Windseed can sometimes reach Kimek. He told Mother in dream-speak that as yet, the Cobra Sages do not know how powerful Kimek is. But that won't last if they begin..." She made a warding sign.

Tai had been trying not to imagine what the Cobra Sages would do. Tormenting himself with possibilities gained nothing. "In this plan, Waha and I are the house servants, but that scrawny boy and Eight are the possible recruits for your imperial guard? Shouldn't we be the guards?"

Odval sat back on her heels. "The Baris Khasha would *love* to get the likes of you two—they are overworked and spread too thin, as the First Prince took all the best for second-stage pacification once he conquers your rice island. So if you two were to volunteer, they would whisk you straightaway to training, and might even send you right out as reinforcements. Whereas the weedy, skinny, barely-acceptable candidates will be put to work in the least crucial posts possible, to free up overworked men, or better trained ones if reinforcements are called for. Such as guards for the outer areas of the ring."

"Then they are to be posted along the escape route?"

"Precisely. We've worked very hard to set that up. You two, as Angja house servants, we can put wherever we need. Such as, carrying Kimek, depending on what his condition is when the Cobra Sages do release him. Now, let's get some food into you, while I run my errand." Which meant, check with her mother for news of Windseed and Mek.

And at the same time, over in the garrison, four candidates, including Ze Eight and Salamander's volunteer, had been put through a very rudimentary test to see if they knew which end of a sword to use, and if they could lift a boulder and carry it across a training court.

Then they were sent to interview.

The Khasha duty desk captain and the obsidian throne's household steward each tipped their head as they eyed the four candidates before them.

"At least that one's clean," the duty desk captain commented finally, turned his head, and spat. "Somebody scrubbed him up good. These others? Stink of fish guts and brine."

"That they do, most honored captain, that they do," the steward responded, though not with any enthusiasm. "Still, we can use the deaf one."

The "deaf" one stood there impassively. His black hair had been skinned so tightly into its topknot that his eyebrows seemed pulled into a perpetual expression of shock. His arms dangled from the worn sleeves of his smelly robe, which was belted over sagging trousers.

The steward poked the new recruit and made exaggerated "follow me" gestures.

"Why is it we get the duckweed?" the duty desk captain asked, ignoring the fact that the three remaining recruits stood right there listening. "All right. We'll send you over to guard the ring."

Salamander's recruit mumbled, "Why don't we get to guard the palace? Why did that other rat get to go?"

"Listen Duckweed, with those warts there's no chance of you getting anywhere near the palace. They want guards whose faces don't give them nightmares. This is your last warning—next time you speak without being spoken to gets you a beating."

The recruit bowed, followed by the others.

"You're lucky you know which end of a sword to use, or you'd be emptying chamber pots all day. Now let's get you kitted out and shown around. Then you can relieve men who'd had to serve three watches back-to-back…"

And while the new recruits shuffled after the duty desk ensign, covertly assessing their surroundings at every step, Mek lay on the other side of the fortress. He had no notion how long he had thus lain frozen as stone; he had been isolated except for welcome visits by Windseed when he dared. Days? Months? Years? His efforts at Coral Island, which had felt at the time like a hard day of work, had actually been longer than a full season.

It was almost worth it to have met Windseed—who despite their very different circumstances was so very like Mek. "We will never meet," Windseed had said. "I cannot even risk seeing my family: I must remain where I am, a meek functionary, too crippled to take a Rider." Though Windseed's control was far too good to leak sensory images and memories as did Ardal, Mek had caught impressions that Windseed had deliberately shattered one knee in order to avoid being assigned a blood demon—what they called Riders. His life as a Cobra Sage was as a low-level scribe.

Therefore both of them cherished deeply the rare conversations they had within a bubble of deflection charm in the mental realm, while the Cobra Sages' Riders were all focused eastward.

Then, quite suddenly, he was back. "Mek. It will be soon. The empress has chosen the dueling ring for you—and we are ready."

Mek discovered that he was conflicted. Of course he must escape! But he did not want to lose this brave soul who worked quietly for the good of his world, and nothing but danger as recompense.

And Windseed felt the same. "I read more of your Kanda," Windseed said. "There is more similarity with us than difference, in some regards."

"Are you surprised?" Mek asked. "Aside from the blue eyes among your people, we are much the same: two of everything except noses and our organs of generation. Then fingers and toes. If we had beaks and ate clouds and your people had tentacles and breathed water like the krakens, I'd expect vaster differences in what causes pleasure and pain, delight and longing."

"This is so, this is so," Windseed responded. "Though I might suggest that some pains — and pleasures — would still be shared, common to all creatures under the roof of heaven."

"Harmony," Mek said in that silent realm, the word a plea, a prayer, suffused with the sweetest incense.

"I was reading your Kanda in search of wisdom on matters of life, and after life. Such as our shared belief that we come back again and again in a new life, yet no one ever remembers the previous. Jhax was recently asking, if that is so, what do the ancients say could be the purpose? Or is there a purpose, to have to relearn the most fundamental things, which is a very inefficient path to wisdom?"

"Ar Laq said that we cannot know Purpose until we shed the human form for the last time before becoming like the gods."

"I saw that," Windseed said. "But what if we actually become demons? Or are they different altogether?"

"The word 'demon' — what does it really mean?" Mek returned. "There appear to be so many kinds. What if there are demons of honor, and of art, as well as of bloodlust?" He thought of Sagacious Blade, who he sometimes thought might be a demon of music. But he dared not call to his sword while he was frozen in this stone charm.

"Our shamans in some banners, the ones who pass their lore by song and not by scroll, insist that there is a purely demon world beyond this, but — hai-yee, they come. To you. *Now.*"

SIXTY-FOUR

"BE SMALL, BE SMALL, be small," Mek reminded himself.

A burning sensation rippled through Mek's meridians, restoring blood flow and heartbeat so suddenly that his entire body felt as a thousand beginning healers were each jabbing him with blunt needles. "Uhhhhh," he groaned.

"*This* is an Essence expert?" someone said in the Western language.

"I'm telling you, he flies as well as—"

"Any idiot with a little air affinity can learn light skills," retorted the first voice. "Especially on a charmed sword."

"But not every idiot can set a broken leg by only touching it," persisted the second voice.

"Hai-yoo, if you're talking about Jhax of Ganis, that leg was mangled, not healed. He's got an ugly limp—he shoulda been thrown in the ring years ago."

"That was the father's fault, ignoring the instructions after the bone was set because he wanted to chase Haxu—"

"Irrelevant!" a third voice broke in. "We must be seen to cooperate until the Sun returns. The empress's people are out there, waiting! Get him on his feet."

"I want to test again," the first voice insisted. "Now that he's awake."

"If he had any talent that we could use, he would have responded to our *first* tests," the third stated wearily. "This is just a low-level Essence healer who managed to escape Diamond Kian because she has more ambition than sense. Sidax, if I hear any more claims of high powers out of you, I'll kill you myself. As it is, Diamond Kian demands a tribunal over your actions. Go."

"*I* found him. I insist on seeing the test myself."

Mek left his arms and legs to wobble as he kept his mental door walled shut. Something or someone attacked from the outside, applying a painful combination of blinding light and a miner's pickaxe. It seemed to go on forever, then the mutter, "Either his affinity vanished entirely, due to your poison, or else he's got better control than star level."

"And I say he does," protested the second voice. "I think this Kimek is the one who took out—"

"Nonsense! There's no sign of a Rider. None!"

The voices died away in the distance.

Impatient hands pulled a cloth bag over Mek's head, cutting off what little light there'd been. "Can't have the condemned polluting our sacred precincts with your dirty eyetracks," Mek was informed with grim joviality.

Hard hands gripped Mek's upper arms and he was force-marched along some sort of stone corridor. He let his head droop, but as his body moved, a little strength and life trickled back. It was going to take time—that he didn't seem to have. At least it seemed to prove to his unseen captors that he was the pitiful object he wanted them to see.

They reached a place in which the air currents moved about, icy cold but pure. "…assign a couple of plank-levels who need practice in stripping life force. This one won't afford much beyond practice," First Voice said, a door unlocked—click-click-clank!—and Mek was shoved into someone else's hands.

Different voices spoke past him. "I thought so dangerous a criminal wouldn't be so scrawny."

"Hai-yoo, the snakes will wring the life out of anyone. We all knew that."

More walking, and presently, the bag was abruptly pulled away, leaving Mek's snarled topknot to flop over one ear.

He squinted around. A cluster of other miserable people stood behind him, fear emanating from them. This was no practice duel, but execution, then. A gate opened to the ring, where raked snow glittered with sand. It didn't hide the tang of old blood. The stands were not filled. The spectators sat in clumps, muffled in coats and hats, vendors selling fermented hot milk. Mek sensed a weak expectation mixed with apathy.

"You. Get. To. Have. Weapons," a tough-looking Westerner bawled in Mek's face. "Understand, Mud? Wea-pons. Which?"

Mek had been ready to summon Sagacious Blade, but the sight of those terrified victims changed his mind. Windseed had promised rescue for him. But no one seemed to be ready to rescue them. If he could save even one…

"Flute," Mek said — or tried to say. His voice was a husk, his mouth dry. "Fan." He added as an afterthought.

"Flute?" one repeated incredulously. "He doesn't understand."

"Do the Muds have the same word for flute?"

"Flute. Bamboo," Mek said.

Someone snorted. "Yoo! He won't last long, but it'll be worth a laugh or two, at least. Give him what he wants."

"A flute? We don't *have* musical instruments in the weapons racks."

"Ask one of the bell ringers, dolt!"

Mek blinked around, aware of desperate thirst. He caught the bored eyes of the guard standing nearby. "Water?" he croaked.

The man snorted. "Patience, Mud. You soon won't be thirsty — or anything else, ha ha ha!"

They stood in silence after that, Mek trying to swallow and failing.

Footsteps pounded up, and a young guard thrust a flute into Mek's hand, and a fan into the other. He mumbled something in a whisper that Mek didn't catch, then backed away instantly when the guard frowned at him.

Then the guard opened the gate and pushed Mek through. He stumbled into the ring, scarcely aware of the icy air working its way into his grimy clothes and summer sandals. The fan was limp and soiled. The flute, a battered object with actual teeth marks on it. Clearly used by beginners who must have had scarce interest in playing.

But a flute was a flute.

He walked out to the center of the ring, and stumbled again as an almost unbearably sweet, pure, crystalline sound shimmered through the air. He stopped, open-mouthed with wonder as his opponent came out, a youth perhaps sixteen or eighteen, carrying one of those glittering black knives.

Windseed had explained the ritual before each session in the dueling rings. The ritual was guided by the playing of frost bells — in ancient time they had truly been formed of ice, but now were made of fine crystal. Their ringing began with blowing across the top, a whisper of sweetness, then the tapping began, in counterpoint at first as unseen voices chanted words before battle — meant to heighten the bloodlust for the Cobra Sages. And for Father Dragon's Chosen, to elevate the duel to a contest of honor and strength, meant to gain glory for the warriors, whether in winning or dying well.

Mek turned to his opponent, meeting an anxious gaze, the youth's thought beating against Mek's skull like moths against the oiled paper of a window to get at the lamp inside: *I won't kill you, don't kill me. It has to look like death...*

Mek remembered Windseed's promise — that if his unnamed co-conspirators succeeded in getting him released to the military side, they Had A Plan. He would probably get cut, but not killed: the military would claim his body once he fell, and the conspirator would let him know when to fall.

He didn't question that plan. He could feel the hidden Cobra Sages somewhere around; inside one, the blood demon Rider. He knew that demon from the dock at Icecrown, and firmly warded it as he lifted the flute to his dry, cracked lips, and played a long, breathy note. Oh, music at last, after the long silence!

As soon as the ritual died away, Mek began to echo it, only shifting the register to a haunting, melancholy purity that evoked longing for something greater, wider, higher, than mere human limitations. Essence began to drift up from the earth, and fall from the air, and rise from snow in glittering droplets as Mek drew out of the hearts of all the spectators the fire of anger, of resentment, of angry lusts for vengeance and pain.

He sensed one of the Cobra Sages recoiling from the strength of an emotion so long denied there was no defense against it. The blood demon sparked to angry flame — and Mek's opponent jerked as if someone had prodded him. He swung his weapon at Mek's head.

Mek sidestepped, one hand using the fan to deflect the sword. He played on, the same compelling melody, fresh snow on the parched earth of anger and sorrow.

Someone began to sing, up there in the stands. Another wept.

Harmony, harmony, harmony, sang the flute —

The opponent came in again, and Mek deflected him, residually aware that the swings looked fierce, but whooshed right by him, barely touching the fan.

From behind, a derisive voice shouted, "*I* captured him, let *me* kill him!'

Needles hissed through the air, striking first Mek's opponent, and as his limbs gave way, leaving Mek standing alone in the center of the ring, an open target. Mek's music faltered, for he had to use both hands to deflect the tiny missiles using fan and flute. Then a needle tore through the fan and struck him in the one leg. And as he paused to fight its poison, another hit him in the knee. Then in the wrist of the hand holding the flute.

He stumbled, the flute clattering from a nerveless grip, his arms and legs like noodles, though his mind—honed now at detecting and seizing poisons—remained preternaturally clear as one set of feet approached from one direction, but then another set ran faster, and hands seized Mek's helpless body by the armpits. "Call the sword." It was Tai!

Tai's hard arm clasped Mek against his chest, and his free hand gripped Mek's own hand, fingers twined with his from the back, so that Mek's palm was bare—

Mek instinctively swiped the deflection charm over himself before the poison reached his arm, and called to the sword.

Sagacious Blade smacked into his palm. Mek, using Tai's strength, used the sword to strike downward, sending healing Essence into his young opponent, who sat up, sucking in a sobbing breath. Mek lost the battle with this new poison and his body sagged noodle-limp to the ground as Tai raised the sword high, drawing attention from Mek.

"It's a *king's* sword," someone screamed.

"A ghost sword!"

"...out of the air!"

"Now!" Tai shouted.

Now? Mek struggled against the poison, but he was still too weak. But then Sagacious Blade's entity flashed into the mental realm with a thunderous eruption of silent lightning, torching the towering hunger full of thousands of eyes and teeth—

Sun's blood demon burst into uncounted embers. Mek abandoned his prone body, and with Sagacious Blade shot through the mental realm extinguishing those embers with the speed of lightning as Tai's breath hissed in. "It's too hot to hold!"

Mek's head fell back as Tai threw the sword into the air. The glowing blade shot into the sky, flashing into blue light.

When that light faded, spectators and guards alike began screaming and scrambling to escape. Out of the midst of the chaos, someone drew away the other condemned people; Mek caught a drifting thought, recognizing Odval. He shut out awareness of his body, and as Waha appeared at Mek's other side.

He and Tai hauled Mek up and began to run, jolting Mek between them until they found a rhythm.

Mek fought to hang onto consciousness, and heard a nasal voice saying, urgently, "We opened the back doors, and threw the bars, just as we were told to do…"

Mek faded again, floating in the mental realm *Did we get them all?* He threw the thought toward Windseed. To get no answer.

Which was an answer.

He drifted, this time in a whirlpool of disconnected sensories, rousing to fierce barking. A brown dog hurled itself at Mek and Waha, until Waha exclaimed, "Yes, yes, we get it. Not that way. Lead on."

"We were right in there not half a gong ago," protested the nasal voice. "We set up the escape route just as we were told!"

"Something's gone wrong," Tai said. "Do you want to test it in this city full of enemies out to get us?"

"No."

"Then follow the dog…"

More running. Brine. Spicy perfume. Chimes. Feet, running away. Dog barking in the distance. The clash of weapons, Tai breathing hard, then: "He's down. Go!" Boots and hooves, slush, slush, slush. Bump! Wood against dock. Breathing. Oh, blessed relief—water, to his parched lips. He drank and drank, gasping, then drifted,

A woman's soothing voice, "You're with us, now. We're going to hide you below. There'll be a search, but we've been searched before…"

The poison was fighting to get to Mek's mind. He withdrew all awareness of his physical self to the old citadel behind the wall, and set his mind to neutralizing the poison. When it was gone, and awareness slowly returned, he found himself lying on soft pillows, the fresh, acid-sweet scent of citrus in the air, not quite covering the stink of stale spiced goat's milk right under his nose.

A man's and a woman's voices nearby. Very near, as if

sitting on either side of him.

Sharp voice — that's what roused him. "…her?"

Her?

"She's drunk." A soft hand brushed over Mek's forehead.

"Was there something else, Circle Sage?" Hadn't Mek met that voice before? But pain hazed. Younger. Much younger. Jhax of Ganis! His voice carried the ring of authority now. "I'm already waiting for answers concerning my house guard in his first duel. He was to fight against an eastern prisoner."

The sharp voice lowered to a semblance of submissive politeness, "I beg patience, Bar Than Ganis. In the chaos after the outlander king attacked, we lost the prisoner. *All* the prisoners. We were ordered to search…"

Jhax said, "Is your missing prisoners *my* problem, Circle Sage? No? If you have no information to offer about my missing house guard, then I would very much like to return to more pleasant distractions. And I shall be speaking to the empress about this intrusion."

The sound of retreating footsteps presaged Snowhawk's appearance. "They're gone." And, to Jhax, "We depart at the top of the tide, Bar Than Ganis."

Mek's awareness widened. He lay on cushions in a luxurious cabin, surrounded by gorgeous hangings. The heavy scents of spiced goat's milk and incense hung in the air. At his shoulder sat a somewhat familiar face, a pretty one, now matured to a keen gaze from large, dark-fringed blue eyes. Odval, Ardal's sister!

"Then we can let the mysterious Sagacious Blade out," Odval stated cheerfully. "Is that what we're saying now? That Jetai is Sagacious Blade, imperial king and killer of demons?"

"From the sound of it, the rumors are taking care of themselves, blooming with every repetition." Snowhawk flicked her fingers outward.

"I like that," Odval stated with satisfaction.

Snowhawk moved aside a colorful woven screen at the side of Mek's vision. Mek groaned, struggled to sit up, then fell back, only turning his head as a narrow door opened behind one of the screens, and Tai stepped out, braids swinging about his upper arms. In Western clothing, he looked like an obsidian blade warrior.

Mek's memory was returning. He remembered Tai throwing his hand high, and Sagacious Blade blazing like a star, then winking out. A pang of heat flashed in his palm. Was the sword…yes, he sensed her presence beside him. Still humming with Essence. He drew Essence into himself, washing the last of the Cobra Sage venom from his meridians.

Then sat up on his elbows, and discovered that someone had undone his hair, braiding it with chimes. He looked down, his gaze checking momentarily at two lumps of padding, then past to layers of flimsy fabric in crimson, blue, and gold, embroidered with swallows and lambs.

Then he looked up at Tai, who sat down next to Jhax. "They said I was too long to be the drunken woman," Tai explained to Mek in their own tongue.

"Aish," Mek said, blushing.

"Siu and Waha changed you," Tai added.

"I'll thank them when I see them. It must have been a noisome task."

"They did say you smelled of dungeon," Tai admitted. And then—as though continuing a conversation, he turned to Odval. "You're putting it about that I am Sagacious Blade. What does that gain you?"

"A worthy foe," Jhax said mildly. "Kimek was identified as a musician by eyewitnesses. Defeat by a musician in the ring would be considered humiliating. But what people remember was you."

Ayah! Mek remembered putting the deflection charm on himself, pure instinct.

"The Cobra Sages claimed that Kimek was a rogue Essence wielder, but no one is heeding them, especially after their resounding defeat. Many loathe the Cobra Sages as much as they fear them. To see a number of them actually fall down in a faint was exceedingly gratifying, if also terrifying. Why did you play music instead of pretending to fight?" He turned to Mek.

"An experiment that I *wish* would work: healing by drawing anger from people. So that they would lose the motivation to continue that execution."

Jhax appeared meditative. Tai noticed the unblinking way that Odval gazed at Jhax, her mouth tender, and thought, ah. But the friendly gaze Jhax turned her way was too tranquil for a shared passion.

Mek closed his eyes. They were on a ship, that much he could feel. They had to be on the *Dachi* again. As soon as he had a little strength, he would reach for Anise. He could feel here there, bright as the sun below the horizon. Brighter, somehow.

Jhax began running his finger around the rim of a gold cup as he considered. "If only you, as Sagacious Blade, or some other suitable rank, could be there for Prince Toshan — or someone else — to treat with, we might..."

"Win. Here," Odval said softly. "Or at least gain enough merit to impose a compromise, and maybe unite against the war-bent princes. Especially if the Cobra Sages lost as much as we hope when you destroyed their demon Riders."

Mek closed his eyes, and there was a flash of awareness from Windseed. Mek translated it into words: "Not all the demons are gone. Also, many Cobra Sages don't have Riders. They lost power, but they are not defeated, according to..." He remembered then that the name must not be spoken.

Odval gave Mek a tiny nod. It was clear then — and so very sad — that though Windseed and his mother, Odval and Jhax, all strove against the wickedness of the blood demons poisoning their culture, they seemed so burdened by lethal secrets that trust was tentative even between allies.

Mek sat all the way up, his chimes ringing, a sweet sound that evoked the yearning magnificence of those frost bells. What a cruel paradox, that such beauty was bound to a ritual built around the shedding of blood. *We are such creatures of conflict.*

Mek rubbed his eyes. "If Tai could be where your First Prince's fleet is. How would that help you here? I thought that the empress can't end the war — that she can speak, but she cannot hand out edicts."

Odval said, "But she has influence, which she wields by giving the speaking stick to those she believes must be heard. Until recently it was always the Sun first, though she loathes the Cobra Sages, but the Sun knew *everything*. Could kill at a glance. Had to be listened to, except in purely military matters."

"But military matters — war — gains the Cobra Sages the lifeblood they feed their power on, so they cooperate with whoever is bloodiest," Jhax said. "The princes want the war for so many reasons — to gain loot, to capture rice for the storm-battered islands. For glory, of course. War has been the traditional way to unite the squabbling banners under one cause. The First Prince — with the Sun at his back — promised an easy win if all the banners united in a monumental slaughter before the gain of your rich imperial islands."

"If the slaughter goes against the west, only the Cobra Sages win," Mek said. "Yes? But the princes lose…credence?"

"Stature." Jhax tapped his golden cup with a nail so that it rang. "But what a cost in lives! That's why I wish we didn't have at least a couple of Mother Moon months of sailing between us and the fleet! I don't think you understand the effect of what happened yesterday. A warrior came into the ring waving an ancient Jun Suai king's sword sword brighter than the sun, that is so powerful the Cobra Sages dropped unconscious. It's *never* happened, at least not in living memory."

"I have no authority to negotiate," Tai said. "I'm an advisor."

"If only you were there, you could *scare* them into retreat," Jhax said. "It's been *centuries* since the Sages lost so many Riders. And if they think one man was responsible…"

Odval blinked, and raised her palm. "The chief says that we ought to use the Cobra Sages' immediate knowledge against them. In other words, the First Prince's Cobra Sages had to know about the sword, here, and Sun broken into shards, almost as soon as it happened. The faster we can get word to the fleet, the weaker the princes' hold without the power of the Cobra Sages."

"You could have that," Mek said. "The same man who defeated the Cobra Sages in the ring in the capital could be at the battle site soon. Now. Could he cause a retreat?"

Everyone turned his way.

Tai said, "I thought you could not carry another person even in Essence flight, much less that…I don't even know what to call it."

"*I* can't," Mek said. "Right now, certainly. Maybe never again. Don't know. But right now Sagacious Blade is so full of Essence that I believe I could send you with her. She accepted your touch yesterday. Whether because I needed you, or it was her decision, I cannot know. But I could try to send you, and then call her back."

Tai stood. "Do it."

"It'll be painful. If you survive it. I think you will," Mek amended quickly. "But you might wish you hadn't."

"I'll risk it." Tai said to Odval and Jhax, "How is this? Settle your affairs here. Do what you must to stop the fighting on your side. I'll wave Mek's sword — if it will let me — at that end. I will do anything to stop that war." Tai bowed to Odval and Jhax, then left in search of his carryall — and Waha.

He found Waha below, talking to Siu. They both looked up, Siu unhappy, Waha's expression shuttered.

"Are you staying?" Tai asked Waha.

"That's what we're discussing," Waha said with a rueful smile. "No. In this empire I am always a runaway slave." He ran his hand up his sleeve, over the forearm tattoo. "A presumptuous one. But I have no place in yours either."

"Perhaps not among gallant wanderers, but if you need a place, I'll see that you have one. Here's my request. Mek is weaker than he'll admit," Tai said to Waha. Purpose. This man wants purpose. "Will you see him safely to our capital?"

"Yes." A trace of Waha's old smile appeared. "Then I'm yours to command."

SIXTY-FIVE

IT HURT AS MUCH as Mek had warned.

Mek had said it was vitally important to be able to imagine exactly where the sword would take him. Tai remembered that Anchor island had been the Western fleet's first target, and they'd lost it again to the Supreme Commander's vanguard. If they were not there now, at least he'd be able to find out where to go without having to sail for months.

At Anchor Island's west harbor, his clearest memory was of weather-warped wharf planks at the foot of the broadest pier where capital ships lay. The spot where he'd met Zan and Siu—it had seemed a general meeting place.

Tai drew the sword cautiously. Nothing happened. Mek laid his hand over Tai's. He closed his eyes, summoned Essence, then opened the door to Tai's thoughts, fixed firmly on that image—

Odval and Jhax recoiled as sunlight flashed where Tai had just been as the air stirred crazily in the cabin.

At Anchor Island, Tai stumbled to his knees, his entire body throbbing before the pain narrowed to his chest. He felt a sneeze—no, it was too painful to sneeze—he struggled to breathe—and wiped his nose, to find blood trickling.

The rushing noise in his head gave way to shouting voices and the ring of swords being pulled. He looked up at imperial guards—and past them, straight into the surprised gaze of Supreme Commander Nu.

A quick glance disclosed the westering sun limning banner bearers at either end of two groups of battle-ready warriors, armor glinting. Half the banners were black, with various devices on them. The rest were the imperial standard. He'd appeared in the middle of a parley of some sort.

Everyone turned Tai's way. Without a cloth at hand, he pulled off his headband to stanch the nosebleed as he forced his still-throbbing body to move toward the supreme commander. The smell of gunpowder and smoke drifted on the air, and he saw damaged warships at the dock and in the bay.

Mek's thought was there in the mental doorway: *Windseed says the parley is to gain time for repairs. This remaining prince wants to avenge his dead brothers, encouraged by the Cobra Sage with him. Tell them the Cobra Sage Sun is dead.*

Tai's gaze swept over the Westerners at the forefront of their group as he tried shallow, careful breathing. Which was the Fourth Prince? The Dragon's Chosen all bore obsidian knives, and they wore leather-and-plate armor, but one's armor was more elaborate, worked in black. He appeared to be about sixteen.

Tai met this one's gaze, then he lifted his voice to be heard as he spoke in their language, "I have just come from Baris Tharan, where I defeated your Cobra Sage Sun yesterday while I stood in the palace dueling ring."

The ringing shock of silence met this. Then the masked and robed Cobra Sage behind the Fourth Prince gasped, and murmured a command to the stunned teenager.

Tai raised Sagacious Blade, which caught that sinking sun, lancing a sun-shaft of reflection across their faces. Yes, the Cobra Sages still standing knew what had happened: their instant knowledge worked against them now. The prince looked uncertain, as if all the walls governing his life had disintegrated.

Tai drew another painful breath. "Your empress, who holds the speaking stick until all your banners choose an emperor, listens now to Ganis and Angja banners. Go home, Dragon's Chosen."

Throw Sagacious Blade into the air, Mek whispered outside Tai's mental door.

Tai obeyed, and fought against a weird bubble of laughter at how all those blue and gray and greenish eyes followed the sword as it spun high into the air. Then—with a flash of golden light—it vanished back to Mek. At the same time the Cobra Sage stiffened. *Something* had happened in the mental realm.

The young prince's jaw jutted in decision, and when the

masked one in gray laid a hand on the boy's shoulder, the prince pushed it off. Then whispered to the banner bearer next to him. The man puffed out his chest, put a horn to his lips, and blew a long, mournful note.

The Westerners wheeled about and marched to their longboats, to be rowed to the fleet lined up on the horizon.

When the last of them climbed into their boats, Tai made an immense effort to turn toward Supreme Commander Nu, who began to close the distance between them, then the darkness that had been pulsing at the edges of Tai's vision closed over his eyes and he dropped to the ground in a faint.

In the *Dachi*, Mek lay back, troubled by Tai's loss of consciousness, even though he'd warned Tai. They both knew he'd agreed to it, whatever the cost. Both would make the same decision, if there was a chance they might be able to circumvent resumption of a war.

He opened his eyes, to find Odval looking concerned.

"He's there," Mek said, making an effort to slide Sagacious Blade into her sheath. "But he's going to need rest." And I'm never doing that again, for either of us, he added silently. Sagacious Blade was innocent, still learning the limitations of human bodies. Also, too much Essence had been required to perform such a charm; it might be that ranging freely in the mental realm was the pinnacle of Mek's reach. "Me, too," he added.

Jhax put fist to chest and limped out of the cabin, Odval with him. Then the *Dachi* floated out on the flood tide as Mek slept. Snowhawk ordered her people to work around Kimek, who lay in his song and dance outfit until he'd slept himself out.

When he woke feeling as if he could face a day while upright, he ate, drank, and changed. And when those did not defeat him, he composed himself and reached for Anise —

Her joy and relief and surprise suffused him, not quite hiding the anxiety of long waiting. Her joy was inarticulate, a series of vivid images: his family, four babies born to two brothers and two cousins, the kitchen garden, which — once it had been planted — had turned Ten Leopards from a temporary watch-post to home.

And finally! A shy, somewhat embarrassed but very proud awareness that Anise herself was well along in child, and that they would be seeing this child in early spring. *Your parents are here, and as soon as you come back, we shall have a proper wedding,* she said, so clear in the mental realm he knew she was speaking the words aloud. *Come home as soon as you can!*

A child? Anise's child? *His* child?

He'd promised Tai a visit to the capital, but that was going to have to wait.

Tai took much longer to recover.

The supreme commander had caused Tai to be carried aboard her flagship, and to the best cabin. She checked on him twice a day, ordering ensigns to see to his care, and to call her if he wakened.

As soon as he did, she sat down beside him. "You'll want a report, no doubt."

Tai nodded incrementally. His chest still hurt when he tried to speak.

"I left behind a defense force. The Westerners have definitely sailed for home. We don't know if they will be back again in spring—I've issued orders to be prepared for that—but permanent orders on our side of course belong to the emperor. He will no doubt have all kinds of questions once we reach home, but I've sent ahead a preliminary report on what I witnessed. You can give me your end when you recover a little more. Which you are to do. The chief naval physician says your pulse is still erratic."

Aish! Mek had warned him. He'd accepted the danger—as Mek had known he would. As Mek would, and had. Though Tai did not recollect passing out, his memory of those moments beforehand were very clear, including that shared thought that could have come from either of them: *I will do anything to stop that war.*

He mustered enough strength to thank her, then closed his eyes and slept. And kept sleeping, until he rose without feeling as if his body had been turned into the heaviest stone. His chest still hurt if he moved too fast, but it felt good to exercise slowly in the simplest fundamental.

As he walked about the ship, he became aware that winter did not actually appear everywhere at the same time. It had been winter for some weeks at Baris Tharan, but here to the south, there were still warm days, though the nights were increasingly chilly. About halfway to Mountain Peony, winter overtook them at last, announcing itself with a short blizzard.

Despite the increasing cold, the imperial fleet had been busy with repairs and then preparation for the reception that awaited them. Tai and the supreme commander had plenty of time to exchange information. He found out that the damage had been considerable in the two days of fighting, before the Westerners sent their parley; the first day had been the worst, but that second day, when the Cobra Sages lost their demons, the empire had pushed the Westerners back away from Anchor Island, causing a slaughter that included the eldest princes, who had to fight to the end: princes did not surrender. They won, or died. And the Cobra Sages tended the dying, using their fading life Essence to strengthen themselves.

After some weeks, Mek appeared at Tai's mental door to report that Snowhawk's crew had treated him like a mixture of royalty and dying patient, with Diggy appointing himself steward in charge of food (lots) and visitors (Crew Six with priority, except for Zan and the dog), and that he was in excellent health. His first act was to destroy Sidax's poison in Waha's dagger tattoo.

Waha had accompanied him until Mek was close enough to fly north the last little distance to Ten Leopards on Sagacious Blade.

Mek explained that he still received very occasional visits from the mysterious Windseed, who reported that the Fourth Prince had most of the banners provisionally behind him. "But the warmongers among the banners are trying to win favor by claiming that now they can return to the old ways, the honorable Jun Suai ways. They must win honor by retrieving that sword."

"Are they talking about war again?"

"Some are. Others warn that the king's sword might come with more Essence warriors."

"Then nothing is really decided."

"You don't change centuries of custom and tradition overnight."

Tai's mood was sober when Benevolent Peony appeared on the horizon. "Get ready," Supreme Commander Nu observed wryly, as the sound of clanks and clinks surrounded them, the upper command climbing into full armor, with all weapons at hand.

He wasn't the only one in a sober mood.

Noble Prince Ji Venshai's mood was positively grim as he readied for the parade and grand banquet that the emperor had ordered for the returning heroes.

"Heroes," he said, and spat as he held out his arms for his body servants to begin sliding the layers of silk over his arms before the final, gloriously embroidered brocade was brought in, fragrant from being aired with incense. "They didn't win anything. They just managed not to lose. And yet we're to go forehead to the floor for these so-called heroes."

His sarcasm carried across the hall to the imperial crown princess's dressing room as she got ready.

The crown princess cared little about the details of a distant war that had not resolved anything. The question that kept her awake, though she never spoke it: would Je Tai be at the interview with Imperial Father?

Rumor had it he was instrumental in getting the Westerners to retreat—though Ji Venshai repeated loudly that it was far more likely that the Ghost Eyes just prudently retreated to wait out the winter. She found that lack of family loyalty unpleasant, but then everything about Ji Venshai was increasingly unpleasant. Sometimes when Little Dragon shrieked and fretted, she imagined that he'd shrieked and fretted the same way, and her instinct was to shut herself at the other end of the imperial heir's wing until the nannies could soothe and jostle him to quiet.

"The parade is coming," the steward said quietly at the door.

She had to join Ji Venshai. In silence the pair went out to the Grand Viewing Balcony to be seen as the parade wound its way up to the palace for the reception in the throne room.

The sight of Je Tai riding beside the Supreme Commander—not at the back with the ensigns and lower ranking functionaries, but beside the commander—caused a roil of hot acid inside Venshai. To Imperial Crown Princess Lam, the heat was just as strong, a giddy, glorious sunglow at the sight of him.

The emperor on the other balcony meant that Venshai must sit like a noble prince and smile down grandly, forcing him to mutter through stiff, smiling lips, "Look at that puffed-up peacock. As if he single-handedly won a war."

Part of Venshai's ire was that he had not been included in the reports. "As your vital duties do not place your noble highness in the military chain of command," he'd been told respectfully, "his imperial majesty does not wish to burden your noble highness with matters that would only take away from the vital importance of your many duties."

All nonsense, of course: he was deliberately being kept out, whereas Lam got copies of military reports, as if she knew a cannon from a tea dish. But this was yet more evidence of the vast divide between being a *noble highness* and an *imperial highness.*

Venshai glared at Tai. "Prance away, Cousin. You'll soon take that 'qilin's talent' to grace the Silks for the rest of your heroic life," he muttered as he pretended a smile so wide the icy air chilled his teeth.

He caught the sharp glance his wife shot toward him, and scowled, remembering that she still persisted in that childish passion for Tai's pretty face. If she couldn't see that Tai was just as oily and sly as her grasping uncles—he remembered the silent servants, and coughed. "I'll lay you a wager on how much of a peace we actually won. My guess is, none."

A clash of gongs, and the high screel of suona drowned whatever he said after, though his profile remained pinched with utter disgust. That expression only intensified as Tai rode below them, straight-backed and self-possessed, leaving the supreme commander to respond to the cheering crowd. Finally the parade passed, the signal to leave the balcony and make their way to the throne room.

The imperial crown princess watched Je Tai during the interminable speeches whose components she had been hearing repeated all her life. His manners were impeccable, modest, and withdrawn as the supreme commander praised him for having been instrumental in the defeat of the sinister Cobra Sages, and grateful when the emperor said, "I want to hear a fuller account, Supreme Commander Nu. That includes you, Advisor Je."

And then, after waiting so long and patiently, at last the imperial crown princess was going to be in the same room with Je Tai. Hearing his voice. Seeing him speak to Imperial Father.

Perhaps even to her.

She was oblivious to Ji Venshai scarcely hiding his irritation when court was dismissed, and he had to file out with the rest of the ministers. She paced behind Imperial Father, who leaned heavily on his graywings as they crossed the short distance to the interview chamber behind the throne room.

Imperial Father then invited everyone to sit, and asked after the supreme commander's and Je Tai's health as the graywings served tea and honey cakes. When the servants were gone, the supreme commander said, "Your imperial majesty, this humble servant has furnished her report, and stands ready to explain anything unclear. But if a worthless opinion might be ventured on, it is Advisor Je Tai's report that might be of primary interest, as he was in the Western capital himself."

The imperial princess shuddered at Tai's description of the barbarians' dueling ring. But what struck her deeply was Tai's description of Ki Mek's Essence skills beyond the mental door. She and the emperor both listened intently when he said, "It was Ki Mek, about whom this ignorant one has already spoken to your imperial majesty, who had been destroying blood demons with his Essence skills."

"Then blood demons are real?" the emperor murmured.

"Yes, though they can take many forms. It seems that the Cobra Sages harness them as riders, to enhance their powers. But these demons are not single entities as are human beings. They can combine, or move from one person to another, I am told. The more life Essence they absorb, the stronger they become. Ki Mek, a healer, was able to defeat them by what he describes as dousing a lamp, or popping a bubble. But there is a tremendous cost, and he is still recovering."

"I want to meet him," the emperor said mildly. "Will you convey my wishes, Advisor Je?"

"It would be this humble servant's pleasure," Je Tai said, bowing.

The imperial crown princess swallowed her horror; if this Ki Mek did come to the imperial palace, would he invade her mind, and discover her secret—that she was not of imperial blood at all? She had to prevent *that* if she could!

All this time, Imperial Father looked searchingly at Tai, whose account was simple, as direct as courtly speech permitted, without any of the fawning and flattery that courtiers employed more fulsomely when hiding their enmity for one another, or when they wanted something. Like Ji Venshai, whose every word was honey mixed with incense when he was least trustworthy.

Finally, the emperor said, "My understanding is that the Westerners—with the contrivance of these individuals within their own court—are seeing you as the Essence wielder who defeated their Cobra Sage demons?"

"Yes. This your servant was told that to the Westerners, a defeat by a worthy foe—one with vastly more powerful skills—preserves their honor, or face."

"A treaty might possible, if we send you back as Envoy?"

"That was this servant's poor understanding."

The imperial princess stirred, and the emperor turned her way. "Imperial Daughter? You have an observation?"

"If this ignorant daughter may put a question?" And at Imperial Father's gesture of invitation, she spoke to Je Tai for the first time, aware of the sound of her blood rushing in her ears. Even Mother's horrible poppy tincture could not ease the drum of her pulse. "My own poor understanding is that one of the motivations for this war was the need for rice. Because of the devastation of the demon storms."

Je Tai bowed. "It is true, your imperial highness."

"Our empire never sends tribute," she stated with a glance toward Imperial Father—who nodded back reassuringly. "But we do send silk as gift when we treat with the Easterners over the Great Ocean. Might we extend our generosity to the Westerners before this treaty—a gift of rice, as a gesture of good faith on our part?"

The emperor, to her gratification, smiled her way in approval. "I believe this gesture is in some sense morally required. It was, after all, our own ancestor who created the problem of the demon storms—though it was never intended."

He leaned to pat her hand with his thin, wrinkled one. She saw the slight tremble in his fingers that he tried to hide, and sorrow harrowed her heart.

Imperial Father said to her, "Now that you have reformed the provision conduits for refugees, and secured the release of hoarded stores, we might put those same hoarded stores to good use." To Je Tai, "I will send you as Envoy to treat with them, carrying these gifts. And with a suitable title, to enhance your stature among them."

Je Tai bowed, and Imperial Father said, "All your other merit has not been forgotten. Nor has the rest of your esteemed family. I shall issue an edict raising you and yours to the fifth rank, making you a commandery prince. But, unless these unmet advisors of yours say otherwise, I see no need to send you straight back in the teeth of winter. Take some time. Enjoy the liberty you have earned. Further, I believe we must find a suitable wife for you, one who will both enhance the esteem we feel for you, and also contribute to your standing in the eyes of the Westerners. Daughter, you are best acquainted with suitable unmarried women of court. I require your aid and advice in this matter!"

The imperial princess bowed, chilled to ice.

Je Tai also bowed, uttered formal gratitude, then said, "If this your servant may make a request, your imperial majesty?"

The emperor raised his brows. "Speak informally."

"Might I rejoin Su Inke and my former staff, in order to provide what aid I can? I know that time in that matter presses. Then I wish to visit my home—I have scarcely seen my parents in recent years, and it grieves me to be so unfilial, your imperial majesty."

The emperor uttered a soft laugh. "Commendable, commendable! You are not afraid of work, I find, Prince Je Tai. You will discover that Su Inke and the staff are now at the stage of collating the requirements of the ministries, against the final schedule. They—enlightened by your leadership—made great progress during your absence. Then by all means go home, and carry news of your promotion to your estimable parents. Daughter? If you will conduct our guest to the guest wing..."

The imperial crown princess walked at her most sedate pace. Je Tai did not look directly at her, preserving the proper distance of an unmarried man. His profile looked tired. Sober.

She tried to prolong the walk by telling him how excellent she had found his sister's company, and—with a sharp stab of guilt—how much she missed Je Lei. She won a brief glance at this, and the smallest smile. It was a victory more heady than anything she had ever felt.

Then she said, "That Essence Healer Ki Mek. Is there any limitation to his...his ability to reach past anyone's skull to their thoughts?"

Tai—mistaking the context of her question for physical distance—said, "None that this ignorant one is aware of, your imperial highness."

And here they were, with servants waiting to open doors.

He bowed respectfully and vanished into the guest wing, leaving her to return to the quarters she had begun to hate. She longed for her old tower, and for Je Lei's gentle, soothing presence. She longed for more talk with Je Tai. But here was Venshai, ranting about something. Even the sound of his voice filled her with revulsion. That caustic sarcasm, the complaints that never ended.

She reached her rooms to find her mother there, pacing back and forth. "What happened? Tell me everything," the Sixth Imperial Consort demanded, then her eyes narrowed. "Lam, why are you flushed? Did you drink your elixir today?"

"I did," she said.

"Drink some more," her mother ordered, and summoned a maid to bring it.

Nanny Alk entered then, and bowed.

The Sixth Imperial Consort noticed her, and said, "I see that look, Nanny. Don't trouble yourself to waste breath warning me about poppy. We've had no incidents since she began taking the elixir, have we?"

Nanny Alk bowed again. "Your noble highness, this your most humble servant only seeks to do her duty in issuing a warning about the dangers of adding poppy to medicine daily—"

"You have. Repeatedly. But we have had no problems. Have we?"

And the imperial princess had begun to crave it. The maid appeared then, and the imperial princess obediently drank down the mixture, which at least tasted mostly of pomegranate, with a few spices. The poppy was mainly present by the feel of it inside the nose, like a brush of numbness. In flooded that deliciously cool sense of floating on a cloud above the exasperations of the world.

"Now. I want to know what exactly happened in the west."

The imperial princess began repeating what Je Tai had said—and sure enough, after a short time, the Sixth Imperial Consort lost interest. "Never mind. It's unresolved, and unlikely to affect us here. Nothing in it for my uncle or my brothers. Go visit your son. I hear him fretting. And think about another child! We need to insure the dynasty."

She walked out, but no sooner had the rustle of her silken train vanished beyond the door than here was Venshai. "What exactly did my cousin claim to accomplish in the west?"

His caustic tone was thin, an echo of the baby's fret. She had come to hate the sound of that fretful cry—the only escape was to go to the other side of the imperial heir's wing, and shut the door until the nannies could soothe Dragon to silence.

"He didn't claim to accomplish anything," she said to

Venshai. "He said, quite properly, that the barbarians retreated, and there's some trouble around their throne that might affect the making of a treaty. Imperial Father will send him back as Envoy, and rewarded him with the rank of commandery prince—"

"For doing *nothing?*" Venshai demanded, his voice even more strident. Even through the thin layer of the soft poppy blanket she felt her head throb. "How does he *do* that, reap rewards in heaps for *nothing*, while the rest of us toil from phoenix dawn to turtle last, striving for little more than empty words?"

"You want to exile him to the Silk Islands for nothing?" she retorted.

Venshai glared at him. "I'll make sure he goes farther than that if you chase after him and make a scandal. There's half the court would love to see that—and the other half would be laughing behind their fans."

"I don't chase after *anyone*," she retorted, all the good effect of the poppy gone.

"Not what I saw when that parade dragged by." He sneered. "You were drooling like a dog behind the butcher shop. If the entire court isn't laughing now, it's because all the women were drooling, too. Why is it that women are so...*common?*"

He meant 'predictable', but 'common' came first to mind, with the added fillip of implying servants and street-sweepers. For once he was not thinking of her birth secret—in fact, he'd done his best to put it out of his mind, as revealing it would only ruin the Ji family, too.

But she—always aware of it now—heard that as slur aimed at her, and withdrew, shutting the door between them. Wishing with all her strength that he would never speak to her again. Never enter a room she was in. As for another child, that was never going to happen!

She marched back to her room, and send her maid for another dish of poppy elixir, as he'd ruined the effect of this one. Worse, with the incessant sound of that baby shrieking in the background, sounding just like him.

Impatient, she followed Tigermoth to the auxiliary kitchen, watched her mix the dose, and drank it right there.

A little calm seeped back. A very little, ruined by anger. Silk Islands, for someone Imperial Father clearly respected.

Imperial Father. He was her father, in all important ways! Common…what if someone heard that? And guessed? What if he started blabbing when he was with those brothers of his, and all their women, and…

She pressed her fingers to her eyelids.

And to the maids, just so she could be *alone*, "Prepare me a bath." There was Nanny Alk, hovering like a shadow. "I need contemplative poetry. No, something mild, and amusing. 'When Sun Departs the Mountain Peaks'—that one. It's in the library."

It wasn't in the library. It was still in her room, buried in the trunk where she'd thrown it after she stupidly sent Je Lei away. But that would get rid of Nanny Alk, who acted as if all the medicine in the palace belonged to her.

The imperial princess then picked up a lamp and sped to the kitchen auxiliary, where she went straight to the jars she'd seen earlier. She heaped together the same ingredients, only more of them, added the hot water always simmering, and then choked down the mixture, which was intensely bitter.

But the result was immediate, and a blessed relief. This time the soft cloud spread, cool and soothing, over all the irritations and thunderous emotions that brought her so much trouble. Leaving such lucidity! Everything was sharp and clear, wondrously clear! She looked around the plain room, with its gleaming jars of teas and spices and elixirs.

Something for every problem. Wouldn't the simplest solution be to treat the problem, rather than herself? She considered it from every angle. It would be so easy, as if fate had long ago put everything within reach.

Common. And yet *he* was the toad who wanted to eat the swan.

She reached up to get the ground foxglove seed, which she knew was part of Nanny Alk's medicine, a scant pinch. She added a good dollop. It smelled bitter, which required flavors to counterbalance, mostly cinnamon spice. To that she added a big dose of poppy, mixed it with rice wine, and added just enough boiling water to heat it.

Then she crossed back to Venshai's room, calm and serenely sure.

"What is it? I'm waiting for Gentian."

"I can't sleep," she said, not hearing the latest consort's name. "Until we resolve our disagreement."

He eyed her. "You're the heir," he said in that tone she loathed, part oil and part intimidation, as if she did not know that as soon as Imperial Father was dead, the fight for the crown would begin. He would fight her family, and then he would fight her. Why not resolve it now, and have peace?

"Peace," she repeated as she poured out two dishes of rice wine. He smelled the cinnamon, a spice he relished, and raised his dish. She touched hers to his, saying, "To peace and resolution."

"Resolution," he repeated, sipped, shuddered. She must have mixed it herself. He saw her with her dish to her lips, and downed his in a gulp, head back—while hers went into the potted bamboo shoot beside her.

"Here's more," she said, unsure how much it would take to work.

But she'd put enough foxglove in to drop a patrol of imperial guards, even without the enormous dose of poppy. To which she had become slowly inured over the past months, but to him it was like a great wave washing over him.

He tried to set the dish down, missed the table, muttered something, stumbled—and crumpled soundlessly to the center of the carpet depicting four-toed dragons chasing one another.

An eternity later, or maybe it was only a few breaths, he had gone limp, his soul having fled, unburdened at last of a lifetime of imagined injustices.

She walked to her room and lay down to sleep, drifting pleasantly into dreams, so that not even the sudden screaming of Venshai's fourth and newest consort woke her.

SIXTY-SIX

BETWEEN RETIRING TO A sumptuous bedchamber and waking the next morning, something had changed for Tai. He did not pretend to any awareness beyond the confines of his skull, but he sensed a tension he did not remember from the previous day. Had it to do with a vague memory of running footsteps beyond his door, and the flash of lanterns past the windows, or maybe he'd just been too tired?

Except that the servants who entered that morning were a bit more terse than they'd been the previous evening. And when he asked for directions to Su Inke's current whereabouts, he was told most politely that a message would be sent, and that he was to have anything he desired to eat or drink, and could they bring him something to read?

"I would like to take a walk," he said. He still wasn't quite ready for vigorous exercise yet; he didn't trust the brief but sharp pangs he'd get in his chest and left arm, or the way his breath would shorten.

"I will ask permission," the graywing said, bowing himself out.

In other words…was he supposed to sit here, as if he were a prisoner?

He ate, drank, read what he found, did some very slow fundamentals, and then took another nap, obedient to what the naval physician had said: until his pulse returned to normal, he'd be wise to rest when his body wanted to rest.

That night, he woke to a graywing bringing in lamps, and then another man, utterly nondescript, bowing himself in. Politely he asked if he might post some questions to his highness. Tai had to look about before he remembered that *he* was now 'his highness.

The first question surprised him considerably: "What did your highness discuss with the imperial crown princess yesterday, following the interview with his imperial majesty?"

"Her imperial highness honored me with polite conversation," Tai said, searching his mind. "A question or two about my recent journey as advisor to the naval commander — ay, it was about Essence healers, I think. Then she said many kind things about my sister, who was — or had been, I gather — her assistant or secretary."

"How did you feel about Miss Je's removal from that post?"

"I hadn't known she had been appointed or removed," Tai admitted. "Until the imperial crown princess said she missed her. I was sequestered on a matter according to imperial orders, then sent straightaway to the west, so I actually have seen very little of my family in the past few years." Tai paused, then said reticently, "These are excellent quarters, and I am grateful for imperial generosity, but I am accustomed to keeping busy. The emperor did say I could catch up with my staff, if I did not misunderstand."

The man bowed, rose, said, "I will find out, your highness." And off he went — leaving servants at the door as before, who were polite but firm: stay. Rest. Eat. Read.

Another day passed — bringing a welcome surprise: Waha.

"I've actually been here two days," Waha said. "But first I was sent to Ji House. I think they mistook my accent, hearing Ji instead of Je. Their steward recognized me. Told me you were in the palace, but before I could ask where I might dig you out, imperial guards carried me off to interrogation."

"About?"

"You. Where I'd been. Where you'd been. Why I hadn't come with you. I told them you'd sent me to see that our Essence healer made it home, thinking that 'Essence healer' would sound better than 'gallant wanderer' to imperials. Then they sent me up here. I guess it's lucky the Ji House people had already identified me as your man." He shrugged. "I don't know if this is customary for imperial palaces, but this place seems more locked tight and silent even than the obsidian throne's roundhouse."

Tai admitted that he didn't know either. They spent the remainder of the day catching up. Then speculated on what

Jhax of Ganis might be doing. And Odval and her mysterious mother.

Finally Tai said, "It's taken them a very long time to find out where Su Inke is. Can you do some checking around?"

"Give me some laundry or dirty dishes. The best sources of information are the launderers and the dish washers," Waha said. "And they're less likely to question me further if I'm carrying out an order."

"I have both."

Waha departed with Tai's laundry under his arm. Not half an incense stick after that, the same ageless, nondescript man who has questioned him, knocked softly and entered. "Your highness," he said, and Tai had to swallow the urge to ask him not to use that meaningless title, "you are summoned."

To? But he knew.

Bewildered — wary — he followed the man out. When they reached a hallway, the man looked in both directions. Someone at a distance, mostly hidden in the shadows, raised a hand in an 'all clear' gesture, and the man with Tai gave a short nod, then said, "Your highness, it relieves me considerably to have proved to our satisfaction that you are exactly who you claim to be."

"There was a question?" Tai asked.

"We have had to question everything," the man said. "Before I take you before his imperial majesty, there are two things you had better hear from me, so that you have a few moments to compose yourself. And so that you will not put the emperor to the distress of having to explain: first, your cousin, his noble highness Ji Venshai, is dead."

"Dead? But I just saw him — wasn't that Venshai on the palace balcony, the day of the parade..."

"He was poisoned that night. By the imperial crown princess."

Tai's jaw dropped.

The man took in his undisguised shock with a tiny nod of conviction — almost satisfaction — and said, "The blow to his imperial majesty was considerable. He is..." The man's lips compressed into a tight line. "Not doing well as a result. Please be prepared."

"I will do anything within my limited abilities," Tai began.

Another tiny nod. "That, you must say to him."

Other quietly dressed men closed in, along with a pair of

imperial guards. No one spoke until Tai was bowed into the interview room he now recognized.

He saw the emperor, looking old and worn and very sick, bent over a gilt table inlaid with five-clawed dragons. On it lay divination sticks. Tai recognized the combination.

The emperor glanced up as Tai performed a profound bow. "Leave us, chief," the emperor said, and then, to Tai, a trembling finger indicating the divination sticks as he said, "'The *Book of Wisdom* identifies this reading as 'The cunning rabbit plays dead, and the bow is put away. The rabbit escapes.' I have been contemplating the meaning. What would you suggest?" He waved to the other chair. "Please. Speak plainly."

Tai sat on the edge of this chair. "I do not know the context of the question, your imperial majesty, so I cannot interpret aspects. But I would want to know first, whom do you consider the rabbit to be?"

The emperor dipped his chin. "Exactly. Exactly." He sat back, too weary to stay upright. "The year of the rabbit is over. The dynasty of the rabbit," he murmured. "The dynasty of the dragon has come. I dreamed about you last night, Je Tai."

In augury they taught you to listen past the spoken words. Tai made a slight bow.

"You do not ask about the dream?"

"I will listen if it pleases your imperial majesty to describe it," Tai said.

"Do you believe dreams are prophetic?"

"I...believe that the things that we think about during the day are likely to turn up in dreams," Tai said. "And dream-speakers do sometimes appear. As for prophesy, I would consult an Essence augur. I know they are rare."

"They might be less rare than we think. But who would want to tell the future to those who will not welcome the hearing? I suspect they go mad, or pretend to go mad, or fill their minds with other matters to drown out the future sorrows." The emperor looked up, and said huskily, "Save the empire, Je Tai. I beg you, save the empire."

The words at first had no meaning. Then they detonated like a bomb inside Tai's head, leaving his thoughts scattered to the winds. But the man sitting opposite him regarded him steadily, and Tai heard the labored breathing, and knew that he hadn't the luxury of running when it seemed that for some wild, unfathomable reason, the emperor seemed to be choosing him—not anyone else in that entire court, but him—to take on a burden that was crushing the life out of him.

The emperor looked at him, his expression bleak, but there was compassion in his tone when he said, "You are the scholar on the ice."

Tai bowed his head: if the emperor said it, it was the truth.

"I have no living relatives. Except..." The emperor looked away, then up, and Tai was grieved to see liquid gathering along his lower lids. "Remember what I said about true augurs? There are some questions that would do no good to put. To resume. I have no relations. I did have a son-in-law, but I had not wanted him from the beginning. His single qualification was birth. And he did seem strong enough to hold the court, though the more I began to learn the truth, the more I was coming to detest as well as distrust his methods."

Tai sat silently, unwilling to say anything about the cousin he'd never liked.

"I see that you do not defend Ji Venshai, though he is your blood. They all lie to me, Je Tai. For many reasons. The most benign being to save me pain. But they do not understand that mere physical pain is nothing. I've had it as my constant companion since childhood. The real pain has always been the fear that the empire would disintegrate into fire and blood if I could not hand it to someone who would be able to hold it. I sought, without success, someone to refine the gold in it, and rid us of the dross—I wanted a prince because who else is trained to rule? Before Lam poisoned Ji Venshai, I was willing to accept the dross because he had been trained to rule. But I knew, increasingly, that he had been raised to reign, and not to rule."

He bent, swept up the divination sticks with shaking hands, threw them in the porcelain container painted with cranes and qilins, and then shook it.

He plucked out more sticks, cast them down, and glanced. "What is this? It's not one I'm familiar with."

Tai said, "'Geese carry the yearnings of families far away.'"

"There are songs with that one. Usually sung for those exiled. Or sent to fight far away, by those left at home. I will interpret that as the geese carrying my burden to my ancestors, unresolved. Resolve them, Je Tai. Promise me you will resolve them."

"Your imperial majesty, I am no courtier."

"That," the emperor said, "is your main qualification."

"I've no powerful family backing. No backing at all."

"Your second qualification is the lack of a grasping family. I do not number the Jis among them, as they apparently did not number you. I expect you, even command you, to separate the houses."

Tai managed a bow, wondering what his father would say to that.

"Change the dynasty name. What is your mother's family?"

"Han."

"That's right. A meritorious family. Je Han. Jehan? It sounds well! You would know if it were an auspicious name. As for backing, my dear boy, you do not seem to be aware, but you have the entire navy behind you."

He paused, closing his eyes as he coughed softly, and Tai — whose own chest still ached from time to time — recognized that lack of force as an avoidance of pain.

The emperor said, "I will try to live as long as I can, but I've seen the King of the Underworld waiting for me in dreams and in waking." He drew in a breath. "You are probably wondering how to ask about my daughter."

Tai bowed, for that was exactly what he'd been thinking.

"My dynasty began on a monumental lie. It could end on a smaller one, for the sake of continuity. I've told the Ji family only that the crown prince consort died in an accident. Their house is in mourning now, his consorts sent to their homes as they had no children; I suspect that Ji Venshai had made so many enemies that few will risk my displeasure questioning what sort of accident."

Tai bowed again, his mind catching up with that suggestion to change the dynasty name. Did that mean that the secret about the imperial princess's birth had been exposed? But that was Deceiving the Emperor, a capital crime, requiring a terrible death before the entire city!

The emperor said in his dry, husky voice, "The Yimus are right where I want them; my ferrets found them carrying Ji Venshai's corpse from the site to arrange a false scene, while Yimu Bo was in the process of trying to force the rest of Lam's poison tea down the latest consort's throat. I assume to make the death look like a murder-suicide out of jealousy — a ruse that I would expect of street wolves promoted far beyond their capacity. But the young consort was putting up a spirited fight."

Tai said, "May this your servant trouble you by asking why it happened?"

The emperor drew another husky breath. "Ji Venshai was your blood relation—you have the right. The precipitating incident was an argument, though that is only part of the reason. Lam had been dosed for months with tincture of poppy in secret by her mother, who is sequestered at present. And will remain so, while I investigate the extent of their lies. I shall have more to say on this and related matters once you have become my heir."

Tai heard the quick flow of words, beginning to comprehend what was coming.

The emperor shifted in his seat, waved off a watchful, hovering graywing, and fixed his gaze on Tai. "Marry Lam. For the sake of the empire, I am disinclined to make a spectacle of those who conspired to take my throne; I recognize my part in permitting them to get this far." Another shift. "Lam has worked very hard as crown princess. She is respected. Even loved, by the storm refugees, when she went against her mother's family to clear the corruption from the granaries and distribution, which the Yimus had striven to hide."

Tai thought of the thoughtful face of the young woman who had paced beside him. Her fond words about Lei.

"What I ask is a peaceful transfer of power, just when we need it the most, for I never lose sight of the necessity to move back to the imperial capital as soon as possible. Though I do not expect to make it—nor do I desire to uproot my dynastic parasol tree. If you marry Lam and share the burden of ruling, I can leave this life contented."

Tai bowed a third time. "I vow I will obey to the best of my ability."

"Accepted." The emperor tipped his head back. "Chief." His voice was too frail to be loud. But it was loud enough; an unmarked door opened, and that same nondescript man entered, bowing.

"Chief Ar Pahin, this is Je Tai. Begin now with taking orders from him."

The chief of the ferrets met Tai's gaze, then his face eased and he bowed. "Your imperial majesty. Your *imperial highness*."

Tai dreaded making his memorial visit to Ji Mansion, knowing the truth about Cousin Venshai's death. He did not want to lie to his relations. But no one questioned him. They hadn't the least interest in where he'd been, or what he'd been doing. Kandashai, the most bearable of his cousins, seemed completely lost. Torshai was sullen, ignoring everyone.

The dowager princess had died the year before. Tai's aunt, a gentle woman married very young, had closed out the world, burning spirit money and staring vacantly into the fire, QiQi sitting beside her — still unmarried, having successfully resisted being wed to one of Venshai's enemies in order to get eyes into his house. She still intended to take the imperial examination.

Tai discovered his sister just leaving as he arrived; after he'd paid his respects, he found her waiting out in the courtyard. "Mother and Father ought to arrive tomorrow," she said to him. "They will be here in time for the funeral procession." She added, searching his face, "Have you been ill?"

"In a sense." He hesitated, then said, "It seems that our lives are about to change. Do you want to hear about it now?"

Her expression altered from question to a kind of determination that — though he did not know it — matched his own when faced with a problem. "What can I do?"

"Begin by telling me what you can about the princess. It seems I will be marrying her as soon as the mourning days for Cousin Venshai are over."

Her lips parted in shock, then her eyes narrowed. "What happened?"

"You had better hear it all," Tai said.

SIXTY-SEVEN

IMPERIAL CROWN PRINCESS LAM woke slowly out of the stupor left by so much poppy tincture. No one was about; she discovered when she rose, dizzy and dry-mouthed, that she was now confined to her suite by servants she did not know, one of whom said that all her staff lay in the ferrets' inner prison, waiting for interrogation and execution.

That was when memory caught up with her swimming senses.

The tincture dissipated, but the mood was still with her—only horror had replaced the righteous anger. It wasn't someone else who had prepared that poison tea, though in her memory it felt so much like she'd watched another pair of hands mix it, carry it to Venshai's room, and someone else had spoken, inviting him to drink it.

And someone else had watched him die.

She fell back on her bed, and for an uncounted time could not eat nor drink. Nanny Alk was not there to administer the proper medicine to her, so the princess lay as if stunned. And who knows what might have happened had not the ferret chief come to get her confession.

Thoroughly alarmed—for the emperor had made it quite clear that she was not to be harmed—she was at last roused by imperial physicians, after which the entire story rushed out in a cascade. She begged for mercy for her innocent servants, but there was no response.

After two more wretched days of silence, Tigermoth returned, her eyes swollen from weeping nonstop. She described how she had come out of the bath chamber to discover his noble highness dead, Consort Gentian shrieking, and suddenly the Sixth Imperial Consort and two of her noble brothers rushed in. Then the real chaos began—ending abruptly when ferrets appeared and swept everyone to prison. "All within half an incense stick," Tigermoth finished.

That was the first whiplash to the princess's spirit, the bewilderment in the blameless maid's face. "But for his imperial majesty's mercy," Tigermoth croaked, "we all would have died, instead of those secretly reporting to…" She stopped, clapping her hand to her mouth before falling forehead to the floor.

"To my mother, or my uncles," the princess said wearily, and dismissed her. How stupid she'd been!

The subsequent silence from imperial father lay heavily on her. What could she expect, except execution? That silence was surely prelude to a white cloth with which to hang herself, or a tiny golden cup on a tray, full of a poison that had no poppy in it to ease her through the gate of life to the waiting King of the Underworld.

She was trying to compose herself to face execution with dignity, whatever had or hadn't been revealed about her blood, when her unknown new steward announced that his imperial highness Je Tai requested an interview.

His *imperial* highness?

She scarcely had time to request Tigermoth (she only had the one personal maid) to pin her hair and change her outer robe before there he was, entering her interview chamber, where once his sister had sat day after day.

He wore fine silk in a sober dark brown embroidered with bamboo shoots and acanthus, with pale green and white beneath. The tassel at his belt was no lover's knot or elaborate pattern claiming fidelity or eternity, but the modest scholar's knot.

He bowed with respect, and said without any flattery or polite prelude, "If your imperial highness permits, his imperial majesty desires us to marry one another. I am to say that he believes this will help to insure a peaceful change of dynasty."

"Marry," she whispered—then the import detonated in several remorseless bombs: Je Tai was not asking, he'd been ordered; "change of dynasty" meant that Imperial Father knew the truth? It definitely meant that Je Tai was the new heir. Not her. And Imperial Father was not speaking to her directly.

But…marriage meant, surely, that she wasn't to be executed?

When she was sure she had control of herself she looked up to find he was waiting. He said, gently, "If your imperial highness is unwilling, I will go to his imperial majesty and refuse."

"I'll do it," she said quickly. "Tell Im...tell his imperial majesty that this..." She stumbled on the word "daughter" and continued, "this his lowliest subject is quite willing." She must not presume to address the emperor as Imperial Father. Or even think of him that way...

Through the tears that last blow brought, she saw Je Tai rise. "Then I will speak plainly, if I may," he said. "We shall meet again as soon as your mourning days end. I've several tasks he wants carried out between now and then."

She said, "I do have one request. No, I beg and implore..."

"Please."

"If you could send—no, she will be elevated as well. It's your sister. If she would..." How to express it now, with everything changed? "...care to visit me."

Another polite bow, and he said, "I will pass on your request." Not, *I will send her.* Lei would be a princess now; sister, it seemed, to the next emperor. Whereas she herself...what exactly was she now?

But he was gone.

Imperial Crown Princess Lam had at last what she most desired, but she understood that she had grasped the outer form without the vital inward part. As if she'd caught hold of a swift's tail feather while the swift flew free.

Did she deserve better? With sobriety had come sanity, and now she must face the consequences of actions that she barely remembered. It truly felt as if someone else had done the deed.

But no one else had.

That winter of the dragon year, the imperial court became accustomed to the sight of Je Tai's tall, commanding presence in purple robe standing beside the place reserved to the heir to the throne. Everyone who saw the empty space assumed that the imperial crown princess chose to grieve for her dead consort in private.

The new imperial highness was an object of interest to all, especially after rumors began to spread that not only had he singlehandedly killed off the blood demons ruling the Westerners, he also had something to do with Essence charms on such a scale that the demon storms had at last been cured.

Orioles and swallows—the women of highest rank in the imperial court—made it their business to flatter Tai with invitations to every poetry contest, every gathering to view the earliest plum blossoms, and every court banquet.

More often than not, the noble games offered to entertain the guests included, besides the usual Circle (played with markers and boards of jade, gold, precious woods, and the like) the embroidered ball. This ball, made of brocade pieces and embroidered with silk talismans of romance, was not a mere game: it was understood that whoever caught the ball had an auspicious connection to the thrower. Which—many hoped—could lead to visits from matchmakers. But he never caught the ball, and whispers began to circulate that he would be marrying the imperial crown princess after her mourning.

"What could be more natural?" People nodded wisely. Those who caught the eye of the emperor, as the saying went, soared with the cranes or drowned.

His parents had come to attend Venshai's funeral and found themselves elevated to royal rank as a reward for having raised a son whose excellence had gained the notice and trust of the emperor.

His noble highness Prince Je Pan took his consequent retirement with equanimity, and very soon became a welcome sight in the emperor's room, playing quiet games of Circle as they debated the ancients' wisdom on judicial matters. The emperor liked the slow-spoken, austere former magister, who could not be more different than the late and unlamented Left Chancellor Ji Houduo. The emperor liked the unassuming magister so much that he had decided to send him on ahead to the imperial capital to take charge of the shift to the Hall of Justice, for the vital business of government must not pause.

Lei was not forgotten, though she soon secretly wished she had been. In the time it took to hear Tai's account of his adventures during their walk after visiting the Ji house of mourning, she'd begun to comprehend that her own life was about to change forever. As it did.

It was useless to resent it. That would be unfilial at the very least. But her mother, overjoyed at this elevation in rank and wealth now put all her mind to finding an advantageous marriage for Lei. And Lei found herself courted for all the wrong reasons; worse, when she tried going back to her former room-mates, hoping to go with them to the local entertainment house to see their favorite players in the new play about Lu Frei's Owl and the three silly scholars, they circled around her, every remark requiring a glance to see how she reacted.

And when her silly bunny of a roommate Chrysanthemum found a chance to whisper, "Can you find me a rich husband, Princess Lei?" Lei understood that their relationship had changed forever. Rank had ruined the old, easy friendship.

When Tai came to ask if she would like to visit the imperial crown princess, Lei said, cautiously, "I would."

And when the princess said slowly and even diffidently, "I wish you would call me Lam," Lei looked her fully in the face, saw the suffering there, and said, "I would be honored, Lam."

Waha returned quietly right after the first thaw, and took some time to do a little listening around the capital before being inter-cepted by the imperial guards. He was shunted promptly to the ferrets, who had been investigating *him*.

"Where have you been?" Ar Pahin, the chief, asked.

Waha said, "Je Tai sent me to Benevolent Winds to take a look around."

The ferret made no reaction to his lack of protocol-required honorifics. "And?"

Waha considered, then decided that Tai would not mind this man getting a full report—in summary. "The Yimus are waiting for anyone coming in. The harbor has explosive devices hung below the surface of the water, and cannon emplaced to cover approach. My guess is that someone managed to get word to them before the emperor bottled up the Yimus here in the capital. Yimu Ban plans to fight to hold the island."

The ferret chief looked at Waha with a minute chin dip of approval, and in short order he, Tai, a military captain, and Supreme Commander Nu gathered in a splendid room in the heir's wing.

Tai said, on hearing Waha's unsurprising report, "Yimu Ban is holding the island hostage, no doubt planning exorbitant demands, as he knows the emperor won't want to throw the entire eastern fleet against him, bludgeoning the entire city to the rubble. Is there a weak link in his command chain?"

Waha said, "Exactly as you'd suspect: devotion to gold, if not to his person, at the top rank, and below, a shared hatred of Yimu Ban and his grasping rats and wolves."

Tai turned to the military captain. "I have scant experience in this sort of exercise, but would it be possible to find a way into the city, take out those commanders, and arrest Yimu Ban before he discovers us?"

Us. The captain turned to Supreme Commander Nu, who gave him a thin smile. He said to Tai, "We have discussed these possibilities for…some time now. The best entry-point would be from upriver, through the marshes. The garrison is along this ridge, and the mines are…"

Later that night, the supreme commander was told that the emperor was well enough for an interview. "But if this humble servitor may offer a request," murmured the chief graywing, who was not humble at all, but quite firm in his righteous conviction, "please keep it brief."

Supreme Commander Nu made her way softly into the chamber, where she found the emperor in bed. He begged forgiveness for receiving her in a way that did not suit her dignity, she demurred, then she said, "If this servant of yours is to offer an observation—"

"Please."

"—she would say that his imperial majesty could not have chosen better than Je Tai. He *listens* to the experts you have given him. I expect that the empire's primary gunpowder store will be secure by next Phoenix Moon."

The emperor closed his eyes, his face relaxing. Eyes still closed, he whispered, "Let him choose a replacement governor. Let us see what kind of man he picks."

"Man." Supreme Commander Nu could name three women who would make better governors of that vital island than most men she knew—but now was not the time to put that idea forward.

Tai sailed with Waha, a company of elite warriors, and five fast warships; the warships remained hull up off the bay. Just out of cannon shot, and while Yimu Ban's force focused on preparing for their onslaught, Tai's elites ghosted under cover of a sleet storm into the reek of the lower city.

By dawn, a team of six, Waha, and Tai surrounded Yimu Ban in his sumptuous bed. He got up, clutching layers of silken brocade around him, then out came a knife and he charged Tai in street-wolf style.

Waha had trained Tai in street fighting. Three blows and Tai had him on the floor, hampered in his welter of bedclothes. "Finish me off," the man snarled. "Better than being a spectacle on the execution block."

"Where the blood is scarcely dry from your latest victim?" Tai asked, hiding the slight strain he still felt in his chest at the sudden, violent exertion. "No, everything to be done according to the laws."

And it was, that day, an unpleasant business that left no room for gratification.

Then the last person Tai had brought was rowed in: Su Inke's cousin Tuke, who had been in the scribes while Cousin Inke was studying augury. He'd joined Tai to help with the Great Transfer plans after Tai found out that Su Tuke had been trained to bookkeeping for the military; a brilliant accountant who had no family connections, so no one of higher rank had been aware of how much of the smooth operation of military funds was due to his tireless labor.

Tai walked Su Tuke through the fabulous palace that Yimu Ban had built with imperial tax money and stopped in a great hall with a high seat much like the imperial throne, but without a golden five-toed dragon behind it.

Here the entire household had been gathered, forehead to the floor. "See what you can do to straighten out this rats' nest," he said, and handed off the seal that Waha had found in a chamber he'd called a pirate's treasure den. "Keep any of these people who seem to be honest. For the rest, those not guilty of capital crimes, turn them off with only what they stand up in. The guilty go to the magistrates the emperor sent."

Su Tuke bowed, still expecting to wake up and find himself back in his tiny cubby aboard the troop ship in the harbor, coping with the pile of ledgers from all the eastern fleets.

When Tai left, the entire city turned out in the miserable weather and cheered him all the way to the wharf and beyond, until he could no longer be seen in his launch on the choppy green-gray seas.

Then Su Tuke wandered through that palace, clutching a carryall with his two robes, his patched and worn underthings, a pair of house slippers. his inkstone, brushes, and inks, and blinked around that vast bedchamber full of treasures.

Tai sailed back to face his next task.

Sixty-eight

Every time Tai returned to Mountain Peony, it seemed to him he'd accumulated in his absence a larger number of people whose primary duty was to see to all the details of his ever-complicating life.

He lived in the palace now, in the heir's wing. There was no sign of Ji Venshai left except his baby, a small, round-faced, fretful child who wailed a lot, in spite of an army of servants trying to pacify him.

"Is he always like this?" Tai asked Lei when the two of them were alone at breakfast.

"Mostly," Lei said.

"Doesn't his mother comfort him?"

Lei considered what to say, and Tai gave her a narrow look. "That should be easy to answer. She hates children? Or is it just him?"

"I think…she doesn't know what to do with him. But also there's some resentment. She and Cousin Venshai did not get on very well, according to her. Poor little mouse," Lei added sadly. "A prince no one seems to know what to do with. I think you know the emperor has rescinded his title of First Imperial Prince. No one calls him 'Little Dragon' anymore. I feel so sorry for the poor little boy that I'm the one who spends most time with him—I have little else to do, except exercise with Waha, and read to Lam."

"The baby is no longer in line for the throne?" Tai said in surprise—usually dynasties were grasping for heirs. Who then, too often, grew to be the biggest threats to the throne. Aish! That was a future concern. He had enough to do right now. His days had become so filled that he had yet to catch more than a glimpse of his future wife.

"The emperor doesn't want the Ji family making claims to the throne."

That explained the disinheriting. Tai sighed. "What does the imperial princess feel about any of this?"

Lei wasn't certain how much to tell her brother about what Lam had poured out when they were alone. She settled for, "I think you ought to speak to Nanny Alk. Besides the emperor, who still cares for her very much, it was Nanny Alk who understands her best."

Tai had not missed that "still." But he was not certain what his sister knew, and he felt that though this dangerous secret might no longer get him killed, it wasn't truly his.

He said, "Where can I find this Nanny Alk?"

Lei chuckled silently. "Elder brother, you still don't realize that you don't have to seek anyone. You summon them to you."

He raised his voice. "Tourmaline?"

A graywing appeared in the far door.

"Please ask Nanny Alk to come as soon as it is convenient." He could not bring himself to baldly summon an older woman.

At that moment, Waha poked his head in the nearer door. He took the two in, then said to Lei, "Second phoenix?"

Lei put her hands together in assent.

Waha vanished.

"What was that about?"

"Second phoenix?" Lei looked surprised. "Isn't this the usual time for your martial skills training?"

"If I had the time free, it would," Tai said. His eyes narrowed. "You mentioned exercising. When did this begin?"

"Back at our old home, when Mother took you to poetry parties. It felt invigorating once I was used to it, so I kept learning, except when I was in the palace. I started again when you two got back from Benevolent Winds."

Tai scowled. "He's not flirting with you, is he?"

Lei gave him a skeptical look. "Yes. But it's just flirting. He told me when we first met — when I was barely sixteen — that he was never serious. I liked how honest he was. So very welcome." Lei tipped her head. "Waha also teaches me some of his language as we spar. I began studying Western history after you were sent west. It's fascinating…"

And as she went on to outline some of the customs that the

imperials had adopted from the long-ago Jun Suai princess, the instinct to become protective vanished like mist before the sun. Lei didn't look any older than she had at sixteen, except her manner was no longer the diffident teen of those days. She was still quiet, but self-assured rather than reclusive.

Before Tai could say anything, there was a quiet knock, and Nanny Alk entered, bowing deeply. Lei made a movement toward the door, but Tai stayed her with a glance.

Lei moved back to sit quietly as a dignified woman came forward. She was much younger than the white-haired granny Tai had been expecting. But there was such sorrow carved into her face.

He said to Nanny Alk, "I learned from my sister about the princess's Moods. Speak plainly, please. What can you tell me about these, and what exactly were you giving her? I understand from the report that the poison she made that killed Ji Venshai came from your medicine stores. Included were foxglove and poppy."

Nanny Alk stated, "About the medicine, your imperial highness, it must be understood that I only gave it to her when she needed it. There could be weeks between doses. Months, sometimes, when things were calm. I did use foxglove, but only three or four grains as small as grains of sand. It slows the heart from thundering. The poppy, also, a tiny dose, to soothe the nerves so that the rest of the herbs could circumvent whatever it was that caused the humors to spark to fire, or to stone. Cooling herbs — water affinity — for the first, and fire affinity for the second."

"When did the problems begin?"

"I was not present, your imperial highness, but according to what I was told, her noble highness the Sixth Imperial Consort had issued orders to…to wheedle her into tractability, until my arrival. She was terribly spoilt — no one ever said no. When the Sixth Imperial Consort grew tired of her, she was handed off to servants to be coaxed into quiet. The imbalance of humors was not trained much less treated, but smothered with sweets and soothing drinks and she was permitted to do anything she wanted."

"Does her baby have the same imbalance?"

Nanny Alk hesitated, then bowed her head. "I have spent scant time with him. There might be Essence talent of some sort, is all I can say."

Tai then said, "If I can find an Essence healer to restore balance. Would you wish to stay and preside?"

At that Nanny Alk raised her head, her expression bleak. "Your imperial highness, this humble servant would request permission to be sent, with her children whom she scarcely ever sees, to someplace as far from imperial courts as possible. Somewhere there might be a need for a healer and a scholar."

She left then, and Tai turned to Lei. "Is she always like that? It's as if she expects me to have her executed."

Tears stung Lei's eyes. "I almost think that she would want that, but for her children. You might not know this, but before the Yimus were rounded up, they sent assassins, in the emperor's name, to murder the families of Lam's chief servants—they assumed the ferrets would be killing the servants themselves. So they wouldn't talk. The ferrets were just able to save Nanny Alk's two children, only because the instructors at their school refused to admit which children were hers—and the assassins didn't dare kill them all, as some of them belong to ministerial families."

"That's appalling," Tai said on an exhaled breath. "I believe then that the only reward I can give her would be to find a suitable post somewhere. Maybe I can get her to take Lam's little boy to foster? But I want Ki Mek to examine him first. And her imperial highness."

In the past days, Lei had conquered her fear of the emperor, after seeing him together with the imperial crown princess. Lam had confessed the truth of her mixed blood to Lei, saying, "I found out that my Uncle Bo tried to use the secret to win freedom for himself, after he was caught trying to kill Venshai's consort. But they got it out of him anyway, before he was executed." She'd looked away, gripping her elbows with her fingers. "At least they spared my little cousin, and Uncle Chen. Who had always taken my part. But he was exiled, so I don't think I'll ever see him again."

Lei noticed that she did not mention her mother, who Lei knew had been offered the choice between poison or being sent to a distant temple to write sutras and work for the poor. Yimu Lily—stripped of her title, jewels and silks—had at first chosen the temple until she heard that she would be expected to cut off her hair, at which point she grabbed the poison herself and dashed it down her throat.

Seeing father and daughter together heartened Lei. There

might not be shared blood, but it was plain that there was shared love and devotion.

She looked up at Tai. "I think the emperor would like that, if your Ki Mek really is a healer." She would not reveal Lam's passion for Tai, but she added, hoping to make things easier between the soon-to-be emperor and empress, "Healing is also what Lam wants the most."

Six days before mourning for Ji Venshai was to end, Tai woke to Mek's familiar voice at his mental door: "Tai? Windseed has news. The Fourth Prince has been displaced, and Jathyam is now on the obsidian throne."

Disgust suffused Tai—then he remembered that it was Jathyam's father Gatslan who had earned his hatred. He scarcely recollected the son, except that Ardal had seemed to like him. "Not the father?"

"Gatslan of Angja died with the First Prince while you were rescuing me. Jathyam is a compromise between the military raiders who want the old ways, and Jhax of Ganis's faction, whose main purpose is to curtail the power and influence of the Cobra Sages."

"Is he another Gatslan?"

"Not so. He closed the goldmine at Ardal's request. He lets her manage the cull. She chooses those to send."

"That sounds good," Tai murmured out loud, sitting up in bed. It was easier to speak and think than to try to form sentences mentally when he was so tired. "It sounds very good, yet am I hearing reserve? They don't want a treaty?"

"They do want a treaty, but they cannot settle for abject surrender. They want to meet halfway—Anchor Island has been suggested—and also to go back to the custom introduced during the second Kun Dynasty."

"That was..."

"A swap of princesses. Do you see? It puts both empires on equal footing."

"Swap *princesses?*" Tai threw off the covers—as a soft-footed graywing came in, bearing a lamp. Tai realized he'd exclaimed out loud. He was going to have to get used to this life.

He waved off the graywing, who left the lamp and withdrew, then shut his eyes, and whispered under his breath. "What princesses?"

Mek said diffidently, "Don't you have a sister? As for them, Jathyam would be sending you Odval, who is now their chief princess."

Tai was going to flatly refuse, then hesitated. Lei had been learning the language…yes, but that was idle interest. Not to be taken as desire to be hurled into the enemy empire. "She'd be marrying Jathyam?"

"Yes. But he prefers men, so I'm told she'd be free to pick her side consorts. Windseed, and Odval's mother, are for it because they think it's the only way to get a treaty that will stick."

Tai cursed mentally—then remembered that Mek would hear it. "I'd hoped you could come here first. See if you can help the emperor. He's in such pain from early poison. He's borne it all his life. Also, his daughter…"

Tai stopped, letting Mek pick up images from his memory.

"I don't want to leave," came Mek's somewhat diffident thought. "Anise is due to have our first child any day."

That caught Tai by surprise; he was always going to think of Mek as a boy, he suspected, even when they were old and white of hair.

"I'll come after the baby is safely born," Mek offered.

It was that word "safely" that caused Tai to hesitate. Mek wasn't giving him a specific time, but a condition. Though he'd never been around babies, he remembered what Mek was like with small animals, especially wounded ones. An infant—his infant—might very well take months, even years before a fond father considered it "safe." And the emperor likely did not have that much time. Though that would not mean much to a gallant wanderer, who could point out (rightly) that emperors could afford all the healers the world contained.

"I have an idea," Tai said. "The treaty party could stop at Eagle Island on the return trip. The baby should be in the world by then, and past the 100 days. If you feel it's safe to leave, you could sail in comfort. I'll send you back whenever you wish."

Mek agreed, and vanished. Tai got up to write orders about the logistics of the treaty. The sooner they sailed, the better.

When the sun had brightened the windows, he went in search of Lei, and found her out on one of the terraces in the balmy spring air, walking about with Lam's and Ji's baby. The child was quiet for once, gaze intent on a fuzzy bee crawling over a flower, as Lei held him and murmured "Bee…bee…see the bee on the flower?" She looked up at Tai's approach.

"I wanted to discuss something with you before I take it to the emperor," he said, and quickly explained what Mek had said. He finished, "If you hate the idea I can speak to Cousin Qishai, or one of the Han cousins. I'm sure the emperor would not mind raising her to a princess—"

"I'll go," Lei said.

Tai stopped mid-sentence. "Don't you want to consider it longer?"

"I don't need to. My life is already like a dropped cauldron. If someone has to go, why not I? At least I'm interested, whereas QiQi still has her heart set on taking the imperial examination this year. I'll do it if you meet two conditions."

"Which are?"

"One, if I hate it, and I decide to leave, you won't force me back."

"Done," Tai said. He didn't know Jathyam, but Jhax had seemed reasonable, for a Westerner noble. He might even discuss this contingency in private.

"And second, I can take him along."

"The baby?" Tai exclaimed. "Why?"

"I like him. He likes me. He doesn't cry as much with me. And I'm afraid if I leave him, Lam might…have a Mood."

"Ay." Tai winced. "We really need to get Mek here. Though the case might be beyond him. Anyway, if Lam gives permission, as she's the mother, I don't mind. The emperor will probably be sending an army of servants either way."

Tai then sent a servant to request an interview with the emperor, who granted it immediately. Already those in service around the throne sensed the shift of power from the old to the new, for it was the emperor, struggling to survive from day to day, who immediately dropped everything whenever Tai wished-ed to speak to him.

Tai went to the imperial bed chamber, where the emperor was most comfortable. "Your imperial majesty, I heard from Ki Mek," he said, and related everything—including Lei's willing-ness to go west in trade.

The emperor flushed a mottled color, murmuring, "As I would expect from your family. We shall raise her rank imme-diately, so that she will be received with the respect due to an imperial princess. The only thing I had hoped for was to see you and Lam married first. But it would not do to be too hasty, not good at all. No, we shall prepare a splendid wedding— better than the last one—and it will take place as soon as you return in glory with the treaty."

SIXTY-NINE

THE EMPEROR'S WORDS ECHOED in Tai's ears. He'd always known that eventually he must marry and carry on the family; it was part of filial obligation. And the emperor was father to all his subjects.

Ever since his mistaking Han Anise's friendship for his own passion, the idea of finding someone he wanted to be with had intruded on his thoughts. He knew in himself the urgency that drove people together at Spring Festival; he'd recognized what it looked like in others, but he had extinguished his own fire the way he smothered a hunger for candied haws, or a persistent but mild itch after an insect bite. It was a matter of self-discipline.

When he dutifully went to Imperial Princess Lam to discuss what the emperor had said, he was astonished to recognize that passion in her as she said, "Whenever you and Imperial Father think the most auspicious."

Then she twisted her fingers together, and added, "I don't know if Imperial Father is aware. I am afraid to ask. But you ought to know: my mother was pregnant before she met his imperial majesty. He was just a guard. Low-born. Like my uncles. And my mother," she added deliberately, when he didn't react.

She knew by now that he had the honor — the integrity — she'd begun to believe non-existent, so she was braced for disgust, even repudiation of her tainted blood and false beginning.

He said, "I already knew this, Lam."

She flushed. "Venshai told you. Didn't he." It was not a

question, but a bitter, defeated statement.

"It makes no difference," Tai said. "Your birth father was a man. Like me. It seems he did not get to live long enough to find out if he'd be a good man. If the gods give you and me children, it's their fate to come into high titles from birth, but it will be up to us to raise them as Kanda teaches. Don't you think?"

Tears gleamed along her eyelids, but she blinked them back. "Yes, yes. That is exactly what we must do."

He was going to bow himself out, but something more seemed to be called for, something to acknowledge both what she had confessed in words, and more importantly, perhaps, what she had revealed without words. What? He had learned from watching Mek with small creatures how the power of kindness begot trust. He knew he would never entirely trust her, for reasons not her fault. But he must be trustworthy.

He crossed the distance between them, cupped her cheek, and when she leaned into his hand, he thumbed away the tears. "I will try to be a good husband," he promised. "First, I've got to bring a treaty of peace back to his imperial majesty."

She grasped his wrist, and pressed a kiss to it, then let him go.

He shut the door softly, and left, pausing when he saw the new steward. He remembered then that Nanny Alk and her children were on the way to a small island above Great Ran. "You have her proper medicine, yes? No poppy?"

The steward bowed with wooden countenance, then spoke with firmness, "She was sick for nearly the entire mourning period, craving poppy. She now refuses to have it anywhere in our pharmacy."

"That is a relief to hear." He went to take leave of his parents.

And the next morning, the fleet departed, Lei with Waha at her shoulder, and the baby in arms. The baby, sometimes heard, rarely glimpsed. "What is his actual name?" Tai asked.

Lei said, "Anek."

"Anek," Tai repeated, hoping to get that into memory: here was another blamelessly complicated life he must take responsibility for.

He turned to Supreme Commander Nu, who stood outside the command center up on the third level of the tower ship. She raised her voice, "Set sail!"

Gongs clashed. Horns blew. Anchors rumbled. The sails rattled down, and ship surged on the waves.

The least fulsome of the archivists, you no doubt have seen, wrote that the Grand Imperial Fleet departed in spring airs that branched into nine-colored clouds as the sun rode a six-dragon chariot through the skies. The emperor and his daughter graced the auspicious occasion from the highest balcony of the palace.

The journey west was marred by only one storm—and though the wind howled, and the waves rose to green-gray mountains, it was no demon storm.

As for the meeting at Anchor Island, historians invariably liken it to the Treaty of Swallows at the beginning of the second Kun Dynasty, when the Jun Suai exchanged blade and spear for silk and jade by trading the sisters of the monarchs.

The intent to exchange weapons for peace was the same, symbolized by the exchange of brides, but there the similarities ended. It's true that Je Tai had brought a sister, but Jathyam of Angja brought a cousin. Je Tai had not yet become Emperor Jehan Taiyan, and Jathyam of Ganis was so new to his obsidian throne that he was aware at all times that his hold could fail.

He still could not believe that he could fund his family's wealth on *trade* with the east, rather than raiding. He watched as the easterners, true to their word, began to unload and cart from the east harbor to the west cartloads of silk and rice. And from his own ships, cartloads of bluenose bolsters and blankets, and the porcelain stoves that kept all but the meanest roundhouses warm in the depths of winter, went the other way.

He had two challenges facing him: convincing the bannermen that there was honor in trade, that wealth was honor, and the second challenge, to keep the Cobra Sages restricted to healing and the management of slave tattoos and the like. He had begun by forbidden any high-ranking Sage to be present for this momentous occasion.

The young emperors left their ships to meet.

The moment Jathyam saw Je Tai, he recognized those glittering black phoenix eyes. Je Tai had also chosen to leave off his customary headband, and there was the tiger eye, fierce and stylish, above that phoenix gaze. Jathyam could see beneath the outer strokes the two simple ones belonging to Dragon's

Chosen slaves. He understood the challenge immediately, for this man had not only rid himself of the slave-binding, he had also defeated the Cobra Sages with a single strike of a bespelled sword. The sword of a king.

Jathyam respected such prowess. So did his fiercest bannermen. Peace with a worthy foe! New era, with the Cobra Sages strictly leashed!

Or so he believed.

Among his many galley slaves and scut laborers carting those bolsters shuffled a tall slave whose beautiful tattoos of climbing roses were hidden beneath his rough slave clothing.

Sidax had been ordered by the surviving Cobra Sage elites to redeem himself by the capture of that bespelled sword. He knew that Kimek had wielded it before the Day of Defeat, but in the dueling ring this taller, stronger Jetai had clearly taken the sword away from him.

All during the journey he did the lowliest chores, meek and apparently simple. No one troubled to examine or question slaves—they were *slaves*. Interchangeable. Bound to obedience by the marks on their foreheads—and there was the mark on his forehead. He went unremarked until the last load of gifts went to the easterners, at which time he slipped the deflection spell over himself, and catfooted away from the head-bent line trudging back to the raiders.

He sighted the meeting place, an ancient three-tiered, eight-sided pagoda, about the only building that had survived the demon storms undamaged. He watched, weighed down by an arsenal of poisoned flechettes, and talismans bespelled to burn targets from within. His plan was to fight his way past the expected formidable guards around Jetai, then face the man himself and take that sword, or die trying.

But…Jetai was not carrying the sword! What warrior went out of his private chamber without his weapons?

After staring in astonishment, he surveyed Angja and Ganis lords, and saw that they, too, had left off their weapons. Hai-yoo! This was a peace treaty! Apparently they had agreed to leave behind weapons. That meant the sword had to be on the Mud flagship.

He ghosted away, rapidly altering the plan from attack to covert search of the Mud flagship, as, unaware, the two parties met in the newly-swept ground floor of the pagoda.

Je Tai retained enough residual resentment of Gatslan of

Angja and his never-forgotten, careless comments about unmanning Tai to present a formidable countenance to the Westerners—which eased somewhat when he recognized Jhax of Ganis among them. Jhax leaned on a fine caved walking stick, his ready smile dimpling thin cheeks, as he placed his fist to his heart in greeting.

Lei, walking beside Tai, found her attention arrested by this tall, slim man whose face bore the lineaments of pain. *Jhax of Ganis*, she caught out of the whirlpool of introductions. And as the carefully worked out ritual of discussion and agreement began, the sea breeze toyed with silks and tassels and courting chimes as Lei tried not to stare, intensely aware of that reflective gaze resting on her from time to time.

When she stole another look his way, she saw him whispering to the oval-faced woman her own age whose many dark braids were decorated with beads and sweetly chiming golden ornaments. What a pretty fashion! Was she a consort? No, there was no proprietary air about either of them. She had to be Odval of Angja, as new to her lofty title as Lei was, who would take her place in the imperial palace. Lei laughed inwardly at the image of this Westerner at home in rooms she'd scarcely lived in before this sudden turn in her life.

"Lei," Tai whispered.

She started—ay, it was time for the first shared meal.

The whole was carefully contrived politesse, each side mirroring the other. But ritual was a part of life. Civilization.

The seating was as carefully arranged, the two monarchs at the eastmost and westmost points in the circle, their new princesses to their right, and advisors, interpreters, and commanders disposed around them.

Tai tried not to stare at Odval of Angja as she gracefully dropped cross-legged onto the cushion next to him. He knew that she had been part of the preliminary arrangements, worked out between Jhax, Ardal, her cousin Jathyam, and conveyed from the mysterious Windseed through Mek to Tai and the emperor, but he had not previously noticed how much he liked seeing that posture instead of the knees-and-toes-together kneeling that his sister and mother had modeled all his life.

"I hoped it would be you coming here, and not some bearded old envoy who would lecture me all the way to your end of the world," Odval murmured in her home language.

"I've already learnt a few words of Mud—that is, imperial." She flashed a quick grin. "Windseed got some of it from Kimek."

"His name is Ki Mek," Tai said. "You'll have to get used to family names then personal names."

"Ki. Mek. Did he come, too? Or did they confine him in one of the many rooms of your floating palace because he isn't a man of rank?"

"He's not here," Tai said. "But we will get him on our way back."

"He made a winsome girl, that day," she whispered. "Oh, how angry the snakes were! I still love to think of that. Especially when I consider how much danger my brother is still in." Her expression clouded for a heartbeat.

Tai caught Jathyam's eye, and shifted easily to a discussion of the weather, using the Western language.

Conversation limped along, Lei struggling to speak to Jathyam while hoping that she would be able to talk to Jhax of Ganis—whose gaze she caught once. Twice…

And aboard the floating palace, Sidax ghosted from chamber to chamber, exasperated at how much space there was when the principal mode of power was shifted from the oar to the wind. How arrogant, to depend on the fickle wind, whereas oarsmen could always be counted on, motivated by pain.

The search was not easy, which made the prospective triumph sweeter. These imperial guards, for all their tight line-of-sight patrol, were not looking for deflection spells. One day that might be as common a thing as it was in the world of Father Dragon's Chosen—but that day was not now.

It was a limited triumph, though, because when he finally attained the rooms that had to belong to that Je Tai, weapons he found—but not the pearl-handled sword.

He searched twice. Then began grimly on the adjacent servant rooms…

In the pavilion, the meal was ending. Silent servants hung colored paper lanterns painted with phoenixes and dragons collectively adding a warm, golden glow.

It was time to write out the treaty agreement and apply the seals. Lei was not needed for that. She slipped away, thinking of retreating to the ship to see how Anek was getting along with his nannies—all of whom had been carefully chosen for their kindness—when here came the other princess, leading Jhax of Ganis.

"Princess? "You wait?" Odval asked tentatively, as her few words in imperial seemed to desert her. It was the sudden impact of those long, tilted black eyes, so very much like those of Jetai. Now an emperor?

"Friend," Jhax enunciated self-consciously. "My friend. Kimek friend. Your friend?"

When meeting his pale gaze, Lei found her own Western vocabulary on the verge of fleeing, but then he stumbled over an obviously-prepared sentence in charmingly accented imperial. His voice was soft, his laugh even softer.

Emboldened, she ventured into a couple of sentences that Waha had coached her in.

Odval watched in satisfaction. She had just about conquered her passion for Jhax, who alas had treated her with the careful courtesy of a brother for a sister. She'd assumed he was passionless, but passion there was now in the way he stared at Jetai's admittedly gorgeous sister. Odval sustained a pang, then consciously let it go. She was on her way to a new life. If Jhax, so solitary and meticulous, liked this sister of Jetai's, it would be best for everyone. As long as she was not horrid. But there was nothing smirking or cruel in her voice or her manner, and the three stumbled through an attempt at conversation, switching languages back and forth as eyes met eyes, searching…

And on the flagship, Sidax cursed heatedly as he examined room after room, having to freeze and hide until footsteps passed. Could that pearl-handled sword possibly be stashed among the ordinary warriors' armory? How stupid that would be! Unless these ignorant Muds knew how to bespell their weapons to kill if the wrong hands touched them. But he distinctly remembered seeing that weakling Kimek lose the sword to this Jetai without anything happening.

Grimly he kept searching. First he had to scour this entire flagship before he sneaked to the military vessels. These had to be the princess's chambers—female trinkets lay in carved boxes. A good place to hide a sword, actually. Unexpected. Two maids entered, and he faded against a bulkhead, then saw an open door…

Tai found himself having to work around lying to Jathyam. After lying to the emperor the first time they met, he had sworn a vow to never permit politics to force another lie. That was the path his uncle and cousin had trod, an easy one to get lost on.

Yet Jathyam, gesturing Tai to the side, was so earnest in asking if Tai could give him any spells that would help him keep the Cobra Sages from regaining their hold. That meant Jhax and Odval had not told Jathyam the truth about his possessing no Essence power. It seemed that these friends and allies still kept secrets from one another out of necessity.

"I wish I could," he said, infusing his voice with the regret he truly felt. "I hate the Cobra Sages as much as you do." He almost said 'More' but withheld it. "What you call spells, or charms, in our language, are…restricted to the individual." There, that much was true.

"That means you cannot lend me that sword of yours, just until I can rid myself of the last of them? I swear on my heart's blood and my blade I would return it."

Tai thought about the Three Blessings, and the idea of glory being bound up with bloodshed. And slavery. He shook his head. Making a peace treaty was not the time to point out that the Dragon's Chosen had a lot more problems than the Cobra Sages.

And we are not much better. The imperial court had let itself become infested with the Yimus and the Jis. And a dynasty ago, a general had had to invent a disaster in order to prevent civil war from tearing the empire apart.

Tai shook his head slowly. "I could hand it to you, but it would remain just a sword. The Essence-charms are truly part of the individual."

"Hai-yoo, it was merely a dream," Jathyam said, white teeth flashing in a laugh. "We lost much when the Sages took over matters of Essence from us, leaving us with the obsidian blades. Or so my sister Ardal says." A quick glance. "And our brother."

He knows about Windseed. Tai made sober bow. "He's a hero who can never be acknowledged. I hope he will be sung in your history."

"I will see to that," Jathyam promised. "If I survive long enough."

Odval walked up then, with Lei and Jhax, bringing hot rice wine for Jathyam to try.

And on the flagship, Sidax was able at last to search the princess suite in spite of the many maids coming and going. He nearly skipped the adjacent chamber, where he heard a baby babbling, but the thought occurred that a clever mind would expect exactly that.

Cursing anew, he slipped into the chamber, which smelled of honey. But he scarcely noticed that when he sensed the chamber imbued with Essence potential. His gaze went to, then dismissed, a young woman bent over a piece of cloth, stitching quickly. His attention arrowed to a baby sitting on the floor.

First, the sword. Sidax began to ease along the wall, his gaze sweeping the room for trunks, shelves, the seams in woodwork that would indicate hidden or inset compartments. Then the baby dropped whatever it had been gumming, and let out a fretful "Buh."

Sidax froze, trusting to the deflection spell as the maid said something brightly in imperial—the word for milk was the same—and whisked out the door. The baby paid no heed, reaching toward a basket with intent, as Essence potential swirled around him. Sidax stared, aware he only had moments before the maid returned. But he knew how the Cobra Sages tested the very young. He carefully drew a talisman in the air, and a honey-smeared corn cob leaped up from the basket, dangling. *That's right, baby, see the possibility…*

The baby's brow furrowed, then he gave a grunt. Reached. And the cob flew from the air to his hand. The baby let out a pleased and surprised "Buh!" and began gnawing the cob, fingers sticky.

Sidax gloated. A very rare talent, to manifest so early, and these stupid easterners had no idea. His plans changed in an instant. Moving catfooted toward the baby, Sidax bent swiftly to touch the top of his head. A starburst nearly blinded him, and he caught himself before his breath hissed in. He straightened up and fingered his blade as he faced the doorway through which the maid should enter at any moment.

No—there were too many people coming and going. Nowhere to hide a body. He'd never get the brat off the ship before someone put up a squawk. He needed to do this cleanly, with as much time as he could win. He crossed the room and ghosted through the open window.

At the pagoda, Lei conscientiously tried to speak to Jathyam with her limited vocabulary, mostly to see how much effort he put in trying. Jhax was there, looking encouraging.

It was a stultifying attempt at converse, but they both tried, as the rice wine and the spiced, fermented goat's milk flowed. She made herself sip some of the latter, though she did not like the smell any more than she did the taste. But she would be leaving behind rice wine forever.

The cumulative effect made her muzzy, but she felt hopeful overall, as she made her way back to the flagship for her last night within imperial governance. On the morrow, they would hold the betrothal rituals, and then she would be moving into Odval's cabin aboard Jathyam's flagship under the golden banner with the black dragon on it.

This was real. This would be her new life. She would even be wearing new clothes soon, and would that include chimes in her braids? She was trying to form the question in the Western language when she got back to the flagship.

She washed up, changed for sleeping, then tiptoed into Anek's chamber, where he slept soundly. She gently kissed the soft, warm fuzz on the top of his head, and went to try to sleep, her head aching a little from the rice wine and the fermented milk, and her stomach was uncertain.

Sleep wouldn't come. It was a relief when dawn finally arrived. Remorselessly, the sun moved up in the sky, and she dressed for the last time in her imperial silks, then faced the farewells. Anek was hardest because he couldn't know she was leaving. He stared into her face, then let out a shriek as angry and miserable as those awful days when Lei had first come to the palace. Could he possibly know?

"He's teething," said the older nanny comfortingly. "They get fractious. I'll rub some calendula on his gums."

Lei kissed him a last time, swallowed past the tightening in her throat, then descended to where Tai was waiting. He searched her face. "Regretting your decision?"

"No." She firmed her voice. "Anek was fretting. I don't want to remember him that way."

"The nannies will spoil him," he promised, and unexpectedly grief pulsed in him at the prospect of never seeing his sister again. "Is there anything I can do for you?" he asked, low and a little husky.

She was blinking back tears. "Nothing for me. But Cousin Qishai. If she passes the imperial examination well—and I believe she will—I hope you will give her a good position. I know she will work hard."

"I promise, what she earns, she will have," Tai said. The rest of the Jis would also not suffer—though Lekshai would remain in the north with the Tiger Claw Army.

Then it was time for the ritual; Lei saw Odval looking as

tense as she felt, and ready sympathy made it somewhat easier. When the time came to part, she did not look back, feeling slightly better when Jhax appeared and paced beside her until they reached Jathyam, who closed in on her other side. His hand was warm and kindly as he walked with her to the ramp of the big galley ship, where rows of eyes stared. She straightened her spine, lifted her chin, and walked into her new life.

Tai watched her go, then turned to Odval, who looked a bit misty-eyed. "Set sail," Tai said, and the command was relayed up to the command tower.

For the rest of the day, he exerted himself to make things easy for Odval, translating everything until they finally parted late at night. Once the fleet was underway, he went to rest at last, relieved that he would not be expected to drink any more wine.

Midway through the night, he became aware of lights bobbing past the windows, and rose to light a lamp. At his door he found a graywing hovering anxiously. "Feldspar?"

"Your imperial highness," the graywing gasped, flinging himself forehead to the deck, "the child is missing!"

"Missing? He can't be missing—he doesn't even crawl yet!"

Tai ran across to Anek's chamber, to find it completely empty. No sign of any disturbance.

Soon the entire flagship was lit, as everyone searched from the deepest hold to the top of the tower. How could a baby be missing? There was no staff missing. The weeping, terrified nannies and servants were all interrogated, but nothing anomalous had been reported. He had gone down to sleep, as always, the night nanny sleeping in the cubby adjacent. She would have woken at the first cry…

Odval appeared, long hair streaming down. "What is it? Pirates?"

"The baby is missing," he said.

"What baby?" she asked blankly.

Tai realized that the Westerners hadn't even known about Anek. There went a suspicion that had not even formed a bud yet. Could Lei have taken him? No—the Western ships had departed before his own fleet had set sail.

As for the Westerners, a scut worker was eventually reported missing, but Jathyam assumed he'd deserted. It was not worth turning back for a slave who wanted his freedom, and they sailed on. He had his treaty—a new era!

SEVENTY

TAI SENT A SCOUT back to scour the island. When they caught up with the fleet a month later, they were empty-handed. The baby had just vanished.

Odval showed sincere concern, and Tai—whose inexperience comforted him with the thought that the baby couldn't be in danger, as there had been no signs of violence—was aware that the subject gave them something to talk about. This bridged the initial awkwardness of their situation. He apologized frankly for his lack of social skills, to which she replied, "Remember what sort of people I live among. If a conversation doesn't include raids or knives, it's not a conversation. We'll have to learn together."

He liked her quiet humor. As for the missing child, since the scout had found no sign of the baby, he would throw the question onto Mek, who might know some Essence-related method of searching for missing people.

The plan was to turn north once they stopped at Great Ran—but to his surprise, when they floated into the harbor cleared for their arrival, a figure appeared in the air, approaching the flagship.

"Hold your arrows!" Tai called, and heard the order relayed along the flagship and outward.

Mek soared overhead on the scaled sword glinting like gold in the sunlight and landed on the deck, the wind blowing his wispy hair straight back. Tai was distracted by the high arcs of brown skin at his temples: Mek's hair was thinning already, though he was not quite halfway through his twenties.

His expression caused cold to pool in Tai's gut. "Come

inside," he said, and Mek followed him, unaware of the affronted glances from graywings and sailors and ensigns for his lack of respectful protocol. But then a man who could fly on a sword could get away with most anything.

Mek said abruptly, "The Cobra Sages got him."

"Him?" Tai repeated.

"The baby. Didn't your fleet sail with a baby?"

Tai stared. "We did. He's Princess Lam's and my cousin Ji Venshai's child…"

"Apparently he's a Talent. Like me. The Cobra Sages found out somehow. Windseed reached me ten days ago."

Anger flared through Tai. "Jathyam—"

"Did not know. None of them did. This was the Cobra Sages, acting on their own."

"I can turn this fleet around and sail for their capital," Tai began.

"And then what? Fight against the very people trying to get rid of the Cobra Sages? You won't be able to get at them. If it was easy to get at them, don't you think Jhax or even Jathyam and his bannermen would have done so by now?"

Tai gritted his teeth. "What do you suggest I do, then? This is unforgivable."

"It is," Mek said, looking destroyed. "I feel I am most at fault. I ought to have come when you asked me to. If I'd been able to meet the baby, I'd have known he was a Talent, and I could have taken him. Or found him a safe place. But that accursed Sidax is trained for that sort of thing—the Cobra Sages steal babies with Essence talent wherever they find them."

Tai expelled his breath. "I guess I must leave it to you, then. Are you coming with us?"

"Yes. I came south to save you time. I owe you that much. And more." Mek looked grim. "As for what to do, we can only trust to Windseed. He is going to try to rescue him if he can."

"While being in danger of discovery himself."

"Yes."

Tai was then called away by the relentless press of decisions to be made, leaving Waha and Mek alone. Waha said, "I'll go after Sidax. I'll take him out if it kills me."

"It would kill you," Mek said, his gaze pleading. "Don't do it, Waha. If it were just your fighting skills against his, it would be different—and even then, what would that change, really? Sidax was made that way by a vicious form of cultivation. If he's gone, he'll be replaced by another like him. It's the Cobra Sages that have to change. I see that as my fight," he added, lower.

"If you discover a task I can do, send for me. Anywhere. I promise on my soul I'll do it."

Mek's brief smile was a wan semblance of the sweet one that he'd had as a grime-faced boy taking Diggy's huge, ugly head in his small hands before easing his vertigo. "I'll remember that," he promised, then he looked up when Odval ran up to join them. They fell into conversation with the comfort of familiarity, but Mek's mood stayed wretched for the remainder of the journey.

When they reached the capital, it was to find the entire city draped in white. There was no parade.

Lam met them at the dock, with an entourage. "Father Emperor died right after Kraken Festival," she said after greeting Tai and Odval. "He received word of the treaty, and was gone by morning, when they carried in his medicine."

They rode in carts up to the palace, then Tai turned Odval and Mek over to his parents, and faced the princess alone as he told her, with difficulty, about what had happened to Anek. "I don't think Lei knows," he finished. "She might by now, if Windseed and Jhax are able to dream-speak to one another. I don't know how that works."

She did not react with grief. It was more like defeat. "I am at fault," she said dully. "I ought to have kept him." But there was no love in her voice.

Tai hid a pulse of pity for that baby he'd only glimpsed once or twice. A troublesome father—murdered—a mother who didn't really want him, and then to be taken by the worst of enemies...*What did you do in your last five lives to have so much against you so early in this one, Little Dragon?* he thought, then took Lam's hand. "There are others who will try to rescue him, Essence experts, which neither you nor I are. Meanwhile, the empire is looking to us to carry on."

She stiffened her back, her chin coming up.

He said, "It's probably as well that the emperor has been properly buried. In all our history, in spite of our ritual wish that the emperor would live ten thousand years, none do, and the new has to replace the old as quickly and smoothly as…"

"As the scholar on the ice," she finished. How often had she heard that?

Tai smiled. "We cannot alter duty. But we can make our wedding and coronation a joyous spring celebration, shall we?"

She looked thoughtful. "And your Western bride?"

"She must be included. I think you'll like her. She and Lei made friends at the treaty meeting."

The princess had been raised to expect consorts, as dynastic continuity was another aspect of "the scholar on the ice." But she had never been able to have friends. Until Lei. "I hope so," she said. "However, you and Imperial Father had both said that the announcement about having to evacuate the capital would be your first command."

"I have an idea about that," he said, his tone musing. "If I present it as evacuation, there will be all the expected angry reaction and resistance. But what if I announce that the new dynasty is returning to the home of our imperial ancestors on the slope of Mt. Lir? The ministers have known the necessity for some time now. It will be no surprise to them."

Lam uttered a small laugh. "Every shopkeeper and carter and player will want to follow!"

"Especially if I let it be known that anyone who wishes to accompany us will be conveyed at crown expense."

"Which we were going to have to do anyway," she said, and there was the dawn of a smile at last. "But if we make it sound like a…"

"The grandest party in history?"

"Ayah, I like this idea. Let us do that."

"Then may I turn the planning over to you, with Su Inke under your command?"

She agreed, not just with pleasure but with a sense of purpose, and when later he brought Mek to diagnose her, she submitted, braced for all her sordid secrets to be aired—which was no more than she deserved.

But the experience was nothing like she'd expected. There was no monstrous ransacking of her inner thoughts, just a sense of warmth inside her head. When she opened her eyes, this neat, unobtrusive man in the plain, gallant wanderer garb said with a kind smile, "I used Essence to clear the scars, you might say, left from the poppy. If I did it right, you shouldn't feel the craving anymore. Or, it will be very small."

She had never told anyone of that daily fight against getting more of that soothing blanket between her and the howling ghosts of her emotions—she had assumed that was her punishment for what she had done to Ji Venshai. "I...don't," she said slowly, her awareness sharpening. "It's a memory. But not a want." She said softly, "My...my moods?"

He said apologetically, "I've done what I can. There might be better Essence healers than I. I'm still learning! If I find one, I'll send that person, but human minds are much like light and shadow shifting on water. It's not like mending a bone."

"Or a muscle," he said later to Tai, who had at first tried to wave him off when Mek said that it was his turn now. "I'm fine," he'd said. "Except for being always behind in my waiting tasks. Which I ought to be doing right now."

But Mek waved *him* off. "Tai, when I sent you by Sagacious Blade, I'm afraid I damaged your heart."

"I'd do it again," Tai retorted, mouth tight. "Without hesitation. You should have seen those captains behind Jhax and Jathyam. They looked at me as if they expected me to smite them with my thoughts only."

Mek gave him a brief smile, more like a wince. "I know you would. Listen, Tai. I've tried to renew some of the...the tiny sparks, I guess I could call them, the ones I used in myself when nullifying poison, and stone. Sparks is right, yet wrong in that there is no fire. What I'm saying is, the sparks will renew the damaged ones—*if* you rest enough to let them. You have to find time to rest, especially if you feel any pain."

Tai agreed, but inwardly he was thinking it was all very well for a gallant wanderer, whose days were completely his own, to demand rest for those without that luxury. But again, he had chosen this life. He must meet its demands.

"I'll come back when I can," Mek then said. "And I will let you know if Windseed has any success with rescuing Little Anek."

The next morning, he was gone.

You have no doubt read the official archives, which all agree that the combined wedding and coronation was legendarily splendid, but from all private accounts, it really was an occasion for widespread joy, aided by the fact that most of the rest of the Yimu hoard was used to fete the entire city. Entertainers from all over the empire flocked to the capital and were promptly hired, so that anywhere one went, there was music, and dancing, and free food—paid for by the crown.

The announcement of the return to the imperial island, coming on the heels of such glory, was better received that any in the imperial palace had expected. Some was due to generations of inherited expectation that emperors were wont to make changes on imperial scales, but there was also the fact that the imperial island was there in all ancient works and poems, the center of civilization. To return, in order to begin a new era with a new dynasty seemed to all as if the gods smiled on the world at last.

Su Inke—future Left Chancellor—and his officials had done a magnificent job with the logistics of preparation, resulting in a fleet larger even than that at the beginning of the Tan Dynasty. The exodus going from Mountain Peony to the ancient capital was no frightened flight, but a glorious parade of celebration, with music floating over the waters from ship to ship—an impression so lasting that, once the new imperial family had settled in, Empress Lam at last got her wish, and the Journey to the Clouds once more saw the caravan of elegant sampans enjoying the wonders of the most fabulous orchids in the world.

As you know, Odval had two daughters, and in due time Imperial Prince Lanek was born to the emperor and empress— nicknamed Mao at the military school he was sent to, for Tai had agreed with the emperor that to be a good commander meant learning first to obey. The emperor had stated that spoiling princes and princesses was to ruin them. Tai agreed. His own introduction to martial arts had done him so much good.

This is what you might not know. Lam and Tai were both so wary of more sons, due to the abysmal record of fighting princes in history, that Lam decided she would bear no more children.

Occasionally they heard from Empress Lei of the Dragon's Chosen, whose unofficial consort was Jhax of Ganis. She gave him a son, and a brother who could inherit Father Dragon's Empire, if the banners chose. Which eventually they did choose. For those three generations, the West seemed to be slowly improving in that there was no war—but the old problems had not gone away.

Ten Leopards was now the permanent home of the Ki family, or a part of the Ki family. With their numbers being so large, and only a few Bians, between intermarriages and other comings and goings, there were soon two branches of the Ki family, Eagle Island led by Anise and Mek's eldest son, and Ten Leopards by their second son. They freed Mek—now Grandfather Ki—to travel as Sagacious Blade.

Eagle Island continued to hold the spring competition; Mek usually won any contest he competed in. Uncle Ze had told him to continue to win, for it gave the others a goal to aim for—not subduing all other gallant wanderers, but becoming one's best self. The Sky Mirror competition was now famed not just in the northwest, but all over the empire, though the rules still held: no death duels.

It was to be expected that Anek would gradually be forgotten by all except Ki Mek, who continued to learn Essence healing, and who with Sagacious Blade fought blood demons and those bent on destruction. But he, and Windseed, were never able to find Anek in the mental realm in order to extend a healing hand.

Ki Mek was also unable to help Mao (eventually Emperor Maoyan), who took violently against him in his one visit—and issued an edict for all Essence flyers to be killed on sight.

There was a spiritual price to be paid for these labors, and defeats, in the Essence realm. He began to need solitude; as he and Windseed acknowledged in their sporadic, vital-to-both conversations. Their conversations were all the more precious for being rare, for both had to exert extreme vigilance to sustain them as the Sun blood demon slowly recovered its strength and malevolence.

Grandfather Ki found his secluded valley, where once some unknown hermit had lived. He cleaned out the cave, replanted the garden, and dwelt there from time to time, cultivating in peace. He occasionally took this or that youngster over the years—not just his own, but any likely young gallant wanderer who wanted to cultivate Essence skills as well as martial.

He was there when Windseed contacted him to say that Anek had tracked down and killed Sidax. Ten years later, Windseed was suddenly silent, and Ki Mek knew that he'd been discovered, and assassinated, but it was another ten years before he found out that he'd been murdered by Anek.

Anek—or that which had been Anek—had as a Rider the

revitalized Sun, and in taking command of the Cobra Sages, now called himself the White Dragon. Once again, the Cobra Sages exerted force over the obsidian throne until the White Dragon took it himself, and that ended all communication between the empires.

Ki Mek required a long sojourn in his sacred valley to recover, but when he emerged, he made a vow that though he was like the ant shaking the parasol tree, he would guard the world against the return of the Cobra Sages, until Sagacious Blade chose her next wielder.

Before Ki Mek left his valley, he poured out wine to celebrate the friend who never took the time to rest. He played his flute, then sang:

> *The seas are eternal, but old friends are gone.*
> *Like the tides, we wait for them to return.*
> *Will we be together again?*

AFTERWORD

"SAGACIOUS BLADE CHOSE ME? Grandfather Ki didn't?" Ari asked. She carefully laid the scroll down, emotions autumn leaves in a wind.

"They both did. But he chose you first," Waoji Lion's Mane said.

Ari's eyes burned. "But…that's when Sagacious Blade's Essence protection left him, and came to me? Is that why he died?"

"He chose you fully knowing it was a possibility. He accepted that. You must remember that living so long a time means that he had outlived everyone he'd known when young," Waoji Lion's Mane said. "Han Anise had received Essence healing through his love and care, and lived far past a century, but she had to see her children die before her, and finally desired peace from a never-ending old age a few years before you came to Ten Leopards. Her last breath was a promise that she would wait for him."

Ari laid her hand on the scroll. "Tai—Emperor Taiyan—was Shigan's ancestor, the first Jehan emperor. I read about him in the emperor's archive, but it was all his meritorious deeds, and nothing of him himself. What happened to that coded record of his?"

"Apparently he burned it when he felt his end coming. But he had shared some of it with Odval, who shared with her daughters. Their descendants showed me some old letters."

Ari accepted that, mentally trying to equate the Tai in Waoji's record with that distant figure in the annals. "And he suffered heart damage from the very first Essence transfer? No, not the first. Ki Mek's was the first, when he went to the Jade Island. But he could heal himself with Essence. Is that why Taiyan didn't live past forty?"

She rubbed her breastbone. Though it seemed the sword finally learned how to get it right, or had gained enough Essence to transfer people—because she sensed the cost in Essence—there was definitely a physical cost as well, even if minute, now. And she knew that Jion, like his forefather, on finding out, would still pay it, if he thought the empire required it of him.

"Forty is so young," she finally said with a rueful smile, struggling with a sense of grief for someone dead so long ago. Who might have already come back at least once, though not as Je Tai, friend to Ki Mek. "Ayah! If you'd given me this scroll when I first met the sword, I would have thought forty very old."

Waoji Lion's Mane smiled at this mild attempt at humor. "Mek had warned the emperor that rest was vital for one with a damaged heart, but Taiyan never could take the time to rest, until time took him away—but at least those were very happy years."

"I'm glad of that," Ari said.

"Maoyan was far too young to be an emperor, and I believe you know the problems of that reign. That was when Ki Mek truly became Sagacious Blade, traveling constantly fighting blood demons in the west, and doing his best to mitigate Maoyan's increasingly terrible reign from within, even after he was declared an outlaw. It was a relief to him when Maoyan at last died."

Ari remembered Shigan's grim stories about that forefather. "Did Maoyan inherit his mother's Moods?"

"I cannot say, for Ki Mek never wrote anything down about people he healed, or tried to heal. I had to learn what you find there through other sources—except in a few cases where he shared memories directly, especially toward the end when he was failing, and had difficulty speaking. He would wander in dream-memories, with me as companion."

Ari slowly began to roll the scroll again, trying to fit together the legends of Sagacious Blade with family- and animal-loving, patient Grandfather Ki, and with the Ki Mek she'd just met in Waoji Lion's Mane's scroll.

She said, "I used to try to correct people when they talked

about Firebolt's exploits and exaggerated them. Until my brother Yskanda pointed out that legends were like art in that he did not attempt to recreate the people in his pictures exactly as they are. He groups them in settings that please the eye, and elevate emotions."

Waoji Lion's Mane smiled a little. "My wife used to tell me not to correct any stories about us, because how people told them added their own hopes to them, and their desire to be a part of great things. Bi insisted that storytellers are transformative, and every single person who retells a story becomes a tiny part of that story."

"I can see that," Ari exclaimed.

He chuckled. "Perhaps there's something in it, even for the persistence of stories that are not great things." He mimed wielding an ink brush, his smile widening. "But why people tell the stories they tell is far beyond my understanding. I wrote down this one because I made a promise. Now that I've kept that promise, I can retire to bore my grandchildren with the stories that *I* like best."

Ari laughed. "I'll take this precious scroll to Shigan. I know he'll be interested. He always regretted not getting to spend more time with Grandfather Ki, though he thought of him as a musician who happened to be good at martial arts."

"I think Ki Mek would have liked being remembered that way. He was never a great musician, but somehow he could bring out great emotions." Waoji Lion's Mane pressed a fist to his chest, then gathered his things. They both bowed to Grandfather Ki's grave, poured out wine, then they traveled down the mountain together, trading some of those stories.

She made her way back to the imperial island by way of Te Gar (finding out that the baby was another grandson, welcome as they all were, but Petal still had hopes of a future granddaughter) where she arrived as autumn reached its most glorious color.

Yskanda was still tall, ethereally handsome in spite of his silver hair. He was always out in all weathers, sketching madly as he tried to capture ephemeral qualities of light that only he seemed to see, but when Jion had finished reading the scroll, and insisted that Yskanda also read it, he did not ask why. He laid down his brush and paints, ignored the smudges on his long, clever hands and his plain but finely woven robe, and commenced reading.

"You seem very determined to get Second Brother to read it, too," Ari remarked when she and Jion were alone.

Jion's gaze went to the sword resting on the rack in their bedchamber, the pearl in the handle glowing softly in the lamplight. "I am," he said.

"Are you ready to tell me why?"

"Partly," he responded, surprising her. "Though Yskanda never wielded the sword, he understands the Essence realm better than either of us."

"So he does."

The next evening, while a huge, round Phoenix Moon ruled the sky and the empire was celebrating that with round cakes, lanterns, circle dances, and harvest banquets, Ari, Jion, and Yskanda met in their favorite chamber, where Yskanda handed back Waoji Lion's Mane's scroll.

"First, it makes me wonder what has been going on in the west, since the White Dragon's defeat."

"I pay a great deal to people watching from a distance," Jion said with a grim smile. "My hope is one day to start up trade again."

"My second impression is this. I kept wanting to pull Ki Mek out of the pages and speak to him," Yskanda admitted. "Both when I learned something I had not known about Essence, and when he seemed ignorant of something that I could have told him." He turned to Jion. "I think I understand a bit more about the burdens of people born with metal affinities. They seem to make very good organizers and chiefs, but at such a cost, either to themselves or to others around them."

"Emperor Maoyan," Ari and Jion said together, then looked at once another and laughed.

Yskanda smiled vaguely, then said, "You asked me to read it for a purpose?"

"Yes." Jion regarded his two best beloveds. "I am used to thinking ahead. It's something I tried to teach our children, but only Samu truly grasps it. Though they are all excellent people, and we've done our best, people are individuals."

Ari waited. In her experience, when people began by telling you what you already knew, and they knew you knew it, it usually meant something big was coming. Something that you might not like or want.

Yskanda's gaze was unblinking, and Ari suspected he

might be thinking something similar.

Jion said slowly, "My forefather Taiyan said it there, toward the end, referring to the old Kanda quotation from the *Conversations Among the Scholars*: 'Even the condor must flap his wings, and the whale must blow water: just so the scholar who slides on the ice will have to run again.'"

Ari let a little of her impatience slip. "It simply means we have to keep striving to do our duty, but we all know that."

"It means more than that, Ryu," Jion said tenderly. "We, the Empire of a Thousand Isles, are the scholar on the ice, the condor soaring in the air. The whale in the deeps. The empire is at peace, and has been for our entire reign, but it did not start that way. We all—I include your excellent First Brother Muin—work very hard for that peace. We are doing our best to pass it on."

Both Ari and Yskanda smiled at this mention of their elder brother, now a venerable general. All his sons and grandsons had gone into the military. Yet none were warlike; their affinities tended toward earth. Solid and practical.

Ari looked puzzled. "Are you saying that you're having reservations about Samu inheriting, on a chance resemblance to Je Tai in the scroll? Not merely looks, but the metal affinity? And so we're *not* going to hand off the throne when you turn seventy-seven—an auspicious number, you were the one to say so!—so we can sail through all the islands? That's three years away!"

"No, no, no. No changes to our plans. I'll come at my idea another way. I have faith in Samu. But, just as our children, though raised similarly, turned out to be quite different, so it is in the world. We appreciate peace because we know what it was like before we won peace. Samu's grandchildren might well find peace dull, even tiresome."

Ari brought her chin down. "This is very dispiriting to hear. I don't want to talk like this. I know we cannot control the future, but is that a reason to predict it will be bad?"

Yskanda held up a paint-smudged hand. "I think I understand," he said slowly. "It's the same reason we keep debating ethical cultivation, and the cardinal virtues, and we study Mana Ta and the Sage Empress, because the scholar has to *push* to keep sliding on the ice. It's what we teach the students, we must keep striving—and each one hears it differently."

Jion gave a sober nod. "That's partly it. Maoyan strove. If you don't believe me, you've only to read his writings. And my sister Manon, who I admired more than anyone, was inspired by them. For what I felt was all the wrong reasons. I'm very certain the White Dragon also worked very hard."

That shocked Ari to silence. Jion saw her expression, and put out an apologetic hand. "I see I'm failing yet again. Another try. I believe that if my own father had permitted his children to learn martial arts, I would have done much as I did, because dance and music were most important to me, and our little sister would have struggled and escaped as often as she could to her flowers and her pets, but Manon would have excelled. I believe she would have become another, more warlike Maoyan, perhaps conquering the Westerners for their own good, and no one could have stopped her without a horrendous cost."

Ari took his hand. "So…you're saying we were wrong to permit those who wanted to learn martial skills to get training?" Sorrow chilled her at the idea—she loved martial arts.

"I'm misspeaking again," he exclaimed, squeezing her hand. "You are a living example of what I'm trying to come to: in you, like your elder brother Muin, martial skills are exemplary. I trust Muin to oversee the imperial army. I trust you."

She smiled at last. "Go on."

"*Anything* can be jade and poetry, or cracked walls and ruin. All any of us can do is our best, because humans are individuals. And Kanda was right that the best path is training in the virtues. But…"

He held out his right hand away from the other two, and Sagacious Blade flashed from the far wing and the hilt smacked into his palm. "I have read all the records concerning the sword. Have you?"

Yskanda gave his head a shake. "Only the oldest one, when the sword was first imbued with the soul of the chief musician. It was the descriptions of the music of that time that I found most interesting. How musicians in some ways hear their handiworks the way artists see theirs."

Jion laid the sword down before them, stroking it gently with his fingers. We have thought of this blade as…someone. That's where I think the danger is."

Ari's eyes widened. "I see. The demon in it is not the blade, though for all this time she has made herself, or itself, part of the blade. And a blade, even in the hands of someone like Ki Mek, is still a weapon of war."

Yskanda said, "Ahhhh." He smiled. "I've had to listen to the two of you talk endlessly about who should have it when you go on to the next life — supposing you can even choose. Ari, you keep saying that emperors do not need any more power than they already have. I think you're right. And you, Jion, point out that handing it off to some random gallant wanderer isn't much different than just throwing it onto a path somewhere and letting it lie until someone picks it up — which might be someone with malice in their heart. And I agree. Because a sword is still a sword."

Jion lifted his hands. "I have to admit that I have found it very convenient to use the blade over the years. Especially to join you on your travels." He brushed his hand over Ari's. "But I sometimes think that it would be better if the sword was *just* a sword."

"Whereas I would love to see all that vast Essence potential go into a book," Yskanda admitted. "Oh! Or maybe a brush." His expression brightened at that thought.

The corners of Jion's mouth turned up, and he tipped his head back. "Are you listening, YinYin? That is you, is it not? We cannot know what you are cultivating toward, or why, but we appreciate deeply the benefits you've brought to humankind over the centuries."

"And to you and me as individuals," Ari pointed out.

Jion smiled again. "But do you think that maybe a powerful sword is not what humans need the most right now?"

"I still like the idea of the brush," Yskanda said softly. "It makes words, and art, not war —"

He stopped, gazing into the center of the room.

Ari and Jion peered in the same direction, and Ari thought she saw the vague outline of a human form, with darker shadows drifting like smoke around the pale oval of a face. But then it was gone, the flames in the candles streaming then steadying. A trick of the eye?

Jion gave a soft exclamation. He looked puzzled as he touched the sword. Then lifted his hand, and shut his eyes…and nothing happened.

Ari leaned over to touch it, and knew in a heartbeat that the Essence was gone. Sagacious Blade was now a well-made bronze sword with overlapping scales, a milky white stone set in its hilt.

"I thought…that was a discussion," Jion said, holding back laughter. "YinYin? Is this what you wanted? Could you talk to us?"

They all stilled, studying the air expectantly, but nothing happened, and Ari said, "I guess I can take her—it—when I travel now."

"And when we get too creaky to travel, it can go in the treasury," Jion conceded. "Unless you want to put some charms on it to protect the bronze from tarnish?"

They chatted on as the sword lay inert before them, until they noticed Yskanda gazing into space with his eyes-half shut.

"Second Brother?" Ari asked.

"Yskanda?" Jion murmured.

Yskanda stirred, then said, "I was just trying to imagine the wonderful arts that might happen if all that charm went into a brush."

Was that the autumn wind in the redbark trees, or was it the echo of a laugh?

Author's Note

My gratitude to my Patreon readers who faithfully read and commented on the rough draft, and especial thanks to Rachel Neumeier for her excellent comments on beta-reading, and to Brenda Clough for being willing to do a fast proof on this juggernaut.

This wraps up the Sagacious Blade circle. I'd like to write more in this world if readers would like to read it. In any case, if you've the time and inclination, even a one sentence review is a real help for me, as well as for all the other indie writers out there. Word of mouth is powerful — for some of us, our only PR!

ABOUT THE AUTHOR

Sherwood Smith studied in Europe before earning a masters degree in history. She worked as a governess, a bartender, an electrical supply verifier, and wore various hats in the film industry before turning to teaching for twenty years. To date she's published over fifty books, one of which was an Anne Lindbergh Honor Book; she's twice been a finalist for the Mythopoeic Fantasy Award and once a Nebula finalist. Her YA fantasy novel *Crown Duel* has been in print for over twenty years.

She reviews books at Goodreads and blogs intermittently at Dreamwidth, and can also be found at Patreon.

Visit her website at https://www.sherwoodsmith.net and sign up for her newsletter to learn about new books!

ABOUT BOOK VIEW CAFÉ

Book View Café is a professional authors' publishing co-operative offering DRM-free ebooks in multiple formats to readers around the world. With authors in a variety of genres including mystery, romance, fantasy, and science fiction, Book View Café has something for everyone.

Book View Café is good for readers because you can enjoy high-quality DRM-free ebooks from your favorite authors at a reasonable price.

Book View Café is good for writers because 90% of the proceeds goes directly to the book's author.

Book View Café authors include New York Times and USA Today bestsellers, Nebula, Hugo, Lambda, Chanticleer, National Reader's Choice, and Philip K. Dick Award winners, World Fantasy, Kirkus, and Rita Award nominees, and winners and nominees of many other publishing awards.